Praise for the delectable Culinary Mysteries by Nancy Fairbanks . . .

"Clever, fast-paced . . . A literate, deliciously well-written mystery."

—Earlene Fowler

"Not your average who-done-it . . . Extremely funny . . . A rollicking good time."

—Romance Reviews Today

"*Crime Brûlée* is an entertaining amateur sleuth tale that takes the reader on a mouthwatering tour of New Orleans . . . Fun."

—Painted Rock Reviews

"Fairbanks has a real gift for creating characters based in reality but just the slightest bit wacky in a slyly humorous way . . . It will tickle your funny bone as well as stimulate your appetite for good food."

—El Paso Times

"Nancy Fairbanks has whipped up the perfect blend of mystery, vivid setting, and mouthwatering foods . . . *Crime Brûlée* is a luscious start to a delectable series."

—The Mystery Reader

"Nancy Fairbanks scores again . . . a page-turner."

—Las Cruces (NM) Sun-News

Three-Course Murder

Nancy Fairbanks

BERKLEY PRIME CRIME, NEW YORK

THE BERKLEY PUBLISHING GROUP
Published by the Penguin Group
Penguin Group (USA) Inc.
375 Hudson Street, New York, New York 10014, USA
Penguin Group (Canada), 90 Eglinton Avenue East, Suite 700, Toronto, Ontario M4P 2Y3, Canada
(a division of Pearson Penguin Canada Inc.)
Penguin Books Ltd., 80 Strand, London WC2R 0RL, England
Penguin Group Ireland, 25 St. Stephen's Green, Dublin 2, Ireland (a division of Penguin Books Ltd.)
Penguin Group (Australia), 250 Camberwell Road, Camberwell, Victoria 3124, Australia
(a division of Pearson Australia Group Pty. Ltd.)
Penguin Books India Pvt. Ltd., 11 Community Centre, Panchsheel Park, New Delhi—110 017, India
Penguin Group (NZ), Cnr. Airborne and Rosedale Roads, Albany, Auckland 1310, New Zealand
(a division of Pearson New Zealand Ltd.)
Penguin Books (South Africa) (Pty.) Ltd., 24 Sturdee Avenue, Rosebank, Johannesburg 2196, South Africa

Penguin Books Ltd., Registered Offices: 80 Strand, London WC2R 0RL, England

This is an original publication of The Berkley Publishing Group.

These are works of fiction. Names, characters, places, and incidents either are the product of the author's imagination or are used fictitiously, and any resemblance to actual persons, living or dead, business establishments, events, or locales is entirely coincidental. The publisher does not have any control over and does not assume any responsibility for author or third-party websites or their content.

THREE-COURSE MURDER

First edition: January 2006

ISBN: 0-425-20764-1

This book has been catalogued with the Library of Congress.

PRINTED IN THE UNITED STATES OF AMERICA

10 9 8 7 6 5 4 3 2 1

Contents

Crime Brûlée

Acknowledgments

Many thanks to my editor Cindy Hwang, who suggested that I start a culinary series; to my literary agents Richard Curtis and Laura Tucker; to John Shoup of Great Chefs Publishing for granting permission to use material from *Great Chefs: The Louisiana New Garde*, a book that was as helpful to Carolyn Blue as it was to me; to good friends Mike and Carol Eastman of Northern Arizona University and Larry and Dawn Scott of Boston College with whom my husband and I roamed the French Quarter and even the swamp in search of adventure and good food; to Carol Lee Griffin and her late husband, Gary, whose hospitality gave us an early introduction to the delights of New Orleans; and to Joan Coleman for her friendship, encouragement, and time in reading this manuscript.

Grateful acknowledgment is made to John Shoup of Great Chefs Publishing for permission to reprint recipes and use material from *Great Chefs: The Louisiana New Garde* by Nancy Ross Ryan with Chan Patterson, and to the New Orleans chefs whose recipes are used. Their names are listed in the recipe index.

Visit the author's World Wide Web site at
http://www.nancyfairbanks.com

For the Gourmet Group

1982 to 20–

In celebration of
good food,
good wine,
and good company

Lillian Mayberry
Jack Bristol
Becky Craver
Lionel Craver
Doris Drow
Gregg Drow
Nancy Herndon
Bill Herndon
Joyce Keller
Randy Keller

Author's Note

Characters and events in this book are inventions of the author. Although real restaurants, meals, and New Orleans scenes are described, the action is fictitious. Any resemblance to actual people and events is purely coincidental.

Nancy Fairbanks

Prologue

Life doles out the most amazing surprises, not all of them pleasant. For instance, who could have imagined that I would find myself in New Orleans trying to solve a mystery, which no one, including the police, seemed to find mysterious at all?

To point out how incongruous the situation was, I should introduce myself: I am Carolyn Blue, a forty-something professor's wife, mother of two, and novice food writer—not a promising résumé for even the most amateur of detectives, and my adult life heretofore contains nothing to recommend me for my self-imposed assignment, the location of a missing person.

How astounded I would have been at the age of twenty had I been able to foresee myself enmeshed in a mission that ultimately proved to be quite terrifying. As an undergraduate, I believed, with my contemporaries, that thirty was the age at which adventure and commitment to ideals ended, the age when one, if still alive, became a fuddy-duddy. Which is not to say that Jason and I were rebellious types, storming administration buildings, occupying the offices of deans, and shouting unpleasant epithets at police officers. We were much too busy for that, he working on a doctorate in science, I pursuing an undergraduate degree in medieval history. We didn't even smoke pot or take hallucinogenic drugs.

I'm sure our children are profoundly appreciative of that abstinence, since they are both normal, intelligent young people with no sign of chromosomal damage. Also they are now away at college, the beneficiaries of generous scholarships that save their gratified parents from being dragged into poverty by the weight of onerous tuition payments.

Jason, my husband, is a university professor and respected scientist. I, having resisted the feminist impetus to go out and accomplish something in a high-powered job, spent my twenties, thirties, and a bit of my forties raising my children and giving charming dinner parties for my husband's colleagues, both foreign and domestic.

Although I was quite content during those years, I must admit that I no longer have much interest in elaborate gourmet projects. In fact, I have become quite addicted to OPC (other people's cooking). I'll eat just about anything that isn't prepared in my own kitchen by me.

Being a semiretired mother and hostess, I have become an Accompanying Person. Perhaps you're not familiar with the term. An Accompanying Person is the spouse or significant other of a scientist attending a conference away from home, perhaps even in another country. I find travel a delightful pastime, one of its greatest benefits being that the traveler is not expected to cook. Entertainment and even meals are provided for Accompanying Persons by the scientific group hosting the conference. I am showered with tours, lunches, and banquets in exotic places.

Even more amazing, this new freedom to accompany my husband has provided me with a career, one that is beginning to generate an income. I haven't had a paying job since I fell in love with Jason, who was the graduate assistant in a perfectly deadly science course the university forced me to take. We married after a year's courtship and were supported by my family and his fellowship while he completed his doctorate and I my bachelor's degree in a subject that was, although fascinating to me and approved by my father, not one with much appeal to prospective employers.

I had Christopher, my first child, while Jason was a postdoctoral fellow and Gwen, my independent daughter, when he became an assistant professor at another institution. After he became a full professor and the children had gone off to college, Jason decided, to the astonishment of all, including me, to take a different job in an unlikely place, but that's another story.

Not a very exciting history, you might say, until I took it into my head, after a trip to Spain, to write an article for the newspaper in El Paso, Texas, our new location. The story was entitled "Goats are Tastier than You'd Think," and was probably accepted for publication because people in El Paso and Mexico actually eat goat. My inspiration was a mildly amusing series of events, or mishaps, if you will.

In Madrid, Jason and I went to a charming restaurant that had a menu in many languages, English among them. I ordered lamb, of which I am very fond, and there was some confusion with the waiter, who didn't speak English or understand it and couldn't read the English menu when we pointed to my selection. Then the entrée arrived, a dainty leg of something crisscrossing my plate. Knowing what leg of lamb looks like, I was sure I hadn't gotten it. Nonetheless, I was inspired to adventure by the novelty of eating in a new country and sampled my mystery entrée. The meat was very rich, somewhat greasy, and had an ambrosial marinade on the skin.

"What can it be?" I marveled.

When I gave Jason a bite, he informed me that I was eating goat, or *cabrito* (baby goat), as it is called in Juarez, Mexico, where Jason ordered and enjoyed it while entertaining a seminar speaker from Belgium. You can imagine how taken aback I was. Jason, however, expressed envy. During the second half of our trip, when we were attending a meeting in Catalonia, a province on the eastern coast of Spain, I once again ordered lamb. This time Jason ordered goat, but when our plates came, I had received another goat's leg, and Jason had been served fish. We were both frustrated and complained, not that our protests registered with our non-English-speaking waiter or influenced his employer, who settled the dispute by pointing to the menu entries we had chosen and then to the entrées we had received. As far as the owner was concerned, I had ordered goat and my husband had ordered fish. Jason admitted that his fish was very tasty but claimed half of my goat to assuage his disappointment.

I found the whole incident much more amusing than Jason, although I never did get to sample lamb in Spain, where I had assumed it would be not only excellent but readily available. I have read that many immigrant shepherds in the western United States were Basque. Actually, I don't suppose the Basques consider themselves Spanish. For that matter, the Catalans don't either, and they speak a different language, which may account for the fact that I missed getting lamb a second time.

But as I said, I submitted an article about eating goat in Spain to our local newspaper. For a wonder, they published my contribution, which was then picked up by other papers in the chain and evidently appeared all over the country. One day while I was loading the dishwasher, I received a telephone call from a literary agent in New York who said that she had read my goat piece and asked if I did much traveling.

"Well, yes, a bit," I said modestly. "I travel with my husband."

"I wonder if you'd be interested in writing a book of anecdotes about eating abroad?"

Needless to say, I was quite astounded and replied, "My next trip is not abroad. We're going to New Orleans."

"Even better," she said. "I know just the publisher for a book on eating in New Orleans." As it happened, she did. The publisher was duly contacted and offered me an advance to write the book, which is why, as I said, I have a sort-of job and why I found myself searching a strange city (and New Orleans really is strange) for Julienne Magnussen, although none of our friends seemed to think she was actually missing. However, I knew that my childhood friend would never have missed the crawfish Etienne, much less the seafood gumbo, unless something dreadful had happened to keep her from the table.

1

The Menu at Etienne's

Any cook who aspires to duplicate Cajun or Creole cooking must be willing to master the art of making roux, that seemingly simple mixture of flour with oil, butter, or—horror of horrors!—lard. To produce a cup of roux, begin with a cup each of all-purpose flour and of the oil or fat of choice. Place the oil in a large, heavy-bottomed skillet, and whisk in the flour. (Traditionalists and those who have sufficient upper-body strength recommend a cast-iron skillet.) Then cook slowly, stirring without pause while keeping an anxious eye on the mixture. If your roux burns, it must be discarded. Otherwise, it will ruin whatever dish you add it to—unless you happen to favor food with a bitter taste. How long must you stir? That depends on the color at which you're aiming. For tan, 10 to 12 minutes; for medium-dark roux, 15 to 18; for dark-brown roux, 20 to 25 minutes.

In these days of public consciousness regarding repetitive motion injuries, one must wonder if New Orleans doctors are keeping statistics on such ailments as *roux elbow* and *roux-induced carpal tunnel syndrome.* I'm told that a treasured gift in Louisiana is a jar of roux made by a master of the art. Perhaps you can make friends with such a person. I, for one, would be delighted to exchange an artfully arranged Christmas assortment of Mesilla Valley pecans for a jar of New Orleans roux.

Carolyn Blue, Eating Out in the Big Easy

The opportunity was a meeting of the American Chemical Society to be held in New Orleans, the occasion a dinner, which I would arrange for three other couples, companions from our student days. I was somewhat nervous about my plan, although the eight of us were the closest of friends when we attended the university together, working on graduate and undergraduate degrees. But I haven't seen most of them in over twenty years. Of course, Jason, my husband, runs into those who attend the same scientific meetings, but for me it's been a matter of garnering news of the others at second hand, and my husband isn't given to collecting personal details and passing them on. He's much more likely to tell me about a paper given by one of our friends and the questions asked by the audience.

There have been notes at Christmastime, to be sure, and they sometimes included pictures of children and pets, and I have kept in closer touch with Julienne Magnussen. We talk by phone several times a year, send letters and E-mails, and get together when we're both home to visit our families. Julienne and I have been best friends since childhood. Several times a week for the last two months, she has E-mailed me to add to the list of sights she plans to show me when we meet in New Orleans, the city of her birth. But the other five people, including Julienne's husband Nils, are in the nature of friends one remembers with affection from youth, friends whose lives are familiar in outline, although when one thinks of them at all, one wonders whether they might not have changed into entirely different people over the years. Several of them have.

Julienne and Nils, for instance, were passionately in love both before and after marriage. She told me that they once made love on the sofa in the office of the math chairman, who had left the campus and his graduate students to participate in deer-hunting season. However, I now get hints from her that things aren't as rosy as they once were. I've wondered whether their problem, if there is one, might not be professional jealousy. Julienne is now a full professor with many papers in prestigious journals. She's been an invited speaker at important professional meetings, chair of sessions, editor of journals, recipient of government research grants, and mentor to graduate students. Moreover, Julienne served as chair of her department (an honor about which she complained constantly during the five years of her tenure) and was even proposed as dean of the college, an appointment she firmly declined.

Nils, although he's had a perfectly respectable academic career, is still an associate professor and not nearly as well known in his own field, mathematics, as she is in hers. And Nils tends to be depressed because everybody says mathematicians do their most brilliant work in their twenties, which he is, of course, long past.

Then, I'm somewhat uneasy because the other three women all obtained graduate degrees and made their mark in their chosen fields, while I've drifted through motherhood and helpmate-hood, coming only now in my forties to start a career outside the home. It's entirely possible that I'll be viewed with some disdain by my female friends, while, ironically, the males will probably envy Jason his full-time wife.

Oh well, such are the ironies of gender competition. (I have at last given in to the use of *gender* as the indication of a person's sex rather than a grammatical term, *sex* having too many libidinous connotations these days.)

Then there is the dinner, which I suggested and planned, having established myself as the group's culinary expert. Everyone is coming a day early to attend and will, if I remember them at all, have no hesitation in telling me if they don't find the meal worth their time and trouble. That's not to say that they are rude, just outspoken. But even in the matter of the dinner, I had to work with the restaurant that Julienne insisted on. She pointed out that she has often been in New Orleans, having, in fact, moved from Louisiana to Michigan as a child, and knows where to order the best gumbo, her favorite dish.

I like gumbo myself but rather resent having to organize a whole meal around some stranger chef's expertise in making roux, a talent that I personally never mastered, even in the days when I wasn't addicted to other people's cooking. I've always hated the idea of spending long periods of time stirring flour over a fire in the faint hope that it won't burn.

The owner and chef, Etienne something-or-other—his last name is French and completely unpronounceable—has been rather cavalier and even impatient about my desire to choose the menu, which he would much rather have chosen himself, quite possibly from the leftovers of the previous night's offerings. However, when he learned that I am a food writer, he became extremely charming and loquacious, at my expense. I was tempted to insist that he call me back so the long-distance charges would be billed to him. It cost me $21.25 to plan the following menu, which I hope, and Etienne assures me, is the epitome of New Orleans cuisine.

We are to start with deviled alligator puffs and drinks. The deviled alligator will be followed by gumbo, then avocado stuffed with shrimp remoulade, crawfish Etienne as the main course, and finally bread pudding, which I detest but was bullied into by Julienne, the chef, and even my husband Jason. Appropriate wines and brandies are to accompany each course.

Thank God, Jason and I don't have to foot the bill for this dinner. The cost is to be divided evenly among the couples, as long as I keep it below $60 a person, bargained up from $35 in an E-mail negotiation with Broder McAvee, who teaches Calvinist theology at a small but highly regarded liberal arts college on the West Coast. His wife Carlene is a microbiologist and department head in a bioengineering company and has been invited to the meeting to give a plenary address on computational something-or-other. I'm sure she makes lots of money, but Broder doesn't and says Carlene might be able to afford $200 dinners, but he personally thinks $50 is outrageous; he can eat all week for $50. Well, maybe he can, but it makes one wonder *what* he eats and whether he makes Carlene eat the same things, and especially what they served their four children when the children were at home.

Incidentally, the alligator puffs, which I chose as a conversation piece and to satisfy my own curiosity, have generated a veritable blizzard of humorous E-mail notes among the group. Everyone is now calling our reunion "the alligator dinner."

2

Deviled Alligator Puffs

Whatever man's original motivation for eating a creature as ugly as an alligator (perhaps it was an eat-or-be-eaten situation), I can certainly recommend deviled alligator puffs. Alligator meat may well have a nasty reptilian tang; if so, it's completely disguised by the herbs, spices, breading, and frying that go into making the puffs, which are light, crispy, and very flavorful (in a non-frightening way). The alligator meat is also low in calories and cholesterol, although the breading and frying undoubtedly negate any health benefits.

Not the least of an alligator puff's charms is that it breaks the conversational ice at a cocktail party or before a dinner when the guests haven't yet imbibed enough alcohol to be easy with one another.

However, I am not including a recipe for alligator puffs because it is unlikely that the reader will be able to find alligator meat, ground or otherwise, in the local supermarket. I certainly couldn't, but at that time I foolishly imagined alligators being captured in the swamps by daring hunters called "alligator wrestlers."

Silly me. Alligators have evidently become domesticated. There are over one hundred alligator farms in the state of Louisiana, so I can only surmise that the delicacy is consumed in cities more sophisticated than my own. In fact, I am told that in New Orleans the much favored turtle soup is often made with alligator meat. However, I have never seen turtle soup on a menu in El Paso.

Carolyn Blue, *Eating Out in the Big Easy*

Our reserved private dining room at Etienne's was gold and cream with French doors opening onto a patio we couldn't use because rain was falling steadily on the lush shrubbery, the flagstones, and the ornate, white-painted, wrought-iron furniture. Jason and I arrived early to monitor the preparations, but we were joined before eight by Lester and Miranda Abbott.

I remember Lester as a husky young graduate student; now he is the fat dean of a college of science with, to hear him tell it, a very active research group. He wore a brown, double-breasted suit that didn't particularly flatter him.

Ever so slight a smile touched my husband's mouth as Lester bragged about his fourteen graduate students and three postdoctoral fellows and the twenty-six papers his research group had placed during the last year in the very best journals. That little twinkle in Jason's eye was a reminder that Lester Abbott is garnering a reputation as the king of irreproducible results, in all probability, according to Jason, because Lester doesn't monitor the research in his labs closely enough; he's too busy wheeling and dealing at the administrative level.

Jason harbors a mild prejudice against interfering administrators, not to mention the fact that his own research group has published more papers than Lester's, and Jason has aged much more gracefully. My husband is a runner, swimmer, and racquetball player. He is still slender, his hair still dark and thick, with just a touch of distinguished gray at the temples and in his neatly clipped beard. Poor Lester, although he and Jason are both forty-seven, has become rather pompous and self-congratulatory and isn't at all attractive anymore. It's hard to believe that we once called him Les and considered him one of the jolliest persons in the group, especially when he'd been drinking, and he did a lot of that in the old days.

Miranda, his wife, who had once been slender, has grown stocky and developed a thriving practice in tax law. She let us know within two minutes of arrival that she was now billing $350 an hour. Can you imagine? She'd make almost as much in a day as I received as an advance for writing a whole book. Having come straight from taking depositions in a "very important" tax case, she was festively attired in what I took to be a power suit. The garment was so well cut that you could hardly tell she was overweight and so severe that no one could ever accuse her of attempting to make points with feminine wiles.

I felt decidedly frivolous. I was wearing one of those new, almost full-length dresses whose straight-line tailoring belied the pretty flowers on the cream background. Miranda's hair is iron gray and cut very short. Mine, still blonde with the help of a biweekly rinse, is curly but rather carelessly tied back with a scarf whose color, that evening, matched the flowers on my dress.

For all our differences, the conversation was amiable enough, the reminiscences pleasant. Then Julienne and Nils arrived, and suddenly the room hummed with the antagonism that flowed between them. Jason shook hands with Nils, who towered over him. Nils is six three, while Jason is what I consider a perfect height, five seven. He sometimes teases that I chose him because his height gave me an excuse to eschew big hair and high heels, and I'd be the first to admit that such considerations certainly increased his husband-desirability quotient during our courtship. High heels, in my opinion, were designed by males to hobble females who might desire to flee. Nils still had that Nordic blond hair, although thinner than it once was, and the Viking chin and body had softened with the years. He now seemed somewhat indecisive and sulky, while Julienne was as vivacious as ever.

She kissed Jason on the cheek and said, "How are you, you handsome thing?" to which Jason replied, "Never as gorgeous as you, Julienne." Nils scowled at them.

Then Julienne turned to me, breaking into infectious laughter and hugging me. "You look wonderful, Caro!" she exclaimed. "I'll bet if we took a vote, everyone would agree that you're the youngest-looking person here."

"I *am* the youngest person here," I replied, "even younger than you by a month and a half."

"Oh well, rub it in," said Julienne. She was wearing a dress that I'd never have dared to buy: bright red, sheer floating fabric, with one bared shoulder, one covered with a short, flared sleeve, and a low-cut, crisscross bodice with a full, layered skirt falling in an uneven handkerchief hem that flirted with her knees.

"You look gorgeous, Julienne," I said admiringly. "What a wonderful dress."

"Just what any high-priced call girl would wear for a special customer," muttered Nils.

I couldn't believe my ears and didn't know what to say. Julienne, however, said quite clearly, "Screw you, Nils."

Then she turned back to me, as if her husband had never made that ungentlemanly remark, and said, "I hope you're ready for the grand tour of New Orleans, Caro. First, we're going to meet every single morning for chicory coffee and beignets at Café du Monde."

"Wonderful!" I agreed, imagining the taste of delicious, deep-fried donut squares dusted with powdered sugar, a New Orleans delicacy about which I'd read but had never experienced.

"And we're going to the voodoo museum. You don't want to miss that."
"I don't?"

"You don't. And the swamp. We have to take a swamp tour, and don't give me that dubious look, Caro. You'll be perfectly safe. Daddy and Philippe and I went fishing in the swamp lots of times."

Philippe was Julienne's older brother, who had, as older brothers are wont to do, pretty much ignored the two of us. I couldn't imagine the oh-so-serious Philippe fishing in a swamp with his little sister. Still, I didn't want to seem a complete coward. If Julienne could brave the swamp when she was just a tyke, surely I could face it on a tourist boat in her company. "All right," I agreed. "We'll visit the swamp."

"And the French Market and Lafitte's Bar and the tacky clubs on Bourbon Street. You haven't lived until you've seen the tassel twirlers."

She was bubbling with laughter, and I had to wonder what a tassel twirler was.

"I'm sure, my dear wife, your department chair will appreciate your skipping sessions to watch a bunch of overage strippers," said Nils sarcastically.

"And if no one else tells him, you will? Is that your plan, Nils?" she retorted. Nils flushed with anger while Julienne turned her back on him. "And Le Bistro for crème brûlée. That's a must, Caro. You and Jason and I can go for dinner one night. It's at Maison de Ville on Toulouse, very romantic. We won't invite Nils since he's being such a shit." She sent him an angry look.

"Crème brûlée sounds good," I agreed in a weak voice. Marital discord in public places always makes me uneasy.

"Miranda! Lester!" Julienne hugged Miranda and patted the stolid Lester on the cheek. Jason, ever the diplomat and always ready to move the conversation into areas scientific, said to Nils, "If you don't mind my picking your brain, old friend, I have a couple of projects that need input from a mathematician."

"Why not," Nils replied. He picked up a flute of champagne from the tray a waiter was passing and tossed down half. "Ask away," he said. "It's common knowledge that chemists don't know dick about math."

I was about to pass him the alligator puffs, but since he'd insulted both my husband and my best friend, I passed them to Lester, who had two, probably to make up for the fact that he'd refused alcohol. When Miranda explained that he was now in AA, Lester didn't look particularly pleased to be exposed as a reformed drunk. For a moment, I was afraid that they might embark on a quarrel, too, but Carlene McAvee breezed in at that moment with Broder plodding behind, looking anxious; no change there.

What a surprise Carlene was: very California, with long, frizzy gray hair and a gauze skirt topped by a shirt that looked to have been made by Southwestern Indians who favor the colors black and turquoise. She radiated enthusiasm. Broder wore a black suit and looked like the Calvinist theologian he was: serious, responsible, and weighted down with the consciousness of a sinful world. His hair had receded, his middle thickened, and the creases deepened between his eyebrows.

Miranda was saying, "Lester Junior has his degree in law. Now he's going for a doctorate in chemistry."

"Trying to please you both?" asked Julienne.

Miranda ignored the question and continued with evident satisfaction, "Do you have any idea how much money he's going to make over a lifetime with those two degrees? Millions!"

Carlene laughed. "I'll bet Broder and I haven't produced a millionaire in the bunch."

"What *are* your brood doing, Carlene?" Miranda asked. "If anyone had told me you'd have four children, and a full-time job, well, I—"

"Nothing to it," said Carlene. "I've got energy to spare. Everyone pitches in on the boring domestic stuff, Broder keeps us all virtuous and out of jail, and I make the money and do the childbearing." She linked her arm through her husband's and squeezed affectionately. "Broder's a daddy in a million. Our oldest girl is in seminary."

Lester looked astonished. "I'm not sure I approve of women pastors."

"What are the rest of them doing, Carlene?" Julienne asked, laughing. "Any other shocking career choices?"

"The eldest boy is in a Central American jungle doing a post doc in archaeology, and the two younger kids are studying microbiology. How far along are they, love?" she asked her husband. "Do I have to get them jobs yet?"

"Jason, what about your two?" Miranda asked, turning to us.

"Undergraduates," he replied. "Gwen in drama, Chris in chemistry."

"Drama!" Miranda exclaimed. "Good lord, you'd better hope she finds a wage-earning husband, or you'll be supporting her for the rest of her life."

I felt rather resentful on Gwen's behalf. "She's already supporting herself, Miranda, and she's only a freshman," I said.

Jason nodded. "Gwen never ceases to amaze us. She talked someone last summer into giving her a job computer programming. She's been a trigonometry tutor and a—what else, Caro?"

"Well, she directed a children's theater and served as an assistant to a muralist working in a downtown bank. She's very talented." I suppose, as a proud mother, I can be forgiven for bragging a bit.

"Takes after my mother in her politics," Jason added. "If she'd gone to school in the sixties, she'd have been out burning her bras."

Jason's mother is a feminist critic and professor of women's studies at the University of Chicago. She finds me a most disappointing daughter-in-law. But Jason is wrong about Gwen and bra-burning. My daughter isn't loath to trade on her beauty, and she wouldn't think of going without a bra.

"You've got a child don't you, Julienne?" said Broder.

"And only one," Nils muttered.

"Diane," Julienne replied, ignoring him. "She's in prep school in New Hampshire and doing very well."

"Since her mother can't be bothered to keep her at home," said Nils.

"Oh?" retorted Julie combatively. "You want to put a sensitive, intelligent girl into the public schools?"

"Since we took her on—and God knows where she came from." Nils turned to the group at large, ignoring his wife. "Julie simply arrived with this baby one day and said she was going to adopt it."

Julienne whirled on him in a flurry of red skirts, and I knew that trouble was imminent. "Well, you *did* want a child, Nils," she snapped.

"Of our own," he retorted.

"Of course. The child-of-my-loins syndrome. If you were so set on begetting your own—" Her voice dripped with sarcasm. "—maybe you should have gone to a doctor to find out why we weren't having any."

"The problem was that you've always been more interested in career than family, Julie. That's the problem." His eyes, usually so blue, seemed to bleach with malice.

"Nils, you wouldn't know a problem if it bit you on the ass," she sneered. "The fact is, you don't want to hear about problems unless they're your own."

"Case in point," he persisted as if she hadn't spoken, "you can't be bothered to keep Diane at home with us. You—"

"That does it, Nils." Julie slammed her champagne glass down on the dinner table, splashing golden bubbles across an unoffending white linen napkin. "I've heard just about as many of your complaints as I can stomach." With red skirts whirling again, she announced that she was going to the ladies' room and stalked out.

Conversation was somewhat stilted after her exit, and Nils said nothing. He was busy sulking over by the French doors.

3

For Lack of Seafood Gumbo

Gumbo tells, in its ingredients, the tale of the many national groups that immigrated to New Orleans and influenced the city's cuisine. With the original French settlers (from aristocrats and soldiers to prostitutes and transported felons) came the recipe for roux, the necessary first step in the making of gumbo. The soup is thickened with filé (powdered sassafras leaves introduced to the colony by the Indians) or okra, the seeds of which arrived in the New World in the hair and ears of slaves from Africa. The Spanish, who ruled for a short time and imposed their most lasting influence on the architecture of the Vieux Carre, provided the spice of peppers. Acadians (Cajuns), who were driven from Nova Scotia by the British, make the andouille sausage found in many gumbos, and Croatians farm the oysters, while the whole, whatever its ingredients, is served over rice grown in Louisiana fields by Chinese settlers.

The gumbo at Etienne's in New Orleans is everything a good gumbo should be—with a thick, flavorful stock and enough rice and seafood to make it less a soup than a stew or dish with sauce. If you know a restaurant in your hometown that serves tasty gumbo, patronize it. Otherwise, it might go out of business and someone might suggest that you make the gumbo yourself. Only a professional paid to do so should have to attempt the difficult and time-consuming task of making the roux that is the basis of a good gumbo.

Carolyn Blue, *Eating Out in the Big Easy*

The alligator puffs disappeared as everyone pretended not to notice that Julienne had failed to return. Then, while waiting for the presentation of the gumbo (the gumbo that had dictated the choice of restaurant, recipe of the chef chosen by the very lady who was missing), I set off to find the rest room and retrieve my friend. If she couldn't face sitting beside her husband, I'd simply change the place cards and move him to the other end of the table. Let Jason put up with him.

But Julienne was not in the ladies' room. After calling her name several times without receiving a response, I peeked under the only closed door in case she was proving to be as sulky as her husband; Nils hadn't said a word to anyone since she left the dining room. The door under which I peeked—and I just bent down to take a look at the shoes—burst open, nearly knocking me over, and an irate lady in flowered lavender silk stalked out and demanded to know what sort of pervert I was.

"I'm looking for a friend," I stammered.

"We in N'Awlins know all about folks who want to make friends with strangahs in public toilets," she retorted disdainfully, bringing home to me how much different indignation sounded in a Southern drawl than in, say, the crisper accents of the Middle West.

"I only wanted to look at your shoes," I responded.

"Mah shoes! Well, Ah nevah! Ah'm goin' to report you to the maître d'." She had been vigorously washing her hands during the conversation and left after making that threat, which, I have to admit, kept me from searching further for Julienne. Instead, I crept back to the dinner, where seven of us sat down to seafood gumbo.

"She wasn't in the ladies'," I whispered to Jason before I took my seat at the other end of the table.

Unfortunately, Nils heard me and said, "That's typical of Julie—inconsiderate to a fault."

He sounded so self-satisfied that I switched his card with Broder's so that I wouldn't have to sit beside him and neither would Julienne when she returned, which she would. I *knew* that she'd never miss the gumbo. Maybe she was making a phone call, perhaps reserving her own room. The Magnussens were staying at the same hotel in the French Quarter where we had reservations, although we hadn't seen them during the afternoon.

As the waiter distributed our bowls, Broder told me how worried he was about his youngest children, who were away at university, no doubt being chased by drug dealers and receiving sexual overtures from lechers with communicable diseases. Poor Broder! He's a dear, but he does fret about sin. I gave him a weak smile and looked down at my gumbo. Where were the crab claws, the sausage, the shrimp, and the oysters? And what were those chopped, hard-boiled eggs doing on top? I frowned, sniffed, then tasted. "Waiter!" I called. "What is this?"

"It's the turtle soup, ma'am."

"What turtle soup?"

"Well, actually, ma'am, Ah believe the chef used alligator insteada turtle, but that's by way of bein' a N'Awlins tradition, an' Ah know you're gonna find it's the best turtle—well, alligator—soup you ever did eat. Etienne is famous fo' his—"

Jason was chuckling and leaned forward to say, "Well, we *have* been calling this the alligator dinner, Caro, but I never realized you were *this* fond of reptile meat."

"I ordered gumbo," I informed the waiter. "My friend insisted on this restaurant because of Etienne's reputation for wonderful gumbo."

"Since the friend who insisted didn't even bother to show up for the course," said Nils, "it doesn't much matter, does it?" He looked smug while he ate his soup as rapidly as possible, no doubt in order to prevent me from having it removed.

"Etienne, he's even mo' famous fo' his turtle soup," said the waiter, who was clasping a tray in a white-knuckled grasp.

"But turtle soup is not what I ordered, and this is not, by your own admission, turtle soup. I want to see the chef."

"For heaven's sake, Carolyn," said Miranda. "This is delicious. Don't make such a fuss."

I gave the waiter what I hoped was a suitably steely and commanding glance, and he was soon back with Etienne himself, a short, round man, wearing a ludicrously tall chef's hat and glaring majestically.

"Madame does not like my famous soup?" he demanded.

"Madame ordered gumbo, as you very well know."

He looked blank for a minute, then slapped his forehead with the palm of his hand. "But of course, Mme. Julienne, who loves my gumbo. How could this mistake have taken place? Discipline shall be meted out to where it is deserved. *Bien?* You will eat my ambrosial turtle soup—"

"Alligator," I reminded him.

He glared at the waiter. "Turtle, alligator. It makes no difference."

"Broder, doesn't the Bible have prohibitions against eating alligators?" asked Carlene, eyes twinkling.

Broder looked thoughtful and admitted that there was a prohibition against eating crawling things, snakes for instance, and alligators might be included, although they did have feet. On the other hand, such dietary restrictions were practiced by Jews, not Christians, and in fact, he thought crocodiles were native to the Middle East, not alligators, so alligators wouldn't have come up, as such, in the Bible.

"Madame will accept my most profound apologies," Etienne ordered, although Broder was still talking about dietary laws, "and enjoy her turtle soup, and tomorrow I will send to her hotel a container of my excellent gumbo. And one for Mme. Julienne as well." He bowed and left before I could protest.

Well, what could I do? I ate the soup, and it was indeed delicious, flavored with sherry, chicken stock, herbs, chopped vegetables, and the meat. (I later discovered that not only could turtle meat be replaced by alligator but by ground veal, as well.) In fact, the next day when I returned from the less-than-exciting refreshments at the American Chemical Society welcome mixer, Etienne's gumbo awaited me, and it was as wonderful as Julienne had promised: spicy, rich, thick, and loaded with delectable crustaceans caught locally. I amused myself while eating it by imagining Etienne himself, chef's hat askew, apron bespattered, scrambling down some muddy bank to harvest crabs.

As the soup bowls were being cleared away and new wine poured, I excused myself to go in search of my friend, but before I could get out of the room, Nils said, "If you're still looking for Julie, maybe you should try locating her hot-blooded Italian stereochemist."

That comment stopped the conversation cold until Lester tried to break the uncomfortable silence by saying, "Wonderful soup, whatever they put in it. Are there seconds?"

"Certainly, sir," said the waiter, who had been in the act of removing Lester's bowl and was obviously relieved that the restaurant's mistake was not causing table-wide anger and thus promising a substantial diminution of his tip.

"Lester, you don't need seconds," snapped his wife.

"Well, what's next, Caro?" Jason asked with an eagerness that was unlike him on any subject other than scientific research.

"Avocado-stuffed shrimp remoulade," I replied and escaped, wondering if Julienne could have discovered when she left for the ladies' room that gumbo was not to be served, upon which discovery she left the restaurant entirely. But it wasn't my fault the wrong soup had been served, so if she left, it was because of her husband or because something dreadful had happened to her.

I checked the ladies' room again and found two women sitting on poufy, low-backed, wire-legged chairs. The ladies were renewing their makeup in front of gilded Cupid mirrors. One other woman stood at the marble sinks, but the stall doors were open, and Julienne was not there. Through a window covered with stirring rose silk drapes, I could hear the rain and studied the window as if my childhood friend might have pulled over a chair and crawled out into an alley. But that was a ridiculous idea. For one thing, anyone who tried to stand on one of those silly little seats would have been tipped onto the floor with resulting bruises.

And if Julienne had wanted to leave, she could have walked out the front door. In fact, and although our hotel was only a four-block walk through the Quarter, she would have called a cab rather than exposing her lovely dress to the rain.

Unless she called the mysterious Italian stereochemist, a little voice whispered in my head. Then the Carolyn who had grown up with Julienne and shared adolescent secrets rejected that disloyal notion, and I went out to question the restaurant staff.

But first I noticed that the hall leading to the rest rooms had a door at the end. What if someone had kidnapped her in the hall and dragged her out through that door? I hurried down to try it and found the door locked. But the abductors might have had a key. *Oh nonsense, Carolyn,* I told myself. *Don't be so melodramatic! She's probably in the bar having a drink, making a new friend, and paying Nils back for being such a pill.* I checked the bar, which was very crowded but harbored no one with curly black hair and a stunning red dress.

Next I tried the maître d'. Was it my imagination, or did he look at me peculiarly? Surely that obnoxious Southern belle in lavender hadn't reported me to him as the lesbian shoe fetishist in the ladies' room. In reply to my query, he said that he had seen Julienne come in with a tall, blond man, but he had not seen her leave, alone or accompanied.

"I'm afraid something terrible has happened to her," I cried, allowing melodrama to overcome me once more.

"Nothing terrible happens to the customers at Etienne's," he assured me in a heavy, if unconvincing, French accent. "Only the most delightful of culinary experiences. Is madam not happy with the meal thus far?"

"Aside from the fact that you served the wrong soup," I replied, "the dinner has been tasty."

Evidently he had expected more enthusiasm, for he eyed me with all the approval he might reserve for a fly discovered in the crème brûlée, a dessert I would have preferred to the bread pudding I'd been coerced into ordering. If Julienne didn't show up for the bread pudding, I'd never forgive her. Unless she had no choice in the matter. "The door at the end of the rest room hall—where does it go?" I asked urgently, once more picturing my friend being shanghaied by swarthy men in evening clothes.

"Outside, madam," he replied, "but she could not have escaped your dinner party in that manner, for the door is locked, and I have the only key."

I went on to the tuxedoed person who presided at a too-precious antique desk, dispensing haughty condescension to those who had come in off the street without a reservation, perhaps not even suitably dressed. I wondered how my friends had been treated when they arrived—Miranda in her business suit (of course, at $350 an hour, she could condescend with the best of them) and Carlene in her California hippie outfit. But then Carlene wouldn't have noticed any but the most blatant snub, say, if the gatekeeper at the desk had refused to let her in.

He, too, remembered Julienne's entrance but assured me that she had not departed past his station, nor had she ordered a cab. "No one has yet ordered a cab, madam," he asserted. "Who would eat at such an unfashionable hour as to be finished with dinner already?"

What could I say to such an incontrovertible piece of logic? I stopped a few waiters and busboys passing between the kitchens and the main dining areas, but no one had seen Julienne, and I had to return to my avocado-stuffed shrimp remoulade. Incidentally, it was superb, the avocados soft and buttery, the shrimp firm, plump, and shrimpy, and the remoulade—ah, it was perfect.

But before I sat down under the disgruntled eyes of the waiter, who wanted to clear that course and serve the crayfish Etienne, I leaned down and murmured to Nils, "I'm really terribly worried. Perhaps you should call the hotel to see if she's safely back."

"Nonsense," Nils retorted testily. "She's fine. Just willful."

Broder didn't help my state of mind when I finally sat down to my second course. Having finished his own avocado, he regaled me with stories about the white-slave trade in New Orleans, the corruption of the police, and various murder and drug-dealing statistics. I was so panic-stricken by the time I had swallowed my last delicious shrimp that I nodded to the waiter to serve the main course and rushed out to call the hotel myself.

Julienne didn't answer.

Carol Lee's Avocado Stuffed Shrimp Remoulade

Combine in a small bowl ¼ cup tarragon vinegar, 2 tbs. horseradish mustard, 1 tbs. catsup, 1½ tsp. paprika, ½ tsp. salt, ¼ tsp. cayenne pepper.

Slowly add ¼ cup salad oil, beating constantly.

Stir in ¼ cup ea. minced celery and minced green onions with tops.

Pour sauce over 2 lbs. cleaned, cooked, shelled shrimp and marinate in refrigerator 4 to 5 hours.

Halve and peel 4 medium avocados.

Lift shrimp from sauce and arrange 4 or 5 in each avocado half.

Serve and pass leftover remoulade sauce.

4
Crawfish Etienne

Crawfish. Not the most pleasant-sounding word for something so tasty, but the natives of Louisiana object to the more inviting *crayfish.* In fact, a popular local name for the crustacean in question is *mudbug,* while I myself prefer *minilobster.* New Orleans mythology tells us that the crawfish is a lobster that walked all the way from its native Maine and arrived in Louisiana seriously diminished in size, a cautionary lesson to dieters: eat crawfish, which are low in calories, and walk a lot. However, if your cholesterol is high, eat oysters. They have fewer calories and one-third the artery cloggers.

Whatever you call its main ingredient, crawfish Etienne is not a dish you can make at home. I did try, but the recipe is the secret of Etienne, the talented New Orleans chef, and I didn't come close to imitating his culinary triumph, even though I shelled all those miserable minilobsters. Actually, they're delicious, but essentially only one bite per creature. Consequently, you have to feel sorry for the poor, no doubt underpaid, serf in the kitchen at Etienne's who cooks and then cracks open hundreds of shells in order to produce all the delicious crustacean bits. The bits are then bathed in a glorious cream and wine sauce enhanced by mystery herbs. Even the direst circumstances are mitigated by the consumption of crawfish Etienne.

Carolyn Blue, *Eating Out In the Big Easy*

Isn't crayfish a peasant food?" asked Miranda, who had moved over to talk to me, filling the seat that Julienne would have occupied had she not disappeared. "I always thought they were something that swamp dwellers, the sort who marry their cousins, fish out of the muck and eat."

"Viva la swamp!" I said, having had quite a few glasses of wine in an effort to drown my worries about my missing friend. I picked up my pen and scribbled more notes, dutifully keeping in mind that I had been paid to write a book about food in New Orleans.

I noticed that Miranda was eating her way steadily through the *peasant food* on her plate. Maybe I should have sicced Etienne on her. It was hard to believe she'd once been a rather radical protestor with waist-length hair and beads—until she'd been arrested and was so horrified by the inadequate hygiene facilities at the jail that she never joined another protest. Somehow or other, her father, a prominent Cincinnati lawyer, managed to get her out of jail without her presence becoming part of the public record.

Having learned her lesson (she was always a good student), Miranda immediately changed to prelaw, went on to law school, and look at her now. She's a Republican!

"At least you're finally working," she said. "How could you stand staying home all those years?"

"I enjoyed it," I replied defensively. "I really don't see why we stay-at-home wives and mothers should have to apologize."

"You enjoyed staying home?" Miranda rolled her eyes. "I'd have felt selfish. I mean, *one* income? And a college professor's at that?"

"Nothing wrong with my income," Jason called from the other end of the table. "The kids and I are the lucky ones, having Carolyn at home." He gave me a very sexy smile, which I returned. Jason really is a love.

"Hear! Hear!" muttered Nils. "Every man should be so lucky."

"Well, I call it financially feckless," continued Miranda. "Because I make a lot of money, Lester can afford to indulge himself in all sorts of esoteric research and administrative skullduggery, and we're still very comfortable financially."

I was beginning to feel a bit beleaguered, although I couldn't see that my staying home had thrown us into poverty. Still, if the children hadn't been so smart and received scholarships . . .

"Oh, knock it off, Miranda," said Carlene. "I think women should get to stay home if they want to. I mean, kids are fun! I wouldn't have minded mothering a couple more, but I just didn't have time for more pregnancies."

Lester looked horrified. "You'd have wanted *six* children? Or eight?"

"Why not?" replied Carlene. "As long as they do their own ironing, the more the merrier."

"They are a responsibility, however," said Broder. "In this world, one thinks twice about having children. And we certainly couldn't have afforded those we have if Carlene hadn't been working. Theology professors are not well remunerated."

Carlene giggled. "Now Broder, when did you ever *think twice?* Unless it was after conception."

Broder turned red. I had to put my hand over my mouth to hide a smile. I wouldn't embarrass him for the world, but the idea of a hot-blooded Broder begetting children with abandon was amusing.

"I suppose your move to El Paso had something to do with your sudden need to become a working woman," said Miranda, evidently miffed because others, even the very successful Carlene, had supported my right to stay home. "Why in the world would you take a job in El Paso, Jason?" She looked at my husband with a mixture of horror and pity. "Some trouble with your previous position? Goodness, you'd been there for *years.*"

"Toxicity," said Jason, looking energized at very thought of a favorite subject. "I was offered a chaired professorship in the chemistry of environmental toxicology. With a mandate to found an institute."

"But in *El Paso?*"

"Where better?" Jason replied. "The toxins in the air, soil, and water are a researcher's dream."

"Still, old man," Lester chimed in smugly, "it is a step down from your old position."

"My research group at this point numbers over thirty," said Jason mildly.

Lester frowned; Miranda added, "But it must be a cultural wasteland. How can you stand it, Carolyn?"

"We have a very presentable symphony, a good opera company, and even a local ballet," I replied defensively. Initially, I had been quite reluctant to leave all my friends and associations when Jason announced this marvelous opportunity that had been offered to him, out of the blue as it were. And the children had been furious. Especially our daughter, who had just been accepted to college. She threatened to stay in her dormitory during all vacations if she had to come home to El Paso. Not that I intended to admit any of these problems to Miranda. "And I do have a maid," I added slyly.

"A maid?" the women breathed.

"In fact, our house has a maid's room and bath."

"A *live-in* maid?" Miranda's mouth dropped open.

"Actually, she lives in her own house," I murmured, "but she has a car. I don't have to pick her up or even pay transportation, and her wages are very reasonable." I didn't mention that Ippolita speaks Spanish and I don't, that we communicate through a Spanish phrase book, and that the book doesn't include the phrase, "The vacuum cleaner is on fire; maybe you should turn it off." Ippolita only understands the instructions I find in the book when it suits her to understand. In fact, she does pretty much as she likes, although she does get the house cleaned. Needless to say, the vacuum cleaner repairman considers me his best customer.

"Well, I still think—" Miranda began.

Broder cleared his throat and interrupted diplomatically, "The owner at our bed and breakfast recommended a gospel brunch that occurs tomorrow in the warehouse district. She says it's very colorful—a black choir and leader, ethnic food. It's rather expensive, unfortunately, but—"

"—but we can afford it," said Carlene. "We heard that the audience is dancing in the aisles by the time it's over. So why don't we all meet there at quarter to eleven? We don't have to register at the convention center until late afternoon. Then there's the reception at the aquarium afterward."

"Complete with cheap wine, American beer, and dubious canapés," said Miranda. "Unless you attend a conference abroad, you never get a decent thing to eat at a meeting of chemists, present company excluded."

"Well, whatever they serve, it will take care of dinner," said Carlene, ever practical for all her offbeat wardrobe. Maybe she only wore things like that when she was away from home, or always wore them because they were inexpensive.

"Sounds fascinating," said Jason.

I was signaling the waiter to clear the table and produce the dreaded bread pudding.

"Nils, be sure to tell Julienne about the gospel brunch," Carlene added. "She'll love it."

"And remind her to bring her camera," said Miranda. "She promised to send pictures to all of us, and now we have none of our reunion."

"Maybe we should try to call her again," Broder suggested, digging enthusiastically into his bread pudding. "She must be back at the hotel by now."

I hope so, I thought nervously.

"As I suggested, you might have better luck calling her favorite colleague, Linus Torelli," said Nils.

"Linus?" Lester looked interested. "Was he named after Linus Pauling?"

"He's young enough to have been," Nils snarled.

"Oh, knock it off, Magnussen," said Carlene angrily. "If you'd work a little harder yourself, maybe you wouldn't have to be jealous of your wife."

"What's that supposed to mean?" Nils demanded.

"Why, that when we were all in school together, you were the fair-haired boy," Carlene replied crisply. "Now it's Julienne who's the star."

Nils stood up, knocking his chair over, dropped his napkin on top of his bread pudding, and stalked out.

I sighed, foreseeing an acrimonious divorce in the future of my dear friend Julienne. It's so sad to see a marriage end, especially a marriage that was once marked by great love; but obviously, in this case, a fragile male ego had overridden a warm female heart. I didn't for a minute believe that Julienne had been unfaithful to her husband. Nils was simply substituting sexual jealousy for professional jealousy because the latter made him look small-minded and exposed his own inadequacies while the former placed the onus on Julienne.

One has to wonder how many modern marriages break up on the rocks of professional competition. Had I become a famous medieval scholar instead of a mom, would Jason have come to resent me? Probably not, I decided. In the first place, Jason isn't like that. In the second, he considers the study of the Middle Ages more in the nature of an indulgence, while the study of chemistry is serious business.

Feeling better, at least about my own marriage, I took a bite of the bread pudding. Oh my. This was not like any bread pudding Mother used to make. In fact, it was a sort of bananas Foster, which I love, plus bread pudding, plus whipped cream. Bathed in a delicious banana-rum sauce, even bread pudding can send a shiver of culinary delight up the spine. I ate every bite, as, I noticed, did all the others, except the bad-tempered and absent Nils. Lester confiscated and ate Nils's serving when Miranda wasn't looking. Would the rum sauce knock him off the wagon? Maybe not. He didn't drain Nils's goblet of dessert wine.

"Wonderful dinner, Carolyn," said Lester, looking as if he'd like to mop up the sauce left on Nils's plate. He was the first to break the uncomfortable silence that followed the angry departure of a second Magnussen.

"Anyone care for a brandy?" Jason asked.

I placed my fork properly on my empty dessert plate and slipped away to call Julienne's hotel room again. Her telephone rang uselessly and ominously in my ear. I could only hope that she was in the room but refusing to answer, anticipating the caller to be her husband.

When I returned, the five remaining diners were preparing to disperse after the expected compliments to me on the menu and an exchange of directions to the gospel brunch. Then Jason exercised his preference for walking in the rain—actually, he would have preferred to jog, but I demurred—and we shared his giant, black umbrella during the four-block walk to the Hotel de la Poste. I don't think we've used that umbrella since we moved to arid El Paso, but Jason, always foresighted, thought to find and pack it.

The trip home was very pleasant as the sidewalks were neither so crowded as to be troublesome nor so deserted as to make us uneasy. My moisture-deprived skin was sucking in the precipitation as we passed under streetlights that glistened on wet pavement. Even the sounds of revelry seemed muted in the fine rain. Or perhaps the visitors were just quieter; I didn't notice as many go cups in festive hands. But then why buy a drink to go when raindrops would quickly water it down?

The hotel glowed warmth into the wet darkness as we approached on Chartres Street. Three flags, of which I recognized only that of the United States, dripped from poles that slanted out above the cream columns in front. What were the others? French and Spanish? Louisiana and New Orleans? I'd have to ask. At my insistence, we turned left into the small lobby with its antiques and its somnolent desk clerk to ask after Julienne.

"Haven't seen a lady in a red dress pass by," he answered. "Sure didn't notice one comin' in here. You all want me to buzz her room?"

I thought of Nils, with his disgruntled attitude toward Julienne. He would take such a call amiss. Therefore, I shook my head unhappily, and Jason and I went off to bed. Our lights were out within fifteen minutes. Inspired by our exotic surroundings, we had had a romantic interlude that afternoon, which sufficed for our first day in New Orleans.

Banana Bread Pudding with Banana-Rum Sauce and Whipped Cream

I will never again speak slightingly of bread pudding after having it in New Orleans. What a treat! The following recipe is actually that of Chef Frank Brigtsen but produces results close to the marvelous dessert I had at Etienne's. Try it if you are long on time and desire a wonderful final course to some special meal.

Preheat the oven to 300° F.

Put *6 cups bite-sized pieces of day-old French bread* in a 9 x 12 x 2-in. baking pan and set aside.

In a blender or food processor, blend *3 large eggs, 3 cups milk, ⅔ cup sugar, 2 large very ripe bananas, 1 tbs. ground cinnamon, ¼ tsp. ground nutmeg, ½ tsp. vanilla extract* until smooth.

Pour mixture over French bread pieces; fold in *½ cup ea. seedless raisins* and *roasted pecans* and let mixture set for 20 minutes.

Top with *3 tbs. unsalted butter* cut in small pieces.

Cover pudding with aluminum foil and place pan into larger pan. Add warm water to depth of 1" in larger pan. Bake 1 hour. Remove foil and bake uncovered for 15 minutes or until set.

In a deep, medium bowl, whisk *¾ cup heavy whipping cream* just until it begins to thicken. Add *1 tbs. sugar* and *¼ tsp. vanilla*. Continue whisking until soft peaks form. Cover and chill.

SAUCE:
Heat a large sauté pan over low heat. Add *⅔ cup unsalted butter* at room temperature, *½ cup packed light brown sugar, 6 large ripe bananas quartered, 1 tsp. ground cinnamon,* and *¼ tsp. ground nutmeg.*

Moving skillet back and forth, cook until butter and sugar become creamy and bananas begin to soften, about 1 minute.

Remove skillet from heat and add *3 tbs. dark rum* and *2 tbs. banana liqueur* (optional). Return pan to heat, tilt, avert face, light liquid with long match, and shake skillet until flames subside. Add *½ tsp. vanilla, remove from heat, and keep warm.*

SERVE:
Place a large scoop of bread pudding in the middle of each plate or bowl.

Place 2 slices of banana on each plate and top with about 3 tbs. of sauce.

Spoon whipped cream over pudding and serve immediately.

SERVES 12.

Carolyn Blue, *Eating Out in the Big Easy*

5
Soul Food

On Sunday morning, while Jason went to buy a newspaper, I called the Magnussens' room in search of Julienne. No answer. Surely Nils hadn't disappeared as well. This was not the reunion of old friends I had looked forward to. Worried and tired after a restless night, I began the slow process of getting dressed for the gospel-brunch excursion planned the night before. Did one dress up as for a church service or opt for casual clothing like the tourists who were already crowding the streets below my window?

Some were even carrying go cups and sipping liquor at ten A.M. This was the Big Easy indeed, and I wasn't sure I approved of street drinking, especially on Sunday morning. Had he known what I was thinking, Jason would have laughed and remarked on the vestiges of a Protestant Midwest background that clung to my psyche like crumbs of Styrofoam to a wool dress.

I chose casual and pulled on beige slacks and a brown turtleneck sweater with a bit of gold jewelry and an autumnal print scarf to tie my hair back. Before I could complete my toilette, a stocky black woman with powerful arms and a gold tooth that winked at me from an amiable smile knocked at my door and entered the room.

Black? Or African-American? I seem to have lost track of which is currently the politically correct designation. Before the Civil War, *black* was the term used to refer to slaves in New Orleans, while free Negroes were *men and women of color*. Of course, *colored* would now be considered old-fashioned, if not downright insulting. It is, no doubt, a sign of encroaching middle age that I am behind the times on modern racial terminology but knowledgeable about the relevant linguistic history.

At any rate, the maid's accent was so Southern as to make me think I might need an electronic translator. One thing I can say for El Paso: the natives do not have Southern accents, although many have Hispanic accents, but those aren't at all hard to decipher, unless, of course, said native is actually speaking Spanish. Maybe I should get an electronic translator to aid in communication with Ippolita. Or maybe not. I have the suspicion that she can understand me perfectly in either language if she chooses to, but perhaps I do her an injustice or give myself more credit than I deserve in my use of the phrase book for communicating with my Hispanic housekeeper. And is *Hispanic* preferable to *Chicano* or *Mexican-American?* I have no idea.

"Please do stay," I said to the maid, hoping that I'd understood correctly her presumed offer to come back when we were gone if that would be more convenient. She began immediately on the bed while I brushed my hair back and tied the scarf. Was she responsible for the Magnussens' room as well? I wondered.

"Excuse me." I had finished fastening conservative gold button earrings to my ears. "Do you make up this whole floor?"

"Mostly, yes, ma'am." She finished the bed and headed for the bathroom with an armload of fresh towels.

I followed to stand in the doorway. "I have friends on this floor, the Magnussens."

"Miz Julienne you mean? An' her husband? Don' know his name. He didn' introduce hisself like dat nice Miz Julienne. Dem as had such a terrible fight yesterday afternoon. Cain't say as I blame her, not comin' home to da likes a him last night."

"She didn't sleep in her bed at all?" I asked, thoroughly alarmed. Then it occurred to me that the maid could hardly know that for certain. If the room had one king or queen-sized bed, they would have shared it, and Julienne might have fluffed her pillow up when she rose. If the room had separate beds, they were probably full or queen-sized, and they might have made up their differences and shared one. "You can't be sure of that," I pointed out anxiously.

"Oh, Ah be sure," said the maid. She stopped work and put both hands on ample hips. "One bed been slept in an' got his 'jamas layin' on de sheets. Other bed ain' even got de spread rumpled. An' dey be twin beds, only twin-bed room on da floor. Hafta ask fo' dem twin beds. Folks do dat don' wanna be sharin' a pilla. Course it ain' none a mah business." She went back to work, but I could see that the woman was beginning to regret having spoken so freely.

"Julienne's been my friend since we were little children," I hastened to explain. "I'm so worried—"

"Yo'all don' sound like you from N'Awlins," said the maid suspiciously. She had turned from cleaning the tub.

"I'm not. Julienne moved to Michigan when she was little."

"Po' chile," the woman commiserated. "Mus' be terrible cold up dere."

"Julienne shivered for three years," I agreed. "Even in the summer." How had we moved from Julienne's frightening disappearance to her childhood intolerance of Michigan weather? "I'm so terribly worried about her," I said to the maid, who was now swishing a brush around the toilet bowl. "She left the dinner party last night, and it seems that no one has seen her since."

"Well, likely she run off, or he done sumpthin' to her. He was a-yellin' so bad Ah couldn' hardly git no one to answer da door when Ah come to deliver dem extra towels Miz Julienne wanted fo' washin' her hair with."

Oh lord, I thought, more worried than ever; Nils and Julienne had been quarreling even before the dinner party. By the time the maid had finished the room and I had prepared to go out, Jason returned with a rumpled copy of the New Orleans *Times-Picayune* under his arm. He couldn't say enough about the delights of having a morning café au lait and a beignet at Café du Monde on Jackson Square. How could I have forgotten? Julienne had said last night that we would meet every morning for breakfast at Café du Monde, and I had missed the meeting.

"Did you see Julienne?" I asked.

" 'Fraid not," said Jason absently.

"Didn't you look for her?"

"Carolyn, why would I? She's probably just getting up. We are, after all, going out to brunch shortly."

"Then why were *you* eating breakfast?" I couldn't resist teasing my husband for having eaten immediately before our eleven-to-one seating at the Praline Connection.

"New Orleans is for stuffing oneself with the local cuisine," Jason replied. "Isn't that the gist of your book?"

I could hardly argue with his logic, but then I wasn't interested in logic; I was interested in the whereabouts of my missing friend. "Julienne didn't come back to the hotel last night."

Jason looked surprised. "Really? Then it would appear that the problems between her and Nils are serious," he said thoughtfully. Then he smiled. "But she'll show up. I imagine she's giving Nils something to worry about, and I must say, he was pretty unpleasant to her last night."

"He was beastly," I agreed furiously. "I'll never forgive him for the things he said and for driving her away. I just hope she's safe."

"Now, Caro. Of course she's safe. She's probably staying with friends or relatives in New Orleans."

Was she? I don't remember her mentioning friends or relatives here, not since her great aunt died several years ago. Julienne and her brother Philippe had come down for the funeral of Beatrice Delacroix, a jazz funeral, which Julienne arranged, over the objections of her brother, and later described in detail to me, along with the cemetery in which her aunt was interred. She had said I'd have to see it. Did she still want to go? I'm not a devotee of cemeteries, although they can be a useful tool for historic research.

I rushed Jason out before he could suggest that we call the Magnussens' room and meet Nils in the lobby. I was so irritated with Julienne's husband that I didn't care to walk however many blocks with him.

Jason obtained a map from the front desk showing the route from Hotel de la Poste to the Praline Connection. How glad I was that I never wear heels; it looked to be a good distance and proved to be worse than I expected. We turned left and walked several blocks on Chartres to Canal, where we turned left again and walked two and a half very long blocks to the confusing five-way intersection that led us to South Peters and the

Warehouse District, where the blocks were even longer. The area gave me an eerie feeling. Once we had left the bustle of the French Quarter, we passed one featureless warehouse after another and in a neighborhood where few people were on the streets. Under gray skies, heavy with the threat of impending rain, I found myself glancing apprehensively into alleys and down cross streets, as if some threat lurked there.

Unable to secure a cab, had Julienne been snatched off the street as she walked home through the rain to the hotel? I shuddered to think of how terrified she must have been, perhaps calling for help and ignored by hurrying passersby, or unable to call out because a dirty hand was clamped over her mouth. Or had her abductors used an ether-soaked rag so that they could drag her, unconscious, into a waiting car?

As my imagination ran amok, I clutched my husband's arm in a death grip, but Jason only glanced at me, briefly puzzled, and patted my hand. He seemed immune to my low spirits. Having met, at the Café du Monde, a fellow scientist whose conversation had lured him away from the sports page of the newspaper, Jason was intent on telling me about an exciting new compound the fellow had synthesized and planned to talk about at the ACS meeting.

"It's a dilemma," Jason confessed. "His paper and Julienne's are scheduled for the same hour on Wednesday."

"Julienne's missing," I reminded him gloomily.

"Believe me, Caro, she won't skip her own paper!" Jason laughed and, having previously disengaged my clutching hand, now took my arm as we crossed the last street and approached the Praline Connection. Miranda and Lester arrived at the same time but from a different direction. They were staying, as Miranda had pointed out last night, at an expensive, high-rise hotel on the riverfront, conveniently situated near the convention center. Personally, I preferred the exotic ambiance of the French Quarter. Why, if one had a choice, would one elect to stay elsewhere? Unless it was because the walk to the meeting would be shorter. When Jason pointed out that we were only a few blocks from the Ernest N. Morial Convention Center ("Dutch" Morial was the first black mayor of New Orleans), I realized what a long walk Jason would have every morning, possibly in the rain. The one umbrella we had brought was not going to suffice when we parted company in the morning.

While giving half an ear to Broder McAvee, who was seven or eight places behind us in the line and complaining audibly about the cost of admission, we paid for our tickets, then claimed a table for eight. Ours wasn't near the stage; those tables had already been taken, mostly by black women dressed as if for church, which made me somewhat embarrassed over my choice of casual, touristy clothes. We *were* near the soul-food buffet. I am, personally, unfamiliar with soul food, but I was prepared to write about it and even like it, although I had heard that collard greens are somewhat bitter. On the other hand, they are supposed to be very healthful. As it turned out, I found that I prefer spinach to collards in the dark-green, antioxidant-rich, healthful-vegetable category.

Oh, for the days when we knew less about the benefits, beyond simple sustenance, of the food we were eating. What would a medieval European peasant make of the advice that one should choose chicken and fish over red meat or suffer the cholesterol consequences? Since medieval peasants rarely had any meat in their diets, they would, no doubt, have been quite indifferent to any diet consideration other than the benefits of having a full stomach.

There was a second buffet with more ordinary offerings—bacon, eggs, sausage—but I decided that it was my duty as a newly minted food reviewer to sample and write about the more exotic, more regional cuisine. The food was just then being set out by platoons of young African-American waiters and waitresses, all wearing black hats that made them look as if they expected to desert the service industry and join jazz bands momentarily. Some of them frowned at me, probably thinking that I wanted to fill a plate before the lines were officially open. A third, and rather well hidden, buffet offered coffee, orange juice, and desserts: cake, pralines, peach cobbler. The room itself was very large with metal rafters in the dark loft space overhead and tiny white Christmas lights twinkling everywhere. It was also very noisy and becoming more so as it filled up.

During my investigations, Carlene and Broder joined the table, Broder still complaining, and as I sat down next to Jason, Nils straggled in, looking as sulky as ever.

"Where's Julienne?" Carlene demanded, even before he could take his chair. The unoccupied seat beside him reminded me, rather terrifyingly, of Banquo's empty chair at MacBeth's banquet.

"Gone," Nils snapped. "I haven't heard from her since she walked out last night."

Before I could quiz him further, the opening of the buffet tables was announced, and the throng in the cavernous warehouse stampeded toward the food. Miranda and Lester refused to try soul food; they opted for eggs and sausage, as did Nils. Jason had some of everything; my husband has a healthy appetite and an appreciation for whatever is put in front of him. When we order something particularly memorable during our travels, Jason will even join me in trying to reconcoct the dish in our own kitchen, although I suspect that he sees the effort as akin to a lab experiment.

Broder and Carlene accompanied me to the soul-food buffet, and we helped ourselves to red beans and rice, which was a traditional Monday dish in New Orleans, slow-cooked on the fire all day while the wife and/or servants did the weekly washing. At home I make a Caribbean recipe that includes not only rice and beans but green onions, salt pork, olives, and various other delicious ingredients. Although I prefer my own recipe, the Praline Connection served a tasty and, I suspect, lard-rich version. Best of all, I didn't have to spend my time cooking it.

Their barbecued beef proved so tender that it disintegrated between the teeth in a swirl of tangy sauce. The jambalaya was packed with chicken, ham, and sausage and left the flavors of thyme, garlic, and chili powder dancing on the tongue. The peppers were so lavishly stuffed that the filling squeezed from the ends and even burst from the side veins. Then there were the bitter greens: perhaps they are so popular with soul-food lovers because they cut the taste of grease, or perhaps some instinct for survival shows itself in the popularity of collards, which the body believes will chase plaque from the arteries and dread oxidants from the cells. Grits completed the menu.

I have had grits before and have never been a fan. I consider them even mere detestable than Cream of Wheat, which my mother served on freezing mornings to protect us from frostbite of the fingers and toes by warming us in advance from the stomach outward. Does that make sense? I never thought so. At Praline Connection I was tempted to seek out their chef and suggest a more interesting recipe. My next door neighbor at home, a seventy-five-year-old Hispanic matron whose husband's company built her house, my house, and hundreds of others, introduced me to a local hominy dish that is easy to prepare and quite delicious.

Vastly amused by the conviction that, like her namesake, Lazarus, she will rise from the dead to terrify her droves of children, grandchildren, and great grandchildren, Lazara has arranged to have this dish served at her funeral dinner. It involves sautéing chopped onion and chili peppers, mixing in the hominy, then baking the whole with grated longhorn cheese on top. You will never mistake this dish for some wimpy breakfast cereal.

Of course, I didn't find the chef, although I wanted to obtain the instructions for his barbecue sauce, but I did take notes on every bite I ate. That practice earned me impatient glances from my friends, puzzled stares from strangers, and a visit from a waitress who asked if I worked for the *Times-Picayune*. She seemed disappointed to hear that I didn't.

While I tasted and took notes, Lester, Carlene, and my husband chatted about the amazing growth of research on "buckyballs," huge, soccer-ball-shaped molecules discovered in the relatively recent past. Broder told Miranda about the lamentable lack of impact made by Calvinist theology on African-American Christians. Miranda responded with the suggestion that Calvinist hymns might not be lively enough to attract converts, a theory that Broder declared frivolous. Never having considered herself a frivolous person, at least since leaving jail in the early seventies and electing a career in law, Miranda refused to talk to Broder any farther and turned her attention to the heretofore silent Nils.

"Did she take her clothes with her?" Miranda asked.

Startled, Nils looked up from his peach cobbler (which tasted of fresh peaches, although March is certainly not the peach season) and barked, "No."

"Isn't that just like Julienne?" Miranda responded. "Running away without a word to her friends, causing us all sorts of worry—"

"Well, she *meant* to worry me," Nils interrupted, "but I'm not falling for that ploy."

"Julienne may be intelligent," Miranda continued as if he hadn't spoken, "but she's always been flighty, thoughtless, and self-centered."

If I hadn't been so worried by the revelation that Julienne had left her belongings behind, I'd have taken exception to Miranda's harsh assessment of my oldest friend. Flighty, thoughtless, and self-centered didn't describe Julienne at all. "Nils, if she were leaving you, she'd certainly have taken her clothes," I pointed out. "Could she be staying with relatives or friends?"

"There aren't any left alive."

"Then you've got to contact the police and report her missing."

Nils glowered at me. "I have no intention of asking the police to find my runaway wife," he muttered. "Why should I embarrass myself when she's probably staying on the riverfront with Linus Torelli?"

I almost exclaimed, "Without her clothes?" but caught myself in time. Such a remark would not have convinced Nils of anything but the presumed sexual infidelity of his wife, a suspicion I didn't entertain for a moment. However, I was considering the idea of contacting the police, even if I had to do it myself, when the lights on the stage bloomed, music drowned out conversation, and the gospel show began. It was an experience! Choruses of young people, featured performers in sequins, and a master of ceremonies/preacher wearing red boots and a gray Ghandi suit with flashing gold chains and medals. By the end of the performance, the audience was indeed clapping, swaying, and dancing in the aisles—well, not at our table. College professors and tax lawyers aren't given to dancing in the aisles, although some of us did join in the clapping, and I noticed that Carlene was tapping her foot.

6

Hurricanes

New Orleans is the birthplace of the cocktail, the first having been concocted by Antoine Peychaud, who escaped the slave rebellion on Santo Domingo in the late eighteenth century and set up a pharmacy in New Orleans. There he sold a brandy-based drink guaranteed to cure whatever ailed his customers. His cocktail, the Sazerac, was served in a *coquetier* or eggcup from which the word cocktail derived. Peychaud himself invented the bitters that, with a dash of absinthe, added flavor to the Sazerac brandy.

One can imagine the traumatized Frenchman, having barely escaped with his life from the violence in the Caribbean, dealing with post-traumatic stress disorder by sipping his new medicinal cocktail from the large half of an egg cup. Would he have approved of the changes made in his recipe over the years? Probably not. The brandy has been replaced by rye whiskey and the absinthe, now outlawed in the United States, by Herbsaint, an anise liqueur, but the bitters still carry his name.

So delighted was I with this delectable piece of culinary history that I determined to sample as many of the famous cocktails of New Orleans as I could. In moderate amounts, of course.

Carolyn Blue, *Eating Out in the Big Easy*

When the performance at the Praline Connection ended, Nils took the opportunity to slip away while Jason and I were saying good-bye to the rest of the party, all of whom had different plans for the time between one and the opening of registration at the convention center. I assume that Nils's plan was to avoid going to the police station to report his wife missing. Therefore, I did it for him.

We asked directions from the young man taking tickets for the second show, and he, looking insulted, demanded to know if we thought something had been stolen from us during our visit. Given the master of ceremonies' many narrations about young people being saved from unfortunate circumstances by embracing Christ and the Praline Connection, I can see that my inquiry was ill advised. I assured the young man that we had been not only unmolested but also pleased with our experience and wanted to consult the police about a missing friend.

Miranda, who was directly behind me, muttered, "Oh, for heaven's sake, Carolyn, give it a rest. Think how embarrassed she'll be when she turns up and finds that the police are looking for her."

I replied, "If you read your guide book, you'd know that female tourists are warned against walking alone at night."

"You got that right, lady," said the young man. "Some female friend a yours been walkin' 'round after dark by her ownsef an' ain't turned up, you best be headin' fo' the Vieux Carre station." His input on Julienne's disappearance was frightening, but he did provide directions to the police department, which had a branch near the corner of Royal and Conti, a little over a block from our hotel. Perhaps the advice of a native convinced Jason, who had not previously been much inclined to make a fuss about Julienne's strange absence.

At any rate, he agreed to make the long walk back to our hotel, although he would have saved himself steps by going to the area of the convention center instead. Fortunately, Jason is not averse to exercise, whereas I, had I not felt that Julienne's well-being was at stake, might have preferred to explore the river area. Back we trudged along South Peters, Canal, and Chartres, past our hotel to the corner of Conti and Chartres, then left on Conti to Royal.

The station proved to be an impressive sight: cream stucco with two-story columns holding up an elaborate roofline, trees and shrubs growing green and healthy outside, and a black wrought-iron fence behind which sleek white police motorcycles were parked on the flagstones surrounding the porte cochere. I found the handsome building reassuring, but once inside, both the decor and our reception were less so. The desk sergeant wanted to know what our relation to the missing person was, and he took the news that we were simply friends as no cause to leap into action. Further questioning elicited the information that Julienne Magnussen had a husband in town. The sergeant wanted to know why the husband hadn't reported her missing. The final blow to our case was the admission that our friend, whose husband hadn't seen fit to come in himself, had been missing less than twenty-four hours.

"Ma'am," drawled the sergeant, "we don' go lookin' for no adults 'less they been missin' forty-eight hours. Likely this lady jus' run off from her husband an' don' wanna be found. No use us lookin' for a woman don' wanna be found."

"You're not going to do anything?" I cried.

"Well, when she been gone forty-eight hours, y'all send in the lady's husband. Then we might—"

"But she disappeared between Etienne's and the Hotel de la Poste," I protested as Jason tugged at my arm. "She must have been kidnapped."

The sergeant picked up his ringing telephone and turned his back on me. And to think my mother always told me that policemen were my friends! I scowled at his back and allowed Jason to escort me out the door, through the lines of motorcycles, and out onto the sidewalk. Where, I wondered, were the policemen who were supposed to be riding the motorcycles and protecting the public from the dangers of the Big Easy? The only policeman I had seen was that recalcitrant sergeant.

"How about a hurricane at Pat O'Brien's?" Jason asked.

"A what?"

"It's a famous New Orleans rum drink." He steered me resolutely along Royal Street toward Saint Peter Street and O'Brien's, which was housed in a delightful, late eighteenth-century brick building with tall windows and a wrought-iron balcony but marked only with a discreet round, green sign. By the time we arrived, I had discovered in my guidebook that the building had originally been a theater built by a Spanish military officer.

Perhaps foolishly, I wanted to sit on the patio, which, even with the ever-impending rain, was crowded with noisy young people. Our waiter, an ancient black man wearing a green jacket with white piping and a black bow tie large enough to dwarf the back of a lady's head, wiped off two seats and served us the largest alcoholic drinks I have ever seen—and the pinkest. However, they were very tasty and just what I needed.

Now searching for information on the drink, I discovered as I sipped that the hurricane was reputedly the result of an imprudent overbuying of rum and glasses in the shape of hurricane lamps by the owner in the 1930s. What fun! I made notes and told Jason I might just order a second. Jason replied that he thought the four ounces of rum in the drink I had ought to be enough for one afternoon. I think he was afraid eight ounces of rum might disable me to the extent that I wouldn't be in any condition to walk out of the bar on my own, and he was probably right, although at the time I thought he was exaggerating the alcohol content.

Fortunately, I took his advice and managed to exit Pat O'Brien's in a ladylike fashion, even remembering to claim the deposits on the glasses. What a strange custom that is. Of course, the management wanted to sell us the glasses as souvenirs, but I didn't want a souvenir of a day when the police refused to assist in finding my best friend. Furthermore, tourists evidently used the glasses to hold beads they acquired during Mardi Gras parades. No Mardi Gras parades would be held during our visit, so we didn't need bead receptacles.

Pat O'Brien's Hurricane Punch

Mix 4 oz. of dark rum with 2 to 4 oz. of Pat O'Brien's Hurricane Mix. (Buy the passion fruit cocktail mix in New Orleans; then try to duplicate it at home—good luck!)

Serve in a hurricane glass filled with crushed ice. (The glass resembles the lamp of the same name, but without lighting apparatus, and is available at Pat O'Brien's, but you won't get your deposit back if you don't return it. Any very large, 12- to 16-oz. glass will do.)

Garnish with an orange slice and a maraschino cherry.

Because the police had not been at all obliging, I decided to investigate Julienne's disappearance on my own, beginning with Professor Linus Torelli, who Nils seemed to believe was Julienne's lover. Therefore, I went to the convention center with Jason, another long walk, and while he was registering at the table that included people whose names begin with B, I sidled over to the T table. Rendered ultragregarious and none too truthful by the hurricane, I breezily informed a pleasant and helpful young lady wearing a convention badge that I was looking for my friend Linus Torelli. Had she seen him?

Much more obliging than the police, she ascertained that he had already registered; she even provided the name and telephone number of the hotel at which he was staying, the same nearby high-rise where Miranda and Lester Abbott were registered. With any luck I wouldn't run into them. No doubt, they would have disapproved of my mission, as I suspected Jason would, had he been aware of my intentions.

I ventured out with Jason's umbrella raised against a slanting new rainstorm that soaked my shoes and spattered my raincoat. Thank goodness for my New Orleans guidebook, which had advised carrying an umbrella at all times in this season. Jason had read it ahead of time. Otherwise, I would have been soaking wet instead of just damp and squishy of foot when I arrived at the reception desk and asked for Dr. Torelli. The clerk should have taken helpfulness lessons from the T registration lady at the convention center. He would not give me a room number; he would and did call the chemist in question, which is how I came to interview Julienne's colleague in the lobby of his hotel.

Linus Torelli was a slender man of medium height with olive skin and tightly curled black hair without a trace of gray, a good ten years younger than my friend, if I was any judge of age. More convinced than ever that he could not be her lover, I blurted out, immediately after the introductions and not long enough after the hurricane, "What's your relationship to Julienne, Dr. Torelli?"

Not surprisingly, the man was taken aback to be so addressed by a mature female, who was somewhat the worse for rain and totally unknown to him. He coughed and stammered and finally managed to tell me that they ran a combined seminar for their graduate students. Then he seemed to reconsider this innocuous explanation and added, "Of course it goes without saying that Julienne and I are good friends."

What does that mean? I wondered testily. Was he her lover or not? "When did you last see her?" I demanded.

"Madam," he snapped, but got no further for I repeated my question more aggressively. Normally, I am a very low-key person; alcohol and worry seem to have caused an unfortunate personality change. Was I, by any chance, experiencing a testosterone surge? Could menopause be creeping up on me? And did menopause actually trigger the production of testosterone in women? Probably not. While I was worrying about my uncharacteristic aggressiveness, Dr. Torelli was mumbling that he had not seen "Julie"—he called her Julie! Surely that was significant!—since Friday, the day before she left for New Orleans. Did that mean he hadn't left until this morning?

"She's missing," I told him. "She hasn't been seen since 7:30 last night—unless you've seen her." I thought I saw alarm on his face. "Have you? Seen her?" He was taking much too long to answer a simple question.

"No. No, I told you," he stammered. "Not since—ah—at the department. Last Friday."

I didn't believe him, and he seemed to realize as much, for he hastened to add, a slight sneer in his voice, "Why don't you ask Nils? Her husband." With that, Dr. Torelli walked out the front door. Into the rain. Without a raincoat. I'm sure *that* was significant! I just didn't know of what. Or exactly how he had lied to me, although I was convinced that he had. And I didn't like the man. There was something sneaky about him. Not Julienne's type at all. So nothing made sense.

I plopped down onto a deep-cushioned sofa, inexcusably indifferent to the damage my damp clothing might be doing to the expensive upholstery, and tried to reason my way through the evidence I had. Julienne and Nils had been quarreling. She had left the dinner because of his unpleasant attitude. And disappeared. Kidnapped? Off to see the man her husband claimed was her lover, a man who denied having seen her? Before I could carry my thought processes further, Linus Torelli reappeared, brushing rain from his curls and sports jacket.

He planted himself in front of my sofa and said, "She's chairing a session, you know. And giving a paper. No matter where she is, she'll be back for those."

Spoken like a true scientist, I thought as he strode toward the elevators. Evidently, he had changed his mind about escaping from me by going for a walk. Two other people got on with him, but I noted all the floors where that particular elevator stopped: seven, fifteen, and twenty-two. That narrowed down the location of his room, but not much. What if Julienne was up there? I should have rushed after him and boarded the same elevator. Not very subtle, but wouldn't he have been surprised?

Instead, I fished my wallet from my handbag and looked through the pictures until I found an old one of Julienne, her brother Philippe, and myself, taken at least fifteen years ago on the lakeshore when we had been visiting her family's summer cottage. It was the only picture of her that I had with me, so I slipped it from its protective plastic envelope and went to the reception desk where, after waiting through six check-ins and one check-out, I arrived at the head of the line and showed my photo to the clerk.

The woman nodded. "I remember her. At least I think it was her. She was wearing a red dress."

"Yes!" I agreed enthusiastically. "She was. When did you see her?"

"Last night. I worked a double shift yesterday."

"When last night?"

"Oh, eight-thirty or nine. Somewhere around then. She had me call one of our guests."

"What floor?" I asked breathlessly.

The clerk gave me a narrow glance. "I wouldn't remember that. Why do you want to know?"

"She's missing." I'm sure I looked as worried as I felt. "And the police won't do a thing."

"Really?" The young woman's eyes went wide. "Well, he came down—"

"What did he look like?"

"I don't know. Dark-haired. Cute. I figured he was her brother. I mean he was younger and had the same color hair."

I shook my head. "What happened then?"

"They went out and came back after midnight. She went upstairs with him. That's when I got curious because I was sure there was only one person registered to that room. The management doesn't like people having nonguests staying overnight. Still, I thought she was his sister, so I didn't . . . Well, you mean she wasn't?"

I didn't answer, embarrassed that Julienne might have been staying with a lover. I wouldn't have believed it. And maybe she wasn't. "Did you see her leave?" I asked hopefully. Maybe she had come right back down.

"I didn't," said the clerk, "but I went off shift at six this morning. Not his sister? Well, that's New Orleans for you." She still refused to tell me on what floor the dark-haired man had his room. That would be "against company policy."

I turned away, thinking hard. If the man with the dark hair was Linus Torelli and the woman in the red dress was Julienne, she hadn't been kidnapped at the restaurant or off the street, which was a relief. But why had he lied? And what had he done with her? Or was she still upstairs? If so, on which of the three floors? I glanced at my watch and realized that I had to get back to my own hotel and dress for the welcome mixer at the aquarium. The hurricane seemed to be wearing off just in time for the next round of alcohol. Maybe Julienne would attend the mixer.

7

Jug Wine and Tidbits

Very piquant," said my husband judiciously as he sipped his white wine in a plastic glass. *Very piquant* is our wine code for *vinegary but overpriced*. We were attending the welcome mixer at the Aquarium of the Americas with Nils. Since we had run into him in the lobby at the hotel, I could hardly refuse to walk to the foot of Canal Street in his company, especially since Jason did not seem averse to doing so. Fortunately, the rain had abated, and I said nothing more about Julienne after Nils snarled at my first question. I was tempted to mention the desk clerk who had sighted a woman in a red dress in the company of a man at Linus Torelli's hotel, but I held my tongue.

As I kept my eyes firmly on the aquarium's distinctive round structure with its slanted, flat roof, which the three of us were approaching in virtual silence, it occurred to me that Nils himself might have found Julienne at Torelli's hotel. Could he have gone there looking for her the very night she left the dinner at Etienne's? Then, infuriated by her infidelity, real or imagined, he might have attacked her. But if so, where was she?

I resolved to begin calling hospitals as soon as we returned to our room, for I was imagining scenarios in which Nils knocked Julienne unconscious after catching her in Torelli's company. Although the softening process of middle age has begun, Nils is a big man. If he hit his slender wife, he would do great damage. After hitting her, perhaps he stuffed her into one of those taxis that lurk in front of large hotels. Then he gave the driver some excuse (perhaps that she had passed out in a diabetic coma), asked to be taken to a hospital, and left her there in the emergency room while he escaped the consequences of his jealous rage.

All this had passed through my mind as we reached the aquarium and joined the mob of scientists and their significant others attempting to reach the refreshment tables. The frustrations involved were enough to turn my imagination off for the time being.

"Might as well enjoy what we've got," Jason was saying of the hors d'oeuvres. "I, for one, don't intend to wait through any more long lines."

We'd waited fifteen minutes for the wine and even longer for the food offerings, which were not at all up to New Orleans standards, certainly not as exotic as the alligator puffs I had chosen for the reunion dinner. But then the American Chemical Society organizers had probably decided on this menu and were more interested in economy than culinary adventure.

"I'd planned to substitute this for dinner," said Nils morosely. He hadn't even mentioned his wife since refusing to answer questions on the walk over. All the more reason to suspect him of foul play, I decided.

"Jason! And the delightful Carolyn!" The newcomer looked more closely at Nils and came up with his name, too, although Nils is not a chemist. "Dr. Magnussen."

We all shook hands with Corbin Bunster, the eminent theoretician from Cal Tech, a man who has the amazing ability to remember every person to whom he has ever been introduced. For those of us less memory-endowed, Dr. Bunster is not to be forgotten because of his scientific renown and a set of eyebrows that flare from his forehead like the mustachio of an aging Mexican bandido.

"And where is your dear childhood friend, Carolyn?" he asked me. He remembers not only one's name and face but past conversations, no matter how mundane. "Since Dr. Magnussen is here, I presume the brilliant Julienne is as well, especially as she's scheduled to present a very interesting paper at the conference."

"She's missing," I replied, glancing at Nils to see how he'd react when a famous scientist learned of the disappearance.

"Missing the wine, is she? A sensible decision," said Bunster.

"Missing, period. None of us has seen her since last night, not even Nils."

Bunster looked alarmed. "Missing in New Orleans! Good God, man," he exclaimed, turning to Nils, "I hope you've reported this to the police."

Nils gave him a fulminating glance, then turned it on me, and left in a huff. This seemed to be his only method of departure since arriving in New Orleans.

"Irritable fellow," Bunster remarked and strode off to display his phenomenal memory elsewhere. Jason and I went to sample the beer after discreetly placing our half-full wine cups on a table of aquarium literature. Then, beer in hand, we began to wander the Caribbean Reef and Gulf of Mexico exhibits on the first floor. They included towering glass tanks inhabited by multitudes of aquatic creatures. As Jason greeted colleagues, talked of bonds, molecules, and heats of formation, scribbled little pictures of compounds on the program, and generally acted like a scientist, I tuned out the chemical chatter and admired the scene. There were vicious-looking, beaked turtles making rushes at lettuce bundles carried by divers and, my favorites, giant rays, rippling their sueded, winglike bodies, trailing stingers, and looking much more impressive than those who undulated lazily across the aquarium screen saver on my computer.

On the second floor in a humid rain forest with suspended walkways that allowed one to stroll amid lush vegetation and swooping tropical birds, we came across the McAvees and Nils. Carlene was quizzing him about Julienne, surprised that she was still among the missing but convinced that she would reappear the next day for Carlene's plenary address to the conference. Broder interrupted to say that, in such a dangerous and sinful city, Julienne might have been kidnapped by white slavers.

Because that was exactly the scenario I had envisioned the night before when I went to look for her in the Etienne's rest room, that particular set of fears was revived. I turned to Nils and asked if he had checked her belongings to ascertain whether anything was missing.

"I didn't notice anything," he muttered reluctantly, which I took to mean that he had at least looked. "Ask Torelli. He'd know what, if anything, she took with her."

"He says he hasn't seen her," I replied, without thinking. After all, I hadn't mentioned to Nils that I had pursued Torelli to his hotel.

"Well, if you believe that, you're more naive than I'd have thought," Nils snarled.

Actually, I hadn't believed Torelli, not after talking to the hotel clerk, but again I didn't mention that, preferring not to feed Nils's anger about the supposed liaison. On the other hand, when I reviewed Nils's response, I realized that, one, he hadn't commented on my having talked to Torelli, and, two, he'd seemed quite sure that Torelli had seen Julienne. *Had* he caught them together at the hotel? And if so, what had he done about it? I shivered, remembering the violent scenario I had concocted on the way to the aquarium.

"You must be wrong, Nils," said Carlene. "I can't imagine Julienne having an affair. Goodness, I've never had one—well, with Broder—but I married him." Having revealed something that shocked none of us, she went off, long, multicolored skirt swishing, to find another glass of the abominable wine; perhaps her foolhardy acceptance came from a misplaced loyalty to California vineyards. At any rate, she left in her wake a red-faced husband. No doubt, Broder was embarrassed to have revealed, even to friends, his premarital indiscretion. He immediately changed the subject to Calvinist theology.

Within three minutes even we long-time friends were shifting restlessly, so I rescued us all by murmuring, "As a point of historical interest, Broder, didn't the early Calvinists bury those they considered heretics up to the neck and then roll large stones at their heads?" Before he could answer, I turned to Nils and asked him to let me look over Julienne's belongings, explaining that anything found missing would at least reassure us that she had made it as far as the Hotel de la Poste safely. Sulky to the end, Nils refused, exacerbating my suspicions that he himself might be responsible for the disappearance of his wife.

"In that case, I intend to go looking for her tomorrow in all the places we planned to visit," I announced. "I think you ought to come with me, Nils. Since you aren't involved in the conference, you don't have anything better to do, and you might show some concern for—"

"I've already said that I don't intend to chase after her. Go by yourself if you're so set on finding a woman who obviously doesn't want to be found," he replied.

"Perhaps I'd better accompany you, Carolyn," said Broder.

"And miss my paper?" demanded his wife, who had returned with her wine refill in record time. Presumably, after one glass, other attendees had opted for beer.

"Of course not," said Broder. "We'll go after your address. But you'll agree that in a city this dangerous, a woman should not be wandering about unaccompanied by a protective male."

Dear Broder. It wasn't as if I'd be searching the city at night. I wanted to know if anyone had seen Julienne this morning or this afternoon. Still, I made arrangements to meet Broder after lunch on Monday. With any luck, Julienne might have come back before then. I certainly hoped so, not only because I loved her dearly, but because I didn't see Broder, no matter how well meaning, as someone who would help in wheedling information from denizens of the French Quarter.

When we finally left the aquarium, which was still packed with scientists taking advantage of free food and drink, and returned to our hotel, Jason went to the bar in Bacco, the hotel restaurant. He wanted to have a nightcap and draw more chemical structures on napkins with an environmental toxicologist from the University of South Florida who had followed us home. I went straight to our room, gumbo delivered from Etienne's in hand, and ate it while I called all the hospitals and the police stations to see if there had been any reports about Julienne. There hadn't, and I anticipated another night of worry and restless tossing.

How could my best friend have disappeared when I'd spent less than an hour in her company? Was her marriage to Nils so terrible that she couldn't have stayed for my sake? Admittedly, I'd have been angry had Jason treated me the way Nils treated her at the dinner party, but then Jason would never do that. He may be devoted to his work and distracted from time to time, in fact, a good deal of the time, but he's always a sweet man when he returns from the realms of scientific thought. He proved as much when he arrived in our room, pockets stuffed with napkins written over with brilliant ideas and a libido inspired by the sight of me in my see-through lace nightgown. I may be forty-something, but my husband still thinks I'm the perfect amalgamation of physical desirability and culinary expertise.

Poor man. It hasn't yet penetrated his consciousness that, although I still enjoy our marital trysts in the bedroom, I am much less interested in kitchen adventures. I could write a book extolling the joys of other people's cooking. In fact, I am.

8

Beignets and Chicory Coffee

In New Orleans, café au lait means chicory coffee with milk. Among other things that the original French settlers learned from the Choctaw and Chicka-saw Indians was the use of a peppery syrup made from the root of a dande-lion cousin whose new leaves appear in your salad as endive. The chicory syrup in coffee may seem bitter to outlanders, but to New Orleans natives and other aficionados of the blend, it produces a rich beverage with half the caffeine of undoctored coffee. That may explain why citizens of New Orleans can drink more than twice as much coffee a day as the average American and still con-tribute to the laid-back ambiance of the Big Easy.

Carolyn Blue, *Eating Out in the Big Easy*

I truly did mean to attend Carlene's lecture Monday morning but reminded myself that Julienne and I had planned breakfast at the Café du Monde on Jackson Square. Having missed yesterday's rendezvous, I had to be there today and hoped that she would, too. Jason was very understanding about it and consoled me by saying that he wasn't expecting to understand a good deal of the science in Carlene's lecture himself. If *he* didn't know that much about leading-edge biochemistry, why should I? Therefore, with a clear conscience, I set off, raincoat-clad, newly purchased umbrella in hand, for Jackson Square, which was just over three blocks from the hotel.

The skies were gray, the streets wet as I chose a green plastic chair from among many placed on flagstones under the green and white striped awnings of the famous coffeehouse. Naturally, I ordered chicory coffee and beignets, those hot, delicious squares of fried dough lavishly dusted with powdered sugar. The chicory was a research impulse gone wrong. Even generous splashes of cream and multiple packets of sugar couldn't cut the bitter taste enough to suit me. For once I, the typical Midwestern, north-of-the-Mason-Dixon-Line Yankee, felt sympathy for the benighted Southerners that had been reduced to drinking chicory with little or no coffee during the Civil War. In their place, I think I would have surrendered years earlier just to get a less off-putting caffeine fix with breakfast.

As I devoured my beignets and brushed the resulting rain of powdered sugar from my black raincoat (Café du Monde would do well to provide bibs for its patrons), I watched the square for Julienne. I had already cased the café both inside and out before sitting down. The stones were bright with rain, and the trees blew in a gentle wind beyond the iron fence. Old-fashioned lampposts were mirrored on the wet street, as were the trailing images of cars and tourist buses. Across the street, a tiny mule with a bouquet inserted in its bridle turned its head to inspect the heaped blossoms of pink and purple inside the fence, while an egg-shaped woman tried to keep her excited toddler calm as she negotiated for a ride in the little red mule carriage. The vehicle had small wheels in front, larger behind, for all the world like an old-fashioned bicycle.

A man in a yellow raincoat played "St. Louis Blues" on his trumpet, and the sad, mellow notes met scattered applause and the tiger growl of thunder as the sky darkened and a fine rain began to fall. Laughing tourists in hooded jackets and stoic natives, umbrella-topped, passed by. As the rain grew heavier, young people with backpacks ducked under the awnings, and hungry, sheltering pigeons waddled under my table, but amid all this activity, Julienne did not arrive, and my disappointment burgeoned. What should I do? I stared miserably at the three white, shingle-capped steeples of the Saint Louis Cathedral, lifting simple crosses to the sky as if pointing out what a sad, dark day it was.

My waitress, an Asian woman wearing a white cap and long white apron over her black trousers, stopped to ask if I wanted anything else. Having taken up space at her table for over an hour, I felt obliged to order again, a frothy cappuccino this time and another beignet. When she brought them, I showed her the picture of Julienne from my wallet. "I'm waiting for this woman. Have you, by any chance, seen her? Either today or yesterday?"

Obligingly, the waitress peered at the picture. "That's you, isn't it?" she asked, pointing to me on the left. "Must have been years ago."

Had I aged so much? I wondered. Or did I appear dated because of the waist-length hair? "My friend looks a lot the same," I replied. "Have you seen her?"

"Not today," she replied, "and I wasn't working yesterday." She peered at the snapshot again. I must have looked as disappointed as I felt, for she added helpfully, "You want me to show it around?"

I hated to let the picture out of my possession; it was the only photo of Julienne, no matter how outdated, that I had with me. However, I released it, and off she went. *It's really very good of her to bother,* I told myself. And my search was rewarded, for she returned with a young black man, wearing the same apron, cap, and bow-tie costume. "Seen her yesterday morning," he said, handing back the photo. "Couldn't hardly miss her. Wearing a fancy red dress. Stayed about an hour. Left me a fine tip."

Almost limp with relief, I finished my delicious coffee, dusted away more beignet sugar, left my waitress a "fine tip," and then set off toward the convention center. Of course Julienne hadn't been on Jackson Square to meet me this morning! She had gone to hear Carlene talking about computational biochemistry. I had to get there before the end of the lecture. By dint of more jogging than I had done in years, which earned me odd glances from natives, I did arrive while Carlene was still talking, no thanks to the New Orleans Police. At the corner of South Front and Poydras, when I was still blocks from my destination and completely breathless, a motorcycle officer stopped me, evidently under the impression that a pedestrian moving on foot at any pace faster than a saunter must be up to no good. The phrase, "Where are the police when you need them?" hardly applied here. I didn't *want* to be delayed, but I decided to make the best of his mistake.

Before he could arrest me or strip-search me or whatever he had in mind, I gasped, "Could you give me a ride to the convention center? I'm late for a lecture on computational biochemistry."

He must have thought my statement eccentric enough to eliminate me from his list of possible wrongdoers. Instead of arresting me, he said, with no little sarcasm, "The N'Awlins Police ain't in business to give rides to tourists, ma'am. You see an extra helmet here? Any place for you to ride *on?*"

"Well then, thanks anyway," I called over my shoulder as I ran off. He didn't pursue. Lafayette, Girod, Notre Dame, Julia—I crossed them all before reaching even the corner of the huge center. If only I'd known about the Riverfront Streetcar, I could have saved myself such a traumatic overexposure to aerobic exercise. Surely it can't be good for one. I arrived with my heart thundering noisily in my chest and my lungs burning, but I did hear the last five minutes of the lecture and congratulated Carlene with proper enthusiasm on her presentation when it was over.

Fortunately, she didn't expect comments from me on the science. She got plenty of those from actual scientists. We hugged one another, Carlene asked after Julienne, but then took offense that our friend had not shown up. Given her attitude, I didn't mention that Julienne had been seen at Café du Monde yesterday. "She's missing, Carlene," I said firmly. I was only then beginning to realize that the waiter's identification on the basis of an old picture might not be accurate, although he had mentioned a red dress. How many women went to breakfast in a fancy red dress? Well, in New Orleans, there might be quite a few, I had to admit to myself but not to Carlene.

"Don't you think she'd be here if she could?" I asked reasonably. But why couldn't she? That was the question. And why couldn't she meet me as we'd planned? Didn't she know I'd be beside myself with worry? Of course, she knew that.

I saw Linus Torelli at the same time he saw me. He tried to skulk away, but I left Carlene without so much as an "excuse me," which was very rude, although necessary under the circumstances, and chased him into a small lecture room where chemists were beginning to assemble for a panel on something or other. "You lied to me," I said.

Torelli flushed with embarrassment, glanced nervously at three or four men who turned to stare at us, and then hustled me out into the hall.

"You said you hadn't seen her, but the desk clerk at your hotel says you two went out together Saturday night, and that she went upstairs with you when you returned."

"Sh-sh-sh," hissed Torelli. "If this gets back to my . . . to her . . . husband, he'll . . . he'll . . . he's really paranoid about the two of us."

"Small wonder," I snapped. "Where is she?"

"I don't know."

"You do, too."

"Listen, Mrs.—"

"Blue."

"Julienne and I are not lovers." He was whispering, glancing nervously from side to side. "We're colleagues. We run a combined seminar for our graduate students."

"Then why was she spending the night with you?"

"Sh-sh-sh. She didn't. I mean, after she quarreled with Nils, we went out wandering in the Quarter. She wanted to take pictures."

"Did she have her camera?" She hadn't had a camera at Etienne's. She'd forgotten it, probably because she and Nils had been quarreling before dinner.

"Of course. She always has it."

"Fine. But she went up to your room afterward."

Torelli looked downright desperate as a skinny, redheaded man, eyeing us curiously, greeted him and slipped around us into the room. "Please keep your voice down," Torelli begged. "If you don't care about me, you might think of Julie's repu—"

"No one saw her leave your room or the hotel," I persisted angrily. If Torelli was worried about her reputation, why had he started something with her in the first place? If he had. "And no one knows where she is now." I glared at him accusingly. "She didn't even come to the plenary addresses."

"Well, it's not my fault!" Torelli sighed and admitted in a voice almost inaudible, "There are two beds in my room. She asked to sleep in one of them . . . because she was so furious with Nils, she refused to go back to their hotel. She said since he believed we were having an affair, she'd just spend the night with me."

"And initiate an affair?" I gasped. Oh Julienne! And Nils—this was all *his* fault!

"*No!*" exclaimed Torelli. Then, more calmly, "No. But she did say it would serve him right if, when she returned Sunday night—"

"But she didn't!"

"Are you sure? She said she was going to tell him that she'd spent the night with me. Jesus, can you imagine what would have happened if she'd done that? He'd kill me."

Or her, I thought with a shudder. Had she carried out that crazy plan, and Nils—

"I told her that was a really bad idea," Torelli assured me.

"And then what happened?"

"And then she came up with another crazy idea—that we should rent a boat. As if I'd do that. I don't like boats. I don't know how to drive a boat, and she expected me to . . . to run it while she took pictures."

He turned pale at the very thought. Aquaphobia, I deduced, wondering if he knew how to swim. Julienne swam with the ease and grace of a dolphin. We'd had wonderful times at the lake when we were children. Even Philippe had deigned to join us occasionally, although he wasn't nearly the swimmer Julienne was.

"That's crazy, don't you agree? I mean, she's a beautiful woman, and a brilliant chemist, but you couldn't get me into a boat in the daytime much less at night, and certainly not to take pictures on the river or in the swamp. And I hadn't had any sleep. I can't afford to skip the meeting and go dashing off—"

"Do you think she went?" I interrupted. It would be just like Julienne. When it came to photography, I'd seen her hang off cliffs and approach scary-looking bikers. Taking pictures from a boat would be no big deal for Julienne. I could imagine her photographing the river, the docks, the riverboats, the—good grief. What if her little boat had been run down by some huge riverboat or barge, and no one even noticed? Had she gone out and rented the boat right after waiting for me at Café du Monde on Sunday morning? After all, she hadn't known of the arrangement to meet for brunch at Praline Connection. It was made after she left. She probably wanted Jason and me to take charge of the boating while she took pictures, and when we hadn't been there to help, she'd—

"With who?" Torelli was asking disdainfully. "She couldn't handle both a boat and a camera at the same time. And who'd want to go boating in a swamp?"

That's right; he had mentioned the swamp. Surely she hadn't gone into the swamp by herself when she couldn't find anyone to go with her. I was conscience-stricken to have failed her. Not that I'd have wanted to go boating in a swamp, except maybe on a tour. We'd talked about taking a swamp tour, which sounded safe enough. But alone? Well, if we'd met Sunday morning, I could have talked her out of that idea. "So you don't think she actually went?" I asked hopefully.

"Of course not. But we did part on an unpleasant note."

"Did she have any extra clothes with her?" I asked, subdued. She wouldn't have gone boating in that red dress. Would she?

"I don't think so. All she had was her camera and one of those big shoulder bags. They look like pouches. I don't know what she thought she was going to wear to bed. Maybe one of my shirts. And that's a good point. If she hasn't been back there yet, she's probably in her hotel room right now. She can't still be wearing that red dress, even if she did look amazingly sexy in it."

Ah ha! It was obvious to me that Linus Torelli was or had been in love with Julienne, no matter how platonic and colleague-oriented he claimed his feelings were. Therefore, I didn't know how much of his tale to believe, and I couldn't very well demand that he let me look in his hotel room to see if she was still there. Still . . . "Can I look in your hotel room?"

"Why?" He glared at me. "Oh hell, why not? I have to attend this meeting, but . . ."

Attendees had been streaming past as we hissed discreetly at one another. Now a man at the door was giving Torelli an are-you-coming-in-or-not look. "Room 2210. Here's the key. Leave it at the desk." He scooted through the door, which closed behind him, and I was left with his key, in which I was no longer interested. If he'd give it to me, obviously he wasn't hiding Julienne in his room. I did check and found nothing to indicate that she'd even been there, so I went back to my own hotel and knocked at the Magnussens' door, hoping fervently that Julienne would answer, that she had either returned to her husband or was at least packing her clothes in order to move somewhere else. If she'd had clothes in the shoulder bag Torelli mentioned, there couldn't have been many, not enough to last her into a second day.

What a disappointment when Nils opened the door. Still, I barged right in and insisted on looking through her belongings. There was no way to tell whether she'd taken clothes away, and Nils claimed not to know what she had packed.

"She came back last night, didn't she? Why didn't you tell me?" I was watching closely to see what he'd say, whether he'd lie.

"I've already told you. I haven't seen her since she walked out at Etienne's," he retorted.

He seemed more angry than guilty. "Her camera's gone," I said, trying a new tactic.

He shrugged.

"And there's no laptop computer here. She must have brought one. You all bring them with you." I even carry one myself, now that I am a paid writer. Not that I bought it: I haven't earned that much. My laptop was Jason's before he upgraded.

Nils shrugged again. "*I* don't bring a computer with me," he said, as if this was a point in his favor. "Why don't you look in Torelli's room?"

"I did."

Nils gaped at me.

"Nothing of hers, including her, was in his room. But this means that, at the least, she came back here from the dinner at Etienne's to get her camera and computer." It then occurred to me that someone might have killed her on the street to get the electronic equipment. Julienne would have resisted, and then . . . Oh God! "You don't even care, do you?" I asked angrily. "You don't care what's happened to her."

"Nothing's happened to her," Nils replied. "She's ran out on me, and she doesn't care who she worries or—"

"Oh, do be quiet, Nils," I retorted. "I don't for a minute think she was having an affair, but I can certainly see why she wouldn't want to spend the week with you. You're treating her abominably."

I left the room and went to the hotel desk. If Julienne had, in fact, meant to leave Nils, she would have turned in her key card, as any responsible person would. But she hadn't. The desk clerk assured me that both Magnussens had their cards, and if they'd lost them, they should report it.

What should I do next? I asked myself. Have lunch? Or visit the police station?

9

Muffulettas

You haven't experienced the ultimate in sandwiches until you have tried that New Orleans delicacy, the muffuletta. First, it is huge—big enough to feed two men or four women. Second, it contains generous piles of ham, salami, and mozzarella. Third and most important, it is garnished with a piquant, garlic-infused salad made of chopped green olives, capers, celery, and pickled carrots. All of this is encased between the two halves of a round, eight- to ten-inch, seed-covered loaf of soft white bread. Ah, heaven!

The muffuletta is messy to eat; bits of the olive salad may find their way onto your clothing. If you delay too long in devouring your muffuletta, the bun will become soggy. But even soggy, it is a treat. The only serious fault I can find with this treat is that it tastes so good, you'll be tempted to eat it all. Then, unless you're a very large person with a very large appetite, you'll feel in need of a tummy tuck or a girdle for hours to come. Still, what's a little discomfort when the cause is so yummy?

So walk over to the Central Grocery or the Progressive Grocery on Decatur Street and, as you devour your muffuletta, spare a thought for the many Sicilian immigrants who flooded into a crumbling French Quarter in the late nineteenth century, bringing with them new and delicious additions to the pantheon of New Orleans delicacies.

Hint: You can buy a half or quarter sandwich, something I didn't know when I purchased my first muffuletta.

Carolyn Blue, *Eating Out in the Big Easy*

I sat down dejectedly on one of the antique chairs in the hotel lobby, thinking of Julienne, who might have been seen Sunday morning but not since then, maybe not since the previous night. And the bottom line was that no one was looking for her. Not her husband, not her terrified-of-water colleague/lover, and not the police. Just me. And what did I know about finding a missing person? Deciding that I was more worried than hungry, I donned my raincoat, picked up my umbrella, and headed for the Vieux Carre Police Station. I was so upset that I actually found myself looking over my shoulder, responding to that eerie sensation one gets at the back of the neck when convinced that an unseen person is stalking one. Paranoia! At the station, before entering, I turned resolutely, scanned the street, and saw not a single suspicious individual. *Well, Carolyn,* I said to myself, *aren't you embarrassed? After all, you are not the person who is missing.*

Having rescued myself from silly timidity, I marched into the station. There was a different officer at the desk, but he was no more helpful than the sergeant who had sent Jason and me packing early Sunday afternoon. I tried to remain pleasant, remembering my grandmother's advice that more flies are to be caught with honey than vinegar. In this case "honey" did me no good. Perhaps it was my Yankee accent that offended the officer.

Finally, abandoning the gentle and ladylike persuasion I customarily espouse when not overcome by the effects of rum and Pat O'Brien's hurricane mix, I said forcefully, "I thought this was supposed to be a city that welcomed tourists. I do not consider your lack of concern for a missing professor, a very prestigious professor I might add, either friendly or helpful, and believe me, if anything has happened to Dr. Magnussen, I intend to start writing letters to every newspaper and travel magazine in the country to warn tourists of exactly how little protection they can expect from the New Orleans Police Department. In fact, I'm here to write a book about the city, a book for which I've already received an advance, I might add—just in case you think I'm some deluded nincompoop who couldn't get a book published if—"

"Ma'am." My tirade was interrupted by one of those deep, drawling Southern voices that are guaranteed to send a shiver down a female spine. I looked up to see, standing beside me, a very tall, very handsome man of a certain age, which is to say about my age. If I hadn't been a happily married woman, I might have melted into an adoring puddle at his feet. As it was, I simply stammered into stillness.

"Lieutenant Alphonse Boudreaux, ma'am." He smiled at me as if I was the woman he'd been looking for all his life.

I swallowed and steeled myself against such charm. I had Julienne to find. I didn't have the time or lack of wifely propriety to let myself be sidetracked by a man, even a police lieutenant, who undoubtedly left swarms of swooning females in his wake. "My friend, Dr. Julienne Magnussen, is missing," I said, "and this is the second time that I have reported as much without arousing the slightest interest among the officers of your department."

"Reckon they must be blind then," said the lieutenant. "Ah sure do find you mighty interestin'." Before I could reproach him for flirting with me when I had a pressing problem to solve, he said, "Why don't you step this way, Miz . . ." He glanced at my ring finger. "Ah don't think Ah caught your name, ma'am."

He put his hand under my elbow and gently shepherded me toward a door that led to an inner part of the station I had not been able to access before. "B-blue," I stammered.

"Beg pardon?" He pulled out a chair for me in his utilitarian office and seated me with a courtly flourish.

"My name is Blue. Carolyn Blue."

"Yes, ma'am. Ah thought for a minute there, you were referrin' to your state of mind. Well, now, Miz Blue, why don't you tell me about your missin' friend. Whatever impression you might have got, Ah wouldn't want you to think N'Awlins doesn't care about the safety an' happiness of her visitors."

I stared at him. He really was a fine-looking man, dark-haired with a hint of gray at the temples, nicely weathered skin, and a physique that flattered his uniform rather than the other way around. Of course, he wasn't any better looking or built than Jason, just eight or so inches taller. And there was no chance that he was anywhere near as intelligent, or humorous, or sweet-tempered, or—

"Miz Blue?" he prodded, evidently realizing that he'd lost my attention to distracting inner thoughts. Good thing he couldn't read them. He'd either be amused at my interest or irritated that he had come off second best in comparison to my husband. "Could you tell me when the lady disappeared? She one of those tooth-straighteners we got in town this week?"

"I beg your pardon?"

"The orthodontists at the Superior Inn."

"Dr. Magnussen is a chemist. Here for the American Chemical Society meeting."

"Oh, sure. At the convention center. They're a lot less rowdy than the dentists."

"I'm delighted to hear it," I replied. "Now, having established my friend's credentials, could we—"

"Talk about her bein' missin'? Yes, ma'am. When did she—"

"She disappeared Saturday night . . . well, actually she was seen Sunday morning. By a Professor Torelli, but that was really in the middle of the night, depending on the hours one keeps, I suppose. And possibly Sunday morning around breakfast time, although that's not—"

"Why don't you just start right at the beginnin' an' tell me the whole story," he suggested. "Plus anythin' you can think of that might help me."

Help him? He was really going to investigate Julienne's disappearance? I felt as if a suffocating veil had been lifted from my spirit. Finally, someone who saw what a dangerous situation this might be! I smiled at Lieutenant Boudreaux and began to talk. And I told him everything, my suspicions about Nils, about Linus Torelli, about white slavers and muggers and camera thieves, about the possibility of Julienne being run down while boating on the river or becoming lost in the swamp. The lieutenant nodded with a serious expression and even made some notes. By the time I got to Julienne sightings at Torelli's high-rise hotel and at Café du Monde, the lieutenant interrupted me to say that he'd had no lunch and was getting "mighty peckish."

I was quite hungry myself, so I could imagine how famished a man his size might be. Therefore, I agreed to walk over to an establishment famous for its muffulettas (the lieutenant pronounced it moofalottah), a New Orleans treat of which I had read and on which I would certainly need to write in my book. Seeing no harm in combining sleuthing and culinary research, I rose with alacrity and off we went, although I had to stop talking because it took all my breath to keep up with him. I couldn't even pause to look over my shoulder, although I again had that unsettling sensation of being followed. But who would be following me? And why? If there were a stalker, he certainly wouldn't be practicing his avocation while I was in the company of a very large policeman. So again I was being silly, experiencing a psychological discomfort induced by my friend's disappearance, no doubt.

Much to my surprise, we entered a place called the Central Grocery on Decatur Street in the Quarter, hardly the milieu where I expected to find gourmet food, although it had that mouth-watering bouquet of aromas common to good Italian groceries. There we waited in a long line among milling crowds and ever-increasing noise to buy—and I, of course, insisted on paying for my own—two immense sandwiches. We carried those in paper bags to a bench on the Moonwalk, a charming, landscaped area on the levee by Jackson Square. The area's name derives from the nickname, Moon, of a former mayor. Perhaps he had been a moon-shaped politician as a result of eating too many muffulettas. I certainly felt moon-shaped after we had removed the voluminous wrappings and devoured the contents. But they were wonderful! Also much too big for me to eat. However, the lieutenant was only too glad to finish mine while I finished the story of Julienne's disappearance and my theories of what might have happened.

Once Lieutenant Boudreaux had disposed of the bags and wrappings, he sat down beside me again, and we watched traffic on the river for a time while he considered all the implications of my tale. "You may not know it, ma'am, but we're not supposed to look for adults until they're gone forty-eight hours," he began.

I'm afraid that the look I gave him was not only disappointed but also somewhat unfriendly.

"An' your friend's been spotted, so that runs the forty-eight-hour time period to at least tomorrow mornin'."

I positively scowled at him.

"Still an' all, Ah hate to disappoint a pretty lady who likes muffulettas almost as much as Ah do."

I began to feel hopeful again. "So you'll—"

"Ah'll check the police reports, an' the hospitals, an' call some friends Ah got on the river patrols."

"But—"

"An' Ah'll do it mahself—the callin' that is. Then, if that don' turn up your friend, an' maybe in this case, no news is good news; better an inconsiderate friend than a dead one; that's mah feelin'. Still an' all, if she don' turn up, then tomorrow, if you can get her husband to report her missin', Ah'll put out an APB on her so every cop in the city'll be lookin' for her."

"But what if he's the reason she's missing?" I protested. "He thinks she's unfaithful."

"Lots a that goin' 'round these days. Not too many husbands doin' away with their wives because of it, 'specially not professors with professor wives. Mos' smart folks would consider killin' a wife a bad career move."

"I suppose so," I had to admit.

"Don' mean it might not be the case. Happens he won't come in, Ah'll have to consider that suspicious. Might be Ah'll have to talk to him mahself. Would you say this Dr. Magnussen is a violent man?"

Was he? Until lately I wouldn't have thought so. "He spoke to her very angrily, even cruelly. And in public as well as in the privacy of their room. The housekeeper told me about a terrible argument they had at the hotel before dinner."

"Lotsa mean-mouthed folks around. Don' mean they take to hittin' or shootin'. He got a gun?"

"If he does, he couldn't have brought it with him. They came by plane. Wouldn't he have been arrested for carrying a weapon on an airplane?"

The lieutenant ran a large hand through that thick, black hair. "If security turned it up. Wouldn't be smart to chance takin' one on a plane. You know what kinda camera an' laptop the lady was carryin' when she ran off?"

I searched my mind desperately. As for the laptop, I was simply assuming its existence and had to tell him so, but I finally dredged up the name of the camera Julienne favored.

The lieutenant nodded, took out a notepad, and scribbled a few lines. "That's an expensive one, for sure. Can't hurt to put it on the pawnshop lists. Thief took it off her, he's gonna try to get money for it. It'll turn up. Then we'll have somethin' to go on."

I shivered when I actually had to face the implications of what we were discussing so theoretically.

"You sure you want to pursue this?" he asked kindly.

"Yes." I had to interrupt our discussion because I had actually been observing, while we talked, someone who looked suspicious, a bearded man sitting on the opposite bench and watching us over his copy of the *Times-Picayune*. I put my hand on the lieutenant's sleeve and whispered urgently, "Don't stare, but do you see that man across the way wearing the cap and rumpled tweed jacket?"

"Uh-huh," said the lieutenant.

"He's been staring at us," I whispered. Of course, the man wasn't staring at us now, but he certainly had been. During my conversation with Alphonse Boudreaux I had taken several peeks to confirm my suspicion.

"Could be," the lieutenant agreed.

"Don't you find that suspicious under the circumstances?" I asked.

"No ma'am. Likely he thinks you're pretty—Ah sure do—or he's someone Ah arrested sometime or other."

"A criminal?" I whispered.

"City's full of 'em," the lieutenant agreed casually. "Also full a men starin' at pretty women. Don' let it bother you, Miz Blue. If he's lookin' at you, he's not gonna come over an' invite you to have a drink with him, not when Ah'm here, 'cause Ah'm bigger'n he is. An' if he was lookin' at me . . . Well, there he goes, headin' off toward the street. Most likely he was lookin' at the cathedral. Got a good view of it from his bench."

I breathed a sigh of relief as the man in the cap disappeared into the crowd. I was being a ninny, and it occurred to me that this sudden attack of paranoia would not impress the lieutenant. He might think I'd imagined the whole thing about Julienne. I gave him my most earnest look and said, "I do appreciate your offer to make inquiries about Julienne. We're so worried about her. Well, not Nils, but then he's not thinking straight, or else he's—" I stopped, wary of continuing to accuse a man, whom I had known for years, of doing goodness-knows-what to his wife.

"Glad to do it, Miz Blue." He glanced at his watch and I glanced at mine, noting that I had only twenty minutes to get back to the hotel where I was to meet Broder for our search of the quarter.

"Well," I said, standing up, "I, for one, intend to put the afternoon to good use."

"What good use?" the lieutenant asked, looking worried. "Hope you're not plannin' any foolish—"

I had to laugh. "Believe me, Lieutenant, I'm not given to foolish ventures. Faculty wives are notoriously sedate." I smiled reassuringly at him. "I'm just rushing off to meet a professor of Calvinist theology. What could be more innocuous? I'm going to show him the Quarter."

"Well, y'all have fun," said the lieutenant, looking as if he doubted that would be possible, given the companion with whom I planned to spend the afternoon.

10

Cajun Bloody Mary

Poor Broder was in shock. We'd passed The Unisex World Famous Love Acts/Men and Women, where the male and female genitalia in the drawings were discreetly screened by black patches, and then a place called The Orgy. Now we were standing in front of Wash the Girl of Your Choice, one of the choices being a merry-looking damsel with pancake breasts and wet hair. She was standing under a shower, laughing. Presumably, the customer was invited to join her there. Photos of other naked females in various poses surrounded her. Most were wearing high heels. Did the customer wash the lady of his choice while she was still shod? Did the establishment or the performers have to pay for soggy shoe replacement?

I didn't share these speculations with Broder, who was stammering and red-faced. I heard him mutter something about Sodom and Gomorrah. Fortunately, Julienne had not mentioned showing me any of these particular clubs in the city of her birth. I did take pictures (which I knew Jason would find amusing; Broder didn't) before hustling my protector away toward less bawdy surroundings, if I could find them. As I scouted out the Absinthe House, a favorite of Julienne's, Broder went on and on about the decadence of New Orleans and all the horrible fates that could have befallen our old friend: rape, murder, rape and murder, kidnapping by white slavers and incarceration in a house of ill repute where debauched customers might even now be . . . I had to stop listening and vowed never again to go anywhere with Broder McAvee. I'm sure he is a well-meaning man, but he was herding me in the direction of a nervous breakdown. How could he think of nothing but sin when all around us were marvelous old brick buildings with their lusciously ornate grillwork balconies? How did Carlene stand living with him? Maybe she took Prozac.

The Absinthe House, which Julienne had mentioned, has two incarnations, one in an 1806 building, the second down the street. The second has "Bar" tacked on its name and features the original marble-topped bar on which rests the original brass water-dripper once used to add water to absinthe, no doubt to slow the progress of poisoning the absinthe drinkers. Broder warned me about the dangers of absinthe, but I assured him that no one in this country served it any longer. The bar top, dripper, and other fixtures had been spirited away during prohibition when the historic drinking establishment, then a speakeasy, was raided by federal agents. Both Absinthe Houses encourage customers to tack their business cards on the wall.

In Lafitte's Old Absinthe House, on the corner of Bourbon and Bienville, I did so. Imagine me with a business card! I'd ordered them the very day I signed my contract with the publisher. "Carolyn Blue, Writer," they said in a very discreet format. Black on white. Raised type. They even give my E-mail address, about which I still feel amazed—that I have one. My husband and children may have used computers for years, but not I. I more or less edged into the computer age. First, I wrote a letter to my father on Chris's computer and at Chris's insistence. He was a sophomore in high school at the time and perhaps embarrassed to have a mother as backward as I. I was so enchanted with revision capabilities that did not involve erasures or bottles of White-Out that I continued to use the computers in the house for letter writing and even for that first article on eating goat.

Then Gwen, my daughter, called long distance to announce that she had found a Web site called "Medieval Feminists." Well, I could hardly pass that up, so I ventured out on my first www adventure. And finally, my agent, on hearing that I had no E-mail address, insisted that I get one. Jason added me as a second user on his home computer. Gwen is now saying that I need my own web page and has threatened to set one up for me.

Young people are amazing, aren't they? I can remember thinking that an old-fashioned, manual typewriter was a magical device. Of course, I was four years old at the time, and my father, when he caught me adding letters to a manuscript page of his, forbade me to enter his study again. By the time I was once more allowed in, to dust the furniture after my mother's death, he had an electric typewriter, which I was still forbidden to touch. A psychiatrist would probably say that my reluctance to use computers is the result of psychological damage done to me at an early age by my father. My father, of course, would say, "Rubbish," and I rather imagine he'd be right.

Well, I put my card on the wall, hoping Julienne might see it.

Broder refused to produce his, but who can blame him? I didn't find any business cards identifying Calvinist theologians. I did find a few cards from

Roman Catholic priests, and I found Julienne's card, but couldn't tell whether it was new or old. I also found a bartender who, on studying her picture, thought he might have seen her sometime Sunday. She had been wearing jeans and a jean jacket.

Since the bartender asked me three times during the interrogation what I'd have to drink, I studied the menu and ordered a Cajun Bloody Mary, prepared to take notes for my book. However, I wondered wistfully what the bar's most popular drink in the nineteenth century, the absinthe frappé, would have tasted like. It sounded too delicious to be poisonous. Broder, after some prodding, ordered Jell-O shots. Evidently, he thought he was getting dessert. My drink was amazingly spicy and filling. Even though I have become accustomed to the chili peppers that imbue the Mexican food in El Paso with its unique flavor, my tongue was burning after the first sip, no doubt from Tabasco sauce, that staple seasoning of Cajun cooking.

Legend has it that Louisiana boys off fighting the mid-nineteenth-century war in Mexico were mustered out with renewed enthusiasm for hot peppers. One such soldier named McIlhenny brought special Mexican pepper seeds home to Avery Island, where Tabasco sauce was born as a result. I suppose one could say that some good comes out of a war, but I'd just as soon my son Chris didn't have to fight in any, no matter what seeds he might bring home to improve our various national cuisines.

Cajun Bloody Mary

1½ oz. vodka	1 tsp. canned beef bouillon
3 oz. tomato juice	1 tsp. horseradish
1 dash ea. steak sauce and	2 dashes Tabasco
Worcestershire sauce	½ tsp. ea. black pepper and celery salt

Combine in a mixer and shake.

Serve over crushed ice in an old-fashioned glass.

Garnish with *a slice of lime and pickled okra or pickled green bean.*

With my tongue still tingling, I left Broder to have a second helping of Jell-O while I went to the telephone to call Linus Torelli and Nils. I wanted to ask if Linus was sure that Julienne had left wearing the red dress and Nils if she had brought a jean jacket with her. Neither was in his room, and I doubted that having Torelli paged at the conference would be productive or, if productive, a welcome interruption. But a jean jacket didn't sound like Julienne. I couldn't remember her wearing any such thing. Her Southern-belle mother, Fannie Delacroix, would never have approved. Was the bartender mistaken in his identification? If not, could Julienne have fitted both jeans and jacket into the shoulder bag Torelli had said she was carrying when she came to his room?

When I rejoined Broder to finish my Bloody Mary, he told me that Jean Lafitte, the notorious pirate/patriot, had used a secret room upstairs, now a restaurant, for meetings.

"Shall we go up for a snack?" I asked eagerly. Maybe Julienne had eaten there. If not, I was, after all, researching a book on New Orleans food. Did they have authentic pirate food upstairs? I took a picture just in case I located any recipes for pirate cuisine.

Broder gave me a reproachful look and reminded me that we had to find Julienne. I must say, he was more cheerful and less likely to terrify me with dire predictions of Julienne's fate in Sin City after his second helping of "dessert." In fact, while we were looking for the voodoo museum, another favorite of Julienne's, we stopped to listen to a black street band that featured a tuba player in shorts, two men on trombone and drums, and a portly woman in a white dress who sang and played several instruments herself. Along with haunting blues songs, she did some gospel, after which Broder actually hopped the street barriers that surrounded the group and shook the woman's hand.

"Finally!" he exclaimed. "A good Christian woman!"

I was afraid she or her companions might take him to be some kind of dangerous religious fanatic. The men were certainly scowling suspiciously. The singer, however, beamed at Broder and asked. "You a man a' God, brothah?"

Before he could launch into a convoluted academic explanation of his calling, I, too, slipped between the barriers and whipped out Julienne's photo. "We're looking for a friend," I said quickly. "She's been missing since Sunday." Even the bartender couldn't place her after Sunday.

"Why you think we seen her?" demanded the tuba player, towering over my shoulder.

"Well, I . . ." Had I somehow offended them? "We're asking everyone."

The drummer abandoned his stool, and the trombone player ambled over to look at my photograph. "Das you," said the tuba player belligerently.

"Yes," I agreed, glancing backward apprehensively. "Taken about ten years ago."

"Honey," said the woman, "Ah don' notice folks when we on da street playin'. You oughta try da po-lice."

"Like sayin' you oughta try da mob," muttered the drummer.

"The Mafia's here, too?" gasped Broder.

"Excuse me," said a paunchy tourist in an embroidered shirt. He was in the act of dropping a five dollar bill into the open trombone case on the street. "Could you play 'The Saints' for my wife and me? We always wanted to hear it played in New Orleans. Somehow it's not the same, hearing it on TV or in Indianapolis."

"Sure we can, honey," said the singer. She smoothed down her tight, white dress and began to sing even before the instrumentalists could play any introductory music. Evidently she wasn't interested in staring at Julienne's picture any longer. So much for one Christian coming to the aid of another.

"Come on, Broder, let's find the voodoo museum." He did not look pleased to hear our next destination and told me it was once thought that white children were captured and sacrificed in voodoo ceremonies.

"What luck our children aren't with us," I replied. I, too, was feeling the effects of alcohol. Unfortunately, Broder's Jell-O shots seemed to be wearing off as new anxieties overwhelmed him. He lectured me on the evils of combining pagan African rituals and snake gods with Roman Catholicism, of which he also seemed to have a horror. I, in my pre-trip reading, had found the whole subject fascinating, although not something I took very seriously.

The museum itself proved to be—well, there's no other word for it—spooky. It was dark and smelled like old houses that need a good airing . . . very atmospheric, I suppose. The entrance fee almost caused Broder to rethink his offer to protect me from evil. However, Christian knightliness spirited the five dollars from his pocket, and in we went, but not with any luck, initially. The attendants could hardly see the photograph in the gloom but were anxious to offer us appointments for cemetery tours, voodoo ceremonies, psychic readings, even voodoo tours that included visits to voodoo pharmacies, a prospect that moved Broder to nudge me and hiss, "Absolutely not. Absinthe was bad enough."

As if we had any absinthe, I thought. I'd had vodka; he'd had tequila in Jell-O.

I was worried enough about Julienne to ask if a psychic reading could locate a lost person, whereupon Broder dragged me away from the helpful attendant and into the gift shop, which had, at least, a higher level of light, not to mention an interesting selection of gris-gris potions and voodoo dolls. I bought, over Broder's objections, a love potion for my son Chris who, in his last phone call from school, had complained that the object of his affection had just dumped him for a marketing major. There's nothing like a joke, which I considered the love potion, to cure a minorly broken heart.

Then I selected a voodoo doll for my daughter. I thought she might find it therapeutic to name it after her American government professor and stick pins in it. He had thrown a blackboard eraser at her in front of some two hundred students when she dozed off during an unusually boring lecture. I hadn't cared much for government myself, except as it applied to things medieval. The organization of the English court system under Henry II, for instance, had once been a matter of great interest to me when I was a young medieval history major.

As the clerk in the voodoo gift shop was wrapping my purchases and Broder hovered nervously, as if to protect me from spells and charms and other unchristian dangers, I fished out the photograph of Julienne, Philippe, and me. "Has this lady visited your shop?" I asked, pointing to Julienne.

"Looks familiar," the girl allowed, passing me my wrapped love potion and pincushion doll. "Looks like a lady came in—Sunday, I think. Some time in the afternoon. Before dusk, anyways. We close at dusk."

Broder muttered to himself. He seemed to find something ominous in closing at dusk instead of, say, 5:30 or 7:00. In fact, he found the dusk closing so ominous that he decided he'd wait for me outside.

"What was she wearing?" I asked, hardly noticing Broder's departure now that I was on the trail of information about Julienne.

"Nothin' fancy," said the clerk. "Don' really remember. Nice curly hair, though. Well, jeans. Yeah, I think jeans."

"And a jean jacket?" If so, her observation would support the bartender's at Lafitte's Absinthe House.

The clerk pulled thoughtfully at one of many long, thin braids. "Didn' notice a jacket, ma'am."

I must have looked disappointed.

"Mighta been over her arm."

I nodded encouragingly.

"Bought a voodoo doll." She pointed to a male doll.

Was Julienne going to stick pins into a representation of Nils? Or even Linus, who hadn't been willing to forgo a night's sleep to accompany her on another photographic session? "Was she carrying a camera?"

"Everybody's carrying a camera." She nodded at mine as a case in point. "Well, except that fella who left just now. You want a book about Marie Laveau? She was the most famous voodoo queen of New Orleans."

"Does it contain recipes?" I asked. That would make a wonderful chapter. Voodoo recipes. If they happened to be tasty. The clerk was giving me a peculiar look. I imagined what Broder would think if he could hear me asking about voodoo recipes. He'd assume I was interested in gris-gris type things, scary potions, while I, practical woman that I am, had been wondering what Marie Laveau had cooked for breakfast. If it was grits, the Marie Laveau chapter was gone!

Still, I took a picture when I got outside, then looked around for my escort. Goodness! He was nowhere in sight. Could Broder, imagining that I had sold my soul to souvenir-dispensing devil worshipers, have deserted me? Instead of Broder, I was approached by a stocky woman wearing a turban, a bunchy, many-colored, ankle-length skirt, and a black knitted shawl. *A freelance voodoo tour guide?* I asked myself. She grabbed my arm and thrust her face, a remarkably ugly face, into mine.

In a raspy, threatening voice, she whispered, "Bad luck you stay heah in N'Awlins, missus. I got da second sight."

"Really?" I pulled back to try for a better look at her, but she had me by both arms now, and her grip was bruising.

"Bettah you go away, missus. Bad things come to you, you keep walkin' dese streets."

It occurred to me that she meant to steal my camera or my handbag. Why else would this peculiar person be trying to frighten me with spurious prophecies?

"Danger. Ah see danger," she intoned in a loud, hollow voice.

"Me, too," I replied as I jerked away from her hands and got a firm grip on both my purse and my camera. "If you don't go away, I intend to summon a policeman."

"You be callin' dem po-lice, you nevah leave N'Awlins alive."

"You stole that outfit from the museum, didn't you?" I retorted, feeling braver each minute because, after all, there were other tourists I could call out to. "I saw one just like it on a mannequin inside." Still clutching my handbag to deter theft, if that was her game, I reached behind me to turn the gift shop doorknob, then flung the door open, stumbled over the sill, and cried, "This woman has stolen your . . . your artifacts."

The clerk who had sold me the voodoo doll and several customers, who must have entered the shop from the museum, gaped at me. The turbaned woman gave me a baleful look over her shoulder as she fled, running down the street and colliding with Broder at the corner. Being a Christian gentleman, he helped her up. Being a rude criminal, she shoved him aside and disappeared around the corner.

It wasn't until I returned to my hotel room that I realized I had lost the gifts for the children. Had she taken them? Or had I simply dropped them on the sidewalk or in the shop during the hullabaloo that followed her departure: Broder's fussing, official apologies from the staff of the museum, and a brief spate of note-taking from a policeman who arrived to investigate the incident.

He told me that the city was full of "nut cases" and I shouldn't let the incident worry me since I was none the worse for it.

11

Risotto Mille e Una Notte
(Thousand and One Nights Risotto)

Before I collapsed on the cabbage rose bedspread in our room at Hotel de la Poste, I called Linus Torelli again and, for a wonder, found him in. "Did Julienne have jeans with her when she left your room?" I demanded, not even bothering to identify myself.

Torelli did not sound happy to hear from me. "I told you she was still wearing the red dress. She had no other clothes with her except some sort of shawl thing and the purse."

Perhaps it was another woman, not Julienne, seen yesterday by the bartender and the voodoo sales clerk. "I hope you're telling me the truth, Professor. It's only fair to warn you that I've already talked to a police lieutenant at the Vieux Carre station, and I mentioned your name."

"I can't believe this!" His voice had gone high with anxiety or exasperation; I wasn't sure which. "All I did was befriend her. That's all! You must be a crazy woman to harass me like this." He hung up before I could pursue the conversation.

Sighing, I propped a pillow against the French headboard on my bed and picked up my New Orleans guide. Where else had Julienne suggested we go together? I thumbed through the book and came upon two more places: the French Market and the swamp tour boats. Julienne loved the swamps; she had always said they were unearthly, eerie, and mysterious. Oh, how I hoped that she'd return to accompany me on a swamp tour. And go shopping for souvenirs with me at the French Market. I'd already missed sharing the Historic Voodoo Museum with her and hated to think of paying another five dollars should she insist on returning to point out things that I might have missed. Of course, I probably had missed everything of interest, now that I thought of it. I'd been focused on finding someone who had seen her, not to mention inhibited by all Broder's carping and the unfortunate confrontation with the pseudoseer outside. With such thoughts spiraling through my mind, I drifted into a light sleep from which I was awakened by the telephone bringing me Lieutenant Alphonse Boudreaux's sexy, drawling voice.

"No news is good news, Miz Blue," he said. "We got no unidentified Caucasian women in our hospitals, jails, morgue, or fished outa the river, so Ah don' know where your friend is, but it don' seem like she's dead or injured in N'Awlins."

"I guess that is good news," I said doubtfully. "I found two people who may have seen her yesterday afternoon in the Quarter."

"Well, that's good news, too. Means she was OK twenty-four hours ago. Ah hafta say it sounds to me like she left of her own free will. That bein' the case, this isn't really police business. Country's full of runaway wives, ma'am. They got a right if that's what they want to do. Like you said, her husband hasn't been treatin' her kindly."

"But Lieutenant, believe me, if she were OK, she would have called me, no matter how angry she is with Nils."

"Maybe. But an angry woman, she don' always think about anything but what's botherin' her. Could be that way with your friend. Like as not, she'll be gettin' in touch when she cools down. Meantime, Ah believe Ah did see your name on a police report came in the end of the shift. You the Miz Carolyn Blue got accosted outside the Historic Voodoo Museum?"

"Oh well, it was nothing," I assured him.

"You weren't hurt?"

I looked down at my forearms, which were beginning to ache, and there I saw the fingerprint bruises made by the strange woman who had warned me of danger. "Did you catch her?" I asked, realizing that I would have to wear long sleeves for several weeks. It was no problem here in cool and rainy New Orleans, but when I got home to El Paso, the temperatures could well be nudging the short-sleeve range. We don't really have much of a winter, except at night. Temperatures do tend to plummet then, but not below zero, as had been the case when I was growing up in Michigan. In El Paso, we're lucky to see temperatures near freezing, and then the local weathermen issue all sorts of plant and pet warnings. What weather wimps Southwesterners are!

"We haven't caught the lady who bothered you, no, ma'am, an' Ah'm sorry to say we likely won't. The museum isn't even sure she stole a dress from them like you thought."

I sighed. A familiar police refrain. Two porch chairs had been stolen from my courtyard at home, and the police had said the same thing, adding that my chairs were probably on their way to Mexico. If my assailant had stolen that outfit or the gifts for my children, those articles would, no doubt, stay in New Orleans, but that didn't do me any good. "I do thank you for your efforts, Lieutenant," I said and bade him goodbye.

"What lieutenant has been making efforts on your behalf?" my husband asked, entering the room and dropping his briefcase on the bed.

"I was accosted in front of the voodoo museum by some crazy woman," I replied, holding out my bruised arms for his inspection.

"Good lord!" Jason exclaimed and dropped down beside me, all concern.

"But I fended her off and managed to keep both my purse and camera."

"Where was Broder during all this?" Jason asked, loosening his tie. "I thought he was supposed to be protecting you from sin and sinners."

"More like protecting himself," I muttered. "He left, horrified, when I asked about Marie Laveau voodoo cookery."

Jason grinned. "I won't even ask you what voodoo cookery is, unless it's something you plan to practice on me."

"You know I don't cook if I can help it now that I'm semiretired in the domestic venue."

"More's the pity," he replied sadly. Then he informed me that Lester and Miranda wanted to meet us at Bacco for dinner. They'd read about the restaurant in some gourmet magazine. Since Bacco was in our hotel, I didn't see any way to avoid the dinner, although the prospect of listening to Miranda talk about the $350 an hour she billed while defending greedy and amoral corporate clients didn't give me much joy.

Nonetheless, I smiled at my husband and ducked into the bathroom to shower and put on something less casual. Maybe the very rich Miranda and the very eminent Lester would pick up the bill. And I could certainly make cuisine notes for my book.

While I was waiting for Jason to fiddle the knot of his tie into a configuration that pleased him, I thumbed through my *Louisiana New Garde* cookbook because the restaurant at which we were destined to eat rang a bell with me. Indeed, I found a number of recipes in the book that were attributed to Ristorante Bacco. What luck! I hadn't previously noticed that such luscious-looking dishes came from our very own hotel. When I pointed out items to Jason, he found several he wanted to try.

Bacco was charming in a number of ways: the wood-fired ovens (I was almost tempted to order pizza), the lessons in Italian piped into the ladies' room (Miranda complained about hearing the same thing when she was put on hold while calling for a reservation), the charming ambiance, the elegant curved ceilings, but particularly the food. Once I had tasted it, I was sorry to have stuffed myself with the muffuletta at lunch, not that the sandwich wasn't wonderful, too—but the food at Bacco—*Viva la Italia!* It almost made Miranda's company bearable and Lester's news less disturbing.

Because I was still suffering from lunch overload, I chose a salad and the oyster and roasted eggplant ravioli (a first course hearty enough to be an entrée.) I myself have been known to make a memorable lobster ravioli, so complicated that I hope never to make it again. Therefore, I choose these time-consuming seafood raviolis when I have the chance. And this one was lovely. I believe I detected in the filling, besides the minced oyster and eggplant, hints of garlic, green onion, breadcrumbs, oregano, and a dash of something spicy. And the sauce—which I confess to finishing with my bread when I had consumed the ravioli—cream, butter, wine, shallots, garlic, the oyster flavor and then the surprise—the taste of some licorice liqueur. I checked when we returned to the room and discovered that it was a favorite of New Orleans chefs: herbsaint. What a charming name! I wondered what saint might have favored anise. My reference books don't say.

While I was eating my salad, Jason and Lester were feasting on polenta topped with squid that had been sautéed in garlic olive oil, highly seasoned, then cooked in wine. I'm not really a fan of polenta, but I sampled a bite of Jason's squid. Delicious! I made notes. I don't remember what Miranda ordered as a first course because she didn't offer me a taste. She did complain about my making notes on the food. The waiter, however, seemed pleased and happily discussed ingredients with me.

While we were waiting for our entrées, Lester said, "Julienne is really causing a stir with this puzzling disappearance. Carlene was highly insulted, as were several scientists whose presentations she'd promised to attend. Of course, I assume that she will stop sulking and reappear tomorrow, since she's responsible for chairing a session."

"Am I the only one who's worried about her?" I asked as I sipped chardonnay.

"From what Lester's told me, I don't think we need to worry," said Miranda with an insufferable air of superiority and disdain.

How could I have liked the woman so much when we were young? I wondered. She'd changed out of all comprehension. Lester I could understand. His jolly personality had evidently been the result of alcohol, which he no longer consumed. According to Miranda, he also had a cholesterol problem, which had not been ameliorated by his drinking problem. How unfortunate for Lester! Although the gourmet world was celebrating the health benefits of red wine, those benefits had not worked for him. Miranda insisted that he order a risotto dish, which she described as well reviewed and cholesterol-free. Poor Lester acquiesced but looked sadly envious when Jason chose veal chops in a chicken liver-balsamic sauce, a dish he had seen in my New Orleans cuisine book.

"Maybe you wouldn't mind explaining that remark, Miranda," I said. "If there's news of Julienne, I'd like to hear it."

"I doubt that it's the news you were hoping for," said Miranda smugly. "Tell her, Lester."

The waiter had begun to serve our entrées when Lester responded to his wife's command. "There's quite a contingent here from Julienne's university," he said. "As I'm on the organizing committee, I was, naturally, aware of that, so I took the trouble to look some of them up." He shook his head dolefully and dug into his rice, then chewed with an enthusiastic smile. "This is very good!" he exclaimed. Miranda looked smugger than ever. "Here, Carolyn, try it," Lester offered.

Naturally, I did, and goodness! It was heavenly! How hard was it to make? I wondered. It seemed like an excellent choice to pass on to my readers if the chef would give me the recipe, which I didn't remember seeing in the book. Later I discovered that I had missed the recipe, probably because of its long Italian name. "What is it called?" I asked, even as I waved to the waiter.

Lester didn't remember. "Risotto Mille e Una Notte," said Miranda.

She would remember, I thought, feeling rather grumpy at the thought that Miranda probably spoke Italian fluently, whereas I knew only the few words I had picked up from operas. Being able to exclaim, "Oh, *ciel!*" which means "Oh, heaven!" isn't really very helpful when reading a menu.

"Here, let me try it," Miranda said to her husband. "I don't know why you'd ask Carolyn's opinion. I'm the one who suggested the risotto."

"Carolyn's the expert," said Lester somewhat plaintively, if a man could sound plaintive while he was eating as fast as he could. And I noticed that he didn't provide his wife any, even when ordered to.

With the waiter heading in my direction, all smiles, Miranda whispered urgently, "For heaven's sake, Carolyn, you're not going to go into another long food discussion with the help, are you?"

I ignored her and told the waiter I was interested in procuring a recipe for a book I was writing on New Orleans cuisine. I mentioned my publisher, in case he thought I was some charlatan trying to gain special attention with little white lies. However, he was delighted. Evidently, the chef and the restaurant owners liked publicity. Miranda would have been horrified had she been able to see the ingredients, which included, as one might expect of a good risotto, a lot of butter and cheese, not to mention all the lovely prosciutto. I didn't show the ingredients to her. Lester was enjoying his meal, and I'd have felt terrible if she made him stop eating. Surely his cholesterol wasn't so high that one meal would kill him. Maybe she was primarily worried about his calorie intake.

Risotto Mille e Una Notte

Wash and pat dry leaves from *1 bunch spinach*, blanch in boiling water 2 to 3 minutes, transfer with slotted spoon to bowl of cold water, drain, puree in blender or food processor.

In a large saucepan, bring *12 cups chicken stock* to simmer

In a large, heavy sauce pan, melt *¾ cup unsalted butter* over medium heat and sauté *½ cup chopped onions* 3 to 4 minutes or until pale golden.

Add *2¼ cups (1 lb.) Arborio rice* and stir 1 minute.

Add *1 cup dry white wine* and cook until almost evaporated, 5 to 6 minutes.

Add *⅔ cup peeled and diced carrots*, *⅔ cup chopped prosciutto*, *½ cup diced fresh porcini mushrooms*, and ½ cup of the hot chicken stock. Cook, stirring with wooden spoon, until broth has evaporated. Repeat, adding ½ cup hot stock at a time until rice is tender, but slightly chewy.

Fifteen minutes into broth addition, stir in *⅓ cup green peas* and spinach puree.

When rice is done, stir in *½ cup unsalted butter*, *1 cup (4 oz.) grated Parmesan cheese*, salt, and pepper to taste.

Garnish six wide, rimmed soup bowls with 12 whole slices prosciutto (2 to a bowl), and serve risotto warm.

Having taken care of my professional duties and tucked the recipe in my handbag, Miranda scowling all the while, I turned again to Lester. "Now, what's this bad news about Julienne?"

"Scandal," said Lester around a mouthful of rice, vegetables, and prosciutto. "It seems that Nils's accusations have a basis in fact. Several professors in her department are under the impression that she and this Italian fellow are having an affair."

"Why? Because they share a seminar for their students? That's hardly grounds for sexual gossip," I retorted defensively.

"Because Torelli has all but told them so."

"But he denies it. I asked him."

"You asked him!" Jason looked astounded. "When did you ask him?"

"I tracked him down at his hotel and asked him straight out, and he denied it. Then, and on the telephone today, he said there's nothing to the rumors. That their relationship was strictly—" Well, I couldn't really say "professional" since he had taken her in the night she left the dinner and her husband. "Strictly platonic," I finished somewhat lamely.

"That's not what he's hinting to his male colleagues," said Lester, "and you shouldn't be surprised that he'd deny it to you. After all, he wouldn't want to tarnish her reputation with her female friends, who might tell her what he was saying about her."

"But he wouldn't care if she was being slandered in every locker room in town?"

"I've met Torelli," said Jason mildly. "I'd be surprised if the man has been in a locker room since he got out of high school."

He smiled at me sweetly and offered me some of his veal, which was excellent. Especially the sauce. I detected not only the flavor of chicken livers (very finely chopped) and balsamic vinegar (a flavorful addition to anything from a salad, vegetable, or fruit, to a soup or meat sauce), but also red pepper and sage. I assumed that a meat stock was added as well.

"Wonderful choice," I said to Jason. If I hadn't lost my taste for cooking, I'd have tried to reproduce it when we got home. Maybe I could interest my husband in conducting a sauce experiment. Instead of looking at the recipe, we'd wing it. How much different could it be from the excitement of creating some new compound in a lab or trying to reproduce some other chemist's work? Except, of course, that in the kitchen you could eat the result of the experiment. Since Jason is mainly interested in toxins, no one would want to eat anything produced in his lab.

"I don't believe a word of it," I told Lester.

"Then why did she run away?" Lester asked. He was waving the waiter over.

Did he want a recipe, too? I couldn't imagine that Miranda devoted much of her $350-an-hour time to cooking. However, Lester didn't want a recipe. He wanted the dessert menu.

"The last thing you need is a dessert, Lester," said Miranda.

Jason evidently saw an argument coming on because Lester looked both stubborn and petulant. "My poor wife, in her search for Julienne, was accosted this afternoon and bruised by some crazy woman," said Jason as he cut and provided me with another bite of his veal. I'd rather have had a bit of the sauce mopped up with bread, but we'd eaten all the bread.

"Yes," I agreed cooperatively. "She said, among other things, that I'd never leave New Orleans alive unless I left immediately."

"You didn't tell me *that!*" Jason exclaimed.

I shrugged. "She really had another agenda; to wit, my purse or camera or both, neither of which she got," I added with excusable satisfaction. "But I do think she stole the love potion and the voodoo doll I bought as presents for the children."

"I consider those very peculiar gift choices," said Miranda.

"No more peculiar than you and Lester giving your son toy guns when he was a toddler," I retorted. "My gift selections were jokes. Were the weapons jokes, as well?"

"Goodness, Carolyn, I certainly didn't mean to offend you. I was going to point out that beliefs in illogical things like love potions and astrology are all too prevalent these days."

Miranda sounded definitely huffy. *Too bad!* I thought.

"Amen to that," Jason agreed. "Just this year I discovered that over fifty percent of a junior-level chemistry class claimed to believe in astrology."

"If you go back far enough, even the Catholic Church acknowledged the uses of astrology," I pointed out.

"Oh, well, the Church," said Miranda dismissively.

"And in Padua, there are astrological signs above the seats of judges, so lawyers weren't immune, either," I added.

"When was that?" she retorted. "The Middle Ages?"

"Of course."

"Back when I was teaching, I certainly uncovered some peculiar superstitions among my students," said Lester.

"You don't teach anymore?" Jason asked, surprised. "All *our* deans teach."

"Perhaps they don't have enough administrative functions to keep them busy," said Lester.

Since I knew he was about to launch into denigrating remarks on Jason's new university, I said quickly, "Before you get into that, could I have the dessert menu, Lester?" The waiter had slipped it to him discreetly.

"Lester!" screeched Miranda.

No more was said about Jason's decision to change his place of employment or my run-in with the ugly, turbaned lady. And the Abbotts did *not* offer to pay for any dinners but their own.

12

Po'boys and Café Brûlot

Another favorite sandwich in New Orleans is the po'boy, which once cost a nickel. These days, the price has gone up and might be too steep for the pockets of poor boys; however, no one, rich or poor, can find fault with the ingredients. In a long, slender French loaf, one can order meatballs, roast beef and gravy, oysters, shrimp, soft-shelled crab, or even plain old ham and cheese. A dressed po'boy adds mayonnaise, lettuce, and tomatoes. Like the muffuletta, the po'boy is a meal in itself.

Carolyn Blue, *Eating Out in the Big Easy*

I awoke on Tuesday morning feeling depressed. Julienne had now been missing since Saturday night and had not, as far as I knew, been seen by anyone since Sunday. Where was she yesterday? Why, if she was safe, had she not called me? And now I had to contend with the rumors passed on by Lester: People in Julienne's department thought that she had, indeed, been the lover of Linus Torelli, who had hinted of the affair to various men friends, although he had vehemently denied it to me.

Well, what else would he have said when I was, in essence, accusing him of being responsible for her disappearance? Was he responsible? The man admitted to quarreling with her early Sunday morning, but he claimed that she had stormed off alone. That part of it could be a lie. A man who tells one lie may tell another, and in his conflicting stories about their relationship, one of the versions had to be a lie.

And there was Nils, who wouldn't report her missing to the police. Even if the Sunday Julienne sightings were accurate, today would see the passing of the necessary forty-eight hours, but Lieutenant Boudreaux insisted that Nils had to make the report, not I. And Nils refused, believing his wife unfaithful, believing her to be with Torelli, no matter what Linus said. Was Nils so certain because Julienne had done what she'd threatened—returned to their room on Sunday night, claiming to have slept with Torelli? And now her husband was refusing to report her missing because he had caused her disappearance, the result of a fit of rage and jealousy. But when had he attacked her? She'd been seen Sunday, and he attended the mixer Sunday night. Had he returned to find her waiting for him? All primed to hurt him by claiming to have fulfilled his suspicions? And then he, furious, had—what?

I stifled further disturbing speculation, rolled out of bed, and padded barefoot to the bathroom. Jason had left earlier to breakfast with colleagues. I would return to Café du Monde in the hope that Julienne, still alive, would take pity on a worried friend and meet me there. She didn't. I made a solitary meal of beignets and café au lait, this time without chicory, while I considered my next stop. Obviously I had to check the convention first. Everyone else thought she'd show up to chair her session. I thought that, if she were able to do that, she'd have called me. And I knew her better than the rest of them.

At the conference information desk I managed to extract, from the young woman answering questions, the location of Julienne Magnussen's session, although Jeanne Rae, as her name tag identified her, took great pains to assure me that, as an accompanying person, I was welcome only to the social events, not the lectures. As if I wanted to hear people going on and on about arcane scientific topics. Much as I love my husband, I am no more enamored of chemistry than I was when he was the graduate assistant in my chemistry class. I did point out to Jeanne Rae that, in fact, accompanying persons were invited to plenary lectures, which were, essentially, public events. Then, having wasted precious time, I had to jog through the corridors of the convention center to reach the appointed room before the session attendees had dispersed for lack of a chairwoman, my second, and no less distressing, attempt at jogging in twenty or more years.

I needn't have run so fast, for the attendees were clustered outside the door of the meeting room with Lester at the center of the group, in midtirade upon the unconscionable, irresponsible, inconsiderate . . . Julienne had not arrived to chair the session, and Lester was appalled. I was appalled as well, but for wildly different reasons. Now I was convinced that my childhood friend had come to grief.

Nils was there, too, although he, being a mathematician and no ACS member, had no more right to attend the session than I did. "Have you heard from her?" I whispered to him. If he was innocent in the matter of her disappearance, surely he was now as worried as I.

"No," he replied curtly.

"You have to report her missing," I said pleadingly.

"Why should I?"

He killed her. The thought flashed through my mind like a tornado warning.

"She's obviously run off with Torelli. You'll notice he's not here, either. Since they're such *close colleagues,* he wouldn't have missed her session."

Misdirection or innocence on Nils's part? I wondered.

"Nils isn't required by law to report Julienne missing," said Miranda, who had joined our whispered conversation unexpectedly.

What was *she* doing here? She wasn't a conference participant, either. And she wasn't whispering. Lester and the several men around him turned when she spoke in that authoritative, courtroom voice. "The police don't want to hear about runaway wives," said Miranda. "They have their hands full with genuine disappearances. And don't give me that reproachful look, Carolyn. Have a little pity on poor Nils. Think of how embarrassing this is for him—to have his wife run off with a younger, more attractive man." Miranda looked almost pleased at the notion of a woman running off with a younger man. Nils did not look at all gratified by her defense of his cuckolded sensibilities.

"Torelli isn't better looking," I mumbled. How could these people, who had known Julienne for years, think so badly of her and show so little concern for her well-being?

"Thanks for that, Carolyn," said Nils sarcastically. "It's nice to know that my wife's best friend thinks I'm more attractive than my wife's lover. Too bad Julie wasn't of your opinion." He turned and walked away.

My impulse was to run after him and beg him to accompany me to the Vieux Carre station, but in my heart I knew it was hopeless. For whatever reason, guilt or male ego, Nils wasn't going to change his mind. "I guess your unkind remarks mean that neither you nor Lester has seen Julienne since last night?" I murmured to Miranda.

"We're not likely to see someone who doesn't want to be seen," said Miranda briskly. "Lester, I find that I'm free for lunch. Would you like to meet me at the hotel?"

Looking officious, Lester said, "I'm afraid that won't be possible, my dear. I am now forced to contend with the possibility that Julienne may fail to show up for her paper, having disappointed us today as she has."

I spotted Jason coming down the hall and walked quickly toward him. "I know. She's still missing," he said quietly. "I've been asking around. No one's seen her. Carlene's worried, too, and feeling badly that she made such a fuss about Julienne not attending her lecture. She told me Broder says you two may have found people who saw Julienne Sunday?"

I nodded.

"Unfortunately, that doesn't explain her absence yesterday, and certainly not today."

"Nils still won't go to the police."

"The man's a fool," said Jason.

I could have hugged him for his support and his good sense.

"Even if she's having affairs with ten different men, she wouldn't abrogate her responsibilities here and risk her scientific reputation."

"Exactly," I agreed. "And I don't think she's having an affair. I didn't even like that Torelli. Julienne wouldn't be interested in him. Not in a romantic way. He's just some emotionally retarded, would-be Lothario. He probably can't get a date, much less a wife, so he's trying to make himself look sexy at Julienne's expense. That's . . . that's disgusting behavior. He should be drummed out of the American Chemical Society."

Jason grinned at me, and that reaction took some of the furious wind out of my sails. "I don't know of any case in which a member was drummed out of the society for his sexual exploits, real or imaginary." He thought a moment. "Well, maybe if he raped a student and got sent to jail for it, but then he'd be drummed out of his university and . . . well, you see my point, Caro. What are you going to do now?"

Jason knew me well enough to know that I wasn't going to go home and have the vapors. I considered my options, then said, "I'm going to start making calls, first to her house and her department, in case she went back. Maybe she was so furious with Nils that she got the first plane home in order to file for divorce."

"Maybe," said Jason dubiously, "but it doesn't sound like her."

I sighed, admitting that it didn't. She'd have contacted me. She'd have warned conference officials that she was going to miss the sessions in which she was chair and lecturer. In fact, she'd have stayed for those and then gone home. "Well, I'll start telephoning hotels to see if she's registered somewhere else. If only that . . . that husband of hers would call the police, I wouldn't have to do any of this." Although Lieutenant Boudreaux had told me that no one of Julienne's description had turned up at a hospital or morgue, I wanted to know where she was and that she was safe. What if she'd been hit on the head by her supposed lover, her husband, or a mugger and was suffering from amnesia?

"That sounds like a sensible plan," said Jason, giving me a little hug.

I returned Jason's hug, an unexpected pleasure since he wasn't given to physical displays of affection in front of colleagues. Then I went back to our room in the hotel, sat myself down on the rose-covered bedspread with my address book and the New Orleans phone book at hand, and began to make calls. No one answered at Julienne's house. Her departmental secretary told me that Julienne was at the American Chemical Society meeting in New Orleans and wasn't expected home until the weekend, and, no, she hadn't returned early. Why would she? Dr. Magnussen was a distinguished scientist whose presence at the meeting was important to her department, to her, and to the other attendees. Some secretaries are so officious. The woman sounded like Lester. Then I began calling hotels in New Orleans asking if Julienne had registered under either her married or maiden name. She hadn't.

What now? Julienne had wanted to take the swamp tour. Both to introduce me to the wonders of the swamp and to take pictures. I telephoned swamp tour numbers in the Yellow Pages. No one of her name or description could be recalled by any of the bookers. Fine! That was a long shot, anyway, I consoled myself. She wouldn't have gone without me. We'd had extensive E-mail correspondence about the grotesque vegetation I'd see, the little aboveground cemeteries on the shores, and the alligators and snakes that would be swimming in the bayous and sunning themselves on the mud flats. If she had actually gone without me, I might have better luck interviewing boat captains, who would be more likely to remember her than would some ticket agent for a tour operator. Should I try to go this afternoon?

I rose to glance out the long windows that overlooked the street below. It was raining again, a light, mistlike rain, but still not good weather for a boat excursion or even for walking from boat to boat on some wooden pier surrounded by dripping vegetation that might well harbor nasty creatures, leeches, or something equally distasteful.

And I really needed a more recent picture of Julienne. And of Linus Torelli and Nils. But how? If I had an Internet connection, I could access the departmental web sites at their university, where there would be pictures of the professors that I could print out if I had a printer. But although Jason and I both have laptops, and his has a modem, neither of us has a portable printer. I called the desk, but the hotel did not offer that service. The desk clerk suggested that I try a computer bar.

Computer bar? People sat around drinking and playing with computers in New Orleans? That didn't sound very Creole to me, not very Cajun, not very French Quarter. Nonetheless, I again used the Yellow Pages and made yet more phone calls. A CompuCoffee representative informed me that his customers came to play computer games and didn't ask for printers, which he didn't provide, but that I'd undoubtedly enjoy CompuCoffee's chicory coffee and their newest game. It had some horrible name like Demise of the Bloody Death Planet. On my fourth call, I found an establishment called Po'Boy Computer Café that provided delicious drinks, sandwiches, and Internet access with printer facilities.

I took a cab and ordered, from a young man who told me that he was a computer science major at the University of New Orleans, a "loaf," which consisted of spicy fried shrimp on buttered, heated French bread. Delicious. I was starving after all those telephone calls. Given my appetite and my new profession, it's more than fortunate that I have an active metabolism.

With my shrimp loaf, I had café brûlot, a strong coffee in which are steeped cinnamon, lemon, clove, orange, and sugar. I asked the waiter and wrote down the ingredients after the first lovely sip. He had poured in brandy and set it afire right at my computer table—well, actually, at the eating and drinking ell on the table. The management discouraged endangering their computers with the food and drink and, in fact, asked us not to take the protective cover off the computer until we had finished the repast.

I was only too happy to comply. After devouring my shrimp loaf and my coffee, which was served in a charming cup on a pedestal, I turned to the computer, whipped off the cover, surfed the web, and printed out, with only two emergency visits from their computer techs, pictures of Linus, Julienne, and Nils—five by seven pictures. Ah, the wonders of modern science.

The whole experience was rather expensive, but the food was deductible; in fact, I used the Po'Boy computer to type up notes on the sandwich and brûlot. Even given the cost, I felt quite merry after my Internet success and my brandied coffee. Imagine! A computer establishment with a liquor license! Only in New Orleans! Or perhaps I am showing my lack of sophistication. Such places may exist all over the country without my being aware because I have never traveled in the circles where one would hear of such a thing. Most of my friends tend to look on computers as technological tools rather than gourmet experiences. How fortunate I am to have become a food writer instead of a scientist. Not that there was ever any chance of my becoming a scientist.

13

Mugging a Mugger

Before leaving the Po'Boy Computer Café, I folded the pictures of Julienne, Nils, and Linus Torelli and slipped them into my handbag, then scanned the street for transportation back to the hotel. As you might expect, there wasn't a cab in sight, but I was not downcast. Cognac will do that for you. Instead of fretting, I set off in the direction of the Quarter with the intention of flagging down a taxi when one appeared. In the meantime, I would simply plot out my next move.

Unfortunately, my next move was, of necessity, the defense of my person and purse. A scruffy little man with wild red hair and sunglasses slithered out of an alley and grabbed my purse. I, in turn, managed to snag the strap before it whipped off my shoulder. "Help! Thief!" I screamed.

"Shut up, bitch!" he snarled and gave my purse, which was clutched in his large, hairy hand, a mighty tug.

"Help!" I screamed and tugged back for all I was worth. Imagine calling me "bitch." Bad enough he was trying to purloin my handbag. "Help! Help!" I yanked harder on the strap.

"You dumb broad. Don' you see dis here pigsticker?" The redheaded criminal swung his left arm, and I felt, simultaneously, a burning on my hand and the departure of the purse strap through my fingers. The scoundrel had cut the purse from my grasp, cutting me in the process, while I, intent on saving my belongings, hadn't even noticed the knife in his hand until the blade was flashing in my direction. Was that what he had meant by *pigsticker?* Thoroughly incensed, I swung my umbrella at his head. I'm not sure what injury I did him, and I really don't much care, but he did cry out, drop my purse, and disappear back into his alley.

"Don't let him get away!" I cried to a male passerby. The man gave me a blank look. "He injured me!" Indeed he had. My hand was bleeding, and the passerby was scuttling away, as were two ladies who had been behind him on the sidewalk. No wonder there are so many criminals. Citizens no longer feel obliged to come to the aid of their fellows, and the police are never there when you need them. However, a cab had finally appeared. I waved my bloody hand, and the driver pulled to the curb. Then a man in a vested suit, dark blue with a fine pinstripe, tried to slip into the backseat ahead of me. I gave him a rap with my umbrella and climbed in.

"Way to go, lady!" said the cabby and asked where I wanted to be taken.

"The Vieux Carre Police Station," I replied. "I've been mugged."

"Tryin' to snag a cab from someone ain't da same as muggin', ma'am."

"I was accosted by a purse snatcher," I replied. "As it happens, I can tell the difference between rudeness and crime, although I imagine criminals are often rude as well as unprincipled. The purse snatcher certainly was."

"Sorry to hear it, ma'am. Makes da city look bad, dat's what Ah say."

"You're quite right," I agreed. "I am not finding New Orleans a friendly place."

"Ain't da same place as when Ah was a chile," said the cab driver, nodding mournfully. He was a black man who looked, given the scar on his cheek, as if someone had taken a knife to him, too.

"Were you mugged?" I asked.

"Me? No, ma'am." He glanced into his rearview mirror and caught me examining his cheek. "Oh, dis here? Mah ole lady done dat. She be as red hot as good gumbo." The man actually sounded overcome with admiration for the violent propensities of his wife, or had he meant his mother? *My old lady* could mean either.

"Um-m," I murmured. I had pulled off the scarf that tied my hair back so that I could knot it around my hand. But what a shame to get blood on that lovely periwinkle blue print, I thought as I pulled the knot tight with teeth and free hand. The color exactly matched my linen shirt and slacks. Then I considered the attack. No doubt, my conduct would be considered foolhardy. Well, it was, and had it not been for the cognac, I would probably have acted in a more sensible manner.

On the other hand, I had saved not only my handbag, a very nice leather envelope with shoulder strap that Jason had given me for Christmas, but also my money, credit cards, driver's license, and, equally important to my mission, the pictures I had printed out at the café. And I thought that I had injured the man with the knife, which he richly deserved. Now I intended to file a complaint against him. I was prepared to give quite a detailed description of my assailant.

"Here you are, ma'am," said the cabby.

I climbed out in front of the police station on Royal Street and paid him, including a generous tip.

"Now you take care, ma'am," he said as he pulled away. It had begun to rain, so I put up my umbrella. It was then that I discovered I had broken several of the ribs while belaboring the purse snatcher, or possibly the man who had tried to commandeer my cab. *Bother,* I thought as I raced under the portico with my umbrella at half-mast around my head. It was the umbrella I had purchased here in New Orleans, perhaps an inferior product produced for hapless tourists.

"Let me guess," said the sergeant at the desk. "You wanna see the lieutenant."

"I want to report a mugging," I retorted severely. I could see that he was already pressing a buzzer to summon Alphonse Boudreaux.

"Who'd you mug?" muttered the sergeant.

"I heard that," I snapped back.

"Miz Blue?" The lieutenant escorted me to his office and listened sympathetically to my story. When I told him that I had hit the attacker with my umbrella, he began to grin. When I showed him my hand, wrapped in the now blood-spotted scarf, he made soothing sounds and came around his desk to unwrap the injury and inspect it. Did lieutenants customarily devote this much attention to female complainants? Somehow I doubted it.

"Well, Miz Blue, Ah don' think it needs stitchin', but Ah can surely have one of mah men drive you over to the hospital—"

"No, no," I replied quickly. "I'm sure a bit of disinfectant and a Band-Aid will do the trick. No functional damage seems to have occurred." I wiggled my fingers to show that they still worked. "However, I do want to describe the mugger for you."

He nodded and returned to his desk chair, from which he made notes as I talked.

"Perhaps you could call in a police artist." I had seen that done on TV. "Then you can put up posters of my assailant in the various substations."

"Happens we don' have a police artist handy," he said as apologetically as if he were personally responsible for that deficiency. He made a few more notes, then looked up. "Miz Blue, you sure do get yourself in a soup pot a trouble."

"Believe me. Lieutenant, nothing like this ever happens to me at home. It's New Orleans. I don't want to hurt your feelings, but I have to consider this a dangerous city."

"Most cities are, ma'am. Now, what were you doin' at Po'Boy Computer? That is a known drug hangout. We have raided that establishment more than once."

"Drug hangout?" I was nonplused. "But it looked perfectly respectable, and their computer facilities are excellent."

"That may be, but those computer geeks sure do like cocaine. Ah wouldn't be surprised to hear they're refinin' it in the back room. On the other hand, the sandwiches are mighty good."

"Indeed. I had the spicy shrimp, which was delicious. And the café brûlot!" I sighed with remembered pleasure.

"Tut tut," he said, grinning. "Drinkin' cognac in yo' coffee in the middle of the day?"

"It's part of my research," I explained defensively. "Café brûlot is considered a New Orleans specialty. I did take notes, you know. In fact, I typed them up and printed them out, along with the pictures."

"Now, what pictures would those be?"

"Of my friend, her husband, and the man she stayed with during part of Saturday night. I can't find her if I can't show the pictures around."

"Seems to me, seein' as trouble jus' follows in your footsteps, maybe you should try stickin' to ordinary tourist activities."

"Perhaps I shall," I agreed cunningly. "I think I'll go on a swamp tour tomorrow."

"Good idea." The lieutenant rose. "Wish I could go with you." He had circled the desk and now touched a finger to my hair, which was no doubt tumbled messily around my face now that the restraining scarf wrapped my latest injury. "Yo' hair sure does look pretty hangin' loose like that, Miz Blue. Mighty pretty."

"Thank you," I replied and left hurriedly. I certainly didn't want to give the lieutenant any mistaken ideas about my availability. Did he think, because I had visited the police station daily, that I was smitten with him? Surely not.

Having walked the short distance back to the hotel, I took out the small first aid kit I always carry on trips, disinfected my cut, and covered it up with three Band-Aids. Then I inspected my handbag and umbrella. The three bent umbrella ribs straightened out reasonably well when I pounded them with the heel of my shoe. As for the handbag, its strap had been cut just above the buckle, so I unhooked and discarded the cut end and gouged a hole two inches above the remainder of the strap with my manicure scissors. Pleased with my makeshift repairs, I then took a well-earned rest on the bed while I studied the pictures of my dear friend, her hardhearted husband, and Professor Torelli, whatever he was to her. Perhaps I should make one last call—to his hotel.

I did that, and you can imagine my dismay when I was told that he had checked out that morning. The clerk assured me that Dr. Torelli had left the hotel alone after having the concierge book him an early return flight on Delta Airlines and requesting that a cab to the airport be called.

Julienne was still missing, and Torelli had fled! Oh God. In a panic, I called Lieutenant Boudreaux, but he had left to attend a meeting at police headquarters. I was forced to leave a message with the derisive sergeant, the one who had acted as if I was the mugger rather than the muggee. Disheartened, I collapsed onto the cabbage roses and worried myself into a restless sleep. I find that even a troubled nap is better for the nerves than no nap at all, especially when one is exposed to the rigors of travel.

At five, the lieutenant called to say that Julienne had not been on the Delta flight with Torelli. It seems that policemen can get any information they seek. Delta Airlines would certainly have refused any request I made to check their passenger lists. But was that good news? That Julienne hadn't departed with Torelli? I thought not.

At five-thirty, Jason returned from the convention center and sat down beside me on the bed to give sympathetic ear to my findings and my fears. I didn't mention my little brush with the would-be robber, and he didn't notice the Band-Aids on my hand. Sometimes having a husband whose mind tends to be taken up with things scientific can be a boon; one doesn't have to worry him with the little things.

"The fact that she didn't leave with Torelli doesn't mean she's dead, Caro," he assured me. "We'll take the pictures you got and show them around the Quarter. Maybe someone has seen her."

Thank God for my dear husband. Although he understood my dismay and sympathized, he did not give way to panic. Instead, he proposed a course of action, and action is always both more reassuring and more productive than fruitless lamentation. I got up to shower and change. Fortunately, the hotel provided a shower cap, which I wrapped around my hand, while my own shower cap protected my hair.

We would search the Quarter from one end to the other with these new pictures, I told myself as I used the perfumed soap provided by the hotel. At home I buy less exotic soap products. I was feeling particularly good-humored because Jason had mentioned how very clever it was of me to think of the university web site as a source of pictures. He had also been most interested in my description of the Po'Boy Computer Café. I didn't mention the drug connection. Since neither of us would be going back, there was no need to bring that up.

14
Crawfish Étouffée

The two historic cuisines of New Orleans are Cajun and Creole, the first the child of Arcadian farmers and fishermen immigrating to the Louisiana swamps and bayous from Canada in the eighteenth century. Why any group of sensible people would travel so far to settle in a swamp is certainly a puzzle, but we do owe them a vote of thanks for their contribution to traditional New Orleans menus. Cajun food is hearty and rustic, spicy and rich in lard, while its cousin, Creole cooking (Creole means native of Louisiana), is more urban, more sophisticated, more delicate, and more likely to employ cream and butter in the French fashion. The original settlers were French, although the charms of French cooking and its innovations had to be reintroduced to the population of New Orleans by the Ursuline sisters who arrived in 1727.

Carolyn Blue, *Eating Out in the Big Easy*

We set out with the idea of eating Cajun and finding Julienne. My first thought was to try K-Paul's Louisiana Kitchen for the food part of our mission. It was just down the street from our hotel, but the line was far too long. Jason was amenable to bypassing Chef Paul Prudhomme's establishment because it was listed as "expensive" in the guidebook. Bacco's, the previous night, had been expensive as well, especially to two people becoming used to the lower eating-out prices in El Paso, Texas. Of course, the self-proclaimed well-to-do Abbotts had not sprung for dinner. Why had I thought they would?

Therefore, in the interest of economy in research, we next headed for the Père Antoine Restaurant on Royal Street, which was also recommended by our guidebook and listed in the "inexpensive" section.

Before we got there, however, we detoured to watch a marvelous street show that featured two hip-high puppets in sunglasses and suits. One played a small piano while the second sang into a microphone—with the help of a sound track. Puppet lip-synching, if you will. When the show was over and the crowd dispersing, having deposited donations in a box, Jason approached the puppeteer, a person in baseball cap, T-shirt, and unlaced, high-top tennis shoes. "Have you seen any of these people?" Jason showed him, or her, the new photo of Julienne, then the old one, then those of Linus and Nils.

"You 'ave not contributed to the box, monsieur," said the piano-player puppet, who was dangling from the hand of the puppet master.

Jason looked embarrassed, whether at the oversight or because he was being admonished by a puppet I couldn't say, but he did drop all the change from his pocket into the box. It made a respectable waterfall of tinkling sounds, but the puppeteer didn't look impressed. Perhaps he/she detected the fall of pennies. Jason hadn't checked to see what he was contributing.

"Don't recognize them," said the puppeteer with hardly a glance at the photos.

I flourished the old photo and asked dryly. "Not even this one?" I pointed to the picture of myself.

"Nope," said the puppeteer and, walking the piano player over to the piano bench, began a spiel for the next performance.

I was disappointed. Julienne would have appreciated that show and would probably have given generously enough to be remembered had she seen it and had the puppeteer been willing to search his/her memory. We had almost reached Père Antoine's when, at the corner of Royal and Saint Peter, I stopped to admire an all-silver figure standing, statuelike, on the sidewalk. In fact, at first glance I took him for a statue but was almost immediately disabused of that notion when we resumed our stroll and he leapt toward us with a shriek. Startled, I shrieked in return. Perhaps I had been more traumatized by the mugging that afternoon than I realized.

Jason seemed not at all taken aback, as if being attacked by a silver-painted man on a city street was an everyday event. He whipped out the photos and presented them to the antic statue, who seemed very disappointed with that reaction. Mine had caused him to grin; Jason's was obviously unexpected. "Have you seen any of these people?" Jason asked.

"Why?" retorted the statue.

"We're looking for this lady." Jason displayed the computer printout of Julienne's university photo.

The statue examined each of the photos carefully while I fretted lest he leave silver paint on the only pictures I had. Finally, he passed back the three computer printouts but held onto my precious snapshot. "That's you," he said, smirking as he looked from me to my image on the picture. I said nothing. "And her I seen, too." He pointed to Julienne. "Same woman as in the other picture but even more of a babe. Younger, right?"

My heart speeded up. "When?" I asked eagerly. "When did you see her?"

"Shit if I know. It was like . . . on the weekend." He still held the old photograph, and I had to restrain the desire to wrest it from him.

"And him. She was with him," said silver skin.

Who? I looked eagerly to see whether he had identified Nils or Torelli. "Saturday? Sunday?" asked Jason.

"I dunno. Saturday?"

I tried to keep the disappointment off my face. The person he was pointing to, as having been with Julienne, was Philippe Delacroix, her brother, who was in the Midwest, not New Orleans. And if the puppeteer had seen Julienne on Saturday, it would have been late at night with Linus Torelli.

"What time?" I asked.

"Afternoon? Early evening?"

"Impossible," I snapped, turning away. Julienne had been arguing with Nils at the hotel or at Etienne's Saturday afternoon and early evening.

"So maybe it was Sunday." The fellow shrugged. "What I know is, I was in my pose—an' by the way you're supposed to show your appreciation with a tip—an' I jumped out at them just like I done with you, an' this guy . . ." He stabbed his finger at Philippe. ". . . he called me an asshole an' pushed me off the curb. If you know the bastard, just tell me where he is, an' I'll—"

"I'm afraid you're mistaken," said Jason calmly and tucked a dollar bill into the silver man's hand.

The statue held it up and muttered, "Damn cheap tourists," but we were already on our way down the street toward Père Antoine's and a dinner that was much more satisfying than the interviews we'd had thus far.

We both agreed that the silver statue had not seen Philippe and, therefore, had probably not seen Julienne either, especially since he couldn't even tell us on what day the alleged encounter had occurred. "He was just looking for a big tip, so he told us what he thought we wanted to hear," Jason guessed. I felt very discouraged. It was more disheartening to be lied to than to get no information at all.

After our disappointment, Père Antoine's was a pleasant surprise, featuring, as it did, a charming decor with flowers in front, large mirrors in back, and modest prices. I had crawfish étouffée, a thick stew made with roux, lard or some other artery-clogging fat, crawfish tails, and spices.

Jason had the seafood platter, which included everything: scallops, catfish, shrimp, crab, and an item called Cajun popcorn (seasoned shrimp, deep-fried). It was a feast to which I helped myself—in the interests of my research, of course. We split an order of red beans and rice to round out our Cajun experience. One wonders if all Cajuns are fat. I certainly felt fat when we staggered out of Père Antoine. If I'd been wearing a belt, I'd have loosened it.

15
Mint Juleps

After our Cajun feast, we wandered up and down Bourbon Street. Even in this unwelcoming weather and on a Tuesday night, it was mobbed. I knew that people lived in the French Quarter, but I couldn't imagine how they endured the noise. Then I saw pictures that rang a bell. Julienne had said I had to see the tassel twirlers, and there they were, or their pictures at least. Presumably, the real performers were inside. I tugged at Jason's arm, pointed to the establishment, and shouted above the crowd noise that I wanted to go in.

"No, you don't," Jason assured me, looking embarrassed.

"Julienne mentioned it."

"But Carolyn . . ."

I ignored his reluctance and urged him inside. The place—whose name I hadn't even noticed, but surely there couldn't be two dens of tassel twirlers in the city—was mobbed, mostly with men. A seedy looking person tried to lead us to a table, but Jason was immediately hailed by a large group of men who had that scientific look about them: rumpled clothes, suede-patched elbows, beards, ACS badges. Voices accustomed to lecturing in large halls to hordes of students roared over the cacophony, inviting my husband to join them in male camaraderie.

Then they saw me behind Jason and looked dismayed, like small boys caught looking at dirty photographs. Julienne and I had once caught our fifth-grade male schoolmates perusing such items. Julienne grabbed a few, and we dashed off, giggling hilariously. Once we had looked at our booty, we were rather puzzled and threw the pictures away, but those boys viewed us with fear and trembling for months, afraid we'd tattle, I suppose.

Having invited Jason, the table of scientists couldn't very well change their minds when they learned that I was part of the package, so I was duly introduced to a number of mighty intellects out on the town. The man by whom I was seated, a professor from Purdue, assured me that their presence here was in the nature of a research project. While Jason ordered a beer and I chose a mint julep, another of the New Orleans favorite cocktails on my must-try list, our tablemates proved their scientific acumen with a learned discussion of the physics of tassel twirling. I sipped the mint julep and asked the waiter how it was made, taking notes for my book as he described the process.

Mint Julep

Make simple syrup by combining *1 cup sugar* with *2 cups water* in a medium saucepan. Bring to a boil, stirring. Reduce heat and simmer 5 to 10 minutes. Cool and store in the refrigerator in a covered jar.

For one cocktail, combine *3 tablespoons of simple syrup* and *6 fresh mint leaves* in an old-fashioned glass. Crush leaves with a wooden pestle.

Add crushed or cubed ice.

Add *1½ ounces of bourbon*, stir, and serve.

Then I turned my attention to the performer, a curvaceous young woman wearing only tassels, which were attached to strategic portions of her anatomy. While noisy men shouted their approval of her talents and the professors discussed, for my benefit I imagine, the rotational forces involved in tassel twirling, I marveled that the young woman seemed to have developed muscles in parts of the breast that I would have assumed to be without muscles, had I ever given the matter any thought.

She could twirl her tassels clockwise, counterclockwise, and both at once: left breast counterclockwise, right breast clockwise. Amazing! She could also execute similar tricks with her buttock tassels. It certainly wasn't as entertaining as the American Ballet Theatre doing *Giselle*, but the performance was unusual. Also, she was a very pretty girl and evidently quite athletic. I, for one, clapped enthusiastically at the end of her number while my husband's colleagues joined me, casting surreptitious glances in my direction all the while.

Then an intermission was announced and the bill presented. My drink cost $20! "Did you see this, Jason?" I asked, horrified.

"Yer payin' fer the entertainment, lady," said the waiter. "Ya thinkin' about not payin', I'll have to call the manager."

"She wasn't *that* good!" I muttered as Jason paid the bill. Fortunately, I didn't say it loudly, for the young lady herself appeared just then at our table and posed seductively as she asked if any of the gentlemen would care to buy her a drink.

The august members of the American Chemical Society looked flummoxed, but Jason, always considerate of the feelings of others, said that we would be delighted to. I must admit that I looked at him askance. The young woman sidled over, pulled up a chair from another table, and pushed in between us, giving me a challenging look. She had the most amazing eyelashes when you saw her up close: so thick and long that one had to anticipate them tearing loose from their anchors at any moment and taking her natural eyelashes with them. I winced to think of how painful that would be.

Poor girl. She was obviously in a profession with dangers beyond the obvious: breast sprains, lascivious men, and the health hazards of dancing practically naked in the cold and damp of a New Orleans winter. Would they let her work if she had the sniffles? A woman, no matter how pretty, is not very seductive with a runny nose. Julienne's mother had always advised us to break a date rather than appear in public with a red nose and a handkerchief at the ready.

The tassel twirler was batting those eye fans at Jason as he asked what she would like to drink. She opted for champagne. I said, "I doubt that the champagne is very good here, but this drink is nice—a mint julep." I gestured to my glass. "I even have the recipe, if you're interested."

The young woman looked flabbergasted. "Well . . . OK," she responded.

"She'll have champagne," said the waiter.

"Nonsense," I retorted. "Since my husband and I are paying for her drink, she can have whatever she wants." I turned to her. "Maybe you'd rather try a hot buttered rum. It *is* a nasty night."

"Tell me about it. I slipped and fell on my butt walkin' over for the first show."

I nodded sympathetically. "That's very painful. I did that once at Disneyland. We were taking our children to see that silly It's a Small World After All thing."

"I seen that," said the young woman. "I liked it."

"I did, too," Jason agreed. "It was the only time our children stopped whining to go on the roller coaster, but poor Carolyn was in agony sitting through that ride. This is my wife, Carolyn, by the way, and I'm Jason, Jason Blue."

"Desiree," said the young woman, who then turned pugnaciously to the waiter and announced that maybe she would have that hot buttered rum. "I ain't never had one," she said to me.

"Oh, they're delicious," I assured her. "And you must be chilly." Although the room was warm with the presence of so many people, the door to the street opened repeatedly to admit new customers and damp, cold drafts. Desiree had goose bumps surrounding her tassels.

"You're very talented," I added, trying to make her feel at ease socially since she seemed to be rather out of her element. Perhaps she wasn't used to being bought a drink by couples. The other professors certainly seemed to be visibly astounded at the situation.

"Say, you two ain't into any kinky threesome stuff, are you?" Desiree asked suspiciously. I presume that was her stage name; what mother would actually name her daughter Desiree? "I'm an exotic dancer. I'm not no whore."

"Of course not," I agreed.

"We wanted you to look at some pictures," said Jason hastily.

"Dirty pictures?" She scowled.

"Hot buttered rum." The waiter slapped it down on the table and presented Jason with the bill.

"Why am I paying for entertainment?" he asked. "Miss Desiree *is* the entertainment, not the entertainee."

"Oh, pay the man, Jason," I said and took the pictures from my purse. "We're looking for my friend." I pointed to Julienne. "And anyone she might have been seen with." I pointed to Nils, then to Linus.

"Well, I got a memory for faces. Men, they only look at tits. Women look at faces." She was gulping the hot buttered rum with obvious relish. "Now this is more like it," she said and bent over the pictures. "Him!" she said quickly. "Saw him here last night." She pointed at Nils.

"With Julienne?" I asked eagerly. That damn Nils. He knew where she was; he'd actually seen her and wouldn't even tell me. No wonder he refused to report her missing.

"Nah. He was with a bunch of guys," said Desiree. "They all had two drinks each, watched my set, didn't want to buy me a drink, but this guy—" She pointed to Nils again. "He said he liked my hair an' give me ten bucks."

Nils had liked Desiree's hair? That was sad. It was black and curly like Julienne's, only much longer, possibly a wig.

"Big blond guy," Desiree continued. "Over the hill, but I'll bet he was cute ten years ago. He coulda put his shoes under my bed. Ya know what I mean? Least he din' sound like none a these mush-mouthed Southerners. Now me, I'm from New Jersey. Workin' the exotic dance circuit an' ended up here 'cause I had a boyfriend wanted to . . ."

I'm afraid I stopped listening to Desiree, who was pouring her heart out to me. Probably she didn't get much attention from mother figures, although it was hard to think of myself as the mother of an exotic dancer. Still, the disappointment in finding out that she had not seen Julienne, just Nils, was overwhelming. As was my anger that Nils would be out ogling twirling tassels on young breasts when his wife was missing and in God knows what sort of trouble.

Desiree wound down and announced that she had to get back and change for her next set. Change? Did she have different tassels for each appearance? Different colors? Longer or shorter? Maybe they operated on batteries, and the batteries had to be changed. I could understand that. Tassels that suddenly refused to twirl would not be conducive to the sexual titillation inherent in her performance. I was dying to ask but didn't want to embarrass her, so I stood up and offered my hand. "It's been so nice to meet you, my dear," I said. "I do wish you continued success in your career." I was ready to go home and give up for tonight. Jason, angry that he'd been levied a cover charge on Desiree's drink, paid the bill, and left the waiter a two-cent tip.

"I've always wanted to do that to a rude waiter," Jason murmured with satisfaction as we threaded our way through the crowd of tassel-twirling aficionados and out into the street.

16
A Salad from Hell

I woke up Wednesday with the sinking realization that Julienne had now been missing since Saturday night. Others might have seen her Sunday, but I hadn't, and I had no idea why she hadn't called and no reassurance that she was safe. Therefore, I had to entertain the suspicion that she wasn't, although that suspicion did not mean I would stop looking.

When my mother died during my eleventh year after an eighteen-month fight against cancer, I had run from the house, grief-stricken and terrified of what the future might hold. Who would look after me now that she was gone? I knew that my father loved me, but his interests were academic, not nurturing. And so I had, in essence, run away from my fears, hidden from them, secreting my afflicted self in a little half cave on the banks of a nearby creek where I sometimes went to be alone. I fled to the place where I had occasionally found comfort in solitude.

And Julienne had found me there. She had not said, "Oh well, Caro's run away. We'll just have to wait until she shows up again." Julienne had come looking for me because she was my friend. And she had found me and taken me home to her own house and her own mother, who was warm and comforting and quite willing to adopt a half orphan into the family. From then on, although I lived in the same house with my father, my comfort lay in Julienne's house with my surrogate mother. Fannie Delacroix was a Southern belle who was as affectionate as my own mother had been but in all other ways so different that her love was not a reminder of what I had lost.

So Julienne had rescued me from grief, and I intended to do the same for her: rescue her from grief, or anger, or humiliation, or whatever emotion had driven her from the dinner party. Since she hadn't flown home, she must still be here in New Orleans. And I intended to find her.

As my first step on this new day of the search, I spent yet another hour waiting at Café du Monde and considering where, if she did not reappear,

I should look next. It seemed to me that the swamp was my best choice. We
had planned to take one of the boats. She had picked up her camera after
leaving the dinner party—a shoulder bag, possibly containing a change of
clothes, and the camera—and she had expressed a desire to Torelli to photograph the swamp. Remembering that, I paid my bill, dusted the sugar
from my jacket, tucked my damaged umbrella under my arm and, map in
hand, set out to purchase a ticket on a Louisiana Swamp Tour van. Jean
Lafitte Swamp Tours, Captain Terry's, Magnificent Alligator Adventures,
Cajun Cap'n—there were many to choose from.

Once on the docks, which were out at the end of a rural road, I went
from booth to booth, waiting through lines so that I could show Julienne's
picture to the ticket sellers. I alternated ticket sellers with boat captains, a
weathered lot, many with barely decipherable Cajun accents. No one remembered Julienne. One captain, who had a stuffed alligator head mounted
behind the wheel of his boat, asked me why I thought he ever looked at the
tourists when he had "snakes, an' snags, an' gators" to keep his eye peeled
for. The last ticket taker, a woman less patient than the rest, glared at me
through the wooden frame of her booth. She had dark, rough skin and a
crooked nose and wore a raveling cardigan sweater buttoned over a flowered dress. "You come to my window, you buy a ticket," she said, a look
of ferocious determination on her face. Obviously, anyone taking up space
in her line was expected to come up with swamp fare. I bought a ticket and
went back to tour with the alligator captain.

I was here; Julienne wasn't, so I might as well see this swamp about
which she had talked so much. I stationed myself at the rail adjacent to the
wheel as we pulled slowly away from the dock. The captain had already
begun his spiel over the loudspeaker system as he piloted his boat, the
Gator Belle, out upon the brown waters.

You may think of a swamp as suffocatingly green. Not in winter, not near
New Orleans. The vegetation was abundant on the shores but ranged in
color from bone white to a brown green that reminded me of desert bushes.
Some of the trees appeared full and healthy; some bare of leaves with thin
branches haloing the trunks like ghost thickets. Some thrust up black and
dead from the water's edge, raising twisted limbs to a white sky, and many
hung heavy with the mysterious, killing moss that blanketed and stifled life.
Occasionally, there was a white, bony skeleton of a tree, leaning precariously
toward extinction, still weighted down with its burden of moss, and the
moss was white, too, having sucked the life out of its host before dying itself. No wonder Julienne had wanted to photograph this. I took pictures myself as we cut through the water, leaving a wide, white wake behind us that
washed into the bushes where the banks narrowed toward one another.

Our captain pointed out a cemetery on the shore, its pure white box
graves and crosses overhung by great moss-laden trees. A rough barricade
of rocks separated the graveyard from the bayou. The greenest sight in the

swamp was the grass in this cemetery, but that grass was not fertilized by the bodies of the dead, for corpses had to be buried above-ground here because the water level was just below the surface. While the captain explained this, I screwed up my courage for a question, afraid that my inquiry would meet with the same brusque retort as the last I had made to him. He was an off-putting sight with his alligator trophy, his mirrored dark glasses, and his camouflage fatigues—more like a mercenary or right-wing, back-country militia person than a Cajun boat captain.

"Do these boats run at night?" I asked timidly, after tapping him on the arm.

He ignored me and pointed out a small shack and tottering pier passing by on our right. I knew that he had heard me, so I waited for my answer. He pointed out a wide-nosed alligator, which looked as if it might slide into the water and head our way. The sight of such an ugly, dangerous creature sent a shiver up my spine.

As we passed a narrow outlet, clogged with fallen branches, I repeated my question about night tours. The captain turned slightly in my direction, mouth grim. "No ma'am. Da *Gator Belle* don't cruise at night."

"Do any of the swamp tour boats?" I persisted. How had Julienne planned to photograph the swamp at night if no boats ran and she could get no one to accompany her?

"Nothin' to see. It's dark," he muttered. Then he pointed out a snake undulating in our direction. As it was the same color as the water, it could only be detected by the path it cut.

"The boat could have a headlight," I pointed out.

He turned into a narrow passage where the river branched.

"Dis swamp is huge, lady. You live here all your life, you might not know all da passages. So you think someone's gonna take tourists in where dey cain't see nothin' an might git 'em lost an' . . ." He shrugged, disgruntled, and began to talk about the creatures, other than man, who lived in the swamps—alligators, egrets, black bears, feral hogs—

My imagination took off at the mention of feral hogs. Were they akin to wild boar? I could hardly forget the terrifying depictions of wild boar, snarling, viciously tusked, hair bristling, as they were pictured on medieval tapestries. And Julienne wanted to go out among such creatures? At night?

"Herons, beaver, deer, osprey—"

"What if someone wanted to take pictures here at night?" I asked him.

"Dey'd be a damn fool," he said shortly. Other tourists were beginning to mutter because I kept interrupting the lecture.

"But if someone did? How would they go about it?"

"Rent a boat, but don't do it, lady. You'd never come back. Only a tourist would think up such a damn fool—"

"This lady is a native," I said hurriedly. "And she wanted to. And now she's missing."

"Raised up in da swamp?" he asked after a few comments on swamp owls.

"In New Orleans."

"New Orleans don' make you no swamp rat. If she's missin', she's pro'bly dead."

I must have looked distraught. Indeed, I was biting my lip to hold the tears back.

"Check da boat rental places," he advised reluctantly.

"Where are they?"

He gave me a few names and directions, which I scribbled on the back of the directions to my camera, the French version. "But if she's a native, she wouldn't be stupid enough to do it. She'd need someone to run da boat, someone who knew da swamp, an' still she'd be in trouble. Now go up front, will ya, lady?" And he began to lecture again as he took us deeper into territory that was more vegetation-choked and more sinister looking. Obediently, I strolled toward the front of the boat, from which I saw more alligators, one actually nosing the boat as we idled in a side channel while the captain talked about raccoons. Somehow or other, raccoons were a comfort to me. We'd had raccoons knocking over our garbage cans when Julienne, her family, and I vacationed at their cabin on the shores of a lake north of home.

Sweet days. Fishing from an old rowboat, gathering wildflowers, giggling over boys, setting off fireworks that burst in dazzling showers above the lake waters, taking home a bear cub. Oh lord, that had been Julienne's idea. Always chasing the wild and dangerous—that was Julienne. Her father had been furious when the equally furious mother bear had torn down his shed to retrieve the cub stowed there by Julienne. In fact, because he was in one of his fierce moods, Mrs. Delacroix had to talk her husband out of shooting the mother bear. If anyone had the audacity to penetrate these eerie swamps at night for photographs, Julienne would. She had taken pictures of the cub, and then of the mother bear battering the shed, and even of Mr. Delacroix, rifle in hand. I'd have to canvass renters of boats.

As I left the *Gator Belle* to catch the van back to the city, the captain called after me, "Your friend wouldna been dat dumb."

Dumb? No. But venturesome? I was afraid she might, or maybe not. Maybe she had been testing Torelli, seeing how far she could push him. That would be like her, too. I remember the Thanksgiving holiday when we were sophomores in college. She was after her father to raise her allowance and suggested that if he didn't have the money, maybe he should play the stock market and get rich. The first two times she made that suggestion, Mr. Delacroix ignored her. He'd been virtually silent during that vacation. The third time, after he'd begun to perk up, Mr. Delacroix got an unholy gleam in his eye and said "Good idea, Twinkletoes."

Julienne and I had taken ballet lessons as children, and for years afterward she had to put up with that paternal nickname. Whereas, I don't think my father ever realized that I was about to put on toe shoes and become the next Maria Tallchief when my mother finally agreed to free me from the hated classes.

But I digress. Three months later, by dint of buying futures, taking out stock options, and other risky ventures, Mr. Delacroix was rich, and Mrs. Delacroix was on the verge of a nervous breakdown. I felt better for having remembered that incident. Julienne had tested her father's courage, with marvelously lucrative results. Perhaps she'd tested Torelli's courage, as well, found him wanting, and left. So who was she testing now by staying away? Me? I hoped not.

Because the van wasn't scheduled to leave for ten minutes and I didn't care to sample any of the uninteresting food offered by vendors in wharf shacks, I stood out of the crowd at the edge of the pier, leaning against a pole and studying the bayou. I could understand Julienne's fascination. There was an otherworldly quality to the brown landscape with its twisted, bearded trees. I had just raised my camera to take one last picture when I was so rudely jostled by a passing tourist that my desperate attempt to grab the pole did not serve to keep me on the boards. Down I plunged into the brown water, my panic-stricken mind conjuring up all the snakes and alligators I had seen on the tour. When I surfaced, slimy, rotting swamp greens, a salad from hell, trailed from my mouth, and I was still clutching my camera in one hand, flailing wildly as my clothing dragged me under again.

17

Potato Galettes

German immigrants, lured to New Orleans with promises of paradise by the financial scam artist John Law, settled down to farm and were soon feeding the less agriculturally inclined French settlers. Often they intermarried with the French or adapted their German names to the local language. One of the ironies of New Orleans cuisine is that its famed French bread and pastries were baked then and are now by German bakers. At La Madeleine, with a bite of luscious cream puff melting in my mouth, I found myself wondering whether Madeleine had once been Minna or Gretchen.

Carolyn Blue, *Eating Out in the Big Easy*

I fought desperately to the surface, where I heard shrieks and a foghorn voice shouting, "Tourist in the water." Then a life preserver splashed down beside me, and I was saved—at least if I could get out before the hungry swamp creatures attacked. I went under, bobbed up, spit out more slimy growths, and hooked an arm through the ring.

"Hang on," the foghorn roared. I clung for dear life and, trailing nasty, rotting fronds, was dragged through the water to rickety steps that had been nailed haphazardly to the wharf poles. Grasping the first crossbar with one hand, I maneuvered to stuff my camera into the handbag that hung from my arm. Now wasn't that foolish? Here I was trying to save a camera that would never function again, when an alligator might even now be cutting a path in my direction.

Arms and legs trembling, dripping liquid mud, I began to climb. When I felt a crossbar tilt under my foot, I almost fainted, but by then a sturdy Cajun on the wharf had grasped my arm. Not waiting for my clumsy efforts, he hauled me to safety, where he proceeded to lecture me in an angry voice. I assume he blamed me for my mishap, but his accent was very thick, so I couldn't be sure.

"I was shoved," I announced, incensed. He paid no attention but dragged me toward the waiting van.

"I cain't take her. She'll ruin my seats," said the driver, a tough-looking woman wearing rolled socks and a skirt far too short for a woman with legs as burly as hers.

"I want the police called," I snapped.

A noisy argument erupted among captains, the van driver, ticket sellers, po'boy vendors, and tourists, who didn't want to ride with anyone who looked and smelled as bad as I did. As they quarreled, I shivered. I was cold, and I was wet and miserable, and I wanted to go back to the hotel. In fact, I wanted to go back to my own house in El Paso and never return to this benighted state again. "If you don't take me home immediately, I'll sue."

A number of the combatants stopped talking, but not the tourists.

I narrowed my eyes at the van driver. "I'll get an attorney and just . . . just sue the socks off the lot of you."

She glanced uneasily at her socks, as if I planned to demand that she hand them over immediately in reparation.

"And I'll file police charges."

People began to back away from me.

"And write to the newspapers about the dangers of this tour." A few more threats of that sort, which warmed me up and evidently alarmed the swamp entrepreneurs, earned me a solo ride to the door of my hotel. I didn't tip the sock lady, either. I was still furious.

And even more furious when the hotel personnel tried to keep me from going upstairs. They didn't believe anyone as disreputable looking as I could be a paying guest. Well, too bad about them. I'd probably caught some horrible disease from that disgusting swamp water, so I didn't care if I dripped mud on all their precious antiques as long as I got to my room and washed myself clean. I even called the desk and demanded that a bell-hop come to carry away my sopping, muddy, swamp-rot-fronded clothes, which I threw out into the hall. I never wanted to see them again. I couldn't imagine that any washing machine would be equal to the task of making them clean enough to wear safely.

Then I spent perhaps an hour under hot water in the shower washing my body, my hair, even the inside of my mouth. Once sufficiently clean and dry, I considered whether or not I needed a preventive antibiotic to protect me from dangerous tropical diseases. It was then that I noticed my most immediate need: food. I was starving.

Forgetting the microbes and parasites that might be attacking me internally, I used the hotel hair dryer on my stringy hair, donned clean clothes, the wearing of which completely ruined my carefully planned wardrobe schedule, and set out for Jackson Square. There is nothing like a terrible fright to make one ravenous, and it took only a glance at my list of eateries that needed visiting to settle on La Madeleine.

It was a good choice. The ravishing French bakery smells were wonderfully comforting to a person in my traumatized state. Nonetheless, I knew that I needed something more nourishing than pastry, so having dragged myself away from the tempting breads, croissants, cream puffs, tarts, éclairs and so forth displayed in the glass cases up front, I bought a potato galette, a salad, and a glass of white wine. Then I sat down by a window to eat, regain my equilibrium, and consider my options.

My galette was unbelievably good—a crispy, thick pancake the likes of which I could eat every day for lunch if I had the opportunity. Unfortunately, I probably never shall. I liked it enough that I even tried to reproduce it at home, but the results were disastrous. I produced a galette that was deliciously brown and crispy on the outside, but inside an unappetizing combination of raw egg and crunchy, uncooked potato bits turned even my husband away from the table. Perhaps I'll find a recipe one day and overcome my aversion to cooking enough to try again. I may well have been so distracted by my terrible experience on the swamp tour that I completely misinterpreted how the dish had been made.

That's quite possible, but I did manage to calm down enough to reject the idea of going home with my tail, figuratively, between my legs. Also I had had an idea, an idea that should have occurred to me much earlier. I would call Diane, Julienne's daughter, at boarding school. If Julienne had contacted anyone, it would be her child. No matter what Nils said about my friend's lack of maternal instinct, I knew that she loved Diane and that Diane loved her. Perhaps Julienne had left New Orleans and flown to see her daughter. Oh, I hoped so. I could forgive her for having caused me so much anxiety if only she was safe.

And there was nothing dangerous about making one long-distance telephone call. I couldn't be mugged or drowned while doing so. I couldn't even be bruised by crazy voodoo priestesses. In fact it seemed to me, on reflection, that an undue number of dangerous situations had befallen me during my short stay in the Big Easy. Easy indeed. Easy to run afoul of the crazy, the rude, and the criminal! Should I call Lieutenant Boudreaux to tell him that I had been pushed off a pier?

Well, probably not. I didn't want him to think I was paranoid. Or disaster prone. People tend to avoid the disaster prone, and I might need his help if I ever uncovered any evidence of Julienne's whereabouts.

18
Chocolate Éclairs

I didn't resist that pastry counter after all. Before I left La Madeleine, I gazed longingly through the glass and decided that I might need more sustenance to get me through another afternoon of investigation. Therefore, I bought a chocolate éclair and carried it back to the hotel, where I put in the first of several calls that yielded surprising information.

A very Boston-sounding lady at the prep school attended by Julienne's adopted daughter reluctantly agreed to call Diane off the soccer field to take an "extremely important long-distance call." That's the way I put it to Ms. Ivy League. Where had she gone to school? Radcliffe? Mount Holyoke? She'd probably majored in something delightful like medieval history, as I had, but she'd been offered jobs while I'd been asked how many words a minute I could type and if I took shorthand. Medieval history wasn't seen as a marketable commodity in the Middle West when I graduated.

But then would I have wanted to teach in a girls' school instead of marrying Jason and raising Gwen and Chris, then beginning this new career to fill my "empty nest"? Career in mind, I took a bite of the chocolate éclair and made relevant notes while I waited: "real cream whipped to a thick, rich froth . . . smooth, dark chocolate shining on lighter-than-an-angel's-wing pastry . . ."

"Hi, Aunt Carolyn. What's up?"

My weight, I thought in silent answer to Diane's question. She sounded out of breath and cheerful. Hurriedly, I swallowed my second delectable bite (although it was a crime not to savor every smidgen) and greeted Julienne's child. "Is your mother visiting you, Diane?" I asked.

"No. Is she planning to?"

"Well, have you heard from her this week? Or anytime since Saturday?"

"Not a word, but she promised me a neat present from New Orleans before she left. Hey, I thought you were there, too."

What should I say to that? I didn't want to alarm Diane, and she didn't seem to have any information on Julienne, which was disappointing.

"Boy, everyone's looking for Mom. Is she hiding out or something? Did she meet some gorgeous hunk and elope?" Diane giggled.

I wondered if Julienne's daughter had suspicions about the relationship between Julienne and the missing Professor Torelli.

"Dad called Monday night asking if I'd heard from her, and I said, 'Like hey, Daddy, haven't *you* heard from her?'"

Like hey, Daddy? Was Diane rooming with some valley girl from California who was having an unfortunate influence on her speech patterns?

"And you know what? I don't think he answered. Aunt Caro, I hope you're not going to tell me they're fighting again. I told them I absolutely would not tolerate a divorce in the family. I mean it. I'll run away from home. Well, from school, and I've got a bunch of tests coming up, so that would really screw up my chances of getting into a good university and . . ."

It was interesting that Nils had called asking about his wife. Did that mean he wasn't responsible for Julienne's disappearance—at least in any physical way? Or was he concocting an alibi for himself? "I didn't do anything to her," he'd say. "Ask our daughter. I called trying to *find* Julienne."

"And then Uncle Philippe called," Diane was saying. "When was that? Saturday, I think. Weird as usual, of course."

Philippe had called? "What time?" I asked.

"What time what? Was he weird? He's always weird."

"Did he call?"

"I don't know. Afternoon. Before we drove over to Exeter for the dance at Phillips Academy."

So Philippe had called before Julienne disappeared. What for? Weird in what way? Just because he rarely spoke to me and never seemed to like me when we were young didn't make him weird—just not my favorite person.

"Actually, now that I think of it, I left a message for Mom at her hotel. I told her what he'd said. I'll bet she got a laugh out of that."

"When did you leave the message?"

"Saturday night," Diane replied. "Eight o'clock or so. Kind of pathetic, don't you think, that my date was so boring I could take time out to call my mom and never worry about missing a thing?"

Had Julienne received that message later? Obviously, she'd still been at Etienne's—or somewhere else—when Diane called. Or possibly she hadn't answered in the room because she thought that her husband was at the other end of the line. But Julienne might well have picked up the message when she left the hotel with the camera she'd come for. I'd have to check. "Tell me about Philippe," I suggested as I tried to put everything together.

"Oh, he's so grumpy and gloomy. You know?"

Well, that wasn't news. No one in the family had ever said so, but as I grew older, I'd begun to suspect that Philippe was subject to bouts of depression.

"He's decided—you won't believe this." She giggled. "He's decided that the laws of primogeniture entitle him to all of Gram's estate, instead of the half he got. Primogeniture? How screwy is that?"

I wanted to tell her what a difference primogeniture had made in the history of Europe, but I managed to restrain myself. As interesting a topic as it was (the accrual of land and power in fewer hands when only elder sons inherited), it didn't really relate to the disappearance of my friend in any way, aside from the effect it might have had on her brother's thinking. Because now I remembered how cavalierly I had dismissed the identification by the silver-statue man of Philippe as Julienne's companion on a street in the Quarter and his description of Philippe pushing him off the curb. Was that the action of someone who was depressed? I had no idea, since I'm not given to depression. And what was that fancy school teaching Diane if not the importance of primogeniture in the history of Western Europe?

"My nutty uncle has decided that Mom should just hand over everything she inherited from Gram. Can you imagine?"

I sighed. Julienne's mother had died just this year in an automobile accident—a matter of a pickup truck running a stop sign on a rural road. It was the second such death in the family, although Mr. Delacroix's accident, which occurred years ago, had involved only his car and been virtually inexplicable. The police had finally decided that he must have fallen asleep at the wheel. Both deaths had hit Julienne hard, and I, too, found her mother's death devastating.

When I went home to visit my father, I'd always ended up spending most of my time with Julienne's mother, even when my friend wasn't in town, although often she was. Such lovely visits those had been. I'd learned to love New Orleans cooking before I ever visited the city because Fannie Delacroix was a wonderful cook and showed off her talents when either of her "sweet girls," as she called us, came back.

"I told Uncle Philippe she was in New Orleans, and he'd have to take it up with her. Like she'd give him the money or Gram's silver or any of that stuff. No way. She's already promised a lot of it to me. Of course, I didn't say that to my uncle because I didn't want to send him into a funk. Anyway, he said he was heading straight for New Orleans to talk to Mom. Can you imagine? It's the middle of the semester, and he's not invited to the ACS meeting, I shouldn't think."

Probably not. Philippe was on the faculty at a medical school.

"So I gave him her address, and I left a message at her hotel warning her that he might show up. Or then again, he might take whatever medication he's supposed to take and get sensible. You never know with him."

And if he hadn't taken his medication and gotten sensible? Had he flown to New Orleans? Was Julienne with him? Maybe he'd arrived, met her, gone completely to pieces, and she'd had to commit him. It had happened before, at least I suspected as much. Her parents had never talked about Philippe's moods. But that scenario didn't explain why Julienne hadn't been in touch with me. It might be an embarrassing situation if her colleagues knew about it, but surely she wouldn't try to hide Philippe's problems from me if they had become her responsibility after her mother's death.

"Aunt Carolyn, you're not saying much." For the first time I heard a note of worry in Diane's voice. "Is something wrong?"

What could I tell her? That her mother was missing and I now had to try to find her uncle to see if he was involved? Or her father? Or her mother's alleged lover? This was not a situation one wanted to explain to a teenage girl. "Diane," I said, rather cunningly I thought, "Diane, I think your mother has skipped town."

"Skipped town?"

"Absolutely. She must have got your message and headed for the hills." Could that be true? I suppose there would be times when one got tired of dealing with the severely depressed, especially when everything else was going wrong.

Diane had started to giggle, which was better than panic.

"Thanks for the information, dear. I'll keep in touch, and you study hard, you hear?" I gave it my best Southern accent, which all Delacroix family members agree is ludicrous.

Diane certainly found it so, for she replied, "Oh, Aunt Carolyn, you don't sound *anything* like my mother or Gram either. You'll just never make it as a Southern belle."

"I am deeply hurt," I retorted. "I thought I was improving."

I finished my chocolate éclair as I considered my next move. M-m-m. The stiffly whipped cream was delicious, and wasn't there a hint of vanilla? Or were my taste buds remembering the way my mother whipped cream before she became ill? With a little vanilla and sugar. Oh, those strawberry shortcakes she made! With wild strawberries we picked ourselves, laughing and eating as many as we picked, each of us in wide-brimmed straw hats to protect our fair skin. Mother had been blonde, too.

Had she used a biweekly rinse on her hair? I didn't know. That was something I'd probably have found out had she lived into my teens and beyond. *Well, enough of that,* I told myself sternly as I popped the last bit of chocolate éclair into my mouth. But still, I thought I'd ask at La Madeleine how they doctored their cream—if at all.

19
Missing Siblings

Having finished my chocolate éclair and dropped the doily and bag into a flowered wastebasket by the French provincial desk, I returned to the bed to think about Philippe and Julienne. If he hadn't come to New Orleans, it didn't much matter whether Julienne had picked up the message from her daughter. Or did it? On the off chance that he might make the trip, had Julienne disappeared in order to avoid an unpleasant interview with her brother? It was possible. I seldom saw Philippe these days, and Julienne didn't talk about him much, but when she did, it was with a sort of weary forbearance. She certainly didn't laugh about her brother as Diane had. But was she afraid of him?

After dialing the long-distance information operator, I asked for the number of the medical school where Philippe taught. Would Julienne skip her convention obligations to avoid a confrontation with her brother? I asked myself. For that matter, were depressed people dangerous? Logic told me that the only danger they posed would be to themselves.

Having obtained the number, I then called the medical school and asked to be connected to Dr. Delacroix's office. Three rings. Four. Soon I'd be transferred to an answering machine, and what would I say? Philippe's failure to answer his phone at the office didn't mean that he'd gone to New Orleans. He could be teaching a class, supervising students, taking a coffee break, gone home for the day. Should I try to get his home number?

"Dr. Delacroix appears to be out of his office," said a pleasant voice, surely the operator who had answered originally, not some recording. "Would you like to leave a message? Or be transferred to the chairman of his department?" the real female person asked.

I made a snap decision and opted to talk to the chair. If Philippe had left town, I'd find out. If he was at home, I could get a number, unless the number was unlisted. Maybe I'd use Julienne's name if the chairman proved unwilling to give me a home number. Maybe I'd even claim to be Julienne. At this point, I was prepared to be shameless in my quest.

"Who's this?" a male voice demanded. "Is that you, Delacroix?"

"No," I replied, taken aback. "I'm Carolyn Blue, but I—I'm looking for Dr. Delacroix," I stammered. So much for impersonating Julienne. I'd never be a successful liar. "I'm a friend of his sister."

"Well, I'm looking for Dr. Delacroix myself," snapped the chairman, or so I presumed him to be.

"He's missing?" I asked, astounded. Both of them were missing? What in the world did that mean?

"As far as I can tell. The man's not in his office, not at home, and not showing up for his classes, his appointments, or his meetings."

"For how long?" I asked.

"Devil if I know. He didn't appear for his Monday class. You say his sister's looking for him, too?"

"Well, I—" Would the chairman be interested if I told him Julienne was missing and that I was looking for both of them?

"If she finds him, have her tell him for me that tenure isn't the guarantee of lifelong employment it once was."

That was definitely a threat. "Philippe didn't mention that he would be absent?" I asked.

"Not a word. To anyone. And he'd damn well better have a good excuse. Just because he's brilliant but too weird to practice medicine doesn't mean we'll put up with this kind of behavior on the teaching end. What kind of example does this set for the students? They'll think they can just take off and leave their patients in the lurch."

I'd known a few doctors who obviously thought that anyway. A case in point was a pediatrician who had moved his office halfway across town without warning me. I discovered his defection when I rushed Chris in one day with his thumb, so I thought, half severed, and found a locked door from which the name had been removed. A janitor, exiting the men's room with mop and bucket, told me that my pediatrician had decamped, although he didn't know to what new address.

At that point I was so terrified that I took Chris to the emergency room—at considerably more expense, I might add, than it would have cost to visit his doctor, had the doctor been considerate enough to tell us he was moving. "Well, good luck trying to teach consideration and responsibility to a group of medical students," I said, an unfortunate remark that just slipped out on the heels of my angry recollections.

"What was that?" demanded the chairman. "Are you one of these ungrateful patients who think they should get unlimited time with their doctors for no money? Well, I can tell you what's going to come of that attitude. No doctors. Or only doctors who can't speak English. Maybe we real *American* doctors should go on strike. Close up the medical schools. Let disease . . ."

Pity the poor patient who looked to this man for sympathy and a kindly bedside manner, I thought. He had the personality of a porcupine. "If I can find Dr. Delacroix, I'll pass on your message about tenure," I said loudly enough to interrupt his tirade. "Do you have any suggestions about where he might be?"

"None," snapped the angry chairman. "If I knew, I'd have tracked him down myself."

And that was the end of our conversation. What had I learned? That Philippe might be in New Orleans. Now I needed to know if Julienne had received her daughter's message about Philippe when she came back Saturday night to pick up her camera. Could Philippe have been in New Orleans even then? I called the front desk and explained that Mrs. Magnussen's daughter wanted to know if Mrs. Magnussen had received the telephone message left Saturday night. The clerk, somewhat dubious over the propriety of releasing such information, finally agreed to check when I assured her that I didn't want to know what the message was, just whether my friend had received it. Having decided to be helpful, the desk clerk informed me that Mrs. Magnussen had actually retrieved two voice-mail messages Saturday evening and made one phone call. The call had been made around nine o'clock.

Was the call she made local? I asked. The clerk didn't feel free to discuss that but suggested that Dr. Magnussen could look at the billing himself and tell me.

Given Nils's attitude toward any queries about his missing wife, I doubted that he would. In fact, it occurred to me that the desk clerk, looking at telephone records, would have no way of knowing which Magnussen had heard the messages and made the call. Still, nine o'clock, she'd said. It had to be Julienne. Nils was still at the restaurant at nine. Then I was reminded of all the calls I myself had made that evening, none of which Julienne had responded to. Oh well. I had to admit that I hadn't left messages. While tapping the telephone impatiently, thinking, I noticed that my index fingernail on the left hand needed filing.

So what did this information mean? I wondered as I fished a nail file from my toiletry bag. Two messages? Well, one was obviously the call from Diane. But who had left the second message? Philippe? Or Linus Torelli? And whom had Julienne called?

She could have ignored a message from her brother and fled to Torelli, arranging the safe harbor by phone. Or perhaps she had called Philippe and agreed to meet him the next day, then set out for Torelli's hotel. Her colleague hadn't mentioned whether her appearance that night was expected, and now I couldn't ask him. So if she had an appointment to meet her brother, it would have been sometime after she waited for me at Café du Monde. Of course, having left Etienne's before the plans were made, she didn't know that I would be preparing for the Gospel Brunch, not café au lait and beignets on Jackson Square with her. Had she been planning to tell me about Philippe's imminent arrival? She might even have been angry when I didn't show up. That would explain why she'd never contacted me. Well, not really. Even angry, Julienne was a considerate friend, no matter what Nils said about her.

I shook off these speculations and returned to my plans. Torelli was gone. I knew that. But I could call around town trying to locate Philippe or at least find out if he had been here. A new telephone search was obviously my next move. I began calling New Orleans hotels, asking for Dr. Philippe Delacroix. Many hotels later and having exhausted French Quarter listings, I found him registered at the Superior Inn. My guidebook said it was "inexpensive" and "five minutes from the central business district."

The more-or-less helpful desk clerk told me that Dr. Delacroix had checked in Sunday at noon and was still registered. In answer to my question about a possible visit from his sister, she remembered a woman, wearing tight jeans, a form-fitting, low-necked knit top, and high heels. "She didn't look like a doctor's sister to me, honey," said the Superior Inn desk clerk. "Showed up Sunday night. I was thinkin' of callin' the house detective when the doctor fella came downstairs to meet her.

Jeans? Well that fit the other sightings, but high heels? Absolutely not. Julienne would never wear jeans and high heels or, for that matter, look like the kind of woman who would inspire a call to the house detective. Had Philippe called a prostitute? What a muddle! "Have you seen the woman since Sunday night?" I asked.

"No, Ah haven't, honey, but Ah'm not on duty all the time, you know. They went out together. Ah remember that. They were arguin'. An' he came back sometime aftah midnight."

"But she wasn't with him?"

"Well, honey, Ah just don't know. Mah shift was ovah at midnight, but mah guess would be she came back with him. She looked the type. He showed her a good time in the Quartah an' she showed him a good time in the room. Know what Ah mean?"

"They were planning to visit the French Quarter?" I asked.

"Where else would anyone go in N'Awlins?" the clerk asked, aggrieved. "We got us free shuttle service to the Quartah 'cause that's where folks want ta go fo' an evenin'."

"And they took the shuttle?"

"Now Ah wouldn't know that, would Ah?"

"Thank you," I said politely. "You've been very helpful." Actually, she'd been downright forthcoming. It's a wonder she managed to keep her job if she always talked so freely about the establishment's guests.

"Why don' you try callin' him, honey. He's bound to answer if he's in, an' Ah haven't seen him leave today."

That would depend on whether he was taking his medication, I thought. A depressed person might not answer his phone.

"Want me to try his room, honey?"

"Yes, please." Could Julienne be staying with him? Or somewhere else under an assumed name? At least she'd been all right Sunday evening, if peculiarly dressed. That is, if the woman in the jeans and high heels had been her, which I doubted. The only person who had ever accused Julienne of looking like a call girl had been her husband.

"Ah'm not getting' an answer, honey. Wanna leave him a message?"

"Yes, please. Ask him to call Carolyn Blue at the Hotel de la Poste." I gave her the number.

Well, it was back to the Po'Boy Computer Café. Even if they were, as Lieutenant Boudreaux had suggested, manufacturing cocaine on the premises, I needed an updated photo of Philippe, which I could print out from the Web site of his university. If offered drugs, I would simply say, "No, thank you," as Nancy Reagan had advocated in her Just Say No campaign.

On the other hand, I'd just as soon not associate with drug dealers. What if the place was raided while I was there? Would the police arrest an innocent, semi-computer-literate professor's wife? Would Lieutenant Boudreaux rescue me? If only Jason and I had a portable printer with us. Our room had a data port and Jason's computer had a modem, but no printer between us. We just weren't as up to date technologically as we liked to think.

Well, I would have to soothe my fears of drug dealers and raids with another sumptuous, flaming café brûlot while I was surfing the net for Philippe's photograph. I would forgo another of their tasty po'boys, however, since Jason would undoubtedly want to eat dinner out.

20

Pralines

Happily, I managed to make the trip to Po'Boy without incident. No New Orleans criminal so much as looked my way. Perhaps my crooked umbrella emitted an aura of menace. I obtained a printout of Philippe's university Web site picture, plus copies of the pictures of Julienne, Linus, and Nils. The originals had become soggy along with the other contents of my purse during my recent fall into the bayou.

Fortunately, I had a backup handbag packed, although it did not match my walking shoes, but then they were too soggy for use, either. I had to wear the shoes I had brought for evening wear, which are not as comfortable as they might have been, and the matching bag, which doesn't hold as much. Still, I couldn't be fussy under the circumstances. I was lucky to have something in which to carry those things we females find necessary to keep at hand. Of course, some of my purse contents were still damp and had to be put in Baggies, of which I always carry a supply when traveling.

I did treat myself to two pralines on which to nibble while I waited for printouts and sipped my flambéed coffee, and I must say Po'Boy's pralines are delightful—rich and creamy, laden with pecans. I include a recipe, which I obtained from a friend, for those of you who may desire to make your own.

Joan's Pralines

Grease waxed paper.

Select a pot large enough to prevent boilovers.

Pour into the pot *1 cup of buttermilk, 2 cups granulated sugar,* and *1 tsp. baking soda.*

Stir until sugar is completely dissolved.

Place pot on low to medium burner and, stirring constantly, let candy boil to the soft ball stage (when a half tsp. or so of the syrup forms a soft ball upon being dropped into a cup of cold water). The mixture will turn a brownish color.

Remove pot from heat, add *2 cups pecan halves, 1 tsp. vanilla,* and *1 tbs. butter,*

Beat mixture briskly until it becomes glossy and very thick.

Quickly spoon onto greased, waxed paper, making small patties.

Let candy completely cool before removing from paper.

Should the mixture harden before you have time to get it all onto the paper, return to the heat for a few seconds to restore the right consistency.

Once I had finished my computer business and my snack, the clerk at Po'Boy sniffed and wrinkled his nose when I extracted my credit card from my soggy wallet in its baggie. Was he sniffing because he was a cocaine addict or because my wallet smelled bad? The latter, I decided, having detected a whiff of swamp odor myself. How very embarrassing! Now I had to wonder whether I had managed to eradicate such odors from my person. I believe I blushed as he handed back the credit card. I couldn't use cash, of course. My dollar bills were drying in the bathroom at the Hotel de la Poste, and my traveler's checks would have to be replaced, the signatures having smeared.

I had taken a bus and had to return on one so that I could pay for my transportation with change, which I had washed off with the perfumed hotel soap and dried on a hand towel before leaving. But before I returned, I spotted a shoe store and stopped to buy myself a new pair of walking shoes. If my wallet retained the swamp scent, so would my shoes and no one wants to be trailed at every step by unpleasant odors.

This was all extremely inconvenient. If I could find the rude person who bumped into me on the wharf, I would certainly give him a lecture on manners. It brought to mind an incident some years ago when Jason and I were attending a performance of Strauss's *Silent Woman* at the New York opera—a lovely theater but a dreadful opera, by the way. Very unmelodic.

Be that as it may, I was bumped from behind by a woman holding a champagne glass, which she spilled on the shoulder of a very pretty teal silk dress I was wearing. The impact unbalanced me, and I fell against a stout, red-faced man smoking a cigar. The cigar burned a hole on the other shoulder of the dress, completely ruining it, and then the two of them snarled at *me*, as if I had been at fault, although I was simply standing in the lobby chatting with Jason and a couple from New York University. We had been immersed in conversation about the soprano, who would probably have sounded wonderful had she been singing some other opera.

Because my attackers didn't hasten away, I got the chance, in that instance, to tell them exactly what I thought of their manners. In fact, I believe I was quite intemperate, demanded names and addresses so that they could reimburse me for my dress. Unfortunately, the bell sounded, and they took that as an excuse to go to their seats without giving me any information other than their opinion of non-New Yorkers. Jason was vastly amused at my display of temper and chuckled all the way through the last act. However, his humor was subsequently tempered by my revelation of what it would cost to replace the dress. Jason is not a miserly man, but then again, he's not given to flinging his money around.

Consequently, he was taken aback when he returned from the ACS meeting to find his wife absent and his bathroom festooned with damp currency, not to mention the errant smear of mud and swamp vegetation that I had missed when I attempted to set the bathroom to rights after my long shower.

"Carolyn, what happened in here?" he asked when I came in.

I must admit that I hadn't been planning to tell him about my mishap on the swamp wharf, having expected to be back before he returned and to use the hair dryer on the money if it hadn't dried out.

"There's mud in the sink," he said. "And wet money everywhere."

I did wonder what he made of these two facts. He might explain the drying money by surmising that I had developed some eccentric fetish for money laundering, but that would hardly explain the mud. I sighed and told him the whole story, and Jason was horrified at my ordeal, except for my ill-considered comment that swamp vegetation tasted like *uni*, which happens to be one of Jason's favorite sushi choices. However, his sympathetic nature overcame gourmet pique as related to *uni*, and he consoled me over my traumatic experience. I felt much better for having confessed and received his sympathy.

Jason then, with some hesitation, told me that Julienne had not appeared to give her scheduled paper, nor had she been in touch with conference officials to cancel. "I must admit, Caro, that I'm very worried about her. Missing Carlene's lecture was a failure of friendship, and missing the session she was scheduled to chair a failure of responsibility, but failing, without explanation, to give her paper . . ." He shook his head. "I just can't imagine Julienne doing that unless something is very wrong."

"I've known all along that she was in trouble," I said. "Does Nils know that she—"

"I haven't seen him, but I believe he's to join us for dinner tonight, and I can't imagine that he'll take the news of his wife missing her own paper as anything but very alarming."

"Absolutely," I agreed. "He'll just have to contact the police now. Unless . . . unless . . ."

"What, Carolyn?" Jason asked.

"Unless he's responsible for her disappearance."

"Surely not," said Jason.

"You know that Torelli left the conference unexpectedly?"

He nodded.

"And I just found out this afternoon that Julienne's brother Philippe is trying to get in touch with her. In fact, he's in New Orleans."

"Well, that's good news. Philippe can insist that Nils contact the police. In fact, Philippe can do it himself, since he's a relative."

"I suppose," I said dubiously, "but I can't get hold of him, and he may have been seen with Julienne on Sunday, the last day anyone saw her. According to Diane, he's got some bee in his bonnet about being entitled to the whole of their mother's estate. You don't suppose—"

"He's her brother," said Jason. "He wouldn't . . . certainly not over money." My husband looked appalled at the very idea.

"Well, you know what they say: most murders are motivated by sex or money."

"Who says that?"

"Mystery writers," I admitted. "And policemen, I suppose."

"We don't know any policemen," said Jason reasonably.

I knew Lieutenant Boudreaux, but he hadn't said anything about motivations for murder.

"And we don't know that Julienne's been murdered. I wouldn't imagine that we know anyone who knows anyone who's been murdered. After all, it's not something that's common in academic circles."

"No," I had to agree. "Did you mean to say that we have to have dinner with Nils tonight?"

"Before we get into that, I was checking for messages at the desk downstairs when the clerk asked if I was aware that the hotel charges for local calls, and that we've made quite a few."

"How much per call?" I inquired, aghast. I had no idea how many I'd made. It could be hundreds.

"Seventy-five cents." Jason studied me, looking a bit puzzled. "It is rather steep, but you can't have made that many. Say you made ten. That would be $7.50."

Say I'd made a hundred; that would be seventy-five dollars. I was going to have to ask just how big a bill I had run up. "I'll try to limit the calls in the future," I promised, knowing that if my search for Julienne demanded more calls, I'd make them. Would they be tax deductible? No, of course they wouldn't. My search for Julienne had nothing to do with a book on New Orleans cuisine.

"Now, about the dinner you mentioned?" That, at least, would be deductible. Unless it was to be held at some restaurant so boring that I couldn't write about it. "Who's going? Not just Nils, I hope."

Jason smiled. "The whole alligator-dinner group."

"And I'm supposed to find them another alligator dish?" I wasn't ecstatic to think of sharing my evening meal with Nils or the Abbotts.

"No one mentioned alligators," he replied. "They're taking us to the Palace Café. In thanks for your time and effort on the reunion dinner."

"You mean they're paying our way?" *Had Broder agreed to that?* I wondered.

Jason grinned. "Reluctantly, in some cases. I believe Carlene had to nudge Broder into participating, but yes, we're the invited guests."

Isn't it amazing how often married people find themselves thinking the same thing? Both Jason and I had immediately realized that Broder would object to another expensive dinner, especially when he had to kick in for two extra people. The Palace Café? I thought I remembered it from my *Great Chefs* book. "Where is it? The restaurant?"

"The central business district, I think. Is that a problem for you? Were you planning on writing only about restaurants in the Quarter?"

"Oh, it's fine." The central business district? Was that near Philippe's hotel? If so, it wouldn't hurt to pop in and try to talk to him. Surely, he'd be in his room by the time we finished dinner.

21
Catfish Pecan with Meunière Sauce

The French and their New World cousins the Creoles are noted not only for gourmet cooking but also for thriftiness. Combine these traits with the periods of poverty that formerly rich Creoles experienced (after the Civil War, for instance) and several famous New Orleans dishes were the result. Gumbo is certainly one—a combination of garden vegetables, leftover meat and seafood, and, of course, roux. Bread pudding and *pain perdu* are two others. In New Orleans, day-old French bread is not wasted. It is used to make New Orleans style French toast (*pain perdu*) as well as the many delicious bread puddings to be found in French Quarter restaurants. Don't decide, as I did, that you dislike bread pudding until you sample one of the exotic New Orleans varieties.

Carolyn Blue, *Eating Out in the Big Easy*

The Palace Café, which specializes in contemporary Creole menus, is another of the Brennan family ventures, and the Brennan family is synonymous with New Orleans cuisine. For a wonder, Carlene had chosen the restaurant. Maybe the "contemporary" label suggested California cookery. Perhaps it was a compromise with Broder, who would have chosen "inexpensive" from the guidebook and had to be satisfied with "moderate." (I had looked the restaurant up before we ventured out.) It was also blessedly close to our hotel, being on Canal Street.

At any rate, the ambiance was delightful. The dining area downstairs was given over to booths in green, cream, and brass with an impressive spiral staircase in the middle. We climbed the stairs. The second-floor dining room had a wonderful mural that depicted famous New Orleans musicians, reminding me that in my concentration on food and Julienne, I hadn't so much as visited Preservation Hall or any of the famous jazz clubs. The visit to the tassel-twirler establishment could hardly be counted as a musical experience, although the bands on the street, when I had the chance to listen, were wonderful, and outside our window at the hotel, we often heard the wail of trumpets and trombones.

At the end of the dining room, we could see the chefs working behind glass. Luckily, I spotted that feature before we were seated and asked if we could be moved closer. Miranda and Lester grumbled, but the maître d' was very gracious. He simply replaced the reserved sign on our table, bowed to me, and led us farther back, where he removed the reserved sign from another table and seated me facing the kitchen. "Madame is interested in the preparation of fine food?" he asked.

"Madame's writing a book," said Carlene, grinning. "So be sure to produce your most delicious dishes for her."

"Carlene," Miranda hissed.

"Our creations are always delicious," the maître d' assured her and then beamed at me. I beamed back. It really is fun to be a restaurant critic. I even got the first menu, which caused Miranda to frown. No doubt she felt that, being the most well-paid member of the group, she should be the diner most catered to.

Two appetizers had been recommended by the guidebook: red bean dip with homemade potato chips and oyster shooters. The shooters are raw oysters served in a shot glass, which did not appeal to me. Truth to tell, I like my oysters cooked and wanted to visit Antoine's for their oysters Rockefeller, a recipe that originated with the restaurant's founder. Rockefeller refers to the richness of the sauce, not some Rockefeller for whom the dish was created.

I chose the red bean dip, which was excellent, especially the homemade potato chips. I wondered, for just a moment, how hard it would be to make one's own potato chips and even walked to the glass wall to see if I could catch a glimpse of the potato chip chef at work (I didn't), but then I remembered that I really preferred other people's cooking and returned to my seat. Miranda glared at me.

Broder was saying, as I replaced my napkin in my lap and made a few notes on the red bean dip, that Julienne's failure to appear for her lecture was a cause of great worry to him. "Yes," Carlene agreed. "I think we all know her well enough to say that this last incident is ominous. Have you heard *anything* from her, Nils?"

"Torelli left. She probably went with him," Nils muttered.

"She didn't," I said. "The police checked that for me."

"You've been to the police?" Nils looked furious.

"Well, you wouldn't," I said coldly.

Nils didn't answer, but he looked upset, as well he might. Jason defused the situation by insisting that I try his crawfish cakes. Spicy, crispy, infused with Romano cheese and the delicious flavor of crawfish—they were wonderful. The waiter and I had a quick, whispered conversation about the flavors; Worcestershire and Louisiana hot sauce were responsible for the extra tang. I had two bites, one to savor the cakes by themselves, the second to appreciate them as they were served, with a lemon butter sauce in which I also detected white wine. I nodded to Jason and whispered, "Superb choice." My husband does have a wonderful way with a menu. Of course, I invited him to try my selection, as well.

"I can't imagine what's going on with Julienne," said Lester. "No matter what your marital problems, Nils, she shouldn't have failed to fulfill her conference responsibilities."

"Don't blame me for that," snapped Nils, "and I couldn't agree with you more. When I go to a conference, I give the paper I'm scheduled to give."

"Have you ever known Julienne not to show up for her lecture?" I demanded. Nils was silent. "Which means something is dreadfully wrong, and you're refusing to do anything about it. Now, Diane says that Philippe is looking for Julienne."

"You called Diane about this?" Nils was obviously infuriated at my interference. "The last thing she needs during midterms is to be worried about her mother."

"She's worried that you and Julienne might divorce," I replied, "and I can only assume that's because she's picked up on your attitude and your unfounded suspicions." At least, I hoped they were unfounded. Why else would Torelli have left so hurriedly? A man who was in love with Julienne wouldn't have left like that. Unless she'd sent him away. Oh dear, I just wanted to stop thinking about it. I wanted Julienne to appear and be fine and have some logical explanation for her disappearance, preferably one that would show Nils to have been unfairly suspicious of her.

Lips pressed together angrily, I turned to my entrée, which had just been served. I had been lured away from guide selections by a dish called catfish pecan with meunière sauce. My anger and worry fled, at least temporarily, as I gazed at my beautiful entrée: a six-ounce catfish fillet, brown and crispy in its pecan crust and topped with pecan halves, parsley, and a lovely, spicy meunière sauce. It tasted as good as it looked.

Since catfish farming developed into a lucrative industry in the United States, I have become very fond of this firm, sweet fish. It is not only tasty, but also low in calories and cholesterol, for those who worry about their weight and their arteries, and best of all, it's available in markets all year round, filleted so that the fish lover doesn't have to deal with all those tiny, dangerous bones.

Catfish Pecan with Meunière Sauce

Preheat oven to 450°. Trim all fat from *six 5- to 7-oz. catfish fillets.*

Grind *3 cups roasted pecans* and *1 cup dried breadcrumbs* in a blender or food processor until fine. Pour into a pie pan.

Place *1 cup all-purpose flour* in another pie pan and stir in *½ tsp. pepper* and *1 tsp. salt.*

Beat together *3 eggs* and *½ cup milk* in a medium bowl.

Season catfish with seafood seasoning. (Mix together *6 tsp. paprika, 4 tsp. ground garlic, 4 tsp. black pepper, 2½ tsp. ground onion, 1½ tsp. fine thyme, 1¼ tsp. fine oregano, 1¼ tsp. basil, 1 tsp. cayenne,* and *salt to taste.* Can be stored in a cool, dry place, tightly sealed.)

Dredge catfish fillets in flour, dip in egg mixture, and coat with pecan mixture.

Film bottom of large, ovenproof sauté pan or skillet with *olive oil* over medium heat.

Add fish and brown on both sides.

Bake in oven for about 5 minutes.

MEUNIÈRE SAUCE:
Cook *2 cups fish stock* or bottled clam juice, juice of ½ lemon, 1 tsp. Worcestershire sauce, dash of Louisiana hot sauce in medium saucepan.

Add *1 tbs. heavy cream* and cook to reduce for 1 to 2 minutes.

Remove from heat and whisk *½ cup (1 stick) unsalted butter* into liquid.

Serve over cooked fish fillets and sprinkle with *roasted whole pecan halves* and (if desired) *chopped parsley.*

Carlene ordered a marvelous crabmeat cheesecake and offered me a bite, on which I made copious notes, and Jason had the seafood boil, which was served on a raised platter. The waiter told me that Paris cafés served in that fashion, and Jason pronounced his seafood so fresh that it must have been pulled from the sea that very day, which the waiter assured him it was. Nils and Miranda didn't offer me any of their entrées, and Miranda and Lester had rather sharp words when his selection arrived, a double pork chop, rotisseried and served with candied sweet potatoes.

Midway through the meal, someone from Julienne's department, evidently someone who disliked Nils, stopped to tell him the latest news. "Just got a call from home," he said. "The dean is in a real snit. In fact, our chair is pissed off, too, because your wife's using departmental funds to attend this meeting and then isn't—"

"Oh, Brad," said his wife, tugging on his arm, "do be quiet and come on. They're holding our table."

"How did the dean hear about Julienne not showing up for her meetings?" Nils asked. When the young professor shrugged, Nils said, "Won't do *you* any good, Forrester." His tone was just as nasty as Brad's had been. "She's the one with tenure. You're the one who hasn't got it yet, and she'll still have a vote on yours, no matter how many papers she does or doesn't present at national meetings."

"Brad," hissed his wife.

Brad yanked his arm loose from the cautioning marital hand, shook a hank of dishwater blond hair away from his eyeglasses, and continued, "You haven't heard the best of it, Magnussen. Torelli took off for Sweden today or last night. No one's sure exactly when. Didn't even get administrative permission. Makes you wonder what's going on, doesn't it?" The young assistant professor then scuttled away with his wife talking to him angrily all the way from our table to theirs, which was back near the stairs and not at all convenient for visiting us. Nils had turned red, then pale.

"Whatever you're thinking, Nils," I said hastily, "Julienne has not run off to Sweden with Linus Torelli."

"You don't know what I'm thinking," he responded.

"You should be worried about her safety. Why is Torelli fleeing the country? That's the question we should be asking. Does he have tenure? Can he afford to—"

"He doesn't," said Nils.

"There. So the question is, what's he done to Julienne that he has to run away?"

"Really, Carolyn, don't you think you're letting your imagination run wild?" cautioned Broder. "Professors don't murder one another and then skip the country."

"Murder?" Nils's voice was faint, his lips trembling. "Is that what you think, Carolyn? That someone murdered her? Did you think I had? Before you heard this latest news about Torelli?"

"I don't know what to think," I admitted. "I'm scared to death. And why shouldn't I be? You've been acting as if Julienne has been unfaithful to you. Torelli's denying any relationship with her and starting rumors about them at the same time."

"What rumors?" Nils demanded.

"And suddenly he's left the country under suspicious circumstances when Julienne's been missing since Sunday, and he's probably the last person we know to see her."

"When was this?" Nils practically shouted his last question at me.

Carlene said, "Sh-sh-sh, Nils."

The waiter came rushing over to ask if there was a problem.

"No problem," Nils snarled. "Go away." Then he turned back to me. "When did Torelli see her?"

How I wish I hadn't said that! "And then there's Philippe," I responded hastily.

"Good heavens," said Miranda. "I remember him. The world's glummest sibling."

"Forget Philippe," said Nils. "When did Julienne see Torelli? Sunday? After she left me?"

"Philippe is a professor in a medical school now," I said, choosing to respond to Miranda rather than Nils. "And he's decided that he should have the complete inheritance from their mother, both his portion and Julienne's."

"So what? He's not here," said Nils. "I want to know—"

"But he is," I interrupted. "He's been here since Sunday, and he won't answer his telephone at the hotel. For all I know, he's disappeared, too."

"Good grief," said Carlene, "I don't like the sound of that at all. I always thought Philippe was somehow off kilter."

"He's all right," said Nils, but he was beginning to look more worried than angry. "As long as he takes his meds, he's—"

"But Diane said he sounded weird—her words—when she talked to him."

"He went to see my daughter?" Now Nils looked thoroughly upset.

"No, he called to find out where Julienne was, and Diane told him. He's not in New Hampshire, he's here in New Orleans, so Nils, you've got to report her disappearance to the police."

"Jesus." Fingers clenched in thinning blond hair, Nils bowed his head over his empty plate.

"Why is Philippe thinking about challenging his mother's will?" asked Miranda, ever the lawyer. "I wouldn't imagine that Julienne's mother was so wealthy it would be worth the expense."

"Oh, the father made a lot of money on the stock exchange. I remember that. It was when we were in college," said Carlene. "Maybe Mrs. Delacroix still had it when she died. Did Julienne inherit a lot of money, Nils?"

"It's none of your business," he muttered.

Carlene looked highly offended. Some people didn't like to talk about money, but Carlene obviously wasn't one of them.

"When did Julienne's father make all this money?" Lester asked. "I thought he killed himself."

"I don't know why you'd think that," I replied. "He did die not too long after his big bonanza on the stock exchange, but his death was an accident."

"Still, it's peculiar when you think about it," said Miranda. "If they were rich, I mean. Both of them dying in car accidents."

All of us stared at our bread pudding. Were the deaths of Julienne's parents connected to the money? I wondered, then decided that was a silly idea. Mr. Delacroix had gone to sleep at the wheel. No problems had been found with his car and no indication that anyone had run him off the road. And Mrs. Delacroix had been killed by that pickup truck. The driver was in jail for vehicular manslaughter. So whether or not they still had the money, it hadn't killed them.

But what about Julienne? If she inherited a lot, had she died because of it? I thought about Philippe, who allegedly wanted her share. Killing her wouldn't get it for him. Nils would be her heir, Nils and Diane. I looked at Nils, who was still looking stricken. He hadn't eaten a bite of his white chocolate bread pudding, which had been served during our discussion.

We'd all ordered the same dessert, for which the Palace Café was famous, and it was excellent. Had you asked me a month ago if it was likely that I'd order bread pudding twice in one week, I'd have laughed, but both the banana rum and the white chocolate bread puddings were amazingly good. Only in New Orleans, I thought as I scooped up another bite.

"I'll go to the police tomorrow," said Nils.

His sudden acquiescence only increased my confusion. And fear. Did he think that Philippe was a threat to Julienne? Or had he realized that Torelli, having fled the country, might be implicated in her disappearance? Or was he now worrying that by refusing to report her missing after all this time, he himself would look that much more guilty of whatever had happened to his wife? "I'll go with you," I announced.

The group broke up on a glum note. Jason and I thanked the others for the lovely meal to which they had treated us, and then we lost sight of them when the maître d' stopped me to inquire about, first, whether I had enjoyed my dinner, and, second, the nature of the book I was writing. Having reassured him on both counts and now being free of the rest of the group, I talked Jason into paying a visit to Philippe at the Superior Inn.

Once there, we had the desk call his room, but no one answered. Then—and it embarrasses me to say what I did next—I asked the desk clerk to try one more time in case Dr. Delacroix had been in the bathroom. While she was punching in the numbers, I craned my neck to make them out: 214.

"Why don't we have a drink, Jason?" I said when the clerk had announced, rather brusquely, that the room still did not answer.

Jason looked puzzled but allowed me to drag him out of the clerk's view and then over to the elevator. "Where are we going?" he asked as I rushed inside.

"To Philippe's room," I replied.

"But she didn't tell us his room number."

"It will be the same as the number she dialed," I explained, exiting on the second floor.

"Carolyn!" my husband exclaimed. But his disappointment in me did not stop me from knocking at the door of room 214. And knocking. And knocking. No one answered.

22
Eggs Sardou

I was a fetus in a womb of amniotic gumbo, my attempts to move thwarted by the murky soup that enclosed me. Blind to anything but brown swamp water, I could see no hint of light pointing the way up. If I lifted a hand to my eyes, the fingers and wrist were ghostly, and they trailed supple bonds that lapped around all my limbs and slid as sinuously as snakes into my mouth and around my neck. My frenzied mind told me I was being sucked down, but that nowhere would my feet touch a firm surface against which I could push off toward safety. All was mud, above and below, and my lungs burned for lack of air. The muscles of my chest trembled with the desire to suck in something. I was dying.

"Carolyn! Carolyn!" I felt a hand clutching mine and heard a voice, so muffled that I couldn't recognize it. The hand drew me upward as, trailing the clutching fronds, I sought to help in my own rescue. When I burst at last into the air, I saw Julienne leaning over the low edge of a boat. She was smiling at me, camera dangling from her neck. Happiness exploded like light in my heart because she was safe.

Then I opened my eyes, and Jason said, "That must have been one hell of a nightmare, Caro." I looked around for Julienne, but I was in my bed at the Hotel de la Poste. Only Jason and I were in the room, and I was trembling, he patting my arm consolingly in the way of men, who never know quite what to do with their wives' tears or terrors.

"It was just a nightmare," he murmured.

A nightmare? Perhaps. But Julienne had been alive. And in the swamp. I hoped it was an omen. Illogically perhaps, I determined right then that the next search I made would include the people who rented boats on the bayous, boats with sides that were low to the water and had motors in the back. I remembered the motor, although I had had only that one glimpse of Julienne and her boat as, in my dream, she saved me from drowning.

I pictured her living in a wooden shack, raised above the mud on stilts. She would be fishing and taking photos, lounging and listening to music on a portable radio, enjoying a respite from the pressures of her job and her husband's unconcealed enmity, thinking today might be the day she went back to it all, or maybe not. Maybe tomorrow. Cajun men in pirogues would stop by her retreat to drop off supplies and news of the world beyond the swamp. Or just to pass the time of day with a lovely woman who made friends wherever she went.

And I would find her. I could almost hear her laughter as we talked of her latest escapade and compared it to the time she had taken her father's boat and set up camp on an island in the lake. From her hideout, she'd watched as summer neighbors rowed about and shouted her name. She'd listened as her father promised at the top of his lungs to return her bicycle if she, in turn, promised not to hitch rides by hanging onto the back of the postman's truck and coasting with her feet stuck out. Her delighted laughter had given her away one afternoon when Postmaster Boggis stopped at a rural box to drop off newspapers, catalogues for winter woolens, and utility bills. How could I have forgotten that incident?

"You'd better get up," my husband said. "Remember? You said you'd go to the police with Nils this morning."

"Rats," I muttered, getting out of bed and reaching for my robe.

"Rats?" Jason couldn't have looked more astonished. I'd been hounding Nils since Saturday night to report Julienne missing, and after all this time, he'd agreed. Under the circumstances, I could hardly go running off to follow a clue that had come to me in a dream; I had to be on hand to introduce Nils to Lieutenant Boudreaux and to be sure that Nils actually filed the missing persons report.

But Julienne had looked so real. I was now sure that she was alive. Should I tell the lieutenant where to look for her? Policemen probably didn't put much stock in dreams, although there was certainly a lot to be said for this one. It wasn't just an omen. It was my subconscious searching through the information I had and telling me what course to take.

Hadn't I always found that, before an exam at college, a good review of the subject material and then a good night's sleep were the surest path to a high grade? I had always awakened with the subject much clearer in my mind and with new insights ready to pour out onto my blue-book pages. And that was just what had happened with this dream.

"Seven-thirty," Jason prompted. He had come out of the bathroom to remind me, a bit of shaving cream still clinging to his throat where he had given his beard an edging. Jason always said that if he were rich, the first thing he'd do would be to find a beard barber and patronize him regularly. Which was a modest enough ambition, surely. Not that either of us expected to be rich. I tried to imagine sales of *Eating Out in the Big Easy* running into the millions, making us disgustingly affluent, but it didn't seem likely. How many people would want to read my opinions of New Orleans restaurants and try the recipes I included? Not millions, certainly.

At eight-thirty Nils and I were waiting in line at Brennan's, although I *had* made a reservation. The restaurant was, conveniently, on Royal Street, a block from the police station. What culinary writer could justify missing breakfast at an establishment that reputedly sells 750,000 poached eggs a year? From their menu I chose eggs Sardou, that delicious dish that nests artichoke bottoms topped by poached eggs on a bed of creamed spinach and bathes the whole in hollandaise sauce. The anchovies are optional, and I opted out.

In 1908, Victorien Sardou, the renowned French dramatist, had breakfast at Antoine's, where the owner, Antoine Alciatore, created this dish in his honor. Since Sardou wrote *La Tosca,* whose operatic embodiment I adore, I naturally ordered Sardou's eggs.

As I savored my choice—sometimes I think I could eat a poached Gila monster if it was served in hollandaise sauce—I worried because I would not be returning that morning to Café du Monde, but that was silly. Julienne wasn't going to return from the swamp for beignets and café au lait. It was much too far. In fact, I would probably have to rent a car to begin my canvass of boat rental facilities.

I told Nils about my dream and my plans, suggesting that he might come with me. Truthfully, I don't like driving around strange cities, much less backcountry swamp areas. I was hoping that Nils would drive. Also I've found, although it is a situation I deplore, that men respond more readily to questions from other men. Oops! I was assuming that most of the boat owners would be men. For all our efforts to effect equality between the sexes in fact and in attitude, I was making sexist assumptions. And I had only caught myself as an afterthought. Progress certainly wasn't impinging much on my thinking.

"You want to rent a car and have me drive you around asking questions on the basis of a *dream?*" Nils demanded in response to my story and suggestion. "I thought that's why we were going to the police—to get professionals hunting for Julienne and Torelli."

"You still think she's with Linus Torelli?" I couldn't believe my ears. "You were told last night that he's gone to Sweden."

Nils shrugged. "Maybe she went with him. Maybe he's lying, and he hasn't gone to Sweden at all. The police can find out. Then you can stop worrying. You'll know she's run away."

I glared at him. There are some men whose opinions can't be changed with a large rock to the back of the head, much less a combination of fact and logic.

"Obviously, it's going to take a professional to track her down," Nils continued. "You certainly haven't accomplished anything."

"At least I tried," I retorted.

"Well, shortly we'll know the truth. Then you can stop nagging me, and I'll have grounds to file for divorce."

Having revealed his plans, he didn't look very happy about them, and I was furious. Of all the cold-hearted, scheming . . . I forked up my last bite and ate it. Then I waved imperiously to the waiter. The sooner we made our visit to Lieutenant Boudreaux, the better. I didn't think I could stomach much more of Nils's company.

It was raining again as we set out for the Vieux Carre station, not a sheeting rain, but still, this obviously wasn't the most pleasant season in New Orleans unless you lived in the desert and craved the blessing of moisture. Nils complained about the weather every step of the way, but underneath the ill temper, I detected a certain unease. In his place, I would have felt uneasy. His wife had been missing since Saturday, and he had waited until Thursday to report it. If he was to be believed, his only reason for doing so today was to get me off his back and obtain grounds for divorce on the basis of desertion.

We were both scowling by the time we reached the station. There, to my dismay, we found that Lieutenant Boudreaux was away on official police business. The cynical sergeant took our information on Julienne—description, age, profession, social security number, home address and phone number, local address and phone number. He didn't seem much interested.

"Dr. Magnussen has been gone since Saturday," I finally interrupted with ill-concealed desperation, "and not seen since Sunday."

"Who saw her?" the sergeant asked.

Nils turned to look at me challengingly, and I hated to answer, knowing that any mention of Linus Torelli would set Nils off. "A waitperson—"

"A *what?*" The sergeant stopped writing and frowned at me.

"She's trying to be politically correct," said Nils sarcastically. "She means a waiter or waitress."

"—at Café du Monde Sunday morning, a bartender at the Absinthe House—"

"Don't sound to me like she's gone missin'," the sergeant interrupted. "Sounds like she's out on the town."

"—maybe someone at the voodoo museum, a street performer that evening—"

"Her lover, Linus Torelli." Nils added to the end of my list the name that my tongue just didn't want to voice. The sergeant stopped writing again and looked up with sharpened interest.

"Torelli isn't her lover," I snapped.

"When did *he* see her?" the sergeant asked with a smirk.

"After she left the dinner party," I replied unwillingly, hoping I wouldn't have to enlarge on that.

"And now Torelli's made an unexplained trip to Sweden, on which my wife undoubtedly accompanied him," said Nils bitterly. "Or maybe that's what he told his chair, and they've gone somewhere else together."

"His chairman is here in New Orleans. Torelli told someone else, who told the dean of science," I corrected. "And Julienne did not—"

The sergeant had closed his notebook. "We don't go lookin' for no folks who's run off with lovers an' such."

"She hasn't—" I started to protest.

"No problem checkin' that out," a voice from behind interrupted.

I turned, and there was Lieutenant Boudreaux. I fear that my relief at his appearance was only too obvious, for Nils inspected him closely as the lieutenant told the sergeant that he would take over the interview and ushered me solicitously into his office. Nils trailed behind. Only when we were seated was I able to introduce him to Alphonse Boudreaux.

"Well now," said the lieutenant. "The missin' husband."

"*I'm* not missing," snapped Nils defensively.

"Took you long enough to report your wife among the missin'," said Boudreaux dryly. "This lady's been frettin' all week 'bout Miz Magnussen. Don' seem you have."

"I'm not happy that my wife ran off with another man, but I don't know of any law that prevents her from doing so." Nils's tone was downright starchy.

"Easy to check out." The lieutenant took down Julienne's name and what passport information Nils could supply after he agreed that she did have a valid passport, the information on Linus Torelli, the probable city of departure, and the probable destination. Then he made a call. To Customs or Immigration or whoever checks passports. "Computers sure have eased our burden, us in law enforcement," he observed as he waited, phone to ear, smiling companionably at me. "How you doin', Miz Carolyn?"

"Very well, thank you, Lieutenant," I replied. Given the expression on Nils's face, I could only wish that I had been addressed as Miz Blue instead of Miz Carolyn. I didn't want any false impressions of my relationship with the lieutenant circulating in the academic community, although it occurred to me that Nils would love to tell Jason that I had an admirer in the New Orleans Police Department. Did I? Quickly, I put that thought aside.

"Been doin' any more sleuthin'?" the lieutenant asked amiably. "Hope you haven' run into any more local crime waves."

"Not today," I replied.

"Uh-huh. Uh-huh," said the lieutenant into the telephone. "Much obliged." He hung up and turned to Nils. "Dr. Linus Torelli's sure 'nuff left for Sweden, but yo' wife hasn't left the country, sir, so maybe we bettah be worryin' 'bout where-all she might be. When did *you* last see yo' lady, Professor?"

Nils sputtered and flushed. "Am I suspected of something?" he demanded angrily.

"Harm comes to a lady, husbands an' lovers are first on the list of suspects," the lieutenant replied. "So why don't you be cooperative an' answer mah question, sir."

Nils glared at me and replied, "The same time Carolyn saw her, when she stormed out of the dinner party Saturday night."

"An' why did she *storm out,* as you say?"

"We had words," Nils muttered.

"About what?"

"I don't know," Nils said, looking unhappy. "We're always having words about something lately."

"About the fella you say's her lover?"

"We didn't talk about that—not Saturday night, anyway," Nils replied in an almost inaudible voice.

"You did once she'd left," I added.

"But Miz Magnussen—she knows that's what you think?" the lieutenant pressed.

"Yes," Nils admitted.

"So what did you have words about?"

"Her dress," I replied since Nils either wouldn't say or really didn't remember. "He intimated that it was—improper. Actually, she looked lovely. And her decision to send their daughter to a private school. Nils said she was an indifferent mother, which is nonsense. Diane is a student at a very prestigious prep school in the East."

The lieutenant nodded. He was making notes. "We'll put out an APB on her an' send all the information to Missing Persons. Since she was last seen in mah district, Ah'll have mah men askin' questions on the streets."

"Thank you," I said, and believe me, my thanks were heartfelt. Maybe now, at last, Julienne would be found. A shiver went up my spine because I was so afraid that she wouldn't be found alive, that someone—some criminal, the missing Torelli, or even Nils—might have hurt or killed her. But I just couldn't let myself consider that terrible possibility. Julienne was the best, dearest friend I'd ever had, and I couldn't imagine life without our phone calls and E-mails and occasional meetings. I just couldn't.

"Bitch," Nils snarled at me as we exited the station. Having expressed his anger at a woman he must be holding responsible for the lieutenant's suspicions, Nils turned and strode away from me. I was stunned. I don't think anyone has ever called me that, certainly not anyone I've known for years. Of course, there was the purse snatcher. I recalled that he had called me a bitch. A stupid bitch, I believe, although one needn't be concerned with the opinions of criminals. And then there are motorists. Who knows what other motorists call one in the heat of that new bane of society, road rage? Sadly, I turned toward the hotel. I don't know where Nils was headed, but it wasn't there.

23
Chocolate Cake and Red Wine

As I stood in front of the police station contemplating Nils's unpleasant farewell, the memory of my dream came back. I was now glad that I hadn't mentioned it to the lieutenant. He was obviously a man who would put more faith in messages from the INS than those from the subconscious. In my dream Julienne had rescued me from a boat in the swamp. Did that mean she had gone there by herself? Or that someone had taken her there? And if so, who?

I went back into the station and asked to use their telephone. The desk officer refused and directed me to a public telephone, from which I called Philippe's room once more. He still wasn't answering. Could he and Julienne be in the swamp together? Philippe had been a fisherman once, morose but often successful. I personally hadn't wanted to share a boat with him because he never said anything and often didn't answer when spoken to. Depression, no doubt. So why didn't he take one of the many prescription drugs that relieved depression? His chairman had said, as an aside, something about Philippe's not being suited to the private practice of medicine. Small wonder. Who would want a doctor who neither spoke nor answered questions?

I tried to imagine being the patient of a silent doctor, one who conducted an examination, wrote a prescription, and walked out. That wouldn't be a successful approach to sick people. When you were telling Philippe your symptoms, you'd never be sure that he was listening. I can remember Julienne warning him that there was a black widow spider on his shirt collar. He never replied. Of course, there was no spider, but that was beside the point. Any normal person would have looked.

And how did he teach his classes if he didn't speak? Obviously, he now condescended to say something. Maybe depression allowed one to lecture but not to answer questions.

"You lost, ma'am?"

Good heavens! A helpful New Orleans policeman, other than Lieutenant Boudreaux. How long had I been standing by the telephone neither using it nor leaving? "Where can I find a car rental agency, officer?" I asked, pleased to have been approached by someone who might know.

He gave me a lecture on hogging public telephones, then directions to a Hertz office, where I rented a car with no trouble. All one needed was a valid license and a credit card. I fear that having completed my transaction,

I took up more than my fair share of time with the personnel, for I also needed maps, directions, and photocopies of the yellow pages that listed boat rental facilities.

A short, stocky man waiting in the office became impatient and left, much to the dismay of the clerk who had been helping me, albeit somewhat impatiently, when I showed no aptitude for map reading and little confidence in my ability to drive their car to any given destination. Perhaps the clerk's attitude indicated a gloomy presentiment that I would wreck their red Ford Escort rather than irritation over the loss of a potential customer. Have you ever wondered why so many rental cars are red? Is it to warn locals that tourists are wandering the roads, lost and befuddled?

At any rate, I set off in my rental car and promptly became lost, not an unusual occurrence for me. I had to make inquiries of several policemen. Some were in cars that pulled up beside me and asked why I was looking at a map instead of crossing on green. Some were on foot. One was on a motorcycle and every bit as sarcastic as the police cyclist I had asked for a ride to the convention center. And the last was directing traffic at an intersection jammed with drivers attempting to visit the drive-in daiquiri establishment.

That incident gave me pause. I did not find it reassuring to think that I was sharing the streets with motorists imbibing daiquiris; the policeman did not find it reassuring that I had got into the daiquiri line by mistake.

Ah, well. Finally, I reached the first boat rental facility. And the second. And the third. I lost count. No one had rented a boat for night fishing or photography to a woman matching Julienne's description, not on Sunday night or any recent night. Or to a man accompanied by a woman. I was driving along a barely paved road in a light rain, heading for the last place on my list, when I saw, in my rearview mirror, a dusty pickup truck roaring toward my rear bumper. Alarmed, I edged my rental car over a bit toward the shoulder, but not too far because I could see, in my peripheral vision, black water among the weeds.

The truck, revving its engine, pulled out to pass, and on a narrow, two-lane road! The driver must have been some mad-yokel type. Or perhaps he was drunk. I glanced nervously to the left and noticed, to my horror, that his truck was only inches from my front bumper and closing in. My heart accelerated madly as I cut the wheel sharply to the right and—the gods must have been with me that day—onto a rutted dirt road. As my car slewed in mud, I caught just a glimpse of a long-billed cap obscuring the head of the madman at the wheel of the pickup.

Then he was gone, and I was occupied with trying to keep my vehicle from flying off first one side of the miserable road, then the other. Because my wheels were sliding in the mud, I dared not brake, so I took my foot off the gas and steered, ultimately bumping to a stop in front of—I could hardly believe it!—the very boating establishment I had been seeking. Were it not for the drunk in the pickup truck, I would surely have missed the turnoff to the only place where I got so much as a nibble.

Shaking like an aspen leaf in a fall wind, I killed the engine and leaned my head on the steering wheel for a moment. Never have I experienced so frightening a near accident. When I looked up, somewhat recovered, I saw the unshaven owner of a rickety pier that had no boats tied to it. He was leaning against the frame of his door as he smoked a very odoriferous brown cigarette. I had to breathe through my mouth when I approached him. Then, before I could say a word, he asked what I thought I was doing, speeding my fancy red car on his private road. If he thought an Escort was fancy, what did he drive?

"I was almost run off the highway—" I waved vaguely in the direction from which I had come. "—by a madman in a pickup."

"Comin' which way?" he asked.

"I turned right into your road."

"Lucky for you, lady, you wasn' run off into dat dere slough along da highway. It's deep, dat one. You'd been breathin' mud by now, you drove into dere."

"Then I was fortunate indeed," I answered in a weak voice. "Doubly fortunate because I believe your establishment is the very place I am looking for."

"Won't do you no good. Catfish is bitin', an' Ah ain' got a single boat left for hire."

I speculated that savvy locals must think fish are put off their guard by rain. Had I been a catfish, I would have assumed that no sensible fisherman would be tooling around the swamp in an open boat on a rainy day. *I* certainly wasn't happy about being rained on. I had to go back to the car for my umbrella since the man in the doorway did not step aside to let me in. There wasn't even an overhang on his porch to protect visitor or inhabitant. His undershirt and the raggedy plaid shirt over it, not to mention his stained canvas pants, were getting wet. He didn't have to worry about his shoes because he was barefooted.

I returned with my new umbrella to inquire about recent rentals. (I had given in to necessity and purchased a new one to replace the one damaged against the purse-snatching mugger's head.)

"You don' wanna rent a boat, you?" he asked, evidently disgusted.

"You don't have any to rent," I retorted. "You just told me that."

Accepting the truth of my observation, he simmered down and answered my questions, ending every sentence with a pronoun. What an interesting speech pattern. Had it evolved from the French spoken by the original Acadian immigrants to the swamps? I didn't recall any such sentence structure from high school French classes or from the bit of conversational French I had picked up from Julienne and her family. Of course, they weren't Cajuns; they were Creoles.

What I found out from the soggy boat owner was that he had indeed rented a boat to a man who wanted to do some night fishing. This was on Sunday.

"Was he accompanied by a lady?" I asked eagerly.

The owner rolled a second cigarette, lit it from the first, which had dangled from his mouth during the rolling, licking, pinching process—quite a feat, I thought—and then he shrugged. "Coulda been."

In other words, he hadn't seen Julienne.

"What was your customer's name?"

The owner didn't remember. He didn't take credit cards, so he had no record, and he didn't worry about customers stealing his boats, because why would anyone want one and where would they go with it that some friend or cousin of his wouldn't see the boat, know it was missing, and reclaim it for him.

"Did your customer return the boat?" I asked.

He hadn't seen the return, that having occurred sometime between ten and dawn, but he'd rented that same boat out this morning to a man hungry for a mess of catfish.

"What did the man look like?" I asked patiently.

"Ray Ralph? Ray Ralph got him a glass eye an'—"

"So you do know the name of the man who rented your boat Sunday night?" I doubted that Julienne would have been with glass-eyed Ray Ralph.

"Ray Ralph Otis dun rented mah boat dis morning."

I sighed. "What did the man who rented it Sunday night look like?"

He stared at me suspiciously. "You a cop, you?" Then he took the cigarette out of his mouth. "Naw, you ain't no cop. Why you care—"

"I'm looking for a friend of mine."

"What yo' friend look like?"

Patiently, I described Julienne. He pointed out that the Sunday renter had been a man, not a woman, and he didn't remember what the man looked like, just that he had cash money and wanted to rent fishing equipment as well. I showed him the pictures. He didn't recognize anyone. Then the roll-his-own entrepreneur closed the door in my face because, as he pointed out, "wrastlin' " was coming on TV, and he had a mess of gumbo in the pot calling him to lunch.

I could smell the gumbo and, being very hungry myself, decided that it would make an interesting chapter for my book if I survived the experience. Cajun boatman gumbo. Did he use catfish in it? However, that plan was not to materialize. He didn't answer when I knocked on his door again. Maybe it was just as well. He really had looked to be a disreputable character. Jason would have been horrified to think I'd invited myself to lunch with such a man.

As I drove back to town, the rain abated, and I let my imagination linger over the little information I had collected. A man had rented a boat, using cash, before midnight Sunday and returned it before dawn Monday. It could have been Linus Torelli, the chemist who had reputedly disappeared into the cold wastes of Sweden (actually, he was probably in Stockholm, but I didn't *know* that). Torelli had claimed that Julienne left his room in a huff because he wouldn't take her into the swamp, but he could have lied, either because something had happened to her there or because she had him drop her off somewhere and swear not to tell where she was. He might even still be in New Orleans, registered at some other hotel under an assumed name, although why he would—oh well, that was a useless avenue of speculation, and Lieutenant Boudreaux's sources said that Torelli had gone to Sweden.

It could have been Nils under the same circumstances, but I couldn't imagine why he wouldn't then admit that he knew where she was. After all, he'd finally reported her missing just this morning. And I suppose it could have been her brother. Maybe he was still in town because he had promised to rent another boat and pick her up from wherever she was hiding out. It might even have been Julienne, disguised as a man, who rented the boat, but then who had returned it? And if she had, where was she now? Not in Sweden. That's all I knew.

I imagined her meeting her brother, perhaps in a rented car, their going somewhere to talk about their mother's will, Philippe agreeing that he'd been out of line to think that everything should be his. "The silver? The china? Do you want those, too, Philippe?" she'd ask teasingly, and he'd have to laugh. Did Philippe ever laugh? How could he help it, at least occasionally, when he had a sister like Julienne, who could coax laughter from a statue?

They'd stop somewhere and have gumbo, which they had both loved since childhood, recall events from their early life in New Orleans, perhaps reminisce about trips to the lake cabin in Michigan. Did Philippe remember those summers with fondness? Then Julienne would say, "Philippe, let's go fishing again the way we used to. Remember going to the swamp with Papa? I'll take pictures, and you catch us some catfish. We'll find a place to cook them up in the morning," and Philippe would smile and agree. And off they'd go, out of the city, stomachs full of gumbo, minds filled with happy memories, traveling bumpy roads they'd taken in childhood until they came to that shack and rickety pier that belonged to the roll-your-own man. I should have asked Mr. Red (his sign said Red's Boats/Cash Only) whether he knew the late Mr. Delacroix. He might have been a fishing buddy or guide of their father's when he was a younger, less scruffy-looking version of himself.

And when they were sitting in the motionless boat, listening to the eerie night sounds of the swamp, watching the permutations of moonlight on the brown water, Julienne would tell her brother about her problems with Nils and how angry and discouraged the situation made her. And maybe

Philippe would suggest that she just take time out, the way the psychologists are wont to say; Philippe had probably visited his share of psychologists and psychiatrists. He'd remember an old rental shack on solid ground out in the swamp where she could kick back, think things over, and take pictures. He probably even knew a place to stop for supplies and knew where to pull in to ask the owner's permission to use the shack. In fact, since he wasn't answering his phone at the hotel, he might be there with Julienne.

No, he'd returned the boat, but he could have rented another, at a weekly rate, picked up the supplies in the morning, and returned. I was feeling almost cheerful when I returned my red Escort to the rental agency. My imagined scenario made sense. I could picture Julienne and her brother sitting lazily on a pier somewhere in the swamp, fishing, taking pictures of the strange trees and the alligators and snakes and other denizens of the mud flats and the water, getting reacquainted after so many years of following their separate career paths.

By the time I reached Jackson Square, I decided I deserved a treat, so I stopped again at La Madeleine's and bought a glass of red wine and a piece of chocolate cake with deep, rich frosting. My snack wasn't for the book; it wasn't particular to New Orleans. It was happy food, and I enjoyed every sip and bite as I sat at the window and watched the passing scene. Red wine and chocolate: food for the gods. Jason thinks it's a crazy combination, but what does he know?

24

News of an Untenured Adulterer

I returned to the hotel after my dose of comfort food on Jackson Square to find a voice-mail message from Jason: "Caro, I talked to one of Julienne's colleagues this morning. The latest gossip from her university is that the dean of her college received an E-mail from Linus Torelli announcing that he'd just accepted a job in Sweden and wouldn't be back. Seems Torelli told the dean he was leaving because he's being blamed for Julienne's disappearance by, and I quote, 'some nosy friend of hers.' " Jason's delighted chuckle sounded in my ear as he asked, "Think you're the 'nosy friend'? Torelli also says he was not having an affair with Professor Magnussen and he resented all the vicious gossip about them, most of which he attributed to her husband.

"Maybe it was a mistake, but I called Nils with the news, and he seemed pretty upset," Jason added. "I don't know how it went this morning with the police, but I think you ought to check on him. OK? See you around five-thirty."

Torelli had resigned? That seemed a bit overboard to me if he wasn't guilty of anything, and I resented being characterized as the "nosy friend," even if the dean, whom I'd never met, didn't know my name. It's rather off-putting to think that one is being unpleasantly characterized on the Internet, which is not, as I understand it, a particularly private means of communication. And what an odd way to resign! Bad enough to disappear and resign in the middle of a semester without notice, but to do it by E-mail! That is hardly proper academic etiquette.

Feeling tired and put upon, I combed my hair and applied a bit of lipstick as I wondered what Nils was upset about. One would think he'd be glad to know that Torelli was gone for good, declaring Julienne's innocence in the process. But of course, that meant—if Torelli was to be believed, and I believed him even if I hadn't liked him—that Nils had been wrong about Julienne. He'd be upset because he was feeling guilty at having misjudged her.

As I put down my lipstick case, it also occurred to me that if Torelli had not been involved with Julienne, he'd have had no reason to do her harm, although he might have agreed to hide her out from her husband before he left. He might have been the renter of the boat. In fact, he might not be in Sweden at all. One can't tell where an E-mail originates. I had to remind myself once more that Lieutenant Boudreaux said Torelli had flown to Sweden. Could that be faked? In truth, I didn't know what to think. My speculations were unaccompanied by proof.

I picked up my handbag and headed for the Magnussen room. At least I didn't have to go out in the rain again, for it was pouring down from low-hanging, gray clouds. Even I, starved for the sight and feel of rain, was getting a bit tired of it. El Paso's perpetual sunshine might look good by the time we got home. I knocked on Nils's door, waited, knocked again harder, called his name, and finally got a response, although not a very welcoming one. Nils opened the door looking rumpled and unhappy, more so when he saw me.

"Did you come to say, 'I told you so'?" he asked bitterly.

"I came because Jason said that you seemed upset after he called about Torelli's resignation."

"Why should I be upset?" Nils retorted sarcastically. "The man's gone to Sweden. He's not coming back. My wife didn't go with him. I'm delighted."

He didn't look at all delighted. His thinning blond hair stood up in ragged tufts, his face seemed bloated, his eyes puffy, and I could smell scotch on his breath. "Do you want to discuss this out in the hall?" I asked calmly. Getting impatient with a man so edgy didn't seem like a good idea.

He shrugged and waved me in. He had one of the rooms that overlooked the courtyard, while ours overlooked the street. I stood for a moment eyeing the greenery below, thinking it must be more peaceful at night than the front of the building where Jason and I could hear the voices and laughter of people on the street. On the other hand, the melancholy sounds of horns wailing in the night were romantic. People our age, parents of grown-up children, can always use a bit of romance in their lives.

Nils had dropped down on one of the twin beds, so I sat down on the other, facing him. He looked the picture of dejection, hands dangling between his knees, head hanging. "We'll find her," I said encouragingly. "Do you want to help me look? Maybe she's rented a place in the swamp."

His head came up abruptly. "Why would you think that?" he demanded.

I felt a stab of panic. After all, the only clue I had about the swamp was the fact that a man had rented a boat to go night fishing. No woman had been seen with him. What if the man had been Nils, and he felt that I was closing in on him, and he—

"You think she's so furious with me that she'd hide out in some moldy swamp so I can't find her and try to patch things up?"

"I . . . I don't know where she is," I stammered. "I'm just guessing." Patch things up? If he wanted to patch things up, didn't that mean he hadn't done anything to her that would prevent them from reconciling?

"I did some investigating myself," Nils continued, low-voiced. "After Jason called me about Torelli's resignation, I called this fellow in her department."

I nodded and guessed, "Mark somebody or other."

"How did you know that?" He looked alarmed, as if I had psychic powers and might be reading his thoughts.

"I remember Julienne saying this Mark always knows everything that goes on. In her department, at any rate."

"Oh. Well, he does."

"What did he say?" I found that I was almost afraid of the answer.

"That she wasn't having an affair with Torelli. The son of a bitch has been dropping those hints in the department to cover up the fact that he was fucking the chairman's wife."

You can imagine my horror. No one that I know uses the "f" word, at least in my presence. Well, maybe some of the younger faculty. And the students. My son Chris used it once, and when I reprimanded him, he said, "Oh, Mom, everyone uses it." I was not happy to hear that. I suppose if I'd been part of the counterculture of the sixties and seventies, I might not have been so disgusted with Nils's language, but frankly I avoid R-rated movies because so many seem to employ a one-word vocabulary, which shows a woeful lack of inventiveness on the part of the scriptwriters, in my opinion.

"Well, aren't you going to say anything?" Nils snapped.

I managed to get my mind off the wording and onto the content of his revelation. In this case, the word in question wasn't just an expletive; it was used to describe an activity: Linus Torelli having sexual relations with his chairman's wife. Good heavens! I never cease to be amazed at the clandestine sexual activities that go on in the academic community. In this case, not just adultery, but adultery of the stupidest kind. Not that liaisons between students and professors aren't madness in these days of proliferating sexual harassment charges, but to become involved with one's chairman's wife was surely a suicidal impulse, professionally speaking. "Did he have tenure?" I asked.

"Tenure? That's your only comment? Did he have tenure?" Nils stopped looking woebegone and looked, instead, irritated.

It *was* a stupid question. Even insensitive, given Nils's obvious misery. Although I'm sure it would come to the mind of any person who has spent many years involved with college faculties. Even if the chairman's wife was the aggressor, the chairman wasn't likely to take that into account if he became cognizant of the affair. Would a chairman's wife seducing an untenured professor be considered sexual harassment? I wondered.

"He didn't," said Nils.

"He didn't what?" I had been lost in my speculations, which only proved that I needed a nap.

"He didn't have tenure," said Nils impatiently. "My God, he was ten years younger than Julienne. He wasn't even coming up for consideration until the end of next year."

"Then why did you think Julienne would be interested in him?" I retorted.

Nils gave me a strange look. "You mean why would she go after someone without tenure when she was married to someone who had it?"

"No!" What a silly interpretation of my question! "I meant why would she be interested in someone ten years her junior? Or, why would you believe it of her?"

Nils sighed. "Because I'm a fool." He dropped his head into his hands. "I've been so stupid."

I had to agree with that, although I didn't say so aloud. "So why did he take off for Sweden in the middle of the semester if he was in love with the chairman's wife? Did the chair find out about it?"

Nils shook his head and mumbled. "Martha found out about the supposed affair between Julienne and Torelli. In fact, her husband called her from here to tell her about Julienne disappearing and Torelli being suspect and so forth, and the wife called Torelli and tore a strip off him, said she was going to tell her husband that Torelli had seduced her."

"Good grief! How do you know all this?"

"Torelli told Mark. So Torelli hopped a plane to go home and pacify the chair's wife and try to talk her out of screwing up his bid for tenure, and she decided that he'd just been after her because he wanted her to support him with her husband."

"Is that likely?" I asked, amazed. What a bizarre story!

"I don't know. Maybe. She's older than Julienne and doesn't look half as good. What the hell would he want with her if he weren't hoping to get something out of it? Anyway, he panicked and went to Mark for advice."

"Which is like telling your troubles to Barbara Walters on national TV. I remember Julienne saying this Mark is a terrible gossip," I mused. "He not only knows all but tells all. If Torelli's that indiscreet, maybe he did need someone to support his bid for tenure."

"Julienne always said he was a good scientist." Nils scowled. "If she hadn't kept saying that—"

"Oh, nonsense, Nils. Don't put your jealousy off on Julienne. Especially now that you know you were wrong about her. And *especially* since your jealousy drove her away, and we don't even know where she is."

Nils looked so guilt-stricken that I almost wished I hadn't reminded him of his culpability in all this. "So what advice did Mark give Torelli?" I asked to get his mind off his troubles.

"He said that Torelli was done for with Martha on his case, and he'd better take the job in Sweden if they offered it. They did, and he did. End of story."

"Surely Martha wouldn't have told her husband that he should fire Torelli because she had been having an affair with him."

"No," Nils agreed. "She'd have said both Julienne and Torelli should be fired because *they* were having an affair, which he'd have believed because he'd already heard the rumors. That way she'd have gotten even with them both."

"Julienne has tenure," I pointed out.

"She'd never have been given another raise. She'd have found herself teaching all the scut classes and lots of them. She'd have gotten all the bad committee assignments. You don't have to fire someone to get rid of them. Julienne wouldn't have put up with that kind of treatment, and Martha wouldn't have stopped nagging her husband until he forced Julienne to leave."

"And Torelli just went off and left Julienne to that fate? How despicable! And this Martha doesn't sound like a very nice person, either."

"Martha's a bitch," said Nils.

I was reminded that he had called me a bitch just this morning. While I was remembering that, Nils was rising from the bed and grabbing a raincoat that had been thrown across the desk chair. "Where are you going?" I called after him as he headed for the door.

"To get drunk," he replied and slammed out.

Well, that wasn't a very fruitful approach to the problem of his missing wife! I sat a minute longer on what must have been Julienne's bed before she disappeared. Without any new ideas about where to find her, I used Nils's telephone to try Philippe's hotel room again. Might as well let Nils pay for the call. Goodness knows, I had spent an insane amount of money on calls before I discovered what they were costing. I punched in the numbers. By now I had them memorized. Without much surprise I listened to the ringing of the telephone. Philippe still wasn't in.

I hoped that meant he was with Julienne. Maybe his failure to answer meant that they had left town together, and he had kept his hotel registration to foil attempts to find them. Was Philippe a loving enough brother that he would risk his own position at the medical school where he taught in order to comfort his sister? Perhaps, if not to the swamp, they'd gone to the family cabin on the lake.

But the weather there would be dreadful, worse than New Orleans.

Then suddenly Nils's words came back to me, or to be more exact, his verb tenses. "She'd never have been given another raise . . . She'd have gotten all the bad committee assignments. . . ." As if nothing the chair's wife or the chair meant to do to Julienne made any difference. Because she wouldn't be around to take the heat for the alleged affair. What was Nils thinking? And why?

25

The Roux Morgue

It was after three-thirty when I returned to my room and sank down on the red bedspread, toeing my shoes onto the floor and stretching out. Although I was determined to have a nap, my mind refused to turn off. Nils didn't expect Julienne to return. Why? It didn't bear thinking on. And Martha, the chairman's wife. A spiteful woman. Would she seek revenge if Julienne did return? Surely, Martha could be persuaded that there had been no affair. Well, none but her own.

Still, that would be a difficult subject to introduce tactfully. What was Julienne supposed to say in her own defense? "I wasn't having an affair with Linus Torelli. You were." Actually, that approach, put more subtly, had merit. This Mrs. Chairman Martha might think twice about accusing Julienne if she knew that Julienne was aware of the jealousy that lay behind Martha's campaign to get rid of someone she perceived as a rival for the affections of a lover.

But there *was* no campaign to force Julienne out. Not yet. And Martha—I was calling some woman by her first name when I had never set eyes on her. This whole wild story about affairs and vengeance might be a figment in the imagination of another person I'd never met. Mark the Gossip. Still, Torelli *had* left the country. And Julienne *was* missing. Oh God, how I hoped that she was with her brother!

But where could she and Phillipe have gone? When did she plan to re-turn? Why hadn't she called me? What kind of job had the amoral Pro-fessor Torelli been forced to take in Sweden? Where should Jason and I go for dinner? Preferably someplace with food interesting enough to write about in my book. I should look at the *Louisiana New Garde,* but I was so sleepy. My thoughts drifted and broke up as my eyes began to close.

The ringing jerked me awake. Time to get up, I thought groggily as I reached for the telephone. "Thank you for calling," I mumbled and swung my legs over the side of the bed. The telephone receiver was on its way back to the cradle when I saw the time. Four o'clock? They'd given me a wake-up call at four o'clock? Light shining through the windows told me that it wasn't morning, and I replaced the receiver against my ear in time to hear a male voice saying, "Miz Blue? Miz Blue?"

"Lieutenant?" Why was *he* calling?

"Miz Blue, Ah'm tryin' to get ahold a Professor Magnussen."

"Why?" I asked.

"Well." There was a long pause.

"Is something wrong?" Suddenly, I was no longer sleepy, but rather short-winded and anxious. "What's wrong?"

"Likely nothin', ma'am. But if you know where the professor is—"

"He's gone out to get drunk."

"Damn!" Another pause. "Sorry 'bout the language, ma'am."

"Why did you want to speak to him?"

"Well." The next pause made me even more nervous than the first. "Well, Miz Blue, fact is, we got this body in the morgue. Jus' came in."

"Oh, my God. It isn't—"

"Probably not, ma'am. We jus' thought, your friend bein' missin' an' all, maybe the professor should take a look."

"Where did you find the body?" He told me in great detail, little of which meant much to me as a nonresident of the area. However, I did gather that the body had been fished from the swamp by a tour boat, much to the dismay of the tourists. "Is it . . . is it . . ."

"Like Ah said, Miz Blue, we don' know who it is. That's why we need identification. Probably someone who lives out in the bayous fell off a fishin' boat or a pier. Somethin' like that. Been in the water a while."

"I'll come."

"Oh, now, Miz Blue, Ah don' think you wanna—"

"Where?"

"Well, the morgue, but—"

"I'll take a taxi. Will a taxi driver know where the morgue is?"

"Yes, ma'am. Likely he will, but Ah don' think—"

"Thank you for calling, Lieutenant." I hung up. *Oh lord, not Julienne,*

I prayed as I stuffed my feet into my shoes and grabbed my handbag. *Not Julienne.*

With a sick dread, I sat on a bench outside in the corridor, waiting for Lieutenant Boudreaux to appear and usher me into the morgue. A policeman and a man in white medical scrubs were smoking cigarettes ten feet down the hall and chatting.

"I don't get it," said the officer. "Why are they callin' it the roo morgue?"

"R-O-U-X. Like you start with for gumbo," said the pathologist or tech or whatever he was. "We've had one sous chef, one maître d', and one waiter brought in in the same week."

"Yeah?" The cop frowned, puzzled.

"You never read *Murders in the Rue Morgue?*"

"I don' read much," said the cop. "It's a book about gumbo?"

"No, man. R-U-E in French means *street.*"

"So?" responded the policeman. He blew a smoke ring and watched it drift away.

"It's a pun," I said sharply, wishing they'd stop talking. Instead, they both turned and stared at me.

"She's right," said the tech. "It's a kind of joke, you dummy."

"Who're you callin' a dummy?"

I turned my back on them as the argument escalated. Then the lieutenant arrived to rescue me from tasteless puns and try to talk me out of viewing the body, which he evidently hadn't seen himself. However, I insisted. I had to know one way or the other, so he escorted me, reluctantly, through the door and into a cold room where an incongruously merry-looking man, his round stomach ballooning in a pregnant mound under a white lab coat, awaited us by a steel table. Shivering, marginally comforted by the support of the lieutenant's warm hand at my elbow, I nodded to the morgue tech, or was he the coroner?

As he began to draw the sheet back, the lieutenant swore. I retched. Because the face was gone, shredded by monster teeth, while the victim's arm had been devoured entirely.

"Ah knew this wasn't a good idea," said Boudreaux, his hand tightening on my arm. "Slater, why don't you—"

But I couldn't wait. Tearing my arm away from the lieutenant's supportive grip, I dashed into the now-empty hall and turned left toward a rest room I had noticed as I came in. Unfortunately, it proved to be the men's room, but I had no time to observe the niceties of gender separation. I catapulted through the swinging door and vomited into the first available receptacle.

"Hey, lady!" cried the policeman who hadn't read *Murders in the Rue Morgue.* Before he protested, turned his back, and zipped up with frantic haste, he had been standing at the urinal next to me.

I retched again. And again, impervious to his demands that I leave the "little boy's room," as he put it. "Lady, Ah'm gonna arrest you. It ain't right for ladies to come in here. Jus' 'cause you're hungover, don' mean you kin—"

Hungover? I gave him an indignant look, staggered to the sink, and cupped my hands under the faucet, then lifted the water to rinse my mouth. By the time I had splashed water on my burning face, the second occupant of the men's room had thought better of arresting me and gone.

Could that have been Julienne on the table? I wondered, appalled, and leaned weakly against the grungy wall tiles. Possibly. The hair—it might have been Julienne's. I scrubbed the tears away from my eyes and walked slowly back to the morgue, where Boudreaux intercepted me at the door.

"Miz Blue, if you'd given me the chance, I'da told you what they told me; there's just not enough left to identify unless you know the lady real . . . real intimately. Maybe we can get a print from the right hand. Ah should never a let you corral me into—"

"I doubt that Julienne was ever fingerprinted," I replied. "And I *can* identify her." In my mind I replayed voices—Julienne's and mine—twelve years old, on a sleepover at her house, giggling and trying on each other's clothes.

"Look at that!" said Julienne, turning away for me and pointing unhappily at a light tan splotch just where her bottom rounded on the left side.

"It's so light you can hardly see it," I had protested. "Besides, nobody's ever going to see it except me . . . and your mom, I guess."

"What about my husband when I get married?" Julienne wailed.

The idea of anyone, especially a male someone, ever seeing one's naked bottom was too much for my twelve-year-old mind; I had suggested we listen to records. But I *could* identify Julienne—by that birthmark she had so detested. I wondered, sadly, what Nils had thought of it.

Slipping past Lieutenant Boudreaux, I walked back to the steel table on which, I prayed, no light tan birthmark would be in evidence on the poor, mangled body that lay there. "Could you turn her over, please?" I asked the potbellied man in his spotless lab coat. How would I have felt, I wondered, had that coat been splashed with blood? It didn't bear thinking on. The body was horrifying enough.

"Ma'am, Ah don't think a nice lady like yourself oughta to be lookin' at the backside a this here—"

"Please," I said, voice wobbly but determined, "if we're going to find out who she is, or isn't—" which is what I devoutly hoped to ascertain, who she wasn't "—you're going to have to turn her over."

Looking resigned, Lieutenant Boudreaux gestured to the man, who then stripped back the sheet. I had to close my eyes. Could that be Julienne? I was unable to tell because the body had been unbearably savaged. Mr. Slater lifted and turned the body. Very gently. I liked him for that. It was touching that, in such a grisly profession, he had maintained his humanity. And then I gasped, because the left buttock, on which I had based my confident prediction of identification was virtually gone, gnawed away. I turned, weeping, and the lieutenant led me from the cold room.

"We're runnin' a fingerprint check right now on AFIS," he said consolingly. "Probably find out it's some woman been in prison for years an' drowned herself because she couldn't make it on the outside. Not much chance it's your friend."

"I suppose not," I said.

He handed me a clean linen handkerchief. It must be a Southern thing, I thought. Julienne had carried linen handkerchiefs, too, while most of us philistines just use Kleenex. At the thought of Julienne and her lace-edged handkerchiefs, I started to cry again and used the lieutenant's. Of course, it had no lace, but I did notice a B embroidered in the corner. And now, having shown so little self-control, I'd have to get it washed and ironed before Jason and I left New Orleans.

26
The Intrepid Gourmet

Lieutenant Boudreaux sent me back in a police car. Still sniffling into his handkerchief, I climbed out in front of the Hotel de la Poste, only to be confronted by Carlene, Broder, and my husband.

"You poor girl," Carlene cried and pulled me into a motherly embrace. "What happened? Were you arrested?"

The policeman jumped out of his front seat and said, "Here. What are you doing?" to Carlene. "This woman's under my protection."

Evidently he thought I was being attacked. How ironic that the New Orleans Police couldn't wait to protect me from a friend's hug but were never in sight when one of the many crazies in the city really was attacking me. I could certainly have used his help yesterday when that madman in the pickup truck tried to run me off a country road.

"Caro," Jason cried, "what are you doing in a police car, and why are you crying?"

"Get your hands off her," the officer said to Jason.

"He's my husband," I protested, fearing Jason's imminent arrest.

"Oh." The officer climbed into his patrol car immediately, saying, "I purely hate domestic disputes."

"What dispute?" Jason asked, but the officer was already pulling away. My protection, needed or not, had been very short-lived.

"I've been to the morgue," I said, sopping up tears with Lieutenant Boudreaux's soggy handkerchief.

Jason and the McAvees looked stunned. I don't suppose any of them has ever been to a morgue. I certainly hadn't until today. "It was horrible."

"Julienne," said Broder. "Was it Julienne?"

"I don't know. I looked at the body, but I couldn't tell."

"How could you not tell?" Carlene asked reasonably. Although Broder seemed to be giving in to fear for our friend, Carlene remained calm. "Either it was Julienne, or it wasn't."

"The woman had been . . . been . . . killed by an alligator." More tears. I couldn't seem to stem the flow.

"Oh, sweetheart." Jason put his arms around me, although this conversation was playing out on the street in front of the hotel, and Jason usually saved demonstrations of affection for private moments, as you'd expect of a long-married scientist with two more or less grown children. I cried some more, and he handed me a Kleenex, having failed to notice that I had a real handkerchief from Lieutenant Boudreaux.

"She was . . . was chewed up," I sobbed. "The woman in the morgue. But she had black hair. I think. It was muddy . . . just like . . . just like mine when I fell into the bayou." Before I could get any further with my description of the body I had gone to view, thunder rolled, drowning our conversation, and rain poured down as if dumped on us from buckets in the hands of angry rain gods. We all sprinted inside and dripped on the antiques in the lobby.

Carlene made me sit down, handed me another Kleenex, and said, "It wasn't Julienne," in a voice of absolute certainty. "Why would Julienne let herself be eaten by an alligator? She was a native of Louisiana. If anyone knows the danger of getting near an alligator, it's Julienne. She would never put herself in a position where an alligator could get anywhere near her."

"But—"

"You can take my word for it, Carolyn. She came to visit us one time and scared my children half to death with alligator tales. You never heard so much squealing and shrieking and giggling in your life. Children do love gore. Don't you agree, Broder?"

"Well, they've grown out of that phase," he replied defensively.

"True, but the point of this story is that Julienne knows all about alligators and how to keep out of their way, so the woman you saw was not Julienne. Now . . ." Carlene, who had been sitting beside me, got up, pulling me with her. "Now we're all going to dinner to have a wonderful meal. You can write about every bite we put in our mouths."

"Why did *you* have to go to the morgue, Caro?" my husband asked. "Shouldn't Nils have been asked?"

"He was, but he's out getting drunk," I replied, beginning to feel angry. There's nothing like a good gush of indignation to dry up one's tears.

"Drunk!" Broder frowned disapprovingly. "Nils's conduct throughout this whole episode has been reprehensible. When a search for Julienne needed to be made through the dangerous streets of New Orleans, you and I had to take on that responsibility because Nils wouldn't. I think—"

"I think you're getting grouchy, love," said Carlene. "Is it the prospect of an expensive dinner? Or are you just hungry?"

"I'm getting tired of rich food," Broder admitted. "I'd like to eat some ordinary—" He paused, trying to think of what might be ordinary enough for a Midwesterner who had been subjected to years of oddball California cuisine and health food by his wife and who had now suffered through a week of French sauces and Cajun spices. "—some plain old steak and potatoes," he decided. "But I don't suppose steak and potatoes would do anything for Carolyn's book," he finished wistfully.

"On the contrary, I seem to remember . . . let me think . . . there was a delicious-looking recipe for filets and mashed potatoes." Broder looked hopeful. "Let's go up to our room to dry off while I look it up." I knew Broder and Carlene were staying at a B & B on the edge of the Quarter, so it wouldn't be very convenient for them to return there before dinner.

"I like mashed potatoes," said Broder, as he and Carlene trailed us up to the room.

I found the recipe under an entry for the Pelican Club, filets mignons with shiitake mushrooms and Cabernet sauce and garlic mashed potatoes with roasted onions. It sounded perfect for a cold, rainy night. I didn't mention the mushrooms and Cabernet sauce or the garlic in the potatoes to Broder, who was busy peering at a map with Jason, looking for the address on Exchange Alley. Carlene was in the bathroom toweling off her longish gray-white hair, and I was calling to secure a reservation for four.

"Oh, I'm sorry, madam, but I'm afraid a reservation for this evening would be impossible," said the person who answered the telephone.

"What a shame," I replied. "I had wanted to include the Pelican Club in my book on eating in New Orleans, but I suppose I'll have to substitute some more accommodating restaurant."

There was a brief pause. "Is this a guide book?" asked the man.

"No, it's a—how should I describe it?—a book about food, New Orleans food. The manuscript is due at the publisher's in six months, and I am due home on Saturday, so I'll just have to skip the Pelican Club, although I did want to sample your filet with shiitake mushrooms."

"An excellent choice, madam. If you'll give me just a minute, I'll see if a table can't be found for your party."

"Oh, good!" I said breezily. "I think I'd prefer the front room, which I'm told is quite elegant, and I do want to look at the paintings. Do you have any of particular interest? That would make a nice addition to my description of the ambiance."

"We have some very fine pieces," I was assured. "Consigned from excellent galleries."

"I'm delighted to hear it." While the reservation person was getting me a reservation, I had to suppress an undignified impulse to giggle at my own temerity. A certain rather crude member of Jason's department would have said that I had "balls." In this case having balls proved to be an excellent thing. We got our reservation, passed around towels to sop up the results of the cloudburst that had caught us in the middle of my personal cloudburst, combed hair, refreshed lipstick, used the facilities, borrowed extra umbrellas from the hotel, and ventured outside again, maps in hand.

Jason and Broder argued amiably over whether we should turn right or left (Exchange Alley runs parallel between Chartres, our street, and Royal, the police station street). Jason won, and we turned left, finding the restaurant at the corner of Bienville and Exchange Alley. Having lost the route debate, Broder argued with his wife about whether they should order courses in addition to the filets and mashed potatoes. Broder was worried about the extra cost of desserts and appetizers.

"We'll skip the appetizers and share a dessert," I suggested. "They're supposed to make a marvelous profiterole. The pastries are served three to a plate, but maybe I can talk them into four," I said cheerfully. I had been thinking about Carlene's statement that Julienne would never have put herself in the path of a hungry alligator. That seemed a reasonable assumption to me.

"They're not going to make the dessert bigger just to accommodate us," Broder complained. "They'll want to sell us four desserts."

"If I talked them into giving us a reservation on short notice, I can talk them into providing one more little profiterole and four forks," I assured him. After all, I told myself, I was a food critic with "balls."

27

Filets Mignons with Shiitake Mushrooms and Cabernet Sauce, and Garlic Mashed Potatoes with Roasted Onions

Somewhat the worse for rain, Jason, Broder, Carlene, and I arrived at the nineteenth-century townhouse in which the Pelican Club was housed. There we were greeted with deference and seated at an excellent table in the front room, which was as elegant as my guidebook had indicated. I felt a bit guilty at the thought of the party for whom the table had originally been designated, but goodness, academics aren't often treated like visiting royalty, so I decided to enjoy the windfall dropped in our laps by my new profession. Accordingly, I whipped out my new camera, purchased to replace the one that fell into the bayou. What an expensive trip this was turning out to be! Perhaps the new camera was tax deductible. While I took pictures, Carlene prowled the room looking at the paintings that were for sale. Other diners were staring at us, which was a bit embarrassing.

Then Carlene cried, "This one. I want to buy this one." It was a very pleasant, fuzzy picture with golden splashes slanting across the foreground. Broder, having leaned forward to see the price, gasped. "Now, love," Carlene chided exuberantly, "I have to have it. It looks just like a compound we're working on in the lab."

"Can't you just frame a picture from your electron microscope?" asked Broder, looking more and more alarmed.

"Broder McAvee, I make enough money that, for once in my life, I can afford to buy an oil painting that I like."

"Acrylic," murmured the female diner behind whose chair Carlene was standing.

"Especially one that looks just like the bioactive compound my team developed," Carlene continued. "Look, Jason. Doesn't that look like . . ." She came out with some long string of chemical designations that I couldn't have deciphered or remembered if I were to be quizzed on them the next minute.

Jason obligingly leaned forward to look at the yellow pools of light in a shadowy field of sometimes-translucent blue and black. "Could be," he agreed. "Certainly there's carbon there."

His vague answer, the twinkle in his eye, and the hint of a grin behind his beard told me that he probably wasn't even familiar with her compound, much less in agreement on the biochemical significance of the painting, and even I knew that there was carbon everywhere.

"Ah hate to rain on your parade, ma'am," said the companion to the female diner who could tell acrylic from oil, "but that's an impressionist renderin' of a New Orleans street at night."

"Nonsense," said Carlene.

"Ah know the artist," said the man, offended at having his expertise ignored.

I couldn't resist the impulse to participate in the fun. "There's a Lyonel Feininger quality to the layering of paint, don't you think?" I suggested thoughtfully.

"It doesn't look like Feininger at all," protested the acrylic lady with knowledgeable indignation.

"I'd call it a postmodern Renoir," Jason chimed in. He was now definitely on the verge of laughter.

"I can't detect a redheaded girl anywhere in that painting," I objected enthusiastically. There's nothing more exhilarating than talking absolute nonsense, something grown-ups so seldom get to do.

"Oh, stop it, you two." Carlene grinned at us, then turned to the maître d'. "I want to buy it."

Poor Broder groaned as if he thought the college educations of his remaining offspring would come to an abrupt halt because of his wife's spendthrift impulses. However, I knew what a broomstick skirt cost. Carlene was wearing another of her collection. She must have saved a fortune on clothes over the years with that posthippie wardrobe. Enough so that she deserved to buy a painting if she wanted to, even if it didn't look like a chemical to me.

Carlene went off to complete her purchase, calling over her shoulder, "Just order that filet for me." The rest of us retreated to our table and perused the menu. Broder was horrified at the price of the steak, so much so he didn't notice that it came with sauce, mushrooms of an oriental variety, and garlic in the mashed potatoes. Claiming to have my book in mind, Jason ordered an entirely different entrée, an assortment of seafood cooked in a clay pot with vegetables. The broth, according to the waiter, was flavored with, among other things, cilantro, which is very popular in El Paso.

"I read in the paper the other day that the Mexican drug cartels have been smuggling cocaine into the United States in shipments of cilantro," I said conversationally.

Broder looked horrified. "You mean there might be cocaine in our steak and potatoes?"

"Not at all," I assured him. "If there's a problem, it will be with Jason's seafood stew. Perhaps we should watch him closely to see if he shows signs of drug overdose."

The waiter looked bewildered.

"Thanks a lot," Jason said dryly. "Maybe we should call one of your acquaintances on the police force to bring in a drug dog to sniff my seafood."

"I assure you, sir—" the waiter stammered.

"You poor man," said Carlene, who had taken her seat during the cocaine remarks. "Pay no attention to these people. They're mad scientists, except for my husband, who is a thrifty Calvinist, and this lady, who is a mad food critic."

Then we ordered three filets in Cabernet sauce, plus Jason's seafood flavored with possibly dangerous cilantro, and fell to discussing Julienne's disappearance. Carlene again assured me that the body I viewed could not have been our friend. She insisted on the logic of her contention. But Broder, surprisingly, made the argument that really resonated with me. He said that had the alligator-savaged woman been Julienne, my heart would have confirmed it.

"I have always felt that there is a continuing bond between the living and the dead when they have been close in life," he told me. "Do you really feel convinced that Julienne is dead?"

Did I?

"What did you feel when you viewed the body?"

"I threw up," I admitted. "In the men's room."

"Caro!" Jason exclaimed. "What were you doing in the men's room?"

"Really, Jason," Carlene chided. "Surely, you've noticed that there are always lines outside ladies' rooms while the men's rooms are always empty. What was she supposed to do? Throw up on the woman in front of her in line rather than use the men's facilities?"

"Insensitive of me not to have anticipated that situation," Jason admitted. "Sorry, Caro."

"I should think," said Carlene, a bit smug at having made her point. "I hope you're supporting the movement for equitable public toilet facilities for women." She was looking at my husband.

"I didn't know there was one," Jason replied.

At this point, I was feeling a bit conscience-stricken. Carlene was berating poor Jason when I had used the men's room because I hadn't seen a ladies' room. And in fact, the men's room hadn't been empty as Carlene assumed. There had been the unfortunate policeman urinating when I reeled in. I had to stifle an unseemly chuckle at the thought of his horror and indignation when he found himself sharing the trough with a retching female.

"At any rate," Carlene continued, "vomiting was simply a result of physical repulsion at a terrible sight. I think Broder has a point. Aside from the horror you felt, did you think you had lost your childhood friend? Do you have the feeling that Julienne is dead? I know I don't. I keep expecting to see her walk around the corner, grinning and apologizing for having missed my plenary address."

Actually, I didn't know how I felt. Having been consumed with worry for five days, buoyed one minute by optimism, then plunged the next into dread, my strongest emotion was confusion, which isn't so much an emotion as a mental state. Carlene and Broder might be right. Surely, I would have recognized my friend, no matter what the condition of her body. Surely, I would have experienced overwhelming grief. "Maybe she *is* alive," I said, feeling my spirits lift.

"Let's hope so," said Jason. He covered my hand with his own.

"We might as well expect the best as long as there's no reason to grieve," said Broder.

"Imagine. Optimism from a man who believes we're all destined from birth for heaven or hell," said Carlene.

"I've never really understood the idea of predestination," I chimed in, glad to change the subject. "Does that mean you can sin indiscriminately, and if you're predestined for heaven, you'll still get there?"

Before Broder could answer me, the waiter began to serve our entrées. Conversation pretty much ceased after that as we concentrated on our dinners, which were marvelous. Jason's crustaceans in a clay pot, the broth flavored with lime, chili, and cilantro, had the intriguing tang of a ceviche

I've eaten in Juarez on one of those rare occasions when the drug wars abated enough for dinner excursions across the border. If any cocaine had fallen off the cilantro into the broth, I couldn't tell. I believe cocaine is supposed to induce a feeling of exhilaration, but I must say I had found our foolish conversation about Carlene's painting more exhilarating than Jason's entrée.

As for the filets—ah, heaven! I had asked for mine medium rare, and medium rare it was. Between us, Carlene and I had managed to convince Broder not to order his filet mignon well done, although medium was the pinkest he would agree to, but Broder loved his dish as well. I even noticed him surreptitiously wiping up the last of the rich, flavorful wine sauce with a piece of bread and eating every mushroom. When he first spotted them on top of his beef, he claimed to be completely unfamiliar with shiitake mushrooms and to be suspicious of mushrooms in general, having heard from colleagues of Carlene's about a group of biologists in the Northwest who had been poisoned by eating gathered mushrooms.

We assured him that the event in question had been years ago and that efficient Japanese harvesters, who wouldn't dream of poisoning a customer, had undoubtedly gathered his shiitakes. I had to signal Jason to silence when he launched into a discussion of Japanese culinary toxins. The subject, which would not calm Broder's fears, was puffer fish or *fugu*, a favorite Japanese sushi, known not only for its nerve toxin, but served to special customers with enough poison left in the fish to give them tingling lips without killing them. At least that is the expectation.

I include the recipe for Chef Richard Hughes's filets with shiitake mushrooms for those who are overcome with a desire to spend several days in the kitchen. Otherwise, fly to New Orleans and visit the Pelican Club.

Filets Mignons with Shiitake Mushrooms and Cabernet Sauce, and Garlic Mashed Potatoes with Roasted Onions

TO MAKE FILETS FOR 4:
Preheat oven to 350° F.

Brown *four 8-oz. filets mignons* on all sides in *2 tbs. of butter* in a heavy, ovenproof skillet.

Bake in oven for 8 to 10 minutes or until medium rare.

Set filets aside and keep warm.

Transfer filet pan to burner on stove top, add *1 tbs. chopped shallots* and *1 cup stemmed and sliced* shiitake mushrooms, and sauté until shallots are translucent.

Add *2 tbs. bourbon*, protect face, ignite bourbon with long match, and shake pan until flames subside.

Add ½ cup demi-glace (recipe follows), ½ cup Cabernet Sauvignon, and ¼ cup Madeira or dry sherry, and cook over medium heat to reduce until thickened, 5 to 8 minutes.

Stir in 2 tbs. of butter, salt and pepper to taste.

TO MAKE 1 TO 1½ QTS. DEMI-GLACE SAUCE:
Place 5 lbs. cut veal marrow bones in large baking pan and roast in a 400° F oven until brown, 30 to 40 minutes.

Add 2 cups peeled, diced carrots, 2 cups diced onions, 2 cups diced celery, and roast 20 minutes more.

Add 2 tbs. tomato paste, stir, and continue roasting 10 minutes.

Place on stove top, pour in 2 bottles Cabernet Sauvignon and 1 bottle Madeira wine or dry sherry, and cook over medium heat, stirring to scrape up brown bits from pan bottom.

Place in heavy stockpot, add 1 gallon water, 8 garlic cloves, 1 fresh thyme sprig, 3 bay leaves, and simmer 24 hours.

Strain through fine-meshed sieve and cook over medium heat to reduce to consistency of heavy cream. Unused sauce may be frozen for later use.

TO MAKE MASHED POTATOES:
Preheat oven to 375° F.

Rub olive oil on 1 unpeeled onion and 2 garlic heads with outer papery husk removed, and roast 30 minutes or until slightly browned and softened.

In large saucepan, boil 3 large white, peeled and cubed baking potatoes in salted water to cover until tender, 20 minutes.

Peel onion and puree in blender or food processor.

Slice garlic heads in half crosswise and squeeze out garlic cloves; combine with onion puree.

Mash potatoes with onion-garlic mixture until soft. Add 6 tbs. butter, ½ cup hot milk, and salt and pepper to taste.

TO SERVE:
Pour sauce over filets and serve the warm mashed potatoes alongside.

While Broder was devouring his last bit of Cabernet sauce-soaked bread and wearing the expression of a man who would have patted his tummy in satisfaction had he thought his wife would let him get away with it, I managed to talk the waiter into a four-profiterole dessert plate. It arrived promptly, a lovely sight. Each profiterole was filled with homemade ice cream and topped with chopped pecans and a creamy chocolate sauce, the whole garnished with sliced, fresh berries. I do love the combination of raspberries or strawberries with chocolate. Combined with the last few sips of my red wine, the dessert was delicious.

"In answer to your question about predestination," Broder said to me over dessert, "I like to think that a soul predestined for heaven shows itself in the admirable behavior of its owner."

"So we can tell that a man like Linus Torelli is destined for hell because he was slandering Julienne while having an affair with his chairman's wife?" I asked.

Three pairs of eyes turned in my direction.

"Where did you hear that?" Jason asked.

"Nils told me. Someone in their department named Mark says that Torelli wasn't having affair with Julienne; he just acted like it to cover up the fact that he was—ah—intimate with his chairman's wife."

"You can't be serious!" Carlene exclaimed and started to laugh. "That must be some exciting department to work in. So why did he take off for Sweden so suddenly?"

"Because the chairman's wife heard he was having an affair with Julienne and threatened to have him fired by her husband."

Carlene nodded. "Hoist on his own petard, as it were. What does that mean anyway? What's a petard?"

"It's from *Hamlet*," I said absently. "A petard is a thing for blowing holes in castle walls."

"I was asking a rhetorical question, not expecting an answer. How in the world would you know something like that, Carolyn?"

"Because I wasn't a science major," I retorted, laughing. "Anyway, this Mark told Torelli he'd never get tenure with the chairman's wife on the warpath, so Torelli took the job in Sweden. Now Nils is feeling terrible because he accused Julienne of being unfaithful when she wasn't."

"I never cease to be shocked at the sexual scandals in universities, where one would least expect to find them," said Broder, shaking his head over the sins of academe. "Happily, we don't have those problems at smaller colleges of religious origin."

"Oh, come off it, Broder," said his wife. "Have you forgotten the dean who used to pinch bottoms at faculty parties?"

"He was very old and somewhat senile," said Broder, "and he was gently nudged into retirement."

"Gently nudged, my eye," his wife retorted. "I saw that he got the boot after he pinched me."

"He pinched *you?*" Broder looked very unhappy to hear it. "Well, I'm sorry you had to put up with that sort of thing, Carlene, but I doubt that you were responsible for his resignation. Our president at that time, a man of great rectitude, got wind of the dean's problem and—"

"The president was moved to action at the insistence of his wife. The last time the dean pinched me, I walked her over to his circle, and of course he pinched her. Voila! That was it for the Dean of Bottoms, as we wives used to call him."

"I see." Broder looked stunned. Evidently, a lot went on at his college of which he was unaware. Hastily, he turned to me and remarked that, having heard about Linus Torelli's lamentable lapses of morality, he now wondered whether the young chemist might not have had something to do with Julienne's disappearance. "A man of loose morals might do anything," said Broder ominously. "And sinners do like to blame their own falls from grace on innocent bystanders. No doubt, he blamed Julienne for the very problem he created himself by slandering her."

I did not find that conjecture very reassuring, having, at that point, managed to convince myself that Julienne was probably safe and avoiding, with the help of her brother, undeserved recriminations from her drunken husband. Therefore, I made my last notes on the dinner with a heavy heart.

"Didn't you enjoy your food, Mrs. Blue?" asked the maître d', looking somewhat alarmed. He must have been alerted by my glum expression.

"If the rest of my visit to New Orleans had been as delightful as this dinner," I assured him, "I would be a happy woman."

The poor man didn't seem to know what to make of that accolade from a food critic who claimed to like his cuisine but looked anything but pleased.

28

The Faux Priest

I sat dispiritedly in the Café du Monde drinking a latte, munching on hot beignets, and wondering what to do. Of course, Julienne didn't appear at the café. I'd given up expecting her to. Philippe didn't answer his telephone. No surprise there. And the truth is, I had run out of ideas. I didn't know where to look next. Once again I brushed powdered sugar from my black raincoat, which, for a change, I didn't need. There was actually a stray sunbeam escaping from the usual umbrella of rain clouds that hung over the city. For lack of inspiration, I took my trusty *Frommer's New Orleans* from my pocket and thumbed through, scanning for likely investigation sites.

The French Market! Julienne had mentioned it. Although I didn't think I'd find her there, it would at least provide a destination. I followed Decatur Street from Jackson Square, entered the French Market, and wandered in and out of stores, looking but not buying, then moving on to the farmer's market portion as I imagined how it had been in the 1700s when it was an Indian trading post at which Creoles could barter for sassafras from the Choctaws. The Spanish had put a roof over it, German farmers had supplied the produce as it evolved, and Italian immigrants sold food in its stalls, structures now swathed in garlic strings and offering, twenty-four hours a day, the most delicious in seafood, fruits, vegetables, and spices. The chef that cooked our meal last night must shop here, as well as many a New Orleans housewife who wanted to buy the freshest of food for her family.

I looked to my heart's content, then purchased some crab boil in cellophane packets. Jason would like that. The text on the label informed me that I could also use it for shrimp, lobster, and crayfish, whatever crustaceans I could find. Good! El Paso had shellfish but not always just what one wanted to buy at the time one wanted to buy them.

Then I spotted fresh pralines and purchased two. Something sweet to nibble on will often raise my spirits. Beyond the farmer's market was the flea market. My enthusiasm began to pick up, sparked by the pralines and the offerings. Table after table covered with merchandise that might or might not please friends and relatives beckoned to me. I'd buy a few mementos to take back home. I browsed. I picked things up and put them down, discovering that putting an item down lowered the price. Interesting. If I wanted to buy something, I'd be expected to bargain, not a talent at which I have any practice. Still, I was game.

On the edge of the pavilion a little Asian lady, wizened and in need of orthodontics, presided over a table of cloisonné pillboxes. Excellent presents for one's aging friends and even those not so old. I picked up a box decorated with a multicolored dragon and pressed the button that released the lid. The proprietor scowled at me. Evidently one wasn't supposed to open the box. I soon found out why. Once opened, it popped open again when I tried to close it. I put the dragon box down. She plucked up a prettier model with butterflies on it and handed it to me. Wiser as a result of my first experience, I persisted in testing the release and locking mechanism. This one worked. "How much?" I asked with a smile.

"Five dollar," she replied.

I put it down.

"Four dollar."

I shook my head.

"Tree dollar."

At two-fifty I bought five boxes in varying patterns, but I had to test eight to find five that worked, and every time I popped a lid open, she scowled at me. Still, they were pretty, and perhaps the pillbox lady had had a very sad life and had forgotten how to smile. Or maybe the state of her teeth made her self-conscious. Or her feet hurt. Mine certainly would if I had to stand behind a table of pillboxes all day. I planned to keep the blue and green one for myself. Maybe I'd keep two. One for Tylenol, a second for antacids. If any more friends disappeared on me, I'd be needing something for an upset tummy.

My next serious stop was at the mask table. Now, very few people actually need a mask, but these were so exotic. Of course, I realized that they weren't as gorgeous as some I'd seen in a Mardi Gras shop during my French Quarter tour with Broder, but those had been very expensive. These, after a haggling session, cost me three dollars each. How could I resist? Especially the ones with feathers. I purchased an orange yellow model with fuzzy feathers surrounding sad, downturned eye slits; a round, red felt mouth decorated with tiny black feathers; and black and yellow feathers trailing down below the mouth. Then I chose a model with red sequins around the eyes and a veritable plume of black feathers shooting up above the head, and last, my favorite, the gorgeous green mask with blue-eyed peacock feathers in an elaborate crown.

I wasn't convinced that I could get them home on the plane in mint condition, and I didn't know what I'd do with them once I got home. It's not as if I attend any masked balls or would feel comfortable with feathers tickling my face and neck all evening. Nonetheless, I was inordinately pleased with my under-ten-dollar collection of masks, so pleased that I wondered if El Paso had flea markets. I'd never patronized one before.

Of course, an El Paso flea market probably sold piñatas and Mexican pottery, and I had no need for a piñata and was afraid of Mexican pottery, having once read about a California family who contracted lead poisoning from a glazed juice set that they purchased in Tijuana. Because of Jason's research interests, I'm always on the lookout for unusual news stories about toxins.

With my pillboxes in my purse and my masks in a plastic bag, I set off toward Jackson Square thinking of lunch. But where? I sat down on a bench and studied my Frommer's. Should I try The Gumbo Shop on Saint Peter Street? Or Saint Ann's Café and Deli on Dauphine, an establishment reputed to have saved the sanity of a person just moving into town? I could use some psychic comfort, I decided, if I could find the place. I thumbed through to a map, pink and white with black lines, and looked for Dauphine. Ah, there it was. Decatur (where I was), Chartres, Royal, Bourbon, then Dauphine. Now where did Saint Ann cross Dauphine?

"Are you lost, my chile?"

I looked up to see a priest with a tanned, somewhat weathered face and reddish gray hair ringing a bald head. He was smiling at me and wearing a black . . . frock? What does one call a skirted priest's garment? Maybe he was a monk. But the gown had a high clerical collar. "I'm looking for the Saint Ann's Café, Father," I replied. If he was a monk, I supposed he'd tell me.

"It's right on da way to mah parish," he said, "if you like to walk along wit me."

How kind! And how charming! A Cajun priest! I recognized the accent. "Thank you, Father." I stood up and accompanied him along Decatur. Soon we were zigzagging through streets and alleys, and I was completely lost. Still, once I got to my destination, I could study the map during lunch and would, no doubt, find my way back to the hotel without too much trouble. It wasn't as if I'd thought of a more useful way to spend the afternoon. If the police didn't turn up news of Julienne, I was stymied.

As we entered yet another alley, this one quite messy, Father Claude was telling me an amusing story about a parishioner who had taken out a restraining order against the church because she was allergic to the flowers that customarily decorated the altar. "Downright disgustin' da way folks dump dere trash in dese alleys," said Father Claude, interrupting his own story. "Makes a mighty poor impression on our visitors."

"Indeed," I concurred, for I had narrowly avoided tripping over a wooden box from which spilled a few remaining salad leaves—arugula, I believe. He had to take my arm to keep me from falling.

"Bettah we stop right heah," said Father Claude.

"Oh, I'm fine," I replied. "I'll be more careful about—"

"Right heah's a good place." He grasped my arm, quite hard actually, and then I felt something poking my chest, for he had swung me around and wore a very unpriestly look, a really sinister look.

I gulped and glanced about desperately. The alley was deserted. I peeked down at the object jammed against my breastbone. A gun! I was caught between astonishment and terror. "You're not a priest!" I exclaimed.

"Got dat right, missy," he replied.

It was then I noticed that the gun was, of all things, plastic. This faux priest was threatening me with a toy gun. That was really the last straw. I'd had quite enough of the criminal element in New Orleans. Without a second thought, I snarled, "Idiot!" and swept my free hand—free except for the plastic bag of masks—up against his hand, the hand clutching the plastic gun. I was planning to tell him I had no intention of giving up my purse to a man wielding a toy, but the gun went off.

Imagine my surprise and fright! Imagine his! He staggered back, blood streaming from his ear, an expression of astonishment and rage on his face. Then he ran away, leaving me in possession of the gun. I leaned over to pick it up and examine it. Could a plastic gun shoot real bullets? Close to tears and shaking like the off-balance ceiling fan in my family room, I tottered down toward the end of the alley where my would-be assailant had disappeared. Several tourists who saw me emerge with the gun in my hand ran away. I can't blame them. Then a policeman approached me, drawing his own weapon.

"Oh, thank goodness!" I cried and fell, weeping, into his arms. It's a wonder we weren't both killed by mistake.

Father Claude's Ear

Officer O'Brien disentangled himself, gingerly removed the plastic gun from my fist, and called for assistance. To me he said, "Ma'am, this may be the Big Easy, but it don't make us cops easy to see ladies runnin' out of alleys wavin' guns."

"I was mugged," I sniffled and pulled out Lieutenant Boudreaux's handkerchief since Officer O'Brien didn't think to offer me one. Having had it laundered by the hotel at considerable expense, I hated to use it, but the lieutenant's clean handkerchief was the first thing that came to hand, and I was in desperate case.

"Well, likely that's one sorry mugger," said the patrolman dryly. "You got a permit for this here weapon, ma'am?"

"Of course not. It's not *my* gun." I gave my tear-filled eyes one last swipe, blew my nose, and stuffed the handkerchief into my raincoat pocket. "Shouldn't you put it into a baggie or something? Since it belonged to the mugger, it may still have his fingerprints on it."

Officer O'Brien evidently didn't have an evidence bag on him. Instead, he appropriated my mask bag and stuck the plastic gun in that. Of course. I protested because I didn't think having a weapon, even a plastic one, dropped in among the feathers would do them any good.

At that moment, a patrol car pulled up beside us, and Officer O'Brien murmured to the two men who climbed out, "Female wavin' a handgun on the street. Claims she was mugged an' disarmed the mugger."

"I didn't exactly disarm him," I tried to explain as they helped me into the backseat of the car, putting a hand on top of my head just as I'd seen it done to suspects on television. Officer O'Brien got in back with me while the other two took their places in the front seat. Because they had my mask bag, I leaned forward and knocked on the screen to get their attention. "Could you please place that gun in an official police evidence container before it damages the souvenirs I bought at the flea market?" I requested, feeling considerably calmer and much safer now that I was under the protection of the police.

After leaning back, taking a deep breath, and trying to get comfortable on the rather lumpy seat, I turned to Officer O'Brien. "Are we going to the Vieux Carre substation?" I asked.

"You been there before?"

"Several times."

"I'll bet," said the officer who was holding my mask bag and searching the glove compartment, presumably for an evidence container. These policemen did not seem to be very well equipped. It occurred to me that we needed an evidence *team* to take care of the mugger's gun, but I'd never seen a crime-scene van on the streets of New Orleans, although one can hardly watch ten minutes of a television police drama without observing one. In this case, it would seem that life did not imitate fiction.

We arrived under the familiar portico in no time and all climbed out, Officer O'Brien assisting me, as if I couldn't get out of a car on my own. Perhaps it was the Southern-gentleman training. Lieutenant Boudreaux had always been very gallant. I nodded to the sarcastic desk sergeant as we passed through the reception area and made our way to a small room where I was left after Officer O'Brien excused himself. I couldn't help noticing that he locked the door behind him, almost as if I was a prisoner. And they had not returned my masks.

I must have waited five minutes or more, staring at the peeling walls of the little room and trying not to notice that some very unacceptable phrases had been scratched on the table at which I sat. Then a black man in civilian clothes unlocked the door and took a seat across the table from me. He was accompanied by Officer O'Brien, who introduced him as Detective Rosie Mannifill. Rosie? What a strange name for a man. Perhaps his mother had named him after a very large football player named Rosie.

Jason, over the years, has watched some professional football on television, so I pick up a few names as I pass through the family room. Rosie Greer was one of those names, although I couldn't say what position he played, or plays, or for what team. The teams seem to proliferate like rabbits. Who but an ardent fan can keep track of their names? In fact, I may have heard the name *Rosie* when I was living at home. Mr. Delacroix watched football. Of course, my father didn't. I introduced myself to the detective and offered to shake his hand. He wrote down my name.

"O'Brien here says you told him you was mugged."

"Well, I suppose that would be the word for it," I agreed. "The man grabbed my arm and shoved his gun against my chest."

"An' you disarmed him?"

I thought about Detective Mannifill's phrasing. "I wouldn't put it quite that way, Detective. You see, when I realized that the gun was plastic, I thought that he was trying to steal my handbag by threatening me with a toy. After all, who ever heard of a plastic gun?"

"Anyone who knows anything about guns," said Detective Mannifill. "I got one myself."

"You do? Don't you consider it dangerous?"

"Dangerous as any gun, ma'am."

"I mean especially dangerous. When I tried to knock it out of his hand in a fit of pique, the mugger's weapon went off. It probably exploded. Western history, when untrammeled by the romantic myths about gunfighters, tells us that weapons misfired or exploded as often as not. And cannon explosions in earlier centuries . . ." I could see the detective's eyes glaze over and had to presume that his interest in history, even the history of firearms, about which I am not really an expert, was minimal. "At any rate," I resumed, "whatever happened, I certainly heard the explosion, and his ear bled copiously."

"You *shot* the mugger?" Detective Mannifill now looked as if he didn't believe me.

"Not in the sense that I pulled the trigger. I just gave his hand a sharp upward blow. However, he may well have been shot. Perhaps you should call local hospitals to check for someone missing an ear, or part of one." I thought for a moment. "And you'll want to check for fingerprints. Mine will only be on the barrel. If the mugger is a career criminal, no doubt his fingerprints will be on file."

Mannifill turned to O'Brien. "She was running out of the alley carrying the gun by the barrel?"

"Well . . . yeah," O'Brien admitted.

The detective rose and started to leave the room, presumably to call hospitals and ask for fingerprint experts. I called after him, "I would like to have my plastic bag with the masks back." He didn't reply, so I turned to Officer O'Brien and remarked, "I bought some charming feathered masks at the flea market."

"Yeah, my wife likes them. She got my little girls some for Halloween."

"Oh, they must have looked adorable. How old are they?"

Officer O'Brien and I were discussing Halloween costumes favored by little girls when the detective returned and sat down. "So maybe you could describe this mugger, Miz Blue." he suggested.

"He looked like a priest."

Both men stared at me.

"Well, I'm not saying he was one," I amended defensively. "But he was wearing one of those ankle-length black gowns with the traditional clerical collar and—" I stopped to picture him. "—and he had reddish gray hair sprouting out around a bald head."

"Anything else?" asked the detective. He was taking more notes.

"He offered to show me the way to Saint Ann's Café and Deli on Dauphine Street. Naturally, I didn't hesitate to accept help from a priest. I mean, one doesn't really expect to be mugged by a priest, does one?"

"Where did the mugging occur?"

"In the alley. I have no idea which one, but Officer O'Brien should be able to tell you that. In fact—" I turned to the patrolman. "—you may have seen him running out of the alley. He was ahead of me."

O'Brien shook his head. "Didn't see no priests with bloody ears." He told the detective where he had first seen me, gun in hand.

"Anything else?" asked Detective Mannifill.

"He was about my height, five-six, and had olive skin, rather leathery, as if he'd spent a lot of time in the sun without using sunscreen." The detective raised his eyebrows. "I hope you don't think that you're safe from skin cancer because you're black," I cautioned him.

He scowled at me. "Anything else?" he prodded.

"He told me that one of his parishioners had asked for a restraining order against the altar flowers in his church. That was just before he grabbed me."

"Courts don't issue restraining orders against flowers," said the detective. "Anything else?"

What an impatient man! I searched my mind. "Only that he introduced himself as Father Claude."

"Well, shit," said Detective Mannifill. I gave him a disapproving look, but he didn't apologize for his language. "Since when is Father Claude mugging tourists?" He said this to Officer O'Brien, not to me.

At this point in what I could now see was an interrogation, Lieutenant Boudreaux entered the tiny room, completely filling up the last bit of space.

"Good afternoon, Lieutenant," I said. "I had your handkerchief laundered, but unfortunately, I've just had a very trying experience and had to use it again. However, I promise to get it rewashed and ironed, and this time I won't cry on it."

"Don't give it a thought, Miz Blue," he replied graciously. "My mama provides 'em by the dozen. Hear tell, you got mugged."

"By Father Claude," said Mannifill.

"Doesn't sound like his usual MO, muggin' tourists."

"Had him a Glock, one a them fancy plastic models," O'Brien chimed in.

Lieutenant Boudreaux looked worried. "Seems to me you're jus' gettin' more than your fair share of criminal attention, Miz Blue. You got any enemies out there? Anyone might have followed you from home with evil intent?"

"Heavens no, Lieutenant. I'm a faculty wife. And a food writer."

"Maybe she give some chef a bad review, an' he put a hit out on her," said O'Brien facetiously. In response, he got a frown from the lieutenant.

"When were you plannin' on goin' back home, ma'am?" the lieutenant asked.

"Tomorrow, I suppose. Have you heard anything about Julienne?" He shook his head. "Or identified that poor woman in the morgue?" Again he shook his head.

How could I go home tomorrow when I didn't know what had happened to my dearest friend? "I just don't know what to do."

"Well, one thing you can't do, ma'am, is leave New Orleans until we get this matter cleared up," cautioned Detective Mannifill.

"Are you saying I'm a suspect of some kind?" I asked indignantly. "I believe that I am the victim in this incident."

"Sure looks that way, Miz Blue," the lieutenant agreed, "but until we catch up with Father Claude—"

"Like that's gonna happen," muttered O'Brien.

"An' we're sure the man with the ear injury's not gonna file charges against you," Mannifill added.

"But that would be outrageous, Detective. I didn't pull the trigger of his gun. I simply—"

"You never read about any a these burglars who wanna file charges when the homeowner catches 'em in the house an' shoots 'em?" asked O'Brien.

"I believe these two incidents would not be at all comparable," I said stiffly.

"An' you'd be right, Miz Blue," said the lieutenant soothingly. "So we'll let you know as soon as we catch the mugger or the evidence exonerates you."

"Oh well, that's all right then." The evidence could hardly fail to exonerate me. One can't shoot another person by holding the barrel of the gun. So unless Officer O'Brien's careless handling of the weapon in question had destroyed fingerprints, or contact with feathers had brushed away those little whorls—

Detective Mannifill cleared his throat to get my attention. "If you'll just write down your local address and phone number, we—"

"We got it, Rosie," said the lieutenant. "Miz Blue is by way of becomin' a daily visitor here." He turned to me. "Miz Blue, Ah'm gonna send you home in a patrol car, an' Ah hope this time you'll jus' stay in your hotel room with the door locked until it's time to go catch your plane. Ah'd be mighty relieved to hear you promise me that's jus' what you plan to do."

I smiled at him and replied that my plans included a nice nap in my room and dinner at some excellent New Orleans restaurant with my husband and at least four friends. He seemed to find that acceptable. They fingerprinted me for elimination purposes with respect to the plastic gun, gave back my plastic bag with the three masks, and drove me to the hotel. En route, I was pleased to discover that the yellow, orange and black mask, my least favorite of the three, was the only one crushed by Father Claude's weapon.

30
The Helpful Sibling

How in the world would I explain to Jason why I couldn't leave New Orleans tomorrow as planned? He had to get back to the university. Should I need to do any further research, we had planned to return here during the next vacation. Now I'd have to tell him about Father Claude with his gun pressed against my breastbone and my mistaken conviction that it was a toy weapon. Instead of Father Claude losing his ear, I could just as well have been killed myself. And now I might be charged with—what? Assault with a deadly weapon? Counterassault with the assailant's deadly weapon? That certainly didn't seem fair.

And why exactly had Father Claude, or whoever he was, pointed his gun at me? One of the officers had said robbing tourists wasn't his usual MO, which means, I believe, *modus operandi*. Surely he hadn't meant to shoot me! Why would anyone want to? Especially a stranger! Perhaps he had mistaken me for someone else. Officer O'Brien had jokingly said that some chef might have ordered my assassination. Was this Father Claude an assassin? If so, they should have told me. And they certainly hadn't seemed sanguine about catching him. "Fat chance of that," O'Brien had said. The situation was confusing and frightening and—yes—surreal. Especially, surreal. Things like this do not happen to faculty wives.

And there was Julienne. I still hadn't located her. Nor had the police. Earlier I had been worried about leaving New Orleans while she was still missing. Now I couldn't leave whether or not she was found. She probably wasn't in the city herself. Very likely her brother had helped her leave. With Philippe in mind, I called his hotel again. No answer. Then it occurred to me that I had been direct dialing his room. He could have left town, and I wouldn't know the difference. I could have been dialing an empty room or some other person now occupying Philippe's old room. I called the hotel desk to explain my problem.

"Oh, he's still here," said the clerk, after leaving me a short time on hold. "But I haven't seen him. Can't imagine why he never answers his phone. Hang on a minute." More time passed while I relaxed comfortably on my bed and thought about a nap. "He's been using room service every day," she said, "so he must be in there. In fact, he's got one whopping big bill, but it says here that he's a doctor, so he can afford it. Reckon he's one of our orthodontists, though why you'd come to a convention and never leave your room is beyond me. They're out there this afternoon at the pool having a high old time."

"Dr. Delacroix is not an orthodontist, but thank you for your help."

Philippe was there, staying in his room, ordering from room service, not answering his telephone? Depression! That explained it all. He'd fallen into one of his customary depressions. Perhaps about Julienne's situation. Perhaps because his chairman was threatening to fire him. Or just some chemical imbalance. But depressed or not, he could still give me news of Julienne. I rose, combed my hair, and grabbed my raincoat, although it wasn't raining, thank goodness. However, that didn't mean it wouldn't start.

Mindful of the money I'd spent on telephone calls and taxis, I prudently walked to the corner where the Superior Inn's free shuttle lets guests off in the French Quarter and caught it back to Philippe's hotel. Without asking the desk clerk to announce me, I boarded the elevator to the second floor and was knocking at his door within minutes. Then I watched the peephole until I saw it go dark. Success! He was in there. If he didn't open the door, I'd just keep knocking. Even the most depressed person would get tired of someone pounding on his door.

However, the door flew open, and Philippe said, quite unpleasantly, "What are you doing here, Carolyn?" while he tugged me into his room and slammed the door. He didn't look depressed to me. He looked angry. In fact, he swore under his breath and said something like, "If you want something done right, you have to do it yourself," whatever that meant.

His attitude made me a little nervous, but I had a perfectly good reason for being here, even if he did consider my visit inconvenient. "Philippe, I'm looking for your sister, and you're my last hope of locating her. Why haven't you been answering your telephone?"

Philippe began to laugh, which I took amiss, and with good reason, given all the unpleasant things that had happened to me during my search. "Well, you may think this is funny, Philippe, but you wouldn't believe all the dangerous situations in which I've found myself this week while searching for Julienne."

Philippe laughed harder, obviously in a better humor than when I first arrived, for all that I found his amusement disconcerting. "I know all about your problems, Carolyn," he said with a final chortle.

"You do?"

"Of course. I know everything."

"Philippe, have you taken too much medication or something?" I knew immediately that I'd said the wrong thing, because his face twisted with rage.

"You're a stupid, interfering woman, Carolyn," he snarled and pushed me into a wing chair that stood in front of gently stirring draperies, which no doubt led to his balcony. *Party Central,* the Yellow Pages ad for the Superior Inn had said. *"Every room with a balcony overlooking our interior courtyard and pool."* I remember thinking that it didn't sound like Philippe's sort of place.

"You should have left well enough alone." He loomed over me in what I took to be a threatening fashion, although why Philippe would want to frighten me I couldn't imagine.

Well, I wasn't about to be intimidated. "Do you know where Julienne is?" I demanded.

"More or less," he replied, suddenly casual as he backed away and sat down at the foot of the bed. "Of course. And I know where you've been all week and what you've been doing."

Well, that was nonsense. He hadn't been out of his room, if the desk was to be believed. "Don't be silly, Philippe. Just tell me where Julienne is, and I'll be on my way."

"It was a mistake, Carolyn. You running around town getting people interested in things that weren't their business. Even you should have realized that by now. Couldn't you feel my power, my control? I'm the spider, spinning his web, pulling in the stupid little flies."

That wasn't depression. That was just plain craziness. Still, I had to approach him as if he hadn't become completely unbalanced. "I don't know what you're talking about, Philippe," I said, trying to sound calm and friendly. "You've been in your room all week as far as I know, but you must have helped Julienne to—"

"Oh, I did. I was very helpful to my sister, much more helpful than she ever was to me. And I've been trying to help you, too, little sister's friend. You were just too dumb to take the hint."

"Philippe, that's the second time you've called me stupid, which I'm not, and as for controlling me, that's silly. I haven't even seen you in years. If you didn't look so much like Julienne, I wouldn't have recognized you." He had Julienne's wild black hair but little else. In fact, he looked sick: terribly thin, his skin sallow instead of the rich olive that ran in the family, and he had great black circles under his eyes, as if he hadn't slept in weeks. "Are you ill?" I asked. "You don't look at all well, Philippe."

"How foolishly maternal of you to ask," he responded in a nasty tone. "But actually, I've never been in better health. If you didn't recognize me, it would be because you've only seen me when they were forcing me to subvert my real persona with medication, but that's over. I'm drug free and at the height of my powers now. I'm winning it all."

"Winning what? And what drugs? Antidepressants? Admittedly, you don't seem depressed."

"But that's what you'd like, isn't it? To see me whining and miserable?"

"No, of course not."

"So I couldn't control you."

"Why do you think you control me, Philippe?" Again I was trying to be the calm, reasonable faculty wife I usually am instead of scared stiff and confused.

"Were you afraid when the voodoo woman told you to leave town?" he asked.

"How do you know about her?"

"I sent her."

"You—"

"I'm watching you, Carolyn. My agent knows everything you do. Every ridiculous, futile move you make. The man with the knife who grabbed your purse. Remember him?"

I was speechless for a moment, then rallied to say, "He didn't get it."

"He didn't?" Philippe frowned. "You're lying. You're probably still trying to get your credit cards canceled and reinstated."

"I hit him with my umbrella."

"And falling into the bayou? Remember that? Too bad you didn't drown."

"If he got my purse, where did the money come from for the bus ticket to the bayou?" I asked sharply. I hadn't seen whoever pushed me into the water, but I *had* been pushed. And the purse snatcher, whom I hit with my umbrella, could he have been the same man? And the voodoo woman— well, she was a woman. Or not. She'd certainly been ugly enough to be a man.

"If you hadn't got here first, you'd be dead on the street, Carolyn, another tragic victim of random violence."

A shiver went up my spine. Father Claude. Philippe had meant to have me shot?

"Now we'll just have to wait."

"Wait for what?" My voice was quavering. I could only hope he didn't notice.

"He'll be back when he can't locate you, and since he obviously failed today, he'll have to do it here and find some way to dispose of the body."

Was that *my* body Philippe was talking about? He obviously didn't know that I had shot Father Claude's ear off, in a manner of speaking, and I certainly wasn't going to tell him. On the other hand, I had to get out of here before Claude plastered a bandage on his ear and reported in to "the spider." I glanced surreptitiously at Philippe. Now was the opportune time say my good-byes, since it seemed that Philippe wasn't prone to doing his own dirty work.

"Nothing to say, Carolyn?" he goaded.

"I have to be getting back." I stood up. "Jason will be expecting me."

Philippe leapt up and pushed me into the chair. "You're not going anywhere, and Jason won't be expecting you for at least several hours."

"It's the last day of the meeting. Sessions end at three."

"No, they don't, not till five, and then he'll have a drink with his colleagues and doodle little chemical structures on cocktail napkins and trade academic gossip. Why, he probably won't be home until at least seven, by which time you'll be long gone. So don't try to lie to me, Carolyn. It won't work."

I gulped and settled into the chair, not even a particularly comfortable chair. What to do? It is very hard to make plans while in fear of one's life. Talk. I had to keep him talking. And hope Father Claude had become tired of failing in his missions, hope he wouldn't want to tell Philippe that he had been shot with his own gun by a forty-something wife, mother, and food critic.

Since he was known to the police, Father Claude must be a career criminal. In which case, this whole debacle would be professionally embarrassing. It would probably ruin his reputation if it got out. The police were looking for him. Maybe they'd find him. So I just had to—what? Get away from Philippe before he decided that he was crazy enough to do his own killing. Perhaps I should remind him of his Hippocratic Oath: *Do no harm*. But oh God, what had he done to Julienne? Or paid Claude to do to her?

"You're uncharacteristically silent."

Philippe was grinning at me with a curve of lip that seemed particularly malicious. That might have been my imagination. His smile had always been humorless, on the few occasions when I saw it, but not malicious. "Well, Philippe, since you don't want me to leave, I was just wondering what might be a good subject of conversation."

"So well brought up, Carolyn. I always admired that about you. Maybe if your mother had lived longer, she could have taught you to mind your own business as well as to function adequately as a good little hostess type."

How dare he bring up my mother? She had been the sweetest, kindest, gentlest, most rational person who ever lived, while he was a crazy would-be murderer. "What did you do to Julienne?" I demanded.

31

An Alligator's Dinner

What did I do to Julienne?" Philippe rose from his seat on the foot of the bed and dragged the second wing chair over in front of mine. When he sat down, we were almost knee to knee, and his proximity sent a shudder through me. Then he leaned forward, arms on knees, hands hanging loosely, and thrust his face into mine. I could smell the faint odor of his breath, toothpaste overlaid with alcohol.

"I gave her another chance," he replied, seeming to take pleasure in the ambiguity of his answer.

"I don't understand." Did alcohol explain his strange behavior? He might be drunk instead of crazy, although I didn't find that a reassuring possibility, either.

"Of course you don't, Carolyn, because you know next to nothing about Julienne and me, especially about me."

"That's true," I agreed. "What kind of chance did you give her?"

"That sounds like an accusation."

"No, Philippe, I was just asking for clarification of what you said, that you gave her another chance."

He nodded. "I did." Much to my relief, he settled back in his chair. "I made some requests of my sister, and she refused, so I gave her a chance to reconsider. I think that was quite generous of me. Considering."

"Considering what?"

Anger swept across his face, blazing in his eyes and tightening his thin lips, but just for a second. Then he became calm again. "Considering how much Julienne has taken away from me over the years."

Was he talking about his mother's estate? Diane had said he wanted it all because it was his right. "Primogeniture, you mean?" I asked hesitantly. "The estate?"

"That's part of it. I *am* the eldest son, the *only* son. Julienne got a dowry so she had no right to the estate."

A dowry? He *was* crazy. "Julienne had a dowry?"

"Of course. Mother gave her half the household stuff, not to mention all those bonds, when she married. I wasn't given any bonds when I married, no sheets, no dishes, no—"

"I didn't know you had been married," I stuttered. Had he? Julienne never mentioned it.

"That's because you don't know anything, even your own field. How could you have majored in medieval history and not know the rules of inheritance? Don't you know about primogeniture? And dowries?" His tone was hectoring, and he leaned forward again as if to intimidate me. With some success, I might add.

"Yes, of course I do, but . . . but Philippe, that was centuries ago."

"Oh, really?" Now his tone was scathing. "My mother didn't seem to think so; she's the one who talked about her daughter's *dowry*."

Now that he mentioned it, I did remember Fannie and Julienne joking about a dowry, but that's what it had been: a joke.

"Or maybe you want to talk about modern law? Or moral law? Or ordinary fair play, about which I'm sure you know nothing either? Well, Mother always favored Julienne unfairly over me, and Julienne exerted undue influence on her in the years after my father died. Any court would find in my favor."

"But Philippe, your mother wasn't of . . . of unsound mind."

"And I am? Is that what you're saying?"

"No," I whispered, because he really was frightening me. And how sound was his mind? This wasn't simple depression. Or clinical depression. It wasn't depression at all. It was something else entirely, something for which he refused to take medication, as he'd said himself.

"And the estate was the least of my sister's sins."

Keep him talking, I told myself, even though his mood seemed to bounce frantically from calmness to rage with each change of subject, each new thought that came to him. "What did she do?" I whispered.

"When my wife died . . ." His face became grim. "When my wife died . . ."

He couldn't seem to get beyond that phrase. "I'm sorry. What happened?" I prompted.

"She committed suicide."

How terrible! She'd committed suicide? And Philippe had always been prone to depression, at least in his youth.

"Oh, don't look so tragic. It was a whim."

"A whim?" I stammered.

"Yes, a whim. Postpartum depression, they said. She could have waited it out if she'd had any sense. I told her that."

Postpartum depression meant there had been a baby.

"And I protected her from their medications."

Good lord. His wife had been seriously depressed, and he hadn't allowed her doctors to relieve that depression? Perhaps repressed guilt over his wife's suicide had unbalanced his mind.

"But she was just as dead as if she'd had a good reason to kill herself. And then my sister—my *sister*—" His voice dripped venom. "Julienne, ever the helpful, greedy sibling, had me committed and took my child. With my mother's connivance. They said I was bipolar, a danger to myself and others, but that was just an excuse to dope me up and deprive me of the good times. My father . . ."

Bipolar. Manic-depressive, in other words. The new terminology was probably the result of some politically correct desire to mask the real nature of the disease. And he was in the manic phase right now, unmedicated. Because he *liked* the manic phase. He considered mania the *good times*. That explained all the talk of power, of being the spider who controlled the flies that ventured into his web. I was a fly. Had Julienne been a fly?

Now he was talking about his father. I concentrated on this new subject.

". . . just because he had periods of brilliance. Do you remember when he made all that money on the market? I'm doing the same thing right now, but I, fortunately, don't have my mother following me around, terrified that I'll lose the family savings." He laughed exuberantly. "I'm going to make more than my father ever did with no one to nag me to death the way she did. 'Promise me you'll nevah do that again, Maurice.' " His voice had assumed a feminine quality in a scathing imitation of Fannie Delacroix. " 'If you don't promise me, Maurice, Ah'll have to have you committed.' "

Oh my God! Was he saying that his father had been bipolar as well?

"She drove him to his death with all her nagging, but she never managed to control him, did she? No pills for my father. No loony bins."

Was Philippe saying that his father had committed suicide rather than submit to treatment?

"You're speechless, Carolyn. You didn't know all these things about your favorite surrogate mother, did you? The charming Fannie. My mother hated men. She'd rather have had you for blood kin than me."

"You're wrong, Philippe," I cried, hoping to head off the rage into which he was working himself. "She was very kind to me, but you were her son. She *loved* you."

"Shut up!" He was shouting in my face. Then his voice dropped abruptly back into the normal range. "But let's talk about Julienne. Your dear friend. How much did you ever know about the estimable Julienne? Nothing! Did you know that she couldn't be bothered to have a child of her own? And why should she bother when she could appropriate mine? And keep her."

"Diane?" I whispered.

"Diane. *My* daughter. Julienne wouldn't even let me tell her that I was her father."

I wouldn't have, either.

"Wouldn't let me have any say in her upbringing. When I wanted her back, Julienne shipped her off to that girls' school. So I gave my sister a choice—about the money, about Diane—and she refused."

"When was this?" I asked with dread.

"When *she* wanted something from *me*, I always agreed. Even the last time I saw her."

"What did you agree to, Philippe?"

"To take her out in the boat, of course. You knew that. You were driving hither and yon asking about boat rentals, weren't you?"

"She agreed to go out in a boat with you?" Why would Julienne have done that? He was obviously dangerous.

"Of course she agreed. I was on my best behavior; she thought I was taking my medication. She thought boating would be good for my nerves, remind me of those happy times when we were children, sailing around the swamp with crazy old Dad, fishing poles in our hot little hands and all that crap. So I took her there."

I didn't want to hear what happened next, but I couldn't get away from him, and I couldn't—

"Don't you have other questions, Carolyn? I'm sure you do." He was leaning forward again. Crowding me.

"What happened that . . . that night? In the swamp?"

"Why, she fell off the boat. Always taking chances in order to get the perfect picture. Don't you think that's just like your friend Julienne?"

That malicious smile spread across his lips, and I felt as if a permanent chill had entered my bones. "She fell out of the boat?" I repeated.

"Do you doubt me? You think I gave her a push when she flatly refused to do the right thing? I did her a favor. I gave her the chance to reconsider."

"You mean you'd have helped her back into the boat if she—"

"No, little sister's friend, I mean if she made it to shore, she'd have time to think over my offer while she was slogging her way back. All she had to do was come here and tell me. I've been waiting. But she hasn't come back, has she? Always resisting me. That's my sister."

"Philippe, you know that those waters are full of . . . of . . ." I saw in my mind that poor savaged body on the morgue slab. An alligator's dinner. And I knew it must have been Julienne. Tears began to trickle down my cheeks because I finally had to admit that she was dead. That Philippe had killed her.

"Tears, Carolyn? What for? Julienne was always a strong swimmer. Better than you. Better than me. Girls' champion all those summers at that wretched lake with our parents fawning over her. She could very well be alive. Probably is."

"Philippe, she's dead! I saw her body at the morgue," I cried.

His eyes narrowed. Had he really thought she was waiting in the swamp, planning to come back and expose him? Or agree to his terms? Or perhaps he was afraid that I had been able to identify her. I hadn't.

"Well, that's all right. If she's dead, I can claim my daughter and my daughter's inheritance, which should have been mine, anyway." He looked quite pleased with the outcome but then frowned. "Did you identify her?" he asked sharply.

"No, but—"

"Well!" Philippe stood up. "I know about your trip to the morgue. Claude told me. And if she's dead and you think you know it, that's the end of our conversation, isn't it?"

"What do you mean?"

"Claude's obviously not coming back, so I guess it's up to me to end this." Before I could panic or try to push him away, just a second after I lurched to my feet, Philippe swept me up in his arms. As if I were Scarlett O'Hara and he Rhett Butler about to carry the heroine up the broad staircase.

"What are you doing?" I tried to struggle free, but he was surprisingly strong for such a thin person. Surely, he didn't mean to rape me, I thought in a panic. But no. He swung around my chair and brushed right through the drapes. They were dusty and, in sweeping over my face, filled my nose and throat with fine, dry grit. Once past the drapes, he lifted me high and tossed me away, as if he were launching a kite into the air.

Then I was falling, terrified, with the sun in my face.

32
Mardi Gras King Cake

I was spread-eagled in the sky while my clothing fanned out in a vain attempt to buoy me up in the unresisting air. Turning my eyes desperately to the balcony, I saw Philippe's back as he disappeared without a backward glance through the door and the drapes, whose dust mixed in my throat with the acid of terror. I thought of Jason and the children. I didn't want to die! And I was so afraid of the terrible pain I'd feel, even if only momentarily, when my body slammed into the courtyard below.

And then I did hit, but I bounced. It was like playing on the trampoline in the backyard when the children were little. I could almost hear their screams of delight and my own laughter as we bounded on our feet and our bottoms. However, the second time I bounced, I heard the harsh sound of tearing canvas. Then I was falling again, my second of relief and remembrance gone as I plummeted once more and jarred into stillness.

Oh, I hurt! But worse than the pain and fear, I couldn't breathe. There was no air in my lungs, nor could I draw more in. This must be death, even though I had fallen into something that offered little initial resistance. I opened my eyes to look one last time at the sun. Instead, I saw men surrounding me, grotesque faces peering down from odd angles while some drew back and turned to one another in an uproar of unintelligible babble. Glasses and goblets in hand, laughing, talking, frowning, the men began to look less surreal as I blinked my eyes; then the babble separated into understandable speech, understandable in its separate words, if not in its meaning.

"Hell, Alistair, how come she didn't pop *out* of the cake?"

"Couldn't you a found us someone younger?"

"Better yet, someone *nekked*."

"She squashed da hell out of da cake, her."

"Ole Alistair always did have a flair for the dramatic."

"That li'l lady put out the Tooth Fairy Candle with her butt." Uproarious laughter followed most of the remarks from these men. I now saw that they were wearing sport coats, tieless shirts, and casual trousers. Then I was able to drag in my first breath and knew that I wasn't dead and that this wasn't some all-male hell peopled by a swarm of aliens with abominable taste in clothes—checked jackets, yellow pants, even a pink sport coat—all drinking and obviously the worse for liquor.

One staggered forward to peer at me and spilled beer on my face. When

I tried to push myself away from him, my hands sank into the surface upon which I had landed. When I tried to wipe the beer from my face, I saw that my fingers were covered with green, gold, and purple grit. I was dazed, still unable to breathe deeply enough to satisfy oxygen-starved lungs, and evidently very messy.

"Did you fall from heaven pretty, overaged, lady?" asked a leering fellow in a lime green sport jacket and dreadful green-striped pants. All he needed was a straw boater and cane to be dressed for vaudeville.

"I was thrown . . . off a balcony . . . by a madman," I croaked.

Some of the men laughed. I saw one pounding another's back and shouting, "That's a good one, Alistair." Alistair, for all he was wearing a frightful golf shirt with an emblem of an alligator eating a golfer, looked sober and confused. Again I reassured myself that I wasn't dead, just surrounded by ill-dressed, drunken ghouls. But Julienne was dead. Tears of grief and shock began to roll down my cheeks, and the men stopped laughing. One even tried to comfort me on the failure of my appearance in their conference cake.

"I need to call nine-one-one," I replied, reluctantly employing what little breath I had to speak.

Alistair offered me a cell phone. Others, realizing with surprise that my abrupt descent through the canvas of the tent and into their cake wasn't a bizarre convention act, fished out their phones as well. Within seconds, I had my choice of at least twelve cell phones. I took the nearest. Men on either side of me seized my elbows and sat me up, causing clouds of Mardi Gras–colored powder to swirl around me. Cake and icing squished out from beneath me and oozed onto the tablecloth which, much to my horror, was decorated with teeth of many colors. The act of sitting elicited a groan.

"Don't move her, Mort," cried Alistair. "You want to get sued?"

"She's covered with frosting and sugar," Mort protested. "That's not gonna be good for mah cell phone."

Alistair tried to push me back into the cake. "The police wanna see the body jus' wheah it landed."

"Yo' not supposed to disturb a crime scene, fella," said another person.

"I'm not dead," I protested. "Not moving the body is for dead people." My breathing had evened out. Obviously the breath, not the life, had been knocked out of me.

"How about a nice margarita, lady?" The man in the pink jacket tried to thrust a salt-edged cocktail glass into my hand, but I resisted both the margarita and the attempt to lay me out once more on top of the cake.

"You got real nice teeth, ma'am," said the man in the lime green outfit. "Musta had a good orthodontist." He bent over to study my teeth at closer range. "Real good bite there."

Of course, I thought. I had landed in the midst of the Southern Orthodontist Society conventioneers. Which reminded me vividly of Philippe, although he was not one of them. Still, he'd be getting away while I was being ogled and cosseted by dentists. I ignored Mort's fears for his cell phone, which I still clutched in one sticky, multicolored hand, and dialed 911.

Then, taking a deep breath and steeling myself to make a brief, cogent statement of the facts, I said, "My name is Carolyn Blue. I am at the orthodontists' convention at the Superior Inn, and I have just been thrown out a second-story window by the man who killed Dr. Julienne Magnussen. Her body, I believe, is in your morgue. The killer's name is Dr. Philippe Delacroix."

"Damn conventioneers!" said the 911 operator, which I thought very unprofessional of her. The orthodontists were all protesting loudly that no orthodontist would throw a lady out of a window. They were making the same mistake made by the desk clerk who had assumed that any doctor at the Superior Inn was an orthodontist.

"Could you please send the police?" I requested.

"You need an ambulance?" asked the operator, her voice sounding doubtful and suspicious.

"I don't know," I replied. My arms and legs moved, although I had a number of aches and pains. "I haven't tried to stand up."

"Well, don't move. Help is on the way. This isn't some kind of drunken joke, is it?"

"I assure you that I am neither drunk nor amused by being thrown off a balcony. And the . . . the perpetrator is dangerous."

"He armed?"

"I don't know, but he is certainly unbalanced." And probably already gone during the time wasted with questions from the orthodontists and the operator. "Couldn't you just send the police before he gets to the airport and flies away?'

"They're already comin', ma'am. How far did you say you fell?"

"Two stories."

"What did you light on?"

I eyed the remains of the cake, a huge artifact made of twisted brioche dough, formed in a circle, frosted, and covered with the aforementioned purple, green, and gold sugars. "My research would lead me to believe that I landed on a traditional, if giant-sized, king cake." Absently, I stuck a frosting-and-sugar-covered finger in my mouth. Interesting. The frosting contained a touch of anise flavoring and bits of candied orange peel. A very nice combination. Was that traditional? I thought not. But how ridiculous that I should be assessing the flavor of frosting when I had nearly lost my life and my dearest friend had suffered a terrible death. Tears began to seep out of my eyes while the operator said, "Well, honey, if you got the baby Jesus, you have to give the next party."

"I think not," I replied severely. I had no intention of giving a party for the Southern orthodontists, no matter what New Orleans king cake traditions might apply.

A man in a sensible, dark business suit was standing beside me saying to

Alistair, "We do want our guests to enjoy their stay with us, but we deplore damage to our facilities. Not only do I fail to see why the Superior Inn should pay for the destruction of your cake, but somehow or other, your members have ripped a hole in the tent we provided, and we will expect to be reimbursed for the repairs."

"Damn Yankee," said Mort to the manager, who sounded like a fellow Midwesterner. Then to me, Mort said, "You think this fella will be comin' after you? The one threw you off the balcony?"

"I doubt it. Sir, do I take it that you are a representative of the hotel?"

The dark-suited man turned to me, and his face lighted with a smile. "Let me guess," he exclaimed. "You're from Wisconsin."

"Michigan."

"I'm from northern Illinois."

"Carolyn Blue," I said, extending my hand. The two of us looked at it, he obviously reluctant to make contact with the multicolored icing, even for the sake of a fellow Midwesterner. I withdrew the hand and fought off the temptation to sample the interesting anise and orange flavor again. "If you have a security person or persons, could you send them to room two fourteen to detain Dr. Philippe Delacroix? He's the man who threw me off the balcony."

"Close personal friend?" asked the manager. "Significant other?"

"Madman," I replied, aggrieved that he would think my predicament the result of a lover's quarrel. "And if he's not there, my raincoat and handbag are. I'd appreciate their return." Then the siren wailed in the distance, moving ever closer. I hated to greet my rescuers while sprawled in a cake, but I was really afraid to move in case I did myself some further injury than to my pride.

The king cake is a Mardi Gras tradition, a sweet brioche-like confection, iced and dusted with sugars in Mardi Gras colors: purple, green, and gold. It is first served on Twelfth Night in honor of the Three Kings and continues to be served at parties and even at coffee breaks during the Carnival weeks that lead up to Mardi Gras or Fat Tuesday, the day preceding Lent. A prize, either a plastic baby figure representing the Christ child, a ring, or a gold bean, is baked into each cake.

In Europe, the person who is served a slice of king cake containing the prize must play one of the three kings. In South America, the partygoer who gets the Christ child figure also wins a year of good luck. But in New Orleans, the receiver is considered "king for a day" and may be expected to give the next party. One wonders how many New Orleans prizewinners conceal their good fortune in order to avoid the expense of hosting a Mardi Gras party.

Entering the words *king cake* into a search window on the Internet will provide you with a recipe. Even better you can put your order in to Mam Papaul's for cake mix, plastic baby, filling, glaze, and colored sugar in one handy package.

Carolyn Blue, *Eating Out in the Big Easy*

33
She Jumped?

The paramedics arrived, tested me, and helped me off the cake table after declaring me free of broken bones and spinal cord injuries. When I was upright, frosting and festive sugar from my shoulders to the back of my knees, the orthodontists gave me a standing ovation, and Mort again offered me a margarita. I took it, but a paramedic snatched it away from me. "You might have a concussion, ma'am," he pointed out.

"I didn't hit my head," I replied and retrieved my drink. However, it was an inferior version of the margarita I had first tasted at Martino's in Juarez during a lull in the drug wars. Jason and I took a German scientist to dinner there, at his insistence, and ordered a pitcher. The New Orleans margarita was too sweet and was undoubtedly made with those large, pulpy, flavorless limes instead of the tiny, flavorful, nut-hard Mexican variety. Or perhaps—I sipped again—this one had been made with—horror of horrors—a mix.

While I was assessing the margarita on a scale of one to ten—I gave it a five because at least it had alcohol in it, and I was in need of calming—Mort discovered the good luck plastic baby Jesus stuck to my posterior and presented it to me. I assured him that I did not intend to host the Southern Orthodontists at their next party.

Alistair assured me that they wouldn't expect it and ordered a table knife from a passing waitperson in order to scrape frosting from the back of my clothes. Ordinarily, I wouldn't have welcomed such familiarity from a male stranger, but being plastered with frosting tends to skew one's perceptions of propriety. Also, if the hotel security people returned with my raincoat, I didn't want to ruin the lining with king cake remains. When the scraping of my back wasn't particularly successful, Alistair—I never did learn his last name—prevailed upon the hotel manager to provide me with replacement clothes. I changed in the pool house, since the orthodontic festivities were being held in the patio that contained the swimming pool.

You'd think the manager would want to placate a woman who had been tossed off one of his balconies, if not for humanitarian considerations, then to avert a lawsuit. Not so. Either he had no suitable female clothing available, or he was being deliberately offensive, for he provided me with a dun-colored skirt and jacket sized for a woman who weighed several hundred pounds. I emerged from the pool house looking like a bag lady.

Fortunately, the security people arrived with my raincoat, umbrella, and handbag shortly thereafter, and I put on the raincoat. "What about Philippe Delacroix?" I asked anxiously. "Did he escape?"

"Who's that?" asked the house detective.

"The guest registered to the room where you found my raincoat," I replied impatiently. "Tall, unruly black hair, gaunt face, black circles under the eyes, very strong, dressed in black, arrogant. He'd have been acting like a megalomaniac."

"Guess they didn't get him," said the detective. "All I saw was some cops trying to talk to a guy who was sitting on the floor in the clothes closet. He was crying."

Crying? That didn't sound like the Philippe I had encountered upstairs. Having heard the answer to my question, the orthodontists were staring at me suspiciously, and the manager looked smug. What were they thinking? That I had *jumped* off that balcony and then blamed Philippe when I survived? I myself interpreted the security man's news to mean that Philippe had locked some terrified hotel employee in the closet and then escaped, which meant that he was still at large and could come after me. The thought of being thrown off another balcony or possibly fed to alligators, as he had done to his sister, turned me cold with fear.

"I don't think Dr. Delacroix seemed the type to throw anyone off a balcony," the manager murmured to Mort. "A very respectable person, that's how he struck me. However, if he did, I shall hold the Southern Orthodontists responsible for the damage to the tent."

"He's not one of ours," Alistair protested. "You seem to have forgotten that our cake was ruined when she tore through your tent."

Before I could argue with such a self-serving apportionment of blame, plainclothes detectives arrived, spotted and identified me, and asked for a statement. Having donned my raincoat to cover up the clothes provided by the hotel, I retired with the detectives to the manager's office for the interview.

"You made the nine-eleven call, ma'am?" asked Detective Dennis Mc-Crow after inviting me to take off my raincoat. Naturally, I refused, given the abominable suit I was wearing. Detective McCrow was a redheaded youth in his midtwenties with a face scarred, in all probability, by a serious case of teenage acne. Why don't more parents avail themselves of the many treatments now available to prevent such disfigurement? Chris had been so plagued in his teens, and we promptly took him to a dermatologist. Although Chris persisted in referring to the specialist as Dr. Zit, he did cooperate in the rigorous skin-care and medication routine prescribed. Now twenty-one and acne-free, Chris has hardly a mark on his face. But poor Detective McCrow! Of course, one can't commiserate with a scarred person. One can only ignore the problem. I smiled and started to reply.

"We need to establish her identity first," said Detective Virgie Rae Boutaire, a short, anorexic black woman with hair clipped to within an inch of her skull. She looked as if a passing breeze would blow her away, but I surmised that she was all wiry muscle, enabling her to deal with violent malefactors. At least, I hoped so. As for the haircut, it was rather startling, but I could see the advantages: coolness in hot weather, time saved in hair styling, and so forth.

"You got a problem with mah hair?" she demanded.

"I was thinking how pleasant it must be during hot and muggy weather."

"You got that right," she agreed suspiciously. "Name?"

"Carolyn Blue."

"ID."

Surprised, I fumbled through my handbag and produced my wallet with my Texas driver's license. Detective Boutaire took the whole wallet and called in the information on the license as well as my social security number. She had a cunning little microphone pinned to the shoulder of her jacket.

"What are you doing?" I asked with interest. Up until this week I'd had very little to do with the police and found myself intrigued by their work habits.

"Checkin' your record."

"Oh, I imagine you'll find me listed a good deal in your files," I said. "I was in several times to report a friend missing and once to try to identify a body at your morgue." I had to blink back tears when I said that, because I was now reasonably sure that the body *had* been Julienne. "Also, I was accosted by a female practioner of voodoo; I was the intended victim of a purse snatcher; I was pushed off a pier in the swamp boat tour area, almost run off a country road; and finally, a man attempted to shoot me."

"An' today you claim someone threw you off a balcony," Detective Boutaire finished for me. "You been havin' a real bad week." As she talked, her shoulder mike squawked at her, and she checked off the various attacks I had mentioned. "Anyone actually see any of these incidents?"

I must admit that I was quite taken aback by her question, which seemed to imply that she thought I was making all my troubles up, including the plunge into the tent and the cake below. "They were all orchestrated by Dr. Philippe Delacroix," I replied. "With the help of someone named Claude. Philippe told me so before he threw me off his balcony."

"An' why would he do that?" asked the detective.

"Because I wouldn't stop looking for his sister, and he had pushed her off a boat in the swamp Sunday night, after which she was . . . was eaten by an alligator." The thought of Julienne's fate sent a wave of nausea over me, and the two detectives, foreseeing an unpleasant event, teamed up to push my head down and advise me to breathe deeply. However, that was as far as their concern went.

"An' why would he dump his sister in a swamp?" Detective Boutaire asked once I was upright again.

"Because she wouldn't turn over her half of their mother's estate and give him back his daughter, whom she had adopted while he was in a mental institution."

The two detectives exchanged glances of such skepticism that I was forced to review what I had just said. It did sound peculiar. "I believe that Philippe is manic-depressive, that is to say, bipolar. He was certainly manic this afternoon. He talked as if he controlled the world from his hotel room, and . . . well . . . he threw me off the balcony because Father Claude hadn't succeeded in killing me. That's hardly the action of a sane person."

"You say this Father Claude tried to kill you?"

"Yes, he had a gun, but since it was plastic, I assumed, incorrectly as it happened, that his weapon was a toy. I hit his gun hand and, during the altercation, he lost his ear. Or so I assume. It was bleeding profusely when he ran away."

"You shot a priest in the ear?" Detective McCrow asked disapprovingly.

"I doubt that he was a priest, and, no, I didn't shoot him. The gun—"

"The *gun* shot him? So you're one a them gun-control people? Guns shoot people, not people? You probably don't think citizens got a right to carry arms or hunters to—"

"Oh, shut up, Dennis," snapped Detective Boutaire.

"I guess you're one of those NRA people," I said angrily to Detective McCrow. "Well, for your information, I am quite unfamiliar with guns. If I belonged to the NRA, I'd have known that Father Claude was carrying a real gun. Then I wouldn't have tried to knock it out of his hand, and I'd be dead. And in answer to your first question, I *am* the person who called nine-eleven. The orthodontists were too busy making facetious remarks about ladies jumping in and out of cakes and trying to give me a margarita."

"What orthodontists?" asked McCrow.

"Can we get back to the interrogation?" Boutaire interrupted.

"If that's what this is," I exclaimed indignantly, "maybe I need a lawyer."

"Get one if you want," said Boutaire, "but we don't usually bother to prosecute suicides. We might try to have you committed."

"Me? You want to commit *me*? I assume you mean to a mental institution. You should be looking for Philippe. He's the one who needs help."

"Far as we know, we found him," said McCrow. "All curled up in a corner of his closet and didn't hear a word we said to him, jus' kept sobbin' like a big baby an' sayin', 'she jumped.' Didn't seem too dangerous to me."

"Shut up, McCrow," said his partner. "Now, ma'am, were there any witnesses to these alleged attacks on you?"

"An' how come you're out shootin' priests?"

"Shut up, McCrow."

"I don' know why you keep tellin' me to shut up. Jus' because Ah'm new on the squad don' mean I don' git to ask no questions."

I took a deep, calming breath. It was hard to believe that somehow I had become the suspect after all my close calls with Philippe's minions. Or minion. For all I knew everyone who attacked me was Father Claude. "May I suggest the following," I said, trying to sound as calm possible. "One. Check mental health records on Dr. Delacroix. He's unstable and has been for years. Two. Compare DNA between the body in your morgue and Philippe. You'll find that they are brother and sister. Three. Check the will of their mother, Mrs. Fannie Delacroix. That will provide you with Philippe's motive, other than insanity, for pushing his sister off the boat. He wanted all the money."

I didn't mention Julienne's daughter having told me that and wouldn't unless I had to. The poor child didn't need to know that her uncle—no, her natural father—had killed her mother—well, adopted mother. Oh lord! It then occurred to me that Diane was the natural daughter of a man suffering from bipolarity, and that her father was fathered by a man who had probably suffered the same mental condition. The periods of silence, the wild plunge on the stock market, the car accident that might have been suicide—Maurice Delacroix had probably been bipolar just like his son Philippe. What did that say about Diane's chances of escaping the family curse? The situation seemed more tragic every time I thought further on it.

With difficulty, I pulled myself together and went on. "Four. Show a picture of Philippe to Mr. Red at Red's Boat Rentals, or have Mr. Red pick Philippe out of a lineup. He rented Philippe the boat. Five. Check the fingerprints on the gun I turned over to the officers at the Vieux Carre substation to see if the prints match those of a criminal named Father Claude. Six. Check Philippe's sleeves for fibers from my clothes, which are in the pool house downstairs because, Detectives, I did *not* jump! I changed clothes in the pool house because I was covered with cake frosting and had to—*why are you laughing?*"

Both detectives were convulsed with mirth. I couldn't imagine why. I thought all my suggestions not only practical but impressively technological, perfectly in line with criminal investigation methodology I had seen on TV.

"Lady, do you know what it costs to do DNA tests?" asked Detective Boutaire. "You think the department's gonna spring for that? It's not like we got a murder here. An' even—"

"Julienne's been murdered," I said and began to cry again. At that moment, and much to my relief, Lieutenant Boudreaux walked in, checked us all out, and handed me a handkerchief. I was so embarrassed. I hadn't yet returned the last one.

Then the interview started all over again. While I was getting myself together with the help of the lieutenant's handkerchief, he interviewed the two detectives, who treated him with much more deference than they had me. They didn't have that much to tell him. Philippe was in custody, but he wasn't talking now, not even to say, "she jumped." As far as anyone could tell, he wasn't even hearing. Did that indicate deep depression, catatonia, or deception? I wondered.

Then the lieutenant interviewed me, showing every indication of sympathy for my ordeal and great interest in what Philippe had told me about Julienne's death. "If we can't get him to talk, we'll have to do a DNA match on the two of them," he mused. His fellow officers looked shocked. I tried not to look smug. "Better yet, we can probably identify her by dental records."

"Am I under suspicion?" I asked my police friend and champion.

"No, ma'am, Ah wouldn't think so," said the lieutenant, patting my shoulder.

"Say, she could be making the whole thing up," said McCrow. "If it turns out the body is this Julienne, maybe Miz Blue pushed her off the boat an' then blamed it on that poor nut upstairs. Maybe she made up all those attacks. No one saw nothin'. We only got her word."

"Except that the fingerprints on the Glock are Father Claude's," said the lieutenant. "Hers are only on the barrel. You can't shoot someone while you're holdin' the barrel of the gun. Anyway, the gun was stolen two years back in the robbery of a pawnshop, an' she's a professor's wife from El Paso, Texas. Not likely she was here two years ago holdin' up pawn shops, but that bastard—'scuse the language, ma'am—we got his fingerprints at crime scenes all over the Quarter. Nevah got him, not even a mug shot, but we're lookin', an' now we got a bettah handle on what he looks like. All those disguises not gonna hide the fact that he's missin' an ear, not when we catch him."

Detective McCrow looked crestfallen that I was not guilty of killing my friend, manufacturing attacks on myself, and attempted suicide. I suppose he had believed Philippe and thought I'd been overcome by my guilty conscience and jumped. But then, even his partner, Detective Boutaire, didn't seem to value his intelligence highly. And what had Philippe meant when he said, "she jumped"? The antecedant of "she" could have been me, but it could also have been Julienne. Either way he was lying.

"So detectives," said the lieutenant heartily, "Ah think you all bettah take yo' nutcase downtown an' see if you can get a confession out of him, an' Ah'll take charge of Miz Blue here, who's lookin' mighty peaked. She's had her a real hard week."

Amen to that, I thought and left willingly with Lieutenant Boudreaux. When I thanked him for his kindness, he said, "Think nuthin' of it, ma'am. An' call me Al. You evah had crawfish boil an' hush puppies?"

"I don't believe so," I replied.

"Then Ah'm takin' you to the best place for crawfish an' hush puppies in the whole city, an' that's sayin' somethin'."

34

Crawfish Boil and Hush Puppies

The lieutenant's car was parked squarely in the middle of the taxi zone in front of the hotel and guarded from ticketing by a uniformed officer. "They seemed to think I might be guilty of something," I said, amazed. Lieutenant Boudreaux nodded, helped me into the car, then took the wheel himself, and pulled out into very heavy traffic.

"Most people we deal with are guilty of somethin'," he replied mildly. "They jus' din' know the background a the case."

"But I told them."

"Sure, but you're a civilian. Don' take offense, Miz Carolyn. Cops get lied to so much, they come to expect it, an' Ah'm not gonna let you be arrested. So you jus' try not to think about all that bad stuff. Think about hush puppies and crawdaddies."

But that was hard. As depression settled over me, my interest in food disappeared. I was sure the crawfish and hush puppies would be delicious, but I was about to ask that he take me back to my hotel when Lieutenant Boudreaux said, "Sorry fo' the loss of you friend, Miz Magnussen. Reckon we're gonna' find that's who our unidentified body is."

I nodded. How terrible that Julienne, so beautiful and vivacious in life, should be lying in a drawer in a cold room, unrecognizable even to me, her best friend. "They won't let Philippe go, will they? He might hurt someone else."

"Not from what Butaire and McCrow had to say. Man who won't move or talk, he's not likely to—"

"He could be faking. When I was up there, he was . . . he was like a . . . malicious spider. He called himself a spider, luring us into his web, using that . . . that Claude—"

"Claude was workin' for him? He said that?" The lieutenant glanced from the traffic on a narrow neighborhood street we had entered to my face and caught my nod. "Wonder what their connection is?"

"Goodness only knows. Philippe did live here until he was almost a teenager. Maybe they knew each other from childhood."

Boudreaux nodded. "Could be. We don' know hardly anythin' about Claude ourselves, jus' talk among criminals an' crimes we think he committed. Don' even know if that's his real name, but if Delacroix called him that, maybe we can trace them back."

"Is he a . . . a . . . killer?"

"He seems to do whatever comes to hand long as there's money in it."

"Then Philippe was paying him to stalk me?"

"Likely, unless Claude owes him favors, somethin' like that."

He swung the police car into a bus zone near a small neighborhood grocery store that had a hand-lettered sign offering Best Crawfish Boil in Town—Take Home a Pound or Four. While talking, I had forgotten to ask for a ride to the hotel instead of lunch. What did the lieutenant expect me to do, stand in the aisles of the store eating crawfish with my fingers? Maybe he planned to go back to the Moonwalk, sit on a bench as we had with the muffulettas, and eat the repast. If so, I hoped the crawfish were shelled. Otherwise, we'd make a spectacle of ourselves and ruin our clothes.

He came around and handed me out of the car and into the little store, where he was greeted with enthusiasm and jokes by the proprietors, two short, rounded people, an Asian female and a Cajun male.

"This here's Miz Carolyn. She's a woman had a real hard week. What she needs is some of your fine, spicy crawdads an' a bag of de-licious hush puppies, Pierre."

Pierre swept me a bow and told me that his "crawdaddies" were good for whatever ailed me. I doubted that, although the place smelled enticing. His wife, giggling girlishly behind her hand, began to scoop hush puppies from a deep pot of bubbling fat and drop them into a bag.

The lieutenant snatched one from the bag and held it out to me. "Blow on it first so you don't burn your mouth," he cautioned.

I felt very foolish and not a little self-conscious about blowing on a hush puppy held in the fingers of a police lieutenant while the lady, whose name was Yashi, beamed maternally at us. However, her hush puppy was amazingly good: hot and crunchy outside, light and oniony inside. The tears came to my eyes when I thought of how Julienne would have loved this experience.

"Why she cry, her?" asked Pierre, who had been fishing spice-encrusted crawfish from the crab boil.

"She jus' lost a friend," said the lieutenant, who then peeled and fed me a crawfish. "Best crawdaddy you're ever likely to taste," he announced, smiling.

I nodded. It really was, and I wanted to ask Pierre for his recipe, but somehow I didn't have the heart because I'd never be able to pass it on to Julienne. I could imagine the conversation we'd have had. "You couldn't possibly have a better crawfish recipe than I have," Julienne would have said, and I'd have replied, "Winner has to do the rowing next summer?" The tears rolled down my cheeks at the thought that we'd never have that conversation, never go out together on the lake again on a fine summer day.

"She still cryin', her," said Pierre.

"Better you buy beer, too," Pierre's wife advised Lieutenant Boudreaux.

The lieutenant went to inspect the beer selection. "Well now, we got Turbo Dog, Voodoo. Here we go . . . How about a Dixie longneck?"

"I've never tried any of them," I replied, sniffling. However, I certainly should. German immigrants had been the primary brewers of beer in New Orleans, a city proud of its local brands. In fact, the word *Dixie* was of New Orleans derivation, having come from an American mispronunciation of the French word for ten displayed on one side of a ten-dollar bill printed in the 1800s for circulation in the city. "But I choose the Dixie longneck," I added, always interested in things of historical significance.

The lieutenant pulled a six-pack from the refrigerator and paid for the two sacks and the beer while I used a corner of his handkerchief to stem my tears. "Well," he said, once we were back in the car with the enticing odor of his purchases wafting through the grill from the backseat, "where shall we go to eat this?" He put the key in the ignition and turned to smile at me. "My place all right?"

Oh, dear, oh, dear. Somehow or other, the lieutenant had gotten a very wrong idea about our relationship. Kind as he had been, I had no intention of . . . no desire to . . . I glanced, panic-stricken, at my watch. Worse and worse. It wasn't lunchtime. It was five-thirty. Jason would be arriving at the hotel just about now, wondering where I was, and now this handsome policeman evidently expected me to accompany him to his place.

Unfortunately, I couldn't take that to mean the Vieux Carre substation. He expected me to join him for a private feast of crawfish, hush puppies, beer, and goodness knows what else. I closed my eyes and wished myself elsewhere. What an absolutely dreadful week this had been, and somehow or other, I had to write a book about it. How would I ever manage? How would I ever manage to explain to Lieutenant Boudreaux that I wasn't amenable to . . . to New Orleans cuisine followed by late-afternoon adultery?

"Ah can see you're jus' speechless at mah suggestion," he said, his tone somewhat wry.

Reluctantly, I opened my eyes. "Lieutenant, I'm a happily married woman. Very happily married. If I have somehow given you the impression that . . . well . . . well, I'm so sorry. And embarrassed. And—"

"Mah mistake," he said, sounding perfectly amiable.

Thank goodness for that. What if he'd made a scene? Which perhaps he had a right to make. But what had I done—

"Saw you look at yo' watch," he continued. "Reckon yo' husband might be comin' home to the hotel jus' about now? Not stayin' fo' any talk about teeth an' such?"

"He's with the American Chemical Society," I replied earnestly, glad to get away from the topic of afternoon trysts, "not the Southern Orthodontists Society." Hadn't I told the lieutenant that before? Yes, I thought I had, which only goes to show that men don't really listen to women. "I only know the orthodontists from falling into their dessert," I continued. "Well, actually, I don't know them at all, although they were reasonably gracious about the destruction of their king cake."

"And so they should be," said the lieutenant gallantly. "A pretty lady like you. Ah hate to think what bad memories you're gonna have of our city." He shifted and pulled out into traffic. "When you leavin'? I recollect you said somethin' about tomorrow."

Oh, he remembered that, did he? Just like a man, even a pleasant one. He had been looking forward to a one-night stand, with the lady in question, me, conveniently disappearing the next day on an airplane.

"Tomorrow afternoon," I replied.

"Well, you'll need to come on over to the station tomorrow mornin' to make a statement."

"Another one?"

"Formal statement. Signed statement. You wanna tell her husband the news?"

"I don't even want to see him," I said bitterly. "If he hadn't berated her at the dinner, she wouldn't have left, and then—"

"No use, thinkin' that way, Miz Carolyn. If her brother was set on killin' her, likely he'da found another opportunity. Anyways, we'll take care of notifyin' the husband."

"Thank you." We were back in the Quarter. In fact, we were on Royal Street, and I wondered if he planned to make me walk home to the hotel from the substation.

However, that thought did him an injustice. He drove me right to the Hotel de la Poste and even insisted that I take the dinner he had purchased. Of course, I protested, and, of course, he insisted. "Jus' so you remember us kindly," he said, smiling. He didn't offer to escort me inside.

35
The Last Crème Brûlée

Le Bistro Crème Brûlée

Preheat oven to 325° F. In a medium saucepan, scald *1 qt. heavy whipping cream* and *2 vanilla beans, split lengthwise,* over medium heat.

In large bowl, whisk *6 egg yolks* and ⅔ *cup granulated sugar* together until thick and lemon-colored. Remove vanilla beans from cream. Slowly whisk hot cream into yolk mixture until smooth. Strain through a fine-meshed sieve.

Fill ten 4-ounce soufflé dishes to ¼ inch from top. Place cups in baking pan and add 1 inch warm water to pan. Cover cups with aluminum foil or baking sheet. Bake 30 to 45 minutes or until set. Remove from oven and cover each cup with plastic wrap. Chill for at least 8 hours.

To serve: Preheat broiler. Evenly spread *5 tablespoons raw or brown sugar* on top
of custards. Place under broiler about 4 inches from heat until sugar is caramelized.
Let custard cool and tops harden before serving.

SERVES 10.

When I opened the door to our room, Jason was lying on the bed with his shoes off, watching the national news on TV. He took one look at my face as I came in, my arms loaded with paper bags, and clicked the remote to turn off the program. "What's wrong, Caro?"

"She's dead." I set the bags down on the dresser in front of the ornate mirror. By the time I turned, Jason was there to put his arms around me. He didn't need to ask who had died.

"Does Nils know?" he asked after a minute.

"Not from me. The police will tell him. I couldn't bear to talk to him . . . I guess because I hold him partly to blame."

Jason led me over to the bed and sat down beside me, his arm around my shoulders. "What happened?" he asked quietly.

"She and Philippe went out together on a boat. He pushed her overboard, and an alligator got her." I swallowed a sob.

"My God." Jason sounded horrified. "I guess that means they found the body?"

"Yes."

He remained silent for a moment, then said firmly, "They'll need someone to identify her. I do *not* want you to volunteer, Caro. Let Nils do it."

"I've already seen the body. I just didn't know it was her."

He thought a moment. "When you went to the morgue? That was . . . well, of course it was. Still, Nils can damn well be the one to go over there a second time."

"He won't be able to tell, either."

"That bad?"

"Yes. They'll have to use dental records. Or a DNA comparison between her and Philippe." I was beginning to feel numb, as if the real me was standing back watching this Carolyn Blue as she answered questions with little apparent emotion.

"But why would Philippe—"

"Because he's sick . . . mentally ill. Bipolar, and paranoid too, I imagine. He thought their mother had unfairly favored Julienne over him in the division of the estate. And he claims Diane is his daughter and Julienne wouldn't give her back."

Jason looked astonished. "Could that be true?"

"About the money? Not really. About Diane? I just don't know, but, Jason, if she is Philippe's daughter, we'll have to think long and hard about telling Nils or her."

Jason nodded. "It's not news either one would be happy to hear, especially not after he killed Julienne. What an awful mess."

"I know." It made me even more miserable just talking about the situation, and I tried to change the subject. "I brought home dinner. A police lieutenant took me to this little grocery store."

"Good idea," said Jason absently. "You probably don't feel much like eating out again."

"No," I agreed.

"You realize that even if we say nothing about Diane and Philippe, he probably will."

"Right now, according to the police, he's practically catatonic. Maybe he'll never recover." I spread newspapers across the bedspread, unloaded the paper bags, and pried the tops off two Dixie longnecks. "In fact, I hope that's what happens. I hope they commit him to some archaic mental institution and never let him out."

Jason looked somewhat taken aback at my vehemence, but he said nothing and accepted a helping of crustaceans and hush puppies. Lieutenant Boudreaux might be given to hitting on married ladies, but he did know his "crawdaddies." They were delicious, although I had to page through one of the tourist magazines the hotel provided to find the directions for eating them.

"All right," I said to Jason. "First, twist the tail off." He did so. "Now, hold it by the bottom and peel off the top ring." Jason peeled. The juices dripped. I read further. "Now, pinch the bottom of the tail between your forefinger and thumb, and pull the meat out with your teeth."

Jason did that and smiled at me. "Terrific," he said.

I nodded and rose to take off my raincoat. I didn't want to get crawfish juice, no matter how delicious, on the garment that had been the most useful to me during this dreadful visit. My mind was on Diane, that sweet girl in boarding school who didn't know that her mother was dead and her biological father—I shook my head and devoured two crawfish in the prescribed manner. Nils obviously didn't know that his adopted daughter was also his niece-in-law. With any luck, neither of them would have to face that dilemma.

"Why are you wearing that awful suit?" Jason asked.

"My other clothes were ruined."

"How?" He looked puzzled.

"Philippe threw me into a cake." I didn't mention from what height, anticipating that Jason would be upset that I'd been thrown from a two-story balcony. Time enough for the whole story later, when neither one of us was in shock.

"A *cake?*"

"A big one. It belonged to a bunch of orthodontists."

"Maybe you could explain that?" We were both cracking open the crawfish and sucking the tender, spicy morsels into our mouths.

"Well, I told you Philippe was crazy. I wasn't exaggerating. He's not only crazy, he's violent." Did Nils know that his brother-in-law was bipolar and probably his father-in-law as well? Evidently it was a genetic disorder.

"Good lord! He attacked you, too?" Jason exclaimed in response to my remark about Philippe. My husband shook his head and opened a second round of beer for each of us. We were drinking straight from the bottles. I suppose we could have used the glasses in the bathroom, but it didn't occur to us. My mind returned compulsively to Diane and Nils. Perhaps, after all, I was obligated to tell him that his daughter might be at risk? But then he'd watch her like a hawk, looking for signs of abnormality, perhaps seeing symptoms that weren't there. He could ruin her life. Everything about the situation made me want to weep, to hide my head in the sand, to pretend none of it had happened and I knew none of the tragic details.

"My paper got an excellent reception," Jason told me. By that time we were finishing off the last of the hush puppies.

"I'm glad."

"Now, you think of something good that happened on this trip."

It was an old game of ours. When everything was dreadful, we tried to think of good things. "Well," I said listlessly, "a handsome police officer asked me out."

Jason looked surprised but, on consideration, remarked, "Just goes to show the good taste of the New Orleans Police Department. What's his name? I'll file a complaint."

"No need. I didn't accept the date."

"That's good news." He opened the last two bottles of beer and handed me one. "Want to drink a toast to Julienne?" he asked.

I set the bottle down. "No, I have a better idea. Do you remember Julienne saying that the three of us should go together to Le Bistro for the crème brûlée?"

"When did she say that?"

"At the alligator dinner." Oh God, I'd have to stop thinking of it by that awful name.

"I like crème brûlée," said Jason.

"Correction. You love crème brûlée! So let's go there and have dessert. In her memory."

"But do you think they can fit us in? At this late hour, and just for dessert?"

"I'm a food critic! Of course they can!"

And they did.

In Memory of Julienne Delacroix Magnussen
Brilliant Scientist
Best of Friends
We loved the crème brûlée, and you, Julienne.
Carolyn Blue, *Eating Out in the Big Easy*, Dedication

Truffled Feathers

Acknowledgments

Grateful acknowledgment is made to author Sharon O'Connor for permission to reprint copyrighted recipes from *Dining and the Opera in Manhattan,* Menus and Music Productions, Emeryville, California, 1994.

For Bill, My Dear Husband and Fellow Traveler

Prologue
Champagne on the Plane

Champagne, bubbly and delicious in a flute or tempting in a cocktail glass as a Bellini, a Kir Royale, or a Champagne Cocktail, is a favorite both here and abroad. However, this wasn't always so. In New York City in the 1790s, it was very *unpopular*, quite possibly because it was heated before serving. How unpalatable does that sound? Wouldn't the heat have dispersed the very bubbles we are so fond of?

Carolyn Blue, "Have Fork, Will Travel," *Tampa Sun Times*

Carolyn

Forebodings, premonitions: Some people claim to have these before appalling events, but I have never had a premonition in my life, at least not one that bore fruit. I don't even believe in dreams anymore. And my husband, Jason, derides all such things. He is too much a man of science, and I am too much given to the sane and ordinary. Perhaps this is a good thing. Otherwise, the two of us could not have basked so innocently in the pleasures of traveling to New York in first class on American Airlines that Monday. We might not have fully appreciated the comfy blue leather seats, the extra legroom, the early boarding, or the obsequious service of food and alcohol. Needless to say, we are unaccustomed to traveling in such a luxurious and expensive fashion. Few academics are. Not that I am an academic. I am an academic's wife and, having received an advance for a book to be called *Eating Out in the Big Easy,* a "self-employed person."

This is my first venture into the ranks of wage-earning women; for years I stayed home raising my children and giving charming dinner parties for my husband's colleagues, but now my children have gone off to college, and I avoid the kitchen if at all possible. I find it more fun to write about food than to prepare it.

"Champagne?" asked a perky stewardess. "Or orange juice?"

Jason looked up from his copy of the *Journal of Environmental Toxicology,* which, needless to say, was not provided by American Airlines, and smiled at the young lady. "We'll have both." Before I could protest, the smiling stewardess had provided the makings for mimosas, two screw-top bottles of champagne and two glasses of orange juice,

"I wasn't going to have a drink," I said to Jason. No use telling the stewardess; she was already wending her way down the aisle, tempting other passengers into the midday consumption of alcohol.

"I suppose you were hoping for something tastier with your champagne," Jason responded. "Kir? Peach schnapps?"

"It's not that." I could feel the pressure of my waistband. After a recent trip to New Orleans, I had discovered that the pursuit of material for my book had provided not only reams of notes but also an unwelcome inch or so on my waist. I, the lady who prided herself on an active metabolism, had gained weight! I can only explain the dismaying outcome of my new profession by blaming my age. I am over forty, alas. "I've been thinking of going on a diet," I admitted to my husband.

"You can't be serious!" he exclaimed.

"Toasted nuts?" Another American Airlines temptress appeared beside my husband, who had taken the aisle seat so that, without jabbing me in the ribs, he could draw little chemical pictures in a notebook when the impulse overcame him. The stewardess didn't wait for us to accept. She simply deposited small white containers of mixed nuts beside our mimosas.

I sighed. Champagne I might have been able to resist, but nuts? Never. I love nuts. "Don't say a word," I murmured sternly to my grinning husband as I selected a cashew and pondered how nice a combination it would make with a mixture of champagne and orange juice. Oh well, it was all grist for the mill of the busy culinary author; I could type up notes on eating toasted nuts, *hot* toasted nuts, at 36,000 feet.

"You are absolutely the last woman in the world who needs to watch her weight," Jason assured me as he reopened his journal, preparatory to reading fascinating things about his favorite subject, toxins.

"You're not wearing my slacks," I replied and bit into a smooth, salty Brazil nut before sipping my orange juice down far enough to add champagne.

"I don't think your slacks would become me," Jason said dryly. Then he was gone, lost in the realms of serious science, leaving me to my interrupted thoughts and my snack. I poured champagne into my depleted juice glass after opening my computer on the tray table. Imagine a computer that fits into one's handbag! Jason had found it on the Internet. I created a file for New York notes and entered my thoughts on champagne and toasty nuts. Then I saved and opened the second chapter of the New Orleans book. Immediately my spirits plummeted.

My visit to New Orleans had been very traumatic, so traumatic that I couldn't think about it without having to repress tears. But I could hardly write chapter 2 without considering its subject, so what was I to do? It had occurred to me that I could use this trip to collect material for a second book, *Eating Ethnic in the Big Apple*. But if I couldn't write the first book, the publisher would hardly want to hear my ideas for a second. And I was to meet my editor for the first time. Would he be sympathetic to my problems with the New Orleans book, for which I'd already accepted an advance? Doubtless he expected something other than weepy excuses in return for the publisher's money.

Then there was my agent. I'd never met her, either, and she already had 15 percent of the advance. Even if I returned my portion, she wouldn't want to give her share back. And by not producing the book, I'd be ruining my budding career as a cuisine writer. Three articles in the local newspaper, some picked up by other papers, do not a career make. What a pickle I was in!

"Something wrong with the computer?" Jason asked.

"No, it's working beautifully." To prove it, I typed in my opinion of the joys of making roux, base of gumbo, and other New Orleans delights. Fledgling food writer or not, I've never made a decent roux in my life. I don't like to make roux. I don't even like to cook.

"I like other people's cooking."

I stared at what I had just typed. Although it was quite factual, it did not belong in chapter 2 of my book. And why did I want a career, anyway? I didn't need the money. Not really. Our children have scholarships. We'd actually made money on the sale of our previous home because real estate in El Paso is so much cheaper than it was in our former location. We have no mortgage! And we were going to New York because a big chemical company was interested in hiring Jason as a consultant.

Although Jason had no intention of giving up his teaching position at the university, he wasn't averse to earning a decadent amount of money by answering questions for Hodge, Brune & Byerson (Cleaning the Environment Through Chemistry). Especially since the consulting involved toxins. Jason loves toxins. I glanced over at him. I'd venture to say that the little drawings he was busily sketching into his notebook would, if in their natural state, kill everyone on the airplane, or at least mutate their DNA or cause their cells to reproduce wildly. Unchecked cell reproduction equals cancer, in case you're not familiar with the concept.

At any rate, we don't need my small advance on royalties or any royalties I might earn in the future. I could have refused. I could still give the money back and be covered by Jason's new source of income, providing he and the company came to terms. But what would my husband think of me throwing up my new career? Jason has never encouraged me to get a job, but on the other hand, he is a thrifty man. And his mother! The eminent professor of women's studies at the University of Chicago! Well, I can just imagine what she'd say. She'd certainly consider me an even bigger source of embarrassment than she had in the past. I can hear her complaining to some fellow feminist, "I thought my daughter-in-law had finally developed enough gumption to join the workforce, but . . ."

I guess I'll have to write the book. But not this very minute. I closed my computer and reached into my carry-on for a wonderful cookbook Jason had given me for my birthday: *Dining and the Opera in Manhattan* by Sharon O'Connor. It has a CD enclosed featuring opera arias, some by singers of bygone days with voices so beautiful they make me wish I had been old enough to hear them in person. And the recipes! They are so tempting that I actually cooked my husband an anniversary dinner from the cookbook. If I do say so myself, the results were superb, and Jason was beside himself with delight. I fear that I gave my husband unrealistic hopes for the future. Ah well!

I opened the book and thumbed through, daydreaming of visiting some of the restaurants from whose chefs the recipes derived. With any luck, our industrial hosts might take us to one or two, providing me with useful culinary notes at no expense to the family budget.

These culinary daydreams cheered me up considerably. Gourmet food, wonderful museums, maybe an opera, certainly a play (we already had theater tickets)—I foresaw an exciting week in the nation's most sophisticated city. What I didn't foresee was the web of conspiracy and violence toward which we were flying. First class.

CAROLYN'S ANNIVERSARY DINNER
Le Cirque's Sea Scallop Fantasy in Black Tie
Fantaisie de St.-Jacques en Habit Noir

Trim the muscle on the sides of *16 sea scallops (1 oz. ea.)* if necessary; reserve the muscle. Rinse the sea scallops and pat dry with paper towels. Cut each scallop crosswise into four ¼-in.-thick slices.

Preheat oven to 300°F. With a truffle slicer or potato peeler, cut *2 or 3 fresh or canned truffles (1 oz. ea.)* into about 50 paper-thin slices no larger in diameter than the scallops. (If using canned truffles, drain and reserve juice). Place 1 truffle slice between each slice of scallop and reassemble the scallop; for each one there will be 4 slices of scallop and 3 of truffle. Chop scraps of leftover truffles.

In a small saucepan, cook *¼ cup white vermouth, preferably Noilly-Prat,* and any reserved muscles over medium heat until dry. Reduce heat to low, add any reserved truffle juice and *1 tbs. heavy whipping cream,* and whisk in *8 tbs. butter,* 1 tablespoon at a time; the sauce will thicken and emulsify. Add *salt and freshly ground pepper to taste* and place pan over barely tepid water to keep sauce warm.

Melt *2 tbs. butter.* Place *1 bunch spinach leaves (8 oz.), stemmed,* in a bowl, and toss with 1 tbs. melted butter. Arrange spinach leaves on serving plate and place in preheated oven for 2 to 3 minutes or until they are slightly wilted; set aside.

Sprinkle scallops with salt and pepper. In a large, nonstick pan, heat remaining tbs. melted butter over medium heat, and sauté scallops on one side for 3 minutes. Turn over, lower heat, and sauté for another 3 minutes.

If you like, cut each scallop in half horizontally so you can see the layers of black and white. Arrange scallops on top of spinach leaves. Add minced truffles to butter sauce and coat each scallop with sauce. Sprinkle with *2 tbs. minced fresh chervil* and serve.

MAKES 4 SERVINGS.

Lutece's Caramelized Rack of Lamb
Carré d'Agneau Caramélisé

Have your butcher prepare *2 racks of lamb (8 chops each)* by removing most of the fat and the chine (backbone). Have the rib bones French cut (so that they extend from the meat by ¾ inch). Ask the butcher to give you the chine and rib ends along with the racks.

Preheat oven to 375°F. In a small bowl, stir together *2 tbs. honey, 2 scant tbs. Dijon mustard, 2 tsp. dried thyme, crumbled,* and *juice of 1 lemon;* set aside. Brush lamb with *2 tbs. peanut oil* and sprinkle with *salt and freshly ground black pepper to taste.* Place racks in a roasting pan and surround with reserved bones. Roast in preheated oven 4 minutes, then turn and baste the meat. Roast another 4 minutes, then turn, baste the meat, and roast another 4 minutes. Add *2 small onions, cut into ⅓-in.-thick wedges, 2 carrots, peeled and cut into ⅓-in. pieces,* and *2 unpeeled garlic cloves* to roasting pan, and roast for 5 minutes. Turn and baste meat, stir vegetables and bones, and roast another 5 minutes. Place lamb on platter and let sit in warm place for 5 to 6 minutes; leave bones and vegetables in roasting pan.

Meanwhile, preheat broiler. Pour all fat from roasting pan. Add *1½ cups dry white wine or water* to bones and vegetables. Place pan over high heat and boil liquid for a few minutes, stirring the bones and vegetables with a wooden spoon. When liquid has been reduced by half, strain it through a sieve into a sauceboat. Press the vegetables through the sieve with the back of a spoon, but do not attempt to push all the solids through the sieve.

With the lamb racks meat side up, brush the top of the racks with the honey mixture. Place the meat under the broiler for about 3 minutes, or until the top of racks are nicely caramelized. Cut each rack into 8 chops and arrange 4 on each of 4 plates. Pour liquid from roasting pan over, garnish with *watercress sprigs,* and serve with *green beans and potatoes.*

SERVES 4.

Lutece's Pears with Calvados
Poires au Calvados

Preheat oven to 350°F. Lightly butter a dish or ovenproof casserole just large enough to hold the pears.

Peel and core *4 ripe pears.* Halve them lengthwise and cut each half into 4 wedges. In a sauté pan or skillet, melt *2 tbs. unsalted butter* over medium heat and add the pears. Sprinkle them with ¼ cup sugar and sauté the pears until they are lightly caramelized. Add 2 tbs. Calvados, let it warm, ignite with a match, and shake pan until flames subside. Place pears and Calvados mixture in the prepared dish.

In a medium bowl, whisk together 2 eggs and ¼ cup sugar until eggs are frothy and pale in color. Add pinch of ground cinnamon, salt to taste, and 1 tbs. all-purpose flour. Slowly stir in ¾ cup heavy whipping cream and 2 tbs. Calvados. Pour this mixture over pears. Bake in preheated oven for 35 minutes or until top is light golden brown. Serve warm.

SERVES 4.

1

Low-Fat Canapés and Bad News in a Limo

Carolyn

Having been helped into our resurrected-for-the-trip wool coats by the stewardess, we left the airplane, computer cases dangling from our shoulders, and hurried down the freezing umbilical cord that connected our plane to the gate. "Looks like Max isn't here to meet us," Jason said after studying the crowd inside.

He sounded disappointed, although I wasn't surprised. After all, Max Heydemann, the man who wanted to recruit Jason, was the director of research and development. He and my husband had evidently taken an instant liking to one another. Even so, a man with Dr. Heydemann's responsibilities was unlikely to drive out to a distant airport in the middle of the business day.

"So. Cab or bus?" Jason asked.

I knew Jason was hoping that I'd choose the bus, which was much less expensive and possibly much safer than a cab. I'd heard frightening tales about New York taxi drivers. On the other hand, if we had to drag our bags aboard a bus, Jason would realize how much I had crammed into my suitcase.

Fortunately, I spotted rescue from marital discord in the person of a very slender man in a long, black overcoat. He wore a snappy chauffeur's cap and had dark skin with a narrow mustache that looked as if it had been drawn on his upper lip with an eyebrow pencil. While beaming at the disembarking passengers, he held against his chest a sign that was neatly lettered with the words "Welcome, Dr. and Mrs. Jason Blue."

"I believe they've sent someone," I said, nodding toward the driver.

We introduced ourselves, and he folded his sign carefully, as if he might have use for it at some future time. "I am being Radovan Ramakrishna," he said.

Radovan? Wasn't that the given name of a Serb general? Now, Ramakrishna sounded right. With his thin features and dark skin—

". . . driving you to New York City in the limousine of the company which you are visiting, please. Are you having valises to retain from the baggage-go-rounds?"

We agreed that a visit to the "baggage-go-rounds" would be necessary and followed our chauffeur, now festooned with our computer bags, through the corridors of the bustling airport. I personally kept a very close eye on him in case he proved to be a computer thief rather than a limo driver. A professor of urban minority poetry had had her computer stolen in the Newark Airport, and I did not plan to follow in her footsteps. However, my paranoia almost caused me serious injury. I was so fixated on my own computer, hanging from the driver's shoulder, that when he stopped abruptly, I walked right into Jason's computer case (which Mr. Ramakrishna held in one hand), thereby sustaining a painful rap on my knee.

"A thousand pardons, madam," cried Mr. Ramakrishna, looking stricken as I rubbed my knee and blinked back tears. "Are you injured? Do you require a practitioner of medicine—traditional, holistic, alternative, herbal—I know an excellent doctor of herbal—"

"She's fine," said my husband, patting me on the shoulder. "Aren't you, Carolyn?"

"I am begging to differ, sir, for one can see that your good lady has suffered—"

"—the consequences of pedestrian tailgating," Jason finished for him. My husband took my arm and assured me that my knee would feel better once I started using it, which was true. I was hardly limping at all when we got to the baggage claim area. Once there, Mr. Ramakrishna not only refused to give up our computer cases but also insisted on taking our baggage claim checks and dragging luggage off the moving belt at our direction. In his zeal, he also dragged three other bags off by mistake. In one such case, a woman in a purple fur and mauve faille shoes with chic, clunky heels snatched her bag away from Mr. Ramakrishna, threatening to call a police officer and demand a luggage-theft arrest. Our driver took this altercation with equanimity, although he murmured to us, once she had stalked away, that she was obviously suffering from the excess aggressiveness engendered by eating meat. Then he maneuvered our wheeled suitcases outside and left to retrieve his limousine while we thin-blooded desert dwellers shivered in a cold wind.

Once Mr. Ramakrishna returned and tried to heave my huge suitcase into the limousine trunk, I was again attacked by guilt. Jason had to assist in the transfer from sidewalk to vehicle, and our poor driver was panting when the feat was finally accomplished. However, this did not prevent him from ushering us into the plush interior of the passenger compartment and pointing out the refreshment bar. It was stocked, as he proudly informed us, with "a most refreshing and healthful Indian tea," a "delicious" mango and yogurt drink, and a tempting array of vegetarian canapés, all of which had been provided by his cousin's restaurant and catering service in the East Village. Then he handed us a business card for the restaurant, admonishing us to tell his cousin that Punji had sent us and we were to have the honored-client, 15 percent discount.

Was Mr. Ramakrishna Punji? I wondered, feeling a bit dazed by the time he had climbed into the driver's seat and sped abruptly into traffic.

Jason poured himself a cup of tea and sampled a tidbit that looked like a fragment of nan smeared with an unidentifiable orange-red paste. When Jason nodded approvingly and tried another of the offerings, I reached out for one myself. Mr. Ramakrishna, head poked through his open window, which was turning the limousine exceedingly chilly, screamed, "Bloody eater of sacred cows!" and swerved wildly to avoid a hotel van that had cut him off. Jason's tea slopped onto the canapé tray and scalded my hand, which I withdrew hastily. The only topical ointment available was the cold mango-yogurt drink, which I applied.

Having glanced into his rearview mirror, Mr. Ramakrishna nodded approvingly. "Very good for the skin," he enthused. "Not only most delicious on the tongue, but used by temple dancers to achieve skin of satin."

"Peachy," I mumbled. My hand was still stinging.

"Mango," he corrected. "Please be noting the aggressive nature of non-Hindu drivers and be assured that I, Punji, am at your service to protect you from all manner of bloody accidents. Also to recommend fine places for vegetarian consumption so that you, too, can become calm and healthy without blood-carrying vessels compacted with death-dealing and disgusting meat products."

Jason leaned into the corner, out of rearview mirror range, and rolled his eyes. I clapped my hand over my mouth to keep from giggling. "Vegetarianism has a long history in the United States," I said conversationally. "For instance, a vegetarian society met in New York City in the 1890s." I had been reading food history in preparation for our trip.

"Hindus are being vegetarians for many thousands of years," Punji replied, unimpressed by vegetarianism in our country.

"I believe the banquet included, among other things, bread with curry sauce."

"Curry sauce is being very tasty if properly concocted," said Mr. Ramakrishna, "but Western bread has texture to be avoided."

"Ah." Chastened, I munched on a healthful canapé, as Mr. Ramakrishna tore onto a busy highway, causing a wave of outraged honking, to which he responded by sticking his head out the window and shouting, "May the curse of vipers fall on your pig-breath heads!"

I sighed and wished that we had taken a cab. Or a bus. Or any vehicle not driven by this produce lover, who thought his diet precluded aggressive behavior.

Jason leaned forward and said, "When we get into the city, I'd like to be taken straight to Hodge, Brune & Byerson."

"You're going to leave me alone with him?" I whispered anxiously.

To my dismay, Mr. Ramakrishna proved to have very acute hearing. "Do not fear, Mrs. Jason Blue. I am not a danger to American ladies. I am a most respectable man of good but poor family in my native country. Most certainly no harm shall come to you in my vehicle." Then he cut across two lanes and scooted in between a large truck and a small Volkswagen painted Easter-egg lavender with white daisies on the door panel. The driver of the eighteen-wheeler blew his air horn while the driver of the daisymobile brandished his middle finger at Mr. Ramakrishna, who leaned out his open window and shook his fist, shouting, "Lizard-eyed eaters of smelly sheep!"

I wrapped my cashmere neck scarf over my ears, which were freezing in the rush of frigid, automotive-scented air. My husband calmly requested that the window be closed. I myself was not at all calm; in fact, I was considering a leap from the limousine. Had it not been exceeding the speed limit and surrounded by other vehicles, I might have tried. However, I imagined landing on the hood of a speeding car, in which case I would suffer a death of a thousand cuts as I was hurled through the front window into the lap of the driver. *Death of a thousand cuts?* I was beginning to sound like Mr. Ramakrishna.

Once the window was closed, Jason continued, "Before you take me to Hodge, Brune & Byerson, you can drop my wife off at the Park Central Hotel."

"My instructions, sir, are to deliver you both to your hotel, from which you will be picked up by Dr. and Mrs. Sean Xavier Ryan at 6:30 P.M. for a festive evening of dinner and opera, a noisy, Western performance with many loud singers."

"How lovely!" I exclaimed. "*Mefistofele* is playing tonight. We've never seen it, Jason."

Jason completely ignored the desirability of our proposed entertainment and frowned. "I promised the director of research and development that I would come straight to his office to confer on an urgent matter."

I hadn't heard anything about an urgent matter and turned to look inquiringly at Jason, who shrugged and said, rather evasively I thought, "It's about chemistry."

"There's a surprise," I murmured, wondering what was going on beyond the consultancy interview that was Jason's reason for this trip.

"Would the gentleman who is to meet you be Dr. Maximillian Frederick Heydemann?" asked our driver.

"Yes, and he's expecting—"

"I am most sorry to inform you, Dr. Jason Blue, that the unfortunate Dr. Maximillian Frederick Heydemann is no longer among the living."

Jason looked stunned. "You must be mistaken. I talked to him yesterday." I hadn't known that.

"Yes, he met his tragic end over a large sandwich piled high with a very fatty and odoriferous meat called pastrami. No doubt, the meat killed your friend Dr. Heydemann, as meat is being most frequently guilty of doing. You would be wise to insist that your hosts take you to a safe and healthy vegetarian restaurant this evening. By doing so, you will avoid early and calamitous death, both you, Dr. Jason Blue, and your good lady, Mrs. Jason Blue. My cousin's restaurant serves not only a healthy and delicious vegetarian menu, but also the vegetables are organically grown. No pesticides or unhealthy chemical fertilizers are used in the production of my cousin's vegetables."

"I've read some very interesting research," said my husband, "showing that a person eating vegetables and fruits ingests many more natural pesticides produced as a defense mechanism by the plant itself than any pesticides sprayed on by man. In the meantime, because effective pesticides are outlawed, malaria is flourishing and killing millions of people."

"Jason," I whispered, "I don't think Mr. Ramakrishna is interested in—"

"Malaria?" sharp-eared Mr. Ramakrishna interjected. "Many people in my native land are dying from malaria. Nonetheless, Mrs. Jason Blue, they have otherwise healthy bodies and nonaggressive characters because of their vegetarian diets."

"When did Dr. Heydemann's death occur?" asked Jason.

"Over his meal of pastrami," replied the driver. "This very day, I am hearing, he went, as was his custom, to a meat-eating establishment and ordered an inordinately large sandwich. Then, while consuming this unhealthy meal, Dr. Maximillian Frederick Heydemann fell over into the plate of the person beside him. It is a most horrifying tale, is it not? The person whose meal was contaminated by his meat-eating neighbor embraced the unfortunate Dr. Heydemann from the rear and punched him in the stomach. Then, it is said, he attempted to kiss Dr. Heydemann, perhaps to atone for having attacked him, but it was too late. Your friend was dead, as was soon discovered by men in a siren-bearing vehicle with stretchers and electric shockers. A most sad and bizarre tale, which I am sorry to tell you."

Jason was silent for the rest of the wild ride into the city. Mr. Ramakrishna, perhaps as a mark of respect for the dead, perhaps because his window was closed, no longer belabored other drivers for getting in his way. However, when provoked, he did murmur things like "Pig-breath worshipper of Allah" and "Devourer of rancid intestines."

I was left to consider his bizarre story. Did it represent a misinterpretation of events? Or were the strange happenings described to us symptomatic of widespread psychoses induced by the stress of life in large, overpopulated urban areas? I remember, as an undergraduate, reading an article about the deteriorating behavior of rats when too many are confined in too small a space. Whatever had happened, my husband's friend and mentor at Hodge, Brune & Byerson was dead.

Not an auspicious beginning to our visit. Nor did the situation improve.

2

All-You-Can-Eat Sushi and Shocking News

In case you haven't run into it, sushi is a sticky rice ball spiced with a line of wasabi (red-hot green paste) and wrapped with thinly sliced raw fish and sometimes seaweed. For the uninitiated, that sounds disgusting, but it isn't; it's delicious, and often quite expensive. Therefore, an all-you-can-eat sushi bar is a source of wonder and delight to those of us who live in the country's interior, away from sources of fresh fish.

With sushi, fresh is very important. After all, old fish smells bad, and the idea of eating old, raw fish is insupportable, which makes New York City a good place for sushi, because there's no dearth of supply; the Fulton Fish Market sells 90 million pounds of fish a year. The all-you-can-eat sushi chef can rush down to the market early in the morning and order, on a handshake, whatever he needs for the day.

But what if the fish doesn't show up? A chef at Versailles named Vatel is said to have thrown himself on his sword over an order of fish that failed to arrive for a banquet. Having lost face because he had no fish for his sushi customers, one might anticipate that a Japanese chef would commit ritual suicide with the family samurai sword. Right there in the restaurant. So steel yourself for possible violence, but don't miss the all-you-can-eat sushi in New York.

Carolyn Blue, "Have Fork, Will Travel," *Butte Miner's News*

Carolyn

Who is Dr. Sean Xavier Ryan?" I asked as I put the finishing touches on my coiffure. Since we would be going to the opera, I had created a French roll instead of staying with my customary, tied-back-with-a-scarf hairstyle. And I was wearing an evening dress, something I rarely get to do at home. Straight-line black silk with an embroidered jacket. Black is always a safe choice in New York and for two months a year in El Paso. The other ten run from pretty summery to hellishly hot, and only the young care to wear black when it's hot, so I have a full-length green silk for the other ten months. El Paso has only two opera performances a year.

I turned to inspect my husband, who looked very distinguished in his dark wool suit with his dark, silver-touched hair and close-clipped beard. Jason had been ready for ten minutes and was reading a journal article, from which he looked up when I inquired about our hosts for the evening.

"Ryan's an inorganicker. Particularly interested in heavy metals. Good chemist." He sighed, gathering from my overly patient expression that I expected something more personal. "Well, young. Actually, the fact that we're being entertained tonight by one of the junior researchers may be telling. If they were serious about making me an offer, they'd send along someone higher on the food chain."

Jason didn't seem particularly concerned, which was surprising, since he found this company so interesting. Hodge, Brune is less than twenty years old but very successful with its emphasis on environmental chemistry. They were looking at lots of intriguing toxins, according to Jason. On the other hand, my husband is, after all, an academic. He likes to do his own thing without being pushed to consider the potential for profit in his research.

"Well, whatever happens, we're being provided with first-class airline tickets and a hotel room, although it is rather small and plain." I looked around me and compared the room to the limousine. "Not to mention dinner and a night at the opera. Maybe they'll take us to one of these famous restaurants." I pointed to *Dining and the Opera in Manhattan,* which rested on the nightstand.

"I don't see Ryan as the fancy-restaurant-grand-opera type. I imagine Max got the opera tickets. He and his wife went regularly. Now, suddenly, he's dead." Jason shook his head, obviously baffled. "I'd put him in his early fifties, and he seemed to be in excellent health."

I stuck a few jet beads into my hair and studied the effect of black against blonde hair. Hair ornaments are such fun. "What do you think of this?" I inserted a fan of black and gray pearls attached at the ends of almost invisible wires. They projected several inches above the back of my head.

"You look like a flamenco dancer but without the ruffles," Jason replied.

Needless to say, I removed the pearl fan. However, I did leave the beads in. "You're feeling bad about Max Heydemann, aren't you?" I asked sympathetically.

"I liked and admired him," Jason replied. "And I'm not sure that I'm interested in Hodge, Brune now that he's gone, even if they do make an offer."

"Whatever you decide." I smiled and dropped a kiss on the top of Jason's head. He has such thick, springy hair.

When the telephone rang, Jason answered, then rose and collected our coats. "Don't you find the lobby here peculiar?" he asked as we headed for the elevators. I myself rather liked the lobby: very Art Nouveau with purple or green swoopy-backed velvet sofas and armless chairs with fringe, black and white diamond-tiled floors, and a lushly flowered beige and purple area rug.

Once there, we came upon a lively family argument. "Look, Patsy," Dr. Ryan said belligerently, "if I have to spend the evening at the fucking opera, I'm God damn well going to eat someplace I like." He was a short, wiry young man with a long Irish face and muted carrot hair.

I remember an excellent carrot mousse of that color at a French restaurant in Chicago. The occasion was the celebration of our tenth anniversary, which occurred during a visit to Jason's mother. I chose the restaurant; my mother-in-law complained about the new fetish for gourmet food among yuppies, which saddled working women with extra time in the kitchen. That was in the days before gen-Xers came along expecting to pick up their gourmet food at the local supermarket on the way home from the office.

Mrs. Ryan retorted, "The company's paying, Sean, so could we, for once, go someplace to eat that prides itself on quality rather than quantity?" She was a petite brunette, unfashionably curved, rosy-cheeked, and irritated. "And stop complaining about the opera. If you had a smidgen of sensitivity in your mean Irish soul, you'd be glad for me. I may never get to see another opera unless I divorce you. Maybe I *will* divorce you."

"Nonsense. What would you do with the kids?"

"Give you custody, move to New York, make a fortune at an ad agency—"

"—and languish all your days missing your sexy husband."

I could see that Jason was trying to think of a tactful way to break into this scene of marital discord, which was being played out between a man with feet planted pugnaciously on a flowery carpet and his wife, who had plopped herself down on a purple chair that towered about three feet over her head. To rescue Jason, I approached the wife. "It's so wonderful to meet a fellow opera lover," I said and extended my hand. "I'm Carolyn Blue. You must be Mrs. Ryan."

She bounced off the chair as if she were a cheerleader being tossed to the top of a pyramid. "Now see what you've done," she hissed at her husband, then smiling hospitably at me, "I'm Patsy Ryan. Welcome to New York. We're so pleased to be chosen to entertain you tonight."

Ryan shook hands with Jason, not a whit embarrassed to be caught complaining about opera within earshot of two opera lovers. "Don't pay any attention to my wife. She knows damn well we'd never have been here if it weren't that Max died this afternoon."

"We heard," said Jason grimly.

"Yeah. Well, can you believe that? Fucking New York! It's worse than Philly."

"Oh, surely not," said his wife sarcastically. "But it *is* awful about Max."

"Good a scientist as they come," said Ryan. "Better."

"I was certainly impressed," said Jason.

"Well, he was with you, too. Said you'd be invaluable if you'd come aboard. Some of the assholes in the group feel threatened by academics. Think professors read too many journals. So how do you feel about sushi?" He was hustling us toward the entrance and a cold, driving rain. We had seen snow over the Middle West. In fact, we made it out of O'Hare just before flights began to be canceled. Once in the New York area, there were patches of snow in New Jersey, but New York seemed to be clear. I hoped that it would continue that way.

"Sean!" wailed his wife at the mention of sushi. He ignored her.

"Love it," said Jason. "So does Carolyn." He introduced me to the irrepressible and foul-mouthed Dr. Ryan. Had I been his mother, I'd have washed his mouth out with soap years ago. But of course, he probably doesn't talk that way in front of his mother. My children don't.

"Great!" said Ryan and hailed a cab, ignoring the doorman and ushering Jason, Patsy, and me into the backseat so quickly that we didn't have time to put up umbrellas. Ryan took the seat beside the driver. Since Patsy looked mutinous, I suppose I could have intervened, but fair is fair. She was getting the opera. He was getting the sushi. Maybe they'd take that into consideration and stop squabbling. Not that they didn't seem to relish it.

"We're going to this great all-you-can-eat sushi place up near the Met," Ryan announced.

"I've never heard of all-you-can-eat sushi," said Jason. "It's a novel idea."

"Damn right. Everywhere else you pay through the nose for each piece or order some plate, the Hirohito Special or whatever, and half the stuff on it you don't like anyway. At this place only the *uni* costs extra, but hell, Hodge, Brune is paying, so we can eat all the *uni* we want. You like *uni*?"

Jason loves *uni*, which I call, to myself, swamp paste. We were going to reek of fish by the time we got to the opera, and there was always the danger of green wasabi splotches on clothing. On the other hand, I do love sushi, and an all-you-can-eat sushi restaurant should make an excellent subject in my embryonic second book. If I got to write it. Well, I wouldn't think about that. "Have you ever seen *Mefistofele*, Mrs. Ryan?" I asked.

"Oh please, call me Patsy. No, I haven't, but the cast is supposed to be wonderful. I used to work at an ad agency on Park Avenue, and we'd walk up to the Met and buy standing-room tickets after work."

"You're a writer?" I asked, assuming she'd been a copywriter at the agency.

"Artist. Freelance now. Imagine trying to keep up a home-studio career with little kids underfoot. Not that they're not adorable."

"How many children do you have, Patsy?" Jason and Sean Ryan were talking chemistry, of course.

She didn't get to answer because we arrived and had to dash through the rain into a long, narrow establishment with rosy lavender tables and black leather booths on two sides of the long sushi bar. Behind the bar, six sushi chefs, some of whom looked like Japanese bandits, patted, molded, and wrapped their lovely delicacies with deft grace and arranged them artistically on plates and wooden boards with piles of crispy, pink, pickled ginger. My mouth watered at the sights and smells as my eyes took in the clientele.

The place was mobbed with a crowd notable for its cultural diversity. Next to us a gray-haired, middle-aged Hispanic man with the expansive gestures and voice projection of an actor talked to a beautiful young woman. In the back was a table of broad-faced, brown-skinned natives of some Pacific island. A Caucasian couple in front of us at the sushi bar kissed and exchanged soulful glances while popping sushi into each other's mouths. Had you told me when I was a girl that I'd be eating raw fish, much less enjoying it, I would have gagged. Now I ordered enthusiastically: *ebi* (shrimp), *hamachi* (yellowtail), *sake* (salmon), *maguro* (tuna), and *unagi* (eel), not to mention an avocado-eel roll and a California roll, a bowl of miso soup, and a pitcher of hot sake. Jason and Sean Ryan were even more adventurous in their choices. They ordered things that I knew to taste fishy, plus *uni*, which tastes swampy. Patsy, looking pained and admitting that she could never remember what was what, said she'd have the same thing I was having.

"Why don't you have the same thing *I'm* having?" her husband asked combatively.

"Because you'll eat *anything*," she replied.

Our miso was served, rich and hot, perfect on a nasty winter night during what should have been spring. In El Paso, summer was blowing hot breath down the backs of our necks, and air conditioners were being turned on.

"It's cloudy," said Patsy, staring down at her soup. "It looks positively toxic, and the spoon is unusable. What kind of spoon shape is that?"

Before Jason could launch into discussion on possible toxins in miso soup (I'm sure he could find some; he says anything can kill you if you eat enough of it), I said, "It's perfectly acceptable to drink it from the bowl," and I demonstrated by doing so. The soup was followed by wooden boards with the sushi pieces, the wasabi, and the ginger, plus shallow porcelain dishes on which to rest the chopsticks and in which to mix the soy sauce with dabs of wasabi for dipping—very carefully. Too much wasabi will send an electric shock right up one's sinus passages.

"For heaven's sake," exclaimed Patsy. "How am I supposed to eat those?"

"Like this, babe." Sean, wielding his chopsticks with dexterity, dipped a rice ball with a pile of pasty orange *uni* on top into his soy sauce and popped it into his mouth. Jason did the same.

"If I try to eat with chopsticks, I'll end up with rice and fishy bits in my lap," Patsy wailed.

"I can't believe I married a woman who can't use chopsticks. Everyone knows how to—"

"Just pick it up with your fingers," I murmured and demonstrated with a piece of eel sushi, held daintily between thumb and forefinger. I dipped it in the soy sauce with just a brush past the wasabi, and ate it, as if I ate messy things with my fingers every day. I do love eel. It has the most wonderful rich, sweet sauce on it and crunchy little seeds. Patsy followed my example, even to the choice of eel. Then we both tried, inconspicuously, to get the sticky rice off our skin. I was regretting my own magnanimity in suggesting fingers to save her from chopstick humiliation.

"It is tasty," she admitted.

"You just ate eel," said her husband, looking smug. I suppose he didn't dare make fun of the finger wielding, since I had suggested it.

"I did not," his wife protested.

"Try the tuna next," I suggested, pointing to it. "You'll wonder why you ever liked your tuna canned."

"When is Max's funeral to be?" Jason asked. "I'd like to attend."

"Beats me." Sean was devouring *hamachi,* piece after piece, and answered with his mouth full. "I don't suppose Charlotte can make any plans until the police release his body."

"The police?" Jason and I spoke in shocked chorus.

"Sure. Since he was murdered, there has to be an autopsy."

My husband and I exchanged stunned glances. "Our driver didn't say Max was murdered," said Jason. "He seemed to think Max had died over a plate of pastrami."

"He did, but the pastrami didn't kill him. He was stabbed. They don't know what with, last I heard."

"It was probably some crazy street person," said Patsy. "I've seen very disreputable men hanging around the front of that deli."

"They're delivery boys," said Sean.

"No matter what the mayor says," she continued, "this is a dangerous city. Crazy people talking to themselves on the subway, the homeless attacking innocent pedestrians with bricks. Thank God we've moved to Connecticut where the children can grow up in a safe, sane environment."

"Oh, right!" said Sean. "Now they're out in the backyard eating dirt and getting lead poisoning."

"They're not eating dirt," his wife protested.

"There's a parkway two lots over, been there forever," Sean said to Jason. "Hundreds of thousands of cars speeding by every day for God knows how many years."

"It's walled off," snapped Patsy.

Jason was nodding over a bite of raw shrimp. "Unleaded gasoline."

"Bet your ass," said Sean. "More green space you got in an urban area, the more lead settled into the ground before lead-free gasoline. That's why New York has less lead poisoning than Philly. Philly has more green space."

"Well, I'm not paving over the backyard." Patsy had poked her unused chopstick into the wasabi. Before I could stop her, she raised the chopstick to her mouth and sampled the hot mustard paste, then emitted an agonized shriek. The roar of conversation stilled, and the rail-thin, black-garbed manager with his shaved head came rushing over.

Sean grinned at him. "White ghost female eat wasabi."

The manager glared at both of them and bustled away. He handled everything from greeting guests to reprimanding waiters, waitresses, and sushi chefs and running the cash register.

Jason ignored them all. "Max was murdered?"

"Looks like it. Fucking New York." Sean waved the waitress over to order more sushi.

Murdered? How terrible! And frightening! I hardly noticed the rest of the meal, or the hullabaloo when Sean, paying the bill in the crowded aisle by the cash register, turned and swept an order of sushi, board and all, onto the floor with his briefcase. After that we ran—not my favorite activity—in pouring rain to Lincoln Center, where the fountains were shrouded by tents, but the huge arched windows fronting the Chagall lobby murals beckoned to us. At the sight of those sparkling lights, the excitement of opera at the greatest house in the world overcame my gloom.

3

Mefistofele at the Met

Jason

I could see that my wife was appalled. How ironic that the company should send, as a substitute host, Sean Ryan, whose speech is, admittedly, somewhat "contemporary," although he is as promising a young scientist as I've met in recent years.

So there we sat, through an excellent sushi dinner and an opera performance that Ryan hated, while my wife winced every time he opened his mouth. Caro takes special offense at the use of the word *fuck*. It's fortunate that she doesn't have to spend much time among today's college students. I remember with amusement the occasion when our son Chris complained to me that his mother had reprimanded him for his language, which he, as a college student, felt was no longer a matter under her control.

Happily, my son is a logical person with a sense of humor. I responded, "Then you won't object if your mother, having come under your linguistic influence, says to you at Christmas break, 'Chris, get in there and clean up your fucking room.' " My son looked shocked, then laughed, and has never since offended his mother with unacceptable language. I doubt that strategy would influence Sean Ryan.

At any rate, in the Ryans' company Boito's *Mefistofele* is not a performance that I am likely to forget. Caro was enraptured with the Chilean soprano, whom neither of us had ever heard, and the bass and tenor were equally good. However, it was the staging and the audience, at least our small portion of the audience, which were so memorable.

Patsy Ryan, a woman who makes me appreciate my own wife even more than usual, took it upon herself to arrange our seat placement, ladies in the middle, Caro beside Ryan, me beside Patsy. Obviously, Ryan's wife did not want to sit next to him while he made audible comments such as: "Look at this sucker" (in reference to the back-of-seat subtitle screen, with which he experimented during the first ten minutes of the performance before he fell asleep) and "Why do they think heaven looks like a God damned opera house?"

Leaning forward to glare at him, his wife hissed back, "What do *you* think it looks like, Sean? A chemistry lab?"

Then in a peculiar scene onstage, during which Faust was seducing Margharita in a pseudo-apple orchard on a tilted grass platform, which was turned by an old woman with a hand crank, Ryan said to Carolyn, "I'll be damned. They're playing boccie." Carolyn replied, "Those are apples, not boccie balls. The apples are probably another facet of a symbolic Adam and Eve theme. Now please do hush up, Dr. Ryan."

An ancient gentleman behind her became quite animated during intermission in response to her remark on Adam and Eve and offered a long dissertation on the influence of various Christian sects on the Faust story. His companion, a handsome woman of middle age, who never took off her fur coat during the performance, interrupted him to say that it was just the same old story: libidinous men blaming illicit sex on women and making them pay the price. "Look at poor Margarhita!" she exclaimed. "She refused to run off with Faust and was hung."

"Her soul was saved," snapped the old gentleman.

"So was Faust's," said Carolyn acerbically, "and all he had to do was think up some pie-in-the-sky, benevolent monarchy scheme, to be presided over by himself."

"Exactly," agreed the lady in mink.

"I read the other day," Carolyn added, "that Jenny Lind refused to sing in operas because the heroines were so often impure."

"Lind would never amass a following today with that attitude," sniffed the befurred lady. "Unless it was with the Christian right."

"Maybe not, but around 1850, she was so popular in New York that people of all persuasions fell off the pier in their eagerness to greet her ship."

My dear wife, always the purveyor of some curious historical tidbit.

"I need to go to the ladies'," complained Patsy.

"Tough, babe," said Ryan, who had just returned from fortifying himself with a stiff drink. "They're hauling up the chandeliers."

One of the interesting innovations of the new Met at Lincoln Center is the elaborate and retractable chandeliers. I wonder how many people still think of it as the "new Met." My mother took me to what she calls "the real Met" when I was a boy, an unimpressive, yellow brick hulk close to a gaggle of pornography shops, from whose fascinating windows I was dragged away. That particular building replaced the Academy of Music, which did not have enough boxes to satisfy the demand in 1883 from new millionaires like the Rockefellers and Vanderbilts. Carolyn had apprised me of this information before the performance began; it was evidently part of her New York research. To Ryan this most recent seat of New York opera would undoubtedly be remembered as the "damn Met" after the night's experience.

At the next intermission, Carolyn allowed herself to be talked into accompanying Patsy Ryan to the ladies', and both returned incensed, partly because Ryan greeted them by saying, "That must have been the world's longest piss," but mostly because, in the face of formidable lines of women waiting for the facilities, there were evidently only four stalls available. I offered my sympathy, knowing from recent experience that "potty parity" is a sore topic with women.

Ryan's final and most amusing faux pas occurred during the Helen of Troy sequence when Faust offers Helen one red rose, they pledge their love, and then plan a bucolic future together. One has to wonder about Faust. Why would a scholar want to spend his life lounging in a meadow among sheep and agricultural types—even in the company of Helen of Troy? During the scene, Ryan, having been awakened by the snores of the elderly gentleman behind us, turned to Carolyn, and said, "That's not me doing the fucking snoring."

"Not this time," murmured Carolyn through gritted teeth.

I might have been more amused by the interplay had I not been so uneasy. Among her many conversational gambits, Patsy Ryan bemoaned Max Heydemann's "pastrami habit." "If he hadn't insisted on going off once a week to eat pastrami in that deli, he'd never have been murdered. Max was a creature of habit," Patsy assured me. "Every Monday at twelve-thirty he went out for pastrami. You couldn't get a meeting with him around lunchtime on pastrami day, isn't that right, Sean?"

Ryan shrugged. "He went there to think."

"How could anyone think in a place that crowded and noisy?" she demanded.

"He claimed he had his best scientific ideas with his mouth full of pastrami."

I hadn't known that about Max.

"He wouldn't even schedule a trip if it interfered with pastrami day," said Patsy. "He never took a vacation longer than six days. Charlotte told me so." Patsy sounded indignant on Charlotte's behalf. "I don't know how she stood it."

I could see my wife digesting this information. Perhaps she was wondering how angry a wife might be (angry enough to commit murder?) if all her vacations were limited to six days by her husband's love of pastrami and science. I could understand Max's devotion. Even we scientists are given to superstitions in the matter of idea generation. I know a photochemist who does his deep thinking in a particular pair of socks, which he does not allow his wife to launder. I myself find pistachio nuts conducive to scientific inspiration, although I've always meant to investigate the compounds in them for psychoactivity. Perhaps Max knew something about pastrami ingredients the rest of us don't. He was fond of saying, "It's all chemistry," as an explanation for just about anything that happened. As for his wife Charlotte, I've met her several times, and she never expressed any irritation with her husband about pastrami or anything else. They seemed quite devoted. I would need to mention that to Carolyn before her curiosity led her to investigate Charlotte Heydemann.

Whatever had happened to Max, I was sure that it was not a random street or, in this case, deli killing, and the news that Max's Monday visits to the deli of his choice were predictable did not change my mind. Of course, I hadn't mentioned my last conversation with Max to Carolyn. My poor wife was still recovering from traumatic events in New Orleans, about which she had spared me the details, although a policeman there did tell me about her many close calls. But Max had telephoned before we left El Paso. He said that a serious problem had developed at Hodge, Brune & Byerson about which he hoped to use my contacts and expertise, a problem that he did not want to discuss on the telephone. Now Max was dead, and I was left wondering what this problem had been and what relation it had to his murder.

No, this was not something I would mention to Carolyn. I had no wish to place my wife in danger, and I fear if she knew there was a mystery afoot, she might naively put herself in harm's way out of curiosity or indignation. Carolyn likes to think of herself as a sedate, retiring faculty wife, but in truth, time is bringing out a forceful side to her personality. Still, I did not want my wife mixed up in whatever was going on at Hodge, Brune. She has her own problems, namely the meetings with her editor and agent. That should keep her busy this week, that and culinary research and cultural activities. Carolyn loves museums almost as much as she does classical music and interesting historical data. How many women can name all the medieval kings and queens of England? In order?

4

Breakfast at a Crime Scene

Although smoked salmon is appreciated all over the country, more is consumed in New York City than anywhere in the world—possibly ten thousand
tons. If piled up, how many stories of salmon would that be? New Yorkers eat
lox, the salty, brine-cured and smoked variety of Eastern European ancestry,
with their bagels and cream cheese or, on a canapé, the more expensive,
lightly cured Nova caught in Canada and processed in Brooklyn. The rest of us
are probably buying our smoked salmon frozen.

A delicious and easy-to-make canapé for a cocktail party or predinner nibble requires only a loaf of dark Russian rye, smoked salmon, a half and half mixture of mayonnaise and Dijon or horseradish mustard, chopped red onion, and
capers. Cut the bread into finger-food sized pieces, top with salmon, dab with
mayonnaise/mustard, sprinkle with capers and onion, and serve on trays with
wine or cocktails.

Carolyn Blue, "Have Fork, Will Travel," *Macon Dixie Messenger*

Carolyn

Imagine liking to run so much that you'd do it in a strange city when the
temperature is below freezing. Yet that's just what my husband must have
done. With any luck, the exercise lifted his spirits, which had seemed low last
night when we returned to the hotel. Runners do something called "hitting
the wall." I take that to mean they eventually get so tired that they become
giddy. The giddiness is called "runner's high." I've experienced giddiness
from flights of fancy, but I can't imagine any outcome from running other
than exhaustion and injury and any reason to run other than flight.

I glanced at my watch as I combed my hair back and tied it with a scarf.
Jason was breakfasting with people from Hodge, Brune, and I had been
warned last night to expect lunch and a museum visit with someone named
Sophia Vasandrovich, the wife of a senior scientist. In the meantime, I could
consider my waistline and skip breakfast or . . . really, I shouldn't . . . give
in to curiosity and trot down the street to the deli where Max Heydemann
died. Patsy had mentioned that it was close to our hotel.

Hunger and curiosity won. I called my agent, whose name is Loretta
Blum, confirmed our ten-thirty appointment at her office, declined with regret her invitation to lunch, bundled up, and set off with Loretta's New

York accent echoing in my ears. "Just be sure you're free on Friday. We're eating with your editor, the big-time gourmet."

The deli, which was only a block away, didn't look that prepossessing, even if it did serve fabled pastrami, and I certainly wouldn't be having pastrami for breakfast. I almost turned away, but as I glanced down the long corridor beyond the front counters, I saw a plate of bagels, lox, and scrambled eggs. Lovely, almost translucent salmon beckoned to me from atop a rich, whipped mound of cream cheese. The sunny yellow of the scrambled eggs, still emitting steam, was too much to ignore. I let the door close behind me and entered the close warmth of the room.

On each side of a middle aisle, rows of tables were wedged together with chairs on either side. There was no privacy offered here. Diners would be elbow to elbow with strangers. However, the place was not crowded. I walked in quickly and claimed a place at the aisle end of a row, unwrapping my heavy woolen scarf and draping it over the chair, removing my coat, stuffing gloves in the pockets. Other customers were eating in their outerwear, even in this hot room, which is a strange custom of the natives that I had observed before. How can they expect to be warm when they venture back into the cold wind if they sit inside sweltering in their woolens? I draped my coat over the scarf-covered chair and sat down.

"Coffee?" asked a waitress. She was a square-shouldered woman with heavy breasts, overpermed blonde hair, and big black-framed glasses. I accepted the offer of coffee, ordered lox, bagels, cream cheese, and scrambled eggs without looking at the menu, and speculated as she walked away on whether she was wearing a girdle. No woman, even a young one, could have a bottom that flat coupled with such generous breasts unless she was wearing a girdle. I judged her to be in her thirties; she didn't have the delicacy of skin younger women have.

The waitress returned immediately to pour my coffee. "You from out of town?" she asked.

"Yes." Did I look like a tourist?

"How'd you hear about us?"

Now there was an embarrassing question. I'd feel like a ghoul admitting I'd come here because of the murder.

"Lemme guess? You read about the guy who died an' wanted to see where it happened?"

"Actually, the victim was a friend of my husband's," I said a bit defensively.

"Max was?" She looked surprised. "He was a regular here, you know. Came every Monday. Ordered the same thing. Sat right where you're sittin'."

"Here?" I was learning more than I wanted to know. "In this chair?"

"Yeah." She bustled off. I stared at a poster that demonstrated the Heimlich maneuver and wondered how many customers here had required it. Max hadn't, but possibly the fist in the stomach, as described by Punji, had been a fellow diner's attempt to administer it. Almost before I realized what I was doing, I glanced surreptitiously at the floor and the table, looking for bloodstains. How could I do such a distasteful thing? I don't stop to gawk at accidents or read the violent stories first in the newspaper.

A platter appeared before me, but now I wondered if I would be able to eat.

"He keeled over sideways," said the waitress, sounding chatty, as if she were gossiping with a neighbor. "Face first into the lox an' cream cheese plate next to him. Shook up the guy who ordered it. I can tell you that." She laughed, a sort of good-natured bray. "That sort of thing's no good for business. Likely to cut my tips. An' now my ma's scared an' wants me to quit an' move back to Jersey with her."

"I can understand that she'd be worried," I said.

"Well, it's not like people don't get offed in Jersey, too. Ma's got MS. She thinks someone's gonna break in an' tip over her wheelchair. Like anyone would think she's got anything worth stealin'."

"I'm sorry to hear about your mother's condition." Wouldn't that be terrible? To be confined to a wheelchair, anticipating attacks from criminals?

"Oh, she does pretty good. Runs this apartment house. Gets her own place free. Tenants go to her apartment to pay their rent. They don't pay, my cousin comes over an' hassles 'em. He's connected, so he don' take no shit from deadbeat tenants."

Connected? Did the waitress mean that her cousin was a Mob person?

"An' he knows all the union guys, so Ma don' have no trouble gettin' repairs done when the place needs 'em. Works out real good for her. Aren't you gonna eat your lox?"

"Oh. Oh, yes." I cut myself a bite: bagel, lox, and cream cheese. It was wonderful.

"Good, huh? You oughta come back for lunch or dinner. Try the pastrami. Your husband's friend, who got snuffed, he always came for the pastrami. Never left a scrap. My ma would have liked that. She can't stand people to waste food. Poor guy died before he finished his last sandwich. Damn shame."

"Did you see what happened?" I asked, forking up some of the eggs and enjoying them immensely.

"Well, I saw him keel over. I was headin' that way when the guy with the lox plate jumped up and tried to Heimlich him. Course, no one knew then that he wasn't chokin'. Though you'd think the guy next to him woulda noticed he wasn' coughin' or nothin'. Then some other guy hauls off the lox guy an' lays Max out on the floor. 'This man's not breathin',' he says an' starts blowin' in his mouth an' poundin' on his chest. Puff, push, push, push, or whatever. You want some more coffee?"

"Yes, please." After her graphic description, I needed it. I felt as if a bite of bagel might get stuck in *my* throat before she could pour again into my cup.

"So then the boss comes back from the cash register an' says to the guy givin' artificial respiration, 'What the hell did you do to him?' an' the artificial respiration guy, who turns out to be a doctor—kind who does nose jobs, but still that's a doctor, right?—He gets huffy an' says he's tryin' to save a life here an' don' bother him. An' the boss says, 'Man's bleedin' onna floor.' "

"Dr. Heydemann was bleeding, and no one noticed it until then?" I asked.

"Max was a doctor, too?"

"Research scientist," I replied.

"Well, he wasn' bleedin' a whole lot, but by then it was seepin' out from under him."

She pointed to the aisle floor with her shoe, a sensible shoe, I might add. Why would a woman wearing a girdle be able to overcome vanity to the point of wearing sensible shoes? Maybe the girdle supported her back, while the shoes supported her arches. Waitressing must, after all, be a physically taxing job.

"So the boss calls EMS," she continued, "but the guy, your husband's friend, is dead by then. For all I know, the Good Samaritans killed him."

"But I thought he was stabbed."

"You'd have to ask the cops. They didn' tell us. Ask a hunnerd questions, don' answer none."

"And no one saw who killed him?"

"Place was mobbed. It was lunchtime." The waitress strode off to wait on an elderly man who had taken a seat across the aisle and two rows back from me. I was left to wonder how a man could be murdered in a crowded restaurant and no one see the murderer. I pondered that conundrum as I continued to eat my lox and cream cheese, which were so-o delicious. I suppose lox is carcinogenic. I believe all cured meat has nitrates, which turn into nitrites, which cause cancer, or the other way around. Jason would know. For that matter, and because of my husband's research interests, I know more about such things than anyone who likes to eat would want to know. Wasn't pastrami a cured meat, too? Maybe Dr. Heydemann had cancer as a result of eating pastrami, and a minor hemorrhage had killed him when well-meaning fellow diners administered fatal, life-saving measures. Wouldn't that be ironic?

"Actually," said my waitress, returning to scoop up my empty plate, "this is probably the safest place in town. What are the odds of another murder happenin' here in our lifetimes?"

"What indeed?" I replied and handed her my credit card.

"Pay up front," she instructed, "an' we don't take credit cards, so you'll wanna leave the tip in cash before you head up to the register."

5

Blue Mountain Coffee and Arsenic

Jason

My first interview of the morning was with Frances Striff. Instead of taking me out to breakfast, she provided Blue Mountain Coffee and Viennese pastries in her office. While I breakfasted with good appetite, as a result of my run, Dr. Striff had tea and dry toast. I couldn't see that she needed to diet, so she may have preferred Spartan fare. Her personal appearance was certainly Spartan: a brown pants suit that hung off her gaunt frame, no makeup, blunt-cut hair, and lace-up shoes that would have done her great-grandmother credit. Of course, I have seen my own fashion-conscious daughter in footwear that is equally grim, but hers, she once assured me, was stylish. I doubted that Frances Striff worried about fashion. I made a mental note of these things because Carolyn likes to hear about my day but becomes discouraged if I can only tell her what scientific topics were discussed.

"I guess you've heard about Max Heydemann," Striff said, setting her teacup into its saucer with an angry clink. "You can bet that whoever takes his place won't even try to hire another woman. Max did try, but I'm the only one who could stick it out. Probably because I look like one of the boys and mind my own business."

"Maybe you should consider academia," I suggested, at a loss as to how to respond to her description of herself. "Women are doing very well at a number of universities."

"When I hear of one that offers lucrative stock options and a generous retirement plan, I'll consider it. In the meantime, I've sacrificed two marriages to this company, so now I'm avoiding legal commitments, making a bundle here, and piling up retirement money. Maybe I'll get out early and take an adjunct professorship somewhere so I can do whatever I want in the lab and travel when I feel like it. Isn't that why you're considering us? The money?"

Frances Striff's personality was as blunt as her haircut. "Actually, I'm interested in the toxin research," I replied.

"Well, I wish I could tell you about mine, but as of five last night, we can't say anything about anything related to Hodge, Brune to anyone, even you. But please don't take that as evidence that we're not interested in hiring you. After Max's recommendation, upper management is salivating at the prospect.

"Except for the unlovable Vernon Merrivale, former scientist, present security fanatic for R and D. The man's paranoid, and I've heard him say that academics are notoriously loose-lipped about their research. He thinks that about women, too. The man's always skulking around my labs asking questions." She took a bite of her dry toast, which she had popped out of an ancient toaster on her desk after pushing the pastry plate in my direction. "So-o-o. I can't talk to you, but—"

"Am I to take it that this new wall of silence is related to Max's death?" I asked.

"Oh, no. The police think some street crazy knifed him. Merrivale is just using Max's death as an excuse for more security measures. We already have to be debriefed after outside conferences to be sure no one asked us nosy questions or got into our briefcases where we'd stashed secret papers that shouldn't have left the company. It's worse than having a high security clearance with the government."

I was, at this point, beginning to wonder if I really wanted to consult on any regular basis with Hodge, Brune. Free discussion among colleagues is not only one of the joys of science but also an impetus to new ideas—a sort of intellectual cross-pollination. But even if I didn't take this position, I felt I owed it to Max to find out what had been worrying him and see if I could do something about it. "Did Max say anything about a problem before he died?"

"What problem?"

"I don't know. He . . ." Since Max hadn't even been willing to talk about the matter on the telephone, I felt bound to keep his confidence by being at the least circumloquacious. "He seemed . . . worried . . . that last time we talked."

"Did he? Well . . ." She considered the topic. "At the Thursday meeting he was acting strangely. He'd stare at each of us as we talked and then ask odd questions. It was almost as if he thought people were fudging their results. It made me nervous, I can tell you, and I've never falsified data in my life. Made us all uneasy. Calvin Pharr got testy and actually took a belt from his flask at the meeting. Usually he's more discreet, by which I mean he only drinks in his office," she added dryly.

I must admit I found the idea of a scientist drinking on the job highly unusual. That would certainly be a problem to a research director, although I couldn't see how my "connections and expertise" would be of any use in this situation. Dealing with alcoholism would seem to be a medical problem and quite outside my experience.

". . . Vasandrovich was frowning, and poor Fergus McRoy started babbling when he was put under the gun," Striff continued, "but that's typical Fergus. The man's a good scientist, but he's a first-class worrier. What was so unusual was Max's attitude. I've never seen him act like that before, suspicious and nitpicking. Did he tell you—"

"It was just a feeling," I replied quickly. Given the extreme secretiveness now imposed on the scientists here, I might never find out what Max had wanted my help on.

"So do you want to tell me about *your* research?" Frances Striff asked. "Merrivale can't object to that."

What scientist doesn't want to talk about his work? "I've got three students doing an interesting arsenic pollution problem."

"Really?" She leaned forward to listen, dropping the remains of her toast into a wastebasket. For the next thirty minutes I told her about ground and water pollution by arsenic, the result of smelter operations in the past, and what we hoped to do about it. When I finished and had answered a number of intelligent and provocative questions, she pulled a telephone forward and punched in a number, saying, "You've got to talk to Calvin Pharr. He'll love this. He and Sean Ryan do heavy metals. Calvin, Frances Striff here." In minutes she had changed my schedule and was leading me to another office, saying before she departed, "I'm your host tonight. What do you want to eat?"

"Something unusual," I suggested vaguely. "My wife is a culinary writer; she—"

"I know just the place. Patria. Nuevo South American. My partner and I love it. Might as well let the company pay for a return visit. Your wife won't faint if I bring a lover along, will she?"

"No, of course not." I must admit that I wondered whether the lover was male or female, and what Carolyn would think if it were a woman. Even so, Patria sounded familiar to me. Carolyn must have mentioned it when she was looking at the Zagat guide to New York restaurants. She'd be pleased.

"Arsenic?" Calvin Pharr was saying. He was a fat man with a square, bald head. "I've got just the problem I want to talk to you about." He reached into his drawer and pulled out a flask, then thought better of the impulse and replaced it, saying, "I just remembered I can't talk to you about anything scientific. Hell! Listen, I hope you sign on so we can have a two-way conversation. Max would kill Merrivale—that's the prick in charge of security—if he knew what was going on now."

Max and this Merrivale, whom I had never met, hadn't gotten along? Did that have anything to do with Max's death or the problem he wanted to discuss with me? I shook off that thought as bizarre. "Maybe you'd like to hear what we're doing in El Paso."

"Absolutely. I purely love heavy-metal pollution. New Jersey is a gold mine, which I could probably get fired for saying, even if everyone in the country knows it."

I had another fruitful conversation with Pharr, although he evidently forgot about his previous discretion and took swallows from his flask at twenty-minute intervals while we talked. When we had finished discussing arsenic, I asked him, as I had Frances Striff, whether he knew of any problem that had been bothering Max Heydemann.

"What? You mean like a premonition of his own death?" he asked dryly, then thought better of his response. "Sorry. That was a serious question, wasn't it? Which makes me wonder why you asked and what you know that I don't. Well." He took another hit of brandy.

Given that it was not yet noon, I had to surmise that Pharr, no matter how brilliant on heavy-metal chemistry, really was an alcoholic.

"I heard him yelling at someone in his office. That was unusual for him. Max wasn't the noisy type. He could cut you up into little pieces and spit you out with words, and he did to a few us, but I can't remember him yelling at anyone."

Us? Max had attacked Pharr verbally? About his drinking? Or about something else? "Who was he shouting at?" I asked.

"Dunno. I was on my way out to a long, liquid lunch and didn't stop to listen."

"When was it?"

"Friday? I think so. It must have been Friday."

The day before Max called me. How could I find out at whom he had been angry? "What was the fuss about?"

"Dunno. Why are you asking?"

"I liked him."

Pharr received a phone call and said he had to head for his lab. Before he left, he called someone named Morrie to come and get me. Pharr had hardly left when a man with thinning hair and a rumpled suit appeared in the doorway and asked, "Dr. Pharr?"

I introduced myself after saying that Pharr was out.

"OK, you'll do," said the man and took the second visitors' chair, from which he stared at me wearily. "You know any reason anybody'd have to kill Dr. Heydemann?"

I shook my head, because I really didn't know anything concrete about the matter.

"How about his wife? Did they get along?"

"May I ask who you are?"

He scratched his ear. "Sorry. Worski. Detective." He pulled a shield from his pocket. "The wife?"

"I've only met her twice, but they seemed to have an amiable relationship."

"Kids? Did he have problem kids?"

"I don't know if he had children."

"How long you been with the company, anyway?" he asked, looking irritated, as if I were withholding vital information.

"I'm not with the company. I'm being interviewed for a consulting position."

"Well, shit."

"How exactly did he die?"

"His heart was punctured by a long, narrow, pointed instrument. Like an ice pick, only longer. Perfectly placed."

"Does that sound like the work of a crazed street person?" I asked doubtfully.

"Maybe. Could have been a pro. Who the hell knows? An' what do you care if you hardly knew him?"

"I liked and respected him." I considered telling this policeman my concern and decided that I should. "And before Dr. Heydemann died, he called me and asked for my help on some serious problem."

"What problem?"

"He didn't say. He seemed to think his phone was tapped, or someone was listening. At least that's what I assumed, bizarre as that sounds, because he said he didn't feel that he could discuss it on the phone."

"Well, these people are worse than doctors claimin' doctor-patient privilege when it comes to discussin' what the company does. No big surprise to hear he was paranoid. Makes you wonder what they *are* doin'. Makin' illegal drugs or something? You know anything about illegal drugs?" He gave me a narrow, suspicious look.

"The company has made its name in research on environmental toxins."

"Yeah, but how do they make their *money?*"

"I would have assumed the same way," I replied.

"Well, I'm not assumin' anything, an' no one is tellin' me anything. Christ. Guy got stabbed in a crowded restaurant over a pile of pastrami, an' no one saw a thing. No one around here knows a thing. No one at his house knows a thing. His wife's sedated. We can't even talk to her."

Detective Worski rose, handed me his card, and told me to call him if I discovered what the victim's problem had been. I agreed.

6

Green Tea on Commission

Carolyn

When Jason and I travel, we each carry hundred-dollar bills and travelers' checks. The occasion of buying New York's fifteen-dollar subway and bus pass seemed a likely opportunity to use one of my hundreds. Therefore, I stealthily slipped the bill from my handbag as I stood in line. When I slid the money into the opening, the tall African-American in his bullet-proof glass enclosure said, "WE DON'T TAKE HUNDREDS, LADY," his voice booming over the loudspeaker system. I gulped, feeling all eyes turn in my direction as I stuffed the bill into my purse and fumbled for a twenty. That bill he accepted, I received my pass, and then he counted out my change: "SIXTEEN, SEVENTEEN, EIGHTEEN . . ." As I hastily thrust the five one-dollar bills into my handbag, I imagined that every purse-snatcher in the city had been listening and was now heading in my direction, bent on violent robbery.

Only the subway car ad for 1-800-DIVORCE took my mind off my fears as I rode, white-knuckled, toward Loretta Blum's office. Under the telephone number the ad said, "Finally an affordable lawyer. We take Visa, MC, and Diner's Club." I remembered someone telling me that holders of Diner's Club cards experience the highest percentage of divorces. Perhaps that credit card company offers a special, low interest rate for the maritally challenged.

Do you picture people before you meet them? I had pictured my agent rather vividly: an older woman, slim and chic, gray-streaked hair, charming. In person, Loretta Blum was younger than I, sported a wide circle of dense, jet-black curls, and was screaming at someone named Simon on the phone when I was ushered into her office by a young woman with a pierced eyebrow.

"What the hell are you thinking of, Simon? You keep her away from the damned computer, you hear me?" She waved me to a seat. Evidently Simon's answer was not satisfactory because she threatened, if he didn't get Rachel under control, to provide him with a second and more radical bris. Was Rachel an author? I wondered. And why didn't Loretta Blum want her near the computer? Perhaps Simon was someone from the agency sent to monitor the activities of the troublesome Rachel.

"She puked on the keyboard?" shrieked Loretta. "Put Ellie on. I want that computer cleaned up and locked up immediately, and, Simon, don't you dare put any disks in the drive, you hear me? No disks! The last thing I need is some damn virus or crash."

Ah, Rachel was drunk and endangering the work stored on the computer. Perhaps Simon was a husband, lover, or son, who was prone to introducing disks into Rachel's computer, disks that had not been scanned for viruses and caused disastrous hard-drive crashes that deleted whole novels. Jason won't let the children use his laptop for just that reason. However, they have their own computers; whereas, I was never allowed to use my father's typewriter, and he did not provide me with one of my own until I was a college student. Ah well, old resentments do persist in one's psyche.

My agent, as yet unintroduced, slammed down the telephone. "Kids!" she snarled. "I should have drowned them at birth." I must have looked confused because she shrugged. "I got two on vacation, one with the flu, and my mother-in-law won't come over to watch them. She says they don't treat her with respect. Hell, I'm happy as long as they don't burn the house down."

"I'm Carolyn Blue," I said, trying not to think about her threat to provide Simon, evidently her son, with a second circumcision. Would my agent be considered a "castrating mother"? Would her mothering techniques produce a serial killer? Men are extremely testy about their genitalia (pun intended).

"Right," said Loretta. "*Eating Out in the Big Easy*. Have some green tea." She poured a singularly vile liquid into a dainty china cup and pushed it toward me. "How's the book coming?"

"Well, actually—"

"Don't tell me you've got problems, writer's block or some damn thing. I don't want to hear that. You've got the advance. Now you write the book."

"Unfortunately, I had a very stressful, even dangerous week in New Orleans. I'm finding it extremely difficult to write about—"

"So get over it, whatever happened. And I don't want to hear about it. You think you know hard times? My mother was born in a concentration camp. My Uncle Bernie got her into this country. Only one to survive in the German part of the family. Now *that's* something to be upset about. That's hard times. She named me Loretta because someone told her she looked like Loretta Young. That was some movie star from way back when. My poor mother, she thought looking like a movie star when you got numbers tattooed on your arm was pretty neat, so she named me Loretta. You can bet I didn't name any of my kids after movie stars. Maybe I should have." Having established her superiority in the recognition of genuine hard times, she slapped her hands down on her desk and stared into my eyes.

"So you'll write the book. You've been paid; you write the book. You're a professional now. Stress?" She snapped her fingers. "We all got stress. Get over it.

"Now, we're meeting the editor for lunch this week, and he'll want to hear all about it: the recipes, the restaurants, all that gourmet stuff. Believe me, Rollie won't give a rat's ass about your personal problems. All he cares about is food, and books about food, and people who want to talk or read about food. So when we go out to lunch with Rollie, you tell him about all the great stuff you ate in New Orleans. I wouldn't give you two beans for that town myself, but Rollie likes it.

"And let him do the ordering. I don't have to let him order for me, but I'm Jewish, thank God. You're not, right? If you are, don't tell him. He's got nothing against Jews except we don't eat stuff gourmets love. He orders you pig liver or some disgusting thing, you love it. Got that? And don't order a cocktail. He thinks cocktails ruin the *palate*. The man's a pain in the ass, but that's OK. You drink wine with whatever he gets you to eat. Let him pick the wine. He'll love you."

"About the New Orleans book," I persisted when she stopped to take a breath. "Perhaps I could replace it with one called *Eating Ethnic in the Big Apple.*"

Loretta Blum actually gave my suggestion two or three seconds of thought before she resumed her monologue. "Good idea."

I felt a welling of relief.

"Tell Rollie about it. Run it by him. First, *Eating Out in the Big Easy.* Then, *Eating Ethnic in the Big Apple.* Catchy. You got good instincts. I bet he'll go for it. You got a synopsis with you?"

"No, and I meant to substitute it for—"

"Forget that. The contract says New Orleans, but it can't hurt to negotiate for a second book. Maybe they'll give the first one some publicity if they've got another one in the pipeline.

"Now, about stirring up some interest in the book and in you. After all, no one knows you from Jane Doe. We need to get your name around, so I had a great idea. I wangled you an appointment tomorrow with a guy named Marshall Smead, works for a syndication company. You already had some columns on food published in newspapers, right? That's how I found you. No reason you shouldn't do that regularly, make a little money, get your name spread around. It's not big bucks, unless you get real well known. I wouldn't even handle that—syndicated columns. It would be a deal between you and the syndication company, if you can swing it." She began to stir through the litter of papers on her desk. "Address. Where did I put that address?"

When her phone rang, she picked up and snarled, "I'm talking to someone in here, Marsha. What are you doing out there? Getting your brain pierced to go with your belly button? I said no calls." She listened briefly, then said, "Put him on. I'm gonna kill him. . . . Simon, why are you still bothering me at work? . . . So Ellie's throwing up, too? What do you expect from me? I'm here. You're there. Call your father. See how he likes it. . . . OK, put Ellie on. . . . Ellie, I forbid you to throw up anywhere but in the toilet. You got that? In the toilet . . . Don't tell me you're sick. You're not. You're throwing up because your sister did." She hung up, retrieved an address written on the back of a business card, read the printed front, and muttered, "Who the hell is that?" Then, thrusting the card at me, she said, "Tomorrow at ten. Think you can find the address? Take a cab. Then you won't have to worry."

I stared down at the scrawl on the back of the business card of someone she didn't remember. Marshall Smead. His office was on the twenty-first floor of some building that I took to be farther downtown. The idea of writing a regular food column sounded appealing. What would I call it? "Eating Out with Carolyn?" "Other People's Cooking?" That was the only kind I really like these days. "Have Fork, Will Travel?" I felt an overwhelming desire to laugh but doubted that my bossy agent would be amused.

In fact, I didn't get the chance, because she was off on a new subject. "Now, about your clothes."

I glanced down at my tailored, blue wool dress. It looked perfectly appropriate to me. Not as flashy or as expensive as her red and black suit, which would have been stunning had she been built less like a cement block.

"You need something with more flair. You know what I mean? Something that says *designer rags*."

"I really don't think my advance will cover *designer rags*," I said dryly.

Loretta Blum snorted with laughter. "You never heard of buying wholesale? You know who to go to, you can dress sharp without touching the inheritance from your grandmother or whatever. So you'll go to see my uncle, Bernie Feingold. He's in the rag trade. I'll call and tell him you're coming; he'll take care of you." She ripped from a pad a note page that was engraved with her name and wrote down another address. "Don't put it off. Better you go before your appointment with Smead.

"Absolutely turn up looking like you been in the big city more than once in your life when we have lunch with Roland DuPlessis. After food and wine, he notices clothes. You'll see when you meet him. Fat as a pregnant cow and dressed like some fag artist type. You never know what he'll turn up wearing, so don't stare. Wouldn't hurt to say something nice about his outfit if you can do it with a straight face."

She stood up. "So that's it. Go get a few outfits from Bernie, then go home and think about a sales pitch for Smead tomorrow at ten. Tell yourself, it's not just a little extra money; it's free publicity. You're gonna get paid for having your name in the paper. You can even plug your own book when it comes out. Pure gold. One of my best ideas. I'm counting on you to follow through. OK?"

Numbly, I agreed, put down my teacup with its disgusting brew virtually untouched, and allowed myself to be sent away. Loretta Blum was overwhelming, to say the least. With any luck, I'd never have to meet her again in person after the lunch with the food editor. She did seem to have the success of my career at heart—if she had a heart. She certainly didn't want to hear my problems. Or even the problems of her children. I hoped my next appointment, lunch and a museum visit with some scientist's wife, proved to be more pleasant. I wouldn't be visiting Uncle Bernie today, no matter what my agent advised. Mrs. Vasandrovich this afternoon and Mr. Smead tomorrow would just have to put up with me in my country cousin clothes.

7

The Caesar Chicken Burrito as an Objet d'Art

I love museum restaurants. The food is usually acceptable and often very good, but best of all, a museum restaurant allows one to sit down on something other than a bench. Walking in one of those revered temples of art is worse than an uphill climb on a rocky path. The slow pace and the marble floors result in aches, pains, and exhaustion. Therefore, falling into a chair in the restaurant is pure luxury, delicious relief. One does not have to rise and move on after three minutes in order to make way for other weary art lovers or to prove that one is an art lover oneself.

I had my first bruschetta in the balcony café at the History of Women in the Arts Museum in D.C. The bruschetta was wonderful, and the interior views of the elaborate old house that hosts the collection, lovely. One day at MoMA, the Museum of Modern Art in New York, I sat down in their austere black, gray, and silver café with its fascinating modern chandeliers. From my chair I could gaze out huge windows at the sculpture garden while I feasted on thick, nicely herbed tomato soup and finished with a delicious chocolate tart. In the garden, snow was falling on the ground, on the black metal sculptures, and on the black and white birches. It was as beautiful a scene as any museum-quality painting.

Carolyn Blue, "Have Fork, Will Travel," *Spokane News-Ledger*

Carolyn

I arrived at Hodge, Brune, half frozen. A cold wind whistled off the water surrounding the island and howled through the stone canyons of the city, crystallizing my blood. (Although I meant that metaphorically, Jason once told me about research involving fish that live under the arctic ice. They have ice crystals in their blood. Isn't that a strange thing?) Jason, unfortunately, was nowhere in sight at Hodge, Brune, and according to a secretary, the husband of my hostess, Dr. Vaclav Vasandrovich, was now occupying the office of the late R and D director, Max Heydemann.

Having profited from a colleague's death, was the new director considered a suspect by the police? I wondered. Probably not. I have heard of some very unpleasant scientific quarrels but no murders motivated by chemistry.

The secretary advised me to wait in the R and D office, where the visitors' chairs were more numerous and comfortable. I dutifully shuffled off on icy feet and approached a second secretary, who looked decidedly tearful. She was obviously another of the late director's many admirers. After telling her that I was here to meet Mrs. Vasandrovich, I took a seat beside a grammatically impaired man wearing an olive green topcoat.

"I ain't got all day," he said to the secretary.

"Dr. Vasandrovich is still on the telephone," she replied.

That was obvious. I could hear him through the door, shouting in a foreign language. Russian, I think. When I was an undergraduate, my roommate took Russian and frequently begged me to quiz her on vocabulary lists.

The man in the olive topcoat, which looked like army surplus to me, or possibly some trendy new style, muttered angrily to himself. "It's obviously a long distance call," I said by way of consolation. "It must cost a fortune to call Russia."

"Russia, my ass." He eyed me with disfavor. "Vasandrovich is probably callin' his bookie in Coney Island. Or he jus' don' wanna talk to the police."

Upon discovering that I shared the sofa with a policeman, I introduced myself and asked if he was investigating the death of Dr. Heydemann.

"I'm Worski," he said. "Did you know Heydemann?"

"No, but my husband did. In fact, he came here to be interviewed by Dr. Heydemann for a position and was exceedingly upset to hear of his death, which I gather was not only tragic but bizarre." Detective Worski did not find any death in New York City bizarre. He had seen it all, or so he said. "But how did a street person manage to get into the restaurant, much less stab someone without being noticed?" I asked.

"Who says it was a street person?" retorted the detective. "Your random murder—that's not the usual way of it, lady. This Heydemann, the killer got him with something like an ice pick, only longer an' thinner, an' he knew just where to put it. Does that sound like some homeless schizoid? No way. But try to get these people to talk to you about why he might have been killed. You'd think they was sellin' plutonium on the black market the way they clam up about company business. Worse today than yesterday."

I stared at Detective Worski, aghast. "Do you think someone *here* killed him?"

"Naw. More like they hired it done."

"A professional assassination?" And my husband wanted to work for this company? "Dr. Heydemann did go to that particular restaurant every Monday," I confided. "If someone wanted to find him in a public place, that would be an obvious choice, although it seems peculiar to me. Wouldn't a site less public be preferable?"

Worski shrugged. "Hit men got their own fetishes. Anyway, thanks for the tip, Mrs. Blue. That's more than anyone else bothered to tell me."

We both turned when the office door opened and a distinguished man with thick silver hair, dark skin, and startlingly blue eyes waved the detective into his office, apologizing in an offhand manner for the delay.

"Yeah," said Worski, rising with effort from the soft cushions of the sofa. "This lady says you was talkin' Russian in there."

The man, presumably Dr. Vasandrovich, asked, "You speak Russian, madam?"

"Not really," I replied, embarrassed, and introduced myself.

"Ah. Jason Blue's wife. And my own dear Sophia is late for your afternoon together. I must scold her for her tardiness, and you, dear lady, for mistaking the language. I was speaking Czech, to my Aunt Elizabeta, as a matter of fact. Still, perhaps it is a natural mistake, for my name must sound Russian to you, whereas I am actually Polish and Czech. A graduate of Charles University. You may have heard of it."

"Of course," I replied. "Founded in 1350 in Prague by a Holy Roman Emperor."

He gave a slight bow. "I am gratified by your knowledge of my country's history. Well, Sophia, finally you are here. This is Mrs. Blue. Your absence has kept not only Mrs. Blue but the very impatient Detective Worski waiting."

Maybe I should have visited Loretta Blum's Uncle Bernie after all. Compared to this very sophisticated, very tall lady, I did indeed feel like a country cousin. Mrs. Vasandrovich swept me away, ignoring her husband's reprimand, courtly though it had been. She declared it a shame that my appointment had kept us from eating somewhere more chic than the museum restaurant, which was now our only option in the short time left. Obviously, we had to see the *Picasso in Clay* exhibit, to which she would be so pleased to introduce me, Picasso being a special favorite of hers, as he was with most art connoisseurs, etc., etc., etc.

I found myself rather irritated to be blamed for Mrs. Vasandrovich's missing an elaborate lunch when she was the one who was late. My hostess and I ended up in the cafeteria line at the Metropolitan Museum of Art because there were no tables available in the restaurant. Mrs. Vasandrovich was unhappy with the choices. I spotted a Caesar salad with chicken on French bread and reached for it, only to have a burrito-like packet wrapped in plastic shoved in front of my choice by a stout cafeteria employee wearing a hair net.

I sighed and took the burrito, along with a small bottle of white wine and a $2.75 cookie. The cookie was delicious, but at that price it should have been. The burrito was filled with chicken bits and an approximation of Caesar salad, but the dressing—well, in my cooking days, I had done much better and still could in a pinch. The wine was a disaster. Mrs. Vasandrovich, who invited me to call her Sophia, toyed with her lunch and discussed the tragedy of Max Heydemann's untimely death, the violence of life in the United States, and the qualifications of her own husband for the position that he now filled on an interim basis. She assured me that her husband would give mine every consideration in his search for employment with Hodge, Brune, particularly because Max had thought so highly of him. "Max was Vaclav's mentor, you know," she confided. "They were as close as father and son."

Since Max had been in his fifties, and Vaclav looked to be of the same generation, I found her description rather peculiar, but I did manage to keep my thoughts to myself.

Sophia then told me that Max had been responsible for bringing Vaclav to the United States while the Czech Republic was still in communist hands. Having seen in her husband such great potential, Max managed to arrange his escape right under the nose of the communists, who would never have let Vaclav go had they known of his intention to defect. Of course, Vaclav would never have left her behind to be imprisoned, but Max had arranged for her escape as well. Sophia herself had been most unpopular with the detestable red regime because of her noble, in fact royal, lineage. An excellent scientist, Max, she concluded. Vaclav was taking his death very hard.

I was by then eating my lovely cookie, all creamy chocolate and crunchy nuts, and feeling much more charitable, so I asked with genuine interest, "Hapsburg or Premyslid?" referring to her "royal lineage."

My question evidently won Sophia's heart. She beamed at me and exclaimed, "You know Czech history?"

"Some," I agreed as I pressed a finger onto the last crumbs of my large cookie and lifted them to my mouth.

"My family is descended from the true Bohemian kings," she replied proudly. "We predate that upstart, John of Luxembourg. Ottakar II is my progenitor on my mother's side."

"Ah, the one who brought in the German settlers in the thirteenth century. A canny political move at the time, but the source of much ethnic strife thereafter," I murmured and winced over a sip of vinegar masquerading as wine.

"Yes, well, he was a very successful king." She touched her lips with a napkin. "Much more admirable than any of the Hapsburgs, who weren't even Bohemian, or for that matter John of Luxembourg, who was responsible for the massacre of our nobility on the field at Crecy. What a shame my ancestress, Elizabeth, was forced to marry such a foolish man."

"Ah, but you have to be fascinated by a king who would lead his knights into battle even though he was blind. And he *was* the father of Charles, the Holy Roman Emperor, who was certainly a credit to the Bohemian crown," I replied.

"Indeed." She nodded enthusiastically. "But I regard the brilliance of Charles's reign as a credit to his Premyslid blood. His father, through neglect, left Prague in ruins." She pushed her goblet away, having evidently found the wine as detestable as I did. "I noticed that you were talking to that ill-dressed policeman. Have they caught the crazy person who killed poor Max?"

"I think they're leaning toward the idea that it was a hired assassin," I replied.

"Really?" She looked taken aback but recovered her aplomb quickly. "How interesting. A scandal in the making, perhaps. His wife, Charlotte, his second wife, was simply a nobody, even by American standards, before he married her. A failed ballet dancer."

Now that was interesting, I thought. I'd never met a professional ballet dancer, failed or otherwise.

"Who knows what such a woman would do?" said Sophia. "His children do not care for her, which is understandable. Their own mother came from a fine family. Family is most important, don't you think?"

"Um-m," I replied, wondering how she would characterize mine.

"I tell you this in confidence, but I saw her, Charlotte Heydemann, in a hotel with a young man. Perhaps the lover killed Max!" She stopped talking long enough to notice that I had finished my lunch. "Shall we go now to enjoy the Picassos?"

She certainly did, exclaiming over every silly plate and pitcher. Picasso must have been hooting with laughter when he made those ugly things: plates with fish and vegetable lumps on them, garishly painted; and the pitchers, whose curves were the breasts and bottoms of fleshy women. And I had to nod politely at Sophia's many admiring exclamations. What fun the exhibit would have been if Jason and I had gone together. We'd have been helpless with giggles . . . well, not Jason, but he would have been amused.

I do love modern art. It so often exhibits a marvelous sense of humor. We saw a picture that afternoon, part of the regular collection, called *The Critical Eye*. The artist had painted a scene in which a real cow was examining a portrait of a cow while a number of serious, black-clad scholars seemingly awaited the real cow's critical opinion. One man held a notebook to take down the cow's impressions while another had a mop in case the cow soiled the museum floor. Sophia was not amused.

But the afternoon wasn't a total loss. The news that Mrs. Heydemann had a lover was certainly intriguing. Detective Worski would be interested, if anyone thought to tell him. In fact, perhaps it was my duty to do so, but how to get hold of him? Maybe he was still at Hodge, Brune. I called, and he was. At first, he seemed surprised and not too pleased to hear from me, but when I mentioned the story I'd heard that afternoon, he said, "Good lead, Mrs. Blue. Murders usually lead back to sex or money."

I had read that somewhere.

"And family members are first-class suspects. Thanks for the tip."

"You're very welcome," I replied, not sure that my husband would thank me for getting involved.

8

Ominous News in Patria

Jason

When I returned from lunch with several Hodge, Brune scientists, the atmosphere at company headquarters had changed from one of restrained grief to one of near panic. Upper management and senior scientists huddled in twos and threes in offices and hallways, talking in undertones, falling silent when lower echelons or outsiders approached. I was evidently an outsider, because the prevailing alarm was never explained to me.

The seminar that I was to give that afternoon was postponed, and I was suddenly shuffled off to spend the afternoon with Fergus McRoy, a nice enough fellow, although neither of us really knew why we had been thrown together. McRoy's interest was in coal and its by-products, and company paranoia prevented him from discussing his research. In fact, he seemed distracted, and Striff had described him as nervous during the last meeting with Max, so I studied McRoy as we talked but saw nothing more sinister than anxiety in him. Was that anxiety indicative of a guilty conscience?

I had rather expected to spend at least some time after my seminar with Vasandrovich, who had become interim director of R and D. It did not happen, which made me suspect that the company, all protestations to the contrary, was no longer interested in working out a contract with me. McRoy also expected to see Vasandrovich and even mentioned that he might have to leave me abruptly. Neither of us was summoned, so we ended up talking sports, as men are prone to do when at loss for more interesting topics. McRoy was a soccer fan, not an interest on which I had much to say.

I arrived at the Park Central earlier than expected to find my wife napping but quite willing to awaken, hear about my day, and tell me about hers. Her tale centered on her take-no-prisoners agent and her afternoon with Vasandrovich's wife, a woman with whom Carolyn had not been charmed beyond some interesting medieval family connection. I, in turn, said that something was going on at Hodge, Brune, beyond or perhaps even connected to Max's death, and we discussed what it might be. Carolyn suggested that people were afraid of losing their jobs when a new R and D director was brought in.

These downsizing and housecleaning operations that go on in contemporary industry make me appreciate universities and the tenure system. One may have some anxious early years in academia but, if granted tenure at a compatible institution, life can be very pleasant thereafter. Of course, too much ease can be stultifying, which is why I left a very good position. My colleagues thought I had lost my mind, but I wanted new challenges instead of an easy slide into middle-aged complacency.

"We're eating at a place called Patria tonight with Frances Striff and her companion," I told Carolyn. "I assured her that you wouldn't be horrified at the presence of her lover."

"Of course I won't," Carolyn replied. "On the whole, it sounds rather exciting, and Patria is very chic."

"Even if the lover is another woman?"

"They're a lesbian couple?" she asked, intrigued.

"I have no idea, but Striff has had two failed marriages and is quite plain. Even I noticed that, so I thought—"

"Don't be ridiculous, Jason. I'm sure science is responsible for many divorces, and *plain* fends off sexual harassment. Being a woman in the world of science isn't the most comfortable position."

"There are many successful female scientists," I replied rather defensively.

"How many at Hodge, Brune?" Carolyn demanded.

What could I say? Dr. Striff herself had pointed out that she was the only one. Our speculations about her companion proved to be moot. In fact, my description of Dr. Striff was embarrassingly off the mark. If she hadn't approached us in the lobby, I wouldn't have recognized her. Wearing makeup and a very skimpy black dress, she looked more like a former model than a frumpy scientist. Carolyn raised an eyebrow at me after the introductions. Striff's companion, Paul Fallon, was a charming fellow, possibly younger than she, whose profession, if any, I never learned, but he and Carolyn hit it off immediately with common interests in things cultural. Fallon had seen the *Picasso in Clay* exhibit and remembered as many ugly ceramics as Carolyn: plates of bacon and eggs, a pitcher depicting a fat man in a green hat. We became a very jolly group over a round of mangolitas, a concoction of champagne and mango juice, not to mention bits of mango that tended to lodge alarmingly in the throat.

Once I had developed a strategy for avoiding mango strangulation, I divided my attention between the restaurant decor, on which my wife was busily making notes, and my menu. I am a fairly well-traveled individual, but few scientific meetings are held in South or Central America. Therefore, but for the explanations, the menu would have seemed to be in a foreign language. What, for instance, is *fufu*? Obviously, I was in for an exotic experience.

Carolyn was discussing dishes with a hovering waiter, who could evidently recognize a food professional when he saw one. I reluctantly passed up the Oysters Rodriguez because of the *fufu* and Huacatay sauce in the description and chose an eggplant empanada. I know what an empanada is, a small pastry. They are served in El Paso, although usually with fruit rather than eggplant inside. This empanada came with "adobo roasted lamb tenderloin and *sarsa* salad." Both Carolyn and I agreed that my appetizer was excellent—rare lamb, crusty empanada, and a fine chili tang, which came, I presume, from the *sarsa*.

She ate half of mine, and I finished off her Pastel de Choclo, a mushroom potpie with corn bread on top, spicy shrimp on a skewer, and a sweet sherry vinaigrette on some leaves. Although I've never been a fan of corn bread, one can hardly go wrong with mushrooms.

I had no trouble choosing the Seafood Parihuela as a main course. How could any seafood lover pass up grilled lobster tail surrounded by clams, mussels, rock shrimp, bay scallops, and calamari? It was served on a white bean cake and cooked with tomatoes, *chorizo* and *panca* pepper. Carolyn remarked that the sauce had a lovely beany flavor, which was quite true.

She was more venturesome and ordered Sugar Cane Tuna described as a "coconut glazed loin with *malanga* puree, chayote, and dried shrimp salsa." Other than the tuna, I probably failed to identify the ingredients. I thought I was sampling a sweet potato puree, but perhaps *malanga* is something else entirely. Whatever it was, it contrasted nicely, as my wife pointed out, with the chopped vegetables marinated in lime and the crust on the rare tuna, which was rich and sweet. This unusual fish was served on a frosted aqua platter. Carolyn liked the platter so much that I was struck with the idea of buying her something similar for Mother's Day. Maybe if I do, she'll cook me another meal like the one she prepared from her new cookbook.

God knows what Frances and Fallon were eating. We weren't well enough acquainted to exchange portions, and they weren't interested in discussing ingredients. However, our waiter was, and some other fellow, when Carolyn had filled many pages with notes, came over to ask if we were happy with our meals. We chemists nodded, mouths stuffed with alien food. Fallon said the Churrasco Nica was better than ever (it appeared to be beef), and Carolyn absolutely beamed at this new representative of management, swallowed, and asked for copies of the menu. She was also sampling from their alcohol offerings—not only the mangolita but also a mojito, which was a rum drink with lime and mint. I had Cabro, a Guatemalan beer recommended by Fallon. My wife said that it tasted like sweat.

Over our appetizers (we all ordered from the three-course prix fixe menu), Frances and Fallon argued about who had discovered the place. Fallon said that his hairdresser had recommended Patria. I wondered what a hairdresser could do for him that my barber couldn't at a more reasonable price. Frances insisted that she had read about it in *The New York Times* and suggested they go, and didn't he remember the fellow on the subway who had been complaining in song about the cultural inadequacies of males?

Any conversation was difficult because of the noise. The two-story room was huge, with towering, green-framed windows and, over the door, a lush collection of plants and a mosaic. Of this, we had a good view because we were seated on the balcony above the main dining room and bar. Carolyn was particularly taken with the waveform banisters and the twisted spindles that held them up. She lamented not having brought a camera to take a picture of the place. Frances looked taken aback. Evidently, taking pictures of the interior of a restaurant would not have been chic, although, as I said, I was astonished that Frances Striff could look chic.

Over the entrées, Carolyn asked Frances whether she thought Vaclav Vasandrovich would be welcomed as the new R and D director.

"Good God, you had lunch with his wife, didn't you?" Frances replied and began to laugh.

Fallon murmured to me that Sophia Vasandrovich was a notorious snob. Then Frances got control of her hilarity and advised Carolyn not to judge Vaclav by his wife. "I think the poor man was initially impressed by her royal ancestry, but none of the rest of us are. I suppose, if we can't have Max, Vaclav will do as well as anyone."

Sighing at the thought of Max's death (he had been a man I thought might become a close friend), I turned back to my lobster. Carolyn and Fallon began a spirited argument about which Picasso sculpture was funnier, the pregnant goat or the lollipop-head baby in the stroller. My wife takes great delight in modern sculpture, while I prefer Bernini, Michelangelo, or even Canova, although his male figures are on the effeminate side. Carolyn maintains that the models were just younger.

When we were presented with the dessert menu, my wife ordered That's da Bomb, which I promise you was the name on the menu. She is, unquestionably, a chocoholic, and That's da Bomb is a chocolate dish. However, she was taken aback when it arrived because it looked rather like a space machine: chocolate mousse in a chocolate shell with hazelnuts, ice cream landing legs, and a crispy, chocolate cookie-like thing in the shape of an isosceles triangle thrusting up from the ship. Mine wasn't much less bizarre because she talked me into ordering the Chocolate Cigar. The cigar itself contained chocolate mousse wrapped in a chocolate almond cake with mocha ice cream, but the cigar also came with a ring—not edible—and a book of lighted matches that wafted the smell of caramelized sugar under my nose.

Fallon had lime jalapeño sorbet, which does not sound very appetizing, but he seemed to enjoy it, and Frances had a pear tart with pistachio and blue cheese ice cream. Carolyn had been considering that dessert—for me— until I refused to try it unless the blue cheese could be eliminated from the ice cream. I personally prefer to have my blue cheese on a salad, or even a cracker, but in ice cream? That sounds like something you'd use as a threat when your child refused to eat his broccoli.

Frances had taken two bites of her dessert and laid her spoon down when I decided to introduce the subject that had been nagging at my mind all evening. "A lot of people at Hodge, Brune seemed worried this afternoon," I said around a spoonful of the ice cream. "Is something going on that I should know about?"

Frances looked hesitant. Fallon said, "The man is thinking of hiring on. He should be told what just happened."

Carolyn looked alarmed and blurted out, "Has someone else been murdered? If so, I think we should go straight home, Jason."

"You haven't seen your editor yet. You have to stay until Friday," I replied.

"Not if you're in danger."

"It's not that," said Frances. "We had some very disturbing news today. Another company just announced the development of a process we've been working on for five years, one we were ready to patent."

"That's a relief," Carolyn murmured. She was nibbling on the wing of her spaceship.

"It won't be to our stockholders, if it gets out," said Frances grimly.

"May I ask what kind of process?" I asked.

"It has to do with a method for eliminating pollution from coal-burning power plants."

"That should be a very lucrative breakthrough."

"They've filed for an international patent," she said gloomily. "Did it just before making the announcement, the thieving bastards."

"You're sure it's your process?"

"Pretty sure."

"What company?"

"Some small Ukrainian outfit no one ever heard of. For heaven's sake, the Ukrainians don't even care that their coal miners keep getting killed. Why would they care about air pollution?"

"No doubt because they stand to make a fortune if their, or your, process works," I replied thoughtfully.

"It works."

"Without costing a fortune?"

"That's the great thing about it," said Frances. "The power companies won't be able to say they can't afford it, and our stock has already been rising on the rumors that we're about to make a big announcement. When this gets out, shares will plummet, and there goes my early retirement."

"And people at the company think the research was stolen from Hodge, Brune rather than being a parallel effort that neither of you were aware of?" I asked.

"I'm guilty," said Fallon, grinning. "I don't want Frances to retire and move away to some leafy campus in some uninteresting section of the country, so I engineered a stock disaster."

"Not funny, Paul," Frances snapped. "A lot of people are going to be hurt by this unless we can prove that they stole from us. Take Charlotte Heydemann, for instance. I imagine a lot of what Max left her is in company stock."

"You know Mrs. Heydemann?" Carolyn asked, suddenly interested.

"Of course. Max finally lucked out in the family sweepstakes with her. She adores him, as opposed to his crazy first wife and their obnoxious offspring."

"Really?"

Now why was Carolyn interested in Max's family? I wondered. That question was eclipsed when it occurred to me that Max's death might somehow be connected to this expensive piece of industrial espionage. Carolyn calmly continued to demolish her That's da Bomb. She hadn't seen the implications and, when back at the hotel, I mentioned them, she said, "Now, Jason, industrial espionage? That's crazy."

Of course, my wife has never had to deal with industrial paranoia about the open discussion of science.

"I imagine the police are more likely to look at the family situation, especially if it's as dysfunctional as Frances seems to think."

I eyed Carolyn narrowly. "Well, you don't need to look into it, my love," I said. "You didn't even know Max." The last thing I wanted Carolyn to do was put herself in danger. However, *I* intended to make some inquiries, and not about Max's family. Perhaps I now had the answer to what had been worrying Max when he called me over the weekend.

9

Besting the Syndicate

Carolyn

Before I went downtown to keep my appointment with Marshall Smead, I again stopped for breakfast at the deli where Max Heydemann was killed. Again, Thelma of the black-rimmed glasses and bouffant hair waited on me. I had thought of a possibility for relieving my husband's mind about industrial espionage, at least as it might relate to Max Heydemann's death. Although Jason hadn't mentioned that piece of deduction, I know my husband well enough to make accurate guesses as to how his mind works, by application of relentless logic to socially unlikely situations.

"Good morning, Thelma," I said and gave her my order for coffee, juice, and a roll, no butter, no cream cheese.

"You sick?" she asked.

"Just mindful of my waistline," I replied. "I made a recent trip to New Orleans."

"Not much theater there," she remarked, apropos of nothing, unless she wanted to remind me that I was now in the theater center of the country and should take advantage of my opportunities. Jason and I planned to. We had tickets to an off-Broadway play, whose premise was, according to the Internet review, "In the beginning God made Adam and Steve." I anticipated that it would be outrageously contrary to the principles of political correctness, and political correctness, which can be admirable, does become wearing at university campuses. A bit of outrageousness had sounded good to both of us.

When Thelma returned with my breakfast, I asked my question: "Did you ever notice Max meeting any Eastern Europeans here?"

She looked surprised. "He never met anyone here that I saw. How come you're asking about Eastern Europeans? That's like Russians?"

"Just idle curiosity," I replied. Then mindful of the company fear about stock plunges, I added, "Actually, one of his closest colleagues and friends was Czech. I was hoping that they got to spend some time together before Max died."

"Not here," said Thelma and strode off to wait on an elderly, bearded patron.

Probably because I arrived on time and he kept me waiting forty-five minutes, I was predisposed to dislike Marshall Smead before I ever met him and even more so at first sight. He looked . . . devilish. V-shaped eyebrows and hairline, which would probably leave him, in a year or two, with a tuft of hair in front, a bald spot around it, and the remaining hair too far back to be noticeable except from the rear. Perhaps that's why he was so rude, because he was anticipating the future temptation to comb that remaining forelock in silly strands across the barren field of his head. And I might add that I did not judge him solely on his looks and inability to keep appointments on time; when I entered his office, he was glaring at me, as if I, not he, had been late.

His first words were, "Is your name really Blue?" While I puzzled over that, he added, "Don't bother to answer. Whatever your name is, you should change it."

I replied that I had no plans to change my name or my marital status, for that matter.

"Let's see your portfolio," he snapped.

"What portfolio?"

"If you don't have a portfolio, why are you here?"

"Because my agent, Loretta Blum, sent me, and she said nothing about a portfolio."

"I thought you'd written food columns for newspapers."

"I have. Three. For the El Paso paper."

"Oh, great! I'm overwhelmed. Three columns for a small-town newspaper."

"The metropolitan area is over two million." I didn't mention that I was including Juarez, Mexico, in what we laughingly call the El Paso Metroplex, a little joke that would undoubtedly go unappreciated among Juarenses.

"And I suppose you forgot to bring your three columns along?"

"I didn't forget. I had no idea I'd need them."

"How do you figure I'm going to judge your work if I can't see any of it?"

"Look, Mr. Smead—"

"Look, Mrs. Blue, you're wasting my time. Call for an appointment when you have something to show me. Better yet, just send me something." Then he got up to open the door for me, his first, and not very convincing, sign of courtesy. After all, he was showing me out. And I was delighted to leave and furiously angry at both Mr. Smead and Loretta, who had gotten me into this embarrassing situation without the least forewarning of what would be expected of me. Just send him something indeed!

"That was short," said his secretary, smiling at me. "I'll walk you out."

Good grief! Were they afraid I'd refuse to leave the building?

"I'm taking an early lunch today."

"Are you?" The sight of her soon-to-be-unused computer sparked a delicious idea. "I'd like to use your computer while you're gone." She looked at me askance. "Mr. Smead asked me to write him a column. If I do it here, I can leave it and save myself the trouble of coming back." Since I never planned to speak to him again.

"Well . . . I guess." She looked dubious and glanced at the closed door to his office.

"Shall I bring him out to give you permission?" I asked generously.

"Oh, no," she replied and left as fast as her high heels could tap-tap out the door.

Teeth gritted, I dropped my coat over her chair and sat down to write. "Advice for a First-Time Visitor to an All-You-Can-Eat Sushi Restaurant." I paused only a second before continuing.

Five minutes into my off-the-cuff column effort, someone came in and asked, "Where's Marshall?"

"In his office, if he hasn't slipped out the back way," I replied, continuing to type.

"Carolyn? What are you doing here?"

I looked up to find Paul Fallon walking toward me. "I'm writing a column for Marshall Smead," I said, continuing to type ferociously.

"No kidding. You should have told me last night you'd be coming here today. I had no idea you did columns as well as books." He was now standing behind me.

"I had no idea you . . . well, do you work here, or are you visiting?"

"I'm the VP." He had been reading over my shoulder and started to laugh. "That's delightful, Carolyn. I'll look forward to seeing the rest." Then he walked into Smead's office without knocking and closed the door. I recovered from my surprise and concentrated on the column, which I was sure Marshall Smead would hate. Had Paul Fallon hired the ultra-rude Mr. Smead? I wondered. After changing the title, I was just printing out copies when the two men left Smead's office.

"What are you doing here?" Smead asked sharply.

"You asked for a sample of my work. Here's a column." I placed it in his hand and picked up my coat. Paul Fallon hastened to assist me while Smead looked surprised.

"Take a good look at it, Marshall," said Fallon. "It's great! How about lunch, Carolyn?"

Because Smead seemed so unhappy to discover that his boss was asking me to lunch, I immediately accepted, just to spite him. I had originally planned to return to the hotel for a snack and a nap before the memorial service for Max Heydemann, about which Jason had called from Hodge, Brune before I left the hotel.

"Send that column on to my office, Marshall," Fallon called over his shoulder as we left. "I want to see the rest of it." To me he said, "How would you like to eat at a very popular restaurant behind a butcher shop?"

"Sounds like meat for a column," I replied blithely.

"Was that a pun?" asked Fallon.

KEEPING YOUR HEAD IN A JAPANESE RESTAURANT

1. DO NOT visit a Japanese restaurant with a sushi bar if you believe, as my Aunt Beatrice does, that raw fish bits introduce death-dealing parasites into your body.

2. DO NOT attempt to converse in Japanese with your waitress on the basis of having listened to language tapes from the Japanese for Commuters series. She will giggle behind her hand and rush off on her little feet to tell her father that the elephantine, round-eyed barbarian at table three is too stupid to speak properly even the simplest Japanese phrase. Then the whole family may gather by the cash register, staring and giggling.

3. If you are so venturesome as to order *uni*, DO NOT smell before tasting unless your salivary glands are stimulated by swamp gas.

4. DO NOT complain about the miniature size of your sake cup. Remember that the Japanese are a small people who do not tolerate alcohol well. You can always order a second carafe of sake, but chances are you won't need to. At one swallow per cup, it takes a while to finish the first carafe, or whatever they call that little stoneware jug.

5. If you do order two jugs of sake, DO NOT become amorous and pinch your waitress's bottom. She will report any sexual overtures to her grand-

mother, who will dash out of the kitchen swinging her ancestors' samurai sword and attack you in the name of family honor. Since she is only four foot six, you may be able to fend her off, but you will be charged the dreaded family-honor gratuity on your bill and be banned forever from the restaurant.

6. If you are unable to handle chopsticks with dexterity, by all means pick your sushi up with thumb and forefinger. This method may earn you the disdain of management, but it is preferable to leaving the restaurant with wasabi and soy sauce stains on your clothing. Neither condiment is easy to remove.

7. While eating sushi with your fingers, you will discover that the sticky rice adheres stubbornly to your skin. Use your chopsticks to scrape it off, then ask for a cut lemon to remove the fishy odor. It is not polite to suck the rice off by putting your fingers in your mouth, and politeness aside, you will be embarrassed to find rice adhering to your chin, where it is harder to remove.

8. DO NOT sample the wasabi (green paste served on a small plate). Any amount introduced into the mouth unaccompanied by soy sauce and food will cause flames to shoot up your sinuses and out your nose. Then other guests will crowd around to stare, assuming that you are the floor show.

9. DO NOT pick the little seeds off your eel. You will insult the chef who has gone to great pains to concoct the eel sauce, and it is only sensible to remember that a sushi chef always has large knives at hand.

10. When eating a hand roll, clutch it firmly in the fist to keep the contents from trickling out the bottom of the cone; then open wide and empty it into your mouth. The seaweed cone is reputed to be edible, but it isn't.

11. By following these simple instructions, your visit to the sushi bar will be a safe and exotic experience. Raw fish is delicious, no matter what your Aunt Beatrice says.

Carolyn Blue, "Have Fork, Will Travel," *Louisville Star Times*

10
"You're Not Hired Yet!"

Jason

When I arrived at Hodge, Brune, having stopped for breakfast, I had already made plans. If I was to find how a little-known Ukrainian company had managed to steal the results of a long research project here in the States and how, if at all, that theft related to Max's death, I needed to know who had information on the project to sell or trade. Such knowledge would rest with the men on the team that had developed the process. The only Hodge, Brune coal chemist I knew was Fergus McRoy, who had said nothing about industrial espionage the afternoon before. If Frances Striff knew what had happened, surely he did. Consequently, I went in search of him, avoiding receptionists, secretaries, and chemists who might have other activities in mind for me.

I found Fergus in a state of extreme anxiety. "Have you heard what happened?" he asked. "No, of course you haven't. I didn't hear until the end of the afternoon. I was supposed to have an appointment with Vasandrovich. I told you that, didn't I?"

"Yes. I expected one myself."

"Right. I'd forgotten. Sit down." He waved toward a chair.

"I guess you mean the Ukrainian thing," I added as I accepted his offer.

"Then you do know? I'm the project leader, and no one told *me*. How'd you—"

"Gossip last night at dinner," I replied.

McRoy dropped his head into his hands. "Five years of work," he moaned. "My biggest project. How the hell could it have happened? You know some bunch of Ukrainians couldn't have come up with it. It was my idea! Mine! And why isn't anyone talking to me about it? There are all these meetings going on, and I'm not invited."

This did not seem like a man who had sold the company out, but I've been fooled by colleagues before. I told myself to reserve judgment. "Well, my advice, Fergus, is that you start thinking about who on your team could have—"

"—given my project to some other company? Ruined my future? Taken the food from my children's mouths?"

"And gotten paid very well for it, I would imagine, so you should think about those who knew enough to turn the research over." I reached across his desk and pushed a legal pad in front of him. "When I've got a problem, I always find it helpful to get it down on paper."

McRoy stared miserably at the sheet and mumbled, "I can't believe any of my people—"

"It could have been someone who had access to the research. Not even a scientist," I suggested.

He shook his head in disbelief, but finally he began to write. Every time he stopped, I made new suggestions, for I had thought quite a bit about the matter while I jogged through the frigid streets near the hotel, zigzagging around other early risers. Scientists, lab assistants, computer programmers, computer repair people, secretaries who might have typed up reports, or conversely people above him in the management chain or colleagues who might have shown a particular interest in the project. On the basis of my suggestions, McRoy managed quite a long list, but he assured me that security was tight. The detestable Merrivale saw to that, although he, Fergus, was beginning to appreciate the man's vigilance.

"Does anyone on this list seem to have more money lately than you'd expect?" I asked.

"I don't know who has money," he said woefully. "I work here. I live at home."

"You must have lunch with colleagues."

"Fiona packs my lunch."

"Don't you socialize after working hours with these people?"

"Not really." He grimaced. "There's the Christmas party of course, but I don't remember anything out of the ordinary."

It occurred to me that had anything out of the ordinary taken place at the party, Fergus McRoy might well have missed it. "Anyone from this list quit just recently?"

He ran a finger down the page. "Waller. He was a lab tech. Went to some gas company in Louisiana. You think he—"

"It's a possibility," I said. "Does he seem like a good source for some-one wanting to steal the process?"

"Well, he didn't have the combinations to the safes. And he was rotten on the computer."

"Could have been faking that," I suggested.

"I suppose." He studied the second page of his list. "Angie Mottson. She got pregnant and left."

I frowned. "Many young women these days work until just before delivery. What was her financial situation? Could she afford to leave when she did?"

"Her doctor said she had to quit . . . some kidney problem and high blood pressure. Fiona, that's my wife, insisted that we send flowers. If I bought those flowers for someone who sold me out—"

"You need to talk to these people. Ask them questions."

"What would I ask?" McRoy looked completely bewildered.

"Do you want me to help?" I wasn't sure what I'd ask either, but McRoy looked pitifully grateful for my ill-considered offer. While running and thinking, I had barely gotten to interrogation techniques before my ears went numb and I had to turn back to the hotel.

"Let me make you a copy of the list." Fergus called his secretary to do the job before I could stop him. She was, after all, on the list. If she were the culprit, she'd be forewarned that he was conducting an investigation himself, one in which I was involved. However, she didn't seem to be at all alarmed when she returned with the photocopies. In fact, she was gossiping with another woman who followed her in.

Fergus took the copies and passed one to me while the second woman was saying, "Dr. Blue? My, I've had a time chasing you down. You were supposed to be talking to . . ." She looked at what was evidently my sched-ule, although I didn't have a copy. "Well, no matter. Dr. Vasandrovich would appreciate your coming to his office."

"What about me?" asked McRoy eagerly.

"He didn't mention you, Dr. McRoy," she replied and held the door for me. Evidently, it was to be a command performance. McRoy gave me a conspiratorial look, as if to say he would begin talking to suspects immediately.

Mindful that Vaclav Vasandrovich was on the list of people who had access to information on the coal project, I thought about things I might ask him, tactfully, during our meeting. There was, however, little time for idle, if intrusive, chitchat. He apologized for not having seen me earlier. I said that I understood, considering the bad news the company had had from the Ukraine. He frowned at me, seemingly surprised that I knew. I asked if he, with his Eastern European connections, had any idea who might have passed the information on. He replied that I needn't worry about the problem, that the company would survive, and an investigation into possible espionage was already under way, headed by their security officer, Dr. Merrivale.

Then he changed the subject by informing me that a group of senior scientists would be gathering for lunch in the boardroom with Vice President Charles Mason Moore before the memorial service for Max. If I'm not mistaken, his eyes glistened with tears when he mentioned Max. I found myself moved as well. A memorial service may bring closure to some mourners, but there is a finality that makes us face, once and for all, the fact of the one memorialized is incontrovertibly dead.

"The body has been released by the police?" I asked.

"Not that I know of. The burial will be later," said Vasandrovich gruffly. "God knows why they have to keep him so long. The trauma to family and friends is terrible. We at the company organized this service in the hope that it would bring some comfort to all. But as I was saying, we would like you to attend the luncheon and, of course, the memorial, if you wish to."

"Yes," I agreed. "As intermittent as our acquaintance was, I was an admirer and, I hope, a friend."

"Those who wish to say a few words will be invited to do so. You are welcome to join in. Max spoke very highly of you."

"That's gratifying," I murmured. What a strange man Vasandrovich was, on the one hand rather cool and formal, on the other sorrowful to the point of tears over the death of his superior.

"Then, if you feel you can do it on such short notice, I was hoping you could give your seminar after the service. I'm sorry that it had to be postponed, although I'm sure you understand."

"Under the circumstances, of course."

"Then can we count on you for the lunch and the seminar? Possibly the interest of your research will serve to take the minds of our scientists off this tragic event."

"Certainly," I answered. "My papers and slides are in my briefcase. I'll be glad to oblige, and to attend the luncheon as well. Max spoke several times of Dr. Moore. I look forward to meeting him."

Vasandrovich said, "Don't expect too much. He has a lot on his mind."

With that, I was dismissed and hastened away to begin making casual visits to people on McRoy's list. I learned that the gone-south lab tech had saddled himself with a demanding Southern belle who swore to divorce him if he didn't immediately move to warmer climes. Would my wife tire of warmer climes and demand that we move back north? Carolyn is not a complainer, but I know she's finding the climate of El Paso burdensome. She has to spend an inordinate amount of time rubbing lotion into her skin to keep from peeling, and in New Orleans last month, she absolutely basked in the rain.

The pregnant secretary, according to McRoy's secretary, had been given maternity leave, although not yet delivered of her child, and was lounging at home in bed with a visiting nurse and company medical insurance to cover her vacation. "Some people have all the luck!" the young lady exclaimed. I wouldn't have considered high blood pressure and possible kidney failure "all the luck," but perhaps this young, unmarried woman had never heard of preeclampsia. When Carolyn was carrying our son Chris, she had been warned of the possibility. However, the urine tests had been switched with someone else's, and the high blood pressure had been temporary.

A computer person, eager to talk, as such people often are, told me, over his special blend of African coffees, that research data on computer hard drives was locked in safes nightly. Only the big shots had access, which was a "pain in the ass" because the disks had to be reinstalled each morning, sometimes causing crashes, data loss, and bouts of painfully itchy hives for him personally because of the stress.

At that point in my investigation, Vernon Merrivale swooped down on me and hustled me off to his office, which was furnished with agonizingly uncomfortable furniture, except for his own cushy leather chair. The room also had no windows, cameras in all corners scanning back and forth, and locks on everything. He had to press a fingerprint pad before he could get into his own office.

"Your wife was seen talking to a police detective yesterday in Vasandrovich's outer office," he said accusingly.

I must admit that his tone immediately irritated me. "So what?" I snapped. "I talked to one myself."

"About what?" Merrivale demanded.

"Max's death, of course. He asked me questions because I happened to be there. That was probably the case with my wife, as well." *Or not,* I thought, but kept that possibility to myself. I could imagine my wife running into the detective, discovering that he was investigating the murder, and quizzing him rather than the other way around.

"Since you and your wife are here at the invitation of the company, we would appreciate your not talking to the police."

"Why?" I asked. "When the police ask questions in the course of an investigation, good citizens try to be helpful—or ask for a lawyer," I added dryly. "I hardly think Carolyn or I would need a lawyer since we were aboard an American Airlines flight in midair at the time Max was killed. On the other—"

"Exactly. Therefore, you have no information to offer the police," said Merrivale triumphantly. "So don't volunteer information on matters you know nothing about, and tell your wife to stay out of it, as well."

Why was Merrivale trying to impede the investigation? I wondered. I had no time to pursue this question because he continued by saying sternly, "Why are you asking people about the coal project?"

"Because the research has evidently been stolen," I replied.

"I don't see that that's any of your business."

"Then you'd be wrong. Max called me last weekend to say he had a problem he couldn't discuss on the telephone but on which he hoped to recruit my help."

"Did he mention the coal project specifically?"

"No."

"Then what makes you think his concerns had anything to do with the Ukrainians?"

"That's the only problem I've run across except his untimely death. Surely, you've had the thought yourself that they might be connected."

"In what way?"

"If I knew that, I wouldn't have to ask questions." I thought a minute. "Well, actually I would. Even if Max's death *was* unrelated, he did want my help on something. If this was it, I want to give that help. I thought very highly of him."

"Coal isn't your field."

"No, it isn't, but he mentioned my connections."

"You have connections in the Ukraine?"

"Not there specifically, but in other areas of Eastern Europe."

"But they'd be academic?"

"Mostly."

"Not likely to be of much use," said Merrivale. "My information is that you've talked to several people connected with the coal project."

"Yes, I chatted with various people this morning."

"Amateurs in the field of industrial security, bumbling around, asking questions, can only impede the professional investigation."

"Has it occurred to you that Max might have had suspicions about who was responsible for the leaks or sale of information and was killed to keep him from revealing the person he suspected?"

"I assure you, Dr. Blue, I do not need your assistance to formulate rational hypotheses about this case, and I must ask you to keep away from the investigation. It is not your concern."

"I beg your pardon, Merrivale, but as Max wanted to bring me in as a consultant, I feel honor bound to—"

"You haven't been hired *yet*, Dr. Blue. Keep that in mind." Vernon Merrivale eyed me coldly over a high-bridged nose and stood up, indicating that the interview was at an end.

I have to admit that I was happy to leave, not that I was intimidated by Merrivale, but I resented having to sit in an uncomfortable chair that was unusually low to the floor. Had he ordered the legs shortened in order to look down on visitors to his office? I wouldn't be at all surprised.

And what was *he* up to? As the man in charge of security at Hodge, Brune, he should welcome anything the police could discover and encourage cooperation with them. Instead, he almost seemed to be engaged in a cover-up. Why?

11

Salade Niçoise in a Butcher Shop

Ah, those French! They invented haute cuisine. They invented the bistro. They even gave us the word *restaurant*. In the eighteenth century, *restoratives* or *restaurants* were soups sold in Paris by Monsieur Boulanger. Within several years, the word having become popular, another culinary entrepreneur, Monsieur Beauvillier, was selling not just soup but a menu of popular dishes to visitors who knew better than to eat at a Paris inn.

And the French at home and abroad continued to be the purveyors of good food. In New York during World War II, when meat was rationed and hard to come by, wonderful beef could still be eaten at Au Cheval Pie by those hardy enough to brave the screaming arguments, smashing bottles, and physical assaults the owners launched at one another. But where did the volatile French restaurateurs, Marcel and Louise, get their meat?

One night, a mysteriously muffled figure actually stalked through the dining room with a live sheep in his arms. Perhaps there were farmers of French descent throughout the Northeast willing to make special trips into the city in order to uphold the honor of French cuisine in hard times. Or perhaps the owners of Au Cheval Pie had a network of lamb and cattle rustlers.

Carolyn Blue, "Have Fork, Will Travel," Lake City Post-Telegraph

Carolyn

Paul Fallon took me to a place called Les Halles, so named for the market in Paris, which was torn down by the city fathers to make room for the Centre Pompidou (that amazing museum that looks like a chemical factory. I remember thinking, when I first saw it, that the museum, with its exterior pipes painted in bold primary colors, must have been designed by Joan Miró; it wasn't.) Les Halles is now just a subway stop in Paris but also a bistro on Park Avenue between Twenty-eighth and Twenty-ninth Streets in New York, a reasonable walk from the building that housed the syndicate. However, we took a cab. Perhaps Paul hadn't noticed that I was wearing flats. Men tend to think that women wear heels unless they're home barefoot and pregnant in the kitchen.

And it was, indeed, a butcher shop with glass cases full of meat and crowds through which we wove our way to the dining room in back. The dining area was even more crowded and roaring with conversation, bustling waiters, and clattering crockery. Paul had a reservation at a tiny table. Every other seat was filled. I wouldn't have been surprised to see people sitting on one another's laps.

When I looked at the menu and ordered salade niçoise, Paul said, "You can't order a salad. This is a meat place. Have the cassoulet or the steak with *pommes frites*. Or they serve a wonderful sausage here with garlic enough to ward off a vampire. Do you read Anne Rice?"

"No," I replied, "and I'm in the mood for salade niçoise. Because of those tiny green beans. I can't get them at home. Besides I have to attend a memorial service. I can't go reeking of garlic."

"Well, I can," said Paul, and he ordered the sausages.

"We'll share a cab. Maybe my breath will take Charlotte's mind off her grief."

I had to laugh. "Are you sure she's grief-stricken?" I asked. "Has anyone found out yet who killed Max?"

He looked surprised. "Well, I doubt that Charlotte did it."

"You've never heard rumors that she has a lover?"

"Have you?" When I nodded, he looked surprised. "I can't imagine who said that. Care to confide?"

"I had lunch and visited a museum with Sophia Vasandrovich."

"And she said Charlotte had a lover? No way."

Our lunches were served at that moment, and Paul attacked his meal with gusto. I could smell the garlic across the table and see the glistening fat as he cut into his first sausage. In truth, it looked delicious. Perfect for an icy day with a stiff wind blowing through the crowded streets. Why had I chosen a cold plate? But then I looked down at my salad and those lovely little green beans, perfectly cooked. I moved the anchovies to the side and began to savor ripe, peeled tomatoes, sweet and moist (where did they get them this time of year?); meaty black olives; raw, thinly sliced onions; hard-boiled eggs with no green ring inside the whites (I have problems doing hard-boiled eggs, and what an embarrassing thing that is for a woman who was once reputed to be a gourmet cook); and last, flaked tuna, oily and flavorful, not the wimpy kind packed in water. *Oh Carolyn, what about your waistline?* my conscience asked.

Paul was grinning at me. "You're really enjoying it, aren't you? Does that mean you don't want to sample my sausage?"

"Of course I want to sample your sausage, but I don't know you well enough to ask." He cut off a piece and deposited it on my plate. "Um-m-m," I murmured appreciatively.

"Sorry for not taking my advice?"

"Not a bit," I replied, popping a black olive into my mouth and following it with a deliciously red wedge of tomato. "Do you want to sample my tomato?"

He laughed and shook his head. "I'm more into red meat than red vegetables. Anyway, we were talking about the big question: Who killed Max? Believe me, I'd pick Sophia over Charlotte any day."

"Why Sophia?" I asked.

"Don't tell me she wasn't dripping furs and jewels. She probably had him killed so Vaclav could take his job at Hodge, Brune and rake in the big bucks." He took a long draught of beer while I sipped my white wine. "Or maybe Calvin Pharr did it after Max warned him about his drinking."

"You mean this Pharr person got drunk and killed his superior?"

"Nah. Hired it done. If Calvin had showed up at the deli, Max would have recognized him, or at least someone would have remembered him. He's really bald and really fat, so you could hardly miss him. In fact, he'd have a hard time getting into the aisles between the tables."

"Max was seated at the end on a cross aisle," I replied.

"How do you know that, pretty lady?"

I didn't much like being called "pretty lady." To me it seemed either condescending or flirtatious. "Because I had breakfast at the deli in question and talked to one of the waitresses," I replied.

"What are you, an amateur detective?"

"Of course not," I replied uneasily, knowing that Max's death wasn't really any of my business.

He grinned at me. "It's that writer's curiosity. You've all got it."

"Even food writers?" I asked dryly.

"OK, so we've got Sophia and Calvin. Who else had a motive? Well, his children and his first wife. *She* hated him."

"Really?" That was interesting.

"But she's probably locked up at the very fancy country-club-type sanatorium her parents spring for every time she goes off the deep end. Still, that leaves the kids: Junior, better known as Rick, who keeps running up debts at Dartmouth, and his charming sibling, Fluffy, who doesn't even bother to go to school."

"Max had a daughter named Fluffy?" I asked, astounded. "If he thought of that name, she did have a motive for murder."

"Actually, I think Fluffy was the name of Charlotte's cat. Junior wrung its neck when Max refused to pay any more gambling debts. The daughter's name is—what?" Paul Fallon popped a French fry into his mouth as he tried to remember. "Ariadne. She hated it. I've forgotten what she calls herself now, but she's expensive to maintain and has the morals of an alley cat. They say she's already had two abortions, and Max refused to pay for the second. Then Charlotte stepped in and wrote the check. Probably thought she'd get stuck with a cocaine baby while sweet Ariadne went on screwing her way through the smart set. She even had a shot at me during one of the gala company Christmas parties, but Frances rescued me before Miss Heydemann could get her itchy little fingers on my zipper. Are you horrified?"

"Fascinated," I replied. "Who'd have guessed at all this scandal?" *And widely known at that!* "So why did they kill their father?"

"Money. Maybe they heard he was going to change his will, so they had him assassinated. Or Rick went into the restaurant in drag and did it himself."

As I whisked a piece of tuna through the lovely vinaigrette and savored the morsel, I shook my head in amazement at the breadth of his imagination.

"You don't buy that scenario? Well, maybe Max was mad at Charlotte for crossing him on the abortion and threatened to disinherit her, so she hired a hit man before Max could get to his lawyer."

"You should be a novelist instead of a vice president."

"That one sounds more likely to you?"

"Not really."

"OK, so he was killed by the thieving Lithuanians."

"Ukrainians? Now that would really make a good plot."

"I give up. Maybe Blind Harold did it." He called to the waiter and ordered cheesecake, without even asking me. "New York is the birthplace of cheesecake," he told me.

"Nonsense. Cheesecake was being baked in Europe in the fifteenth century. Now, who's Blind Harold?" Since Fallon was paying, I didn't protest being cheated out of the delights of picking my own dessert. Probably the cheesecake would be good. New York might not be the originator, but its renditions are famous.

"Blind Harold was this old guy Max gave five dollars to every Monday before he went into the deli. Maybe he forgot to come up with the money, so Blind Harold followed him in and killed him. Was Max missing five dollars when his body was found?"

"I don't know, but if Harold is blind, how could he find Max in a crowded restaurant, much less drive the—whatever it was—into the right place?"

"Maybe he's not really blind. Just because his eyes are weird and white when he takes off his dark glasses doesn't mean he hasn't been faking it all these years."

I had to laugh, but when I did, Paul Fallon beamed at me and took my hand. "You have one nice laugh, Carolyn," he said.

I snatched my hand away without even being subtle about it. Within the last month or so, I'd had one man get the wrong idea about my availability, and I really didn't want to find myself in that position again.

"Whoa!" said Fallon, looking surprised. "I'm not coming on to you. I'm just a guy who touches people. Bad fault, hmm?" He waved to the waiter and paid the bill. "If you go to work for us, promise you won't charge me with sexual harassment."

I was thoroughly embarrassed and once again felt like the country cousin in the big city.

"Well, let's get to that memorial service. That is, if you're not afraid to share a taxi with me."

"No problem," I retorted. "You can sit in front with the driver."

"I am properly chastened." He helped me into my coat and then led the way through the throngs of customers still waiting for seats in the packed restaurant.

12

In Memoriam

Jason

Luncheon in the board dining room was excellent, but then I love raw oysters, and six were served to those who wanted them. I met more chemists and listened to talk about the subject on everyone's mind, the fact that some little-known, Eastern European company had beaten Hodge, Brune to the patent on a very lucrative antipollution process. It was obvious that Vernon Merrivale, the security chief, was trying to keep people from talking about the subject in front of me and to me. Also, I finally met Charles Moore, the vice president. Although I did not sit by him at the table, I found him to be a very serious man, little given to smiling or idle conversation. He addressed a few comments and questions my way and remarked that the company was very pleased that I had been able to spend the week here. Then he fell into discussion with Vasandrovich, and I turned my attention elsewhere, although not without thinking Moore's enthusiasm for my visit rather lukewarm.

After the meal he stopped me at the door and asked that I come to his office for a conference following my seminar. As I rode to the memorial service with several other chemists, I considered the probability that Moore's message that afternoon would be Hodge, Brune's inability to offer me a contract at this time. So be it. My connection had been Max, who was now gone. Since I dislike teaching the summer session, I'd have to scare up some grant money.

The memorial service was held at a midtown club, very well appointed and sedate. Had Max been a member here? It didn't seem to fit his Brooklyn background, and I wondered idly whether he had been religious. That was not a topic that had ever come up between us. Much as I had liked and admired the man, I really knew very little about him personally or what in his life could have led to his untimely death, unless it was connected to the theft of proprietary information from the company.

I got a surprise when Carolyn came in, cheeks red with cold, in the company of Paul Fallon. She explained that, New York being such a small world, Fallon had proved to be the vice president of the syndicate where she had had an appointment that morning. I replied that I'd heard connections were all in the publishing world. Carolyn murmured back, "What good's one friendly connection when the man who interviewed you is a rude, snide, obnoxious—"

"I hope you're not talking about Marshall," Fallon interrupted; he had been waving Frances Striff over to join us.

Carolyn flushed, but Frances remarked that she couldn't stand Smead herself. "The man thinks all women are incompetent and doesn't even have the good manners to keep his attitude to himself."

When my wife gave Frances her own special glowing smile of approval and sisterhood, Fallon groaned. "I hope that doesn't mean you've crossed us off before I even get to read the rest of your column," he said to Carolyn.

"Not at all,", she replied. "I intend to send Mr. Smead several examples of my work, all written in whatever spare time I have while I'm here. No doubt, you'll be able to find them in his wastebasket if you want to see them, Paul."

Then we were called to our seats by the appearance on the podium of a man I had not met. Whether or not Max was religious, this man evidently was, for he spoke of Max's great soul and the hope that he would find as much happiness in the life hereafter as he had in his work and in his personal life. At that moment, the speaker smiled at a woman in the front row. She wore a wide-brimmed hat with a veil, but I could see the gleam of her chignon through the veil and knew it was Max's wife, Charlotte. Her thin body, entirely clothed in black, almost disappeared from sight in the cloak of her widowhood. I glanced at Carolyn, sitting quietly beside me, and hoped that I would have a long life with her before death separated us.

Many members of the audience rose to speak of Max, as I myself did, saying that I wished there had been more time to know him better because he had been a person to be admired. Some mentioned the brilliance and innovativeness of his mind, others the great influence of his guidance on their research. Vasandrovich had tears in his eyes as he spoke of how Max had changed his life by bringing him to this country and how much Max's friendship and support had meant. I noted that Vasandrovich's wife sat stiff and expressionless through her husband's remarks and wondered whether she would have preferred to stay in Czechoslovakia. Carolyn had said she was of royal Bohemian blood, so she may have felt that she left her identity behind when she came here.

It was an interesting service, over and above the grief that shrouded the room, and I listened to and watched carefully each speaker in turn, looking for clues to the mystery of his death, I suppose, and to what had been bothering him that last weekend when he called me. There were shocking things said, as well, for his children were there, his son, Rick, and daughter, Ariadne. Max had never mentioned them to me, and I began to see why, for they spoke of their father with barely concealed enmity. What a source of sadness and disappointment they must have been to him, for I did not see Max as a man who would have been indifferent to his children.

The son was slender and condescending in a black suit that evidently cost ten times anything I own; I wouldn't have realized that, but Carolyn poked me and whispered that she saw London tailoring there. How do women know such things? This Rick stood up and said that although his father had not been an understanding man or a generous one, he hoped that Max would make it up to him and to his sister Ariadne in death. The girl said that Max had been beastly to her mother, deserting her when she needed him most. At this, she looked directly at Charlotte Heydemann as if she blamed her for the divorce. Still she, Ariadne, had loved him, she claimed—he was her father, after all—and she hoped he realized in the end that he owed something to a daughter who had had little from him but criticism and unkindness. Then she sat down, her face mirroring satisfaction, her body fashionably clothed but thin to the point of boniness.

Carolyn murmured, "Anorexia." I found myself wondering whether the young woman's unpleasant personality was formed by a pathological fear of food and whether she thought she looked beautiful in her skeletal way. Appalled, I flashed to my own daughter, wishing I could call and ask what she'd had for lunch, just to be sure Gwen hadn't begun to waste away since Christmas break.

When the service was over, we joined the receiving line to offer sympathy to the family. Carolyn murmured, "Someone ought to look into those two children. They probably killed him for his money." Then she sailed right by said children in the line with me in tow, only able to mumble a few words as we passed, and up to the widow. Charlotte had lifted her veil and, at the sight of the barely controlled anguish on her face, Carolyn put her arms around Charlotte, whom she'd never met, and said, "You don't know me. I'm Carolyn Blue."

"Of course, Jason's wife. I'm pleased to meet you," Charlotte murmured.

"I'm so sorry for your loss, Mrs. Heydemann," Carolyn continued. "My husband thought the world of yours, and if there is anything I can do for you while I'm in New York, please let me know."

Women never cease to amaze me. I don't think I could hug a stranger in public no matter how much sympathy I felt for her.

Charlotte Heydemann bit her lip and muttered something about the kindness of strangers, and Carolyn replied, "I'm sure you have as many friends here as your husband. You need to cling to them now."

Charlotte shook her head sadly. "Haven't you heard? Widows become outcasts. We're no longer burned on the pyre, but we are excluded from the lunch-in-town and the day-shopping circuit."

"Then have lunch with me," said Carolyn. I could see that she was speaking on impulse; we didn't have that much time left in New York. She evidently realized that herself because she said, obviously regretful at the thought, "Well, I have tomorrow, but I don't suppose, with all you have to see to . . ."

Charlotte lifted her chin. "Tomorrow would be lovely, Mrs. Blue. The coroner—" Charlotte seemed to choke on the words. "They're keeping Max's body."

"I'm so sorry. That's terrible."

Charlotte nodded. "I hate it, and the will won't be read until Friday, so if you really have tomorrow free—"

My wife's face lit with a smile. "I'll look forward to it. Where shall we meet?"

"Well . . ." Charlotte thought a minute and said, "Sfuzzi. We can eat light, but still, Italian is always comfort food." She smiled at me. "She's every bit as lovely as you said, Jason."

"Did he say nice things about me?" Carolyn asked, giving me an affectionate look.

"Indeed, he did. We could go to the Guggenheim afterward if you have the time. There's a *Picasso in the War Years* exhibit that's supposed to be delightful."

Carolyn looked doubtful. "I just saw *Picasso in Clay.*"

"Oh well, that's just one of his pranks. You'll love the hats on the women in the Guggenheim show. A friend in our . . ." She swallowed hard. ". . . in my building loved it."

"Good. That's what we'll do," said Carolyn decisively. Then she glanced back. "We're holding up the line. Is twelve-thirty all right?"

"Perfect," said Charlotte. "Jason, Max and I were so looking forward to taking you and your wife to the opera Monday night. I hope you got to go. I heard the Ryans were tapped since Patsy was the only company wife who claimed to like opera."

Jason smiled. "I don't think Sean did. Charlotte, I can't tell you how . . . how very—"

"I know," she said, patting my arm, and it was as if we'd said it all about the loss of Max. "Thank you for coming today. Max was so determined to bring you into the company. I hope it will work out."

"We'll see," I replied, thinking but not saying that I doubted it would.

Once we were free of the line, Carolyn leaned to whisper in my ear, "Who's that strange man?" She darted her eyes expressively. "He keeps lurking about eavesdropping on people's conversations."

I followed her glance and spotted Merrivale, who was indeed standing close to Fergus McRoy and listening to his conversation with Francis Striff and Paul Fallon while trying to look as if he hadn't even noticed them. However, Striff noticed him, took Fallon's arm, and walked away, after slanting Merrivale a poisonous look.

"Goodness, what was that about?" Carolyn asked. "I thought Frances was going to kick him in the ankle, and that redheaded fellow talking to her caught sight of him and blanched."

"The eavesdropper is Vernon Merrivale," I murmured, "head of security. He's running the investigation into the industrial espionage."

"Really?" said my wife. "Well, the way people react to him, you'd think they're all guilty, and I seriously doubt that Frances is. She's the one who told us about the problem in the first place."

"Yes, and Merrivale wants us to keep our mouths shut about it, especially where the police are concerned."

"Wants who to keep their mouths shut?" she asked.

"You and me."

Carolyn turned astonished eyes on me. "Of all the nerve. I can talk to anyone I want. Who is he to . . . well, did he mention me specifically?"

"He said you'd been talking to one of the police detectives."

"I was sharing a sofa with the man. What was I supposed to do? Ignore him?"

I sighed, checked my watch, and told Carolyn that I needed to get back to Hodge, Brune because my seminar was scheduled in less than an hour.

"Goodness, can't they even wait until the man's buried before returning to business as usual?"

I was surprised at the sharpness of her tone. "Are you saying you think I should refuse to give the seminar?"

"No, of course not, Jason. I guess I'm still peeved at those two . . . two . . . Did you see the look the daughter sent Charlotte? They must have been a trial to her."

"Stepchildren often are," I replied in a low voice. "Can you get back to the hotel on your own?"

"Of course," she replied. "I'll just catch a bus or a subway. I'm getting quite good at it. Do you think it was all right to ask Charlotte to lunch?"

My wife looked doubtful, so I said quickly, "I think it was a very kind thing to do. Probably just what she needed."

"But still, I didn't get Mr. Merrivale's permission," she added snidely. "Maybe you should ask him what I can talk to her about."

I chuckled and replied, "I'll definitely ask him and get back to you."

Grinning, she brushed her lips across my cheek. "You do that. Are we going to be on our own tonight?"

"As far as I know."

"Good. I'll choose the perfect restaurant for a romantic dinner." She gave me a smile that still, after all these years, stirs my blood and then headed for the front door. Before she reached it, she stopped to talk to the detective I'd met my first day at Hodge, Brune, possibly the same one Merrivale had been complaining about. Ah, Carolyn. I could only hope her remarks would be tempered by discretion rather than prompted by pique.

Vasandrovich paused beside me and said there was a limo waiting for us behind the building. The last thing I saw as I turned to follow him was the sad face of Charlotte Heydemann as she left the hall talking to Calvin Pharr, who looked quite sober and almost as unhappy as she. Still, I wondered how much cognac he had consumed that morning in preparation for the services. I did know his wineglass was refilled a number of times in the company dining room.

13

A Ride-Along

Carolyn

I must admit that I was surprised to find the police in attendance. "Hello, Detective Worski. Did you know Dr. Heydemann personally?" I asked when I spotted the detective I'd met in Vaclav Vasandrovich's office. Worski was still wearing that peculiar green overcoat and was now accompanied by a tall black man who was better dressed.

"Never miss the memorial service of a murder victim," Worski replied. "Surprisin' what you pick up when people start talkin' about the deceased."

"Really? Has anyone ever confessed at one?" I asked.

"Not that I've heard," said Worski. "You know of any, Ali?"

The black man said, "Why ask me? I've spent more time in white-collar crime than homicide, so I don't attend a lot of memorial services looking for evidence."

We were out on the street by then, and I asked where I might find the nearest subway entrance, a question that earned me the offer of a ride to the hotel in their unmarked police car. Was the arrogant, security-conscious Mr. Merrivale watching me? I wondered. Was he fuming because I chose to defy him by talking to the police? Too bad. I also chose to accept the ride and was soon sitting in the backseat.

"Well, Mrs. Blue," said Detective Worski, "you still like the wife for the murder? I saw you talkin' to her."

"Oh, absolutely not," I replied. "She's very nice and much too miserable about her husband's death to have killed him. But those children. If they didn't kill him, they probably wanted to. Did you hear them?"

"Oh, yeah," said Worski. "Glad they're not my kids. Still, when there's money involved, it's usually the wife. She gets the biggest cut. You think he's leavin' a lot?"

"I have no idea, but I'm having lunch with her tomorrow, and she mentioned that the will's to be read Friday. If you have a formal will reading, that probably means there's a substantial estate. Wouldn't you think?"

"Well, if you're havin' lunch with her, keep your ears open, Mrs. Blue."

I couldn't really tell whether the detective was humoring me in a jocular way or seriously asking for my help.

"Here's my card." He slid a wide-palmed, short-fingered hand inside that green overcoat and plucked out a business card, which he handed me, even as he negotiated a rather terrifying traffic maneuver between two taxicabs, both of which honked angrily. "You give me a call if you hear anything," he added.

I took the card and slipped it into my handbag. "Actually, I had lunch with someone who knows all the gossip: Paul Fallon. Maybe you should talk to him."

"What did he think? He got any ideas about who might have done it?"

"Well, he doesn't think Charlotte Heydemann did, but he mentioned the children. They've evidently been every bit as greedy and unpleasant to their father as they seemed today and weren't on the best of terms with him, mostly over money. Also they resent the breakup with his first wife, their mother."

"How about her?"

"He said she's probably in a mental institution. Evidently, she spends quite a bit of time there."

"Interestin'. I'll have to look into that. Anyone else?"

"Oh, he mentioned the Vasandroviches, because Dr. Vasandrovich has stepped into Max's job and they might need the money, but I think he was joking about that."

"Vasandrovich. That's one of a lot of guys at that company I didn't like."

"What did you think of a man named . . . what was it? . . . Calvin. Calvin Pharr, I think. He evidently has a drinking problem that Max warned him about, although that doesn't seem a good reason for murdering someone." I had shifted to the middle of the backseat, the better to carry on the conversation. "And I suppose there's the espionage angle, although really—killed by Ukrainian spies? That's a bit far out."

"I'd like to hear about that," said the black man, speaking for the first time.

"I don't believe we've been introduced," I murmured. He'd been so quiet, I'd almost forgotten he was there.

"Sorry. My partner, Mohammed Ali," said Worski. "Great name, huh?"

"Really," I agreed. "Detective Ali, are you by any chance—"

"—related to the boxer?" he finished for me. "No, ma'am."

"Well, actually I was thinking of an Egyptian ruler . . . sometime in the last hundred years, I think. The one who invited forty of his enemies to dinner and poisoned them all."

Detective Ali turned around and stared at me. "Do I look like an Egyptian?" he asked.

Indeed, he was very dark. "Well, Aida, the opera heroine, was supposed to be dark-skinned," I said, feeling a bit foolish.

"Wasn't she Ethiopian?"

"What the hell are you two talkin' about?" Worski demanded. "It don't sound like it's got anything to do with our case. Why don't you tell him about this espionage, Mrs. Blue? It's the first sign of interest he's shown since we partnered up."

Embarrassed at my faux pas, I was a little more forthcoming about what I'd heard from Frances Striff at dinner last night than I might have been otherwise. "But I doubt that would be connected to his murder, do you think?" I finished lamely.

In reply Detective Ali gave me his card and suggested that I call him if I heard any more about the Ukrainian connection. "Nobody's talking to us about anything connected to company business over there." Then he murmured something to Worski about the Russian Mob. Worski snorted.

I wished I'd held my tongue. With Hodge, Brune being so secretive about the theft of their research and their security person making threats, I had undoubtedly done my husband a disservice by mentioning it. Should I call Jason and tell him what I'd done? Well, no, I couldn't do that. He was giving a seminar. Maybe tonight when we had the evening to ourselves for a change.

14
Tea with the VP

Jason

My seminar was well received, even attended by Charles Moore himself, who congratulated me afterward on a very interesting piece of research and reminded me of our meeting at four-thirty. As he left the seminar room, Vasandrovich approached me and said, "I hope that you and your wife can join Sophia and me this evening. My wife so enjoyed meeting yours. Mrs. Blue evidently has what, in an American, is a surprising interest in and knowledge of Czech history."

"Carolyn mentioned a discussion they had about medieval history." But I doubted that she'd relish the prospect of being entertained this evening by the Vasandroviches. "Actually, we—"

"Ah, please don't tell me that you have made other plans, Dr. Blue. I feel quite remiss in not having entertained you before now."

I wondered, perhaps unfairly, whether his sudden interest didn't stem from the vice president's compliment on my seminar and reminder of our scheduled meeting.

"Sophia has managed to procure four tickets to the opera. *Il Trovatore.* She tells me we can expect an excellent cast. Of course, we'll have dinner somewhere close by. I hope the restaurant will please your wife who, I believe, is a culinary writer."

"I'm sure she'll be delighted." At least with the opera. Carolyn loves *Il Trovatore.* She is particularly fond of the aria "Il Balen," sung by the Count de Luna, and, for that reason, holds the peculiar opinion that the villain, rather than the hero, Manrico, should win Leonora. Not that it matters. Whoever wins the lady will die with her in the last act, as is expected in grand opera. Vasandrovich expressed his pleasure at my acceptance and went off just before a tall black man, who introduced himself as Mohammed Ali, accosted me. *Mohammed Ali?* Had some poor lunatic managed to get into the building? I wondered. He looked respectable enough.

"No," he said, "I'm not related to the Egyptian who poisoned forty enemies."

"Actually, I was thinking of the boxer," I replied. "What poison did the Egyptian use?" Toxins always catch my interest, even when mentioned in such unusual circumstances.

"I don't know. Ask your wife. She thought I might be related to some Middle Eastern murderer."

I had to laugh. Trust Carolyn to introduce an arcane piece of history into a conversation. "Where did you meet my wife?" I asked.

"Detective Worski and I gave her a ride back to her hotel. Now what's this business about industrial espionage, and why would a bunch of Ukrainians want to steal research about coal?"

Obviously, my wife had not bowed to Merrivale's demand that she keep her mouth shut about company business, and in response to such a specific question, I could hardly remain silent either. "It's a process for stopping pollution from coal-fired power plants," I replied. "Because of global warming and the spread of environmental laws, such technology would be extremely valuable."

"Excuse me, but I'll have to put a stop to this conversation. It involves proprietary information," said Vernon Merrivale, who had spotted us talking from down the hall.

Caught in the act, I thought.

"He doesn't work for Hodge, Brune," said the detective, "so—"

"But he has an appointment to keep," said Merrivale and gave me a hard look. I glanced at my watch and saw that I was, indeed, due in Charles Moore's office.

"I'm afraid that's true," I said to the detective.

"Another time then," he replied. "We are conducting a murder investigation here." He stared at Merrivale. "And we expect cooperation. Or is Hodge, Brune trying to cover up something about Heydemann's death?"

I left Merrivale to answer that question, about which I was beginning to wonder myself, and went to my appointment. Charles Moore, ensconced in a large corner office with a breathtaking view of the city, offered me a cup of English tea, which I accepted reluctantly. I am not an enthusiastic tea drinker, even when assured that this blend was one of the best he had found in his lifelong search for fine tea. We had a brief discussion on recent medical research that revealed the protective properties of tea and then got down to the topic that evidently brought me to his office. Moore wanted to assure me that, despite the disarray in which the company found itself, there was still interest in employing me as a consultant. "Max thought very highly of you, Dr. Blue," said Moore.

"And I of him," I replied. "His death came as a great shock, but perhaps not so much after I considered the telephone call he made to me over the weekend."

Moore's glance sharpened. "I'd appreciate hearing about that."

"He said that he was worried about some problem the company faced and was hoping for my input."

"He told you what the problem was?"

"No, he didn't feel free to discuss it on the telephone. Strange, don't you think?"

"Perhaps not," said Moore. "What input did he want from you? Did he say?"

"Only that he hoped to avail himself of my expertise and academic connections. I'm surprised Merrivale hasn't told you about this."

"What connections?" Moore asked, taking no notice of my mention of his security chief. "Was Max specific?"

"No, but in the light of the Ukrainian debacle, I assume he meant connections in Eastern Europe."

"Which you have?"

"Yes, but I certainly don't have any particular expertise in coal research, so I may be wrong in my assumptions."

"No, I think that you're right. What I'm about to say to you, Dr. Blue, must be in confidence. Are we agreed?" Intrigued, I nodded. "Max feared just what has happened, the theft of our research, and he expected to nail down over the weekend who was responsible. We were to meet Monday morning, but he postponed until that afternoon, and then . . ." Moore sighed. "And then he was killed."

"Good lord!" I thought over what I'd been told. "Someone mentioned (I think it was Calvin Pharr) that Max was overheard shouting at someone in his office. If you determined with whom he had an appointment—"

"We've tried."

"Surely his secretary—"

"She was out with the flu, and the temp who replaced her must have been in the copy room at the time the argument occurred because she heard nothing."

"Have you talked to the police about this?"

"That's exactly what we don't want to do," said Moore. "Too many people know already. It could have a disastrous effect on our stock if it gets out. We've sunk a lot of money into this project over a five-year period, and we want to salvage our investment before the news hurts us more than we've already been hurt. Merrivale will handle the investigation; the man's a pit bull when he gets on the scent, although unfortunately he has a personality to match." Moore smiled ever so slightly, the first smile I had seen from him. "And any help you can give us will be much appreciated. If you could, discreetly of course, make inquiries of your connections in Eastern Europe . . ."

"Of course," I agreed. "Anything I can do to find out why Max was killed." I stopped, having had a thought that would not please Moore. "On the matter of the police, however, I'm afraid they already know about the theft. A Detective Ali questioned me just before I came up here."

"What did you tell him?"

"Why the research would be worth stealing, although nothing specific about its nature, with which I'm not familiar."

"Yes." He sighed. "Well, it can't be helped. I'll have to talk to them myself and beg for their discretion. I hope I can count on the same from you, Dr. Blue."

"I understand your concerns, although it seems to me that you might make more progress if you took the authorities into your confidence and used their resources."

"I rather believe our resources are more extensive in this area than theirs. After all, it has to be someone here who assisted in the theft."

"Yes." *And the murder,* I thought, not happily. "I'll see what I can find out."

"Good. I'll assign you an office, a telephone, a fax, whatever you need."

"I'm afraid this is somewhat outside my area of competence, both the research and investigating a crime."

"Well, we all have that problem, don't we?" said Moore. "Still, we must do what we can."

As I left his office, I was glad to remember that my wife considered the idea of industrial espionage outside the realm of sensible consideration. Her remarks to the police had probably been facetious in nature. In fact, I could easily imagine her laughing about bizarre theories of espionage and murder. That being the case, I hardly needed to tell her what I'd just heard and put her into danger, not that I felt threatened myself. I was just going to make a few calls, which no one but Moore and I and perhaps Merrivale need know about.

The thought of Merrivale reminded me that he evidently hadn't passed on to Moore the news of my last conversation with Max. Why would he keep that to himself? This was obviously a complex situation, which I did not fully understand. Still, I'd make inquiries, and if I found out anything, I'd report directly to Moore, in whom I had more confidence than in the security chief. Then Moore could take the information and the investigation from there in whatever way he thought best. I'd be out of it, and Carolyn, if she felt the need to think about the murder, could think about Max's obnoxious children.

15

How to Pronounce Gelato

What place could be more enchanting than Italy with its splendid churches and castles, majestic Roman ruins, fabulous works of art, glorious music, charming people, delicious food and wine, and, most enchanting of all, its gelato? Everywhere in Italy from the humblest corner grocery to the most sophisticated *ristorante*, one can purchase that paragon of ice creams, gelato. So smooth, so rich, so intensely flavorful. Made fresh every day. One's first taste of gelato is a transcendent experience. And the second taste. And the third.

Can we Americans, you might ask, enjoy gelato in our own country, where Italian restaurants abound? The answer is yes. Americans can eat gelato, without ever crossing their own borders. Therefore, in a New York restaurant that serves delicious Italian food, wouldn't one expect to be able to order gelato? Certainly. Instead of looking puzzled, wouldn't one's waiter, even if he had a peculiar accent (Serbian? Guatemalan? Bornean?), have immediately assured us, when asked, that the house served gelato?

One could excuse him for not recognizing the word *grappa*, even though it has become exceedingly chic and, in its more expensive manifestations, can even be considered acceptable for human consumption. It no longer *always* tastes like a petroleum product. My husband is very fond of it, but he had to call the head waiter in order to learn that the restaurant had grappas for every taste. He chose one.

But in the matter of gelato (which is pronounced with a soft *g*), our waiter looked blank. I tried a few of the simpler flavors on him: *cioccolato, fragole, caffe, pistacchio, limone*. He looked frightened. Italian ice cream, my husband translated. "Oh, gelato!" exclaimed the young man. He pronounced it with a hard *g*. Of course. They had vanilla, he assured us.

Would it really be gelato, I had to wonder, when so egregiously mispro-
nounced? Gelato has eggs and cream in it, not to mention the freshest fruits,
the tastiest nuts. I didn't want plain old vanilla ice cream. Used to more exotic
flavors in my gelato and suspicious that I might not get the real thing, I gave
up and ordered tiramisu, the choice of which our waiter approved, probably
because he knew how to pronounce that.

                        Carolyn Blue, "Have Fork, Will Travel," *Toledo Star-Signal*

Carolyn

I can't say that I was pleased to hear we were having dinner with the
Vasandroviches, although his tears at the memorial service had given me
a better opinion of him. Still, as Jason said, who could pass up *Il Trovatore?*
And I had hopes that the snobbish Sophia would pick a famous restaurant.

Instead, we went to a place I had never heard of: Coco Opera. It was
charmingly decorated: brick walls, wood floors, fat columns of a mottled
dark red, red drapes with gold fringe, elaborate Venetian carnival masks on
the walls and opera posters on the columns, even sheer screens with ex-
cerpts from opera scores hanging from the ceiling. No question we were
meant to attend the opera after dinner. Of course, Sophia had hoped for
something more famous, "but last-minute reservations are so hard to get,
you understand," she explained, "even when you have good connections.
We're fortunate that I was able to obtain the tickets to *Il Trovatore.*"

We all agreed that we were fortunate indeed and studied our menus. I
ordered roasted salmon, which was rare and moist, set on top of creamy
mashed potatoes and surrounded by grilled zucchini and cherry tomatoes
whose bite contrasted nicely with the delicious sweetness of a wonderful
balsamic reduction sauce.

My husband ordered, of all things, liver. The dish was called Liver
Venezziana, and the dreaded liver arrived cut into small pieces, perfectly
medium rare, as Jason had ordered it, accompanied by sliced caramelized
onions and grilled polenta, which Jason described, smiling, as grilled grits. The
whole swam in a dense liver sauce, which was slightly sweet. At his insistence,
I ventured to dip a bit of bread in the sauce. I believe Sophia was shocked.

She certainly looked askance when I discovered that I had forgotten to
put a pen in my handbag and had to ask the headwaiter for the loan of his
in order to take notes. Our waiter, although anxious to please, was not
knowledgeable either about the menu or Italian cuisine in general. I gathered that he, I, and the restaurant were a source of embarrassment to
Sophia, even though the food was very good, and the wine . . . well, it was
a so-so Chianti. Then Jason had a terrible time ordering grappa, and I was
forced to select tiramisu for lack of a more exotic dessert choice. Cheesecake, which the waiter was pushing, is not on my list of Italian delights. The

tiramisu, however, was just as good as he insisted. I felt that I was consuming rich, sweet, coffee-scented air.

Evidently, while Sophia and I were making the obligatory trip to the ladies' room, Vaclav had a little talk with Jason, because as we walked over to the opera, Jason asked me why I had been talking to the police again about Max Heydemann, whom I didn't even know. "Not just Merrivale but other Hodge, Brune executives seem to have security concerns about us now," Jason said dryly.

"Really? Well, if they don't want me talking to the police," I said tartly, "they shouldn't leave me stranded in the company of the police." Too late to confess my indiscreet revelations to Detective Ali; obviously my secret was out. "Since no one thought to offer me a ride back to the hotel from the memorial service, I accepted one from both the detectives on the case, and—surprise, surprise—I talked to them while we were in the police car."

Jason laughed. "Ah yes, Detective Ali, the one you thought might be related to a mass poisoner." He still didn't seem to be particularly worried about the company's perception that I might be a security risk. And I felt that any citizen has a perfect right to talk to the police if she wants to. I rather liked Detective Worski, even if his overcoat was frumpy, and Detective Ali was very well dressed and amazingly lacking in the cynicism of his partner, but then he was the younger man.

The opera was a delight. I do love *Il Trovatore*. There's hardly an aria or chorus that you couldn't sing in the shower if you were so inclined. I rarely do, but I've been known to hum arias in the kitchen. Of course, Manrico treats Leonora abominably in the last act, accusing her of being unfaithful, and that when she's dying from the poison she took to prevent the Count de Luna from having his way with her in return for the release of her imprisoned and ungrateful true love. Opera plots do sound nonsensical when you try to summarize them. Still, the music is thrilling.

But before we got to that piece of high melodrama, we encountered another at intermission, for a strange-looking woman with wild eyes and wilder hair, wearing an expensive gown and diamonds, shrieked across the gaggle of operagoers to Dr. Vasandrovich, "Congratulations, Vaclav. You got the job, didn't you?"

Vaclav looked horribly embarrassed, as well he might, but the woman ploughed through the crowd in our direction, calling, "The demise of my ex is cause for celebration, don't you think, Vaclav? For both of us! Let me buy you a drink! You too, Sophia. Wouldn't you like to be seen drinking at the Met with someone like me, from such a *fine family?*"

Jason and I were speechless. Vaclav, too, but Sophia collected herself and said, purring, "Melisande, how lovely to see you."

Over the strange woman's shoulder I could see a young man shoving people aside as he headed toward us. He looked familiar.

"You're surprised?" the bejeweled woman purred back, her voice a nasty imitation of Sophia's, accent and all. "I'll bet you thought I was back in the sanatorium, didn't you? Not at all. I wouldn't have missed this for the world. I can't think of anyone who deserved killing more than Max."

The young man clutched her shoulder. "What are you doing?" he hissed.

She ignored him. "Well, I did miss the memorial service, didn't I? No one thought to invite me. I'd have had some remarks to make about Max. Stop pulling on my dress, Ricky."

I had recognized the young man: Max Heydemann's son.

"Oh, and Vaclav, you can tell that tacky chorus girl he married that she's not going to get his money. No, indeed. We can count on Daddy to see that my children get what's coming to them."

"Mother, let's go." Rick put his arm around her. "Dad will have done right by us."

"Max neglected you for that bitch, and now they'll both pay."

The intermission bell had rung, and Vaclav was edging away, but she screeched after him, "You tell her that. You hear me? If Max hasn't done the right thing in his will, she'll spend the rest of her life in court trying to pry a crust of bread out of the lawyers."

"Shut *up*, Mother."

"Don't you shush me," she snarled back. "You owe me *money*, dear Ricky, and I expect to be repaid."

We hastened after Vaclav and managed to disappear into the grand tier, where the starburst chandeliers were rising like receding galaxies, but I hated to miss a word that might be passing between those two.

To Sophia I whispered, "Was that—"

"Melisande Heydemann. Max's first wife," Sophia whispered back. "She's obviously overwrought, but as I told you, she does come from a very prominent family."

As *Trovatore* soared to its tragic conclusion, I confess to some distraction. Surely, if Max's children hadn't had him killed, his ex-wife had. Or perhaps she followed him into that deli and killed him herself. And for what did her son owe her money? Maybe she had financed the hiring of an assassin, and Ricky had done the hiring. She was a truly frightening woman. Talk about dysfunctional families!

Because I couldn't sleep when we got back to the hotel, I took hotel stationery from the desk drawer and diverted myself by writing a column in longhand about the waiter who had served us that evening.

"Where are you going?" Jason mumbled from bed as I opened the door to the hall.

"Downstairs to fax this column to that rude Marshall Smead," I replied.

16

The Designated Babysitter

Carolyn

When Jason woke me up on Thursday morning, it was still dark. "What's wrong?" I asked, alarmed. "It must be the middle of the night."

My husband replied that it was eight o'clock and snowing. Accordingly, I squirmed back under the covers, unable to believe he'd awakened me to give me a weather report, and at eight o'clock! That meant I'd had less than seven hours' sleep.

"Carolyn!" He gave my shoulder a little shake. "I can't find my telephone book."

"Who do you need to call?" I mumbled. "Maybe I know the number."

"It's in Eastern Europe."

"What in the world for?"

"The Ukrainian espionage thing."

"For heaven's sake!" I opened one eye and stared balefully at my spouse. "Surely after seeing Melisande Heydemann, you don't think the Ukrainians killed Max."

Jason shrugged. "I didn't say that."

But did he think it? Or was he just trying to help Hodge, Brune on the possible loss of their research efforts? "Did you look in the inside zipped pocket of your briefcase? No, actually, you put it in mine because you didn't have room in yours with all those slides. Did they like your slides?" I was sliding away myself—into sleep.

"They loved my slides," he assured me and leaned over to kiss my forehead. I assume he found the address book, but I wasn't able to get back to sleep, after all. Grumbling, I rose to shower and dress. At eight-thirty I was calling my agent's office to complain about being sent, unprepared, to Marshall Smead. The secretary said Loretta wasn't in yet. Hadn't I noticed that it was snowing? Then she suggested that I come over in an hour or so. They'd fit me in. She hung up before I could protest.

I pulled on the fur-lined boots I had brought with me, bundled up, and headed out into the snow to get breakfast. Because the hour was earlier, the deli was crowded with red-nosed, overcoated New Yorkers, wolfing down huge platters of hot food. Max's ill-fated seat on the aisle was open; maybe all the customers knew someone had died there. I took it and was again served by Thelma, who asked me how the memorial service had gone.

"His children were horrible," I replied. "Only interested in inheriting money from him."

Thelma nodded. "How sharper than a serpent's tooth it is/To have a thankless child!"

Good heavens, I thought. *A waitress who quotes* King Lear. "His widow seemed very nice. She was a professional ballet dancer before she married Max."

"Second wife, right?"

"Oh, yes. I had the misfortune to meet the first Mrs. Heydemann last night. She's a terrifying woman."

"So who do they think killed him? One of the wives?"

I had to laugh, remembering Jason's plans for the morning. "I suspect that my husband thinks it's some industrial espionage thing. Can you believe that?"

"How come?"

"I don't know. Evidently someone in the Ukraine stole their research before they could patent it. Jason's going to call friends in Eastern Europe. They'll probably think he's crazy." And there I went again, talking about Hodge, Brune's secrets.

"How come he knows people in Eastern Europe?"

"Oh, professors. They all know each other."

"Yeah? Well, not likely they'll know anything about the killin'. Mark my words. It was one of the wives. Marriage makes people crazy." She laughed her raucous laugh. "Wouldn't catch me doin' the bride thing." Then she was off to another table, leaving me to wonder if her declaration meant that she was a man hater or just commitment-shy.

When I'd finished my breakfast, I headed for Loretta Blum's office, resenting every step I took in the blowing snow. Nonetheless, I intended to give her a piece of my mind about the horrid visit with Marshall Smead, a disaster for which I considered her responsible. After that confrontation, I was off to look at area rugs farther downtown. Our house has tiled floors, and I wanted to put something pretty and softer underfoot. A few hours of rug shopping, and I'd return to dress for my twelve-thirty appointment with Charlotte Heydemann. But in this weather, would she make it to the restaurant? Would I?

I found Loretta's office in a state of war. Her two daughters were still sick, and her mother-in-law had agreed to look after them, but not their brother, Simon. Consequently, Simon, a sullen twelve-year-old, was sitting next to Loretta's desk (Marsha, the much-pierced secretary, refused to keep him in her anteroom) playing a noisy electronic game. His mother screamed at him to turn it off several times while I was voicing my complaints about Smead, but Simon ignored her.

Finally, Loretta gave up on her son and, catching the drift of my anger, said, "Oh, that's vintage Smead. He's a rude bastard, but did you get a contract? That's the important thing. Think publicity. Think—"

"I'm faxing him columns as fast as I can write them, and I really don't care what he does with them," I replied, taking malicious satisfaction in my anti-Smead campaign.

"Bad attitude, Carolyn. First rule of publishing: Learn to get along with the assholes."

"I'd rather get even, which I may do. Smead hates me, but his boss, Paul Fallon, whom I know socially, is interested in my work."

"Good girl. Second rule of publishing: Exploit your contacts. Contacts are everything. Call Fallon. Invite him to lunch. You can use my phone."

"I have to meet the widow of a friend of my husband's for lunch."

"What can *she* do for you? Does *she* have contacts? By the way, have you been to see Bernie? It doesn't look like it." She eyed my wool slacks and cable-knit sweater. "Simon, turn off that damned machine. You gotta get some decent clothes, Carolyn. We're meeting Rollie tomorrow at Le Bernardin. It's on West Fifty-first."

Well, finally a restaurant from my book on dining in Manhattan. I should be able to get a column out of that. Or two. Or three. I smiled, thinking about inundating the detestable Smead with columns.

"So go downtown to Bernie's. Tell you what. Simon here's bored. You can take him along. He'll show you how to get there. How about that, Simon?"

"No," said Simon.

"Don't tell me no," she snarled. "I got a meeting in—" She looked at her watch. "Fifteen minutes. I'm going to be late. And you, Simon, Marsha won't let you stay, so you'll go with Mrs. Blue here. Take care of her. She's new in town."

"I told you I have a luncheon appointment," I protested. "And it's snowing out there."

"Simon doesn't mind snow, do you, Simon? Just drop him here before noon. I'll be back by then."

With that she left, pulling on her coat, leaving me to eye Simon morosely. "I'm not going to your Uncle Bernie's," I said.

"Wasn't my idea," Simon mumbled. "So, where are we going?"

"Rug shopping." I thought that might discourage him, and he'd insist on staying here with the reluctant Marsha.

"Man!" cried Simon. "Rug shopping? What did I do to deserve that?" But he was putting on his coat, then pulling a knitted cap over his ears. Evidently, I was stuck with him.

17

Telephone Detectives

Jason

Charles Moore was as good as his word. At Hodge, Brune the receptionist directed me to a small office equipped with telephone, computer, notepads, and a memo from Moore informing me that I was to be paid for this week at double my usual consulting rate, which was good news. Carolyn planned to look at rugs today. If she picked something extravagant, it wouldn't propel us toward the poorhouse.

The receptionist also provided a chart that showed the time differences between New York and various cities in Eastern Europe. I glanced at my watch, calculating that it would be the end of the afternoon in most of the cities I planned to call. Some of my contacts could be reached at universities; others would have to be called at home. Therefore, I chose to call first those who were more colleagues than friends. Friends would be less likely to resent being interrupted at home. Also on the first-to-call portion of the list were those who might not have telephones at home, always a problem in countries where the effects of communism have not yet abated.

As might be expected, I found people who were unfamiliar with the claim by the little-known Ukrainian company to a cutting-edge environmental process. A professor in Romania assured me that no cutting-edge environmental research was going on in the Ukraine, certainly not on coal pollution. "My dear Professor Blue," he exclaimed. "They mine coal and burn it; they don't worry about its effects. The miners die, the coal is used, but no one worries about smoke. Much worse are the effects of Chernobyl radiation. So that's what they worry about in the Ukraine."

A friend in Budapest assured me that no one in the Ukraine knew enough or had the funding or equipment to do the kind of research I was talking about. "They're bluffing. They have no process. Maybe they hope to do a bit of blackmail. Sell the rights to what they do not have. Tell your friends not to worry, my dear fellow."

It wasn't a bad theory. Word of the hopes for this research could have leaked, perhaps during the casual discussion that goes on at conferences, hints of great things to come by men who are drinking and chatting after long days of meetings, just the sort of careless talk that Vernon Merrivale deplored. In such a case, might not some impecunious scientist from a faltering economy go home to a dreary apartment and hatch a plan to take advantage of what he had heard? It was worth suggesting to Moore.

I picked up one more bit of information, negative, but still interesting. An industrial chemist in Krakow had actually seen the announcement and, intrigued, asked around about the company. He found the whole story exceedingly peculiar. This was a very small company, I was to know, very few people employed, scientists of no note, and no one knew where the capital investment had come from. One fellow, a colleague at his own company, said that the Ukrainian outfit, which consisted of one building in a poor area of Kiev, had only been in existence eighteen months, perhaps less.

If his information was correct, the Ukrainians could not have developed the process in such a short time and with minimal resources in space and personnel.

"Could there be government or university research behind this announcement?" I asked.

"If that were the case, my friend would be aware. He goes often to Kiev. Something does not smell good. I see this immediately, but not why your interest in this."

"I am making inquiries for friends," I replied. "Friends with an interest in such research problems. If you should come across the name of a scientist associated with the Ukrainian endeavor, my friends would like to talk to him."

"I do not think exists such a Ukrainian. But is like Russians, no? They invent everything and before everyone." He laughed heartily. "Some things never change." He inquired after the health of my wife, whom he had met at a meeting in Germany. We exchanged personal tidbits—Carolyn's new career, the birth of a child to his daughter, my surprising move to Texas— and parted on friendly terms.

Carolyn

Loretta's secretary managed to be away from her desk when Simon and I left. Therefore, I really had no choice but to take him with me, for I remembered very clearly what twelve-year-old boys are like. If I left him, he might disappear or cause chaos in his mother's office. Goodness knows what he might get up to.

"The place I want to go is on Twenty-third Street." I mentioned the address. Simon shrugged and led the way into the whirling, wet world outside, where snow clung to my coat and my eyelashes and squished wetly and with slippery tenacity under my boots. I put up my umbrella. Simon insisted that no one used an umbrella for snow. Much he knew. When I had to, I slipped into a doorway and shook the clinging snow from the umbrella, but I kept it open and thus prevented my coat from turning soggy.

He said we'd take a bus first; I had to pay for his ride, but I had my

Metro pass, which was good on buses. So we rode across town, standing in a crowded aisle with my umbrella dripping on my boots, and exited to climb down into the bowels of the city to catch a subway that still left us many steep steps and two blocks from A.B.C. Carpet. During the subway ride, Simon studied the advertising cards displayed above the seats and asked in a loud voice, "Exactly what is an abortion?" The card said, "Need an abortion? We're here for you." Then a phone number for Planned Parenthood.

I knew just what he was up to and had experience in circumventing such embarrassing tactics on the part of obstreperous youngsters. "How interesting that you should ask that, Simon," I replied. "Are you familiar with the *Oxford English Dictionary?*" He turned to me suspiciously. "The stem *abort* is from the Latin *aboriri,* to miscarry or disappear." I had myself looked it up once in childhood, having heard some older girls whispering and giggling about abortions. Naturally, I used my father's compact *OED* because I loved the little square magnifying glass that came with it. "By the way," I added earnestly, "there is a fascinating book on the making of the *Oxford English Dictionary,* which, as you may know, is the most impressive lexicographic endeavor of Western man. The book is called *The Professor and the Madman.* It seems that a major contributor was, in fact, a madman, who spent many years in an asylum in England, although you'll be interested to hear that he was actually an American, a naval officer, if I remember—"

"Oh, forget it," Simon interrupted. An older lady across the aisle was listening to this exchange and laughing behind her hand when we exited the car.

As we walked the two blocks, Simon jumped into piles of slush that were accumulating on the sidewalks, while I stepped, flatfooted and with care, around them. "We're both going to catch something, a cold or the flu," I mumbled. I should have skipped this trip and gone back to my cozy, dry hotel room.

"*I* won't get the flu," Simon assured me. "I've had my flu shot."

"Kids don't get flu shots," I replied grumpily. "*I'm* not even old enough to need flu shots."

"I get them. I've got asthma."

Oh perfect, I thought grimly and began to watch for signs that an attack might be imminent. I remembered all too clearly a time when I was a young mother and Chris had croup. The wheezing and gasping for breath had terrified me. "Do you have your inhaler?" I asked anxiously.

"Sure," and then he was running ahead of me again, making splatting jumps that sent dirty, semiliquid snow spraying from around his feet, often onto my boots and the bottom of my coat.

I considered what the state of my only coat would be when I met Charlotte Heydemann at Sfuzzi. I doubted that she, no matter how inclement the weather, would arrive with her hem splattered by muddy snow. "Stop that!" I said to Simon in my quietest voice.

For a wonder, he did. Perhaps he was so used to being yelled at by adults that a quiet command got his attention. What a relief to finally step inside that huge room at A.B.C. Carpet, with its dry warmth and its towering racks of hanging rugs. There were gangs of men who, at the command of sales folk, flipped the carpets onto the floor, building up wild overlapping patterns and then rolling them away. I would have felt overwhelmed by comfort if not for the strange, dusty, rubbery air that prickled my nose and brought on sneezes. I fished a Kleenex from my purse and gave said nose a good blow to clear away the odor.

Simon sneezed, too, but he wiped his nose with his hand instead of fishing for a handkerchief. Or perhaps, as the designated, if reluctant, babysitter, I was supposed to provide him with Kleenex. Too late.

Instead, I flipped hanging rugs until I found one with an indefinite green and blue pattern that had the faint lines and hues of a watercolor painting. When it was laid out on the floor for me, it proved to be both too small and, as Simon so succinctly put it, "bor-ing." But on the rack it had seemed huge and mysteriously lovely. Ah well. I looked at a carpet in green, yellow, and white with raised O'Keeffish flowers. It was gorgeous, although I had no idea where I'd put it, just that I wanted it very badly. And it was marked down! Really quite reasonable. Then it went onto the floor, and I saw that it was *very* small, and that dust had caught on the raised edges of the flowers, making the whole look bedraggled and secondhand.

"It's been very popular," said the saleswoman.

I looked at it askance. "Do you have a clean one?"

"We probably do, but truthfully, that model dirties up pretty rapidly."

Even though I didn't need that rug, I was disappointed. It had looked so pretty, so green and springlike, on the rack. It would have been a reminder, in stark El Paso, of landscapes more lush. I sighed and continued to look. Simon fidgeted, wandered off, picked out strange and dangerous-looking patterns in black and brown to show me, looked at rugs with cartoon characters embossed on their surfaces as if ready to leap off and grab some passing child by the ankle. He went to the front of the store to press his nose against the large windows. "Don't go outside," I called. Even though unfairly saddled with this child, I didn't want to lose him and have to explain the loss to his mother.

"If the snow doesn't let up soon, we won't be able to go outside," he called back. "We'll be stuck here. Marooned in a boring rug store on Twenty-third Street! Starving to death."

"It's not even lunchtime," I replied and pushed back more carpets. And more. But then I saw one I couldn't take my eyes off. "Oh my!" I said.

"A very popular design," the saleswoman assured me.

"Does that mean it picks up dirt like a magnet?" I asked.

"Cool!" said Simon, coming to look at my discovery.

"Even your son likes it." The saleswoman beamed at the two of us, while Simon and I, two strangers in the storm, exchanged a rueful glance.

"So buy it, and let's get something to eat," said my charge. "If you don't feed me, I'll starve to death. And then my mother will send out for some crappy chicken soup or something because I'm sneezing."

"When did you sneeze?" I interrupted anxiously.

"Same time you did. When we walked in here."

"That odor disappears within days," the saleswoman assured us.

"I think I'm going to have an asthma attack," said Simon. The saleswoman looked alarmed. "Something to eat would help," he added hopefully.

"We don't serve refreshments," she apologized.

"Just give me your card with the name and price of this rug," I suggested.

"You mean after all this looking, you're not going to buy one?" Simon stared at me with indignation.

"Doesn't your mother consult your father before she buys a rug?" I asked.

"Probably not. Probably he's the one who buys the rugs. How would I know? Nobody consults me about rugs."

I asked about shipping costs, length of time to delivery, and other practical considerations, all the while staring at the rug of my dreams with its op art, many-colored pattern. It was definitely large enough for the space and even contained some of the right colors, not to mention some colors that had never been seen in my living room. Oh well.

Once free from the rug store, the snow having abated somewhat, Simon began to make suggestions about places he'd like to go. I consulted my watch and reminded him that I had to be back at my hotel before noon. Dancing around me as I slogged over the slick sidewalks toward the subway entrance, Simon reminded me that he was hungry and he was my responsibility. Then I slipped! *Broken hip!* my mind screamed. But I did not break anything because Simon, skinny young fellow that he was, caught me.

"I saved you," he pointed out. "So shouldn't you—"

"What do you want to eat?" I interrupted. "It will have to be something you can carry back with you."

"A hot dog," he replied instantly. He even knew where to get one, so I bought Simon a huge hot dog doused with sauerkraut, smelling to high heaven, and dripping out of its wrappings. Then I took him back to his mother's office.

Alas, Marsha had left a note saying that she had taken an early lunch, and, good mother that I am, I did not feel comfortable leaving Simon by himself in the office. I consoled myself by using her absence to appropriate her telephone. When I'd fished my Metro pass from my purse during the ride back with Simon, I also came up with Detective Worski's card, reminding me of two things he should know relative to the investigation of Max Heydemann's death. After all, the detective had said to call him if I learned anything useful. Therefore, I settled Simon in the chair beside Marsha's desk where I could keep my eye on him and called the detective.

He didn't sound very excited to hear from me. Perhaps he was busy. Nonetheless, I persisted. "Two interesting things happened last night at the opera."

"Hard to believe," said the cynical Worski, who evidently didn't care for opera.

"First, an official at Hodge, Brune remonstrated with my husband because I've been talking about the case to you. I thought perhaps that might be significant."

"Who?" asked Worski.

"Vaclav Vasandrovich."

"Yeah, him. No big surprise there."

"He doesn't want my husband to speak to you, either."

"OK."

"Not that the admonition says anything in particular about Dr. Vasandrovich personally," I admitted. "Secretiveness seems to be company policy, which I consider peculiar when a murder investigation is involved."

"Yeah. Same here."

"More important, I met Max Heydemann's first wife. Now there is someone who might well have murdered him! She was absolutely jubilant over his death."

"At the opera?"

"During intermission. Noisily jubilant. And ready to go to court if her children don't inherit most of his money. But most important of all, detective: She's crazy!"

"Uh-huh."

"No, I mean psychotic crazy. Frequently institutionalized crazy. I'd have no trouble believing she paid to have her ex-husband killed. She could have done it herself."

I detected a definite interest in the detective's response to that information and felt the pleasant warmth of having been useful to the authorities, as any citizen is bound to do, even if that usefulness should bring the wrath of the frightening Melisande Heydemann down upon my head. Reconsidering my courageous public-spiritedness, I hastily added, "Please don't mention to her that I told you about last night." He promised that he wouldn't.

Only after I'd hung up did I notice Simon's eyes on me, round and fascinated. "Cool!" he breathed. "You know someone who got murdered?"

"My husband does," I admitted reluctantly.

"And you're helping the police?"

"Just with a bit of information," I replied modestly.

"And you know a crazy woman who did it?"

"I don't *know* that," I hastened to assure him. "I just consider her a . . . a suspect."

"That is so cool!"

It seems that, inadvertently, I had earned Simon's admiration. Not so his mother's when she discovered him finishing off his large, messy hot dog. I hurried off before she could turn her dismay from him to me.

How did a sausage between halves of a bun come to be called a hot dog? you might ask. As the result of a little research project, I discovered that a New York newspaper cartoonist drew a picture of a dachshund encased in a bun and labeled it a "hot dog." Then, as hot dog stands proliferated in the city and price wars ensued, the public began to question what was actually in a sandwich that could be purchased for five cents. Dog meat, perhaps?

Nathan's Famous, the hot dog emporium, pacified public concern by offering free hot dogs to interns from a Coney Island hospital. The crowds of white-coated customers made Nathan's "the place where the doctors ate" and the hot dogs the entrée of choice.

Carolyn Blue, "Have Fork, Will Travel," *Peoria Farm Sentinel*

18
The Marriage of French and Japanese

When eating in a famous New York restaurant, those of us from the hinterlands are understandably fearful that our clothing may not meet the standards of the house, that we may even be asked to leave for reasons of fashion deficiency. Stories have been printed about people who have been ejected. My favorite concerns the campaign against women in trousers conducted by La Cote Basque. Two ladies wearing mink coats arrived to exercise their reservations and were told that the one in trousers could not enter. Alas, the poor lady had a broken leg in a cast over which she felt trousers were appropriate. Management stood firm; no trousers; they must be removed. To be replaced with what? asked the embarrassed ladies. Wear your coat, said hardhearted management. Defeated, the crippled woman limped to the ladies' room, struggled out of her trousers—no small feat when one pant leg had to be dragged over the cast—and ate her lunch swathed in mink and perspiration.

The French are known not only for their wonderful food, but for their unwavering sense of propriety.

Carolyn Blue, "Have Fork, Will Travel," *Des Moines Clarion Monitor*

Carolyn

When I arrived at the hotel, having sprinted up the subway steps, I found a message from Charlotte Heydemann. "Overcome by a desire to eat

French. Got reservations for 1:00 P.M. at La Caravelle. French. You'll love it." I probably would, I thought with dismay after I'd researched it in *Dining and the Opera, Zagat,* and *Access New York City.* It looked wonderful and *very expensive,* and I had issued the invitation, so I would be paying.

Well, at least I'd have an extra half-hour to change. Hurriedly, I stripped out of my snow boots, slacks, and thick sweater and donned a dress, the very dress my agent had thought not chic enough for my editor and Le Bernardin. Would I be snubbed for fashion deficiency at La Caravelle? I then inspected my coat and used a washcloth to rub a few splashes, courtesy of Simon Puddle-Jumper, from the bottom. Jewelry, shoes, handbag, lipstick, French twist rapidly constructed, and I was ready to find a cab; I couldn't wear decent shoes in this weather and take the subway, so cab fare would add to the cost of my Good Samaritan instincts and natural nosiness.

Charlotte and I arrived simultaneously but in different taxis at the Shoreham on West Fifty-fifth and made our way to the restaurant. Quiet elegance, pink banquettes, murals of Paris: I was enchanted. The owner greeted Charlotte with an embrace. I was treated like a valued client, acceptably outfitted for their very beautiful dining room. As I studied the menu, I quickly decided that I would have to stop checking the prices.

Charlotte, looking it over with casual pleasure, said, "By the way, this is on me." Before I could protest, she added, "No arguments. I chose the place, so I'll pay. Believe me, it's worth it to me, a back-to-my-roots indulgence." She laughed softly. "I'm French. Well, my parents were. Oh, how they wanted me to become a great ballerina! But after all the financial sacrifices they made (my father owned a small French patisserie near Columbus Circle, never very successful), I just didn't have the talent. I loved dancing but never progressed beyond being one of the four members of the corps de ballet, mimicking each other's steps or twirling separately across the stage in turn. Are you very hungry, three-course hungry, or do you want something lighter?"

"Lighter," I responded immediately. At least I didn't have to pick the most expensive things on the menu, since she seemed set on paying. I studied the appetizer list and found an intriguing entry: Little Flutes of Curried Escargots. The ingredients were unusual, to me at least: Oriental plus French. I presumed that I was seeing "fusion cuisine," the product of famous chefs raiding the menus of ethnic restaurants.

Charlotte mentioned a Japanese chef in the kitchen of this bastion of French comestibles, so presumably fusion cuisine snatched up not only recipes but also actual people. "And you have to try the Chair de Crabe de Caravelle," she insisted.

Again I tried to protest.

"You're a food writer. You can't leave without having sampled this dish," she announced. "It's dressed with a lovely herb sauce. Now, what about entrées?"

I laughed. "This is supposed to be a light meal. We still have the Picasso hats to view."

"Well then, I'll order the crab, you order the escargot, we'll share those, and then we'll have desserts. And wine. I know just the thing. A wonderful white burgundy."

"At least let me pay my half."

"Absolutely not. It's *my* psyche that needs comfort." She did indeed look like a woman who needed comfort. I was sure she had been crying as recently as this morning. Even under the careful makeup, grief showed in the slight puffiness of her eyes and the drawn lines of her mouth.

We ordered, and Charlotte's forced merriment failed her for the moment. "It's so strange," she confessed. "The police have been back several times. Not to tell me about the investigation. To ask me questions. It's almost as if they think I had something to do with Max's death. That's so ironic. I'm the one most destroyed by this, and they think . . . well, I don't know what they think. Or why."

My conscience smote me because I had a good idea what lay behind the police's suspicions. Sophia's gossip about a lover, and my repetition of this tidbit, not to mention the perception that widows profited from the deaths of husbands who were well to do. Charlotte had told me that her family was not. "Perhaps they think . . . because you're the widow . . ." How could I put this delicately?

"That I stand to inherit a fortune because Max died? Well, I won't be penniless. I know he set up a trust for me, but beyond that, I have no idea what's in his will. Tomorrow's the reading, and obviously, his children are expecting big things." She shook her head. "The trust for me, that's because Max was afraid his first wife's father would go to court, if anything happened to Max, and try to arrange for the kids to get it all."

"But surely he couldn't do that," I protested. "I mean he couldn't win."

"He's done it before. When Melisande, that's Max's first wife, was finally committed, her father went to court to take custody of the children away from Max, and he managed to get shared custody until she was out. You heard them at the funeral; they're dreadful, and they needn't have been. If Max could have kept them away from the D'Vallencourts, he might have made something out of them."

The herbed crab and the escargot flutes arrived, and we shared. The food was amazing, exotic, thoroughly unforgettable, the white burgundy the best wine I'd ever tasted. I've read that in the 1820s only women in New York ate at French restaurants. Men considered the food too effeminate for masculine tastes. I glanced around and noted plenty of male patrons today. How lucky for them that perceptions of manliness had changed.

"Her family is French, too," Charlotte continued as she bit into a spicy flute filled with escargot, mushrooms, and exotic flavorings. "Melisande's. Old money, unlike mine, the no-money family." Charlotte laughed. "When

Max and I met (it was at a ballet benefit; I'm not even sure why he was invited, since he'd already divorced Melisande). Anyway, when we met, I couldn't believe he was interested in me. He was so wonderful, so funny, so brilliant, and there I was, a mediocre dancer nearing the end of an indifferent career."

"Charlotte," I said, "I'm sure he loved you dearly."

"He did," she agreed. "And I, him. I can't imagine life without him." She bowed her head, fighting for composure.

"I met . . . well, saw . . . his first wife last night. It's no surprise he wanted you. I can't imagine any man being saddled with a wom—"

"I thought she was locked away." Charlotte looked alarmed. "Where did you see her?"

"The opera," I replied. We were forking up ambrosial bites of the crab Caravelle. "We went with the Vasandroviches, and she accosted us."

"*Accosted.* That's a perfect word to describe being approached by Melisande. I'll never forget the first time she *accosted* me. I thought she meant to kill me. What did she want? Last night?"

"To celebrate Max's death, I'm afraid."

"That bitch." Charlotte's eyes filled with tears. "The best man who ever lived, and she's happy he's dead. I shouldn't be surprised. And I suppose Sophia couldn't say enough nice things about her. She's such a silly snob." Then Charlotte looked embarrassed. "Sorry. I think grief is making me catty and judgmental. Sophia's—" She seemed at loss for a kind word.

"No friend of yours, actually," I said impulsively, unable to leave Charlotte unaware of the gossip that Sophia was spreading about her, which I now totally disbelieved. "She told me—"

"What?" Charlotte looked curious. "What could she say about me? I've never done anything to her."

"She claims she saw you with a young man at a hotel."

Charlotte looked astonished. "A young man?"

"Whom she took to be your lover."

Then her face cleared. "That's rich. I know who she saw me with. My trainer. He does one-on-one sessions in the gym at the Westchester Suites Hotel on Park Avenue. I go every week to stay in shape. Since I stopped dancing, I have to work at keeping thin. Although now . . . with Max gone . . . Well, who cares about thin? But that does explain the questions from the police," she added bitterly.

"Not exactly." Then I confessed that, not knowing her, I had passed on Sophia's remark to Detective Worski.

"The one in the loden green overcoat? Poor man. He makes you want to take him to Bloomingdale's and buy him something decent to wear."

I apologized for having caused her added grief by repeating Sophia's gossip.

"I'm just glad to know where that came from," she replied, waving to our waiter for the dessert menu. "You can't miss the dessert here. There's the opera cake, which is amazing." The waiter said that wasn't available. "Well, what about the *tarte tiède à la banane*?" He smiled approvingly; most definitely that could be ordered, he replied. "Warm banana tart," she translated for me. "You'll love it."

What could I say? And I did love it.

After banana tarts and the last of the white burgundy and rich coffee, after the paying of the bill, which she would neither let me see nor share, we took a cab through another fall of snow to the Guggenheim, where we peeked out at Picasso's pregnant goat, dusted with snow in the sculpture garden, and I told Charlotte about the bizarre staging of *Mefistofele,* which forced the chubby tenor and soprano to climb up and down ladders while singing at full throat. We feasted our eyes on wild Picasso portraits of women wearing silly hats with stars sticking up at odd angles, and Charlotte laughed and then cried a little because Max would have loved *Picasso in the War Years.*

Finally, we said good-bye in a cab in front of my hotel, promising to renew our acquaintance if and when I returned to New York. "Max did so want Jason to come aboard. I hope he does," said Charlotte in parting. I wasn't sure what I hoped. Hodge, Brune did not seem like that nice a place to work.

Once in my room I found a message asking me to call Marshall Smead. *Not likely,* I thought and sat down to write a column about hot dogs sold on a snowy street. I had just launched into a second on Japanese-French food and Picasso chapeaux when Detective Worski called me to ask what the story was on Charlotte Heydemann and Sophia Vasandrovich. Charlotte had called him to say that she definitely was *not* having an affair with her trainer or anyone else, and that Sophia Vasandrovich probably knew it, and that he might consider that it was Sophia's husband who was taking over for Max while Charlotte was left without the love of her life, so stop bothering her! I had to bite back a smile. Detective Worski sounded as if his feelings were hurt by her anger.

"I had lunch with Charlotte Heydemann," I said soothingly, "and believe me, she is not the sort of person to kill someone, certainly not a husband she adored."

"How do you know she adored him?" Worski asked. "Just because she said—"

"Women can tell these things."

"Great. And I can take that to court?" he asked sarcastically.

"As for Vaclav, he doesn't really have the job yet. He's *interim* director. Really, you should consider the first wife. Her maiden name was D'Vallencourt."

"Well, shit," said Worski without even apologizing for his language. "That's a very influential family."

"Which doesn't mean they might not be behind Max's death, for whatever reason: hatred, revenge, arrogance, psychosis, greed—"

"OK. Mrs. Blue. I get the idea. You think I should go after the rich folks."

"Goodness, Detective Worski, I wouldn't try to tell you your business," I replied.

"Uh-huh. That's just what my wife was always saying. Before she divorced me."

He hung up, and I finished my second column, which I then took downstairs to fax. No doubt Mr. Smead hated getting longhand communications, although I have excellent and legible handwriting, if I do say so myself. He had probably called to say he wouldn't accept any more samples of my work unless they were typed. Just for spite, I faxed both columns to Paul Fallon, too, in case Smead wasn't passing them on.

Then I went upstairs and had a nice nap.

Little Flutes of Curried Escargots
Petites Flutes d'Escargots aux Épices de Madras

As a prelude to your next dinner party or a delicious hors d'oeuvre with cocktails, try this unusual recipe from Sharon O'Connor's Dining and the Opera in Manhattan. It's on the menu at La Caravelle in Manhattan:

In a large sauté pan or skillet, melt 1 tbs. butter and sauté 1 tbs. minced shallots and 1 tsp. minced garlic over medium heat until translucent, about 3 minutes.

Add 1 cup (3 oz.) ea. thinly sliced white mushrooms and thinly sliced stemmed shiitake mushrooms and sauté for 2 more minutes.

Gently stir in 7 oz. canned snails, rinsed, drained, and minced.

Add 1 cup dry white wine and cook to reduce until almost dry.

Add 1 cup chicken stock or canned low-salt chicken broth and cook to reduce again.

Add ½ cup heavy whipping cream, bring to a boil, immediately remove from heat.

Stir in 1 tsp. curry powder, ½ cup peeled, seeded, and diced tomato, 1 tsp. minced fresh chives, and 1 tsp. minced fresh parsley.

Set aside and let cool.

Preheat oven to 400°F.

Lay 12 spring roll skins, cut into quarters, on a lightly floured work surface.

Place 1 tsp. of filling on each spring roll skin and roll up one turn, fold in the sides, and finish rolling.

Transfer to baking dish, and bake in preheated oven for 5 minutes.

MAKES 48 PIECES (SERVES 8 TO 10 PEOPLE).

19

A Greek Port in the Storm

Jason

Carolyn was napping when I arrived in our hotel room, but she had much to tell me as we dressed for dinner with Calvin Pharr and his wife: the wonderful rug she had found, which I would see Saturday; her indignation at being bullied into babysitting her agent's twelve-year-old son, even though she hadn't lost her touch in dealing with recalcitrant youngsters; her superb lunch with Max's widow at a very famous restaurant, better than anything Hodge, Brune had provided; the delightful Picasso exhibition at the Guggenheim, so much better than that silly pottery sideshow about which Sophia Vasandrovich had been so excited; and finally the two columns she had faxed to the abominable Smead before taking her nap. With all this information from my wife, there was no time to tell her about my own investigation, which was fortunate, because I didn't want to bring Carolyn into it.

The Pharrs awaited us in the lobby, Calvin having secured a drink from the bar, his wife, Grace, who was much taller and much thinner than he, preoccupied with brushing snow from a long black coat that covered the tops of her black boots. To me, she looked like a Siberian army officer, although Carolyn later told me that three-quarters of the women she had seen in the city were wearing those long coats.

"It's a frigging blizzard out there," said Pharr in greeting. "Does this place have a restaurant?"

"I have no idea," Carolyn replied. It was obvious to me that she had hoped for better than a meal in her own hotel.

"Well, Calvin, I think we can at least make it across the street," said his wife. "There's a good Greek restaurant directly opposite."

"On your head if some crazy cab driver skids into us," said Pharr and threw back the rest of what looked like a martini. "Let's go."

As it happened, there were remarkably few cars braving the weather. We jaywalked straight into the warm precincts of Molyvos, a long, narrow establishment with rose velvet benches along the walls and those uncomfortable rush-bottomed chairs, so typical of Mediterranean restaurants, lining the aisle side of the tables. Carolyn may have been disappointed that she was not going to one of the restaurants in the book on dining in Manhattan, but the menu was promising. I was very happy with a selection of spreads that came with wedges of pita bread and with my lamb shank, cooked in clay and dropping off the bone. My wife was even luckier in her order of Rabbit Stifado, a stew in a rich wine sauce with sweet pearl onions and topped with crispy fried onion shreds. She said it was like *boeuf bourguignon,* but with rabbit. Three of us enjoyed a dry red wine called Agiorgitiko, of which I'd never heard, and Calvin ordered a bottle of retsina, which he finished on his own.

My wife's notebook was out from the first course onward. When our waitress told us she was new and didn't know that much about ingredients, Carolyn lured a male employee over to detail the ingredients in my dips. For instance, the eggplant spread, which I liked but didn't analyze for content, contained not just grilled eggplant, but yogurt, plum tomatoes, red onion, garlic, red wine vinegar, lemon rind, and lemon juice. And so it went. Calvin drank. Carolyn asked questions, and Grace told anecdotes about her experiences in other Greek restaurants, where servers had warned her, variously, not to dip her fingers in the bowl because it contained olive oil, not water, and not to eat the parchment that wrapped her lamb dish because it wasn't filo dough. "As if I'd never eaten in a Greek restaurant!" she exclaimed indignantly.

"Can I use those stories in a column?" Carolyn asked.

"Feel free," Grace replied. "Calvin, is that your third glass of wine? You'll have to order another bottle." Then she turned to us. "Calvin's an alcoholic; you've probably noticed. I've given up trying to change him. I just say, 'As long as you keep up your insurance payments, go to it, my love.' "

Calvin snorted. "And Grace is a one-glass-of-wine-a-night stockbroker. She makes more money than I ever will."

"Maybe if you'd stop drinking, you'd get a raise," she replied tartly.

"So many interesting professions among women these days," said Carolyn, always a diplomat. "What does Sophia Vasandrovich do?"

"Spend money," said Pharr. "How the hell Vaclav affords her, I'll never know. Maybe she had Max killed so Vaclav could get his job."

"Sophia's much too self-involved to plan a murder," Grace objected, "and too snobbish to deal with an assassin, whose family probably wouldn't meet her exacting standards."

"Right," Calvin agreed. "You're absolutely right, my love. And how would she ever explain it to Vaclav? The man loved Max. Cried when word came that Max was dead. Ol' Vaclav is one tough bastard, but he cried for Max."

"Still, you never know about people," Grace temporized. "Didn't they have a child before they immigrated?"

"Yeah." Calvin poured the last of the retsina into his glass and signaled the waiter. "They had to leave the boy behind with Sophia's mother when they escaped. Max had made arrangements for the grandmother and boy to follow when the Commies let up the surveillance, but before the plan could be carried out, they disappeared."

Carolyn looked horrified. I remembered Sophia's cold face at the memorial service and speculated on whether she blamed Max for the loss of her son.

"I wonder if Vaclav would cry for Sophia," Grace mused.

Then we all ordered baklava, for which the restaurant was famous, baklava with sugared pistachio nuts and spiced honey. I could feel my mental processes becoming more acute as I ate my dessert and mulled over the significance of the Vasandroviches' lost child, of Vaclav's love for Max, of Sophia's spendthrift ways. The only conclusion I could reach is that Vaclav could not have been culpable in Max's death. But what of his wife? Even that seemed a stretch of the imagination. And what about Calvin Pharr, our host, who was now drinking ouzo, a strong Greek liqueur, on which he had started as soon as he finished his bottle of wine.

Finally he said, tossing off the final swallow, "Well, that's it. I loved Max, too, and he wanted me to quit drinking, so I am. Call AA, Grace. I'm on the wagon."

I looked toward Grace to see if she believed him. From the expression of shock on her face, I gathered that she did. Which perhaps eliminated Pharr as a suspect. Why would he have Max killed to keep his own job if he could accomplish the same thing by doing what Max had wanted in the first place? Or had the shock of what alcohol had driven him to changed his path? If, of course, he actually stopped drinking. Surely, for a man who started with cognac in the morning, abstinence would be no easy matter. Very likely, Max's death had indeed been linked to the stolen coal project, not to any personal motive beyond greed.

The Pharrs caught a cab; Carolyn and I pushed our way through snow to the door of our hotel, and she announced that she'd had two wonderful ideas for columns, one on pushy New York waitresses, the other on Golf Course Rabbit Stew. I couldn't imagine what the second entailed, but my wife intended to write both and fax them that very night. I suppose she did it. I myself went to bed, hoping the snow would abate enough overnight to allow me a morning run before going in to Hodge, Brune for double compensation and more questions by phone and in person. What an odd pursuit for a professor: investigation of a murder.

Golf Course Rabbit Stew

I first tasted Rabbit Stifado in a New York restaurant on a miserably snowy night. However, I had in my freezer at home two rabbits, if one could call such large animals (they were the size of small dogs) by the name I had always associated with Peter Cottontail, as read to me by my mother when I was a toddler. These rabbits were provided by friends of ours who live on a golf course in Santa Teresa, New Mexico. The husband, while having a margarita one evening by his pool, spotted a huge jackrabbit hopping off the course toward a plot of shrubs that our friend had particular feelings for, having planted them himself. To protect his vegetation, he put down his drink, walked in to his desk, removed a pistol, for which he had a permit, walked back to the pool apron, and shot the rabbit. He then gave it to me with the mistaken idea that I might like to make some wonderful gourmet dish.

The second rabbit was killed, inadvertently, by his wife, who hit it with a golf ball and thereby lost a birdie on the eleventh hole. She was so indignant that she wouldn't have the rabbit in the house. Again, the husband gave it to me. And what was I to do with it? I'd never cooked a rabbit.

Here is a recipe for Rabbit Stifado that I found in a Greek cookbook. It may not be as good as what I had at Molyvos in New York, but, even made with golf course kill, it's very tasty.

Cut a *medium-sized hare* into serving pieces. Wash well in *vinegar and water*. Place in an earthenware baking dish.

Mix together *4 tbs. olive oil; 1 carrot, finely chopped; 2 medium onions, sliced; 1 stalk celery, finely chopped; 2 bay leaves; 2 whole cloves; pinch of thyme; 2 cloves garlic; several peppercorns; 2 wineglasses dry red wine; 4 tbs. vinegar.* Pour this marinade over the hare pieces and allow to marinate in the refrigerator for one to two days.

Drain the hare pieces and sauté them in *1 cup hot olive oil* with *1 large onion, finely chopped.*

Strain the marinade and add to the pot with *5 to 6 ripe tomatoes peeled and put through a food processor or mixer, 2 mashed cloves garlic,* salt, and pepper.

Cover the pot and cook slowly for one hour.

Peel and wash *2.2 lbs. tiny onions* and cut a small cross in their root ends. Put them in the pot with the hare and continue to cook over low heat for another hour.

MAKES 6 TO 8 SERVINGS.

Carolyn Blue, "Have Fork, Will Travel," *Sacramento News Leader*

20
Hot Dogs, Folklore, and the Old Testament

Carolyn

Loretta awakened me Friday with an indignant telephone call. She wanted to know why I would endanger her son's health and religious convictions by feeding him that disgusting hot dog, which undoubtedly contained prohibited pork and God knew what other dangerous things. Having been up late the night before, firing off columns to Marshall Smead in lieu of the requested telephone call, I was very sleepy and not a little confused by this unexpected attack.

"If he's not supposed to have them, why did he ask for one?" I mumbled.

"Because he's a kid," Loretta replied, as if any reasonable person could have figured that out.

Actually, she had a point. "I guess I didn't realize you kept kosher," I apologized.

"Oh, kosher!" she exclaimed dismissively. "It won't kill him to break the dietary laws, but think of what he might catch from those things. Everyone knows they're made from floor sweepings, pork entrails, and parasites. That's why the Jews prohibited pork in the first place. Trichinosis."

"From what I've read—let's see; that was in *Folklore and the Old Testament* by Frazer—the Jewish prohibition against pork grew out of older pagan rites in which pigs were considered sacred and eaten only on high feast days."

"Horse hockey!" Loretta exclaimed. "I ought to report you to the Anti-Defamation League."

"Report the author of the book," I suggested. "It wasn't my idea."

"Have you been to my uncle's place? Today's the lunch with Rollie, and we're eating at a very classy restaurant."

"I know. Le Bernardin, and no, I haven't, but I'll try to get by this morning." I was tired of being nagged about my wardrobe, and I did want to make a good impression on my editor. But what would I do if I hated Uncle Bernie's fashion offerings? That would be seriously embarrassing, because Loretta expected me to buy something. I heaved a great sigh. This was turning out to be a wearing trip.

Loretta was asking, why the big sigh? Here I was being offered the chance to spruce up my image at fabulous wholesale prices, and I couldn't even be bothered. Tuning her harangue out, noticing the snow had stopped, I was relieved that I wouldn't have to feel like an arctic explorer while hunting for Uncle Bernie's establishment. And I'd now be going to two restaurants where I could sample recipes from *Dining and the Opera in Manhattan* without having to cook anything myself. The chance to avoid cooking was the greatest gift of all. Of course, that is not a proper attitude for a culinary writer, but so be it. "I'm going, Loretta," I said, breaking into her monologue. "If you'll let me get dressed and have breakfast, I'll take the first bus or subway that will deposit me at your uncle's place. Is that good enough?"

It evidently was, although Loretta urged me to take a cab. What if my selections needed alterations? Did I expect Bernie's people to drop everything so that I could be properly attired by lunchtime? I told her that I never needed alterations and hung up. Within a half hour I was at the deli, where I found not Thelma but Detective Worski. He sat down at my table, helped himself to a bite of my Nova and scrambled eggs, and said accusingly, as if her disappearance were my responsibility, "This waitress you told me about. She quit. She's not even at her apartment. Landlord said she moved out last night. Boss here says she quit last night."

I nodded. "Probably her mother's idea."

"What's that mean?"

"Her mother was worried about her working in a place where a customer was murdered. The mother wanted her to move back to New Jersey."

"Where in New Jersey?"

"Teaneck, I think she said."

"Got an address? No one else has one."

"I don't know her *that* well, detective. In fact, she didn't say anything to me yesterday about leaving, but . . . let's see . . . she told me her mother has MS and runs an apartment house in Teaneck. Maybe you could locate the mother by calling a local MS support group. All the diseases have support groups."

"You pick up anything else about her?"

"Well, she said her mother didn't have any trouble collecting rents or getting repairs done because their cousins were connected. I took that to mean that they had Mafia connections with enforcer/debt-collector types and corrupt labor unions. Isn't it amazing to think I may have actually met someone with organized crime ties?"

"Why the hell didn't you tell me about that in the first place?"

"It didn't seem relevant," I replied, surprised by his irritation. "Goodness, I told you about the ex-wife and the children. Now *that's* a clue."

"Huh!" said Detective Worski and rose, buttoning up his tacky overcoat. "Last thing I want to do is go lookin' for some woman in New Jersey."

Jason

Thinking of the telephone bills I was running up and grateful that the charges wouldn't be on my bill, I dialed a fellow in Dresden. He knew nothing about the announcement or the company in the Ukraine but said Kiev had been a favorite city before it began to glow in the dark. With a hearty laugh and best wishes to colleagues at my old university (he didn't seem to realize that I had moved), he rang off, saying he was entertaining his postdoctoral students at his apartment that evening with beer, bratwurst, and pointed questions about their research notes.

I renewed many contacts, some with people I hadn't spoken to in some time, some with people I didn't even know very well but who seemed glad to talk to me. The scientific world is somewhat inbred. If you don't know a researcher personally, you probably do know the scientist with whom he did graduate work or a postdoctoral fellowship or someone from his department. There is a traveling mathematician who has written papers with hundreds of other researchers. Now mathematicians have a number indicating that they wrote a paper with him or with someone with whom he's written a paper and so on over a whole network of interconnected men and women. Even I have an Erdich number because I collaborated with the postdoctoral fellow of a man who collaborated with the peripatetic math genius.

I'm afraid my thoughts had begun to wander as my calls yielded less and lunch with some air and water pollution experts approached. Then I got a call from the Polish industrial chemist with whom I had talked yesterday. "Dr. Blue," he began, accent thick and sibilant, "I have been intrigued by your inquiries and have done research among my contacts."

"That's very good of you," I replied.

"Yes. I have come on an interesting information, so strange."

"Really?"

"Yes. Company in Kiev, it have strange affiliations, perhaps of importance, perhaps not, but is unusual. You understand?"

I didn't but made interested noises.

"Yes, vice president of company is married to young woman whose father is man of power in Russian group which I believe you in United States call crowd."

"Crowd?" I confessed to being puzzled.

"Is not right word? I refer to group affiliated for criminal purposes."

A *crowd of criminals*? "The Mob?" I asked, astounded.

"Yes. I believe that is word. Mob. Yes. Russian Mob. Is most successful adventure in capitalism our old neighbor has yet initiated. Very violent, as I hear by others who know more of such things than I. One hears rumors of their activities in Poland, and my sources say their arms extend into your country. Yes?"

"So I've heard." The Russian Mob? "But would they be interested in scientific research?" I asked, questioning myself as well as my caller.

"If offers much money for little investment, why not? So, my friend, is this something useful for you?"

"I don't know," I replied, "but I certainly appreciate your passing it on to me."

"I am delighted to be serviceable. Poland wishes, as always, good relations with United States. Are we not military allies now as well as allies in world of trade? My company does business in your country and yours in mine."

"Yes," I agreed, although I know little about trade relations with Poland. "The world not only changes but becomes smaller."

"Is indeed so, and no doubt in smaller world I will see you again in future."

"I'll look forward to it." I hung up thoughtfully. The Russian Mob? Well, bizarre as it sounded, it was certainly something I would have to pass on to Charles Moore. I was to see him that afternoon.

21
Never Buy Retail

Carolyn

I found Bernard Feingold's establishment on the third floor at the address his niece had provided. It was a large, open place with people rushing around, racks of clothing rolling on and off the freight elevators, desks piled with paperwork and placed in no apparent order, conversation rising and falling, ironing boards in use, ladies with pins in their mouths, and one small sitting area in a corner fitted out with a worn living room set that looked as if it had come from a discount room store twenty or thirty years ago.

When I managed to catch the attention of a passing middle-aged woman who looked vaguely secretarial, she hustled me over to a tall man wearing a shirt, loose trousers, open vest and bow tie. "From Loretta," she announced by way of introduction and rushed off to a typewriter on one of the desks. There were computers in evidence, but this woman did not use one.

"What is it, dear?" he asked, hardly looking at me. "Loretta sent you? She needs something, my niece?"

Embarrassed, I explained my errand and Loretta's instructions.

"You don't mean to tell me you usually buy retail?" exclaimed the horrified businessman, evidently Bernard Feingold. "Never buy retail, dear." As he looked me over, I studied him, as well. Uncle Bernie was a man of indeterminate age—fifty, seventy, I couldn't tell—but he was very thin and round-shouldered, balding with tufts of colorless hair around his ears, skin splotched with large, irregular freckles or age spots, and wearing a pair of ancient, round spectacles from which one lens was missing.

"Size ten," he announced, having completed his inspection. "I see you looking at my eyeglasses, dear. I got one very good eye, so why would I pay for a lens I don't need? My brother-in-law, the optometrist, he charges me wholesale by the lens."

"I see." The conversation and the place were making me feel like Dorothy in Oz without the introductory tornado.

"Take off your coat, dear. What do you write? She's a go-getter, my niece. You got the goods, she'll sell them."

"Food," I said.

He raised flyaway eyebrows above his peculiar eyeglasses.

"A book about food. Maybe newspaper columns about food."

"Food is good. Who wouldn't want to read about food? Time was, I never saw enough. That was when I was a boy. Now Bernie Feingold always knows where his next meal is coming from. What occasion?"

"I beg your pardon?" Did he mean the occasion of his next meal?

"For the clothes, dear."

"Oh. Well, meals in famous restaurants." Now, that sounded snobbish. "Lunch or dinner?"

"Both, I guess." Presumably, the company would entertain us again tonight. "Something warm, but . . . well . . . dressy. After the desert, I'm freezing in New York."

"Ah, the land of milk and honey. Where we Jews come from." He gave me a sweet smile as he beckoned employees to him and murmured instructions.

"Well, El Paso, Texas, isn't exactly the land of milk and honey," I replied. "More like the land of drought and killer bees."

He laughed. "The eye of the beholder, as they say. Israel . . . now Israel . . . most wouldn't say it's the land of milk and honey, but it looked good to the chosen people. What does your husband do, dear? Is he in the food business?"

"He's a chemist," I replied.

"Try this on." He handed me a green suit with black braided lapels and jet buttons.

I knew I'd never wear anything like that. "What, here?" I asked. I'd seen models change clothes in front of people on shows about high fashion, but I certainly didn't intend to.

"No, there, dear. Ruth, show her the dressing room."

The dressing room was a curtained space in a corner. It didn't even have a mirror. It did have hooks where I could hang my clothes, so I tried on the green suit. It fit wonderfully and probably cost a fortune, but I didn't like it. What if he insisted that I buy it? If there had been a door to a hall in that curtained space, I'd have escaped, leaving his green suit on a hook. As it was, I had to reenter the big room.

Bernie Feingold, benign and ageless, awaited me. "So your husband's a chemist. My son Sheldon, the doctor, he grew up in Brooklyn with a boy who became a chemist. Maybe your husband knows him. Turn around, dear, so I can see the fit."

What difference did the fit make when I hated the color? With a little salt on top, I'd look like a walking margarita. "There are lots of chemists," I replied.

"Not your color, dear. Bring me the periwinkle, Ruth, be a love. She needs a softer shade. Maxie Heydemann. My son's friend. Now there was a fine boy, even if he never got to be a real doctor. How many games of stickball those two played with their mothers shouting out the windows for them to come home to dinner. Mrs. Feingold, God rest her soul, liked the family to be on time for dinner."

"*Max* Heydemann?" Loretta's uncle knew Max Heydemann? This was Oz indeed. "My husband did know him."

"Here, dear. Try the periwinkle."

I staggered off to the curtained space and tried the periwinkle, a suit made with wool as soft as a baby's touch and a color straight from some alpine meadow. And it fit as if it had been tailored for me. *Goodness knows what it costs,* I thought with real regret. I wasn't going to put my husband in the poor-house to have this suit. I hadn't even seen it in a mirror. Maybe I'd hate it. I walked out, feeling the smooth accommodation of the fabric to my stride.

"That's the one, dear. That one you should buy."

"What does it cost?" I asked in a small voice.

"Oh, I'll make you a good price. No worry there. You're my Loretta's client. Her mother was like my own child. So your husband knows Maxie? Here, try this on." He handed me a full-length wool dress, smoke gray with rose accents, so lightweight that I hardly knew when it passed from his hand to mine. "I dress Maxie's wife, Charlotte. What a sweet shiksa she is. Not like the first one who was a schizoid with the mark of the devil on her soul. A Jezebel, that one. Evil-eyed."

I stared at him with a shiver and nodded. "I met her."

"Too bad. A nice lady like you. Much grief she gave our Maxie while he was married to her. Her and her whelps, no-goodniks, both of them. Bad blood drives out good. My mother used to say that. In Yiddish. She never spoke English, my mother. And that Sophia. She's a friend of Charlotte's. Thinks she's the queen of Bohemia." He grimaced, and I had to hide a smile. What an apt description of the lineage-proud Sophia. "Always trying to get me to lower my price. Like I'm not already giving her the dress at cost because Charlotte sent her."

Oh my. He'd think that of me when I found that I couldn't afford these dresses. He'd think I was trying to bargain him down. What was I to do? I liked Mr. Feingold! Better than his niece, truth be told. He directed me to the dressing room with the second dress, which I tried on, having caught a heart-stopping reflection of the periwinkle suit in a mirror propped against a long worktable. Oh, how I wanted that suit! And now I was probably trying on something else I'd long for and have to deny myself.

"Very nice, dear," said Mr. Feingold when I reappeared. "So how is Maxie? Turn around for me. Has your husband seen him?"

"Mr. Feingold, he's dead," I blurted out.

Bernie Feingold stopped studying his beautiful dress on my forty-something figure and stared at me. "Maxie's dead? That can't be! How? He's a young man."

"He was murdered. In a delicatessen."

Mr. Feingold's bespeckled face fell into lines of profound sorrow. "Murdered? I didn't know. And poor Charlotte. How is she doing?"

"Well, she's . . . she's pretty broken up."

"Of course she is. She kissed the ground Max walked on, Charlotte, and why wouldn't she? Those two loved each other like teenagers, except she had to deal with his children. How they hated their papa for marrying her, and her so fine a woman, who made him so happy. Try these, dear. Maxie dead. How can it be that our children die before us?"

At his direction, Ruth handed me a black pants set. The slacks were flared from the knee with widening insets of material, and the top hung in a loosely fitted tunic decorated with insets of teal and, at the waist, a silver and turquoise belt that had a medieval look to it. Guinevere in pants. It must cost a queen's ransom, but I did have to try it on, to see myself in it just once. What a terrible idea on Loretta's part to send me here. Now I'd never be quite happy with my simple, sensible wardrobe. I gave the gray dress one last look and went off to try on another Bernie Feingold choice in the warm-but-dressy category. He was mumbling about Max as I slipped behind the flowered curtain.

"Well," said Mr. Feingold when I returned. "Very smart, and it doesn't overwhelm your coloring, dear. Take my word. It's good on you."

I took his word. I could see myself in the mirror. Another woman would have worn it with high, spiked sandals, but I, if it were mine, would wear flats. Even in imagination, I'll only go so far for the sake of fashion, and hobbling my feet is too far. At the moment, I was stocking-footed. And I had been right to tell Loretta that I wouldn't need any alterations, just an influx of cash.

"At least poor Charlotte will be well taken care of," said Bernie. "Max was a careful man, foresighted."

"We don't know that—that she'll be well taken care of, I mean," I said, turning wistfully before the mirror. "There's a trust fund for her, but the will won't be read until this afternoon, and who knows—"

"Oh, I know. Maxie and me, we got the same lawyer, Jake Blumenthal. Jake went to school with my boy and Maxie."

"No matter what provisions he made, the first wife plans to have her rich father contest the will if her children don't get what she thinks they deserve."

"Jake draws you up a will, no one's rich father's gonna break it. Charlotte gets the most and controls the trusts for the children as long as she lives. That ought to put a stick in their spokes, worthless brats that they are. Now, you want to see more?"

"Oh, no. These are lovely." I shouldn't have said that. "But how much . . ."

He went to his desk, pulled out a scrap of paper, scribbled figures on it, mumbled to himself, scribbled some more. *Oh me,* I thought. *I'll probably turn white when he names a price.* He named one. "For which outfit?" I asked. I could just about afford that. Oh, my goodness! I could justify that much! But which outfit was it that I could afford?

"For all, dear. For the three. I told you I'd make you a good price. For Max's friend's wife, for my niece, little Loretta, wouldn't I make a good price?"

"But Mr. Feingold—"

"So maybe I could come down a little, even throw in a bottle of my signature perfume, but I'd be taking a loss. Still—"

"Oh, I didn't mean that. I mean you're too generous. I can't let you—"

"I can see it's not the queen of Bohemia I'm dealing with here. Do I have to talk you into accepting my offer? You want me to raise the price a little?"

"Oh, Mr. Feingold," I cried and gave him a hug.

"Call me Bernie," he replied, beaming.

22

On Dining with a Famous Gourmet

Wonderful food and lovely decor are to be found in the restaurants of New York at the beginning of the new millennium, but surely they cannot produce the exciting stories and bizarre spectacles of the past. In the eighteenth century, Sam Francis, a well-known patriot and New York tavern keeper, was steward to George Washington, and Sam's daughter Phoebe acted as the housekeeper at Washington's Richmond Hill headquarters. While serving dinner, the girl found her sweetheart, a soldier on the general's staff, adding poison to Washington's favorite dish, spring peas. She carried the dish to the table but then had to choose between her country and her lover. She tossed the peas out the window, and they promptly killed all of the neighbor's chickens. The general survived, Phoebe was a heroine, but her true love was the first American soldier hung for treason.

If Sam Francis's various taverns were the toast of New York in the eighteenth century, Delmonico's was the introducer of haute cuisine in the nineteenth century. Eighteen seventy-three saw the production of the famous (or infamous) swan banquet by Lorenzo Delmonico. It featured a huge, round, ballroom-filling table with a thirty-foot lake in the center where swans floated majestically until overcome by avian lust. The conversation of the diners was noisy, but it was nothing to the cacophonous mating of the swans during the banquet. What contemporary chef could hope to compete with that spectacle? And what did the prim Victorian matrons make of it?

Carolyn Blue, "Have Fork, Will Travel," *Bakersfield Valley Gazette*

Carolyn

Even wearing my new periwinkle suit, I was nervous about meeting Roland DuPlessis. He was a noted gourmet; I was just a woman who liked good food and had once enjoyed cooking. Le Bernardin was a four-star restaurant; I wasn't sure I'd ever been in one. The room, when I was ushered in, featured paneled walls and pictures of ships at sea; I was a land-locked Midwesterner now living in the desert Southwest and about to be confronted with an elaborate fish menu. Fortunately, I don't object to fish, although I'm not as mad for it as Jason. Even so, I did have a lot to be nervous about.

On the other hand, Roland DuPlessis, when I met him, was strangely dressed. He was an immensely fat man, an Occidental Buddha wearing a beret and a vest ornamented with crewel embroidery under a tentlike sports jacket of emerald green. I, at least, looked wonderful. I noticed that the waiter thought so. Even Loretta gave my outfit a nod of approval before introducing me.

"I loved the proposal," said DuPlessis. "Country taste in the big city. What New Orleans recipes will you use?"

I certainly don't consider myself "country," but I held my tongue and named recipes. "Good, good," he said. "Send me copies immediately. I'll want to try them."

I hadn't tried them all myself. I hadn't even wanted to think about that trip. "About the New Orleans book—" I began.

"Menus first," said Roland DuPlessis, accepting his with a grand wave of the arm. "Ah, they have the black bass seviche. I'm sure you'll want that. Very Southwestern. Cilantro. Jalapeños. Loretta, what shall we choose for you?"

"I can choose my own, thanks, Rollie," she replied tartly.

"She's afraid I'll insist that she eat some ocean scavenger, some fearful shellfish." A chortling laugh rolled from his chest.

"I'm Jewish. I'm not eating shellfish to please you, sweetie."

"I think I'd like the Seared Tuna and Truffled Herb Salad," I murmured. Loretta glared at me, but I had the recipe for that in *Dining and the Opera*. It looked like something I could make without taking four days to do it, should I ever be overcome by a desire to cook, say for Jason's birthday.

"Excellent. Excellent," DuPlessis agreed. "I approve of truffles. Did you know that the French ambassador once insulted John Adams by bringing his own chef to a dinner at the vice president's house? The chef served game birds with truffles, much to the disgust of the Americans. We colonials didn't always like truffles; more's the pity. After the Civil War, Ward McAllister, arbiter of taste to the Four Hundred of New York society, said that truffles should never be served more than once at a dinner. Slow progress, but progress indeed. You should go to Umbria if you like truffles, dear lady."

I nodded. "La Rosetta in Perugia. I wonder what game birds were served with the truffles at the Adamses' dinner. During that period, a man named Niblo was offering all kinds of strange things: bald eagle, hawk, owl, swan, although swans were a popular banquet dish in the Middle Ages."

Roland DuPlessis took my hand. I thought he was going to kiss it, so happy was he to find someone who had eaten at La Rosetta and knew snippets of food history. "La Rosetta would make a book in itself," he said enthusiastically. "But Loretta tells me you are thinking of a second book: *Eating Ethnic in the Big Apple.* Charming. Loretta, you can have the yellowfin carpaccio."

"You can't fool me, Rollie," she replied. "That's raw fish."

"No matter, it has fins, so it's not against your religion. Be adventurous, my dear. Expand your horizons. It comes with a divine ginger-lime mayonnaise. I like the ethnic angle," he continued, turning back to me. "Middlewesterner dines Basque, Indian, Thai, Senegalese. I'll make you a list of restaurants."

"He probably wants you to eat chocolate-covered termites," said Loretta, who had been studying her menu and ordered a Chinese spiced red snapper. "I like Chinese takeout," she explained.

"Always the Philistine," said DuPlessis.

"I'm only here until Sunday," I admitted. "I probably won't have time—"

"But you'll come back after the New Orleans book."

"About the New Orleans book—"

"She's dying to finish it," said Loretta, kicking me in the ankle. We exchanged unpleasant glances as Roland urged us to order second courses.

"I want to try one of the desserts," I objected. "And I've done nothing but overeat since I got here."

"It is impossible to overeat if the food is good enough." He plunged a fork into the tuna carpaccio, which he had ordered for himself when Loretta refused it.

"You're living proof of that," said Loretta.

"Ha! Your rudeness is exceeded only by the beauty of your eyes, my dear Madam Blum. And you, Carolyn, how can you associate with a woman as crass as this, a person who refuses to eat shellfish or, say, an excellent loin of pork in a spicy plum sauce, and all in the name of a religion she probably doesn't practice?"

"Who doesn't? Simon's in Hebrew school preparing for his bar mitzvah as we speak. And don't try to come between me and my client, Rollie. We're very close."

I was certainly surprised to hear that.

"She even took Simon for me yesterday when I had a conflict."

"In that case, I hope you lowered your commission accordingly. An hour spent in the company of a child is as bad as a half day in a hot dog factory."

Oh, *why* did he feel it necessary to mention hot dogs? I foresaw another lecture from Loretta on my insensitivity in exposing her child to the dangers of sausages filled with pork and other undesirable meat products. To head it off, I said, "My husband would love this restaurant. He adores fish."

"You should have brought him. *He* could have had the yellowfin carpaccio. Or is he afraid of raw fish, too?"

"Not at all. We eat sushi when we get the chance."

"They have sushi in El Paso, Texas?" Roland looked astonished.

"We even have Japanese people. But Jason couldn't have come." I hastened back into the conversation because I could see that Loretta was about to speak. "He's consulting at a chemical company, and unfortunately, a friend of his was murdered, and—"

"Max Heydemann," said DuPlessis.

I was dumbfounded. "You knew Max, too?"

"I certainly did. Max was the pastrami king of the city. Native of Brooklyn, graduate of Brooklyn Poly and Columbia, pastrami connoisseur. I've enjoyed many a bowl of chicken soup with matzo balls, many an order of Nova or pastrami in the company of Max. We did a research tour of New York delicatessens in our younger days. That was when he was married to his first wife, a dreadful woman whom he avoided by eating out. She never ate *anything* to my knowledge. Absolutely anorexic. And her daughter as well."

"I know Max," said Loretta. "He's dead?"

I told the story. Roland said that he had a theory about the murderer. "A rival deli owner. Once Max made his choice, he never deviated. Every Monday, same place, same sandwich. What better way to ruin a rival than to murder his favored customer over a heap of the house's best pastrami? My second choice would be his abominable son, who once fished a live lobster from the tank at the Grand Central Oyster Bar and let it loose to roam the marble floors, causing a veritable cacophony of shrieking among the female diners. I believe the boy was ten at the time and hasn't improved his manners since then."

After that, we had dessert. I ordered the Chocolate Dome with a Symphony of Crème Brûlée on a Macaroon. I won't give you the recipe because it's really three dessert recipes in one, but it's heavenly, and you can find it in *Dining and the Opera in Manhattan* or on the menu at Le Bernardin.

Seared Tuna and Truffled Herb Salad

To make the vinaigrette: In a small bowl, whisk together 3 tbs. balsamic vinegar; 1 canned black truffle, drained (juice reserved) and minced; 1 tbs. truffle juice; and 7 tbs. extra-virgin olive oil. Season with salt and pepper and set aside.

Season one 12-oz. tuna loin with 1 tbs. minced fresh thyme, salt, and freshly ground pepper to taste. Film a large sauté pan or skillet with oil and sear tuna over high heat until crusty on the outside and rare in the center.

Slice seared tuna into ¼-in.-thick slices and arrange slices on 4 plates. Garnish with 4 cups assorted baby greens and 1 cup mixed fresh herbs such as basil, dill, and parsley. Drizzle vinaigrette over everything and serve.

It was four o'clock when I got home, and the subway ride, which was made charming by the sight of a baby in a stroller wearing a leopard-skin hat and sunglasses, gave me the opportunity to reflect on the things I had learned about the Heydemann family. I considered Roland (he had invited me to call him Roland between his second course and my dessert) DuPlessis's rival-deli-owner hypothesis facetious, but I did think Detective Worski would be interested to hear about Max's will and get another opinion on Heydemann's first wife and his son.

What the detective seized on, when I called, was the will. He wanted to know who had told me and how they knew the provisions, not to mention when the will was to be read. To protect Bernie, I said only that an acquaintance had the same lawyer, who had mentioned the bequests. Worski muttered something about client confidentiality, and hadn't lawyers ever heard of it? Who was this lawyer who went around blabbing the terms of wills?

"I don't think that's the point, Detective," I protested. "The point is that if Charlotte controls the trust funds for the children, they may try to kill her, they or their mother. I think you should provide her protection until this case is solved."

"Oh, great," snapped Worski. "And if she's the murderer, who am I protecting her from? Looks like she's the one with everything to gain. And say, your husband won't talk to my partner anymore. Ali wants to know about this espionage thing, mostly because he's into that white-collar stuff; I don't put much store by that theory."

"Nor do I," I agreed, "but Jason's been asked not to talk to the police."

"Well, he can't refuse."

"I'll tell him." Not a word of thanks for the information *I* had just provided. What a cranky person the detective was. Maybe his had been a very painful divorce.

I had another request that I call Marshall Smead. Instead, I wrote a column on ladies from the "hinterlands" eating in intimidating restaurants with known gourmets, which I then faxed to him. After that, I took a nap.

23
The Mob?

Oysters have always been popular in New York City, but in earlier years, the supply was more varied, more plentiful, and much less expensive. In 1776, two hundred canoes full came into port daily. In 1810, they were to be had from street vendors for one to three cents apiece. In the 1830s and '40s, oyster cellars on Canal Street offered all the oysters a patron could reasonably eat for six cents, although a patron who made a pig of himself could expect to be discouraged from further consumption by being given an oyster that had gone bad. By 1850, New Yorkers consumed more than six million dollars worth of the popular bivalves, and by 1880, Americans were eating 660 Manhattan oysters a year per person; New Yorkers preserved the delicacies fresh in barrels and shipped them to less fortunate parts of the country. And they were large! Thackeray said American oysters were so big that eating one was like "swallowing a small baby." But at the beginning of the twenty-first century, the oysters are smaller and can cost fifteen dollars a dozen. Many things change but not, it would seem, the taste for oysters.

Carolyn Blue, "Have Fork, Will Travel," *Las Cruces Pioneer News*

Jason

I returned to the company offices around two-thirty after a long, pleasant lunch with a group of scientists whom I had not met previously—all air and water pollution men, an enthusiastic and jolly lot. Our lunch venue was an oyster bar that served sixty-five different types of beer and fourteen different varieties of raw oysters, although not all on that day. Nonetheless, the oysters were fresh and varied, the beer cold and robustly foreign, the booths deeply upholstered in soft, dark leather, the clientele almost entirely male, and Hodge, Brune picked up the bill.

My wife would have found the pleased complacency of our group decidedly amusing; nonetheless, we men do like, on occasion, to congregate where large-screen televisions show only sporting events, the atmosphere owes nothing to feminine tastes, and the conversation is decidedly Y-chromosome generated, in this case scientific. I found myself wondering, as I tossed down the liquid left in an oyster shell, whether Frances Striff ever comes here and if she enjoys it.

At any rate, I experienced a bolt of supercharged boredom at the prospect of returning to my small office to make more telephone calls abroad. Whatever my future connection with Hodge, Brune, I wanted to get back to my own labs, students, and scientific problems, which I could discuss as freely as I liked with anyone I cared to confide in. Avoiding questions from the police was a duty I found particularly irksome, yet I knew that Vernon Merrivale would have eyes watching me. He didn't have any power over me, to be sure, but I *was* in his territory. I was also aware that he considered my efforts on the company's behalf of no value and, in fact, likely to do more harm than good to his investigation.

"Dr. Blue. Dr. Blue." A young woman trotted down the hall after me. "Where have you been? Dr. Moore would like you to come to his office."

I turned and headed the other way, the young lady hurrying after me, evidently to see that I did not disappear again before she could fulfill her mission.

"Jason," Moore greeted me with his usual serious mien. "I was afraid you had deserted us." Merrivale sat in a visitor's chair, frowning suspiciously in my direction.

"I was invited to lunch by a group of your scientists."

"Excellent," Moore murmured. "I hope you enjoyed your break." Before I could respond, he hurried on. "I've read the report you sent late yesterday afternoon."

"Nothing much there," said Merrivale.

"What do you think of the idea that the Ukrainian announcement is a bluff?" I asked, ignoring the security director.

"To what end?" Merrivale demanded.

"To claim a percentage of the money you make on the process, I suppose. Or to let you buy them out."

"We've heard nothing from them," said Moore. "Even the feelers we've put out have been ignored."

I shrugged. "Well, yesterday that seemed the best idea I'd heard."

"The important investigation, *my* investigation, is at this end," said Merrivale. "We have to discover who let slip or sold our proprietary—"

"Of course, you want to know, but it won't repair the damage that has been done," I pointed out. "If they really have the process—"

"We'll prosecute," said Merrivale, his face flushing with outrage. "We'll destroy the spy and then the people who hired him."

"You said that was your best theory yesterday," Moore interrupted, addressing himself to me. "Have you learned anything else of note?"

"Perhaps one thing, and I'm not sure of its value. I had a callback this morning from an industrial chemist in Krakow. He tells me that he's found sources who say the vice president of the Ukrainian company is married to a young woman whose father—"

"For God's sake," Merrivale exclaimed. "Wives. In-laws. We're dealing with industrial espionage here, not family sagas."

"As I was saying, the wife's father is reputed to be a power in the Russian Mafia."

Both men looked at me as if I had lost my mind.

"A bizarre twist, if true," I admitted hastily, "but we must remember yesterday's speculation as to who was funding this company. Such a group would certainly have the means, if the project seemed profitable."

"Organized crime isn't *productive*," snapped Merrivale. "They don't *manufacture* things, and they go into legitimate businesses only to launder their dirty money."

"I'm sure you're right," I replied, "but they do engage in theft, threats, bribery, and extortion—or so I'd gather." I hadn't taken this avenue of speculation all that seriously myself, but no one likes to have his hypothesis sneered at. "Your research *has* been stolen, unless this is an amazing and unlikely scientific coincidence. And these criminals may have threatened or bribed an employee of yours into providing the information. Lastly, they may be planning to extort money from you. Just because they haven't doesn't mean they may not yet do so. Theft, threats, bribery, extortion: all within the purview of a criminal organization." I sat back and held a steady gaze on Merrivale. *A cogent argument,* I thought. *Probably wrong, but perfectly logical.*

"Bizarre," said Moore. "But I can't fault the logic."

Exactly, I thought.

"It doesn't matter who's pulling the strings," Merrivale exploded. "We can find that out when we catch the traitor in our midst. We need to ascertain—"

"How did you get along with Fergus McRoy?" Moore interrupted.

"Seems a nice enough fellow," I replied. "He's certainly upset about the theft of his brainchild. He's conducting his own investigation."

"Smoke screen," snarled Merrivale. "He's covering up."

Moore waved a hand to quiet his head of security, looked pensive for a moment, then spoke, each word carefully thought out and articulated. "We have some reason, no evidence mind you, to think that Fergus himself might be suspect."

"Why?" I asked. Of course, that had occurred to me, although instinct told me it was unlikely. But then instinct would undoubtedly lead me to believe that no one I know would have engaged in industrial espionage. I frankly found the concept as incredible as my wife did, although I could not rule it out and so had helped in this investigation.

"Fergus is well paid," said Moore slowly, "but not as well paid as some. And he has seven children. The raising of so many children is a considerable expense. And his wife does not work. She is a homemaker."

"And no one seems to think he's in financial straits," said Merrivale. "So why isn't he?"

"In other words, you think he'd be vulnerable to an offer?" I concluded for them. "That may suggest motive but hardly constitutes evidence."

"Motive explains the inexplicable," said Merrivale.

"Um-m-m." I really didn't care to comment, nor was I impressed. Merrivale's investigation had not progressed beyond wild guesses.

"So what we have in mind," said Moore, "is a social evening between you, your wife, and the McRoys. It's all arranged. They'll take you out to dinner and a play."

"And you'll question him," added Merrivale, "and report back."

"Gentlemen, I am neither a qualified interrogator nor a spy," I protested. "I—"

"We're only asking you to spend an evening with the man," said Merrivale impatiently. "Hell, it's a free dinner and theater tickets."

"*Waiting in the Wings,*" said Moore. "Oscar Wilde's last play, I believe. It's had fine reviews."

I felt like walking out on them, but Merrivale was already placing tickets in my hand. "They'll pick you up at six. That should give you plenty of time to quiz the two of them before you have to head for the theater. Then, if you haven't found out anything, suggest a drink afterward. Nothing like alcohol to loosen a man's tongue. Maybe he'll let something slip. Or she will. Big spending plans or something."

I looked at Merrivale with intense dislike.

Moore, evidently sensing my reluctance, said, "I'd appreciate your opinion, Jason, because I'd hate to think we are holding under suspicion a man who has worked with excellent results for Hodge, Brune for some years."

Put that way, I rethought my impulse to refuse. Maybe it was McRoy, not the company, who needed my help. Perhaps I was obliged to give this plan a try.

By the time I got back to the hotel room and told my wife of our prospective evening out, it was five o'clock, and we had only an hour to prepare. Her first question was: "What restaurant?" She was already reaching for that book I had bought for her birthday. I had to admit that I didn't know. "Well, I hope they pick something I can write about for a change."

"It seems to me that you've been writing constantly since we arrived."

She laughed. "Only since I met Marshall Smead. I just ignored another call from him. Oh, Jason, you'd have loved Le Bernardin. Wonderful, wonderful fish dishes."

"I'd be green with envy if I hadn't had as many raw oysters as I could eat for lunch."

"That would turn anyone green," she retorted gaily, "and not with envy. Ugh." She was putting on a stunning gray dress as I changed my shirt.

"Do you think this is all right for a night at the theater?" She twirled for my inspection.

"My God, you look beautiful, Carolyn. I haven't seen that before, have I?"

Immediately she looked contrite and explained about her agent's Uncle

Bernie, the three outfits, and what they cost. "I know it sounds like a lot, Jason, but they're worth ever so much more than—"

"Just the one you're wearing is worth that price," I replied. "And don't give the money a thought. They're paying me double my usual rate."

"They are? My goodness! I could have bought something else."

"Well, no need to go overboard."

"Oh, Jason, I heard something truly frightening at Mr. Feingold's," and she told me about Max's will and her fear that Charlotte was now in danger of being killed by his ex-wife or children because she controlled the trust funds.

Amazing! The Russian Mafia. Murdering offspring. We needed to get away from this city. Maybe I *didn't* want a job with Hodge, Brune. I'd have to give the matter careful consideration, if the job was offered. Perhaps it depended on my catching Fergus McRoy in some damning slip of the tongue over dessert.

24
The Apprehensive Host

Carolyn

The company was paying Jason double his usual consulting fee? I had to think better of them for that. In fact, it might not be so bad to spend several months each summer in New York. The children would love it. And after all, I was quite sure now that the murder of Max Heydemann had had nothing to do with Hodge, Brune, so Jason would be in no danger.

All these thoughts floated through my mind as I showed Jason my two other outfits while we waited for the McRoys to call from the lobby. I even held out high hopes for the restaurant to which we'd go and for the play we were to see, *Waiting in the Wings*. The review in a magazine about New York provided by the hotel was quite favorable. Lauren Bacall and Rosemary Harris were starring. What luck that the McRoys had managed to get tickets. And where were they? Six-thirty had passed, although they were to have picked us up at six.

Jason began reading an article that compared lifestyles of different types of monkeys, one species in which the males practiced rape, another in which the females controlled the males with sexual favors—lots of them. And if that didn't work, they tore off male genitals. Jason read me choice tidbits, and I wondered what a zoo would do about such behavior, which seemed much too sexual and violent to be viewed by the children who customarily flocked to zoos. And where were the McRoys? At this rate, we'd be lucky to consume one course before we had to hasten to the performance at the Eugene O'Neill Theater. Was this my penance for refusing an entrée at Le Bernardin? We might get no dinner at all, and I was hungry.

"What if they never arrive?" I asked anxiously.

"Well, I've got the tickets." Jason displayed them.

"But dinner," I protested.

"I thought you were worried about your waistline."

Men are so insensitive. Here I was starving, and my husband saw fit to remind me of my waistline.

Our telephone rang at six-forty-five, just as I was taking a tentative sniff of Bernie Feingold's signature perfume. Good grief! It was awful! I hastily capped the small atomizer and dropped it into my purse for later disposal. Then we rushed downstairs to confront our windblown, flustered, apologetic hosts. It seems that they have seven children—seven! Can you imagine? And the babysitter had canceled at the last minute, making it necessary for the eldest to babysit the younger ones, a solution that the McRoys found worrisome, since they rarely went out evenings and had never left the children to fend for themselves. But they—Fergus and Fiona—were so sorry to be late, and now there was nothing for it but that we eat at a restaurant right next to the theater. They hoped we didn't mind. They had no idea whether or not it would meet my standards, my being a cuisine expert. By the time we actually got to the place, which was called the Garrick Bistro, I was feeling sorry for them.

That feeling blossomed as the evening progressed. Fergus, poor man, was distraught. We had no sooner ordered—Seared Sea Scallops and Wild Mushroom Ragout with Truffled Gnocchi for me and Shellfish Bouillabaisse on Lemon Pepper Linguini for Jason—than Fergus announced that the company suspected *him* of being behind the industrial espionage that had led to Max Heydemann's death.

"I would never betray Max!" he cried.

"Of course you wouldn't," his wife murmured soothingly.

"It was my project, my big chance! Would I throw that away? Never. Here I've been alienating everyone on my team, trying to discover how the research got away from the lab, and all along they suspect me."

"Your team?" I asked, confused.

"No, Moore, Merrivale, and Vasandrovich."

"Well, I could tell them that Max's death had nothing to do with industrial espionage," I replied, hoping to calm him. "It was obviously a family dysfunction that resulted in murder."

"You think so?" Fergus looked as if I was about to save him from drowning.

"Of course," I replied. "Didn't you go to the memorial service? You could feel the waves of enmity coming off those children of his. And his first wife—Jason and I saw her at the opera, and she was celebrating his death. She made no secret of that."

Fergus nodded. "She's crazy. And the daughter's a slut."

"And Ricky—the would-be actor—is always in debt and in trouble with his father," Fiona agreed. "So you see, Fergus, you don't have to worry."

All the while we had been dipping a fennel-flavored bread into an excellent olive oil infused with herbs. We also had an amazingly good South African Shiraz, although I hadn't even known they made wine in South Africa. I wrote down the name: Rust en Vrede. Vrede sounded Boer. I found it hard to imagine phlegmatic Dutch farmers making tasty wines whose grapes had been picked, perhaps, by towering Watusi tribesmen. No doubt that is a mistaken picture of wine making in South Africa.

"But no matter who killed Max . . . and I'll never believe it was anyone at the company . . . he was loved. Wasn't he, Fiona?"

"He was," she agreed and asked me what herb that was in the olive oil.

"Tarragon," I replied.

"So no matter who killed him," Fergus persisted, having fallen into anxiety once more, "we've still had our research stolen, and I'm being blamed."

At that point, our dinners were served.

"Why would they blame you?" asked his wife reasonably. "It makes no sense."

I ate a scallop and almost gagged. What *was* that? I poked suspiciously at my ragout. Jason sent me a questioning look.

"Pure prejudice," said Fergus. "It's because we have seven children."

Gingerly, I tried another scallop. And that *was* a scallop. Well, of course. The first thing had been a lump of gnocchi. I'd forgotten about that component of the dish and was very relieved to discover my error. "Surely it's against the law to discriminate against people because of the number of children they have," I remarked. "Like age discrimination. Or sex discrimination."

"I see," said Fiona. "We have seven children, so they assume we need the money."

"What money?" I asked. My scallops were delicious, firm, perfectly cooked, and bathed in a citrusy sauce with greens and mushrooms in it.

"They think I sold the company secrets. That has to be it," said Fergus.

The man was beside himself with anxiety. And my husband looked terribly uncomfortable. Surely, he didn't think this poor fellow guilty of anything.

"Well, that's just foolishness," said Fiona stoutly. "Fergus makes plenty of money. As long as the stock market keeps rising, we'll never have any serious financial problems. The market is his hobby. Other men watch Monday night football. Fergus reads the *Wall Street Journal* and logs onto the financial sites on the Internet." She patted his hand. "You should take your financial records in and show them, dear."

"How can I do that? They haven't come right out and accused me of anything."

"Then maybe you're worrying for nothing." She was eating steadily through her dinner while her husband fretted.

"What do you think, Jason? Do they suspect me?"

"Well, I . . ." Jason looked even more uncomfortable.

"Jason hasn't said a word to me about anyone suspecting you of anything, Fergus," I answered, jumping in with reassurances.

"There, you see, Fergus," said his wife. "All's well."

The music system in the restaurant began to play, of all things, "Don't Fence Me In." They had a terrible selection of boring music, even if the scallops were wonderful. "How's your bouillabaisse, Jason?" Maybe we could distract Fergus from his fears.

"Excellent," Jason replied. "It has not only a good selection of shellfish but octopus as well."

Fiona looked shocked at the mention of octopus. With seven children, it probably wasn't something she was given to serving the family.

"Would you like to try the sauce?" Jason asked. "It's delicious."

I accepted and found it rather fishy, but then my husband likes fishy. I offered him a scallop, resisting the impulse to shock him with a lump of gnocchi. He liked my scallops more than I liked his sauce.

"So don't be glum, dear," said Fiona.

"Why not? Even if they stop suspecting me and find out who did it, the company will never be the same without Max."

"Then we'll move," said his wife. "You've had offers. We can sell the house in New Jersey for a fortune and move somewhere where real estate is cheap and we'll make a profit."

"We did that," I said encouragingly. "Houses are amazingly cheap in El Paso."

"El Paso doesn't have any good industrial chemistry jobs," said Fergus.

"You can take the profit from the house and use it to make more money in the market," said Fiona.

"The bull market won't last forever," said Fergus. "It's already faltering."

"I don't think we have time for dessert," said Fiona. "Not if we're going to make the first act of the play."

We barely gained our seats before the curtain went up on a tale, both funny and sad, about a retirement home for impecunious actors. Fergus hated the play and said so. It reminded him that, for the McRoys, a poverty-stricken old age awaited because there'd be nothing left after they put all the children through college.

"Nonsense," said Fiona. "They'll get scholarships."

"What about Roddy?" Fergus asked despairingly.

"He'll get a soccer scholarship," she replied.

Fergus perked up. "The boy *is* good. A fine goalie. But what if he gets hurt?"

"Well, that was certainly fun," I said to Jason when we were safely back in our hotel room. "Do they really suspect him of being a spy?"

"Yes," said Jason.

"Do you?" I asked, surprised.

"No," he replied. Then we checked our telephone messages. There were four.

25

Room Service and Telephone Tag

Carolyn

As I hung up my coat and began to take off my new gray dress, I said, "I'm still hungry. Aren't you?" Jason was checking telephone messages. "Let's order from room service. Sympathetic as I am to the McRoys, I do think the company owes us dessert."

"Get me something light," said Jason.

I picked up the menu. "How about passion fruit sorbet?"

"Sounds good." He was making notes on the telephone pad. "You've got a message here from Detective Worski. Why is he calling you?"

I shrugged, more interested in the chocolate truffle torte I had just selected than in who had called. "Maybe to say he did provide protection for Charlotte."

"I hope that you haven't been talking out of turn to the police. The company is very worried about news getting out concerning—"

"Jason," I interrupted, "you know I think the whole spy scenario is silly. The other company probably came up with the idea on its own. After all, Hodge, Brune scientists aren't the only people in the world interested in solving pollution problems. As you said, global warming is a matter of international concern. There are probably dozens of companies working on solutions.

"And Detective Worski isn't interested in spy conspiracies. He's probably off in the wilds of New Jersey looking for the missing waitress from the deli." A disturbing thought came to me as I said that. "Oh, goodness, you don't think Thelma's in danger because she saw something when Max was killed, do you? Even if she didn't, the murderer might think she could identify him, or her, and—"

My husband smiled at me fondly. "You can't save the world, love," he said. Then more soberly, "Neither can I."

"In that case, give me the phone so that I can order dessert. I'll even give you a bite of my truffle torte. Do you want coffee?"

"Espresso, if they have it."

"You'll never sleep," I warned.

"Carolyn, I've been up since five; I'll sleep. In fact, why don't we plan to sleep late tomorrow, go out for brunch, and then inspect that rug you're so enthusiastic about?"

What a lovely day he'd outlined: no agents, editors, or worries about making a good impression, just a nice shopping trip with my husband. I dropped a kiss on his cheek as I dialed room service.

"Your second message was from Paul Fallon," Jason added as he loosened his tie.

"Humph," I said. "Maybe Smead complained that I wasn't returning his calls."

Jason stripped down to his shorts; he does have a nice, compact body, no middle-age spread, and his waistline seems to be unaltered by our trip to New Orleans, which is so unfair. I'm sure I didn't eat any more than he did. As he shrugged into his robe, I dictated our order and then looked at Worski's number. I should return his call, although I really didn't want to. What if he had bad news about Charlotte? Or Thelma?

"If you don't mind, I'll make my calls first," my husband said. I went into the bathroom but could hear him having a rather enigmatic conversation with Dr. Moore, the vice president at Hodge, Brune. "Perhaps . . . Nothing concrete . . . No, we didn't. . . . Actually, it isn't a good time. . . . Very well, twelve-thirty, then."

He hung up and went through the intricacies of making an international call from a hotel telephone—the Czech Republic, of all places. I brushed my hair and put on a nightgown and robe. While I was answering our door and accepting delivery of Jason's sorbet and my scrumptious-looking truffle torte (it had a whirl of chocolate cream on top in which was embedded an alluring fresh raspberry), Jason was saying, "Stefan, this is Jason Blue. I'm returning your call. Sorry about the hour, but you did say . . ."

I put the sorbet and espresso down beside my husband and went to the desk to savor my own treat, which tasted as good as it looked.

"Yes, Charles University . . . Really? Now, that's odd. Perhaps I misunderstood."

Where had I heard Charles University mentioned recently? I wondered. And was Jason planning, on the basis of his first call, to desert me at twelve-thirty tomorrow? That wouldn't give us much time for rug shopping after brunch. I felt rather ill used at the thought. However, if he didn't like the rug, I'd be disappointed. Without him, I could take advantage of the situation and buy it on my own. *Not nice, Carolyn,* said my conscience.

"Phone's all yours." Jason looked very thoughtful, even rather puzzled as he stood up, sipping his espresso.

"How's the sorbet?"

"Good."

"Want to try the torte?"

"No thanks."

"Are we still planning on brunch and rug shopping tomorrow?"

"Ah, Carolyn." He looked seriously regretful. "I've got to meet Charles Moore at twelve-thirty. Lunch and discussion in his office. I'm sorry."

"All right. We'll just have breakfast instead of brunch so we can make it to the rug store and back."

"You're an angel."

Not really, I thought. I was feeling decidedly peeved as I took his place on the bed beside the telephone. First, I called Detective Worski at home. The background TV chatter assuaged my conscience about phoning so late. "Are Charlotte and Thelma safe?" I asked.

"Mrs. Blue, I have no idea," he responded. "Mrs. Heydemann's probably at home celebrating all the money she inherited and having got the best of her stepchildren. That's if the will turned out to be what your friend thought."

"I doubt Charlotte is pleased to be saddled with financial oversight of those two. I heard tonight that the daughter is a slut—that's a quotation—and the son a spendthrift, would-be actor. No one has a good word to say about either. You really should take the danger to Charlotte more seriously. Unless you've found out who killed her husband."

"Hell, I can't even find the woman who was probably the last person to see him alive, except for the murderer. I just spent a rotten day with a bunch of New Jersey cops following up leads that didn't pan out. You sure you got the town and the disease right?"

"Yes, I am sure, and I find the disappearance of Thelma very disturbing. What if she saw the murder and was afraid to tell, and the murderer knew she could identify him, so he killed her to protect himself? Maybe you should check for unidentified bodies."

"I thought of that," said Worski. "Why you think I been slogging around New Jersey? It's like she never existed except for that job and a month or two in that short-lease apartment. Maybe she was the last person to see him alive because she killed him."

"Why would she? She was just his waitress."

"We don't know that."

"Are you saying *she* might be an assassin?" What an idea! Gossipy Thelma with her raucous laugh and her mother in New Jersey . . . if she actually had a mother in New Jersey. And what an elaborate story to have made up if it wasn't true. "Do you know where his children were at the time of the murder? Or their mother? Or who they've been associating with?" It was sort of exciting, giving the police investigative tips.

"We're looking into it. If you think of anything more about this Thelma, let me know."

"Who's Thelma?" Jason asked when I'd hung up.

"A waitress wearing a girdle and sensible shoes," I replied. Should I have mentioned the girdle and shoes to Worski? Maybe I had. I glanced down at the Park Central notepad with Jason's neat handwriting on it and decided to call Paul Fallon after all. I was tiring of the game with the newspaper syndicate and didn't feel like writing any more columns. Certainly not tonight. I wanted to go to bed. So I dialed the number and got Paul on the second ring, Paul and enough background noise to convince me that he was at a party or nightclub.

"This is Carolyn Blue."

"Ah, the elusive Mrs. Blue." He laughed. "You're driving poor Marshall nuts."

"Too bad. If he had better manners and developed a more acceptable personality, people might return his calls."

"Does that mean you're not going to?"

"Right. I'm not. And I'm not going to send him any more columns."

"Now, let's not be hasty, Carolyn. Why not have lunch with me tomorrow?"

My impulse was to say no until I remembered that I had no luncheon plans. Because Jason was trotting back to that benighted company to lunch with Charles Moore, I'd probably have to eat by myself in some tacky diner in the neighborhood. "Where?"

"What do you mean, where?"

"Where would you take me?"

He laughed and said he was being blackmailed by a recalcitrant food columnist.

"But I'm not a food columnist," I replied tartly. "Your Mr. Smead definitely gave me the don't-call-us, we'll-call-you runaround."

"I surrender. How about Chanterelle? French, four-star. You'll love it."

"What about Smead?"

"We won't invite him."

Chanterelle was in my book. I was definitely being wooed. "Very well, I accept. Chanterelle at one o'clock."

That settled, I took off my robe and climbed into bed.

"Why is Paul Fallon inviting you to lunch at an expensive restaurant?" Jason asked when I mentioned, a bit smugly, my new plans.

"Because he's madly in love with me and wants me to run away with him," I replied, snuggling against my husband.

"Um-m." Jason put an arm around me. "I don't think it would make a very good impression at Hodge, Brune if you were to run away with Frances Striff's lover. In fact, I'm sure she'd take offense, and we were planning to collaborate on some research, whether or not I take a job there."

"Well, then she won't mind if I collaborate on lunch with her significant other." I was feeling very pleased with myself. If Jason was going to stand me up for a meeting with some old vice president, I had vice presidential options of my own.

26

"The Best Prix Fixe Lunch in Town"

Carolyn

We overslept, a rare occurrence for Jason. Ah well, those who will drink espresso before bedtime against all advice! I personally enjoyed the sleep of the just and decaffeinated. As I had anticipated, we stopped for a standard, perfectly acceptable, but certainly uninteresting breakfast at a diner down the street. Then we made our way by bus and subway to A.B.C. Carpet, where my taste in decorating was affirmed. Jason liked the rug as much as I did and supported buying it because we'd never find its like at home. He didn't even balk at the price or the shipping fee.

"We'll call it a reward for getting through a bad week," he said. My week had had its pleasures, but I could see that he was not happy with his. Poor man. Perhaps he was disappointed that they had not yet offered him the job. He hadn't said much about it. In fact, now that I looked back over our time in New York, Jason hadn't had a lot to say about any of his activities. Or had I been so busy telling him about mine and offering my opinions on the situation at Hodge, Brune that he couldn't get a word in edgewise? I certainly hoped that wasn't the case. I'm not usually a person who insists on dominating conversation.

Once we had purchased our new rug and returned to the hotel, I consulted a city map. I had to go to TriBeCa and felt bound to use public transportation to atone for our extravagant purchase. Jason made a few calls before meeting Charles Moore at his office, so we parted company at the hotel. "Have a lovely lunch and meeting," I said.

He smiled and replied, "I doubt that it will compare with the food at Chanterelle. We'll probably order in sandwiches."

My conscience smote me. Here I had been complaining about the restaurants at which Hodge, Brune entertained us, but my husband was the person being shortchanged. I, at least, had been eating lunch in delightful, memorable venues. I'd have offered to bring Jason a doggie bag from Chanterelle, but I didn't know whether they'd have such a thing. Also, since

Fallon would be footing the bill, I doubted that he'd appreciate my order-ing a lot of food and then taking half of it home. That would not impress him as very sophisticated behavior on my part.

I could imagine him saying to Marshall Smead, "You were right about the Blue woman. When I took her to a great restaurant, she ordered a huge meal and asked to have half of it wrapped up. Can you imagine?" Then he'd go home and tell Frances Striff, which would embarrass Jason, who had said he planned to collaborate with her on a research project. No, it wouldn't do.

Even with the maps, I had trouble making my way to TriBeCa and the address at the corner of Hudson and Harrison. In fact, I got lost, asked di-rections from a native who didn't speak English, asked another who did, and finding out that I was in quite the wrong place, gave up and flagged down a cab. However, once I arrived, I was enchanted by the elegant am-biance of the restaurant. I could hardly take my eyes off the flower arrange-ments as I was led to Paul Fallon's table.

"Look at that pressed tin ceiling," I murmured appreciatively as he rose while I was helped into my seat. "It's amazing." Which it was. Very intricate.

"Look at you," he replied. "That's a stunning outfit."

I had worn the black slacks set with the flaring bottoms, teal insets, and the belt that owed something in design to both Native American and me-dieval influences. Naturally, I was pleased with the compliment. Jason had questioned my choice as a rug-hunting getup. "Save it for a special occa-sion," he'd advised. I hadn't argued because I didn't want to seem to gloat about eating at Chanterelle, which *was* a special occasion, while he was eat-ing in someone's office. I did smile at Fallon and thanked him for the com-pliment.

"A smile!" he exclaimed. "Does that mean I'm forgiven for Marshall Smead's sins?"

I laughed and picked up my menu.

"Now, Carolyn, I hope you're not going to order another salad. Chanterelle offers the best prix fixe luncheon in town, and I expect you to take advantage of it."

"I certainly shall then," I agreed, remembering that I hadn't at Le Bernardin and had gone hungry at dinner. Never again. Goodness knows where we'd eat tonight. Maybe Jason would be kept on and on at Hodge, Brune, and I'd be forced to order from room service or venture out into nasty weather by myself.

"If you don't mind a suggestion, try the seafood sausage to start. It's fa-mous."

I had been looking at the scallops with tomato and thyme, having had such a good experience with the scallops last night, and under not very promising circumstances, but goodness, if I was going to be a knowledge-able food writer, I needed to expand my horizons. Seafood sausage? Well,

Jason would certainly have tried it; therefore, I agreed since he couldn't be here to do it for me.

"I seem to be on a winning streak," said Fallon. "So if you don't have anything against red meat, the Beef with Black Trumpet Mushrooms is— God!—fabulous. Even Frances adores it, and she is not a beef and potatoes sort of girl."

I should think not. Frances was a very thin woman. I couldn't imagine her eating anything as high calorie as beef tenderloin, but to me it sounded wonderful after being pummeled by freezing winds as I tried to find my way here. And I remembered the dish from my *Dining and the Opera* book. Who could forget black trumpet mushrooms? I didn't know what they were, but they sounded intriguing. And I'd have the recipe for a column or book if I wanted to use it.

I allowed myself to be guided in my choice of second course as well, and both were wonderful. I gobbled down the lovely seafood sausages as we made light conversation and drank white wine. Over a bold red and the rich beef dish with its ambrosial flamed brandy sauce and crispy mushrooms, we talked about the investigation into Max's death. Fallon agreed with me that a Heydemann or ex-Heydemann had to be behind the murder. "Did you hear about the reading of the will yesterday?" he asked.

"No," I said, leaning forward eagerly to hear the latest gossip and wondering how he knew what had happened.

"Frances was worried about Charlotte and called to see how she was doing. Then we went over there because poor Charlotte was in shock."

"Oh my goodness," I breathed, alarmed. "Max surely didn't cut her out of the will, did he? I thought there was a trust fund for her."

"More than that," said Paul. "A trust fund, all his Hodge, Brune stock and his options, though God knows what they'll be worth after this Ukrainian debacle, and . . ." He paused dramatically. "He gave her complete control of the money he left his kids. She doesn't have to give them a cent until they're thirty-five unless she wants to, and then she can dribble it out."

"Well, that's just about what I heard." And I explained about Max's lawyer being a friend of Bernie Feingold's son.

"You do get around for an out-of-towner," he said admiringly. "But it's not so much the will as what happened after it was read."

"What?"

"The kids went ballistic. They shouted and screamed at Charlotte. Rick promised lawsuits and scandal. Ariadne even went after Charlotte with claws unsheathed, and the lawyers had to drag her off."

"That's horrible."

"Tell me about it. By the time we got to Charlotte's, her doctor was administering a tranquilizer, and Frances decided to stay the night with her."

"That's so kind of Frances. I told Detective Worski that Charlotte should have protection. I warned him that they were dangerous."

"Did you? Well, good for you. Not that I saw any protective cops lurking around the apartment when we arrived."

We had both polished off our entrées with gusto, and it suddenly occurred to me that I didn't know why I was here. Paul hadn't said a word about my columns. Surely, he hadn't invited me to . . . to chat me up, as the English novelists say.

"And the really satisfying thing about the will," Fallon continued, "is that Max's beastly kids can't do a thing about it. There's a provision that anyone who challenges the will gets cut off with three hundred dollars. Isn't that rich?"

"But if Charlotte were to die . . ." I said ominously. "That's what worries me. If they had motive to kill Max, now they have an even stronger motive to—"

Fallon, looking shocked, interrupted, "They wouldn't dare. They'd be the first people the police looked at."

"Their grandfather has all the money in the world to get them off with high-priced lawyers and the like."

"My God, you're a cheery lady." He picked up the menu produced by the attentive waiter. "Let's order dessert. I thought I was telling you a horror story with a happy ending. Now *I* need reassuring."

So did I. I still didn't know why I was here, but I was feeling uncomfortably full after my first two courses. Accordingly, I ordered the Raspberry Gratin, which, as it turned out, was full of eggs and cream and not all that light a dessert. But it was wonderful. Over dessert and coffee, Paul Fallon set my mind at rest. He did not have designs on my virtue. He had liked my columns and wanted to discuss a contract with me. Feeling a bit peeved that he hadn't said anything earlier, I responded, "Do I have to work with Marshall Smead?"

Paul laughed. "No, not unless you insist."

I grimaced humorously and scooped up more of my luscious, broiler-browned sabayon and raspberries, flavored with just the right amount of muscat wine. Paul had a fig and blackberry dessert. "Fax me a contract," I replied.

"Playing hard to get?" he asked.

"I've had my share of two bottles of wine," I protested. "No one should make business decisions while light-headed."

"I should be so fortunate," he said wryly. "You strike me as more hard-headed than light-headed."

Was that a compliment? I wondered. Obviously I was going to have to take a taxi home. I wasn't fit to find my way through the city's rapid transit system. I'd probably end up lost in Bedford-Stuyvesant. However, if he offered me a good contract (and I did think it would be fun to write newspaper columns!), I could afford the occasional taxi without being attacked by middle-class, Midwestern angst over my spendthrift ways.

Beef with Black Trumpet Mushrooms

Preheat oven to 400°F. In a large sauté pan or skillet, melt *1 tbs. unsalted butter* over medium heat and sauté *1 lb. black trumpet mushrooms or chanterelles, sliced.* When they begin to give off liquid, drain and reserve liquid and mushrooms.

Film large sauté pan or skillet with *olive oil* and cook *3 lbs. beef tenderloin* over high heat until nicely browned. Place beef in the preheated oven and bake for 10 minutes, or until rare. Remove from oven and cover to keep warm.

In a medium sauté pan or skillet, melt *1 tbs. butter* over medium heat and cook sautéed mushrooms until dry and slightly crisp. Remove pan from heat and add *3 tbs. brandy.* Return pan to heat and let brandy warm. Ignite brandy with a match and shake pan until flames subside. Add reserved mushroom liquid, *1½ tbs. beef or veal glaze* (can be made by cooking a good beef or veal stock over high heat until reduced to a syrupy consistency), and *1½ tsp. fresh lemon juice.* Bring to boil, add *¾ cup heavy whipping cream*, and cook to reduce until thick enough to coat the back of a spoon. Season with *salt, freshly ground pepper,* and additional lemon juice if necessary. Add any juices that may have accumulated on the platter holding the beef.

Divide the sauce and mushrooms evenly among 4 plates. Slice the beef tenderloin and place the slices on top of the sauce and mushrooms. Garnish with seasonal vegetables and serve.

MAKES 8 SERVINGS.

Raspberry Gratin

To prepare sabayon: In a double boiler over barely simmering water, combine *6 egg yolks, 1 cup muscat wine,* and *½ cup sugar*; whisk until foamy and very hot. Remove from heat and place the top of the double boiler in a bowl of ice water; whisk occasionally until completely cooled. Fold in *1 cup whipped cream.*

To assemble the gratin: Preheat the broiler. Divide *2 cups raspberry coulis* (made by putting in a blender or food processor and pureeing until smooth: *2 cups fresh raspberries or one 10-oz. package frozen unsweetened raspberries, defrosted, powdered sugar* to taste and *1 tbs. kirsch* or to taste) among 8 shallow porcelain ramekins or other individual ovenproof containers. Add a dollop of sabayon mixture on top. Place an equal amount from *5 cups of fresh raspberries* in each dollop of sabayon. Place under preheated broiler for 2 to 3 minutes, or until lightly browned. Serve warm.

MAKES 8 SERVINGS.

27
Vice Presidential Cookery

Carolyn

When I arrived back at the hotel, somewhat the worse for alcohol and having been roundly cursed for refusing to tip the dangerously reckless cabby, I found that Jason was out. However, there was a message on the bed informing me that we were to have dinner in Greenwich, Connecticut, at the home of Charles Moore and would have to be at Grand Central Station by seven o'clock to catch a New Haven train to our destination.

I was not pleased, and I certainly wasn't hungry. A light evening snack would have done for me. The thought that Mrs. Moore might be home slaving over a hot stove was profoundly depressing. It's bad enough to have to cook without doing it for an unappreciative guest. But did the wives of corporate vice presidents do their own cooking? She might have a live-in chef. In the meantime, I needed to sleep off the wine.

I carefully removed my new outfit and hung it in the closet. Then I called Detective Worski's number to tell him that Charlotte Heydemann had been threatened by her stepson and physically attacked by her stepdaughter after the reading of the will yesterday. He said he'd look into it. I could hear a basketball game playing in the background, but then even police detectives deserve a day off. Had he uncovered any news of the missing Thelma? I asked. Well, if she was dead, he replied callously, they'd obviously buried her, because no bodies matching her description had been found.

Offended by his offhandedness, I hung up and went straight to bed, only to be awakened later by Jason. "How was your lunch?" he asked.

"Superb," I replied. "How was yours?"

"Canceled. Moore had to take his wife to the doctor, so he invited us for tonight. Didn't you get my note?"

"If his wife needed medical attention, how can he expect her to prepare dinner for guests?" I asked.

"I have no idea. Maybe he's going to cook."

"Oh, I'm sure," I replied sarcastically.

"Whatever his plans, he was very insistent that we come tonight." Jason had been divesting himself of overcoat, muffler, and several shopping bags. What had he bought? I wondered. The answer was books. He'd visited a scientific bookstore and found several volumes of great interest. You wouldn't believe how much scientific books cost! Still, I could hardly complain since I had been splurging on clothes.

Then Jason smiled and proffered a little bag. "I bought you these."

And in the small box was a pair of dangly earrings that perfectly matched the turquoise in the belt to my new slacks outfit but also had stones of a deep teal that matched the insets. My dear husband, while I gorged myself at Chanterelle, had gone without lunch and bought me a lovely, thoughtful, perfect gift. And I had been begrudging him a few pricey chemistry books, which were, after all, tax deductible.

"Carolyn, are you crying?" he asked. "I thought you'd like them."

"I love them," I sniffed and put them on immediately, even though I was still in my robe. "I think they're absolutely perfect, and I intend to wear them tonight and admire myself in every mirror at the Moores' house." I gave him a hug. "Jason, I think you are an utterly perfect husband."

"High praise, indeed," he responded, grinning. Then he glanced at the clock and said we'd better dress if we wanted to catch that train.

Jason

When Charles Moore called to cancel our appointment, I assured him that what little I had to say could be said on the telephone. Frankly, I resented having my day with Carolyn cut short and believed that I had done all I could to carry out the investigation that I felt I owed Max, not that my efforts had yielded much. However, Moore insisted that we talk personally and invited us to dinner. He wouldn't take no for an answer. Perhaps he felt badly at having taken so much of my time without offering the consultancy. He need have suffered no qualms on that score; they had paid me well, entertained me, if not royally, at least respectably, and had no obligation beyond that.

Nonetheless, Carolyn and I had to take the train to Greenwich on an evening that did not look promising, weather-wise. She mentioned that snow was predicted. I said I hoped that it would hold off until we got out of the area Monday morning. In passing through Grand Central to the New Haven tracks, I remarked wistfully that I had not been able to visit the Oyster Bar, one of my favorite New York restaurants. "Let's just hope his wife is a decent cook," Carolyn replied. She had paused several times to admire her new earrings in the windows of closed terminal shops.

We were both taken by surprise in Mrs. Moore. Charles picked us up at the commuter station and drove us to a half-timbered Tudor house in a forested area, where an olive-skinned woman in a wheelchair met us at the door. Renata Moore had been crippled ten years earlier in an automobile driven by her son and hadn't walked since. What a family tragedy that must have been, and still was. Moore left us with his wife and hurried off to the kitchen, where he, evidently, was in charge of dinner.

Carolyn couldn't quite hide her surprise at the idea of vice presidential cookery but set herself to be charming to her hostess, who engaged in polite small talk for several minutes and then said, "I understand you're a culinary expert." Carolyn insisted that she was just a novice who could write coherently, a talent being rapidly lost in modern society.

Renata Moore then laughed and said, "I could see that you had your doubts about eating anything prepared by my husband, but you needn't worry. We have excellent gourmet takeout here in Greenwich. Charles brought dinner home before he went to pick you up." An impish smile then lit her face. "But you might compliment him and ask for a recipe. I hear that you're about to enter the ranks of newspaper columnists."

"How did you hear that?" Carolyn asked, amazed.

"Oh, Charles is ever so good about bringing home gossip to entertain me. Sometimes I almost feel as if I still have a place in the lives of my friends and acquaintances because he tells me all the news."

"Ready," said Moore from a doorway that led into a large formal dining room. He was wearing an apron. Carolyn's expression said she thought he was trying to look as if he had actually cooked the meal. I, on the other hand, assumed that he didn't want to spill anything on his suit while transferring food from the kitchen.

"Charles sent the maid home," said Renata as he pushed her wheelchair to a place at one end of the table. "I assume that means you gentlemen have top secret things to discuss over dinner. I sometimes feel that I should have a security clearance myself."

Moore poured wine for everyone and remarked, "I think recent events should convince you, my dear, that Hodge, Brune isn't just another paranoid corporate entity."

They argued amiably while Carolyn and I sampled our *caprese*, which was excellent.

"I'm so envious," Carolyn said to our host. "I can't imagine how you manage to get tomatoes like these in winter. They taste homegrown. And the basil—not a brown spot on it."

"Ah, but you should have tasted the vegetables in the old days when the Italians sold all the produce," said Renata. "Then it was *really* fresh. I even had relatives in Bensonhurst who grew their own zucchini. They used to bombard us with it in the summer, figuratively speaking. Now it's all Koreans selling vegetables in the corner markets."

Carolyn laughed. "Well, even the mozzarella tastes as if it was made today. Surely, the Koreans aren't making the mozzarella." She turned to Charles. "You must tell me, Charles, where you shop. Do you go into New York City for food?"

"Greenwich has excellent markets," said Charles Moore.

I believe I detected Mrs. Moore winking at my wife, and I had to wonder if all women were allied in an underground conspiracy to tease their husbands. Thank God, Carolyn didn't ask him for a recipe.

Carolyn

I liked Renata Moore immediately and admired any woman who could be so cheerful after being confined ten years to a wheelchair. How lonely her life must be, her children grown and gone. And I did wonder whether she was estranged from the son whose driving had resulted in her paralysis. Not that I thought her the kind of person to punish him for an accident. However, guilt, which the boy must have felt, will sometimes lead a young person to avoid the one who is the source of his guilt. I remember that Chris once broke a favorite perfume bottle of mine while playing golf with toy clubs in the house, a forbidden activity. I don't even like Jason to use those putting machines in the den; golf balls are dangerous. At any rate, Chris felt so badly about my perfume bottle that he didn't speak to me for three days.

As I recalled that incident, we were eating veal Marsala with new potatoes and sautéed sweet peppers, fresh out of the microwave, I presumed. The wine, a Barolo, was as good as you'd expect. "I talked to Charlotte this morning," Renata was saying. "There was a terrible scene at the reading of the will yesterday."

"Not surprising, considering how her husband tied up the money," I remarked.

"How is it that you are familiar with Max's will?" Charles Moore asked, giving me an odd look.

"My agent's uncle told me all about it," I explained with relish. "He and Dr. Heydemann have the same lawyer, and Mr. Feingold, my agent's uncle, is a friend of the Heydemann family from years ago in Brooklyn."

"Really?" Moore looked nonplussed.

"*And* I had lunch today with Paul Fallon, who is a friend of Frances Striff, who stayed the night with Charlotte last night. In fact, I had lunch with Charlotte Thursday."

"The day after the memorial service?" Moore looked disapproving.

"She was so sad at the service that I invited her," I replied.

"Good for you," said Renata. "I'm sure that's just what Charlotte needed. I'd have done it myself if I could."

"You *could* drive, Renata, if you chose to," said her husband. "Vehicles are available with hand controls."

"Yes, I could, Charles, but once I got to, say, a restaurant in the city, I'd be in trouble." She turned back to me. "Can you imagine that nasty boy announcing how he was going to spend the money before he even knew whether he was getting any? I couldn't have been more pleased when I heard how Max had tied up the trusts."

I nodded, taking a sip of my wine. Barolo used to be a much more robust wine. Jason says they've changed it so they won't have to age it so long. Too bad, although I don't suppose the old style Barolo would go that well with veal. "What was Ricky planning on doing with the money he now can't get his hands on?"

"Oh, he marched into the lawyer's office and announced that he'd be playing the lead in an off-Broadway play called *And Then Some*. Not a very interesting title, is it?"

"Is he good enough to get the lead in anything?" I asked.

"I doubt it," said Renata. "I believe he's done some amateur theater at Dartmouth, but nothing in New York. Anyway, he said he was quitting school and financing the play himself. With his inheritance."

"No wonder he and his sister made such a scene."

"Yes. They are really appalling people, but then their mother is, too. Fortunately, she's usually locked away."

"Not right now," I said. "We saw her celebrating Max's death at the opera."

"God, I'd like to see an opera again," said Renata. "Charles, I hope you're having your detective—"

"I don't have a detective," her husband replied. He had just reentered the room carrying little round cakes in a red puddle—raspberry or strawberry, I presumed.

They were quite tasty if very small. He'd put the dirty dishes on a massive sideboard, presumably for the maid to take care of when she returned.

"Well, you owe it to Max to hire one and have him investigate that family. I had no idea Melisande was out. You can be sure the three of them are behind Max's death."

"My thoughts exactly," I agreed. "I'll bet that Rick disguised himself and killed his father so he could finance his part in the play."

"Ladies, ladies," Moore groaned. He was pouring Jason a great dollop of cognac and didn't offer any to us. "I'd almost rather espouse the Russian Mafia theory—"

"What Russian Mafia theory?" his wife asked.

"—than your patricide hypothesis," he continued, ignoring her question, which I, too, would have liked to hear more about. "That's just your operatic Italian nature speaking, my dear, and I didn't realize you were pining for a night at the Met. I can certainly see to that."

"Oh, Charles, I didn't mean to make you feel bad. We both know I can't—"

"I must do it in self-defense before you turn company business into a grand opera. Patricide!" He shook his head in a gesture of insufferable male superiority. "Jason, why don't we go to the library? We have things to talk about."

"Oh, you can talk in front of us, Charles," said his wife. "We won't say a word to anyone about your little company secrets."

"Really?" he said dryly.

"Jason and I are going to a play tomorrow and then home Monday, so *we* won't be talking to anyone," I added.

"What are you going to see?" Renata asked eagerly.

"The Most Fabulous Story Ever Told," I replied. "It's playing in the Village and supposed to be very funny."

"You'll love it if you don't mind outrageous homosexual camp. And you'll want to drop in at some little trattoria for lunch. Just walking into one off the street is a lovely adventure." She sighed. "I grew up in Little Italy. After that and the Village, Greenwich seems a bit sedate."

"Care to join me in a cigar, Jason?" Moore asked.

"Bravo, my dear!" said his wife. "If you're going to smoke cigars, I don't think I care to hear your secrets."

The men departed with cognac snifters in hand—talk about sedate! Renata Moore and I settled down to discuss opera in their living room, which looked out through small paned windows on gently falling snow. She was delighted with my description of the staging peculiarities of *Mefistofele* and the antics of Sean Ryan, who had loved the subtitle machine but hated the opera.

"I haven't seen the new subtitle equipment," she said wistfully. "Did you like it?"

"Not much. It is, admittedly, more discreet than super-titles run above the stage, but if you look down at the screen in front of you, you miss what's happening onstage."

"Of course, if the singers are fat and unattractive or terrible actors, that's all to the good. I saw Richard Tucker when I was a girl. He had the most thrilling voice, but his acting was so stilted—you know, the stagger-when-emoting-school?—I always ended up closing my eyes so that I could enjoy his voice without having to look at him."

"I'd like to have seen Richard Tucker," I said with a sigh.

"I have movies. Shall we watch?"

28

Overnight Without a Nightie

Jason

Thank God Charles Moore didn't actually want to smoke cigars in his library. Carolyn, who hates the smell of cigars, would have suggested that I sleep in the bathtub with the door closed. Instead, Moore and I placed the cognac bottle on a table between us while seated in deep leather chairs. "Your wife is . . . ah . . . outspoken, isn't she?" he remarked.

"So is yours," I replied.

Moore looked surprised but had to agree. Then we discussed my dinner with Fergus and Fiona. The gist of my replies was that I did not think McRoy had had anything to do with the theft of the coal research. "The man knows he's suspect. He's been conducting his own investigation among members of his team."

"That could be a red herring," Moore suggested.

"I doubt it. He's troubled because he feels he's destroying the cohesiveness of his group; he's distraught because his years of research have been stolen; and he's particularly hurt because he's suspected by his superiors."

Moore sighed. "If he's innocent, this will all—"

"Unless the problem is resolved, you'll lose him," I cautioned. "He talked of nothing last night at dinner but his dismay at the situation. His wife, who evidently hadn't realized how upset he's been, said he should leave the company and take another job. I gather he's had offers."

"I'm sure he has," said Moore grimly. "Did you get any handle on their finances? Could he have been in such straits that he'd sell us out? That's Merrivale's theory."

"They were quite talkative about their financial situation. Evidently, Fergus has been successful investing in the rising market."

"If he's one of those idiot day-traders, he could have lost every cent they have."

"I gather that he's a careful investor, his wife is a careful husbander of family resources, they're not given to expensive habits, and their children can be expected to go to university on scholarships."

"What? Even that great, lumpish Roddy, who showed up here last year for the Christmas party? He ate everything in sight."

I had to smile. I had never seen "lumpish Roddy," but I remembered how much a growing boy can eat. Chris, for a time, raised our grocery bills

by a third, according to Carolyn. "Mrs. McRoy expects Roddy to get a soccer scholarship."

"Ah. The boy did bounce a ham off his forehead in some sort of demon-
stration. Renata was not amused."

"Has Merrivale come up with anything concrete against Fergus?"

"No, not yet."

I found my suspicions of Merrivale himself on the rise. If he was so intent on implicating Fergus McRoy, might he not be diverting suspicion from
himself? If anyone was in a perfect position to sell the company's secrets and
then derail the investigation, it was Merrivale, who was both a scientist and
in control of company security. As long as he could keep Moore from coop-
erating with the police, he'd be home free, and poor Fergus McRoy, left on
tenterhooks. Of course, I had no more evidence against Merrivale than he
did against McRoy, only suspicion and personal dislike. A course of action
that might at least bring Merrivale under surveillance occurred to me.

"Maybe you should hire a professional detective, not to look into the
scientific aspect, but to investigate the finances and telephone records of
people who had access to the research."

Moore frowned. "Do you know one? A detective?"

"The only detectives I've ever met," I replied, "were on police forces,
but that doesn't mean you couldn't find a reputable agency that is accustomed to dealing with industrial espionage.

"By the way, have you received any demands from the Ukraine?"

"Nothing." He held up the decanter questioningly, then poured into
both snifters.

"Well, you might at least consider an outside investigator if you're determined to keep the police out of the case. I can't see that Merrivale is coming up with more than wild guesses."

"I'll think about your suggestion," Moore replied. "Aside from your
evening with McRoy, have you had any other thoughts about our problem?"

"I did pick up a strange bit of information last night. Someone from
Prague, whom I had called earlier, called me back. He's at Charles University, and I had mentioned in passing that I knew a former graduate student
from Charles, Vasandrovich."

"Yes, Vaclav's Czech. Max got him out quite a while before the Communist regime fell."

"My friend said there's no record of a Vaclav Vasandrovich having received his doctorate from Charles."

"What?" Moore looked nonplussed.

"Could I have misunderstood? Perhaps he did his undergraduate work
there. Or a postdoc."

"No. I remember reading his recommendations. They had to be smug-
gled out. Is your friend sure? Could records have been lost during the Velvet Revolution?"

"I don't think it was all that violent," I replied.

"There seems to be no end to this. First, Max. Then the project theft. Now this news. If Vaclav's credentials are false, I'll have to fire him, and we've been counting on him to take Max's place. In fact, I planned to announce his permanent appointment on Monday. He was the heir apparent. Max had been talking about resigning the directorship and going back to research."

"It's hard to believe that Max would have been fooled by an imposter," I pointed out, "which is to say that Vaclav was obviously educated somewhere. He's brilliant, just as Max said he was. I'm sure you know that. So the question is: If not Charles, where? Was he at Charles when Max brought him here?"

"No, some government research facility, as I remember, and not happy there."

I couldn't see that we were making any progress, so I glanced at my watch. "Considering the time and the weather—" Snow was falling onto the lawn and evergreens outside the study windows. "—I think Carolyn and I should be going. I wish I had more and better news for you, but—"

"Good God, man, you've done more than most in this investigation. At least your queries in Eastern Europe have given us a handle on the Ukrainian company." He set his snifter down with a disgusted thump. "Russian mobsters, false credentials. Makes me wonder what Merrivale has been up to, other than irritating everyone in the labs and holding up the research we still have in our control."

I felt a distinct jolt of satisfaction to hear that Moore wasn't particularly satisfied with his security director.

"And I didn't drag you all the way out here to ask for more information," Moore continued. "In fact, I must apologize for keeping you from your wife today and then canceling our appointment. Renata was watering houseplants, leaning out too far, and fell from her wheelchair. I'm afraid we were both terrified that she had done herself damage. Because she has no feeling below the waist, injuries to that area are not readily evident."

"Really, Charles, there's no need to apologize. I'm sorry to hear that your wife had a fall and hope that she—"

"Oh, she's fine. And I think she really enjoyed the evening until I dragged you off."

I glanced again at my watch. It was after eleven.

"The primary reason for my invitation was to offer the consultancy you and Max discussed. I should have done this earlier, but I have been distracted. Nonetheless, upper management is agreed that we would very much like you to come aboard."

Since I was no longer expecting an offer, it took me by surprise, and I had no immediate answer.

"I hope our present problems won't deter you. We will survive, even if we do lose the coal project, and our research in other areas should be of interest to you, as your expertise is of interest to us." He waited a minute for a reply while I listened to the rising howl of the wind outside and wondered whether we'd be able to get back to the city.

"We had in mind six weeks in the summer," Moore added, "as well as three visits during the rest of the year, to be scheduled at your convenience and our need. And of course, we would expect to be able to call you with questions and perhaps funnel research money and projects to your university labs."

"That sounds very tempting," I replied. "Of course, I'll have to discuss it with Carolyn."

"Of course." He frowned and began to talk money: per diems on short visits, per hours for phone consultations, grants for postdoctoral fellows and research equipment, summer remuneration. It was an offer I could hardly afford to overlook, although with Max gone and having met Merrivale, I wasn't as enthusiastic as I might have been.

"Are you sure Merrivale, for instance, would approve of letting contracts to university entities," I asked, "much less bringing in an academic? My impression is that he considers all professors loose-lipped and feckless."

"Feckless? An odd word to apply to a scientist." Moore produced his little half smile. "Merrivale will have to adjust. This is a serious offer. I'll fax you the terms before you leave, if you like, or if you want to negotiate something else—"

"I consider your offer very generous. Carolyn and I will give it every consideration." I rose, now really worried about the storm and the time.

Moore rose as well. "Having neglected to smoke the cigars I mentioned, shall we join the ladies?" We found them dozing in front of a large-screen TV with an old film of *Andrea Chenier* playing. The photographic quality was poor, but the singing outstanding. I wouldn't have minded watching that.

"You'll get us arrested if you insist on showing people those pirated films, Renata," Moore said as he touched his wife lightly on the shoulder.

She sat straight immediately and replied, "Well, Charles, you've kept Jason so late, and the storm has become so bad that they'll definitely have to stay the night."

"Oh, Renata, we couldn't impose," Carolyn mumbled. I could see that she had been deeply asleep, even though the tenor was singing gloriously on the television screen.

"Nonsense. The guest room is always made up; the last train for the city is leaving as we speak; and this is obviously a night for curling up under a down comforter instead of traveling in the snow. Charles, show them the guest room, won't you? I'm for bed." Calling, "Good night, all," over her shoulder, Renata wheeled herself out of the room before any of us could protest.

"I don't even have a nightgown," Carolyn whispered to me as we walked upstairs, our host having turned on a chandelier in the hall and directed us to the guest room before hurrying after his wife. "And this house is freezing."

Once we were huddled together in bed, Carolyn demanded to know what Moore and I had been talking about so long. I told her the terms of the contract I had been offered. "Good heavens," she exclaimed. "We'll be rich." Then she sniffed. "You dear, you refused cigars. I don't know how to thank you."

"Actually, I wasn't offered any." I pulled Carolyn a bit closer. The sheets weren't warming up as fast as I would have liked.

"It was a ruse? To get you to himself? What were you talking about in there besides the contract? And what was that bit about the Russian Mafia?"

"Just something I heard when I was calling friends abroad."

"Vaclav speaks Russian."

"I'm not surprised."

"I heard him on the telephone, but then he said it wasn't Russian; it was Czech, and he was talking to his Aunt Elizabeta."

"Did he?" I felt a prick of unease. Vaclav had told me that he had no living relatives.

"Maybe he's a secret Russian agent," Carolyn suggested, giggling. She had just kissed my chin.

"Are you trying to start something with me?" I asked, not averse to the idea.

"Of course not." She drew back. "We couldn't. Not in their house."

"I don't see why not. If we could with my mother in the next room in Chicago—"

"But that was our anniversary."

"—we can certainly indulge when our hosts evidently don't even sleep upstairs."

"I forgot to ask him for a recipe," said my wife.

"You're trying to change the subject. We'll be as quiet as mice."

"Or as horny as rabbits," she suggested, now trying to stifle laughter.

"As an internationally known scientist, I resent the indignity of being called horny."

"OK. Then roll over and go to sleep," my wife replied.

"On the other hand . . ." I temporized.

29

A Shock over French Toast

Carolyn

Charles Moore knocked on our door at nine and suggested that we appear for breakfast in a half hour. We showered in the bath attached to the guest room, but we had to put on the same clothes we'd worn the night before and, more to the point, the same underwear. I was not happy.

Then we followed our noses downstairs to a large, sunny kitchen with brick walls, slate floors, a fireplace, modern appliances, and workspaces keyed to the needs of someone in a wheelchair as well as spaces at the standard height. Renata was fixing bacon and French toast while Charles brewed coffee and mixed up a berry, cream, and liqueur sauce for the toast. Immediately, hunger overcame my fixation on twice-worn underwear, and I wrote down his recipe. In fact, I wish that I'd had a camera. Their kitchen was gorgeous, an assessment with which our hostess agreed. "Charles had it put in for me while we were on a cruise. I thought the cruise was my birthday present, but it turned out to be the kitchen."

"If you'll take another cruise with me, my dear, I'll arrange another homecoming surprise," her husband promised. He poured coffee and placed the cups before us on the table of a breakfast nook that looked out over their backyard, snow-covered with sunlight glistening off iced branches. Had there been an ice storm after we went to bed? I wondered if the trains would be running. Lovely as this was, I didn't want to miss the play that afternoon.

Renata was saying, "Oh Charles, you know the cruise didn't work out that well."

"I thought it did."

"You weren't the one in the wheelchair." There was a snap to her voice, and he looked grim as she transferred bacon to a serving platter and handed it to him. "Sorry," she murmured. "It's not your fault I'm such a stay-at-home." She retrieved a plate of French toast from the lower oven and maneuvered her wheelchair to the table while still holding the plate.

Her chair evidently had one-handed electric controls. I'd love to have seen how it worked, but I could hardly ask. Instead, I commented on the delicious breakfast and got Renata's French toast recipe. Jason said he hoped I was planning to use the recipes at home, and I replied that, if I got a second book contract, I'd certainly publish them, with the Moores' permission, of course. Then I added that I'd love to have Jason try the dishes some Sunday in El Paso. We could invite friends.

"Suddenly my wife no longer cooks," he said sadly to Charles. "She talks about food, she writes about it, she eats it, but she doesn't—"

"Who was it who made the elaborate, fantastic, time-consuming, never-to-be-surpassed, gourmet anniversary dinner?" I asked.

"Are you going to do it again next year?" My husband managed to look both hopeful and woebegone.

Renata offered Jason more of the berry topping to soothe his "disappointed chauvinist expectations," as she put it, and Charles rose to answer the telephone. "If it's the office, tell them to stuff it," Renata called after her husband. He looked disapproving, Jason blinked, and we ladies laughed merrily. She was a woman after my own heart, so I told her about Jason's mother, the militant feminist who disapproved of me because I had stayed home raising children and cooking gourmet meals.

"Have I ever failed to defend you when Mother was on the attack?" he demanded.

"Of course not," I replied agreeably. "But then you wouldn't have wanted me to turn into your mother, would you?"

"God forbid," he agreed. To Renata he said, "My mother's a very intelligent woman, and I love her dearly, but she can be hard to take in doses longer than, say, two or three days. She disapproves of half womankind and all men."

"Even your father?" Renata asked.

"They split up years ago," Jason replied. "When we visit Chicago, we spend half the time with him and half with her. Then we all have dinner together on changeover day and quarrel. That's been going on since the divorce when I was twelve, but once I went away to college, Dad moved to a suburb on the other side of Chicago, forty miles away, quit his job at the university, started his own company, married a sweet young thing, and had a second family."

"Jason's half brother and sister aren't that much older than our children," I added. "It was lovely for Chris and Gwen to have an aunt and uncle to play with when they were all growing up, especially since my family's almost nonexistent—just my father, who is not very good with children."

"Amazing!" exclaimed Renata. "I have this huge Italian family. No one ever gets divorced or practices birth control. It's—Charles?" Her husband had returned to the table, his face rather pale. "Is something wrong?"

He shook his head.

"All right." She looked puzzled. "As I was saying, they think Charles and I are absolutely peculiar. Only two children. They were always sympathizing with me and telling me about some new saint who could make me fertile again." She had been smiling, but then she sighed. "Now they keep digging up obscure saints who specialize in making cripples walk. Charles, something is definitely wrong. You look like—I don't know—like someone died."

"She didn't die," said Charles.

"Who?"

"Charlotte."

My hands turned icy. "What happened to Charlotte? I told the police—"

He looked at me sharply. "You told the police what? Why were you talking to the police about Charlotte?"

He looked so fierce that I began to feel defensive. "Because of the will. She controls the trusts of the stepchildren during her lifetime. If they killed Max for money, obviously she would be the next target."

He turned away from me as if I was an idiot, which I really didn't appreciate. Even if he hadn't been at the opera to see Melisande Heydemann crowing over her ex-husband's death and her son trying to drag her away, he had heard the two children at the memorial service. How much evidence did he need that—

"Max must have talked to Charlotte," Charles said to Jason.

"But they wouldn't know that he had," Jason replied.

"They couldn't afford to believe that he hadn't. I never even thought of that."

"What are you *talking* about?" Renata demanded. "And what happened to Charlotte?"

"She was attacked yesterday in front of her apartment building."

"Is she all right?" I asked anxiously.

"She's in the hospital. Stabbed in the shoulder."

We all looked at one another with horror.

"Did they catch the assailant?" Jason asked.

"No," Charles replied. "He got away while the doorman was helping her up."

Within two hours, Jason and I had passed through Grand Central Station, bought some flowers and two books, and taken the subway uptown to the hospital where Charlotte Heydemann was recovering from the attack. A policeman was stationed outside her room, but after consulting her and calling Detective Worski, he allowed us in. Charlotte was propped up in one of those multiposition hospital beds, surrounded by flowers, and looking as pale as the white bandages that bulged out from under the neck and armhole of her hospital gown.

She smiled at us both and thanked us for coming out on such a miserable day. "Not that I'll ever complain about snow and ice again," she added. "We've about decided, Detective Worski and I and my doorman, that if I hadn't slipped on the ice, the man with the . . . whatever it was; I didn't actually see it . . . would have killed me." Then she giggled.

Jason looked quite surprised at her cheery demeanor. I assumed that she was being given painkillers. I sat down beside the bed and took her hand. "Did you recognize your attacker?" I asked.

"Oh, goodness no. He was all bundled up. Knit cap, scarf, bulky, raggedy clothing."

"Really?"

"A stereotypical street person. I told the detective that."

I thought that it could have been Rick playing a part. "But didn't you notice anything—well—familiar about him?"

Charlotte looked thoughtful. "There was something. But what?"

I looked into her eyes, willing her to remember something useful. Actually, her eyes looked odd. Dilated. What had they given her? "Was it his height?" I asked.

"No-o-o. He was average height. Taller than me. He grabbed my shoulder as I was slipping. I thought he meant to keep me from failing, but then—z-z-zip!" She waved her good hand. "For a moment it didn't even hurt. But he missed. My heart. Lucky me. Lucky. Lucky." She smiled sweetly in a blank, woozy sort of way.

Rick was average height, I thought, trying to picture him when he took the podium at the memorial service and then when he chased after his mother at the opera. A bit taller than Jason. Well, good. One clue. "What about his hair?" I asked. Jason had sat down on the other side of the bed and was frowning at me.

"None showing. He was wearing a knit cap, all ravelly. Maybe it was hand knitted. A couple of strands were straggling down the side of his face."

"So it was something about his face that was familiar?" I suggested.

"No, but, I don't think Detective Worski suspects me of killing Max anymore. I couldn't really see his face . . . not the detective's, the homeless man's. The cap was pulled down almost to his eyebrows, and he had a very tacky scarf wrapped around his neck up to the nose. It was so cold! I was cold, too. My ears were freezing. They hurt. More than my shoulder, actually. That's why I was hurrying and slipped . . . because of my ears. That's why he missed. I was falling down. He must be disappointed. Or maybe he doesn't know."

"But the doorman must have—"

"Seen him? A street person, he told the police. He was too busy helping me up to notice much, I suppose. Probably thought I'd sue the co-op association because they hadn't cleared the ice off. When the man let go of me, I fell right down. I have a huge bruise on my hip. Would you like to see it?" She looked as pleased as a child at show-and-tell until she noticed the expression on Jason's face. Then she giggled and said, "Of course, you'd have to leave the room, Jason. In fact, you're probably embarrassed because you know these gowns gape open in back. What if I had to get up and use the facilities? I couldn't. Not with guests. And thanks so much for the flowers. And the books." She looked down at the books that lay on the sheet beside her thigh. "I'll start one as soon as you leave. Not that I'm suggesting you leave. It's nice to have company. Keeps me from thinking about that man trying to kill me.

"First Max. Now me. It's really terrifying when you think about it, isn't it? Even in the big, bad city, and our crime rates *are* down, you know. Isn't that ironic? Nothing ever happened to us when life was more violent, but as soon as things get better . . . well, I suppose good times just remind those who don't have anything of the . . . the contrast. There I was in my warm coat, and this poor homeless man in his rags . . . it probably made him furious. Maybe he was hungry when he saw Max eating all that pastrami." She blinked back tears. "I try not to think about Max. Now I'll have to try not to think about me. But if he's so poor, how can he afford a knife or whatever it was? The detective couldn't answer that."

"But, Charlotte." I was going to make one last try. "You said there was something familiar about him. Had you seen a homeless person like him before?" I supposed it was possible. Some person who should be medicated or institutionalized, who had fixated on the Heydemanns—

"Never," she replied. "I never see them on our block. The doormen chase them away. Maybe our doorman was afraid I'd sue because he hadn't chased the man off."

"So what was familiar about him?"

Charlotte leaned her head back against the pillow and closed her eyes.

"Oh, Charlotte, I'm so sorry. I've tired you out. Maybe we should—"

"Not at all. I was just picturing the incident. It was his smell."

"His smell?" Now, there was a clue. Some distinctive aftershave? She'd certainly recognize her stepson's cologne. "He smelled like Rick?" I asked impulsively. Then how I regretted that question! An odor ID might be no good in court if it was thought that the source of the smell had been suggested to the victim.

"Rick?" She looked quite astonished. "Goodness, no. He smelled like . . . um-m-m . . . garbage. That's it. Do you remember when we had the garbage strike? Well, no, you wouldn't because you don't live here, but the whole city smelled . . . just like that man. Fetid." She shuddered.

You can't imagine how disappointed I was. It might have been Rick, but I certainly couldn't prove it to Detective Worski because the attacker had smelled like garbage, which is not the preferred scent of the sons of prominent families. I sighed.

Jason, who had been strangely silent, leaned forward and asked, "Charlotte, before he died, did Max mention a problem he was having at work?"

"What problem? Max never had problems. His people were very fond of him, and the research was going well. It always did. Max was a wonderful scientist."

"I know," Jason agreed.

"And a wonderful head of R and D." My husband nodded. "And a wonderful husband." She started to cry. "He didn't have any problems until someone killed him," she sobbed.

A nurse bustled in, glowered at us, and gave Charlotte a shot.

"How could you upset her, Jason?" I asked when we had been chased out into the hall. "You're still pursuing that silly spy scenario, aren't you?" Before Jason could answer, I spotted Detective Worski coming down the hall. "I told you to give her protection, Detective," I said very severely. I'm not usually an I-told-you-so sort of person, but in this case . . .

"Yes ma'am," agreed the detective, all muffled up in his green overcoat, "and next time you tell me something, I'm gonna listen extra careful."

"Have you questioned her stepson?"

"We will as soon as we find him."

"He's missing? Well, that's significant!" Jason dragged me away before I could pursue my point.

30

Minestrone at Random

Jason

Only a fool could believe that a husband and wife, on separate occasions, might meet with random stabbings. I was convinced that Max had been killed because he found out who sold the coal technology and that the attempt on Charlotte resulted from a belief that Max confided in her before he died. Max's killer had probably been following Charlotte since Max's death and only yesterday found her in a situation when she was unaccompanied.

I intended to call Moore and urge him to tell the police what we knew. He had obviously had the same thoughts as I concerning Charlotte's situation. That being the case, he couldn't, in all good conscience, allow her to continue at risk. As far as I knew, Merrivale hadn't made any progress finding the culprit, and Moore had seemed to confirm my perception of the situation when he said last night that I had provided more information than anyone else had. I now surmised that Merrivale, for whatever reason, had encouraged Moore's reluctance to cooperate with the police. If that was the case, it would seem all the more reasonable to think that it was Merrivale, a man in a perfect position to stymie the investigation, who had betrayed the company and arranged the assassination.

Unless it was Moore himself. I found that idea even more upsetting, but still, perhaps it had to be considered. Moore? He was the person who had encouraged my telephone calls to Eastern Europe, but when I had mentioned the Russian Mafia, he hadn't been much interested. Merrivale, on the other hand, had tried to cut off that line of inquiry completely. He hadn't wanted to hear anything about the wife of the Ukrainian company's vice president. At this point, I didn't know what to think.

My wife was clearer on her theory that I was on mine. Her questions to Charlotte at the hospital revealed that she attributed the attacks to Rick Heydemann, even though Charlotte's assailant had looked homeless and smelled of garbage. I could have pointed out her illogic, but I doubted that she would appreciate the exercise. First, no matter how he dressed or smelled, Charlotte would have recognized her stepson. Second, as Moore had pointed out, to me if not Carolyn, Max's children came from a very wealthy family on their mother's side. They might have wanted money from their father, but they didn't *need* it, and certainly not enough to risk committing or commissioning murder. That being the case, I had to ask myself whether Moore, if he himself were implicated in Max's death, would defuse any theory of the crime that pointed elsewhere. But maybe that's exactly what I was meant to think.

Carolyn had to prod me off the subway at our stop because I was so wrapped up in burgeoning paranoia, which I found to be a very uncomfortable affliction. How could I accept the tempting offer made to me by Hodge, Brune when I no longer trusted the people who worked there? Rain was turning the overnight snow to slush when we reached our hotel, changed clothes, and set out for Greenwich Village. We were looking for Manetta Lane in order to pick up the tickets I had acquired by Internet. But before that, we had to find a place for a late lunch, and Carolyn was determined to follow Renata Moore's advice, which was to pick a trattoria at random. I myself like to go to places where I've been before or that are recommended by travel guides; Carolyn said she was tired of being a dutiful, preplanning food writer: this lunch was to be just for us.

After much slogging around under an umbrella, we entered the warm confines of an Italian restaurant with a large exposed pipe that traversed a pressed tin ceiling and one of the brick walls. Carolyn assured me that the ceiling didn't compare with the one at Chanterelle, which didn't surprise me. I doubted that the food would, either. I think my wife was drawn into this particular place by the rich smell of fresh-baked bread. I can't say that I remember the name of the trattoria, but the minestrone we ordered was heavy with the flavors of Italy and loaded with white beans, lentils, and vegetables. A more comforting meal cannot be imagined on such an unpromising day. We were both chilled and damp by the time we sat down to our large bowls of soup and a basket of bread slices that sent my wife into raptures. Her nose had not deceived her, and she was so delighted that she insisted on discussing the bread with the proprietor and buying a loaf to take home.

"Carolyn," I protested, "when are we going to eat it?" It was a long object, thicker than a baguette, but just as crusty on the outside. I anticipated, beside the awkwardness of carrying it into the theater, that the aroma would overhang the play, which might not be appreciated by our fellow drama enthusiasts.

"We can nibble between acts," she said. "And at the hotel when we get back. We can buy cheese and wine and have a picnic." She was feeling remarkably jolly, given Charlotte's situation and the abominable weather we faced as we splashed our way to the theater. I suppose she was relieved that Charlotte was expected to recover completely. Carolyn insisted that, as horrible as the attack had been, the police were now looking at Rick, so Charlotte would be safe and Max avenged. I didn't disabuse her of that comforting notion and she went on to chat about how much she liked Renata Moore.

"I think you should seriously consider the Hodge, Brune offer, Jason."

How ironic that our opinions on the matter had completely reversed. I mumbled something appropriate and noncommittal.

"I'd love to meet Charlotte and Renata for lunch when we're here in the summer, that is, if I can lure Renata out of the house. She was certainly right about picking a trattoria at random. Won't we have fun exploring if we come for six weeks? We can eat out every night."

I hated to think what that would cost, even if the price of Carolyn's meals should actually prove to be tax deductible without having to fight the IRS. I am a person who dreads being audited. It happened to me when I was a graduate student. The government decided that my fellowship was taxable, and because I couldn't afford a lawyer, I had to pay up. I'm still resentful and have no faith in the new taxpayer-rights legislation that is being touted by Congress. Carolyn, on the other hand, thinks that we get our money's worth. She's given to ordering those free brochures that issue in great waves from the government printing office. They then pile up in corners, unread.

At the theater we had a surprise. When picking up our tickets at the box office, we were told that the management had exchanged our original reservations in the balcony for better seats on the main floor. While the clerk was locating these new tickets and I was getting wet, Carolyn bubbled over with enthusiasm for the unexpected kindness of strangers in New York. "The civility campaign is really working!" she exclaimed. "They didn't have to bother on our behalf about the tickets. And did I tell you about this nice young black youth, who looked, at first glance, like a gang person and was carrying a huge boom box? He got up on the subway and gave me his seat."

"The effect of encroaching age," I muttered, "our age, not his." Still, it was proving hard to stay grumpy when my wife was so cheerful.

We took our exchanged seats on a left center aisle, one row from the back of the front section, Carolyn with the loaf of bread on her lap. The theater was not at all rough-hewn, as I would have expected of an off-Broadway venue. It had slate blue velvet seats, reasonably comfortable, a carpet in the same shade but marked by the footprints of patrons with dirty snow on their boots, blue painted brick walls, and a red curtain. The play began within minutes, exactly on time, although a chattering gaggle of theatergoers was still entering. What we saw was basically a Biblical history portrayed from a homosexual point of view: In the beginning God created Adam and Steve, etc. It was not subtle, but it was certainly funny.

We both laughed immoderately, although I noticed that my wife became restless about halfway through, twisting now and then to look behind her and tapping her loaf of bread with her head tipped attentively, although not, as far as I could see, to the dialogue. She even dropped the bread at one point and had to retrieve it, not a promising event if it was to be part of our dinner. And she laughed much less frequently later in the act than in the beginning.

I could only surmise that she was shocked to be confronted by husky young actors in skimpy underpants and then naked. They had very large penises. The audience around us seemed to enjoy the display, but I suppose Carolyn was embarrassed. I couldn't help wondering if the naked actors ever experienced unplanned erections onstage. That does happen to us males occasionally, but under normal circumstances, our trousers and anything we may be carrying—coats, books, hats—can be used to conceal the situation until it subsides. No chance of concealment here. Perhaps if an erection occurred, the audience would be even more appreciative.

There was also a lesbian couple as part of the plot. It was an unusual play, but not as unusual as my wife's behavior during intermission.

Having dragged me out into the lobby, Carolyn said, "Let's try the other seats for the second act." She was whispering into my ear as if telling me an important secret. "You just run up there and hold them, will you, Jason? I have to go to the ladies' room."

"But the seats we have are excellent," I protested.

"Here, take the bread with you." She thrust it into my hands and rushed off through the crowd. Could the soup have made her sick? I climbed the stairs to the balcony and found our original seats unoccupied. How fortunate that I remembered the numbers, for I no longer had the computer printout. Carolyn arrived and plopped down beside me just before the second act started, this after studying the other balcony occupants as if looking for a long lost friend. She did not seem herself at all. However, once seated, her expression relieved, she almost seemed pleased with herself.

"Isn't this nice?" She took back the bread.

I didn't see that it was any nicer than our first seats. In fact, if the theater caught fire, our chances of getting out unharmed were radically diminished. Very peculiar, my wife's behavior. But perhaps she had experienced one of those feminine emergencies, which sometimes involve unusual behavior. I was wise enough not to suggest any such thing.

31
Fingering a Suspect

Carolyn

What a shock I had! I'd been sitting there laughing until my ribs hurt when one laugh behind me stood out from all the rest. It plucked some chord in memory and gave me pause. Frowning, I turned my attention back to the play, wondering if the actors playing Adam and Steve had been chosen for the size of their genitals. When I was a little girl, a rather crude neighbor of ours said of a professor at Daddy's university, a man who was given to swimming nude early in the morning, "He's hung like a horse." That phrase would probably apply to those two young men up on the stage, not that I've ever paid much attention to equine genitalia. Still, it was rather interesting to see men exhibited as sex objects: I suppose that's why they were nude. Take that peculiar school of art that posed one naked woman among of crowd of fully dressed men. You never see paintings of one naked man among clothed women. I wondered what Jason thought of all this nudity. Was he embarrassed? I'd have to ask him.

Then my wandering thoughts were brought back by another hilarious line in the play that elicited that strange, good-humored, braying laugh again. It was so familiar. I tried to peek over my shoulder to see who was behind me in the aisle seat, but that was hard to do without being obvious. So I turned my attention back to the stage and a character called "stage manager," who sat at a table at the side of the action and called out such things as "Lights, go! Flood, go!" What an antic imagination the dramatist had. Still, I deliberately stifled the impulse to laugh so that I could listen to the distinctive laughter behind me. And identification was right there, dancing at the edge of my mind.

I dropped my bread on the floor, actually on Jason's foot, hoping that I wouldn't ruin it—the bread. Jason was engrossed in the comedy and didn't rush to pick it up for me. Consequently, I was able to lean forward to retrieve the loaf, then straighten, taking at the same time a good look at the person behind Jason on the aisle. A man. Familiar? I wasn't sure.

Oh, well. Clasping my Italian baked trophy, I again concentrated on the play and was soon laughing myself, but still aware of the familiar hooting behind me. The man couldn't be anyone I knew. Could he? If he was, I'd have recognized him. Then, as my husband and the man behind him convulsed with merriment, I remembered. Thelma! It sounded just like Thelma, the missing waitress.

I turned completely around and stared. Definitely a man. Happily, he didn't notice my interest. Jason did and cut his eyes at me, puzzled. I smiled and turned back to the stage. It could be Thelma. The square shoulders were right. And the face, if you took away Thelma's big glasses and bigger hair. But the generous breasts were gone. Did anyone manufacture a padded bra or breast prosthetics that large? Thelma had had a very flat bottom for a chesty woman; I remembered thinking she must be wearing a girdle. And Thelma hadn't seemed the theatergoing type. No, that was wrong. She had quoted *King Lear*. But why was she here, dressed as a man? Or had she been a man dressed as a waitress?

Then I had the most astounding intuition. Maybe the person sitting behind me, the person who had been Thelma at the deli, was actually Rick Heydemann. I tried to remember what the son had looked like, but the memory was rather fuzzy. I had been so shocked by his remarks about his father that I hadn't looked at him very closely at the memorial service, and my attention had been focused on his mother at the opera. But he had been wearing a very expensive black suit; that I remembered. On both occasions he had been wearing black.

I glanced back at Thelma. Black turtleneck sweater, black trousers. The color of mourning. The trousers had a good crease, more or less the sign of a careful dresser. And other things fit. Heydemann, the would-be actor who expected to star off-Broadway in a self-financed play, was here taking in another off-Broadway play. And he had evidently played the part of Thelma. Why would he have done that unless to kill his father? He would certainly have known that his father patronized that deli each Monday.

This was very strange! Downright frightening. Had he recognized me? Good heavens, I now remembered telling Thelma how horrible Max's children had been at the memorial and that I wouldn't be surprised if they were responsible for his death. What a dreadful coincidence that we should show up at the same play today. Acting on impulse, I yanked the scarf holding my hair back and let the hair fall forward to obscure my face. At the same time, I decided that Jason and I would have to change seats. I only hoped that our earlier reservations would be open.

When the second act ended, I dropped my bread again in order to delay Jason so that Thelma/Rick would have time to leave the auditorium ahead of us. Obviously, my first duty was to call Detective Worski and tell him that Thelma had resurfaced. He could come here and arrest her/him, while Jason and I sat upstairs and watched it happen. That was quite an exciting idea, really.

I had a bit of trouble convincing Jason to go upstairs while I went to the ladies' room, actually the public telephone, to which an usher directed me. While wailing for a man who was talking to his wife, telling her that he'd be late getting back from the office, obviously a lie, it occurred to me that Rick might have followed *me* here. In fact, he might have arranged the seat change so that he'd be seated right behind me, meaning to stab me during the performance because I knew his secret. Goodness, if he could kill his father and stepmother, he was probably getting accustomed to murder, becoming a serial killer, looking forward to doing away with me during the second act, then slipping into the cross aisle and out of the theater while I, dead in my chair, appeared to be napping.

There was one person ahead of me in line, a woman who wanted to call her babysitter. When the man who was lying to his wife hung up, and joined, of all things, another man, whom he hugged, I said rather wildly, "This is an emergency," and snatched the receiver from the worried mother's hand. She was very impatient as I juggled my purse and bread, trying to find the detective's number, but I persisted and actually got Detective Worski on the first ring. He was at his desk, wherever that was.

"I've found Thelma," I whispered, glancing around nervously to see if Thelma had spotted me. I didn't see her. What if she had left at intermission? Well, better that than having her see me sneaking upstairs. "You have to come and arrest her."

"Is this Mrs. Blue?"

"Yes, of course, Detective. I'm at the Manetta Lane Theater in Greenwich Village."

"Who said I wanted to arrest her?"

"Well, at least pick her up for questioning. I thought you'd been combing New Jersey for her. Now, I've found her, but she's dressed as a man. I'm not sure which she is, but I suspect she's really Rick Heydemann. That makes sense, don't you think?"

"If she's dressed as a man, how do you know it's Thelma?"

"Because the laugh is unmistakable, and the shoulders are right."

Detective Worski gave a heavy sigh, which I ignored.

"She's in the left-side aisle seat, first floor, last row of the first section. If you can find Manetta Lane, you can't miss the theater." I stopped to take a breath. The angry mother was eavesdropping and staring as if I was crazy. "Are you coming?" I demanded anxiously. "You did say that the next time I made a suggestion, you'd pay attention."

"I'm coming."

"You'd better bring backup. If she's really Rick Heydemann, she might put up a fight. She might even be armed, although this is a theater performance, so probably not. Still, if she's here to kill me—"

"Why would she want to kill you?"

"Because I told her that I suspect Ricky Heydemann. So hurry, would you?" I glanced around apprehensively once more.

"Yep. I'm on my way. An' thanks for the tip, Mrs. Blue," said Detective Worski, and hung up.

I took another quick look around, then skulked through the lobby as inconspicuously as possible and up the stairs to the balcony, where I sat down beside my husband. "Now, isn't this better?" I asked. "It will give us a whole new perspective."

"I hope you haven't dropped the bread again," he answered. "Maybe we should just leave it behind."

The curtain then rose on another hilarious act of *The Most Fabulous Story Ever Told.* I was happy to see Thelma/Rick in his old seat, but not so happy to see him craning his neck, probably looking for me. How fortunate that I had alerted the police. They'd arrive before I had to leave the balcony and put myself at risk again. I settled down to enjoy the play, and it was *so* funny. I wondered fleetingly if homosexuals found it offensive and if there were any in the audience. Well, probably that man who hugged the other man after telling his wife he was at the office.

Then I wondered whether Rick was homosexual. Of course, being a transvestite didn't make a man homosexual. I remember reading in Ann Landers that men who have perfectly normal marriages . . . well, except for liking to wear ladies' clothes . . . can be transvestites. Sometimes their wives even provide the clothing. I tried to imagine Jason wearing something of mine—my new periwinkle suit, for instance—but I couldn't picture it, and he couldn't get into it. So much for that bizarre thought. I don't think Jason would have been pleased to know what I'd been thinking.

I began to see, as the action on stage progressed, that, aside from its campy humor, *The Most Fabulous Story Ever Told* actually had a message about tolerance for those who are different. And the end was hilarious. The "stage manager," whom Adam decides must be God, leaves in a huff and can be heard stamping out, slamming a door, and hailing a taxi. A female God, washing her hands of the whole ridiculous creation: What a charming idea. I'd have to tell Jason's mother about it. But then why bother? She'd probably read the play.

"Wasn't that a delight?" I said to Jason as we rose from our seats, clapping enthusiastically. I kept a close eye on the aisle seat downstairs, hoping to see Detectives Worski and Ali striding in to apprehend Thelma/Rick. It didn't happen, so I supposed they were in the lobby awaiting their opportunity. "Let's hurry downstairs," I said to Jason. I didn't want to miss the action.

But when we were on the stairs, with me peering anxiously at the exiting crowd, I couldn't see either Thelma/Rick or the detectives. What if Detective Worski had been humoring me and hadn't meant to come here at all? Or he couldn't find backup in time? It was, after all, Sunday. Probably most men were home with their families watching pro wrestling. Have you ever seen pro wrestling on cable TV? It's about as tasteless and histrionic as anything one could imagine. If it weren't for A&E, I'd have canceled the cable service the first time I saw wrestling—quite by accident, I might add.

We were almost to the first floor, part of the slow-moving exit from the balcony, and I still hadn't spotted Thelma. Maybe he/she was changing characters and sexes again, preparatory to killing me as I left the theater.

"This play must be very popular with the gay community," Jason murmured.

"You think so?" I was surprised.

"Surely you noticed all the male/male couples."

Actually, I hadn't, except for the one lying to his wife. "I was wondering if they'd be offended by the play." It was hard to keep up a conversation when I wanted to grab Jason's hand and run for it. Damn that Detective Worski. Where was he?

"Well, everyone was laughing," said Jason. He was now behind me, shepherding me through the crowd so that we wouldn't get separated. Well, Thelma/Rick couldn't stab me in the back with Jason so close behind. But what if he shoved Jason aside? Immediately terrified, I whirled to look behind my husband and saw . . . that black-clad figure with a shining silver spike emerging from his sleeve, his hand lifting toward my husband's back. I screamed.

32

En Garde, Bread Lovers

Jason

I can't begin to convey how surreal events in the lobby of the Manetta Lane Theater seemed at the time. One minute Carolyn and I were drifting toward the exit with the rest of the crowd after the performance. The next she whirled and screamed right into my ear. Then, before I could begin to recover from the ringing in my head, my wife shoved me hard, and I stumbled sideways, falling. Those events in themselves would be cause for astonishment. My wife is not given to screaming, nor is she a violent woman. I can't think of a time when either of us has raised a hand to the other during the years of our marriage.

What followed was even more bizarre, for Carolyn assumed what I later identified as a fencer's stance, one hand raised for balance, the other clutching the end of her long loaf of Italian bread, her fingernails actually digging into the crust for more secure purchase. Then she lunged toward a young man dressed in black. He certainly looked astounded, and I felt as if I were a participant in someone else's drug-induced hallucination. But the action did not end there. Still clutching the bread, the other end of which the young man now seemed to be holding, my wife lowered her free hand into the shoulder bag she carried and pulled out a small cylinder, which she sprayed into the black-clad fellow's face. He screamed, dropped his end of the bread, and raised both hands to his eyes.

Around us pandemonium ensued: The odor of an offensive perfume permeated the air; Carolyn dropped the bread and stepped back; the young man continued to moan and clutch his eyes; and I picked myself off the floor with the help of a stout woman in a brown pants suit. This lady said to my wife, "Did he try to feel you up, dear?" I'm not sure whether she was referring to me or to the young man as the putative sexual predator.

The companion of the lady in brown was a painfully thin female in a full olive green skirt over which trailed a matching tunic that almost reached her knees yet was of so thin a fabric that her nipples showed clearly and embarrassingly on the flat expanse of her chest. She asked, "Was that perfume or pepper spray?"

Carolyn was still catching her breath. My wife is not an athletic person. I believe the only sport she ever participated in after the age of eighteen was fencing, which may explain her strange maneuvers with the Italian loaf, although I doubt that her gym instructor had the students fence with bread. Carolyn only took the class because she had one more gym requirement to fill at the university and had already taken all the dance classes they offered. It was fencing or tennis; being already enamoured with medieval history, she chose fencing. This was before we met; she was a sophomore at the time and still avoiding her science requirements.

At any rate, Carolyn replied to the anorexic woman in olive green, "That was Bernie Feingold's signature scent."

"Carolyn, are you all right?" I asked. I was, I believe, referring to her sanity rather than her physical well-being. After all, I was the one who had been pushed over.

Nonetheless, she replied, "I wasn't injured, and you, thank God, weren't, either."

"Bernie Feingold?" exclaimed the woman who was interested, for no discernible reason, in the perfume my wife had used as a weapon. "Who the hell is Bernie Feingold? They'll have to get a better name than that if they plan to market the stuff." She then pressed her business card on Carolyn. "Agnes Merwyn. Public Relations."

The red-eyed man had evidently been trying to slip away. Small wonder. He probably feared being sprayed again or pummeled with the bread, which now lay on the floor between him and my wife. She was keeping a wary eye on him as she ran a hand over her hair to be sure that it was tidy after her strange exertions. However, he didn't escape because a husky, middle-aged fellow with a bushy mustache and furrowed brow pinioned him from behind and said, "Here you. Stay right where you are. I saw you try to steal that lady's bread."

"Clive," exclaimed a pudgy woman, probably the good citizen's wife, "stay out of it, for goodness sake. Do you want friends to know we attended this disgusting play?"

"I can't abide a thief," said Clive. "They used to hang people for stealing bread."

"That's true," Carolyn agreed, "although evidently it wasn't a deterrent."

"I didn't steal anything." The young man glared at Carolyn, his eyes red and weeping. "This crazy woman attacked me for no reason."

"Other than that you're Thelma," Carolyn replied briskly, "and you tried to kill my husband."

The young man struggled against the advocate of capital punishment for bread theft. "Do I look like a Thelma?" he demanded and broke into strange, honking laughter.

"You see, Clive. He's not Thelma," said the middle-aged wife. "It's a case of mistaken identity. We'll get our names in the papers because of some crazy woman who goes around spraying innocent bystanders with perfume."

"I identified you by your laughter," said Carolyn. "You're Thelma."

Clive let go of the young man. "Men aren't named Thelma," he said.

I had the frightening feeling that my wife, my lovely Carolyn, had experienced some sort of psychotic break. Not knowing what else to do, I put my arm around her, making sure at the same time that her perfume-wielding hand was pinned between us.

"Well, it's about time," she said, further confusing me. Then, as the newly released man in black attempted again to leave, he was grabbed by, of all people, the two detectives who had been investigating Max's death.

"This is Thelma?" asked the older detective.

"Or Ricky," Carolyn replied.

"Ricky who?" asked the young man. "First, you say I'm Thelma. Well, that's crap. You want to see my dick?" He addressed this offer to the detectives. "This woman sprayed something into my eyes. Look at me. I was practically blinded."

He did look terrible, even if Carolyn's weapon had only been her agent's uncle's signature perfume. I foresaw lawsuits in our future. To me, Carolyn said, "He tried to kill you, Jason, although I can't imagine why. He'd have more reason to kill me."

"Who?" I asked. Carolyn didn't look confused, but I certainly was.

"Ricky Heydemann. Look in the end of that loaf of bread," she instructed the detectives, nudging our Italian loaf with the toe of her boot.

The older detective had handcuffed his prisoner. Ali bent down and picked up the loaf. "I'll be damned." He tucked it under his arm, carefully pulled on thin latex gloves, and drew from the loaf a vicious-looking blade, rather like an elongated ice pick. "See that, Worski. I think it clicks out of the handle."

"Bag it," said Worski. He gave his cuffed prisoner a shake.

"I never saw that in my life," protested the man, "and my name isn't Thelma . . . or Ricky."

"I'll bet," said Worski. "But you could sure be the guy or gal who's been targetin' Heydemanns. How come you're after the Blues now?"

"It must be her weapon. She lunged at me with it."

"I was holding the bread end!" said Carolyn indignantly. "You can see where I dug my fingernails in for purchase."

"Yep," said Worski, inspecting the unpapered end of the Italian loaf when Ali held it out.

"The switchblade was on his side," Ali agreed. "And he doesn't have the nails to make those marks on the bread. Look at his nails, Pugh." Another officer was now restraining the cuffed attacker, and he yanked the man's arms up to make the inspection.

"Police brutality!" cried the arrestee.

"Blunt, guy-type nails," Pugh confirmed.

"Thelma had blunt nails, too," said Carolyn.

Police were blocking the front of the theater, keeping the playgoers from leaving. The manager had arrived, demanding to know the reason for the police blockade. He was ignored. Having worked their way through the crowd, several ushers tried to remonstrate with the detectives for causing a disturbance. Worski flashed his badge and told them to herd the theatergoers back into the auditorium. They tried. Then Worski deployed his forces by assigning uniformed officers to take statements from people in the crowd while he and Ali proceeded to headquarters with Carolyn, me, and the man who was evidently under arrest. I was afraid my wife might be under arrest as well, but the police assumption seemed to be that she had attacked in my defense.

As we left, I could hear comments from the people we passed.

"She hit him with a loaf of bread. I didn't see any weapon in his hand."

"No, she sprayed him with mace. Jesus, you can't go to see a play these days without some femiNazi taking offense. Rush Limbaugh got it right about women."

"Rush Limbaugh wouldn't be seen dead at this performance."

"It *was* funny."

"Bunch of queers."

"Did you hear what that homophobe just said?"

And so forth until we were helped into one police car while Carolyn's victim/attacker was helped into another. Had he really been trying to stab me? And if so, why? My God, but my wife was brave! She fended him off with just a loaf of bread and a perfume atomizer!

33

Interrogation with Donuts

Carolyn

Grim and grimy would be my description of the New York police station to which Jason and I were taken for interviews. We were put in separate rooms, as if we might contradict and thus incriminate ourselves if we couldn't coordinate our stories. Or perhaps I was being paranoid. I must admit to feeling more than a little shaky after crossing swords (an unfortunate metaphor, but it sounds ridiculous to say crossing bread and ice pick) with the assassin. Detective Worski did make an effort at hospitality by offering coffee and donuts. Naturally, I accepted promptly with the idea that the repast, although simple, would make a good subject for a column. Then he left me alone with my snack.

Well, no one could ever accuse the NYPD of serving good coffee. The cup in which mine was served wasn't even clean, and the coffee was deplorable. Naturally, I've never tasted battery acid (presumably one wouldn't live through the experience), but this coffee surely was the source of that unfavorable comparison. And then I tasted my donut, which was even more objectionable, a heavy, stale, unhealthy object coated with a sickeningly sticky, tastelessly sweet glaze that clung to my fingers like glue. Had I been a criminal, I would undoubtedly have confessed to any crime to avoid further exposure to the refreshments at Detective Worski's precinct house. I spat the bite of donut into the cup and deposited the whole on the floor in the corner. The room contained only a table and two chairs, and I did not want that snack within sight or smelling distance.

My hands were still shaking from the events at the Manetta Lane Theater, so I laced them on the table and put my head down in the hope that I might catch a nap while I waited. Even a stiff neck would be better than the refreshments I had been served and the trembling stress that was attacking me. I took deep, calming breaths and attempted a muscle-by-muscle relaxation of my body, something that I had read about in a government pamphlet that came in the mail with several others I requested. However, I did not fall asleep. Instead, my mind replayed, like some defective horror movie, the memory of that blade coming out of Thelma's sleeve toward Jason's back.

By the time Detective Worski finally returned, I was not in a very good mood. "Well, was it Rick Heydemann?" I demanded in a snippy tone when he entered the room. By then I was no longer convinced of that myself. Unless the disguise was exceptional, surely I would have recognized Max's son when we finally came face-to-face. The blade wielder had looked like Thelma in drag, if one can use that term for a woman dressed as a man, or a man dressed as a man but sometimes as a woman.

"Don't think so," said Worski. "He's got ID on him, but it's fake. The social security don't match the name."

"Of course he'd have a fake ID, but did you check his face for stage makeup or one of those peel-off masks?"

"That's only in the movies, Mrs. Blue. We did talk to someone claiming to be young Heydemann at the grandparents' house. He seemed kind of flustered when I identified myself, but he didn't admit anything. How come you thought the guy was Heydemann?"

"I don't know," I replied, embarrassed. "It seemed logical at the time. He certainly was Thelma. I'd never mistake that laugh, so I thought, because I'd told Thelma that I suspected Rick, that Rick was coming after me."

"I thought the guy was going for your husband."

"So it seemed. If he'd meant to stab me, he'd have had to go around Jason. And why would he have exposed his weapon before he was in position to stab me, preferably from the back, since I had spotted him? Although he didn't necessarily know at the time that I'd recognized him. And of course, I didn't have any leisure to analyze the situation. I had to protect Jason."

"Well, you did a bang-up job of that." Worski started to laugh. "If this guy is really a paid assassin, he's going to be damned embarrassed when it gets around that a woman with a loaf of bread and a bottle of perfume disarmed him."

"I didn't actually disarm him," I replied modestly. "We both dropped our weapons. I think you should check the box office to see whether he arranged to have our seats changed so that we would be sitting in front of him, whoever he is."

"He's not talking except to accuse you of attacking him. We've put his prints in AFIS—that's the national fingerprint computer—an' we gave him some stuff to wash his eyes out with. Now, what's this about the seats?"

"When we got to the box office to pick up our tickets, they said they'd switched us to better seats. Being the naive out-lander that I am," I continued bitterly, "I remarked to Jason on how helpful New Yorkers are. Now I suppose that young black man with the boom box was hoping to snatch my purse."

"What—"

"Never mind. It's not relevant . . . except as regards my plunge into cynicism. Anyway, the seat change put us right in front of Thelma. That's how I recognized the laugh and got a peek at her. Not what she'd had in mind, I'm sure."

"It's a he," said Worski.

"You checked?"

"Yes ma'am. We checked. Armed suspects always get patted down."

"Perhaps she's wearing some sort of fake male genitalia," I suggested. "During the Renaissance, gentlemen were given to padding their codpieces." Detective Worski was looking at me peculiarly, so I dropped that subject. "Anyway, it would have been quite easy for Thelma to knife me during the second act. Jason would have thought I'd fallen asleep."

"You usually drop off when everyone around you is laughin' up a storm? I heard about that play. Supposed to be real funny if you like gay jokes."

"I often take a nap in the afternoon," I said stiffly. "After my murder, Thelma could have slipped away under cover of the general hilarity. You'll have noticed that her seat was at the juncture of two aisles, just seven or eight places from an exit. Or actually, you wouldn't have noticed because you didn't arrive in a timely fashion."

At that point we glared at one another.

"Think I'll go see if we got a print ID yet," he said.

"What about me?"

"You just sit tight. We haven't talked to your husband yet."

"At the rate you're going, we may have to catch our plane before you get to him."

"Don't get smart with me, Mrs. Blue."

"I can't imagine why I bothered trying to help. You certainly haven't shown any appreciation of my efforts."

"Hey, I appreciate your ramming that guy with your loaf of bread. Everyone here's gonna appreciate that. It's the best story to come out of this precinct in years."

"So glad to have provided entertainment in your otherwise dreary lives," I muttered ungraciously. "And while I have the opportunity, I'd like to point out that the acidity of your coffee is surpassed only by the stale, gluey consistency of your donuts."

"You got that right," Worski agreed as he left the room.

34
The Conspiracy Theory

Jason

"Professor." Mohammad Ali entered and sat down across from me in the small, shabby room where I had been left for some time to worry about my wife. Carolyn had been trembling in the squad car that took us to the police station; I had felt the tremors as she sat in the circle of my arm. Now I was afraid that she, too, had been left alone as I had.

"I'm worried about my wife."

"Mrs. Blue seems like a lady who can take pretty good care of herself. I'd be surprised if my wife could handle the situation at the theater that well. By the way, the guy she perfumed *was* a guy, and we don't think he's Maximillian Frederick Heydemann, Jr."

"He's not," I replied. "I've seen Max's son twice. That was not him."

"But your wife told Worski—"

"My wife evidently jumped to the conclusion that her life was in danger."

"Seems like it was you he was going after."

"Be that as it may, she insisted on moving to the balcony at intermission, after calling the police, an action that she failed to mention to me. She identified the person by a distinctive laugh as the waitress at the delicatessen where Max Heydemann was killed. As to her idea that that person might be Max's son in disguise, the son's abominable behavior convinced her that he, his mother, and his sister were responsible for Max's death. However mistaken she may have been—"

"So you don't think it was a family murder?"

"No, I don't." I had been mulling over the situation while I waited to be interviewed and decided that the police could no longer be kept in the dark about the problem at Hodge, Brune. If Moore and Merrivale objected, so be it. "Just the fact that the man seemed to intend harm to me rather than Carolyn is a good indication that the motive for Max's death and the violence that followed are the result of industrial espionage involving Max's company."

"I'd like to hear about the espionage. You ready to tell me about it?"

He looked quite enthusiastic, making me recall that he had previously been assigned to a white-collar crime unit. No doubt industrial espionage was more to his taste than murder. I told him about the theft of the coal process and the kind of investment in research it represented as well as the profits it promised to any company that patented it, which the Ukrainian company had moved to do.

"And so Heydemann was killed. Why?"

"I believe that he discovered who was responsible for the sale or at least release of the information. He was to have met on Monday with Charles Moore to name the culprit but died before he could do so. The obvious conclusion is that his suspicions led to his murder."

"So he couldn't implicate someone at the company?"

"Presumably so."

"And the attack on his wife?"

"They must have believed that he had confided in her before he died."

"Sounds plausible except for one thing. You don't even work for the company. Why would anyone involved in this plot want to kill an outsider?"

"Again this is a hypothesis, but I have been conducting a telephone investigation for Hodge, Brune by calling people I know in Eastern Europe. Evidently, the criminals think I know something damaging."

"What?"

I shrugged. "I'm not sure. Perhaps that rumor links the Ukrainian company to the Russian Mafia. Perhaps—"

Ali sat up straighter. "Run that by me again."

"I was told by a colleague in Poland that, although the company in Kiev had neither the scientists nor the resources to develop such a process for themselves, they did have a vice president who was married to the daughter of someone powerful in the Russian Mob. There are rumors that this crime syndicate provided the financing for the Ukrainian company."

"I assume you told others at the company about the Russian Mob scenario, so it might have gotten back to whoever the Russians bribed to steal the information in the first place."

"So it would seem."

"Who at the company knew about your investigation?"

"Charles Moore, who asked me to do it and to whom I reported my findings. Vernon Merrivale, their head of security. And whomever they told. Vaclav Vasandrovich, for instance. He's the interim director of R and D, so I'm presuming that he was in the loop. I didn't talk to him personally about my investigation, but all three of them warned us, Carolyn and myself, about talking to the police. One of the three must have been worried about something other than investor reaction to the situation if word of the loss got out."

Ali smiled. "I have to say, the warnings didn't stop your wife. She mentioned a couple of times what she considered a ridiculous spy scenario."

"I see." I must admit that I was angry for a moment at Carolyn's indiscretion and had to remind myself that she had just saved my life.

"OK, so Moore, Merrivale, and Vasandrovich all warned you off. And Vasandrovich is the new director of R and D. Took Heydemann's place, didn't he?"

"Yes, and there's another thing about him."

"What?" Ali looked eager.

"His degree," I answered. "A Czech colleague said Vasandrovich was not a graduate of Charles University, although his curriculum vitae indicates that he was. It may be some problem with the records in Prague dating from the Communist period or the dislocations that followed." Suddenly I remembered something that Carolyn had said while we were preparing for bed at the Moores' house in Greenwich. "Incidentally, my wife mentioned hearing him speak Russian in his office, or so she thought."

"Being Czech, wouldn't it be natural for him to know Russian?"

"Yes, but he evidently denied that he had been speaking Russian. He said it was Czech and that he was speaking to an aunt. However, he told me that he had no living relatives."

"So you suspect him?"

I shrugged. "I have no evidence to link Vaclav and the criminals, and I do know that he was devastated by Max's death. He considered Max his mentor because Max is the man who got him and his wife out of the Czech Republic before the Communists were overthrown. He seems to have felt beholden to Max as well as having a great personal affection for him. Unless he's a very good actor. Vasandrovich looks to be an unlikely candidate for involvement in Max's death."

"And the company hasn't turned up any concrete information beyond what you've told them?"

"Not that I know of," I replied. "Which is what makes me keep coming back to Merrivale. He had access to the stolen research data, and he controls the company investigation of the theft, not to mention being the one most opposed to bringing the police in."

"Which puts him in the perfect position to keep himself from being exposed as the spy." Ali nodded. "Good theory."

"Have you identified the man who tried to stab me?"

"Not yet. His ID is fake, and he won't talk to us other than to claim that the weapon at the theater wasn't his and that your wife attacked him for no reason. We're running his prints and getting a search warrant for the apartment on his fake ID."

"Then, unless we can be of further assistance, I'd like to take my wife back to the hotel. She's distraught, and we have to pack for the trip back to Texas tomorrow. I presume there's no problem about our leaving."

"No problem. We've got your address, and we checked out your credentials. As for Mrs. Blue . . ." Ali grinned. "She may be distraught, but she certainly gave my partner a hard time."

"Did she?" I had to smile and wished that I had been there to see Car-

olyn in action, my wife who can fence with a loaf of bread and disarm a
dangerous criminal with a bottle of perfume.

"Right. And I'm afraid she's going to give us a bad review on our coffee
and donuts, too. Worski said she got downright mean on that subject."

"Well, she is writing a book about food. But the subject is New Orleans
food."

"Yeah? Did she pick on the police there, too, and foil criminals?"

"I believe she did," I replied.

35

Domestic Strife in a Patrol Car

Carolyn

Jason and I were reunited in a patrol car assigned to return us to the hotel.
What a relief to leave that place, although I anticipated even greater relief when our plane was off the ground and heading home. I no longer cared
who Thelma was and what he/she had done, and I hoped to talk Jason out
of having anything to do with Hodge, Brune. I was preplanning my introductory statement on the matter when Jason took me by surprise.

"Carolyn, just who have you told about the espionage problem at the
company?"

He sounded so stern that I stammered, "I-I don't know."

"You don't *know?* You were asked not to mention it at all!"

"Well, Jason, just because Hodge, Brune tends toward the paranoid,
doesn't mean I have to—"

"Why do you think I was attacked at the theater by someone you claim
was a waitress at a deli? Did you tell her about the coal project?"

"I may have," I snapped, feeling defensive as well as indignant. "But I'm
convinced that Thelma meant to stab me, not you."

"Really. And what do you see as the connection between you, Max, and
his wife?" Jason sounded downright sarcastic, as if I was some cotton-
brained student.

"The will and my suspicions about it."

"It couldn't be that Max's killer knew that my investigation was about
to—"

"What investigation?"

He looked taken aback. "I've been using my contacts in Eastern Europe
to—"

"You didn't tell me anything about that."

"You heard me on the phone to Eastern Europe."

"You never said why. First you keep secrets, and then you accuse me of putting you at risk." Really, this was the last straw. I burst into tears.

"Hey, what's going on back there?" demanded the policeman who was driving.

"None of your business," I replied, sniffling.

"If it's domestic violence—"

"The only violence was against me," said Jason dryly. "My wife knocked me over in a theater."

"So press charges," said the policeman, "but don't hit her in my patrol car."

"I didn't hit her," Jason protested.

"And I only shoved him so that he wouldn't get knifed," I added. "I don't know how you can accuse me of domestic violence, Jason, when I saved your life." Both indignant and hurt, I reached into my handbag for a Kleenex.

"You're not going for the perfume, are you?" Jason asked, looking alarmed.

"No, but if I still had the bread, I'd knock you right on the head with it."

"No head-knocking!" The driver slammed on the brakes at a red light and turned around menacingly.

"I'm getting out right here," I said, blowing my nose. It wasn't much of a threat, because I could see the hotel half a block away.

"Good," said the policeman. "More cops get hurt on domestic violence calls than any other—"

"Oh, do be quiet!" I jumped out and ran down the street as fast as I could go, sobbing and being studiously ignored by passing New Yorkers. By the time my husband returned to the room, I had retrieved a contract sent to me by messenger from Paul Fallon, taken the elevator to the room, where I tossed the contract on top of my suitcase, kicked off my shoes, and climbed into bed. Once beneath the covers, I put my head under the pillow and continued to weep. At that moment, I felt that I would never forgive my husband for his unkind words and for failing to appreciate the terror I had experienced when I thought he was going to be killed and the bravery it had taken to defend him.

Well, actually, when I look back on the incident, I hadn't really been brave; I'd just reacted with the only weapons at hand. Still, I had saved his life. Maybe being rescued from danger by a woman had hurt his male ego.

Eventually, Jason entered the room and said in a rather tentative voice, "Carolyn?" I didn't reply. "Caro?" He sighed and retrieved his telephone messages, after which he made a brief long distance call, identifying himself and saying, after a moment, "So he did go to Charles."

Charles who? I wondered.

"Vasandrovich was his patronymic? . . . I wonder why he uses it as a surname. . . . Well, no matter. Probably some immigration snafu. Thanks for calling again."

He hung up and immediately dialed another number. "Charles, this is Jason. I just heard from Prague. Vaclav did go to the university there. It was some surname-patronymic mix-up. . . . Yes, I'm relieved, too."

What in the world was Jason talking about? My body was beginning to relax under the warmth of the blanket, and the pillow blocking light and muting sound contributed to my increasing drowsiness. Defending one's husband from an assassin is exhausting business. The last thing I heard was my husband asking for Detective Ali, but I never heard the conversation. I never heard my husband leave the room. Or return.

What did drag me out of sleep was his voice saying, "Wake up, sweetheart. I've brought home dinner." That and a powerful but tempting odor coming from a bag that Jason had placed right beside my nose.

"Wha . . . ?"

36
Pastrami to Die For

Sometimes the weary tourist, having eaten every meal during the trip in a restaurant, wants to relax and eat takeout in the hotel room. Why? Because it's cheaper, it's less time consuming, no dress code is imposed (one can eat in rumpled or casual clothes, in night clothes, or even, I suppose, nude, if so inclined), and it's relaxing. However, these picnics in the room can bring the ire of the hotel and its patrons down on the head of the culinary miscreant. If you spill red wine on the carpet or mustard on the bedspread, the housekeeping staff will take offense. If your choice of picnic food is particularly odoriferous, people in neighboring rooms may follow their noses and knock on your door to complain. On a trip to New York, my husband brought back wonderful, if overpoweringly aromatic, pastrami sandwiches, and I listened anxiously for that angry knock on our door, even as I ate every bite.

However, visitors less lucky and more famous than us have come to grief by eating in their hotel rooms. After World War II the odor of boiling cabbage prepared by three Russian chefs in the Plaza Hotel suite of UN Ambassador Andrei Gromyko was not greeted with delight. However, he was not asked to leave. Fidel Castro was actually ejected from the Murray Hill Hotel; rumor has it that his staff was plucking chickens and cooking them in a room without cooking facilities. One wonders if the chickens were brought live from Cuba and how the alleged cooking was accomplished. With a hot plate? Over a fire built in the bathtub? Those incidents make our little pastrami adventure look quite conventional.

Carolyn Blue, "Have Fork, Will Travel," *Flagstaff Frontier Ledger*

Carolyn

I sat up and pushed my hair back. "What is it?" I asked, looking at the large, somewhat greasy bag that my husband had deposited beside my nose.

"A peace offering. I'm sorry I was unpleasant about your having talked to people about the coal project."

I sighed. "And I'm sorry if I put you in danger."

Jason smiled. "Well, you certainly did protect me when it occurred."

"I did, didn't I?" It's amazing how much a nap can do for one. I no longer felt trembly and terrified or even on the verge of tears. In fact, I now felt rather proud of myself. After all, I had fended off a professional assassin, and I hadn't even had a real weapon, just wifely instincts, a loaf of Italian bread, and Bernie Feingold's perfume. "So what's in the bag? It's certainly smelly."

"Smelly?" Jason looked somewhat offended. "The desk clerk assured me that this is the best pastrami in New York City."

"And you got it here at the hotel?" That seemed unlikely.

"No, he recommended a deli down the street."

"Ah. Did you, by any chance, have to pay cash?"

Jason looked surprised. "How did you know that? I considered it pretty unusual. After all, credit cards seem to be accepted everywhere. In the heart of New York City, one would expect—"

"You went to the delicatessen that Max visited every Monday, the one where he died."

Disconcerted, Jason looked down at the bag. "Well, I guess we'll find out if it was pastrami worth dying for," he mumbled, pulling from the bag sandwiches piled with enough meat to feed a family of four, sandwiches in which the filling was so thick that the bread slices seemed an afterthought, sandwiches too thick to be bitten into, sandwiches that tended to topple one way or the other. There were also pickles. And Dr. Brown's Cream Soda, which, Jason assured me, was the beverage of choice for these sandwiches. Even before beginning to eat, I was wondering if we could safely save half or more to eat on the plane tomorrow. Then I remembered that we would be traveling first class. Those perky stewardesses would probably be offended if we brought our own lunch aboard.

And the pastrami was wonderful—rich, moist, fatty, flavorful—almost worth dying for.

We ate it all, ate until we were pastrami-dazed and -sated. Then Jason fell back on the bed while I, rejuvenated by my nap, disposed of the leavings, stepped into the bathroom to wash fat residue from my fingers, and returned to type up notes on the minestrone we had eaten in the Village and the difficulties of devouring large, messy sandwiches while sitting on the hotel's bedspread. Then I packed for our departure the next day, showered, and climbed into bed beside Jason, who was already asleep. I was, too, within minutes.

Sometime later, the telephone on the nightstand rang. I must have been having a bad dream because I awoke terrified and, in trying to grasp the receiver in the dark, knocked it off the cradle. I could hear a voice saying, "Mrs. Blue? Mrs. Blue?"

"What?" said Jason, who was now sitting up, his voice sharp.

"Phone," I mumbled. But I couldn't find it. "Turn on the light."

"Tell 'em to call back later." He lay down again.

"Can't find the receiver. Turn on the light."

Jason turned on the light and I, leaning precariously over the edge of the bed, pulled the receiver up by the cord. " 'Lo?"

"This is Worski. Did I wake you up?"

I squinted at the alarm clock that I had brought from home. "It's after midnight, Detective. Of course, you woke us. And we have to be up early to catch our plane. Why in the world are you calling at—"

"So you don't want to know how the case turned out?"

He sounded so smug I could have smacked him, except that he wasn't here, and one can't really smack a policeman. It's against the law. In fact, it's against the law to smack anyone, even one's own misbehaving child. It had probably been against the law to push my husband down, even though I had done it to save his life. "Of course I want to know. It was the Heydemanns, wasn't it?"

"Sort of."

"Sort of? What does that mean? Either it was or—"

"I'm downstairs. Thought I'd drop by personally and tell you what we know. Since you've been helpful an' all that. It's pretty complicated."

I looked at Jason, who had opened his eyes as soon as he realized I was talking to a detective. "He wants to come up and tell us how the case worked out," I whispered.

Jason nodded. "If you want to go back to sleep, I can go down to the lobby and talk to him."

"Ha! And never hear that I was right about Rick Heydemann?"

Jason grinned. "So tell him to come up here."

"But I'm in my nightie."

"And you don't have a robe?"

"Well, yes, but I'll have to get dressed just the same."

"No, you won't. We'll both put on robes and receive the detective in— what's that French word for—"

"I can't pronounce it." French pronunciation has always been a mystery to me, although I love the sauces. I took my hand from the mouthpiece of the telephone and told the detective our room number, then rushed to my suitcase and snatched my robe from the top layer. Pulling it on, I hurried into the bathroom to root through my cosmetics bag for my comb, thinking all the while that I wouldn't have time to put on makeup. Oh well, detectives probably see lots of women who aren't prepared to appear in public. Jason was letting Detective Worski in when I returned to the bedroom.

"I was right, wasn't I? Rick Heydemann hired Thelma. He probably got the money from his mother. She mentioned money he owed her."

"Yeah?" Worski sat in our one easy chair and wrote that in his notebook.

"So how was Rick *sort of* involved?" I asked.

"I imagine, Carolyn, because it was his father who died as a result of the espionage at the company," said Jason.

"Hey, let me tell the story in my own way, OK?" The detective grinned at us in such a way that I had to wonder if we were both wrong.

37

And Then Some

Jason

Carolyn took the desk chair, looking exceedingly impatient, and I sat on the bed, while Detective Worski settled himself comfortably in a small, upholstered tub chair that could hardly contain his bulk, especially since he had not taken off his green overcoat.

"This is one weird case," said Worski. "We go from practically no leads and no clear suspects to way too many. I mean, we start out with this guy whose fingerprints are on the pig sticker, the guy you saw go for your husband, Mrs. Blue. That's all the information we really got, an' he's not sayin' anything except he didn't do nothin' an' he's got a busy day tomorrow 'cause he's got this TV gig doin' a commercial for deodorant. He's an actor, see. That's another thing he tells us. We ask how he supports himself, an' he says he's an actor, not admittin' he was ever a waitress like you say, Mrs. Blue."

"I don't care what he says. He *was* Thelma!" Carolyn insisted. "And an actor—that ties him to Rick Heydemann, who wanted his inheritance so he could finance an off-Broadway play in which he was going to star."

"Yeah, you mentioned that. So what was the name of that play?"

"And Then Some."

"Yeah. Well, funny thing. When Mr. X says about his deodorant commercial he's got to get to an' how he's gonna sue us if we interfere with his blossomin' career . . . that's how he puts it. His career is blossomin' . . . Ali says, 'Don' sound to me like your career is goin' so great. Most actors figure doin' commercials are for the no-talent guys. An' deodorant ads . . . that's like the bottom of the heap. What's that say about you? You're a guy who looks like he's got smelly armpits?' "

Worski laughed appreciatively. "Ali may think white-collar crime is more fun than murder, but he's got one hell of a talent for workin' a skel over in interrogation. He makes that crack about actors who can't get nothin' but armpit work, an' our guy gets pissed. 'You don' know shit,' he says."

My poor wife. I knew she was longing to reprimand the detective for his language.

"You were saying," Carolyn prompted, "that his interrogation bore fruit?"

"Right. So our unidentified suspect says, 'I been promised a part in a very promisin' play,' an' Ali says, 'Where? In Peoria?' an' the skel says, 'Here in New York, smart-ass,' an' Ali says, 'Sure, like Staten Island?' and the guy says, 'Lower Manhattan,' and so forth. They go a few rounds about this big part that's gonna make the guy famous, an' guess what the name of the play is?"

Neither of us replied, and I frankly I couldn't see that the name of the play would have any bearing on whether or not the young man in black had killed Max, who had nothing to do with the theater.

"And Then Some," said Worski triumphantly. "That was the play that was gonna be his big break."

"Rick Heydemann's play!" Carolyn beamed at the detective. "There, what did I tell you? I hope you picked up on the connection while you still had him in custody."

"Well, by then the guys we had searchin' the apartment on his fake ID come back with more stuff."

"His name?" Carolyn asked breathlessly.

"That was later, but the uniforms found the biggest pair of falsies you ever seen under a pile in his underwear drawer."

"Proof positive that he masqueraded as Thelma, who had a bottom too flat for those large breasts. I knew there was something wrong with her figure," said Carolyn.

"Yep." Worski nodded. "An' then they found another one a them pop-out pig stickers. . . . Guess he likes to have a spare. . . . An' his Day-Timer—"

"Surely he didn't enter assassination dates in his calendar," I said. "That would indicate extreme stupidity or perhaps some sort of obsessive-compulsive disorder."

"Let him finish, Jason," said Carolyn impatiently. "Who cares whether he was stupid or neurotic. One has to expect unusual character traits in an assassin."

"You got that right, Mrs. Blue," said Worski, "an' our guy didn't exactly write in his date book that he was gonna kill anyone. What we found was a meetin' with Rick Heydemann the week before Heydemann's dad was killed. He writes that Rick offered him the part of Colin in *And Then Some*. Then he writes, 'Very meaty,' whatever the hell that means. Maybe this Colin character is a fat guy or a weight lifter or—"

"He meant that it was a challenging role," Carolyn interrupted.

"You're saying that he killed Max to get a part in a play?" I objected. "No matter how good the role, that seems an unlikely motive, and I'd imagine a jury would agree."

"It's hard for an actor to get that important first break," said my wife. "I think he might well have been willing to kill for his big chance."

"Jeez, it's hard to tell a story with you two always interruptin'. That's not the only entry in his book. He met young Heydemann the Tuesday after the dad got spiked an' again on Friday that week."

"Friday before or after the will was read?" Carolyn asked.

"They met at a club in the Village late Friday night," said Worski.

"Ha!" Carolyn exclaimed. "They were meeting because Rick wanted his stepmother killed, and the assassin agreed because he wouldn't get the part if Rick didn't get the money to finance the play."

"It still seems unlikely," I insisted. "And why would he try to kill me? Why the meeting on Tuesday, for that matter?"

"Well, the appointment book wasn't all my crew found," said Worski, looking pleased with himself. "There was this bank book. We don' know where the bank is . . . probably some Caribbean island or someplace . . . but he put in ten thousand the day he met Rick before the dad was killed an' another ten Tuesday, the day after the dad was killed, an' another ten Friday, the day before he tried to do the stepmom. That day the book says, 'rehearsals should start in a week, ten days max.' "

"What about today?" Carolyn asked. "He only wounded Charlotte yesterday. What did he say about that?"

"Nothin'," Worski replied. "An he didn't put another ten thou in the bank."

"So he fails to kill Charlotte one day and tries to kill me the next?" I asked. "That doesn't add up. I have nothing to do with the son's inheritance problems."

"It's as I said," Carolyn insisted. "He was actually going after me, but I got him first. With the bread."

"Carolyn!" I protested. "And another thing, Detective, why was he working as a waitress at the deli if he wasn't asked to kill Max Heydemann until the week before he did it? Carolyn, didn't you say Thelma had been there a while?"

"He and Rick could have been talking about it earlier," she replied defensively. "I don't know when he started playing the Thelma role."

"Two weeks before Max Heydemann died," said Worski.

"Were there earlier meetings between the two men?" I asked.

"Not in his calendar," Worski replied.

"That doesn't mean they didn't have earlier meetings," said Carolyn.

"Carolyn, even you thought he was going after me. You saw him over my shoulder."

"Oh Jason, when you see someone with a weapon in a crowded theater, you don't have time for logical thought processes. You can only do that kind of thinking later. If I'd stopped to analyze the situation, one of us would have been dead."

"Well, you got that right, ma'am," said Worski, "but the whole thing's more complicated than young Heydemann needin' money to finance his actin' career."

Both Carolyn and I groaned.

38

Second Act: And Then Some More

Carolyn

W*hat more could there be?* "Have you arrested Rick?" I asked Detective Worski. "And his mother? I'll bet his sister Ariadne was in on the conspiracy, too." Certainly they had Rick and the assassin dead to rights because they could trace the money from Rick to Thelma. Then they might be able to trace it backward from Rick to Melisande, his mother.

"Let's not get ahead of ourselves here, Mrs. Blue."

Detective Worski was obviously enjoying himself, although how he could in the middle of the night, I can't imagine. Didn't the man ever sleep? "All right, Detective, but at least tell me that Thelma confessed."

"Yeah, his lawyer arrived and advised him to take a reduced plea in return for giving us Rick Heydemann."

My husband was looking very disgruntled, but then men, even men as nice as Jason, don't like to be proved wrong. I leaned over to kiss him on the cheek. "It does explain everything more believably than a spy scenario, dear. Maybe now that the murder has been solved, Detective Ali would like to help with the industrial espionage problem. In fact, given that Max's death was a family matter, I'm not opposed to your taking the job offer at Hodge, Brune. If you'd been right, it would have been too dangerous, don't you think? After all, who would want to work for a company where scientists get killed over chemistry?

"Now we both have offers. That envelope was from Paul Fallon, Frances Striff's significant other. His proposal is tempting, and, goodness, the Hodge, Brune offer—"

"Mrs. Blue, could you shut up for a minute?" said Detective Worski.

I was shocked at his rudeness: first, for interrupting me while I was talking to my husband and even more because he'd told me to shut up, which was hardly gentlemanly.

"I'm not through tellin' you about our investigation."

"What else is there to say? You've got the murderer. He's told you who hired him. You have supporting evidence. Surely—"

"Let him finish, Carolyn," Jason interrupted.

Everyone seemed to feel free to interrupt me.

"Thank you, Professor," said Detective Worski. "Does she talk this much at home?" He grinned, noticed that I was frowning at him, and hastened on, probably under the impression that I was planning to keep him from finishing, whereas, I now felt so put upon that I didn't plan to say another word. To either of them. In fact, I'd have left the room had there been any place to go but the hall, which I could hardly enter in my bathrobe, and the bathroom, where I'd have to sit ignominiously on the toilet lid wondering what they were saying.

"Anyway, just about the time we worked out the deal, we got a hit on his photo, which we'd faxed around the precincts the same time we put his prints in AFIS. A detective in Organized Crime called to say we'd pulled in Anton Bashurkov, alias Anton Manners, alias Rory Manners, and so forth."

"The name sounds as if it could be Russian," my husband observed, looking interested.

"Yep. He's never been convicted, but he's in the Organized Crime files as a guy hooked up with the Russian Mob."

"And I heard rumors that the Ukrainian company responsible for stealing Hodge, Brune's coal process was backed by the Russian Mafia," said Jason.

"And Thelma said her mother had relatives who were *connected*," I couldn't help adding. "Of course, I assumed that she meant the American Mafia."

"Yeah, well, Thelma was tellin' you the truth about that," said Detective Worski, "or part of it, anyway. Bashurkov's old lady runs a boardin' house for new arrivals, guys they're smugglin' into the country, but she don't live in Teaneck, an' she don't have MS. That was all a crock of . . . well, it was a crock. You know what I mean?"

"And the deal you made with the suspect? Does that mean you can't pursue the Russian connection?" Jason asked.

I suppose he was right back to worrying that Hodge, Brune was not a healthy company to work for. I certainly had new doubts.

"Hey, any deal we make, it goes down the toilet like so much . . ." The detective glanced at me nervously. "Like so much toilet paper if the guy's been lying to us. So we throw this new angle at him. If he's connected, maybe the Russians, not this Ricky kid, are the ones who want him to off Heyde-mann. Maybe he's a hit man for the Russian Mob. Well, that's when he starts to sweat. When he heard we got his appointment book, he just shrugged; when he heard we got his bank book, he asks for his lawyer an' gives us the son; but when he hears we got him pegged as a Russian hit man, he can't deny it fast enough. No way he's connected with them. Jus' cause his mama's got cousins, don' mean he knows shit about any Russian Mob.

"So Ali, he looks over the Day-Timer, an' says, who's V. that he's had meets with? Bashurkov, he says, it's his friend Victor, another actor. Ali says, OK. Give us the guy's number. Anton, he says, Victor's poor like him. He's got no phone. Ali says, you got one, man, an' all this money banked; you're not poor.

"Then my partner starts lookin' at the bank book. Like there's another twenty thou before Max Heydemann died, he says, an' it ain't the money Bashurkov got from the son. That's a different twenty thou, an' it come in before he got that job at the deli wearin' big tits an' servin' pastrami. An' here's another twenty thou before Mrs. H. was attacked, an' that's besides the money from Ricky boy.

"Anton says that's jus' money owed him. He lends cash to friends; they paid him back. 'What friends?' Ali says. Let's have the names and phone numbers if you got any actor friends you'd lend twenty thou to who could pay it back. Anton refuses to answer on the grounds it may incriminate him, this after he has a little sidebar with his lawyer. They're both noddin' like we'll understand he's not gonna admit to loan sharkin'.

"Bashurkov's not admittin' anything, not loan sharkin', not takin' money from the Russians. He's never taken on a job killin' no one before that stinkin' kid tempted him with big money and the part of a lifetime. He's an actor, for God's sake.

"I say, if we find out he hasn't told us everything, the deal's off. We'll see he gets the death penalty. He's says he's tellin' the truth. I say, so we'll sub-poena his phone records to see who called him or who he's called before he met with V., his actor friend who can't afford a phone but can pay him back a couple of twenty-thousand-dollar debts. Bashurkov don't bite.

"Ali asks how come he didn't get no money for goin' after Professor Blue. Was that a freebie? Or was it because he screwed up and din' manage to kill Mrs. Heydemann so he owed 'em one.

"I say we'll subpoena his mother's phone records, too. Now he looks like he's gonna cry, an' he wants to talk to his lawyer alone."

"V. could be Vaclav Vasandrovich," said Jason thoughtfully.

"But you had that call," I pointed out. "His records from Charles University were all right, after all."

"He did change his name," said Jason. "Sort of."

"But he cried at Max's funeral," I reminded him.

"Who's tellin' this story anyway?" demanded Detective Worski. "If you don' want to hear how it turned out, I'll just go home an' get some sleep. I'm only here as a courtesy."

"And we're being very rude," I hastened to admit. I, for one, wanted to know where this long, long tale was going. Had Thelma lied about Rick? And if so, how could the meetings and payments be explained? "Can we offer you something from the bar?" I asked, inspired by self-serving hospitality.

"What bar?" Worski frowned as if I was trying to lure him downstairs and get him drunk.

"We have this little refrigerator stocked with drinks," I said.

"Those are very expensive, Carolyn," Jason protested, always the thrifty one.

"I wouldn't mind a bourbon if you got it," said Detective Worski. "I'm not on duty."

I busied myself fixing him a bourbon and ice, although the ice cubes in the refrigerator was covered with frost, as if no one had taken them out in years. I even found him a packet of nuts, earning a look of horror from my husband. "Now, Detective, you were saying . . ."

"Right. So we leave Bashurkov an' his lawyer, who's mobbed up, too, we figure. About five minutes, an' when we come back in, Bashurkov's got a new story, but it's got nothin' to do with no Russian mobsters. He don' know any Russian mobsters, he claims, an' if he did, he wouldn't be namin' no names 'cause that's like askin' to end up dead. Right? So don' ask him. He ain' got no information there, but he did get paid twice for the same hit. That much he'll admit."

"Good grief!" I said.

39

The Last Act

Jason

"Then who paid him?" I asked, almost afraid to hear the name. If it wasn't gangsters, it had to be someone at Hodge, Brune, probably someone I had met and liked: Fergus McRoy, for instance, although there wasn't a V in his name. Then it struck me. Merrivale. Vernon Merrivale. In fact, he might be the most likely. All other considerations aside, wouldn't a security person be more apt to know the name of a hit man? "It was Merrivale, wasn't it?"

"Who?" Worski looked half puzzled, half irritated.

"Sorry," I apologized hastily.

"It could be," said Carolyn. "Didn't you say he was a thoroughly unpleasant person? One doesn't picture a pleasant person arranging the death of a colleague."

"You two wanna hear this or not?"

We both answered in the affirmative.

"OK. So he tells us he got this call on the telephone, an offer to pay ten thou if he'd kill a customer at the deli. He claims he took the job there 'cause the tips were good an' women get better tips than men, not that I figure that's true, but it's his story, right? An' this is what he said. We jus' let him talk, no interruptions, unlike some people."

We were both treated to pointed looks.

"So he thinks, terrific, when he hears the name of the guy he's supposed to kill. It's the guy Rick Heydemann already offered him twenty thou to hit, so he says OK to the caller, but ten thou isn't enough. They haggle. He gets the guy up to twenty. Ten before, ten afterward. The guy sets it up so Bashurkov gets the money without ever seein' the caller, who won't give his name."

"Did the caller say how he got Thelma's name?" Carolyn asked. "In fact, did the caller think he was Thelma?"

"So he says, an' Bashurkov didn't know how the guy got his name. It's a weak point in the story, but that don't make no difference."

"Of course, it does!" Carolyn exclaimed.

"I have to agree with my wife. Who'd think to call a waitress to perform a murder?" I asked. "In fact, I'd imagine that female hit persons are rare."

"That's sexist," said Carolyn, giving me a look that would have done credit to my mother. Then she laughed, probably at the expression on my face.

"You think this is funny, Mrs. Blue? This caller put out a hit on your husband a couple of days later."

Carolyn looked properly chastened and stopped laughing.

"So anyway, the caller sets up this electronic money transfer into Bashurkov's account an' ends up hirin' three hits, not all during the same negotiation: Max Heydemann, his wife, an' you, Professor, only since he didn't do the job on Mrs. H., the money is transferred to the hit on you."

"Did the caller say why he wanted me killed?" I asked.

"He didn't say why he wanted anyone killed according to Bashurkov, who says he was figuring by the end of it that if Rick Heydemann couldn't finance the play, maybe he could do it himself and get the lead."

"Can you finance a play with . . . How much did he have by then?" Carolyn asked.

"Forty thousand for Max," I replied. "Then twenty for Charlotte that was transferred to me. That's sixty. But if he had managed to kill all three of us eventually at forty thousand each, that would be one hundred and twenty thousand dollars. Did young Heydemann want me killed, too?"

"I don't think you can finance a play, even off-Broadway, for that amount of money," said Carolyn. "I've read that the Broadway plays cost millions, so surely—"

"Oh shut up, both of you, and no, Professor, Heydemann didn't pay to have you iced," snapped Worski. "He wasn't even after Mrs. Blue."

"Are you saying that assassinating me would be understandable?" Carolyn demanded.

"Jeez, you two are worse than tryin' to talk to the press. You got any more of this bourbon?"

"No, but I think there's a little bottle of Scotch," said my wife, as if those little bottles weren't costing a fortune. Surely she wasn't under the impression that the hotel provided them free of charge or that Hodge, Brune could be expected to pay our bar bill. Whatever she thought, she rose and peered into the refrigerator, naming off the various selections left. Worski chose the Scotch—Chivas Regal, for God's sake. I wanted to ask if there wasn't a cheaper brand in there but thought better of risking insult to the detective, who, by the way, didn't even ask for ice. He just unscrewed the top and poured the scotch into the glass that had held the bourbon, my toothbrush glass, as I discovered the next morning.

"Did you know that Scotch wasn't popular in this country until golf was introduced in 1887 by someone from Yonkers?" Carolyn asked.

"Don' surprise me," Worski replied. "It's not my favorite." He took a generous swallow.

"Small wonder," Carolyn agreed. "During prohibition they made it of industrial alcohol, creosote, caramel, and prune juice, which tells you something about the taste."

Worski looked at the Scotch remaining in his glass with such shock that my wife exclaimed, "Well, I didn't make *that*. It's from Scotland."

"Jeez!" said Worski, then continued his story. "Anyway, he goes on spinning this tale about mystery callers and electronic money transfers—"

"Wouldn't the records of the electronic transfers show who initiated them and what account the money came from?" Carolyn asked.

"Bashurkov says the caller warned him not to get nosy, that the money would be in the form of cashier's checks. Ali says, not good enough; if Bashurkov can't give us a name, it's all on his head because we got no evidence he was paid by this other guy."

"He listed these contacts under V.," I reminded the detective. "If he didn't know the caller's name, why the V.?"

"Yeah, Professor, an' we didn't miss that. We let him talk himself into a corner, an' then we brought that up. Course, we hadn't let him look at his book since we got hold of it, an' he evidently didn't remember what he put down."

"I thought these entries signified meetings," said Carolyn, "not telephone conversations. He was obviously lying."

"Actually, they just said V. on a time line," replied Worski impatiently.

"Sorry," said Carolyn before he could threaten again to leave. At least she didn't seem to notice that the detective had finished his Scotch and was eyeing his empty glass suggestively. "What happened next?" Then she gave him one of her lovely smiles and added, "This is so exciting."

"If it's so excitin', how come you keep interruptin' me?" he grumbled.

"We won't say another word," she promised.

"OK. So we ask what was the V. for, an' Bashurkov says after lookin' like he's forgot his lines in a play, it was for 'value added.' 'Like the tax in Europe?' Ali asks. 'Right,' says Bashurkov. 'So you been to Europe?' Ali asks. 'Eastern or Western?' 'No,' says Bashurkov, 'never been out of the country.' Which could be true. He's got no accent. So how does he know about value-added taxes? Ali asks.

"Myself, I never heard of 'em. Maybe that's something my partner caught in white-collar crime.

" 'I read about it,' says Bashurkov, 'an' it seemed like a good name . . . a joke. Right? . . . Since I didn't know the guy's name.' 'Bullshit,' says Ali."

"I don't believe Detective Ali said . . . that," Carolyn protested.

"Hey, you promised," snapped Detective Worski. "No talkin'. Bad enough my ex-wife was always bitchin' about my language. 'You talk disgusting, Stan,' she says. 'Watch your grammar, Stan,' she says. Shit, I had twenty years of that. I don't need—"

"Our apologies, Detective," I interrupted. Carolyn looked mutinous, but I kept her from protesting by adding, "So you never found out who the second contractor was?"

"Hell, yes, we did. Finally we said, 'You're a lyin' dirtbag, Bashurkov, an' all deals are off.' Then we call in a cop an' tell him to get Bashurkov a ride over to Rikers. The charge is goin' to be capital murder.

"Bashurkov, he turns whiter than an old whore's belly."

My poor wife's mouth dropped open. Grabbing her hand, I squeezed hard in warning before she could offend the detective beyond the point of no return. However, I myself thought his language highly offensive in mixed company.

"An' he squeaks, voice so high you'd think someone had cut his nuts off, 'Vasandrovich. The V is for Vasandrovich.' "

"Vaclav?" I asked.

"I can't believe it," Carolyn murmured. "He cried at Max's funeral. I saw tears in his eyes at the opera. I just don't believe it. Thelma must have been lying."

40

The Last Player

Carolyn

Believe it," said Detective Worski, giving me a superior grin. "We got three actors in this play, the Heydemann kid, Bashurkov, and now this guy."

"Did Bashurkov explain or even know why Vaclav Vasandrovich would want to buy the deaths of Max, Charlotte, and then me?" Jason asked.

"And where did he get the money?" I asked. "His wife must spend everything he makes."

"He gives us this big song and dance about Vasandrovich stealing company secrets to sell to some other chemical company," Worski replied, "an' he's about to get caught, so he's gonna protect himself by having everyone who knew anything killed off."

"Oh." I peeked over at Jason, thinking that he'd always said it was about industrial espionage, but then I'd always said the family was responsible. Now it seemed that we were both right. "Well, I suppose if he was well paid for the spying, he'd have the money to hire a killer, although I can't imagine why he picked someone he thought was a deli waitress."

"You're jumping ahead of me here," Worski warned. "I ain't finished the story."

My husband was shaking his head as if any more twists in the tale would make it totally unbelievable. Worski lifted his glass in my direction. "Got a refill?"

"Gin," I said doubtfully, wondering if combining bourbon, scotch, and gin might not be injurious to his health. "Rum, vodka. Beer."

"Beer." He accepted a bottle of Amstel and continued. "So he gives us this Vasandrovich, an' my partner says, 'A Russian?' Bashurkov can't tell us fast enough that Vasandrovich is Czech. We say, 'Czech, Russian, what's the difference?' 'No, no,' he says, looking like he's about to pee his pants, this Vasandrovich is a scientist. That's all. No Mob connections. The lawyer's backin' him up: a scientist. No Mob connections.

"How does Bashurkov know the guy's got no Mob connections? we ask. 'Ask him,' says Bashurkov. 'He'll tell you he's in this on his own.' So we say OK, we'll ask him, an' we have Bashurkov put back in the cells while we go off to Vasandrovich's apartment. Course, Bashurkov says he don' know where it is; he never got invited, but hell, the guy's in the book—Vasandrovich.

"Meanwhile, Bashurkov an' the lawyer are lookin' relieved. We figure even if Vasandrovich is Mob connected, they think he'll be too scared to admit it." Worski took a gulp of beer. "Them Russians, they're a mean lot. I'm thinkin' if the guy really is a scientist—"

"He is," said Jason. "He's the new head of R and D. He took Max's place."

"He's still temporary, isn't he?" I asked.

"Shut up," said Detective Worski, "or I'm goin' home. Anyway, we figure this Vasandrovich, if he really hired Bashurkov an' did it for the Russian Mafia, he's gonna keep his mouth shut so they don't wipe out him an' his whole family. Like I said, the Russians are a mean bunch. Everyone in Organized Crime wishes they'd go the hell back to Russia an' leave things the way they used to be. Shit, we got the Chinese an' the Columbians an' the Russians an' every other goddam bunch of foreign gangsters. Makes you feel nostalgic for the old dons."

"Vaclav doesn't have any family except his wife, if he was telling Jason the truth," I informed the detective. "He mentioned an Aunt Elizabeta to me, but that was when he was denying that he'd been speaking Russian. Oh, and at one time they evidently had a—"

"I ain't got all night, Mrs. Blue," he interrupted irritably.

"Well, I just thought you might be interested, but maybe Vaclav has already told you about his family."

"Vaclav didn't tell us nothin'," said Worski.

"Are you Russian, Detective?" I asked, then clapped my hand over my mouth. *Think before you speak, Carolyn,* I told myself.

"So Vaclav was afraid to talk?" asked Jason thoughtfully. "Well, as I told you, Detective Worski, I heard rumors about a Russian Mob connection. Or perhaps, Bashurkov made up the whole story about Vaclav."

"Nope. He didn't make it up, an' Vasandrovich didn't tell us nothin' 'cause he was dead when we got there."

"The Russians had already killed him?" I asked, horrified. "What about Sophia? Was she—"

"In hysterics," said Worski, "but not so much she couldn't pull out every paper in his desk. She was lookin' for insurance policies. Said she had to find out if they paid when he'd committed suicide. Then she started cryin' again."

"Did he commit suicide?" Jason asked.

"Yep. He had a gun. Unregistered. He ate it."

"He what?" I asked.

"He stuck it in his mouth an' pulled the trigger," Worski explained, then went on to add information I could have done without. "Bang. Brains all over the wall. It's a pretty sure way of makin' certain no one carts you off to the hospital an' saves your life."

"Did he leave a note?" Jason asked.

"We asked the wife that, since she'd been messin' with the papers on the desk, but she said no. Killed himself without even sayin' good-bye, without even knowin' whether she was provided for, blah, blah, blah. A real piece of work, that one."

"So we may never know—" my husband began.

Detective Worski held up his hand. "I said the wife told us he didn't leave a note. My partner, who's used to these white-collar types, says, lemme look at the guy's computer. All he does is tap a key an' this screen that looks like one a them kaleidoscope things kids used to have disappears, an' there's the note. We printed it out. Printed out a couple of copies while his wife was screamin' at us that she was the only one who should see the note, her bein' his heir an' wife an' so forth."

Detective Worski set his empty beer bottle down on the carpet beside his chair, reached into the depths of his overcoat, and produced a paper, which he handed to Jason. "Thought you might like to see this." I moved over to the bed so that I could read it, too.

To whom it may concern:

I, Vaclav Vasandrovich, now dead by my own hand, do declare myself responsible for the death of my friend and mentor, Max Heydemann. Three years ago, when I had become deeply in debt through personal expenditures, my cousin Boris Petrovich Kovar, the grandson of a great uncle on my mother's side, offered to arrange a loan for me. I was desperate enough to accept without inquiring too closely into the source of the money and the expectations of the lenders.

Before Christmas last year, when I had still managed to pay back only the interest, and had borrowed more besides, a meeting was arranged with the lenders. They said my debts would be forgiven if I turned over to them the research notes for an important company project as it matured. I refused. I was then told that my choices were to pay back the money immediately, accept their generous offer, or face the injury or death of myself and my wife, either of which would be extremely prolonged and painful. I have known such men in my homeland and in Russia, and I believed them. God help me, in fear for my wife and myself, I made a bargain with the devil.

When I had turned over all the material they wanted and thought that finally I was clear of them and their frightening presence in my life, I began to realize that my friend Max Heydemann either knew or was about to find out my secret and my treachery. Questions he asked me and inquiries of his that I heard of over the last week of his life convinced me that I was about to be exposed. I knew then that I would have to bear the shame. I could not ask for help from the men who had bought my honor without endangering a man who had done more for me than any other. I discussed this with my beloved wife Sophia, who was desperate to find an-

other solution, but we finally agreed that I would have to let Max's investigation take its course. As long as I did not reveal my Russian connections, I felt that at least our lives would be safe. How wrong I was.

Max was killed the following Monday. Although I did not kill him, and I did not ask that he be killed or in any way solicit his death, my weakness was the cause. I do not know how the Russians learned that Max was a danger to their plans, but I am sure that they were the initiators of his death. Therefore, I leave a list of their names in the hope that they will be brought to justice. I have meted out that well-deserved justice to myself. May God protect and comfort my beloved wife, Sophia.

Respectfully,
Vaclav Vasandrovich

A list of seven Russian names followed, including that of his cousin.

"So there you have it," said Worski cheerfully. "They all ratted each other out. My case is solved. My partner's excited about the financial trail. Organized Crime's dancing a jig over arresting the Russians. Rick Heydemann's been picked up. We got 'em all."

"Except Sophia," I said.

Jason and the detective looked at me in surprise and puzzlement.

"Sophia made the call to the Russian Mob. How else could they have found out?" I reasoned. "And who else had more to gain? She and Vaclav would be free of the debt she probably got them into, her husband wouldn't go to jail, he'd get Max's job, and she'd get even."

"Even for what?" Jason asked.

"Don't you remember? The Vasandroviches had a son who was left behind in Czechoslovakia with Sophia's mother. Both the mother and the child disappeared. Grace Pharr thought that Sophia blamed Max for not getting all of them out."

"You're right," my husband agreed. "I'd forgotten that."

"I'm sure she hadn't. And she'd never have guessed that Vaclav's conscience would lead him to commit suicide because of Max's death. She probably thought his tears were as fake as those she shed when he died. Look what Detective Worski said about her. She was hysterical because she couldn't find Vaclav's insurance policies. She was only worried about maintaining her lifestyle."

"We got a hell of a lot of people here responsible for one guy's death," said Worski.

"Max was a very special person," said Jason sadly.

"Look at Sophia's phone records," I advised the detective. "I imagine you'll find that she made a call to one of the people on that list."

"Jesus," said Worski. "You got any more suggestions?"

"If I do, I'll call from El Paso," I replied. "Right now, it's past my bedtime, and we have an early plane to catch."

Epilogue

Carolyn

I'm beginning to appreciate El Paso. When we got home from New York, the skies were cheerful and sunny, and no one we know had been murdered. Admittedly, we heard about more drug-related violence across the river in Juarez, but we've never met any of those people and aren't likely to. So we're once more comfortably and safely ensconced in the academic community with spring break to look forward to. "Let's just stay home," I suggested to Jason. "We can offer to buy vacation airline tickets for the children." He agreed.

And we can easily afford the fares, for once our visit to New York began to seem like an improbable dream, we each accepted the contracts we had been offered. Paul Fallon has already sold some of my New York columns to newspapers. Admittedly, these papers are mostly in smaller cities, but, still, I can look forward to checks coming in while I return to work on my book, *Eating Out in the Big Easy*. Writing all those columns seems to have helped me recover from my episode of writer's block.

Jason received a big check from Hodge, Brune for his week there and accepted the contract Charles Moore offered him, so we'll be spending the first six weeks of the summer in New York City. Our daughter Gwen has already decided to join us. Chris plans to attend summer school. Both are still waffling about Easter in El Paso, but we hope to tempt them home.

During Jason's last telephone conversation with Dr. Moore, we learned a good deal about the continuing investigation of the Heydemann case. Sophia Vasandrovich and Melisande D'Vallencourt have both been charged with conspiracy to murder Max, as have the two Heydemann offspring. All of them are out on bail, and Dr. Moore told Jason that the cases against them didn't look as strong as those against Thelma and the Russians, some of whom managed to flee the country before they could be picked up.

A new R and D director is to be brought in from outside. Jason was offered the post and declined, thank goodness. Fergus McRoy submitted his resignation and was lured back with a hefty raise, which will no doubt relieve him of his fears about a poverty-stricken old age. He and Fiona evidently had a more-money celebration because she is pregnant with their eighth, although Renata told me that Fiona says that is absolutely the last McRoy she'll conceive.

I spoke to Renata after her husband and mine had finished discussing things of male interest. She also told me that Calvin Pharr is still on the wagon and his wife Grace has been appointed the manager of a multimillion-dollar mutual fund. Charlotte Heydemann is volunteering as a dance teacher at a settlement house in Harlem and talking about using the trusts of her stepchildren to finance a dance outreach program for inner-city children if Ariadne and Rick are found guilty and lose their claim to the money. If they're not found guilty, she plans to disburse as little cash to them as the will allows. She's even talking about suing them and their mother for depriving her of her husband. All of which makes me very anxious about her safety. If their grandfather gets them off, they just might try again to have her killed.

Hodge, Brune will get its coal process back without going to court, because the international patent office denied the Ukrainian company's request, and the Ukrainian government closed down the factory in Kiev and arrested all the scientists. But not the Russian Mafia father-in-law of the vice president. Both Jason and I find the news about the case somewhat disillusioning. What if the instigators of Max's death all escape punishment?

I do hope the Russians will forget about our part of the investigation. After all, we were only peripherally involved.

Author's Note

Opera and drama performances and museum exhibits mentioned in the novel actually occurred, but over a period of several years rather than in one week. Restaurants and menu items mentioned exist or existed; however, characters and plot elements are fictional.

In addition to making trips to New York City, I used several books as reference sources: *On the Town in New York* by Michael and Ariane Batterberry, *New York Cookbook* by Molly O'Neill, *Access New York City*, *Zagat Survey/New York City Restaurants*, and *Dining and the Opera in Manhattan* by Sharon O'Connor.

I would like particularly to acknowledge the help of Sharon O'Connor, who not only graciously allowed me to use material from her book but also talked to me on several occasions about recipes, restaurants, and operas in Manhattan; of Joan Coleman who, as always, offered encouragement, friendship, and editorial input; and my husband, Bill, who plans our journeys, reads the maps, provides insights into science and scientists, and shares my enthusiasm for travel, food, wine, art, and opera.

NRF

Death à l'Orange

Acknowledgments

Special thanks to my husband, travel planner, companion on the road, and provider of scientific input; to my son Bill, whose computer expertise makes my website possible; to Mary Sarber, who presented me with the fascinating book *Bouquet de France* by Samuel Chamberlain, which she brought home from her own travels; and to my longtime friend Joan Coleman, for her encouragement and her editorial talents.

I found many books useful in the research and writing of this novel, among them: the abovementioned *Bouquet de France, Frommer's Touring Guide to Paris,* the *Michelin Guides to Normandy and Châteaux of the Loire, The Traveller's History of France* by Robert Cole, and particularly the delightful *Food Chronology* by James Trager, not to mention all the tourist books packed with pictures and history of the various towns and châteaux we visited.

N.F.

For my son Matthew,
who knows all about traveling with academics

Prologue

Carolyn

Shortly after my husband and I returned from a frightening but lucrative trip to New York City, we received a phone call offering what seemed to be a wonderful opportunity, a tour of Normandy and the Loire Valley at a cost that no one in his right mind would refuse. Being in our right minds, and enthusiastic travelers as well, we accepted. Who wouldn't? It sounded perfect.

The group would comprise faculty and family from our former university; the tour coincided not only with Jason's spring break but also with our son Chris's (although he'd have to leave France several days early); and our younger child, Gwen, had other plans for her Easter vacation. However, she did say that she expected to go on our next trip abroad while her brother stayed home. Ah, children! You'd think they were grade-schoolers instead of eighteen and twenty, respectively.

And then it was France. Especially Northern France. I was a medieval history major as an undergraduate, and Norman history is as fascinating to me as toxins are to Jason, my chemistry professor husband. I could revisit Paris, see the cathedral in Rouen, visit the abbeys founded by William the Conqueror and his queen, Mathilda, and examine the Bayeux tapestry. The very itinerary of the tour sent shivers of delight up my spine.

And the food! Where better to write about food than France? (I am a culinary writer with a book on New Orleans cuisine in progress and a contract to write food columns for newspapers.) Not to mention the fact that we Blues all love good food.

And when better to travel to France than in the spring, when the weather would be cool and pleasant, perhaps even rainy? Rather than hot and hotter, as can be expected in El Paso in April. Our new location pretty much moves from wimpy winter to blazing summer with a month of dust storms in between.

The only drawback that I could see was the promise I made to look out for the sixteen-year-old daughter of Judith Atwater, the woman whose husband had just undergone unexpected bypass surgery and whose tour reservations we would be assuming. But how much trouble could the girl be? I'd already raised one of my own.

I was ecstatic! And how mistaken my expectations were!

The tour began with an accident and ended with a murder. I can still see those two hands clutching the gun, aiming, as our small group gazed, entranced, at a beautiful cathedral shining with golden light in the darkness of a French town. I hear my own voice crying, "No!" and the shocking crack of gunshots. I see the blood and the bodies. And I feel the guilt. Because I might have stopped it.

1

The Dangers of Luggage Carousels

Carolyn

Paris, Giverny, Rouen, Mont-Saint-Michel, Caen, Saint-Malo, the Loire Valley—a veritable feast for a culinary writer and history enthusiast. So why was I not full of delight and anticipation after landing in Paris at the Charles de Gaulle Airport? Instead, I moped forlornly by the baggage carousel envisioning the horror of days, maybe weeks, without clean clothes, which I consider of paramount concern for happy traveling. It's a preference I picked up from my mother, who was a stickler for clean clothes.

So what was I to do now? I had neither clean clothes nor any faith in my ability to use a foreign Laundromat if I'd had clothes to wash in one. And our luggage still hadn't appeared. In fact, very few bags were left unclaimed, but those that still trundled by looked as deserted as I felt.

My husband had gone off to do battle with Air France over our lost luggage. My son Chris had been sent to find a representative of our tour company and was undoubtedly using his assignment to check out the young ladies of France, all anorexic, black-clad creatures of mystery—at least to young American males. I remained at my station by the moving belt, looking at each piece that came by in the hope that some clever French baggage handler had managed to unearth our suitcases from the bowels of the plane on which we had flown from London. No such luck. For all I knew, the baggage handlers of the Charles de Gaulle Airport had gone on strike in the middle of unloading our plane, as French workers are wont to do. There were a few other woebegone persons staring at the nearly empty carousel with the same expression of waning hope and dire foreboding that was reflected, I am sure, on my face.

I'd not only have no clean clothes, but also no cosmetics, no jewelry, no umbrella, and no washcloth. The French do not provide washcloths in their hotels! How can one wash one's face without a washcloth? Or one's ears? Ears cannot be washed by sticking them under the shower. They fill with water and no longer function properly. They probably develop infections or fungi. Mother was always adamant that I dry my ears carefully after washing. Funny how you remember every word your mother said, even though she died when you were twelve.

Were we supposed to spend our precious allotment of time in Paris shopping for clothes in strange department stores, where the clerks would speak French and pretend not to understand one's attempts at communicating in their language? Not that I can pronounce French, but still . . . And no doubt, French department stores don't even stock washcloths.

My gloomy musings were interrupted when lights flashed, unintelligible announcements burbled over the loudspeaker system, a new horde of passengers came rushing up to surround me, and a whole new avalanche of suitcases thundered into view. Was there even the remotest possibility that ours would be among them?

"Excuse me, sir," I said to a respectable-looking gentleman who had just stopped beside me. He was wearing a suit, rather than the casual clothes in which Americans usually travel. "Do you speak English?"

"Certainly, madam," he replied. "And several other languages as well. Do you require someone to translate from the French for you?" He was actually a fine-looking man, probably ten years or so my senior, average height, stocky but not fat, and possessed of a full and somewhat wavy head of gray hair. And he was an American. The accent was unmistakably American, possibly even Midwestern, like mine.

"No, thank you," I replied. "I just wanted to ask if you came in on Air France from London."

"From London, yes, but ours was a charter from Chicago O'Hare. We passengers are a conglomeration of different tour groups, all setting out from Paris to different parts of France. Not that I am an advocate of tours, but as it happened, the university at which I teach was sponsoring a tour of Northern France at a price that I simply could not pass up, being, as I am, a professor specializing in the history of medieval France. Is something the matter, madam? You look befuddled."

"You're not Professor Jean-Claude Childeric, are you?" Then I felt so silly. That was like saying, "Oh, you're from Chicago. Do you know my husband's mother, Gwenivere Blue?"

However, the gentleman's face lit up, and he said, "I perceive that my renown precedes me. Are you, by any chance, a fellow medievalist, dear lady?"

Now I really was embarrassed. "I am fond of medieval history," I admitted, "although certainly no expert. A friend, whose tickets on the Northern France tour my husband and I are using, because her husband just had bypass surgery, mentioned your—"

"The delightful Mrs. Atwater!" he exclaimed. "And you must be Mrs. Blue."

"Yes." I was astounded. "Evidently we're going on the same tour."

"Ah, but that is the least of the amazing coincidences inherent in this chance meeting, for your friend, Mrs. Atwater, has prevailed upon me to share a room with your son."

"I didn't know that," I said weakly. I had known that Chris was to share a room with someone but had imagined that it would be some other professor's son, maybe even someone Chris had known at our former university. My husband Jason moved us to El Paso, Texas, last year in his pursuit of ever more interesting problems in environmental toxicology.

"I do hope that your offspring is not given to playing loud rock music or staying glued to the television," said the professor jovially, although I detected a hint of serious concern behind this inquiry.

"I'm sure he'll do his best to prove an acceptable roommate," I murmured. Oh dear. Even on so slight an acquaintance, I did not anticipate that Chris would be much taken with Professor Childeric, especially since my son's preferred destination for his spring break had been Padre Island, where half-naked coeds from all over the country would be romping on the beach.

"Dr. Thomas-Smith will be happy to know that you have joined the group," said Dr. Childeric.

"I don't believe I know him."

"Her. She is a professor of nutrition, a spinster."

"And her name is Thomas? How unusual."

"No, dear lady, Thomas-Smith, a hyphenated family name. Be that as it may, Dr. Thomas-Smith's given name is Anna, not Thomas, and she was prevailed upon by Mrs. Atwater to room with the Atwater girl. I'm told that Dr. Thomas-Smith is not happy with the situation, although they have yet to spend a night in the same room. But at least now that you are here, she can relinquish chaperone duties. The girl disappeared at O'Hare, in search of an airport T-shirt, I believe, and caused great consternation."

"Young people do like T-shirts," I replied, hoping that she would not take to disappearing during this tour. Now I began to question my readiness to keep an eye on young Edie in return for a discount on the tour tickets. Judith Atwater hadn't wanted her daughter to miss the educational experience offered by a visit to France.

Surely, I comforted myself, a girl with an interest in French history would soon lose interest in T-shirts and the like when more fascinating experiences were on offer. Our Gwen has always been an inquisitive and cooperative traveler. And even if Edie was a handful, she might become smitten with Chris, my handsome son, who is blond, tanned, and terribly intelligent, although I'm not sure that intelligence is high on the list of desirable male characteristics among high school girls. Still, if she liked him, she might tag around after him. Chris wouldn't be pleased, but I'd always know where she was.

"Why are so many of the bags wrapped in plastic?" I asked. As we talked, I had been keeping an eye on the luggage, but so many suitcases were completely covered with what looked like Saran Wrap that I feared being unable to identify ours if they turned up.

"It is some service offered by the English," Professor Childeric replied. "Perhaps to keep luggage handlers from stealing one's belongings. That does happen, you know. Crime is rampant, even in the most civilized of countries. My wife had her handbag stolen on the Paris Metro as the train approached the Cluny station. I was shocked to think that visitors journeying to one of the world's finest medieval museums have to run such risks."

"It is a wonderful place, isn't it?" I exclaimed enthusiastically. "What a thrill to be able to turn the pages of the Duc de Berry's gorgeous *Book of Hours*."

Professor Childeric beamed at me and clasped my elbow in delight. "My dear lady," he cried happily, "you are familiar with—" But he was unable to finish because he went sprawling onto the luggage carousel, his head slamming into a large, gray, hard-sided, American Tourister two-suiter. Since his hand was on my elbow, I might well have followed him into danger had not my son appeared at my side and saved me from a nasty and undignified spill.

2

Meeting a Gendarme

Carolyn

"Mom, are you okay?" Chris asked as he pulled me to safety. "What happened?"

"Yes to your first question, and I have no idea to your second. We'd better rescue the professor." We pushed our way through the crowd, none of whom thought to do anything but stare at the dazed and groaning traveler being carried away among the suitcases.

"Help!" he cried. His legs were kicking frantically, one foot over the lower edge of the carousel, while he clasped his head with both hands. I could see the blood seeping between his fingers.

"He's hemmed in by the bags, Chris," I said. "You're going to have to grab his feet."

As my son tried, an even bigger bag toppled over onto the professor's shoulder. He moaned and tried to move away. Chris said, "Shit," and reached out again to capture a foot.

"Watch your language," I gasped, breathless because we were both chasing after the victim as he circled the carousel. Chris jumped onto the moving belt himself, heaved off two bags that were pinning the professor, then grasped him under the arms and half shoved, half lifted him free. Jean-Claude Childeric staggered and fell to his knees, continuing to moan. I helped him up and kept him from falling over once he was on his feet. The poor man was not only shaken, but his forehead was bleeding copiously.

By the time Chris had jumped off and come back to prop Professor Childeric up on the other side, we had been joined by a French policeman, heavily armed and very stern looking, who proceeded to lecture my brave son and the unfortunate medievalist.

"This man is bleeding!" I broke in.

"Now, Mother," murmured Chris. "Don't make a scene." For no known reason, offspring become embarrassed when their mothers exercise proper indignation in public places.

The policeman had turned to me. "Madame, is not permitted for travelers to ride on baggage facilities. A fine of many francs can be assessed onto such—"

"For goodness' sake, Officer, he fell! Look at his forehead. And my son got up there to rescue him. Where were you when all this was happening?"

Blood was running between the professor's eyebrows and down his nose like red wine from a *bota*. (This is a Spanish wine carrier with a long spout used in a bizarre ritual that involves pouring wine onto one's forehead in such a way that it will eventually run into one's mouth—or perhaps that's a Basque custom rather than Spanish.) In Dr. Childeric's case, it was running off his chin and onto his clothing. I quickly searched my purse for Kleenex and Band-Aids. "It's bad enough that Air France lost my luggage," I said to the officer, "but for the French authorities to harass visitors to the country, one of whom has just been injured in a completely unintended fall—"

"I was pushed!" interrupted Jean-Claude Childeric. Then he translated that remark for the policeman while Chris and I exchanged surprised looks as I tried to clean the blood away with Kleenex. Why would someone push a traveler onto the baggage carousel? I was now wondering how much wine the professor had imbibed aboard the plane and how appropriate a roommate he would make for my son.

Then I got a good look at the cut on his forehead. It was deep and still bleeding. He must have hit a sharp edge on that suitcase with great force. In which case maybe he *had* been pushed. A frightening thought!

I broke into the discussion between our countryman and the French police officer to say, "This man needs a doctor. He needs stitches. *Dottore. Comprende?*"

"That's Italian, dear lady, not French," said the professor. "Perhaps Spanish, as well. I'm afraid I'm feeling too ill to distinguish."

"Exactly," I agreed. "You need medical attention. Monsieur Gendarme, please summon a doctor immediately."

The policeman produced a cell phone, on which he made a call. No doubt, he said unpleasant things about Americans, but evidently he did summon medical assistance.

"Well, I suppose one can't expect much of the Paris police," I murmured consolingly to the professor as I blotted up more blood from his face with a Kleenex and tried to close the wound and stem the bleeding with two Band-Aids. "They were, after all, founded for the sole purpose of protecting people on their way to and from dinner parties, which seems a somewhat frivolous mission." I used my ministrations as an opportunity to sniff my patient's breath. He didn't *smell* of alcohol. The policeman evidently heard and took amiss my bit of historical information on the Paris police, for he muttered under his breath in French while aiming resentful glances in my direction.

"Frivolous perhaps, but very French, don't you think?" Professor Childeric replied, seemingly cheered by this bit of French history. He then thanked Chris for rescuing him. "I fear that I was quite stunned by my collision with that suitcase. In fact, I may have sustained a second injury. My shoulder is aching abominably. Had you not come to my aid, young man, I might well have been whisked off to some baggage room and arrested as a presumptive terrorist trying to tamper with airplane luggage." He chuckled weakly at his own wit.

"Professor, this is my son Christopher Blue. Chris, Professor Childeric will be your roommate for the duration of the trip." I slipped the first aid kit back into my handbag and turned to greet my husband, who had just arrived on the scene.

"As of now," said Jason, "they don't know what happened to our bags."

"What will we do?" I cried, aghast.

"They've provided us with emergency lost-luggage packets." Jason had three under his arm. "Air France T-shirt and toiletries, I believe."

"What good will a T-shirt do me?" I muttered miserably.

"I'll take it if you don't want it," said a young girl who had joined our group, uninvited. "Hi, Professor Childeric. What happened to your head? You're all bloody. Did you insult that policeman? Did he hit you with his nightstick?"

"Ah, Edie, I see that you have managed to escape once more from Professor Thomas-Smith," said the medievalist. He was sounding weaker. "Mrs. Blue, this is your charge, Edie Atwater."

But the T-shirt-loving Edie was paying no attention to me. She had spotted my son and sidled up to him, eyelashes fluttering. "Hello there. Are you on our tour, too?"

She was a pretty girl, and Chris, from whom I had expected disinterest in high school girls, smiled at her.

Oh dear. Maybe I had a more onerous burden to look forward to with this young lady than trying to keep her from disappearing into T-shirt shops or harboring a secret admiration for Chris. I foresaw having to defend my son's virtue, or hers. This was not a promising introduction to our tour.

Two men in white rolled up a stretcher, and the policeman insisted that

a protesting Professor Childeric allow himself to be put on the gurney and
wheeled away. I felt very sorry for him, but he did need medical attention.
By way of consolation, I called after him that we'd tell the tour director
what had happened to him so that he would be well represented in his dealing with French medical personnel and the police. He raised a hand forlornly as he disappeared into the crowd.

"Carolyn," said my husband, "you've got blood on your jacket."

*Oh dear, I thought. No change of clothes, and I picked this particular
afternoon to minister to the wounded. I don't even have my spot removers;
they're in the lost luggage.*

Travel Journal
Day One, Paris, afternoon at the hotel

Can't believe I did that!

*But then I couldn't believe it when I discovered that Jean-Claude
Childeric was joining the tour group. A man I've hated for years. A man
I'd almost got over obsessing about. Not that I've forgiven the S.O.B., but
at least I haven't been thinking about him much.*

*That's why I signed up for this trip. A first step toward a less dreary
life. Now he's going to ruin it just like he's ruined everything else.*

*Even so, I don't go around shoving people. Not since I was a kid. Must
have been his self-congratulatory manner. Or his offensive flirtation with
that blonde woman by the luggage belt.*

*Suddenly I felt this bolt of Childeric-loathing, and I gave him a good,
hard push.*

No plan, no hesitation. Just whomp, and over he went.

No one in the department would believe I had it in me.

And it was so satisfying!

*To see him sprawling among the scuffed-up luggage of strangers. His
cherished dignity in tatters. Blood all over his head.*

*I would have laughed out loud if I hadn't been disappearing as fast as
I could into the crowd.*

*That's the really strange thing. I pushed a well-dressed man onto a lug-
gage carrier, and no one noticed.*

No one shouted, "Assault" or whatever the French word is.

*No one denounced me to the police. I just drifted away in the other di-
rection and picked up my bag about ten feet closer to the carousel entrance. Then turned to watch the hubbub—the blood dripping down his
nose. He once described it to me as classic. (I ask you: Who refers to his
own nose as classic?)*

*Some young man jumped up on the belt and hauled him off. That must
have hurt. Getting dragged along, hoisted up, and dumped off. He certainly did a lot of groaning. I enjoyed that, too.*

Then the blonde woman came at him with Kleenex and Band-Aids.

Professor Hoping-to-Be-the-Next-Dean must have been thoroughly humiliated.

Good!

Best day I've had in a long time.

If he's badly enough hurt, he'll have to go home.

3

A First Taste of Paris

On a recent trip to France one of the things I looked forward to eating was *pâté de foie gras*. It is not, believe me, anything like American chicken liver pâté. The French version is mild, rich, and creamy; it melts on your tongue in a burst of gentle but compelling flavor—a flavor so delightful one almost forgets that some profit-minded farmer force-fed a goose to produce the swollen liver that makes French pâté.

Given the cost (it's expensive) and the anticipation engendered by good French pâté, it is something one hopes to share with loved ones. Accordingly, I could hardly believe that my husband and son slipped out on our first day in Paris while I was napping, ordered pâté without me, and devoured it all. They didn't even bring a crackerful back to the room for the family culinary researcher. And worse, they told me, in vivid detail, how good it had been.

Because the name is so marvelously French, one would think that *pâté de foie gras* originated in France. Where else? But it didn't. Around 400 B.C. a king of Sparta received as a gift from Egypt some plump geese, whose purpose was to provide what we now know as *pâté de foie gras*. The question is, did King Agesilaus appreciate the pâté? Or did he consider it an effeminate repast, fit only for nonwarrior types? These enlarged goose livers were popular with the Roman nobility as well as the ancient Egyptians, and only in the eighteenth century did a young French chef, Jean-Joseph Clausse, whip up pâté for his ducal patron, then governor of Strasbourg in Alsace. It contained black Perigord truffles and became popular all over Europe.

Carolyn Blue, "Have Fork, Will Travel," *Madison University Banner*

Jason

As she always does when struck down by jet lag, Carolyn collapsed into heavy sleep in the hotel room once she had attended to her most urgent concerns. First, she scrubbed the blood of a clumsy medievalist from her jacket. Second, she took a shower. Then, complaining all the while about the indignity of having no clean clothes to wear for goodness knows how long, she hung the various pieces of her only outfit on separate hangers to air on the balcony. I had to point out that other guests of the hotel used the balcony to get to their rooms.

Our hotel was a very peculiar one. From the public rooms, we had to cross a courtyard, take an elevator to the second story of a second building, cross over a second courtyard by way of a crosswalk, then take a second elevator to the third floor of a third building, where we walked along the balcony in question to find our room.

Fearing that passersby might steal her only outfit, Carolyn agreed to suspend it inside an open window. I pointed out that the room was hot, and if we opened the windows, we couldn't very well use the air conditioning promised in the brochure. I needn't have worried. I never did find an air conditioner.

Then Carolyn fretted because *my clothes* could only be aired after I went to bed for the night. Have you ever noticed how obsessive women are about clean clothes and frequent changes, while we men are perfectly happy to wear the same trousers all week long as long as we haven't left samples of our dinners on them? It would be interesting to see a statistical analysis of the matter to find out whether this clean-clothes fetish was always part of the female psyche or resulted from the advent of the automatic washing machine.

While I was making a second search for the promised air conditioner, Carolyn burst from the bathroom, wrapped in a towel and coughing violently. She had used the spray deodorant provided in the Air France lost-luggage package. As soon as she opened the bathroom door, the deodorant fumes wafted into the room, and I began to cough as well. God knows what toxic gas lurked in the aerosol. I couldn't identify the chemical because it was disguised by perfume, but I would have liked to know its composition.

I felt rather inconsiderate about leaving her in a room scented with possibly dangerous fumes, but she urged me to go, pointing out that Chris would be anxious to have lunch and begin an exploration of Paris and that he was undoubtedly waiting for me in the lobby. I only hoped that his roommate, Dr. Childeric, with whom I had served on academic committees in the past, would not be with him. Despite the heat and the fumes, Carolyn had dropped into deep sleep before I slipped from the room.

"Listen, Dad," said Chris as we walked next door to a sidewalk café for lunch, "is there any chance I could change rooms with someone? This guy I'm sharing with just spent fifteen minutes telling me how lucky I am because my education will be 'incalculably enhanced' is how he put it, by being around him because he knows everything there is to know about French history, especially medieval French history. Like if I really wanted to know anything about it I couldn't ask Mom."

I had been studying the menu during my son's lament. I did, of course, sympathize with him, and I, too, would rather get my historical tidbits from Carolyn, who wasn't given to droning on and on, but I doubted that there was anyone for Chris to change with and said so. "We're supposed to have a welcome banquet tonight," I remarked. "Shall we eat light now?"

"Light?" Chris looked as if I had suggested that we eat bugs. "I'm hungry."

"I was thinking maybe bread, wine, pâté, cheese—"

"You're kidding, right?"

My son, who has more culinary sophistication than most young men his age, loves pâté and good French cheeses, and he is developing a palate for wine—at home. Carolyn is adamant that he not disobey the law by ordering alcohol in public places until he's twenty-one. However, in France he could have a glass of wine without putting either of us at legal risk.

"Can we afford pâté?" he asked.

"I think, considering what I just made during my week consulting in New York, that we can have an order of pâté."

He grinned with delight. "I'm game if you are. You sure Mom won't flip about the wine?"

"We've already discussed it, and since it's legal in France, we settled on a glass at meals if you want it."

"All *right!*" Chris beamed at me and then added, "If we can afford pâté, how about some caviar, too?"

"On the flight over, your mother told me that the Spanish conquistadors discovered the Indians in South America eating, among other interesting things, the roe of water bugs, which they said tasted like caviar."

"Gross," said my son. "Where does she find stuff like that? If I didn't know better, I'd say she made it up." Then he eyed me suspiciously. "Is that a roundabout way of telling me, no caviar?"

"Just a point of information. But you're right. No caviar."

I ordered our lunch, and Chris returned to his discussion of Professor Childeric. "And he's not only a bore; he's a nut. He said—and I'm not kidding about this—that a 'strapping young fellow like me' could make myself useful by keeping an eye out for his enemies. Enemies? Give me a break! He thinks someone pushed him onto the baggage thingamabob at the airport. Well, he did fall onto it, but why would anyone push him? Probably just embarrassed that I had to haul him off before he disappeared through the leather curtains. I wish I'd let him."

Chris spread newly delivered pâté on a piece of crusty French bread, devoured it, followed with a gulp of white wine, and said, "Oh man, if my fraternity brothers could see me now! They think it's a big night when the cook puts meatballs in the spaghetti at the house."

"Jason Blue?" I glanced toward the new voice and recognized a tall, thin, dark-haired man with an angular face and vague eyes sitting at a table near us—Hugh Fauree, a parasitologist at my former university. I had often chatted with him about things scientific before committee meetings. If I remembered correctly, he was a widower with several relatively young children, whom he had probably brought along.

"Hugh, good to see you. This is my son Chris."

On being invited, Hugh joined us, bringing along a glass of beer and a vegetable salad. "I couldn't help overhearing you about Childeric," he said to Chris. "Consider yourself lucky that he doesn't suspect *you* of pushing him at the airport. He accused me just now in the lobby, and I didn't even see the incident."

"Well, at least you're not rooming with him," said Chris gloomily. Then he brightened. "Say, do you have a roommate?"

"No, I have a room to myself, but it's very small," said Fauree, "and I'm looking forward to enjoying my nights in single, if cramped, solitude."

Chris looked disappointed. As I had feared, he must have been planning to suggest himself to fill a spot in Fauree's room. "Look, Dad," he said, turning to me, "couldn't you and Mom have a cot put in your room for me?"

"We don't have space for a chair, much less a cot," I replied. "Be glad you got to come along at all."

Looking somewhat sulky, Chris helped himself to bread and Camembert and muttered something about the missed joys of Padre Island, where no one would have wanted to force-feed him medieval French history and the sands were littered with pretty girls his own age.

I asked Fauree why Childeric would think him capable of an airport assault and discovered that the two were nominees for the position as dean of arts and sciences. "They decided to appoint someone from the faculty, and I'm the science candidate," said Fauree. "Childeric and Laura de Sorentino, chair of modern languages, are the arts candidates." He took a long swallow of his beer and added wryly, "For no discernible reason, Childeric seems to think he has the edge, although Laura and I are chairs, and he's never held an administrative post."

"Congratulations," I said.

"Thanks. I figured if I could stand dealing with the biologists, I might as well take on the rest of the college. The selection committee will want another scientist, don't you think?"

"You're a brave man," I replied evasively. "Many a happy scholar has been turned into an unhappy bureaucrat by accepting a deanship."

"Yeah, but isn't one qualification to be a dean stuffiness?" asked Chris, grinning and devouring chunks of pâté. "I'll bet Professor Childeric's got you beat there, Dr. Fauree. He's the most boring man I ever met, and I've been an academic kid all my life."

Fauree started to laugh. "Maybe if you pointed that out to him, Chris, he'd stop suspecting me of skullduggery in the name of ambition."

"Jason Blue!" I found myself grasped by the face, turned, and given a smacking kiss on the mouth. Oh God, I thought, recognizing my assailant, Dr. Roberta Hecht—a friend of Carolyn's, a world-renowned expert on the art of Joan Miró, and a self-proclaimed serial monogamist. She claims to have grown up in the Church of the Latter-Day Saints and given it up for her own version of Mormonism, one more favorable to women. An attractive woman of Amazonian proportions, she does have a certain Mormon aura of robust health and clean living, but there any resemblance ends. Her post-Mormon period includes four husbands that I know of.

"Robbie," I murmured, thinking, where was one's wife when one needed her for protection against casually affectionate women? Since my defense was in my own hands, I hastily directed Robbie's attention elsewhere before she could progress to the French cheek-kissing ritual, for which she was puckering up. "You remember Chris?"

She glanced over my shoulder, spotted Chris, smiled enthusiastically, and transferred the cheek kissing to him. Chris flushed but rose to the occasion and returned the kisses. "You dear, handsome boy! But then you're not a boy anymore, are you?"

Christ! Surely, she wouldn't go after my twenty-year-old son. That would be distressingly inappropriate.

"And who is this handsome fellow?" she asked, releasing Chris and zooming in on Hugh. I introduced them. Roberta couldn't believe she'd never met such a fascinating man, and at her own university. She kissed Hugh, who didn't kiss her back but did look bemused.

"Well, who are you married to this year, Robbie?" I asked heartily in a none-too-subtle attempt to forewarn my colleague.

"No one at all." She dragged a chair over from another table, earning a disapproving look from a French couple, and slid in beside Hugh. "I have snipped my latest matrimonial ribbons with the golden shears of divorce and am as carefree as a Miró bird, but more mobile."

Carefree and on the prowl for number five, I thought.

"Hi, Dr. Blue," said a sugar-sweet young voice. "I'm looking for your wife."

"Carolyn's trying to sleep off jet lag this afternoon, Edie," I said to Judith Atwater's daughter. "Isn't Dr. Thomas-Smith in your room to—"

"Oh, she's gone off to get tickets for some dreary classical concert tomorrow night at a place called Saint Chapel. Hi, Chris. Can I join you? O-o-o, you're drinking wine. That's *so* cool."

I could see that my son not only agreed with her but also was happy to have his sophistication affirmed by a pretty girl. He purloined the last available chair from the table of the French couple. They responded by glaring at him, after which they slapped down some francs and stalked off with their miniature poodle, which had been yapping annoyingly under the table.

"Can I have a glass of wine, Dr. Blue?" Edie gave me a melting glance.

"You're only sixteen," I replied. "I'm not sure what French law is on the subject, but I'd certainly need written permission from your mother."

Edie looked sulky. Roberta Hecht was telling Hugh that he simply had to see some Miró prints she was carrying because they had little squiggles that were surely parasites. "Think of what a paper we could write together, identifying the actual parasites painted by Joan Miró. Interdisciplinary research is very chic. We might even get an article accepted to *Nature*—Miró prints, parasite photos."

"Did Miró know anything about parasites?" Hugh asked, as any practical man of science would. Still, I could tell that he was already falling under the spell of Robbie's maniacally romantic personality. He'd probably never run into anything like it.

"So, Edie," I said, turning to the teenager, who was now clinging to my son's arm and telling him how "cool" it was that he was a real fraternity man. "The concert you mentioned. Could the venue have been Sainte-Chapelle?"

"Maybe," said Edie cautiously.

"Do you remember anything about the program?"

"Oh yeah. *The Four Seasons*. Boy, does that sound—"

"Mom would love it," said Chris. "Vivaldi at Sainte-Chapelle. I wouldn't mind seeing the place myself."

"Me too!" said Edie. "Wow, Vivalti!"

"Let's pick up some tickets and surprise your mother," I suggested to Chris, and we were soon on our way.

Roberta claimed to love Vivaldi as well, and insisted that Hugh accompany her to the concert—as her guest. When he looked reluctant, she exclaimed, "How could a man with a name like Fauree pass up Vivaldi?" Then she punched him playfully on the shoulder. Hugh blinked. Roberta looked at the shoulder with interest and exclaimed, "Great muscle tone! You could be a kayaker."

"I am a kayaker."

"Me too," said Roberta.

Suddenly Hugh Fauree looked much more interested in attending a Vivaldi concert, and I thought with foreboding that my friend might well be paddling in romantic rapids the likes of which he had never encountered.

"Oh, I want to go too," exclaimed Edie.

"Isn't Anna getting you a ticket?" I asked.

"She said I wouldn't like it. She's going with Professor Petar, who's a real cut-off-their-balls feminist." She looked very pleased with this daring choice of words, then amended hastily, "Well, that's what my dad says, anyway."

4
French Lasagna

I recently found myself in Paris—the font of fine food, the Mecca of Haute Cuisine—anticipating the gala welcome banquet that was to launch an exciting tour of Northern France. Was I subsequently titillated by tasty hors d'oeuvres? Entranced by elegant entrées? Delighted by delicious desserts? I was not. A fish mousse of world-class insipidity greeted us at the table, and we were sent on our way with a boring custard pie. In between these disappointments was lasagna. Not even good lasagna. Wine was not included. To add insult to injury, we paid $15.65 American for a half-carafe of the house red, a mediocre vintage of no pretensions whatever.

My husband is still indignant over that fifteen-plus dollars. He mentions it every time he opens a bottle of wine at home. "This particular Australian Shiraz cost only $10.98," he says, pouring a small portion for tasting. "It's a full bottle, you'll notice, not a half-carafe." He sniffs, then sips appreciatively. "And it's excellent!" My husband likes to get his money's worth when it comes to wine. And I, it would seem, do not like French lasagna. In fact, why would a welcome-to-Paris dinner feature lasagna?

Carolyn Blue, "Have Fork, Will Travel," *Grand Rapids Post-Meridian*

Carolyn

At six-thirty Paris time our group met in a room adjacent to the hotel lobby. Standing among and sitting on bamboo chairs and settees with lavishly flowered, if lumpy, cushions, we introduced ourselves to strangers, renewed friendships with people we had known in the past, and then listened to our guide, Denis. He had a lovely French accent, a dubious grasp of French history, a lively imagination, an extensive wardrobe of black turtlenecks and jeans, and one black sports jacket. Most of this I found out as the tour progressed, but his penchant for lively and fictitious historical discourse was immediately evident.

For instance, he told us that Saint Denis, after whom he was named, had been a native of the Paris region.

"He most certainly was not," muttered Professor Childeric, who had attached himself to me early in the social hour. "He was an Italian sent to Gaul by Pope . . ."

I couldn't help noticing that the medievalist had four stitches holding the wound on his forehead together, that they were sewed with black thread, and that the surrounding area had been painted with a red-orange disinfectant. He looked almost raffish.

"Would you like me to provide you with a gauze pad and clear tape for your forehead?" I whispered.

"You're very thoughtful," he whispered in return. "Unfortunately, the doctor told me to leave the injury uncovered to promote healing and under no circumstances to scrub off the disinfectant. I fear that I must resign myself to looking like some disreputable pugilist until the stitches can be removed."

"The patron saint of our country," Denis was saying, "converted his heathen brethren by introducing them to the use of herbs in their cuisine, thus establishing the French tradition of fine food, which we are about to sample."

Professor Childeric positively growled with indignation and informed me that nothing whatever was known of the saint's preferences in food, except that he was given to fasting.

In my opinion, I whispered back, the advent of haute cuisine in France was the doing of Catherine de Medici, Italian wife of one of the Kings Henri. She brought her own chefs to the marriage.

"Exactly," said Childeric.

"Sadly, the Bishop of Paris was beheaded by jealous pagans who couldn't tell rosemary from hemlock, after which he delighted his followers and converted his enemies by picking up his head and walking off with it," Denis reported in conclusion.

What a delightful story! I thought.

"Balderdash!" shouted Childeric. "There is absolutely no documentation for that fairy tale."

"It is a tradition that is cherished and attested to by all loyal Frenchmen," retorted Denis cheerfully, making a small but graceful bow in the direction of his critic. "The veneration of Saint Denis was a favorite cause of our own Saint Louis, the tenth King Louis of France."

"Ninth," I murmured discreetly.

"Idiot!" cried Childeric, throwing his hands in the air.

My head whipped around in surprise. Was he talking about me?

"The king who particularly favored the cult of Denis was Louis the Pious, not Saint Louis."

Ah, he was still correcting our guide. How embarrassed I would have been had I named the wrong Louis.

Denis the Guide smiled beatifically at the professor and said, "As you Americans say, 'Whatever.' Now, shall we abandon French history for French cuisine?"

Unhappily, the dinner provided at the tour company's chosen restaurant was neither very good nor very French. In fact, our main course was a lasagna distinguished by leathery pasta, a cheese that no Italian would have allowed in the kitchen, bland tomato sauce, and stringy meat. I would be hard put to write a column in praise of French cuisine on the basis of that meal.

Dinner table conversation was as bizarre as the food was dull. Professor Childeric asked me in a whisper over the fish mousse whether I had observed Dr. Hugh Fauree pushing him onto the baggage carousel at the airport. Surprised, I replied that I hadn't seen Dr. Fauree at all until we met for the predinner lecture. Professor Childeric—he preferred *professor* to *doctor* because Europeans hold professors in such "high esteem"—assured me that Dr. Fauree had indeed pushed him, no doubt hoping to cause a more serious injury than had occurred.

"I'm sure you must be mistaken about Dr. Fauree. He is a very mild-mannered person, not at all the type to cause injury to another."

"Ah, but my dear lady, you are obviously unaware that Dr. Fauree has good cause to wish me ill. We are both candidates for the position of dean of the college of arts and sciences, we and a Professor Laura de Sorentino, an excellent French teacher but hardly a serious candidate. I, on the other hand, am, if I may presume to say so, the favored choice of the administration and the selection committee. No doubt Dr. Fauree is resentful, although I hardly think he should be surprised. I am, after all, a preeminent scholar of the Middle Ages in France."

"But pushing you onto a luggage carousel wouldn't advance his candidacy," I pointed out.

"Any public embarrassment is to be avoided by a candidate for high administrative office at a respected university. I have no doubt that he has already telephoned his supporters with scathing descriptions of my humiliation."

"Dr. Fauree spent the afternoon having lunch with my husband and securing tickets to a Vivaldi concert tomorrow evening at Sainte-Chapelle," I replied soothingly. "Does that sound like the sort of person who would push a colleague onto a luggage carousel?"

"Vivaldi? Sainte-Chapelle? Is the tour providing—no, obviously not. I must look into a ticket for myself. How unfortunate that my dear wife, who also loves the music of the Baroque, was unable to accompany me. She is playing in a national bridge tournament. A very competitive player, my wife. You say your husband is friendly with Dr. Fauree? Still, Mrs. Blue—may I beg the honor of calling you by your given name? Still, I hope that you will think well enough of me to keep a wary eye out on my behalf, lest another unfortunate *accident* befall me."

"Of course you may call me Carolyn," I replied without promising to act as his bodyguard. Good grief, the man might be a fountain of medieval information, but the impression he made was of a Victorian gentleman suffering from untreated paranoia. "But I'm sure you're wrong about Dr. Fauree," I added. "Jason thinks very highly of him."

"Then how would you explain my fall, dear lady? I have no other enemies that I know of, and I am not a clumsy person."

"You know, I have given what happened some thought, and it occurred
to me that you might be the victim of air rage. One reads frequently in the
newspapers about passengers and airline personnel being attacked by people driven beyond the bounds of civility by the terrible service, bad weather,
and problems caused by an antiquated air traffic control system."

"That is a delightfully imaginative hypothesis, my dear Carolyn, but I
fear that I have been the victim of promotion rage rather than air rage, as
you so quaintly put it."

Ah well, I could see that I wasn't going to change his mind. Perhaps time
and a good night's sleep would put him in a more reasonable frame of
mind. I smiled cordially and turned to Jason, who sat on my left. He was
poking suspiciously at the just-served lasagna and glad to be distracted.

5

Assorted Tourists

Carolyn

And what of the other tour participants? I found among us an old friend,
Robbie Hecht, Miró scholar and romantic adventurer. While we were
waiting to be seated at the restaurant, she entertained me with the tale of
her latest divorce, during which she and her fourth husband agreed on
every detail in the division of property except who got Buster, the offspring
of a favorite Irish setter (now deceased) owned by Robbie. In fact, she and
the latest husband met and fell in love when he came to buy the puppy.
Robbie was claiming right of prior ownership. That controversy was in the
courts still, although the divorce was final and Robbie was quite obviously
on the lookout for husband number five. She had set her cap with customary enthusiasm for Jason's friend, Hugh Fauree.

I warned her that Hugh had two children, a teenaged boy and a preteen girl,
who might not welcome a second wife so soon after their mother's death. Robbie just laughed and said it was about time that she tried her hand at motherhood and that skipping the pregnancy, childbirth, and diaper stages suited her
to a tee. She and Hugh sat together during dinner, Hugh obviously flattered by
the attentions of a handsome woman who loved kayaking. Evidently women
kayakers are hard to find. Even his late wife had not been willing to accompany
him on kayaking weekends. Also Robbie showed a remarkable interest in parasites; he confided this to me the next morning at breakfast.

Although I thought their blossoming infatuation quite sweet, Jason disapproved. I said, "Robbie's just looking for Mr. Right, and I wouldn't be surprised to find that Hugh is it."

"I'd be surprised," Jason grumbled. We agreed to disagree and stay out of it, always the most sensible course when mutual friends are beginning a relationship. Another attraction more problematical was that between our son and Edie Atwater, underage enchantress. Chris didn't sit with us because Professor Childeric did, and Edie sat with Chris and flirted blatantly.

Denis announced during dinner that all those who wished to participate in the tour of Paris the next morning should sign up in the lobby of the hotel tonight and meet there at eight-thirty tomorrow to catch the bus. Jean-Claude Childeric snorted and announced that he planned to visit the Cluny. Chris immediately opted for the tour, and Edie followed suit. Disheartened, I realized that perhaps it was my duty to go as well. Professor Childeric assumed aloud that I would want to accompany him to the museum, but Jason replied for me that we were going to the Rodin.

I squeezed Jason's hand appreciatively. And after all, what could Chris and Edie get up to while on a bus full of middle-aged professors and their spouses? However, Anna Thomas-Smith sent me a reproving glance and, looking much put upon, said that she supposed she'd have to go on the tour as well, since Edie needed looking after. I assuaged a guilty conscience by reasoning that, as a professor of home economics with a specialty in nutrition, she probably didn't want to go off on her own to a museum anyway.

I was evidently wrong about that because Dr. Janice Petar broke away from a conversation, bits of which I overheard after dinner, with Professors Nedda (English drama) and Macauley (creative writing) Drummond about postmodern novels.

"His wife must be the only person in the world who thinks well of that unintelligible stuff Macauley writes," she muttered as she walked up to me. "I'm Janice Petar. I don't think we met when you and your husband were at the university."

"No," I agreed. "Carolyn Blue." I shook her hand. "Did I understand you to say that Dr. Drummond is a published novelist, or does he critique postmodernism?"

"*Mr.* Drummond. He hasn't got a doctorate, and his dreary little novels are published by small presses and are absolute drivel exclaimed over by critics who wouldn't know a good read if it bit them on the ass."

"Really?" What could I say to that? Since she hadn't kept her voice down, Mr. Drummond and his wife were scowling at her.

"I hope you don't plan to saddle poor Anna with the responsibility for that young twit during the whole tour. She'd never have agreed to room with Edie if she hadn't thought you would be doing the chaperoning. Which reminds me—your name, Blue. That's unusual. You're not, by any chance, related to Professor Gwenivere Blue, are you?"

"My mother-in-law," I replied, suppressing a sigh. This lady reminded me of her, except that Janice Petar was younger.

"Good lord!" exclaimed Dr. Petar. "You have my sympathy. Although she is a powerful voice in my field, the chance of getting a mother-in-law like Gwenivere Blue is enough to keep any woman from marrying."

"Fortunately, I was wise enough to woo Carolyn before I let her meet my mother," said Jason. He had just joined us after escaping a conversation with Manfred Unsell, an economics professor who evidently viewed the tour as an opportunity to observe, while disguised as a tourist, the every-day impact of the European Common Market and the Euro.

His wife Grace, in her quiet way, made it clear that she'd just as soon have been at home, where her daughter was soon to give birth to the Unsells' first grandchild. While in France, Grace Unsell was never without a knitting bag, from which she pulled either some half-finished baby item or a cell phone, on which she solicited information on the pregnancy, the obstetrician's latest advice, the intrauterine kicking and somersaulting habits of the fetus, and so forth. I can't say that I blame Grace. I'd have found expectant grandmotherhood more interesting than the impact of the Euro on citizens and tourists in France. Jason wasn't interested in either.

"In fact, we were engaged before you introduced me to your mother," I said to Jason. "This is Dr. Janice Petar, who knows your mother professionally and who thinks we were remiss in letting Anna Thomas-Smith replace us as chaperones on the tour tomorrow."

"Janice, nice to see you again, and believe me, I never volunteered to be a chaperone," said Jason.

"Just like a man," retorted the feminist. "Leave the children to the women. You'll be sorry if your son gets her pregnant. How do you know that the girl is careful about contraception?"

"How do you know she's even sexually active?" Jason replied. Women like his mother get his back up.

Dr. Petar snorted. "Does she act like a shy virgin?"

"Rest easy, Dr. Petar. Our son does know about contraception, and he doesn't seduce underage girls," said Jason.

Another snort. "I doubt that he'll have to. Edie seems bent on seducing him."

I glanced over at the two young people in question and shuddered. Chris was talking to Denis, and Edie was gazing soulfully up at my son with a proprietary hand on his arm. Before we went up to our room, I took Dr. Thomas-Smith aside and told her how much I appreciated her sense of responsibility for young Edie. Then I listened sympathetically to her tale of the horrors of trying to find the girl in O'Hare Airport. Finally, I assured her that I'd be keeping an eye on Edie myself as I had promised her mother.

"I'm delighted to hear it. You and Professor Childeric seem to be good friends," she remarked.

"Actually, I only met the man this afternoon when he fell onto the baggage carousel at the airport," I replied. "My son rescued him."

"Really? I hope the professor wasn't hurt. I did notice the stitching on his forehead."

"Mostly his pride, I imagine," I replied, smiling. "Fortunately, he didn't sustain a concussion."

"But you did sit together at dinner."

"Yes, we have a mutual interest in medieval history, but mostly he thought he'd been pushed at the airport by—ah—someone on the tour. He wanted to know if I'd seen anything."

"My goodness. Had you?"

"Heavens no. Why would anyone who knows him push a medieval history professor in an airport? It was obviously a case of air rage."

"Yes. I read about a man who actually defecated on a meal tray because he didn't like airline food. A highly unsanitary method of protest." The nutritionist then engaged me in a rather technical discussion of teenagers' eating habits.

One does accumulate a lot of information when associating with academics. Had I been touring with any other group, I might never have learned the name of the pope who sent Saint Denis to France or the postmenopausal effect on a woman's bones of twenty-four ounces of milk a day during her teen years.

Travel Journal
Day One, after dinner in Paris

> *Now that shameless libertine is going after a married woman. Impressing her with all sorts of medieval foolishness. Maybe I should warn her that he's not to be trusted.*
>
> *Or maybe I should just give him another shove.*
>
> *Must put thoughts like that aside and concentrate on ignoring him.*
>
> *Dinner a disappointment. I wonder if the sauce on that lasagna contained horsemeat? It was very lean and tough.*
>
> *Thank God Childeric is going to the Cluny tomorrow. Now I know the place to avoid.*
>
> *If he continues to accuse Fauree of pushing him, that should cause some resentment.*
>
> *Maybe C. will ruin his own chances of becoming dean.*
>
> *I hope so.*

6

Aphrodisiac Art

Jason

On our first night in Paris. Carolyn complained about having to wear an Air France T-shirt to bed. Personally, I thought she looked quite fetching, and pointed out that our daughter liked to sleep in T-shirts. My wife replied that teenagers, being hormonally impaired, would wear anything favored by their contemporaries.

More worrisome to Carolyn was the continuing nonappearance of our luggage. "I am not going anywhere in three-day-old clothes," she declared. "You and Chris will have to buy me something."

"But we're going to the Rodin tomorrow," I protested.

"Not in dirty clothes."

"Carolyn, the French don't even wear deodorant," I argued. "They won't notice."

"The women don't shave their legs and underarms either, but that doesn't mean I'd go out in public covered with hair," she retorted. Needless to say, without the promised air conditioning, the room was very hot, and neither of us slept well. Carolyn awoke the next morning with a tension headache. While she was describing it in terms of a medieval torture that involved tightening a band on the prisoner's head until he or she fainted or died, the desk called to say that our bags were sitting outside our door.

"They'll have been stolen by now," Carolyn exclaimed when she heard. Fortunately, they hadn't been, and she made a miraculous recovery as she pulled out her washcloth and her cosmetics bag with its nontoxic deodorant. My wife has a thing about washcloths. I had to shower second because she was so anxious to use hers.

Our first breakfast in Paris consisted of the traditional croissants and coffee, over which we all discussed our plans for the day. Childeric was going to the Cluny to wallow in medieval artifacts, and no one offered to accompany him, although he made another try at talking Carolyn into it. He even invited me along, but only as a ploy to solicit her reconsideration. I had to wonder whether he was infatuated with my wife. He wouldn't be the first, not that Carolyn encourages or even notices that sort of thing.

Those opting for the tour with the guide, aside from my son and his groupie, were a sedate group: the Unsells, accompanied by her knitting and his long-winded warnings about the dangers of investing in European stocks when the new currency was so shaky; Anna Thomas-Smith, who had little to say for herself but called young Edie *Edwina* whenever her behavior seemed unacceptable (on the third such occasion the girl muttered, "You're not my mother," and Dr. Thomas-Smith replied, "No, but I certainly wish she were here"); Ivan and Estrella Markarov (Markarov is a computer science professor and his wife, a professor of preschool education who was shocked to hear that we'd be looking at naked statues); and Carl and Ingrid Jensen, respectively, an ag professor with an interest in cows and a county home economist who, when she heard that Carolyn wrote about food, gave her a casserole recipe whose basic ingredient was canned cream of mushroom soup.

I had envisioned Carolyn and I wandering through the gardens at the museum, which had been the sculptor's mansion, a formal, two-story stone building with ranks of tall, many-paned windows. These mildly romantic plans for a private day didn't work out. As soon as Carolyn mentioned where we were going, Roberta Hecht invited herself along, which is not surprising since she's an art historian and Miró did odd sculptures as well as curious paintings. That Roberta talked Hugh Fauree into accompanying us was a surprise. I've never known him to express an interest in sculpture. However, he let himself be persuaded—poor fellow! I'm sure he had no idea what she had in mind. I did because I heard her say to Carolyn that she hoped all those naked statues, suggestively entwined, would give Hugh ideas.

In addition to Hugh and Roberta, two other couples joined us. Jeremy and Hester Foxcroft are art professors and New Englanders. He specializes in traditional landscapes and she, in wildly modern art glass, of which the postmodernist Drummonds approved, although they didn't approve of Rodin. They invited Hester to accompany them on a trip to the Jeu de Paume, which had some "very avant garde exhibits." Her husband Jeremy talked her out of avant garde and was called a "reactionary" by Macauley Drummond.

The second couple was named de Sorentino. He is a plastic surgeon and she, the chair of modern languages, a strikingly beautiful woman with the gentle face of a young Madonna and the silver-streaked black hair of an older woman. This lady was the third dean candidate, the one not yet accused of anything by Childeric.

We had a very pleasant day. The others were new to the Rodin, and all were pleased with it. How could they not be? The museum attendants were not on strike, and the house is a beautiful venue for Auguste Rodin's powerful sculpture, which was displayed not only inside, but also outside in a lovely garden. Even the weather cooperated. It was warm, but a light breeze floated through the windows and cooled us outside as well. Much more comfortable than our room at the hotel.

Roberta may have been a bit too obvious in her enthusiasm for the

erotic statues, but Hugh responded favorably to her art-as-aphrodisiac ploy
as well as her art-critic-at-large explanations. The Foxcrofts both sketched
busily, she some of the less representational works inside, he various scenes
in the garden, myself included, unfortunately. There is nothing more embarrassing than being asked to sit for an artist.

Dr. de Sorentino, whose name is Lorenzo, compared his wife's face to
that of every female statue and found Rodin lacking. The man acted as if
he had personally created his wife. Laura de Sorentino seemed enchanted
by the sculptor and carried on conversations in fluent French with natives,
who were obviously charmed with whatever she had to say, or possibly
with how she looked and how well she spoke their language.

She and Carolyn seemed to form an immediate bond and sat together
for some time talking and laughing in the garden, after which we all went
out to lunch at a small, family-owned café that served only chicken dishes.
The special of the day was Poulet Marengo, a dish prepared for Napoleon
after he defeated the Austrians at the battle of Marengo. Carolyn told us
that, since the Emperor had been hungry and the supply wagons had not
yet caught up with the army, the chef was forced to make do with what he
could find in the area: a bottle of cognac, a scrawny chicken, six crayfish,
olive oil, garlic, and tomatoes. She ordered the dish for herself, sharing the
contents of an earthenware pot with the Foxcrofts and me. Lorenzo de
Sorentino insisted on some sort of Italian chicken and became very irritable
when his wife didn't like it and said they should have let Carolyn choose for
them, too.

With Laura's help, Carolyn managed to prevail on the proprietress for
the recipe and ask why her version contained mushrooms instead of crayfish, white wine instead of cognac, tomato paste instead of tomatoes, and
deep-fried eggs. The lady, red-faced from her morning in a hot kitchen,
replied that she was a woman of the Lyonnais and made Chicken Marengo
in the traditional way, as had her mother and grandmother, who knew more
about good food than any army cook, even if the man had served Napoleon
Bonaparte, who, after all, hadn't been a real Frenchman. Carolyn and
Laura dissolved into giggles as soon as the proprietress had returned to her
kitchen.

With our several chicken dishes we had loaves of crusty French bread
and carafes of cold white wine. It was an excellent midday meal, much better than dinner last night.

"Well," Carolyn said later as we took the Metro back to the hotel, "finally some food to write about."

7

The Prozac Dean

Carolyn

I had the most amazing conversation with Laura de Sorentino before we all went off to lunch. We were sitting together in the museum garden while my reluctant husband posed for a sketch by a landscape artist named Foxcroft, who had one of those slow, nasal, Down-East accents. If he hadn't been so completely involved in his sketch and in a verbal color analysis of fall in New England, I'd have taken him for a farmer from New Hampshire or Vermont. The conversation loosened up my embarrassed-to-be-sketched husband, who chimed in with information on the toxins in various oil paints. I'm sure Professor Foxcroft was amazed to learn how dangerous certain paints would be if he chose to eat, sniff, or paint himself with them. Still, he took the information in good part. Not everyone does.

At any rate, Laura introduced our remarkable chat by telling me how strange it was that all three finalists for the dean position should wind up on the same tour. "I realize that you know Childeric and Fauree personally, but you probably didn't know about me. I hope it doesn't make you uneasy seeing that Hugh is your husband's friend."

"Not at all," I replied. "I like to see women advancing into administrative positions. Not that I wasn't a stay-at-home mom for years, but even I'm trying to establish a career. I guess I'd be called the late-blooming, empty-nest entrée to the world of working women," I added wryly.

"The Empty-Nest Writer? I like that." She laughed and added, "If I get the dean's position, I suppose I'll be called the Prozac Dean."

I have to admit that her statement took me by surprise.

"I am a good chair."

"I'm sure you are."

"But I wouldn't have been ten years ago. Oh, I was a good teacher. Isn't that odd? I was horribly shy in any place but the classroom and very unsure of myself socially, for which I can thank Lorenzo. Being married to a plastic surgeon is not, believe me, a bed of roses."

"But I heard him say Rodin never sculpted a female who could compare to you."

"What he meant was Rodin couldn't compare to him—my husband. Every time I got comfortable with my face or figure, Lorenzo proposed some small improvement he could and did make. He considers me his creation."

I'm afraid I just stared at her in shock.

"I got so depressed that I started going to a psychiatrist. I was considering leaving Lorenzo and quitting teaching. Instead my therapist prescribed Prozac, and it made all the difference. The last time Lorenzo suggested a bit of surgery to improve me, I told him to bugger off." She chuckled happily. "Not a very ladylike thing to say. Lorenzo was terribly offended."

"I can imagine," I replied, grinning.

"Anyway, Prozac was a godsend. Suddenly—well, gradually—I was able to talk to people, and then I started heading off disputes in the department. Pretty soon I was being appointed to contentious committees with the idea that I'd make peace so something could get done. And it was so much fun! And people were so appreciative! The department got together, decided that they wanted me as chair, and petitioned the dean. The old chair left in a huff for another university, and everyone stopped squabbling; infighting had been the hallmark of our department. I used to cringe when we had departmental meetings and people started shouting at each other. Now I just speak up and talk them into something they can agree on."

She seemed so amazed and delighted with this new talent that I had to feel happy for her. It occurred to me that she'd probably make a much better dean than Jean-Claude Childeric, who thought he had the position sewed up. As interesting a fund of medieval information as he had, people in other disciplines would probably prefer someone who was interested in them and their problems.

"Of course, I doubt that I'll get the appointment, and that's fine. I'm happy where I am. In fact, just being nominated gives me new confidence. Lorenzo's latest campaign is to get me to dye my hair. Imagine! I don't have time for things like that."

"It's beautiful just the way it is," I said. "What's wrong with your husband? Any normal man would be delighted to be married to a woman as beautiful and intelligent as you," I added indignantly. Then, of course, it occurred to me that I wasn't being very diplomatic about her husband.

However, she was already saying, with remarkable good cheer, "Oh, Lorenzo's just shallow. That's another thing that depressed me in the old days, but now"—she shrugged expressively—"who cares?"

"I never realized that Prozac was so effective."

"It's a miracle drug," she said enthusiastically. "If I become dean, I'm going to organize Prozac Day and invite all students suffering from depression."

I suppose I looked dubious at that idea. "Just kidding," she said. "Our president would be horrified, mostly because he'd be afraid the university would have to provide the pills. They *are* expensive. On the other hand, it takes a whole box of chocolates to accomplish what one little pill will do without making you fat. Maybe I'll just have a sampler embroidered for my office. *Prozac at work here.*"

We were both laughing helplessly when Jason escaped from Professor Foxcroft and told us that we should consider getting some lunch.

The Prozac Dean? She'd probably be terrific!

Chicken Marengo

I obtained the following recipe from the owner and chef at a small restaurant in Paris. Although she took offense when I questioned the historical accuracy of the ingredients, her version of Chicken Marengo is very tasty. It may not have been what was served to Napoleon after his victory against the Austrians, but I have no doubt that he would have preferred it had he been given the choice.

Cut a *small roasting chicken (around 3 pounds)* into pieces.

Heat *3 tbs. olive oil* and *2 tbs. butter* in an earthen casserole or heavy Dutch oven, and sauté the chicken until golden brown on all sides.

Add *1 tsp. chopped shallots, salt, pepper, 1 tsp. dried tarragon, 1 clove finely chopped garlic, 1 cup dry white wine,* and cook until wine is reduced by half.

Add *2 tbs. tomato paste* and *1 cup chicken bouillon or 1 cup liquid from cooking ½ lb. mushrooms* in salted water, reserving mushrooms to add later.

When chicken is tender, place pieces on a heated platter. Reduce sauce and stir in *1 tbs. flour* blended with *1 tbs. butter.* Put mushrooms on the chicken, strain sauce over it, garnish with *parsley,* and serve hot.

To satisfy Napoleonic tradition, garnish with *crayfish (cooked, presumably).* To satisfy the lady from Lyon, surround the chicken with *deep-fried eggs.*

Carolyn Blue, "Have Fork, Will Travel," *San Mateo Messenger*

8

Killer Beef

Carolyn

I'll have beef tartare," I said to the waiter. Since the tour wasn't providing dinner, a number of us met before the concert at a sidewalk café in the neighborhood.

"Is Madame aware that the *boeuf* is—how to say?—not cook-ed?" asked the waiter.

"If it were cook-ed," I replied sweetly, "it wouldn't be beef tartare, would it?"

"Oh, gross," said Edie Atwater. "Raw meat?"

"It's awesome," Chris assured her. "I'll have it, too, and a glass of the house red."

"I'll have what he's having," Edie chimed in, evidently overcome by infatuation to the extent of no longer finding raw beef "gross."

"Without the wine," added Jason.

Edie pouted. Chris grinned. I thought that I'd have to watch those two. She was practically sitting in his lap at the crowded table, and Estrella Markarov, the bilingual preschool education professor, was eyeing them with disapproval. That afternoon Anna Thomas-Smith had hinted vaguely at improper conduct during the tour of Paris.

Anna and I did have an interesting conversation about fat in the human diet. Anna says that Paleolithic man was taller than later Bronze Age man and had no heart disease, unlike modern man, because he had a perfect diet: game meat, occasional fish or shellfish, lots of fruits, nuts, and veggies, but most important, no dairy products and little or no grain. Their diet didn't sound very gourmet to me and certainly not very French.

Anna then gave me a recipe that substituted nonfat evaporated milk for butter and whole milk in béchamel sauce. Since she'd mentioned the sauce, I told her that a seventeenth-century French financier of that name, a man with large investments in the Newfoundland fisheries, had created the sauce himself to make dried codfish palatable to his countrymen, who hated it. If I were still cooking, I might try her version of Béchamel's recipe myself, but would I like it? I comforted myself for having such unhealthy thoughts and tastes by remembering that the French, despite a diet appallingly rich in fat and cholesterol, have a long life expectancy. But I digress.

Carl Jensen, the bovine expert, said in his slow, flat Midwestern accent, "Take my advice, Mrs. Blue. Don't eat any beef at all. They've got mad cow disease in France."

"Indeed," said Manfred Unsell, interrupting an argument with his wife Grace over his desire to order a whole bottle of wine when she planned to drink only one glass.

Unsell was a tall, portly man with a hawk nose and a very red face that contrasted sharply with his black hair. Maybe the red face and nose were an indication that he felt a need for four glasses of wine with dinner.

"The national fear of mad cow disease is having an ominous impact on the cattle industry here," Unsell remarked. "Farmers are facing bankruptcy. In fact, the whole European Union is at risk. Austria has banned imported German beef; the German chancellor had to reassure his constituency of the safety of German sausage—"

"Bo-vine spon-gi-form en-ce-pha-lo-pa-thy," interrupted Jensen, separating the three words into their component syllables. "A terrible fate for an innocent cow. I've seen the poor creatures in England. Staggering, falling down. A pitiful sight. No future but a sure and painful death. It can be passed on to humans, Mrs. Blue."

Jason murmured, "Creutzfeldt-Jakob disease."

I sighed. It was going to be hard to write columns about French cuisine if all these knowledgeable men kept providing unwelcome input.

"Mercy, Carl," said Ingrid Jensen, who was as tall, sturdy, and blond as her husband, "let the poor woman enjoy her beef. As long as it's well done—that's what I always tell my county extension classes," said Ingrid. "Cook it enough, and you don't have to worry about parasites and such."

"Madam," said Jean-Claude Childeric, who had once again attached himself to me, "*boeuf tartare* would not be the famous dish that it is if it were cooked. It must be raw! The beef, as well as the egg yokes that bind it."

"Raw!" Ingrid Jensen looked horrified. She had evidently missed my initial conversation with the waiter. "Why, I'd never let my students use *eggs* that are raw, or even half-cooked. 'Cook 'em hard,' I say. 'Don't take chances.' "

"We don't have that egg disease in the Southwest," I said, then nodded to the waiter and murmured stubbornly, "I will have the beef tartare."

"If you'd seen a cow die, its poor brain turned to mush—" Jensen began.

"I'm not a cow," I replied, "and only three human cases have been reported in France according to the *New York Times*."

"Market conditions are often influenced more by public hysteria than actual statistics," Unsell remarked. "Of course, it all started here on the continent with the export of English bone-meal animal feeds."

"The animals are eating each other?" gasped Estrella Markarov.

"Only in a manner of speaking," said Unsell. "Animal parts that were unusable in any ordinary way were found to make good additions to feed. A very profitable business for the English until the unfortunate advent of mad cow disease. As I understand it, no one is even sure that the feed causes the disease in other animals."

"Oh, I think there's no question that it does," said Jason. "BSE seems to be an offshoot of sheep scrapies. Sheep parts ground up and fed to cows caused BSE, which in turn causes NV—that's new variant—Creutzfeldt-Jakob in humans—all related to one another through autopsy results."

My beef tartare arrived, and I eyed it warily. Even if only three human cases had turned up in France—and the entrée did look delicious—I didn't want to die of some dreadful degenerative brain disease. On the other hand, one little taste—I took it—ah, so yummy. The capers, the onions, the spices, the beef tenderloin—ground and—

"What *is* in question is the mechanism," Jason added. "A lively debate in scientific circles. Some say prions are the infective agent—meaning protein only."

Jason went on to discuss proteins and nucleic acids, but I hadn't the faintest idea what he was talking about. I did wish that he and especially

Dr. Jensen would discuss it somewhere else. Markarov's wife Estrella and Grace Unsell had both turned a bit green as the descriptions of mad cow disease were enlarged. They probably weren't used to unpleasant scientific discussions in inappropriate settings. Unfortunately, I am.

Professor Childeric, sitting beside me and eating something in sauce, obviously hated being left out of any discussion. "These plagues and problems in the food chain have affected European civilization for centuries," he informed us.

"Oh, are you an expert on the science of food?" asked Janice Petar.

She had joined our party, although without her friend Anna Thomas-Smith, who had a terrible headache as a result of spending the day chasing after Edie, or so Janice said. An interesting-looking woman, I thought, glancing at her as she zoomed in on Childeric. She was small and rather muscular with weathered, brown skin and short-cropped hair.

When she mentioned Anna's headache to me before dinner, she had cast me an accusing look. However, it was nothing compared to the malice of the look she shot at Jean-Claude Childeric. It suddenly occurred to me that if Professor Childeric really had been pushed at the airport and the culprit hadn't been an air-rage attacker, Janice Petar might be the person who did it. Not that I had noticed her there, but then we hadn't yet been introduced. I'd have to keep my eye on Dr. Petar.

"Or do you rely on others to provide you expertise in scientific matters?" Janice asked.

Childeric looked quite taken aback at her tone and stammered that he certainly *was* a bit of an expert on French food, especially the cuisine of the Middle Ages. "Take Saint Anthony's fire," he began.

"That *is* an interesting example," Jason agreed. "Fungus on the rye crop that got into the bread, causing erysipelas."

Oh dear, they were off again, and I knew for a fact that Saint Anthony's fire was an unpleasant topic.

Our guide, Denis, was passing the table at the time and said with his mischievous grin, "*Oui.* It was called Saint Anthony's fire because the good saint wished it on those who did not properly honor him."

"Nonsense," snapped Childeric. "It was because the intercession of Saint Anthony was thought to cure the disease."

"I believe Saint Anthony suffered from it," said Estrella Markarov. "That is why it was named for him."

"Cellulitis," Fauree called from their table. "Caused by streptococcus bacteria."

I looked up from my delicious entrée to see Childeric sending a furious glance at his rival in the dean's race. Hugh chuckled and turned away while Ivan Markarov, who had a longish beard and dishwater blond hair, was shoveling in a mouthful of beef tartare and beaming at me. "Is good. No?" he asked. "I think I have Tartar in genes."

I couldn't help adding, "Marco Polo saw Tartars eating various chopped raw meats seasoned with garlic when he visited the Yunan province. Maybe that's where the name of the dish came from."

"Enjoy good food while food is on table," said Markarov.

Was that an old Tartar folk saying? Had the Tartars had tables? I'd always thought they spent all their time in the saddle and slept in the open or, at best, in tents.

"Is interesting problem," he continued, turning dark eyes with a slight oriental slant on my husband. "Genes in cow, maybe in people, make prion infectious. No?"

"I believe so," Jason agreed. "Although I am not a biologist. For instance, I had no idea that Saint Anthony's fire also referred to a bacterial infection."

"Saint Anthony's fire has nothing to do with strep throat," said Childeric. "Fauree has his facts wrong. The scientific name for Saint Anthony's fire is epi—epi something."

"Perhaps everyone is thinking of ergotism," I intervened. "Thousands of people in Europe went crazy and died from that, and nobody knew until the late sixteenth century that it was caused by something on rye wheat."

"Is true," said Markarov. "Russian Tsar, Peter, was going to attack Turks, but whole army gets sick from rye bread." Then he turned to Jason. "I, as computer science person, sometimes work with chemists. You are chemist, no? Who does research on environmental toxins, no? Before I leave Russia, I am noticing many bad air and water. Is serious problem."

His previously thoughtful wife gave him a smile of melting devotion. Then she told us she had just realized that mad cow disease was God's answer to the sins of man. "When our Lord created the creatures of the fields and forests, he made cows and sheep herbivores. *Our greed* has turned them into cannibals, and now we are paying the price. The plague has entered our own houses."

"My little sugar beet is being very holy woman, no?" said Markarov, patting his wife affectionately before he returned to his next bite of beef tartare. "She is making this former atheist into worshipper." He didn't seem worried that his wife's God might strike him down for the sins of man. Personally, I was glad I had managed to finish my entrée before I learned that I might be bringing a holy curse down on my head. The threat of Whatsis-Jacob disease was bad enough.

"Could be God. Who knows?" said Carl Jensen gloomily. "But I can tell you, I worry about our herds in the U.S. of A. If folks abroad don't get a handle on this, we could all end up eating chicken."

But not yet, I thought. I could safely publish a recipe for beef tartare in my column since the American cow wasn't yet infected.

"Did I read recently that chickens may carry the disease as well?" Jason asked.

"We're going to be late for the concert if we don't hurry," I said. No use considering dessert when someone at the table was sure to find a dire consequence of eating whatever I chose. Perhaps I'd write a column on how to ruin someone's dinner.

Do-It-Yourself Beef Tartare Americaine

Beef tartare (also called steak tartare or beef steak tartare) probably originated among invading tribesmen descended from the hordes of Genghis Khan. Some legends say Tartars were in the habit of shredding raw red meat with their knives and eating it. Others claim that they put raw beef under their saddles, where the pounding it underwent during long rides and the sweat of the horses tenderized it. We have more palatable recipes for beef tartare these days. No restaurant chef would consider marinating it in horse sweat.

However, with mad cow disease sweeping Europe, perhaps we Americans should keep the tradition alive while it is still safe to do so. Our cattle do not yet have mad cow disease, and believe me, beef tartare is scrumptious. If you live in a section of the United States where eggs are not infected with bad things, here is my own recipe, which I call Beef Tartare Americaine. If you do have the egg problem, skip the raw yolks, mix the ingredients yourself to your own taste, and serve the dish.

Cut the fat from *2 lbs. raw, top-quality beef tenderloin or fillet*. Grind in a blender or food processor until the meat is finely chopped. Divide into 4 balls and chill in refrigerator until ready to serve.

Finely chop *½ cup onion* and *3 tbs. parsley*.

Serve the beef on cold plates by shaping each ball into a mound and indenting the top to receive a *raw egg yolk*. Arrange *capers*, chopped onion, and chopped parsley around the sides.

Allow guests to mix their own tartare and flavor it to taste with *Tabasco, Worcestershire sauce, Dijon mustard, salt, pepper, cut lemon,* and a good *bourbon whiskey,* all arranged on a lazy Susan in the middle of the table. (For European tastes, you can provide *cognac* or even *port* as a substitute for bourbon.)

To be accompanied by *thin slices of dark bread or buttered toast.*

If you don't want to use raw eggs, you can mix the tartare to your own taste from among the above ingredients, form small balls with the meat mixture, roll the balls in the *chopped parsley,* chill, and serve on a toothpick as finger food.

Carolyn Blue, "Have Fork, Will Travel," *Reno Mountain Times*

9
Vivaldi Adventures

Europeans first came across chocolate when Cortés saw Montezuma drinking a thick, bitter beverage the Aztecs believed was a cure for dysentery and also a purveyor of aphrodisiac effects, which made it the drink of choice at wedding celebrations. Cortés himself wrote to Carlos I that it combated fatigue and might even taste good if sweetened. The Maya used it for religious rituals, and in Nicaragua, cacao beans served as money; ten cacao beans bought the favors of many a willing woman.

Hot chocolate soon became a favorite drink in Spain and Portugal, but the French were not so easily swayed. Two different foreign queens introduced it to the French court, Anne of Austria in 1615 and Marie-Terese of Spain in 1660, but even after the drink became popular and was endorsed by the medical establishment in Paris, shocking rumors circulated that chocolate was an aphrodisiac. Then in 1670 a noblewoman, who had overindulged in hot chocolate during pregnancy, was said to have given birth to a black baby. After the French Revolution, chocolate was considered too aristocratic and Catholic (Jesuits having been accused of trying to monopolize the trade in cocoa) for hardworking, Protestant citizens.

However, at that time the French had never tasted a chocolate truffle. It fell to a Dutch cocoa merchant in 1815 to produce the first edible (as opposed to liquid) chocolate, for which Conrad J. van Houten deserves our thanks. There's nothing more delicious (or addictive) than a chocolate truffle flavored with a tasty liqueur.

Carolyn Blue, "Have Fork, Will Travel," *Oakland Weekly Shopper*

Carolyn

Sainte-Chapelle is to churches what a chocolate-raspberry truffle is to candy—an absolutely delicious, beautiful, inspirational confection of a building. Saint Louis ordered its construction to house the Crown of Thorns, which he purchased at great cost during the thirteenth century from John III, the impecunious Emperor in Constantinople. This building-as-reliquary, completed in only three years, was constructed almost entirely of stained glass, with lovely, narrow windows soaring between pillars to Gothic points in a burst of color that takes the breath away.

What a glorious place to hear the music of Vivaldi, even considering that

I had seated myself between Chris and Edie to head off any possible amorous conduct. She sulked throughout *The Four Seasons,* while behind us Grace Unsell's cell phone rang in the middle of "Spring." Grace had to put down the almost completed baby bootie on her knitting needles to carry on a whispered conversation about her daughter's experiences with false labor. Frenchmen glared. Frenchwomen who understood English eavesdropped and whispered advice. Manfred Unsell tried to take the phone away from his wife, at which she told him that she hadn't wanted to come to France anyway and would be perfectly happy to leave for home this very minute. Then an usher made them both leave before the beginning of "Summer." It was all very embarrassing and detracted from the inspirational nature of the experience.

As did the events that preceded and followed the concert. We were, in fact, late leaving the restaurant because the waiter refused to provide separate checks. Before we left, Roberta, who was seated at another table with Hugh, the de Sorentinos, and the Drummonds, stood up and said to Lorenzo de Sorentino, "Fuck off." Then she gave him a push, almost knocking him from his chair, and strode out of the restaurant. Poor Hugh was caught between his obvious desire to follow her and the need to pay the bill first. I myself don't like the "f" word, although I know that Robbie uses it in moments of great stress, but Estrella Markarov gasped and looked as if she might faint.

As we were all scrambling by Metro and on foot to get to the concert in time, Robbie told me that Lorenzo, the plastic surgeon, had had the gall to suggest that she consider breast reduction in the near future before hers began to sag or cause her back problems. "He actually said that in front of Hugh," she whispered, changing hands on her Metro strap. "I was so embarrassed. You may not have noticed, but Laura didn't take it very well either. She said, 'When will you ever learn, Lorenzo?' and knocked a glass of red wine in his lap. Angry that he was ogling other women's breasts, I suppose." Then Robbie laughed exuberantly. "I don't think they'll be going to the concert."

I felt rather sorry for Laura. She seemed the sort to love Sainte-Chapelle and Vivaldi. Professor Childeric, who had been staying close to me, heard this story and said, "Hardly proper conduct for a dean candidate. Pouring red wine on a spouse in public."

"I'm sure it was an accident," I murmured.

"And where is your spouse. Dr. Childeric?" asked Janice Petar. She was clinging to a Metro strap beside him. "For that matter, why are you, *the* expert on France, going on this very ordinary tour? Perhaps you're hoping to hit on some naïve lady in the absence of your wife. That would hardly be proper conduct for a—"

"Hit on?" Childeric interrupted. "I do not *hit on*—"

"Oh, save it," she snapped and left the car ahead of us when the doors opened at our stop.

"That woman hates me," he murmured, obviously amazed. "And for no reason that I'm aware of. Except—" He nodded sagely at an insight that had evidently just come to him. "Perhaps she's an adherent of one of the other candidates and plans a campaign to slander my good name, to create a last-minute scandal when it would be too late for me to defend myself. Very clever of Fauree."

"I don't think he even knows Janice," I replied. "Science and women's studies are not two fields that—"

"Of course. Exactly! A feminist would be a supporter of the female candidate. Laura de Sorentino put her up to this. She probably had someone push me at the airport, too. Or did it herself. It's a plot to humiliate me at every turn."

He had grasped my arm and was by then propelling me up the stairs at a rate much faster than I cared to climb. Where was Jason when I needed him? Gasping for breath, I glanced around and spotted my husband on the landing with Markarov and Hugh, engaged in what had all the earmarks of intense scientific conversation. Good grief, were they planning to mount a multidisciplinary assault on some arcane problem?

"Professor, you'll have to slow down. I'm going to fall on my face if I don't get a chance to catch my breath."

Childeric was all solicitous apologies.

"And I do think you're imagining plots. These are perfectly respectable, well-meaning academicians like yourself, hardly the sort of people to endanger your physical well-being or your good name." Although after that race upstairs and his wild imaginings, I was tempted to give him a shove myself. When finally we reached Louis IX's lovely chapel, I was pathetically glad to sit down.

Then there was the return to the hotel. Robbie and Hugh did not accompany us. Perhaps she had heard Childeric's accusations and repeated them to Hugh. Having been expelled, the Unsells were no longer with us. Chris and Edie persisted in lagging behind, forcing me to crane my neck in order to keep them under surveillance, and my husband and Markarov continued their avid conversation, leaving me with Estrella, who talked my ear off both riding and walking.

The gist of her conversation was as follows: She was a de la Garza. No doubt I had heard of her family, which was very prominent in New Mexico, an ancient and aristocratic Spanish bloodline, but that didn't keep her from espousing the cause of poor Hispanic children who needed both preschool education, which their parents couldn't afford, and bilingual education, because their parents didn't speak English at home. In fact, she had studied the program at our university and found it most impressive, didn't I?

As I have no preschool children, I'd never heard of it. Then she told me about her first husband, the eminent Professor Arthur Conway, a good Catholic and an internationally renowned expert on communication with autistic children. And I wasn't to believe the jealous critics who claimed that those who assisted autistic children to communicate on typewriters were either stupid, misled, or charlatans. Arthur himself had trained many of the best fa-cilitators in the field, researchers who, by guiding little fingers on the key-board, discovered loving children and brilliant minds inside those mute babies.

Whatever her first husband had been doing, it sounded suspiciously like something Jason read to me from the *Skeptical Inquirer*, Ouija board science he had called it. I politely refrained from mentioning that article to Estrella.

Unfortunately, she continued, God had taken Arthur to his bosom. Her dear first spouse had been struck down on a golf course by the crazed par-ent of an autistic child under treatment, struck down and killed with a nine iron. The attacker was now in a hospital for the criminally insane, and Arthur was undoubtedly in heaven as a result of his own virtue and Es-trella's prayers for him. Then Estrella informed me that, after going through a period of grief when she thought of joining a convent, she had decided that God's plan for her was to remarry and have children of her own, some-thing she and Arthur had been unable to accomplish.

"You may think me too old," she said to me.

"Not at all," I replied politely.

"But I'm only forty-five and have the perfect hips and bosom for moth-erhood."

She did have wide hips and a generous bosom. "Perfect," I agreed.

"How could God ignore my prayers when I have brought my dear Ivan into the arms of the true church, not to mention other converts among my students?"

"How indeed?" I responded, spotting the hotel and wishing I were safe in my bed. Tonight I'd sleep well because I knew that tomorrow I'd have clean clothes to wear. Oh lord, Chris and Edie were holding hands. "Excuse me," I said to the future mother of Russian-Hispanic, bilingual, preschooled, Roman Catholic children, and I hastened back to my son and my duties as chaperone.

10

It's Raining Flowerpots

Carolyn

Did you enjoy the concert?" I asked Chris as I snatched his hand from Edie's.

"It was too hot in there," Edie responded for him. "Seems to me they could put in air conditioning even if that is an old building."

"Not easily," I murmured. "I was really asking if you enjoyed the music."

Edie shrugged. "It was okay. But when Mrs. U.'s phone rang and the French guy kicked them out—now, that was cool. Did you see Dr. Unsell? I'll bet he's never been kicked out of anywhere. Chris and I just about died laughing. Say, Mrs. Blue, would you mind if Chris walked me to my room? Those courtyards at the hotel are creepy at night."

"Indeed they are," I agreed. "And because your mother is such a dear friend and placed your safety in my hands, I'll walk you to your room myself."

"But—"

"Hey, Denis," Chris called as we entered the hotel.

"While you're talking to Denis, Chris, ask him what we'll be doing tomorrow."

"I can tell you that. We're going to see some artist's flower garden," said Edie. "I'll just tag along and talk to Denis, too."

"Nonsense. Jason," I called to my husband, "you and I need to escort Edie to her room. Those creepy courtyards, you know." Jason didn't even hear me.

However, Dr. Childeric came to my rescue by saying gallantly, "I shall be delighted to escort you lovely ladies to your rooms." He linked his arms through ours and led us off toward the dreaded courtyards. Oh well, it was kind of him to offer. The first courtyard was indeed dark and overgrown with shrubbery.

"My room's on the second floor of the next building," said the pouting Edie. "I can get up there on my own. Dr. Thomas-Smith will be waiting for me. She thinks sex-crazed French guys are sneaking around everywhere, looking to jump American girls."

We didn't get to hear the rest of Anna Thomas-Smith's warnings about lascivious Frenchmen because a round object trailing shrubbery plummeted in front of us, caromed off Professor Childeric's shoulder, and burst on the courtyard stones. Edie shrieked. I leapt backward, my stockingless shins stinging, and Professor Childeric staggered. Somehow, a flowerpot had fallen almost on top of us from the balcony above. Had we entered that courtyard just a step or two earlier, one of us might have been dead. I was so frightened that I felt dizzy.

Having heard the crash and the shrieking, hotel employees raced out to rescue us. Edie was found to be unhurt but giggling rather hysterically. I had shard cuts on my legs and even one on my cheek, along with a fine spray of dirt from the pot explosion. Dr. Childeric clutched his shoulder and rocked, moaning. Had the pot been *meant* to hit him? I wondered uneasily.

When Denis arrived and offered to escort Edie to her room, she asked pitifully, "Where's Chris?"

"Gone to bed," said Denis.

Relieved to hear that, I turned Edie over to Denis and let the desk clerk help me to a stone bench.

Professor Childeric joined me there. "Fauree," the medievalist gasped. "He tried to kill me."

"We just saw him in the lobby. He couldn't have got upstairs in time to push a pot over." Could he?

"I didn't see him," the professor objected suspiciously, as if I were part of the imagined plot. "My God, I think something's broken. The pain is—excruciating." He continued to rock. "Or Laura de Sorentino. *She* wasn't in the lobby."

"Laura's too slender to have moved a pot filled with dirt and vines," I objected.

"Then her husband. Or that Petar woman. She looks too muscular to even *be* a woman. I don't remember seeing her after the concert. Or at the concert, for that matter. She probably slipped away to lie in wait for me."

Even in the shadowy courtyard, I could see the sweat on his forehead and the paleness of his skin. "Really, Dr. Childeric," I said as soothingly as I could, "the pot probably fell off on its own." I turned to the two clerks who now hovered anxiously beside us. To one, I said, "This man needs a doctor. Don't you, Professor Childeric?"

"Yes," he groaned.

The first clerk rushed off.

To the second, I said. "You should take care that your pots aren't positioned in such a way that they can teeter and fall off on unsuspecting guests."

The clerk protested that the hotel's pots did not *teeter*. Childeric insisted that the pot had been aimed at him.

"*Oui,*" said the clerk. "I weel call the gendarmes."

"And the doctor?"

"Soon, madame. He eez being sent for."

"Good." A terrible weariness flooded over me. "I think I'll go to bed." I stood up, somewhat unsteadily.

"Excellent, madame. Pierre weel escort you."

"Don't leave me, Carolyn," begged Jean-Claude Childeric, sounding frightened.

"I stay weeth you, Professor, until the doctor, he come. Pierre, he take ze lady away. I theenk she is for faint."

Pierre took my arm, and I was soon in my own room, showering off the shrubbery dirt and perspiration in blessedly cool water, placing Band-Aids on my cuts, which were, fortunately, more painful than serious, donning my full-length nightgown—so much more comfy than a T-shirt. At last I climbed into bed to consider what had happened. I was sorry to have deserted Professor Childeric, especially after he had been so kind as to offer himself as an escort, but I *had* been feeling faint. Also on the verge of tears. The incident had frightened me badly.

Could someone be targeting him? And if so, why? This was his second accident in as many days, and whereas one might, in the midst of a crowd, trip and fall onto a luggage carousel, or be pushed by some impatient and furious passenger, surely being almost pulverized by a pot was not as likely to be an accident. On the other hand, who would *do* such a thing?

I wondered where Janice Petar's room was. She seemed to have a deep-seated dislike of the man. As for an opposing dean candidate, that was silly. When Jason came in, full of enthusiasm for a problem he and Markarov had been discussing, I voiced my fears and speculations to him.

Jason cuddled me sympathetically and listened. Then he kissed my Band-Aid-dressed forehead injury, and said, "Don't let Childeric's paranoia infect you, love. Academics do not try to kill each other with heavy clay pots. But pots have been known to fall off balconies. It happens."

"Umm," I replied, willing to be comforted. "I think there's another cut on my ankle that needs attention."

"My pleasure." Jason tossed off the duvet.

"And on my shin," I suggested. To think Chris had wanted to share our room. What luck it was so small.

11

Monet's Revenge

Jason

After her fright the night before, Carolyn had calmed down and now looked forward to the group's visit to Monet's gardens at Giverny. She even listened to Denis's talk on the bus until he made the mistake of embroidering on the truth. Evidently Monet did not personally plant every flower and tree or nearly drown in a lily pond while carrying on a romantic liaison with a female gardening enthusiast, not his wife. Carolyn snorted at these fabrications and fell asleep, leaving me to chat with Markarov, behind me, and Hugh, who sat across the aisle dividing his attention between me and Roberta.

We three scientists amused ourselves with plans for the investigation of mad cow disease—Hugh to do the biology, Ivan to provide computer programs, and I to design necessary chemical experiments. The challenge lay in the fact that none of us was really an expert on his given segment of the project. However, it passed the time enjoyably and foiled Roberta's attempts to divert all Hugh's attention to herself.

I'm sorry to admit that we continued to chat when we reached the gardens, which are, admittedly, delightful—a riot of colorful flower clumps, exotic trees, bridges, wandering paths, and of course, the lily ponds that figure endlessly in Monet's paintings. Either the man became obsessed with water lilies, or he ran out of inspiration. Carolyn would know.

At any rate, while Hugh, Ivan, and I strolled along the paths immersed in scientific discussion, Carolyn got stuck with Jean-Claude Childeric, whose arm was now in a sling. It seems that the falling pot had dislocated his shoulder. The man was having a serious run of ill luck on this tour.

While he told Carolyn about the excruciating pain he had experienced in the hospital, Carolyn nodded, murmured sympathetically, and took pictures of the garden with such abandon that I considered the financial benefits of buying her a digital camera to save on film and developing. All the while Childeric continued to talk. After he had bemoaned his injury, he regaled her with the name and medicinal or cosmetic function of every herb ever used in the Middle Ages. She did seem interested.

Behind us Roberta Hecht was less good-natured, for not only had I purloined her latest romantic target, but she was being deluged with the names of saints to whom a woman could pray for the blessing of conception, not the least of whom was the Virgin Mary herself. Evidently Ivan's wife wanted to have a child, an unlikely event in my estimation, although I was just guessing at her age and consequent infertility.

Ivan seemed happy enough at the prospect of parenthood. He said, blowing a kiss over his shoulder toward his wife, "My pretty little samovar is hoping we be parents soon. Is not a fine thing for famous American scholar wish to make me a papa?"

Even as he interrupted our discussion with this remark, Carolyn spotted a vista in whose foreground she wanted me. Although she turned away from Childeric to tell me where to pose, he continued to talk. Rosemary was his topic at that moment, and the man has a very penetrating voice. While Ivan and Hugh stood out of range and Carolyn maneuvered to focus me in her camera sights with an arched bridge in the background, Childeric cited references to rosemary in the plays of Shakespeare, evidently to illustrate that medieval interest in herbs continued into the Renaissance and beyond.

Completely self-absorbed, jacket draped jauntily over his shoulders to accommodate his disabled arm, he ambled along beside a bamboo grove saying, "Of course, you will remember, my dear Carolyn, Ophelia's reference to rosemary: 'There's rosemary. That's for remembrance.' A very touching scene. And in *Winter's Tale* there is a reference to rosemary and rue, which keep all winter long, a very desirable trait since castles must have become quite odoriferous in—Agh-g-gh." Childeric had interrupted himself with an electrifying bellow of anguish.

Crouched in an awkward position to get her picture, Carolyn fell over in astonishment and fear. While Ivan stayed to help her up, Hugh and I sprinted along the path toward Childeric, who was bent over, keening, one hand covering his eyes.

"What's wrong, man?" asked Hugh.

"You!" screamed the medievalist. "I recognize your voice. How dare you spray me with some noxious gas and then ask what's wrong?"

Hugh and I exchanged puzzled glances.

"I'm blinded," roared Childeric. "You've blinded me."

Since his eyes were covered, I couldn't fathom how he'd know that he couldn't see. Still, something had obviously happened. I could smell the pungent, lingering odor of some gas or mist. "Insecticide?" I guessed, not at all sure of this hypothesis.

"We are in a garden," Hugh agreed.

Childeric moaned as we led him to a bench and other tourists crowded around. "My God," he said, "not only am I blind, but I'll probably die of cancer. My skin is burning, my eyes are burning, I'm—"

He was on the edge of hysteria, and people surrounding us were saying, "What have they done to him?"

"Water," said Hugh. "We'd better rinse him down. That's bound to help." He spotted a gardener with hose in hand and grabbed it.

"Wait," I cautioned. "Ivan! Find an official and ask what insecticide they use. Do you speak French?"

"*Oui, monsieur,*" Ivan replied and loped off.

Roberta came to join us, took the hose from Hugh, said to Childeric, "Stop whining. I'm going to wash all that stuff off you," and proceeded to do so before I could warn her that she might be turning a chemical to acid by mixing it with water.

Although Childeric leapt up when hit by the stream of cold water and tried to fend her off with his free hand, the dousing seemed to do him no harm. His moaning turned to indignation, and he even admitted that he could see, after all. That being the case, Hugh and I restrained him while Roberta continued to give him a very thorough wash-down, ignoring his repeated complaints about the plot to destroy his suit and his dignity.

"Better a dose of embarrassment than having your skin peel off or your cells mutate," she responded with cheerful pragmatism. "I heard you say something about cancer, and Hugh was talking earlier about cell mutation."

"I knew you were behind this," Childeric snarled at Hugh. "You and your hulking girlfriend."

"Hulking?" Robbie turned the hose on his face, in response to which he yelped and tried to shield himself. "Stop that, you nincompoop," she ordered. "You want to leave it in your eyes?"

At that point a French official arrived, accompanied by Ivan and Estrella, who was explaining the situation in Spanish. Either the official did not understand Spanish, even spoken slowly and with many accompanying gestures by a woman determined to communicate, or he chose not to respond. Ivan murmured to me that the official had stopped understanding Russian-accented French as soon as he heard that a visitor had been attacked, presumably by a gardener.

The official then admonished us for attacking a visitor with the garden's hose. We were to know that all implements for the maintenance of the

Giverny gardens were the property of the Claude-Monet Foundation and not to be used by visitors, who would be ejected forthwith if found—

He got no further, for the lovely Laura de Sorentino arrived with her husband. Lorenzo saw Roberta, wielding the hose, and retreated hastily. A smiling Laura introduced herself to the official, who actually kissed her hand. Then she asked us what the problem was and listened attentively to the story. To Childeric she said, "You poor man. Just let me try to sort this out for you. Are you in pain? Do you need a physician? Lorenzo!"

Her husband, now lurking nervously on the edge of the crowd and, incidentally, talking with suspicious intimacy to my wife, refused to offer any medical attention to someone suffering from insecticide poisoning, about which he knew nothing and for which he did not care to put his reputation and insurance coverage at risk. His wife tossed him a glance of contempt, but de Sorentino didn't seem to notice.

Childeric, rather ungraciously I thought, said that her efforts were not needed here, especially since she was probably a party to the attack. She looked at Childeric with great sympathy and patted his good shoulder, as if his terrible experience had scattered his wits. I was beginning to find the whole scene amusing and glanced at Carolyn to see if she, too, was entertained. She was, but evidently by Lorenzo.

Then Laura turned back to the official, who had never taken his eyes from her. The poor fellow seemed mesmerized by the beauty of her face or, perhaps, by her impeccable command of his language. In my experience Frenchmen can be very picky about the spoken French of male foreigners and inordinately tolerant of a foreign woman's attempt to speak their language, especially if the woman is pretty. Laura had his full attention as she explained that someone had lurked in the bamboo grove and attacked this world-renowned expert on the Middle Ages in France and, indeed, on all things French, with a deadly insecticide spray.

Childeric forgot for a moment that he considered her an enemy and preened, while the official bowed respectfully in his direction. Had these quick-thinking and knowledgeable men of science not intervened with the Giverny hose, Laura continued, no doubt Professor Jean-Claude Childeric would now be dead. Since Fauree was chuckling and translating for me, I found myself highly flattered to be described as knowledgeable and quick-thinking, although it was Robbie who had actually taken charge.

Childeric, on the other hand, turned pale when the probability of his own death was mentioned, and the official breathed *"Mon Dieu,"* no doubt at the prospect of the foundation being held responsible for the death of an eminent scholar. He protested that no gardener in the employ of Giverny would do such a thing.

I then called upon the aforementioned quick thinking to ask what insecticide the garden employed, information that was necessary to the further and successful treatment of Professor Childeric. A gardener was sent for and arrived looking both nervous and stubborn in his Giverny coverall.

Much discussion and translation ensued, Ivan, Laura, the official, and the gardener running on in French and occasionally translating for the rest of us. Carolyn had edged away from Lorenzo and into the group. Childeric was now too busy contemplating the destruction of his clothing and dignity to join in.

It gradually became evident that the fellow who supplied the insecticide believed in organic gardening and had made the compound himself according to a secret recipe inherited from his father (who had worked for Monet) and improved on by himself for the benefit of the foundation and the garden. He refused to reveal ingredients or their amounts in the secret mixture but burst into a flood of indignant French when it was suggested that his spray might injure the eminent scholar. He replied that the spray would not make the professor grow, but that it would keep bugs off him. Furthermore, the ingredients were perfectly safe to ingest or to rub on one's arthritic knees.

"Capsaicin," I surmised. No wonder Childeric's skin and eyes burned. Still, having been rapidly doused with water, thus diluting the chili pepper derivative, he should be safe enough, although it was obvious that he did not feel at all grateful for our intervention and Roberta's decisive action with the hose.

"Shouldn't someone be looking for the miscreant who sprayed Professor Childeric?" Carolyn asked. Laura translated.

"It was Fauree," said Childeric.

"Ah ha!" cried the foundation official. "One of your own countrymen, then?"

"Hugh was with me," I protested.

"You probably helped him." Childeric gave me a furious look. "I see now that the whole science contingent is banding together to destroy me."

"They were behind you on the path, Professor Childeric," my wife explained.

"How would you know, Carolyn? I was talking to you at the time. In fact, how did you escape the deadly spray yourself?" He was now eyeing my wife suspiciously.

"She was taking my picture, not talking to you," I snapped.

The official threw up his hands and advised us to settle the matter among ourselves, unless we wished for a gendarme to take us all in for questioning, which would probably involve incarceration and the confiscation of our passports.

"You're going to arrest us and let the real criminal escape?" Carolyn exclaimed. While Laura translated, the rest of us peered at the bamboo grove. However, it was obvious that no one was lurking there after all the fuss. Grudgingly, the official sent the gardener to investigate. The man found nothing but a spray can, half full of his secret potion, abandoned among the bamboo stalks.

Childeric's accusation had brought to my attention the possibility that my own wife could have been injured had she not fallen back to take my picture. Also Childeric *had* been attacked. That was incontrovertible, just as there was no possibility that Hugh was the attacker. Unless it was the gardener or some other employee of Giverny, whoever had done the spraying couldn't have known that the insecticide was relatively innocuous. The attack might have had serious, even fatal results. Something dangerous was afoot. I could no longer pass off as accidents Childeric's fall at Charles de Gaulle and the plummeting pot in the courtyard last night. Because in each instance, my own wife could have, inadvertently, been a victim instead of Childeric, I vowed to keep her at my side for the rest of the trip and, more important, to keep her away from Childeric.

The gardener spoke solemnly to the official. The official nodded. Hugh began to laugh. "The man says that there is no plot, only the ghost of Claude Monet, returning to protect his garden from rude foreigners, who can never appreciate the splendor the great painter created here. How else could a spray used only by himself, the inventor, have been directed against this stranger? No employee of the foundation would dare to take up the secret spray. He says that we should go away."

While Hugh was translating, the official began to speak angrily in French to the gardener. Laura picked up the translation. "The official says the gardener should shut his mouth and tend to his flowers. It is not his place to drive away visitors to a treasure of France, which is praised and marveled at the world over. The gardener says—"

"What I'd like," Roberta interrupted, "is to find a nice café with a tree-shaded patio, handsome French boys waiting tables, and a good bar."

"Most fine thought," Ivan agreed.

"I think the foundation should provide dry clothes for Professor Childeric, Professor Fauree, and my husband," said Carolyn. "They're all soaking wet, which can't be healthy."

Since the sun was shining brightly on our heads, I rather thought I'd dry out in no time, but Childeric began to complain about his suit, which would shrink in the sunshine. He pointed out bitterly that we scientists had nothing to worry about, being casually dressed, but he had his dignity and his wardrobe to protect. Which is why the three of us, none happy about it, ended the visit to Giverny wearing Claude-Monet Foundation coveralls. Childeric was furious.

12
Young Love Foiled

Carolyn

No wonder Monet's paintings so often featured his own garden. It's gorgeous! I changed film twice because there were so many views and individual flowers I couldn't resist: the lily ponds with willows leaning down to brush the water and cast misty reflections; the dark green bridges, which seem to arch magically from the surrounding trees and shrubs; one particular huge, round, shaggy flower of lavender-pink that I zoomed in on as it perched splendidly among its smaller sisters and large, floppy leaves. I did hope that photo would come out—and a stack of white bells bursting from a stalk, their throats lavender spotted. I'm not much of a gardener, but I loved the place.

It had been a wonderful day, except for the attack on Professor Childeric. I suppose a gardener could have made a mistake and been afraid to own up, what with all the fuss afterward. Childeric seemed none the worse for the spraying, but still I decided to ask Jason how dangerous insecticide could be. I don't use it myself. It smells bad and makes sticky places on the woodwork that attract dirt and become disgusting. I do have a service that sprays outside. That seems to keep down the scorpions, which are the most fearful household bug in El Paso. I screamed and ran out of the room when I saw that first scorpion waving his poisonous tail at me.

As our tour group was making its way to the exit, I glanced down a by-path, half obscured by yellow-green bushes underlaid with purple-hearted yellow pansies. There amid the greenery was my twenty-year-old son kissing sixteen-year-old Edie Atwater. I must admit that she was clutching him like a Venus flytrap devouring a bug. Still, I whirled aside from the main path to confront them, taking my surprised husband with me. He had been sniffing the air and mumbling about what else the gardener could have put in the homemade bug spray. As if anyone cared now that Childeric seemed to have survived the dousing with everything but his suit and self-esteem intact.

I cleared my throat loudly like a stereotypical stage parent, and Chris leapt away from Edie. With some difficulty. She did not seem as embarrassed to be discovered as Chris did. "Jason, perhaps you'd escort Edie back to the group and ask Anna to take charge of her," I suggested.

Jason hurried a scowling Miss Edie down the path toward the disappearing tour group. I turned and said, "Christopher—"

"Oh, oh," he interrupted. "Now, I'm in for it."

"Not funny," I replied. "That girl is only sixteen. And I'm supposed to be chaperoning her. Judith Atwater is not going to be happy if she hears that instead of looking after Edie, I left her to my grown-up son, who has no more sense than to kiss an underage girl."

"Aside from the fact that she came on to me, I can see your point, Mom," said Chris. "I don't suppose you'd accept the argument that I'm just a captive of my hormones?"

"I would not."

"Or that, being male, I'm gender bound to refuse quiche and accept kisses from pretty girls?"

Gender bound? It's hard to give your son a maternal lecture when you're being overcome by a case of the giggles. "Just for that, you don't get to order quiche the whole time we're in France, Mr. Macho. In fact, I think this deterioration in your moral fiber must be a result of the wine you're drinking at dinner."

"Hey, come on, Mom, what was I supposed to do? Give her a push?"

"Only in a gentlemanly way," I answered, turning back toward the main path. "My considered advice is avoid her if you can't fend her off."

Grinning, Chris put his arm around my shoulder. "Makes me sound like a wimp, doesn't it? Can't fend off a sixteen-year-old. Tell you what. I'll hang out with Denis. Maybe if she won't go away, she'll kiss Denis instead."

I sighed. "That won't do either. She'll just have to sit with me. If she wants to flirt, she can practice on your father."

Chris burst out laughing, and I had to join him. Jason is famous for his methods of fending off amorous young things: wedges of wood to keep his door wide open during office hours; serious suggestions that the way to please him is to study hard, these suggestions accompanied by reading lists complete with Library of Congress call numbers and scientific explanations that glaze their eyes. Oh, Jason is a wily one, and I don't suppose I can realistically expect such expertise in my twenty-year-old son, but I could give him advice. "Why don't you try telling her all about chemistry," I suggested.

"Jeez," he replied glumly.

Jason awaited us at the exit from the garden. "Edie's been safely stowed with Anna Thomas-Smith, sulking like a two-year-old and being called Edwina for her trouble." He then glanced inquiringly from me to Chris.

"And I've been duly chastised," Chris answered for both of us. "Mom says you and she will keep Edie under surveillance."

"Wonderful," my husband grumbled. "I'm sure we'll find her conversation very stimulating." He explained that Denis had announced a café break in the village before we reboarded the bus. Chris went off to look for Denis while Jason and I strolled at our leisure and found a charming café with a terrace overlooking the town. The view was lovely; the table, umbrella shaded. A gentle breeze stirred the trees; and best of all, no one sitting on that terrace was from our tour group.

"I'm glad to have a moment alone," Jason said after we had both ordered Kir Royales and been served a little bonus, a bowl of crunchy bits that were garlic infused. I sighed with pleasure, relaxed in my chair, and told Jason that Edie seemed to have been the aggressor in the scene we had stumbled on. My husband nodded, unsurprised. I then said Chris had decided to discourage Edie by hanging out with Denis, which should take care of that problem, although I'd be stuck with Edie.

Finally, I reminded myself that girls Edie's age were not only obsessed with boys but going through that difficult phase of rebelling against their mothers—or in this case, mother figures. I would have to be more sympathetic to her problems. She was, after all, marooned in a foreign country with a group of middle-aged academics. No wonder her interest in Chris was less than ladylike.

"I don't know what to make of the incident with Professor Childeric," I continued. "I don't for a moment believe that Hugh or Laura is plotting against him, but something's going on. Do you think Janice Petar—well, you were behind us. Did you notice her in the area? Or anyone else looking suspicious? Of course, it could have been a mistake, I suppose. Some gardener trying out the spray can or even spraying those stalks—"

"Bamboo," said Jason, who has a penchant for exact designations.

"Yes, thank you." At least, he doesn't know the Latin names of plants and trees. "He might have sprayed Professor Childeric by mistake, after which he was afraid to confess. Didn't you gather that the head gardener felt that only he should use the spray?"

"Carolyn, I have no idea what happened back there, but that's one accident too many for me. Had that been a manufactured insecticide, Childeric could have suffered long-term consequences or even been killed, depending on what was in the stuff and how fast he was treated."

Well, that answered my proposed question, but it certainly didn't ease my mind.

"I'd really appreciate it if you'd avoid Childeric," Jason continued. "I realize the man's full of information that interests you—"

"True, but he can be rather pedantic about imparting it," I added to relieve my husband's mind. "Lectures are nice in their place, and maybe he wouldn't keep giving them if Denis were more knowledgeable and less fanciful, but still, one does like interactive conversation once in a while as opposed to—"

"Good," Jason interrupted with satisfaction. "I was afraid you'd miss his insights. So you will try to avoid Childeric? I don't want you falling victim to some mishap aimed at him. That pot that smashed in the hotel courtyard and even the insecticide could have been lethal."

"Poor man. What can he have done? If everyone ostracizes him, he'll have no one to talk to."

"For God's sake, Carolyn," Jason exclaimed, "surely you don't find that windbag attractive!"

I retorted sharply, "Have you ever known me to chase after other men?"

"Well, I didn't mean—"

"Maybe if you spent less time talking research with Hugh and Ivan—you'd think we were at a scientific meeting instead of on tour—I wouldn't find myself—"

"Would Madame and Monsieur care for another order of drinks?" asked our server.

"Saved by the waiter," said Jason.

"I certainly would," I replied, "and another bowl of those crunchies."

"Madame?"

"I wonder if you could give me the recipe for them," I continued without trying to define the word *crunchies* for him. His eyes bugged out in bewildered consternation. What could be more satisfying than confounding a French waiter? As soon as he had scuttled back into the café, no doubt to seek help from the manager, Jason and I grinned at each other, and our little altercation was forgotten.

13

Conclusions on Sex, Crime, and Revenge

Jason

Although Carolyn had had a talk with Chris, I felt that I, too, should intervene. I took him aside after dinner, not a very memorable one, and said, "About Edie—"

"Come on, Dad, nothing's going to happen between Edie and me. I already promised Mom—"

"It may be harder than you think to keep that promise," I interrupted. "Edie seems to be a very determined young woman, and you're the only person even near her age in this group."

"Are you saying be nice to her, but don't touch?" Chris asked, beginning to look confused. "Or stay the hell away from her? Or what?"

"She's a minor in the eyes of the law, and of her parents, who, unfortunately, aren't here to keep her in line. You understand the term *statutory rape,* don't you? It has nothing to do with consent when it comes to young girls."

"I won't—"

"Be tempted? Of course, you will. She's a pretty girl. And not only infatuated but feeling rebellious and off the leash. At least, she'd like to be. Your mother and Anna are doing what they can. You have to do your part. We'd like to be sure you don't ruin your future, that you don't even put yourself in a position where she could make a false accusation if she takes your rejection amiss."

Chris looked astonished. "I never thought of that." He considered the possibility. "How about this? I won't let Denis out of my sight."

"Good. We'd also like to enjoy this vacation ourselves, so if you have any idea that Denis is getting interested in her—"

"He hasn't really seemed—"

"She hasn't turned her full attention on him."

Chris sighed. "How did I get into this, anyway? I just wanted to enjoy France."

"Didn't we all?" I replied. "It's looking less and less like we're going to."

The Kir Royale

Did you know that before Dom Pierre Perignon discovered that cork was the best substance for keeping the bubbles in sparkling wine, cellarmasters tried bark, rolled grape leaves, and nastiest, a skim of olive oil? Only cork worked, and Louis XIV loved the Benedictine monk's champagne, as did the Sun King's court. Who wouldn't? And a lovely way to drink it is in a Kir Royale cocktail.

Basically the yummy Kir Royale is a flute of *ice cold champagne* with a dash of *crème de cassis* (black currant liqueur). Bartenders differ on whether the *teaspoon of cassis* should be put into the flute before the cold champagne is poured over it or the champagne poured and then topped with the cassis. No one disagrees that the drink should be made flute by flute and served immediately.

There are several nice variations: a *lemon twist* on the rim, a *raspberry or blackberry* floating in the cocktail, or halved *strawberries* sweetened with *sugar* and put in before the champagne and cassis.

My favorite variation is a mixture of cassis and *chambord* (raspberry liqueur) poured in before the champagne. However you fix the Kir Royale, you and your guests will love it; it's delicious and festive.

Carolyn Blue, "Have Fork, Will Travel," *Oak Ridge Times*

Carolyn

Jason was asleep by the time I'd finished writing a newspaper column to send to Paul Fallon, the vice president of the newspaper syndicate in New York. I considered going to the lobby to fax it, but I didn't really want to walk through those "creepy" courtyards alone. That realization forced me to think about the strange incidents that were occurring on our tour. Jason was right. There were too many to ignore, but what was really going on? Obviously, the occurrences were connected to Childeric because he'd been the target two—no, three—times. But did I believe that it was connected to the competition for dean? No. That was ridiculous.

Staring at the lighted screen of my laptop, which displayed the copy of my article, I felt the urge to write down what I could remember of the happenings. Maybe if I did that, I'd see useful connections. In other words, I was again letting curiosity lure me into considering what seemed to be a mystery. Not, thank God, one that involved missing or dead people.

I gave in to the impulse, but in a very sensible and methodical way. I clicked on the Table function at the top of the screen, created a table . . . and found I couldn't get enough words in the little boxes. Computers are so frustrating. Next, I entered items under headings. It wasn't terribly neat. I couldn't even manage to run the bottom line all the way across the page. But still, when I was finished, my information was laid out in front of me.

After studying the chart, two things occurred to me:

First, although Hugh Fauree was Dr. Childeric's prime suspect, no one had seen Hugh at the first two scenes, and he could not have sprayed Dr. Childeric with insecticide at Giverny because he had been behind him on the path, not hiding in the bamboo grove.

Second, in all three instances I could have been injured myself: at

CLUE LIST

Day	Place	Victim	Injury	Means
1	airport Paris	Childeric	head cut shoulder	shove
2	courtyard	Childeric me	shoulder shins	pot
3	Giverny	Childeric	clothes dignity skin	insecticide

Charles de Gaulle, if Chris hadn't pulled me back when I might have fallen with Childeric; in the hotel courtyard, when I had been injured, although not seriously; and at Giverny, if I hadn't dropped back to take Jason's picture. However, the thought that anyone might be after me was silly. I wasn't even a dean candidate.

In other words, I had no idea who might be staging these attacks. If someone was and it was the same person every time, it had to be someone other than Chris, Edie, Jason, and Hugh. Janice Petar seemed to be the only person who really disliked Dr. Childeric, although I had no idea why. Hugh was getting to dislike him, but that was because Childeric was picking on him.

Travel Journal
Day Three, Giverny

Last night I got the S.O.B. with a flowerpot. Arm in a sling. Shoulder evidently dislocated. Must have been painful. Good.

Today he was accusing the other dean candidates of trying to kill him and acting like a wounded warrior in the academic wars. Man's an ass. Wish I'd realized that years ago.

So why did Carolyn Blue walk through Giverny with him? She should have realized by now that his company is dangerous.

It made me very angry. With both of them. Angry enough to stalk them through the garden.

CLUE LIST

Present	Suspect	Motive
Childeric	Fauree	deanship
Chris		
me		
strangers	strangers	air rage
Childeric	Fauree	deanship
Edie		
me	Petar	hates JCC
Childeric	Fauree	deanship
	Robbie	"
	Laura	"
	Jason	"
Jason		
me	gardener	accident?

Beautiful place, but I wasn't paying much attention to the flowers. His fault.

I found this sprayer in a bamboo grove, something in the can. I was thinking fertilizer when I caught him alone and gave him two or three squirts from behind a tree. The sprayer had a good range, but the stuff turned out to be some innocuous bug spray. Well, maybe not completely innocuous. His face and hands were still red tonight. Kind of like he'd been scalded. Not bad, but I'd rather that he got soaked with liquid cow manure. Something that really reeked.

At the time, C. thought he'd been blinded. The others thought it was a toxic insecticide. Then the Hecht woman turned the hose on him. That was fun. C. likes to be well dressed. Good clothes, no wrinkles, hair just so. He looked like a drowned rat. And acted like one. The two scientists got soaked too, and the garden authorities made a fuss. Snotty French. My mother hated that word—snotty—never let me use it. C. is French. Maybe they'll all think twice now about having anything to do with him.

And no one saw me. I circled around and came up behind the big scene he made, no one the wiser.

Maybe I'm invisible, and I never realized it till now.

Childeric did that to me.

Only fair that I return the favor.

Still, I suppose I'd better keep a low profile for a while.

Versailles tomorrow. Heard Denis say thunderstorms predicted. Maybe C. will get hit by lightning.

14

A Feminist Mother of Nine

Carolyn

The plans for day four were a visit to Versailles, a sail at dusk on the Seine, and an evening dinner aboard ship. It sounded charming, but after our first three days, I was wary. Also, it was hard to look forward to the company of Edie. No doubt she would have been thinking the same thing had she known she was to sit with me on the bus and at dinner and enjoy the delights of Louis XIV's palace in my company.

I did try to enlist Anna Thomas-Smith to spend at least part of the day with Edie, explaining with some embarrassment that I had caught the girl kissing my son. Anna's response was a kind but firm no. She sympathized with my problem but pointed out that she was not the person who had promised to take care of Edie. Nor was she getting a tour discount for rooming with the girl. "I do have friends of my own on the tour, Carolyn," she said, "and hope to spend my days, at least, with adults."

Well, she had a point, and I felt guilty for sticking her with Edie yesterday afternoon while I lectured Chris. Anna was quite nice about accepting my apology and responded by advising me to watch out for lecherous Frenchmen, both on my own behalf and Edie's, and to keep an eye on Chris, who seemed a nice boy but was possibly being influenced by the lax morals of the country.

Although I have, of course, read about the amorous and hedonistic French, they've never struck me that way—except in the matter of food and wine. In fact, they seem practical, frugal, and somewhat standoffish, admirable traits when you think about it. I read an article once that advised tourists to refrain from smiling at strangers on the street in France because the French assume that such behavior indicates simplemindedness. Perhaps Charles the Simple, the king who gave away Normandy to the Vikings, had been in the habit of smiling at strangers.

At any rate, Anna and I parted friends, and we all set out on a bus for Versailles. Chris sat up front with Denis and Marguerite, who was to be our special guide in Versailles. Edie sat beside me, refusing my offer of the window seat and suggesting that I might prefer to sit with Dr. Childeric, since I seemed to like *him*. Jason sat beside Ivan, with Hugh across the aisle caught between the intellectual excitement of scientific discussion and the more obvious allure of Robbie.

Edie was blatantly uninterested in anything either Denis or I had to say about Versailles, but very interested in my son's attentions to Marguerite. Then suddenly she announced that, since I didn't want to sit with Dr. Childeric, she would, her idea being that if she had to listen to French history, she might as well get it from the expert. The professor was sitting by himself, when I glanced over. Not only was his arm still in the sling, but his face looked severely sunburned. Was that the result of the homemade bug spray? The red skin had, more or less, erased the antiseptic that had stained his forehead, but his four black stitches now looked loose and even more unsightly. Poor man. Maybe he'd appreciate Edie's company.

While I was debating the matter, Edie hopped across the aisle and informed the astonished medievalist that she'd just *love* to hear about all the lecherous Louis who had lived at Versailles. What history professor could resist an invitation to impart knowledge to an eager young thing, even if her choice of words left something to be desired? I closed my eyes and had a lovely nap.

For the most part, the day at Versailles was overcast or raining, and the gloomy weather was somewhat depressing after the frightening events of the days before. I'm not particularly fond of eighteenth-century history or palaces, but Versailles is certainly memorable—for its size, its ostentation, and its immense gardens. It started out as a hunting lodge built by Louis

XIII so he wouldn't have to sleep out in the cold while galloping about the countryside, looking for animals to kill. On his death, the lodge passed to Louis XIV, who from 1661 on poured money into buildings and interior decorations. After his death in 1715, Louis XV inherited the results.

The tour of all this splendor was punctuated by verbal outbursts from Marguerite, who never hesitated to lambaste Japanese tourists who persisted in taking pictures where none were allowed and to shout angrily at other guides who dared to interrupt her lectures. I personally enjoyed Marguerite's talks enough to resent competing guides, too, even Denis, who occasionally disagreed with her.

When we reached The Queen's Inner Chambers, the fun really began. Louis XV's queen, Marie Leczinska, of whom I had never heard, inhabited these rooms. Because her father, Stanislas I, had to leave Poland and raise her in poverty, she had been thought extremely fortunate to be chosen as a French royal bride, a selection made on the grounds that she was suitably Catholic and unlikely to gain any partisans in court.

However, her forty-three years in France were pretty much downhill from the royal wedding at Fountainebleau in 1725. Before the bridal year had passed, Louis lost interest and began taking a long series of mistresses. Nonetheless, the unhappy Marie of Poland gave birth, in public, to nine royal children in ten years. Denis swore it was thirteen children; Marguerite disagreed in her accustomed aggressive fashion.

Whoever was right, Edie thought having so many children was "gross." Ingrid Jensen voiced dismay at the idea of giving birth in front of an audience of courtiers. Estrella Markarov, no doubt thinking of her own childbearing hopes, said children were a gift from God, no matter what the number or circumstances. Marguerite became peeved at the interruptions and snarled for quiet, after which she went on to tell us that the Polish queen, after the ninth child, announced that henceforth her bedroom door was closed to the king on saints' days.

"That's almost as good as birth control, at least if there's nothing better available," Robbie offered humorously.

"The queen was obeying the church, not practicing birth control," a shocked Estrella retorted. "Roman Catholic women do not use birth control, then or now."

"Church say no sex on saints' days?" asked Ivan, looking worried. "How many saints' days are?"

"The church has changed its position on abstinence," Estrella murmured, blushing.

"Many thanks to Pope for that!" Ivan exclaimed, beaming as he gave his wife a hug. "Sex is like warm stone in cold bed, no? Too much cold nights make mens sad."

"Really, Dr. Markarov!" murmured Anna. "There are young people present."

Her comment went unheard by all but Edie, who sniggered knowingly. The call for propriety had been drowned out by Janice Petar, who said, "That makes the queen an early feminist. I'll have to include her in a lecture. There's nothing more edifying than a woman who turns the rules of the patriarchy against those who thought them up."

"I rather imagine she just got tired of having children," I murmured to Jason, and we all moved on toward our rendezvous with the gardens of Versailles, all of us except Grace, who said it was about to rain. Therefore, she would just sit here beside this nice French lady and knit until we returned. She had found one of the ubiquitous national monument attendants, and the two of them sat down amid the satin and gilt and mirrors for a grandmotherly chat.

The rest of us went out to view the long, long vistas of formal paths and lawns, with statues and fountains, trees and hedges adding decoration. I'm happy to say no one suffered any injuries, although I was keeping my eyes open for the perpetrator.

15

Drenched on Royal Grounds

Orange Bliss

Orangeries were popular with French kings and nobles. At Fontainebleau the sixteenth-century orangerie of the Valois kings began with one tree, planted in a tub in Spain by Eleanor of Castile, acquired by the constable of France, confiscated by the Queen Mother, Louise of Savoy, and moved later to Versailles. It finally died 335 years later without having produced one orange. The few fruits borne by these indoor trees were not tasty. When the trees even blossomed, it was cause for celebration.

The welfare of the Versailles orange trees was inquired after by Louis XIV, even during military campaigns. They provided orange blossoms to decorate the palace, particularly the Hall of Mirrors, and the flowers were admired for their sweet fragrance and beauty. One wonders whether the Sun King inquired as solicitously after the well-being of his queen as he did after that of his orange trees. As for the lack of fruit, faux oranges suspended amid the leaves and blossoms like Christmas ornaments remedied that.

Fortunately, the French were able to import real oranges from countries more favorable to their cultivation. Here is a delicious French recipe, simplified for American use.

Peel, section, and remove seeds and filaments from *4 oranges*. Cut into small pieces and reserve juice.

Whip *¾ cup heavy cream* and mix in *4 tbs. sugar,* 1½ tbs. Grand Marnier, 4 tbs. chopped walnuts, 2½ tbs. orange juice, and the orange pieces.

Ladle into 4 dessert goblets. Use *orange leaves,* if available, or *maraschino cherries* to decorate the individual servings. Chill thoroughly in the refrigerator before serving.

Carolyn Blue, "Have Fork, Will Travel," *Manchester Times*

Carolyn

No doubt the various Kings Louis viewed the park and the buildings with satisfaction, but it seemed to me that Versailles could not have been much fun to live at. Yesterday's sunshine at Giverny had given way to dark clouds. I heard other tourists talking of storms elsewhere, high winds, rain, lightning strikes, power outages, and a man killed when his crane blew over. Thank goodness, I was carrying an umbrella.

Professor Childeric managed to break away from Edie and once more attached himself to me for a chat about yesterday's insecticide attack. "It must have been Fauree," he assured me. "Who but a biologist would think of using bug spray as a weapon?"

"His field is parasites, not bugs," I replied, noting that Jason looked quite irritated, although we were now viewing a lovely five-tiered fountain in the middle of a pond. On every tier there were statues and water spurting. Very nice. Was Jason angry because I hadn't been able to avoid the disaster-prone Dr. Childeric or because Edie had attached herself to him, having lost or abandoned the attention of the medievalist? She was literally hanging on my husband's arm, looking up at him with a melting smile. I heard Jason ask whether her generation was concerned about global warming and the greenhouse effect.

Before she could answer, if she had any ideas on the subject, a sudden wind came up and blew fountain water onto the four of us, not to mention quite a few other unwary tourists. Jeremy Foxcroft, sketching the fountain in pastels, was left with a soggy piece of paper. Edie giggled like a six-year-old running through a sprinkler on a hot day. Jason gave himself a wet-collie shake and eyed the dark clouds rolling in, while Professor Childeric complained bitterly, as if the wind had risen specifically to ruin his day and his tweed sports jacket with the professorial leather elbow patches. Rain then fell, and he crowded under my umbrella, saying that water would spot his silk tie.

I was remarking that we should all be glad the rain wasn't as dangerous here as in other parts of France—he seemed to feel no sympathy for the deceased crane operator—when the wind turned my umbrella inside out, thunder rumbled, and a lightning bolt struck nearby, barely missing a statue of some Greek god. Without even pausing to help me, the professor headed for shelter. Edie, whose wet T-shirt clung and revealed that she was braless, took off after Professor Childeric. Jason joined me, saying, "Saved by a timely storm," and helped with my umbrella.

We took refuge in the orangerie and admired the three thousand orange trees until the lightning abated, then wandered off to look for Edie and view stone dogs spewing streams of water from opposite sides of a runoff basin, a number of really excellent statues from Greek mythology, and finally a huge equestrian sculpture, probably of Louis XIV, where other members of our group were congregated. There we did find our missing foster child.

Carl Jensen seemed to be studying the legs and buttocks of the rearing horse, while his wife remarked that she'd never seen a horse like that at the state fair. "Shapeless head, don't you think, Carl?" Lorenzo de Sorentino seemed more interested in the rider's face, and I liked the king's shoulder-length hair and silly hat.

"So, Sorentino," said Macauley Drummond, "are you considering plastic surgery on his majesty? A nose job maybe? Those French kings were a bit long in the beak."

Lorenzo ignored him, but Drummond persisted. "Take Nedda, what would you propose for her?"

Overhearing Drummond's question, Nedda abruptly ended her disquisition on the brilliance of his novels. Janice Petar turned away from Anna, with whom she had been chatting about how silly Jean-Claude had looked when drenched by the fountain, and snorted, "Brilliant? Drummond's books? More like an exercise in patriarchal rubbish."

"Are you saying you've actually read one of my novels?" Macauley asked. "I'd have thought you stuck pretty much to the drivel put out by the feminist presses, Janice."

"I prefer fiction that says something in an intelligible and literate fashion," she replied.

"Oh really. Whom would *you* recommend?"

"E. Annie Proulx, for one, and so do the critics. If you've won any prizes, I haven't heard about it. Proulx won them all with *The Shipping News*."

"Ugly loser makes it big in the ice and mud of smalltown Newfoundland. Fascinating subject." Drummond turned his back on her and continued to prod the plastic surgeon. "Take a look at Nedda here. What would you do for her?"

Finally Lorenzo turned around. "Well, I'd start off by shaving her head."

"Lorenzo," his wife murmured warningly.

Nedda Drummond did have tightly frizzy, singularly colorless hair, but she was perfectly able to defend herself. "You may not like my hair, de Sorentino, but we scholars don't worry about such trivia. I believe my list of publications and honors speaks for itself."

Her husband's laughter boomed out until de Sorentino continued, "And then I'd paste your wife's Brillo hair on top of your bald pate, Drummond. It would make a marvelous topper for those pretentious ear-to-shoulder locks of yours."

The plastic surgeon walked off; rolling her eyes, his wife strolled in the other direction; and I sighed, thinking that if our fellow travelers became any more disagreeable, maybe I could talk Laura into slipping them all some Prozac. Time for perusing the gardens being over, the onset of another bout of rain and wind sent us hurrying back to meet our guides in the central building. There we found that at least one of us had been enjoying herself.

Grace Unsell had gathered a coterie of four women, two of whom spoke English and acted as translators. They were all offering advice by cell phone to Grace's pregnant daughter, who was getting no sleep because the baby kicked her so hard at night that not only her nightgown, but the covers, bulged with the force of determined little feet. A very chic matron was singing a French lullaby into the cell phone when we arrived. It was guaranteed to calm a child in the womb, we were assured by a Belgian, although she herself recommended herb tea and a gentle rubbing of the wife's stomach.

Female bonding could save the world, I thought, if the men could only be persuaded to let it work.

Well, it hadn't been too bad a day so far. Quarrels, certainly. Wind gusts, drenchings from fountains and rain clouds, a bit of scary lightning, but no physical damage done. Until Jean-Claude Childeric managed to fall down in the aisle of the bus. He claimed that Janice had tripped him in an assault motivated by feminist solidarity with Laura. Janice hooted with laughter. Childeric retorted that his ankle was sprained and he might well sue her.

Sitting across the aisle one seat forward from Janice was Anna, who had relented in her desire to spend her days away from teenagers and boxed Edie in by the window. However, Edie would not stay boxed when she saw a means of escape. She jumped up, climbed over her roommate, and rushed to Childeric's side, giving my son and then me a lofty toss of the head. Then she draped Childeric's good arm over her shoulder and helped him to the back of the bus, while he complained about his sprained ankle and his aching shoulder, which had been jarred by his fall.

Had she decided that she preferred medieval history to science? Or did she think Chris or I or both of us would be jealous of her attentions to Childeric? I, for one, was delighted that she'd found someone to occupy her time without inconveniencing Anna, and Chris seemed to be more interested in Marguerite than the girl he had kissed just yesterday. Yes, it was proving to be a better day than those that preceded it, and we had a lovely cruise and dinner on the Seine to look forward to.

The cruise was very pretty, but there was no dinner on the Seine. In fact, there was no dinner worth mentioning. I wrote an article on indoor orange groves for Paul Fallon, wondering all the while whether he'd found more papers interested in my columns. Since I had to stay up past my bedtime to write them, it would be nice to make more money doing it.

Then I asked myself, did Childeric's fall on the bus merit addition to my clue list? Probably not. Probably he'd tripped over his own feet, and he hadn't been limping much by the time Edie got him to the back of the bus. He had, however, accused Janice, and he had been beside Janice when he tripped. Who was on the other side? Lorenzo and Laura, Lorenzo on the aisle side. Would he do that to forward his wife's candidacy? I sighed, pulled up my clue list, and added Childeric's ankle to the bottom. Hooray! I managed to get the bottom line all the way across.

So what did my list tell me? If all these happenings weren't accidents, they could all be motivated by the competition for the dean's position, but one had to postulate that candidates, their spouses, their friends, and/or one woman motivated by dislike would be willing to hurt someone to influence the selection. Did I believe that?

Travel Journal
Day Four, Versailles

What do I have to do to isolate C.? Shoot the rest of them?
Edie Atwater, of all people, rescued the bastard from having to sit on the bus by himself. Then Carolyn let him under her umbrella.
A lightning bolt almost hit a statue in the park at Versailles but missed C. entirely. Enjoyed watching him fume when a fountain and then a rainstorm soaked him, but that isn't good enough. And it wasn't my doing. Maybe I need to plan ahead instead of acting on impulse.
The best I could do just winging it was trip him. Not very exciting, but it hurt like hell. You could hear him whining about the pain all over the bus.
Then the damn Atwater girl propped him up and spent the ride home fawning on him, telling him what a wonderful scholar he is.
Right! His most successful paper was based on my research, and he never so much as mentioned my name.
My God, but I'd like to get even.
The thing is—how? Nothing works. And here I am, tempted to skip the boat ride and dinner tonight because I can't stand to be in the same room with him.

16

The Dubious Delights of Rouen

Jason

Carolyn had such high hopes for the Seine cruise and dinner, and the cruise was spectacular. We drifted sedately by all those handsome riverside buildings under a white sky. Late in the afternoon the horizon streaked with rose, mauve, and blue, while pink-tinted clouds drifted up from perches atop the statues and towers of the city until finally the sun sank down behind the darkening silhouettes. We took pictures. We mourned the end of the display; then we went in search of Denis, for we had seen no preparations aboard to feed us the promised feast.

He shrugged, smiling, and replied, "Didn't I say? These boat dinners, they are . . . *très* inferior. I have picked a fine café ashore." No one was pleased to hear it. No one was pleased with the dinner that followed. Carolyn's final word on that meal was: "It's not worth so much as mention in my notebook." She was very testy by the time we returned to the hotel, more so when Denis informed us that our packed bags should be outside our doors by 11 P.M. for pickup.

"If you have my suitcase, what am I supposed to do with my nightgown and toiletries tomorrow?" she asked. "Carry them under my arm all day in Rouen?"

"Madame, have you never been touring before? Everyone carries a small bag onto the bus," Denis replied.

"Then where do I put my camera, film, notebooks, pens, and travel books if my small bag is filled with a nightgown and toiletries?" Carolyn retorted.

"Surely Madame's nightgown is not so . . . voluminous?" He treated her to his charming smile. Carolyn did not respond.

"You can have nightie room in my backpack, Mom," said Chris.

"Can I too, Chris?" Edie asked. "My nightie is ever so tiny."

Before Chris could answer, Carolyn grasped Edie by the arm and hustled her off toward the courtyard of the falling flowerpots.

However, Carolyn was more cheerful the next morning. When she awoke, our bags were still on the balcony, so she prevailed upon me to stuff her nightgown into an outside pocket. Then when we were leaving the hotel, she spotted the bags beside the bus and stopped the driver from loading hers until she could dispose of her toiletries. Having triumphed over tour regulations, she said happily, "I can hardly wait to see Rouen. It was a seat of Norman power. William the Conqueror and his queen, Mathilda—"

"Ah, my dear Carolyn," Childeric interrupted, "you must share the ride with me. We can discuss—"

I grasped Carolyn's arm and hustled her away before the hotel marquee could collapse on him and injure her as well. I've never thought of myself as a superstitious person, but this tour was getting on my nerves. Carolyn swept up Edie as we wove through the chatting crowd of academics toward the bus door.

"Well, Dr. Blue," the girl exclaimed coyly, "I do believe you're jealous of Mrs. Blue and Dr. Childeric, but don't you worry. I'll divert his attention." With that, she tossed a glance at Chris, as if to say, *I can have anyone I want. I don't need you,* and she attached herself to Childeric. *Better him than me,* I thought, and settled down to enjoy my wife's company.

Carolyn

I can't believe I slept all the way to Rouen. No wonder Jason likes to spend his time with Ivan and Hugh. When I woke up, he was sitting at the back talking science. I caught Dr. Jensen, the bovine specialist, casting them envious glances, like a little boy who wants to but despairs of being invited to join the other boys in the tree house. Chris had a tree house when he was eight, in which he and his friends gathered to play space war. By the time he was nine, the tree house was forsaken because his sister had sneaked in while he was away at camp and defiled his hideaway with ruffled curtains and Barbie dolls who enacted melodramatic scenes of Gwen's composing.

I took a sip from my plastic water bottle and climbed off the bus, enthusiastically looking forward to the walking tour. Rouen has been here two thousand years or more. Gauls, Romans, Normans, and Frenchmen have walked these narrow streets that now feature elaborate wood and plaster houses leaning precariously toward one another.

"Watch out, Childeric," Robbie called. "That house is about to tip over on you." Everyone but the professor laughed. He clutched his injured shoulder protectively.

We listened as Denis told us that the Butter Tower was built with the offerings of Normans who couldn't give up butter for Lent. I came to sympathize because Norman butter is special, rich and somehow more delightful in flavor than other butters. We visited a plague cemetery that had a courtyard surrounded by typical wood and plaster architecture. Denis said the poor were buried in pits in the center courtyard while the rich were buried inside, with the second floor reserved for bones.

In later years orphan children were housed at one end. To allay their fears of ghosts, black cats were enclosed in the walls to frighten away the dead. The cat skeletons there were found more recently during renovations. Estrella Markarov was distressed to think of the poor little children subjected to such fear and hoped that they were comforted by their faith and by visiting or resident priests.

Ingrid said to Denis, "The poor cats were buried alive? That's—that's barbarous." Denis replied that it was their dying cries that frightened away the ghosts.

Childeric growled, "What nonsense."

I myself had no idea whether or not the story was true, but it was interesting, and creepy. The plague, the corpses, the cats, the children, even the gloomy skies overhead gave me a feeling of impending doom, which I had to shake off to admire the soaring beauty of the cathedral that held, according to Denis, the tombs of such romantic figures as Richard the Lionhearted. "Was that the crusader king?" I asked Denis. "Isn't he buried somewhere else?" Childeric tried to answer my question, but Jason whisked me away when the professor approached.

Other tombs belonged to Rollo, the Norse adventurer to whom Charles the Simple gave the dukedom in return for a cessation of Viking raids up the Seine; and to William Longsword, a later Duke of Normandy, so named, according to Denis, for the "length of his male member."

At this, Professor Childeric was so offended, both morally and academically, that he shouted, "Have you no shame, man? He was called Longsword because his legs were so long that his feet dragged when he rode a horse."

To me it seemed more likely that the duke had wielded a particularly long sword in combat, but it was something I could look up at home, without having to contradict the modern combatants. "Who the hell cares?" Jason muttered. "Why can't the man just shut up and stop infuriating everyone? No wonder things keep happening to him."

Since *I* cared about what the nickname of the Norman duke meant, I failed to agree with my husband's complaint, and he gave me a narrow look. "Don't tell me you feel sorry for that ass?" Such language is not typical of Jason, so I hastened to point out the interesting carvings of biblical stories on the portals as we left. "Hardly anyone could read then, so they had to get their lessons chiseled in the stone. Imagine trying to teach chemistry that way to illiterates."

"We do teach chemistry with pictures," Jason replied, relaxing and smiling at me, "and I've had students who are borderline illiterate. Didn't you hear Nedda Drummond talking last night about refusing to teach freshman English because she had so many students who didn't read and couldn't write?"

We continued chatting happily, trying to take in all the sights while heeding Denis's exhortations to mind the traffic and not cross against the lights because the tour company reprimanded him if cars ran over his tourists. Finally we came in view of the famous clock on the Rue du Gros–Horlage. Childeric came over to give me some "accurate information" on the clock, and I listened absently and admired its beauty. Placed at the foot of the bell tower, it is huge, its face gold and blue with a sunray design and hands that terminate in animal figures.

I squinted, trying to make out what animal it was. Others were speculating aloud. "Looks like a rat to me," said Macauley Drummond.

"How clever," exclaimed his wife Nedda. "How symbolic in a town that suffered so severely from bubonic plague, which was carried by the fleas on rats. The clock tells us that Time brings death to us all."

."Looks like a sheep to me," said Carl Jensen.

"And how do you interpret that, Carl?" asked Drummond. "Sheep bring mad cow disease to us all?" He snickered and added, "Not very poetic."

"No mad cow disease back then," said Jensen. "France only got that just lately."

"Perhaps our knowledgeable guide would care to enlighten us," said Childeric. Then he made a strange grunting sound and, with one hand against my back, shoved me.

I found myself stumbling into the street and falling in front of a large bicycle ridden by a husky, red-faced man in a cap. I couldn't get out of the way, or do anything but continue my fall. Although the incident must have occurred in seconds, it seemed to drag on in slow motion, accompanied by paralyzing fear. The collision with the bicycle flattened me on the cobblestones, and my body shuddered with the shock of the impact.

If you've ever been run down, you know that it's no laughing matter. It hurts! Especially if you're a relatively small woman, small in comparison to a large man peddling his ancient, heavy bicycle with muscular ferocity. I felt frightened and faint as people crowded around me. On his knees beside me in an instant, Jason told me not to move. The rider shouted angrily in French, no doubt protesting my invasion of his right-of-way. Dr. Jensen knelt beside Jason and began to feel my arms, legs, and ribs, all the while assuring me that he'd diagnosed many a broken cow bone.

Someone, Janice I think, demanded to know why Jean-Claude Childeric had pushed me, and as I began to think more clearly, I wondered myself. It was definitely he who had propelled me into the street, not Jason, not anyone else. I had smelled the distinctive cologne he wore as I sprawled forward. The professor insisted that someone had pushed *him*. *He* was the intended victim, not me!

"Well, my wife is the person who was hurt," snapped Jason. "Why don't you stay away from her?"

"Mom, are you okay?" Chris loomed at my feet, peering at me anxiously.

"I didn't mean her any harm," Childeric protested. "We're both victims here."

"I do believe you're a jinx, Childeric, old man," said Macauley Drummond in what I was coming to recognize as his typically nasty brand of sarcasm. "Maybe we'd all better stay away from *you*."

17

The Medicinal Qualities of Calvados

Carolyn

With Jason on one side and Chris on the other, I hobbled toward the Place du Vieux-Marche and a visit to the stunningly modern church of Sainte Joan of Arc. Outside, a dark, conical roof swept up at a slant from its height-of-a-man overhang to a point that seemed to pierce the overcast sky. Lower sections of the roof swooped away from the cone and sent triangular points almost to the ground. The architecture had an original and dark simplicity, but lovely war-salvaged stained glass lighted the inside.

En route Denis entertained the group with the tale of Rouen's patron saint, Romain, an eighth-century bishop who saved the terrorized city from a monster called Gargoyle. Silly me! I thought a gargoyle was an ugly monster head protruding from a cathedral, a carving that drained water from the roof and frightened off demons. Jason and Chris were discussing the best strategy for protecting me from Childeric accidents. They struck on some plan too complicated for my befuddled mind to take in, and Chris went off to implement it.

As a result, when we had lunch at a sidewalk café near the church, I found myself seated with ladies. Childeric was boxed into a table with the men, who could presumably defend themselves against whatever ill fortune might befall. My companions were Robbie, Janice, Anna, and of course, Edie. Liking them all (well, the jury was out on Edie, but I was trying), I was happy enough and ordered seafood crepes and white wine. I have to tell you that, although the crepe and sauce were very nice, the seafood bits were sandy. There is nothing more disconcerting than finding sand in your food by chewing on some. It's not as if you can separate it out like a bone, a piece of gristle, or an olive pit and remove it from your mouth with ladylike delicacy.

My mother advised patting one's mouth inconspicuously with a napkin, thereby transferring the indigestible item into the napkin. With sand-laced food, you must either spit out the whole mouthful, which is hard to do inconspicuously, or swallow it, which makes one fear for the state of one's digestive tract. And to be confronted with this problem while aches were springing up everywhere in my body was really too much.

Robbie had ordered mussels in Normandy sauce and, because she knew about my writing, offered me a taste. I refused a mussel. If my seafood bits were sandy, think of how much sand a whole mussel might contain! I did try the Normandy sauce, and it was excellent, flavored by the rich cream for which the region is famous. To that were added flavors from the mussels, onion, herbs, and other things. I can't tell you everything I detected because my arm hurt, and I didn't make notes. Also, the conversation had begun to command my attention.

"Can you believe that Hugh's room has only one bed, one *single* bed? It's downright inconvenient, I can tell you that," Robbie complained.

I should have changed the direction of the conversation right then. After all, Edie was at our table and listening avidly.

"So it occurred to me that we could shift the room arrangements." Robbie's trademark smile flashed around the circle. "Then Hugh and I could room together. He's such a love."

Anna sent her a warning frown, then glanced significantly in Edie's direction.

Edie said, "Oh, don't mind me. I know that if people my age do it, so do people your age. Married, unmarried, whatever. I think it's cool."

Anna gritted her teeth and said, "You are the most irresponsible girl. If I were your mother, I'd keep you locked in your room."

"Well, you're not my mother, thank God," Edie retorted. "Hey, Dr. Hecht, I'd give you my bed if it would do you any good, but—"

"That's a start," said Robbie enthusiastically. "But Hugh and I can't move in with Anna. On the other hand, Anna, you could move in with Janice, and then Hugh and I could move into your room."

"I think not," said Janice. "Two single women, one a feminist? Ingrid Jensen would love that. The woman has a mortal fear of homosexuality. She'd be telling everyone on the tour that we're gay."

"Wow! Are you?" asked Edie.

Janice eyed her with sardonic amusement. "We're not. Are you?"

"Me? Hey, I like guys." Edie's eyes began to dance. "So how about this? Now that it's settled you're not lesbians, Dr. Thomas-Smith moves in with you, Dr. Petar. I mean, she'd probably rather have you for a roommate than me. She can't stand me! And you probably don't like Dr. Hecht because she likes guys and sex. I mean she's been married a bunch of times, and now she's after Dr. Fauree. So, like she said, she and Dr. Fauree can have my room, and I'll—I'll move in with Chris!"

"And Dr. Childeric?" asked Janice dryly.

"He can take Dr. Fauree's single room. Not likely anyone would want to move in with him if he's as dangerous as Dr. Drummond said." She was smiling broadly as she turned to me. "Gee, Mrs. Blue, you don't want your son rooming with a professor who's on someone's hit list, do you?"

"Since I was the one who had an accident today, I think we can assume that there is no *hit list*," I replied.

Edie shrugged. "Oh well, I think Dr. Drummond was just being . . . snotty. About the jinx business." She turned to Anna and added, "I hope you noticed I didn't say he was being an asshole, although he was."

"You are not moving in with Chris," said Anna. "Carolyn, don't you have anything to say?"

A groan would have expressed what I had to say. My bones felt as if I'd been kicked and trampled by a column of Nazis in jackboots, whatever those are. I'm afraid I didn't acquit myself very well in my surrogate mother role. The waiter approached, and I ordered an apple tart (Normandy is also famous for its apples) and a Calvados.

"Alcohol will not solve this problem," said Anna.

"You're really hurting, aren't you?" My friend Robbie was now studying me thoughtfully. From the look on her face, I gathered that large bruises must have been appearing on mine, not to mention on the clothed parts of my battered person.

"I really am," I agreed.

"Yeah, you look awful, Mrs. Blue," said Edie.

What a source of joy the girl was. I couldn't wait to return her to her mother.

Robbie pulled a bottle of Tylenol from the backpack slung over her chair and passed it to me. "You better take some. They might help."

I snatched the bottle eagerly, fumbled with the lid as the waiter set my Calvados on the table, and washed down four pills with one swallow of the bottled water I carry. Then I picked up the Calvados, which I don't even like, and took a big gulp. I ordered it because one can't write about Normandy without mentioning Calvados, another specialty of the area since it's made of local apples.

"Carolyn, don't do that!" Anna protested. "The combination of alcohol and acetaminophen will destroy your liver."

I don't know about my liver, but the Calvados went straight to my head, perhaps dissolving the synapses, or whatever, that connect pain to the perception of it. "Anna," I said, more relaxed now that I saw a less painful future in the offing, "I really can't worry about my liver right now. It doesn't hurt. The rest of me does." Then I took another swallow, and it burned right down to my tummy. Good stuff!

Anna turned to Edie. "You are not going to room with Chris," she said calmly. "You're staying with me, which does not make me any happier than it makes you, but your only alternative is to go home."

"You can't send me home. I'm too young to travel by myself."

"Yes, you are, although I am sure there are girls your age who could easily and safely make the trip by themselves. You, on the other hand, would miss your plane by running off to a T-shirt shop or never arrive home at all because you saw fit to run off with some drug-addicted biker with a pierced tongue."

"Meany," said Edie and giggled.

She was enjoying the debate. I really should have done something about her sassy way with Anna, but my apple tart arrived—*tarte aux pommes*—and it looked very tasty. There probably wasn't a grain of sand in it. I took an appreciative bite and followed it with a slug of healthful Calvados. I must tell you that the two make a lovely combination. Lovely.

Anna was watching me and shaking her head, feeling very sorry for me and worrying about my liver, no doubt. Nice lady. I took another bite of tart and finished my Calvados.

Robbie said, "You're looking better already. Can I have a bite of your tart?"

"Order your own tart." I waved to the waiter.

"Hey, I'm the one who provided the painkillers."

"Maybe," I agreed, "but I think the Calvados is what's doing the job. I'll have another," I said to the waiter. He didn't blink an eye.

Anna had risen and moved across the café to speak to Jason. Was she ratting on me, telling him I was getting drunk and raucous? Well, I wasn't. I was just feeling a bit better.

"So about switching the room assignments around." Robbie was nothing if not persistent.

"Did you ever consider," Janice asked, "that this open sexual liaison may hurt Hugh's chances to be appointed dean?"

"Now, there's an old-fashioned thought," said Robbie gaily. "No, Janice, that never occurred to me. Anyway, it's the selection committee that counts, and how are they going to know? Are you going to call them up and snitch?"

"Maybe they sent along a spy since all three candidates are on the tour."

Edie giggled, and Robbie joined her. Then Robbie's tart and my second Calvados arrived. Maybe I'd write a column on the gourmet and analgesic properties of Calvados and *tarte aux pommes*. At the time, that seemed like an inspired idea.

18

How to Come Up Smelling Like a Horse

Jason

Dr. Blue?"

I looked up from dessert to find Anna standing beside me, looking worried.

"Ah, my dear Anna," said Childeric heartily, "joining the male table, are you? Had enough of ladies' chatter?"

She ignored him and murmured, "Dr. Blue, I'm afraid your wife is experiencing a good deal of pain from that bicycle accident."

"I'm so sorry to hear it," said Childeric. "How can we be of service to the charming—"

"She's talking to me, Childeric," I said impatiently. "Stop butting in, will you?"

"I certainly didn't mean to interfere." Childeric was now offended. "However, as a friend of your wife's—"

"Pushing her in front of a bicycle is not an act of friendship," I retorted.

"As I was saying," said Anna. "Carolyn is drinking Calvados while taking acetaminophen, not a safe combination and one that I'm sure she wouldn't risk if she weren't in pain. Perhaps she'd be better off resting in her hotel room."

I rose immediately, followed Anna to the ladies' table, and knelt beside my wife. "Anna says you're hurting, sweetheart."

"Well." Carolyn thought about it, then sampled what looked like a tart and sipped the Calvados, which she doesn't even care for. "This is a lovely combination," she informed me. "Actually, I'm feeling better, but I'm afraid I'm getting a bit tipsy."

"How much have you had?"

"One tart and two liqueurs. Works wonders. I may recommend it to my readers."

"How would you feel about skipping the afternoon tour and going back to the hotel for a nap?" I suggested. When Carolyn looked dubious, I added, "You know you like an afternoon nap when you have the time."

"True." She smiled at me and sipped a bit more Calvados. "But I'd miss the res' of the tour. Who knows? We might get something decent for dinner. Something I could write about. Is it a tour dinner? If i's more lasagna, I jus' might go for the nap."

"Carolyn, you poor thing, you're sloshed," said Robbie. "Go home and sleep it off. Maybe the acetaminophen will have worked on the bruises by then."

"Cool," said Edie. "Now if you threaten to call my mom, I'll tell her you got drunk at lunch, Mrs. Blue."

"Isn' she a horrid girl?" said Carolyn cheerfully. "The leas' Judith could do was warn me about her."

"So let's go back to the hotel, Caro," I persisted. "A nice nap—"

"Proceeded by a good soak in a hot tub," suggested Anna.

"Ummm," Carolyn agreed. "That does soun' lovely. But there'll be wonderful things to see, and I won't get to—"

"I'll go back to take pictures if you want," I promised. "I'd even offer to take notes, but it's doubtful Denis will say anything you'd want to pass on to your readers, and I'm not to listening to Childeric any more than I have to."

"He probably didn' mean to push me in front of the bus," said my wife magnanimously.

"Bicycle, not bus," said Edie.

"You didn' get hit. It felt like a bus."

At that point I did manage to fend off Carolyn's idea that another Calvados might be good for her, and having left money on the table to pay her bill, I escorted her back to the hotel before she could change her mind.

Carolyn

The hot soak in the bathtub helped, and the nap was even better. I woke up at the end of the afternoon hurting, but not unbearably. The knock that had awakened me sounded again, and I fumbled for my robe, found Jason's instead, and pulled it on over my nightie. Then rubbing my eyes, I limped to the door, thinking I wasn't that much better after all. Even my hand hurt as I unlocked the door. Had the bicycle run over my hand?

"My dear Carolyn, I just had to stop by to assure myself you were not seriously injured. I'd rather have thrown myself under that bicycle than see any harm come to you at the hands of my enemies."

"Professor Childeric?" What was he doing at my door?

"Jean-Claude. Please call me Jean-Claude." He then stepped around me into the room. "Given the bond between us, surely we need not stand on ceremony, although of course in public your husband might be appeased if you—"

"What are you talking about?" I stammered. I had turned to face him, and he reached beyond me and closed the door.

"Your husband. I fear he suspects our feelings for each other. He seems quite set on keeping us apart."

Childeric still had his hand on the knob of the closed door, thus boxing me in. Finally he pulled the hand back but used it to take mine. He had a warm, damp palm.

"Dr. Blue's feeling insecure, no doubt. It must be hard to realize that your wife has more in common with another man, not to mention a tender regard for—"

I yanked my hand away and edged sideways.

"Ah, my dear, there's no need to be frightened of discovery. He's still with the tour. I must say that it was very insensitive of him to leave you alone, but scientists are not known for gallantry, are they? I'm here now to comfort you."

Then the man actually put his good arm around me. "Let go this instant," I demanded and tried wiggle away. He hung on. The arm in the sling was pressing against my breasts, while his good arm had trapped one of mine to my side as he reached around and clutched my elbow. I don't know when I've been more shocked and embarrassed.

He, in the meantime, was smiling at me fatuously and saying, "Don't be shy, my love. With a rapport like ours—"

"Are you out of your mind? The only rapport we have is a mutual interest in—" Since the lower part of my arm was free, I used it to push at his chest, much good that did.

"Ah, such passion!" he exclaimed.

"A mutual interest in medieval history," I gasped, "does not give you the right to—to—"

"Make a declaration of affection that you have been hoping to hear?" he finished for me. "I knew from the moment we gazed into each other's eyes and you stroked the blood from my forehead so sweetly, that we were destined—"

With a wrench I managed to drag my elbow free, after which I punched him in the shoulder. He howled in pain and staggered back.

"You, sir," I panted, "are a—are a—horse's—patootie! Get out of my room!"

The professor's eyes, which had filled with tears in reaction to the pain of his injured shoulder, then rounded with astonishment. "Carolyn—"

"Out!" Having backed toward the bed, I snatched a silly-looking, ruffled lamp from the bedside table and brandished it at him. Jean-Claude Childeric backed up and fumbled for the doorknob, his mouth still agape with astonishment and his face redder than it had been after exposure to the capsaicin spray. Jason had told me about capsaicin. In concentrated form, it raises blisters on the skin. Childeric bolted out the door. With a shaking hand, I followed to turn the lock, then replaced the little lamp on its table, dropped abruptly onto the bed, and burst into tears.

I was just having a good cry and blowing my nose with Kleenex taken from the travel pack in my handbag, when I heard him tapping at my door again. Indignant, I grabbed up the lamp, rushed forward, and swung the door open, crying, "If you don't go away, I'm going to call the police."

Anna stood in the hallway. "Carolyn?"

I gulped. "Anna?" I didn't know what to say. I'm sure she hadn't expected to be greeted by a tearstained woman wielding a ruffled lamp.

"Was that Jean-Claude Childeric I saw scurrying away from your door?" she asked, an expression of concern on her face.

I'm afraid I burst into tears again, and under her sympathetic questioning, the whole humiliating story poured out. "I don't think I did anything to encourage him," I sniffled. "Discussing medieval history isn't—can't be interpreted as—as flirtatious. Can it?" We were both sitting on the bed, Anna patting my hand consolingly.

"I've never even been alone with him until he forced his way into my room."

"Some men, for all their seeming gentility and charm," she said, "have no real respect for women."

"I don't think he's charming," I responded bitterly. "He's a horrid, arrogant—"

"I quite agree. I think you should—"

"And I called him a horse's—a horse's patootie."

"Did you?" Anna looked—well, impressed, or perhaps amused. "I hope he took it to heart," she said. "Now, I think the thing to do is tell your husband about this—"

"Tell Jason? He'd be furious."

"With you?"

"No, with Childeric."

"And rightly so. In fact, perhaps we should warn some of the other women, just in case he looks elsewhere for female victims."

"Good heavens. Surely, you don't think he makes a habit of this?"

"I've heard rumors," said Anna.

I was beginning to calm down and consider the whole embarrassing event. If this story got around the tour group, I'd feel like a fool. "Let me think about it, Anna." I ran distracted fingers into my hair, inadvertently probed one of my bruises, and groaned.

"The bicycle accident?" she asked.

"The bicycle accident," I agreed. "Robbie's Tylenol is wearing off, and struggling with Professor Childeric didn't help."

"The man should pay for what he's done," she said. "You shouldn't let him get away with this." She glanced down at a tube she held in her hand. "Still, it's your decision, of course." She placed the tube, which was about eight inches long, in my hand. "Dr. Jensen left the tour to find this for you," she said. "He promises, if you rub it into your bruises or anywhere you hurt, you'll feel a lot better."

"What is it?" I asked, unable to translate the French lettering on the plastic.

"Liniment would be my guess," Anna replied.

"I guess that means I've now been treated twice by a vet. If he is a vet."

"I think he's just a cow specialist, but I don't doubt the ointment is safe to use. Lots of country people use liniment on their horses and themselves to ease pain. It can't hurt to try."

"I suppose not. And thank you. Both of you. Well, I'll thank Dr. Jensen myself, but if you see him . . . I'm dithering, aren't I?"

"You're upset," she said kindly. "And undoubtedly in pain. Rub some of that cream on and go back to bed. Maybe by tomorrow you'll be fit enough to dodge the next bicycle." Then her face tightened. "Or the next amorous professor."

"Bite your tongue," I replied, trying to look more cheerful. "I guess you got stuck with Edie again. I'm so sorry. Did she—"

"She had a perfectly boring afternoon, mostly in my company," Anna replied. "Which serves her right. She's an ill-mannered girl." With that, Anna went back to her room and, probably, the company of that ill-mannered girl. I didn't envy her.

The liver-destroying alcohol and Tylenol having worn off completely after my three-hour nap and subsequent visitors, I looked thoughtfully at the large tube in my hand. Then I unscrewed the cap and sniffed. Well, it wasn't French perfume, but my aches and pains were making themselves known. I slipped off Jason's robe and rubbed an experimental dab on an arm that was turning red and purple. Dear Dr. Jensen. Thoughtful Anna. That one spot felt better. Soon I was applying dollops freely—on road-collision areas, on bicycle-collision areas, and on places where my bones simply ached.

Whoever was responsible for my injuries—Professor Childeric or some enemy of his or just some crazy person; after my most recent shock, I blamed Childeric—I wished an equally painful accident on them. With the scent of horse medicine soaking into my skin and wafting through the room, I imagined Jason's expression when he returned. And when would that be? And lord, was I going to tell him about Childeric? I could hardly believe what had happened myself.

Perhaps Jason had decided to join the tour dinner, after all. If so, I'd have more time to decide what and what not to tell my husband. For a wonder, I wasn't even hungry.

19

Suspicions and Quiche

Carolyn

While I waited to see if Jason would return, I thought about Jean-Claude Childeric and all the accidents we'd shared or nearly shared—the airport, the falling pot, the insecticide. Had being endangered together made him think there was a romantic connection between us? Or had he somehow arranged the accidents in order to—what? Scare me to death so that I'd be vulnerable to his advances? He'd certainly had the worst of the first three. So maybe his idea had been to make me feel sorry for him. But this last—I could have been killed. What good would that do him?

And why was he making passes at a married woman? As much as he wanted to be dean, that was hardly the way to go about it. I could have made a terrible fuss and ruined his reputation. I still could, but I'd be too abysmally embarrassed to do it. No wonder men get away with sexual harassment.

At that point in my confused musings, Jason arrived with a bag containing mussels browned in the shell, quiche, salad, and apple tarts. No Calvados, but Carl Jensen's liniment had helped, so I felt able to do without Calvados. And Jason had brought a half-bottle of wine.

"I thought you might rather eat in," he explained as he laid the dinner out on the lamp table. "Are you feeling better?"

"Much better," I assured him. "I've followed everyone's advice, even to rubbing on Carl Jensen's horse liniment. Do I still smell funny?" I held out an arm for Jason to sniff. "Well, I didn't listen to Anna when she told me not to mix alcohol and Tylenol. Do you think my liver is shriveling even as we speak?"

"More likely swelling up," Jason replied. "Pretty soon you'll turn yellow."

"Thanks a lot." I tried the mussels and, surprisingly, they were tasty, but I think it was the stuff on top that made them so palatable. I had two and even looked for a recipe when I got back to the States since I didn't feel up to pursuing one that night at whatever establishment Jason had visited to get our dinner. Jason had the other six. "Is Chris joining us?" I asked.

"No, he's braving the tour dinner."

"Teenaged boys will eat anything."

"He's twenty, but given the food at his fraternity house, you're right." Jason poured me some wine, and I sampled the quiche. Mushroom. Very nice. We sat on the bed eating and discussing what could be going on with the tour. Any topic would do as long as I didn't have to mention Jean-Claude Childeric's visit to my room.

"That bicycle accident frightened me," I admitted.

"Me too," Jason replied. "It *was* Childeric who pushed you."

"Well, bumped into me, but he did say he was pushed." Why was I still defending him? "Obviously, someone is doing these things," I added hurriedly, "but who could it be? Edie? She's peeved with me for keeping her away from Chris."

"Well, if she pushed Childeric to get to you, she didn't accomplish much. Anna made her toe the line this afternoon. Didn't you say Janice dislikes him?"

"No question." The salad had a nice light dressing on very fresh greens. "But I can't remember seeing her near any of the . . . accidents. Can you think of anyone else who seems to have a grudge?"

"Drummond?" Jason suggested. "As far as I can tell, he doesn't like anyone. And de Sorentino. He's a rather unpleasant fellow."

"Could it be a Munchausen syndrome sort of thing? I saw that . . . where? . . . a TV hospital series, I suppose. He hurts someone and then looks like a hero when he steps in to cure them."

"Two problems with that hypothesis. He's a plastic surgeon, and the only medical interest he's shown in any of us is cosmetic."

I had to giggle because I'd had a silly thought. "It's Carl Jensen. He got me knocked into the street so that he could go out searching for horse liniment to cure me. Or Dr. Unsell. He wants to see how the Common Market and the Euro have affected hospital services in France, so he's trying to send us all to the hospital."

"Seriously, Carolyn."

"All right. I had a scary thought while I was soaking in the tub. There's Ivan. He seems nice enough, but he is Russian, and it was a Russian Mafia type who—"

"Take my word for it, Carolyn, Ivan Markarov is not a member of the Russian Mafia," said Jason.

"Oh, you'd think that because he's scientific. You're as bad as Childeric thinking all the scientists are plotting against him because he has a better chance at being dean than Hugh."

"Who says he has a better chance of being anything but an asshole?" my husband demanded sharply.

"Jason Blue. Is that any way to talk in mixed company? I may just have to eat both tarts myself."

Moules Gratinées

Butter was introduced to Western Europe in the fifth century by the Vandals. I wonder if the villagers considered wholesale barbarian rape and pillage a fair trade-off for the delights of butter? And did they realize that, by using it instead of olive oil, they were endangering their health? Those Vandals! After all the damage they left behind, they added heart disease to the toll.

Still, butter is lovely, especially butter made in Normandy. I've come to the conclusion that Norman butter can make anything good, even things you don't usually like—mussels, for instance. Here is a Norman recipe for a first course that combines butter and mussels to advantage.

Vigorously scrub the sand from *2 qts. of mussels.*

Steam in *½ cup white wine* with *pepper to taste* and *several slices of carrots and onions.*

Save the broth and shells after removing the mussels from the shells.

Cream some butter with *chopped and crushed garlic, finely chopped parsley, pepper, and salt (unless the butter is salted).*

Place each mussel in a half-shell, sprinkle with the leftover broth, add to each shell a layer of the butter, and brown briefly in a hot oven.

Carolyn Blue, "Have Fork, Will Travel," *Bisbee Arizona News*

As soon as I had finished writing a column, I tried to pull up my list of clues, to which I certainly needed to add my own injury. The file was gone! I'll never understand how computers manage to devour whole files. I had to start all over again.

After looking over my list, my thought that the first three attacks could have been aimed at me was reinforced; I had even sustained minor injuries from the falling pot. The third, Childeric tripping on the bus, was probably a real accident, and I had been the one hurt in Rouen. Although Edie might dislike me, she couldn't have pushed the pot because she was with me in the courtyard, and I wasn't sure that a girl that slim could have shoved a man of Dr. Childeric's girth hard enough to push me in front of a bicycle.

No one else on the tour seemed to dislike me or would have any reason that I knew of to wish me ill. The idea that Childeric might have set up the attacks under some delusion of unrequited love seemed ludicrous, so I discarded it, while vowing to stay away from the medievalist. Without knowing all the reasons, Jason would be relieved.

That left Ivan. Had he been recruited by Russian gangsters to frighten me or worse? Maybe they had threatened relatives of his in the old country unless he cooperated, and he was cozying up to Jason in order to get close to me and to divert attention from himself. Where had he been during the other attacks? Perhaps tomorrow I could ask a few discreet questions and find out. I saved my clue list, turned off my computer, and slipped into bed to snuggle up beside Jason, terrified at the idea that someone might be stalking me.

Travel Journal
Day Five, Rouen

Pity about Carolyn. I meant to get C., that pompous bastard. What a pleasure it would have been to see him flattened by an irate Frenchman on a rickety bicycle.

CLUE LIST

Day	Place	Victim	Injury	Means
1	airport Paris	Childeric	head cut shoulder	shove
2	courtyard	Childeric me	shoulder shins	pot
3	Giverny	Childeric	clothes dignity skin	insecticide
4	Versailles	Childeric	ankle (probably an accident)	trip
5	Rouen	me	bruises	pushed into bicycle

Still Carolyn's not likely to get anywhere near C. after this. On the other hand, that brainless Edie Atwater reacted this afternoon to Chris Blue hanging out with the guide by trying to attach herself to C. again.

And Hecht. She's ruining Fauree's chances at the deanship. Not that I care who gets it as long as it's not C. But she's dead wrong to think all this public sex isn't getting back to the committee. As soon as they heard that C. had picked up someone's ticket cheap, the way the Blues did, the committee would have got themselves a spy to watch the three candidates, see how they interacted. Wonder who the spy is.

Damn administration. Spies everywhere. Probably why I never made full professor after C. got through with me.

He'll pay.

CLUE LIST

Present	Suspect(s)	Motive
Childeric Chris me	Fauree	deanship
strangers	strangers	air rage
Childeric Edie	Fauree	deanship
me	Petar	hates JCC
Childeric	Fauree	deanship
	Robbie	"
	Laura	"
	Jason	"
Jason me Fauree	gardener	accident
everyone	Janice	hates JCC
	Lorenzo?	deanship
everyone	Ivan Edie enemies of Childeric	Childeric felt I snubbed him? lust? Mafia hates me?

20
Honfleur, Tourist's Delight

French mayonnaise and French fried potatoes—delicious both separately and together. I sampled the combination in Honfleur on the Normandy coast.

Mayonnaise was reputedly invented by the Duc de Richelieu. He named it after Mahon, a British fort on the Balearic Island of Minorca and the scene of his great victory during the Seven-Years' War. When not fighting wars, Richelieu was quite the man about town and is said to have invited guests to dine under his roof in the nude. Perhaps all that creamy female skin inspired the recipe for mayonnaise.

And war has inspired other landmarks in culinary history. Napoleon, for instance, offered a prize for an invention that would preserve rations for an army on the move. Vacuum-packed food was the result in 1808. Napoleon III wanted a synthetic butter for his army, and a scientist produced it from suet, chopped cows' udders, and warm milk in 1867. Sounds disgusting, doesn't it?

As for French fries, potatoes had a checkered history in France once they were brought over from the New World. In 1540 they were considered an ornamental plant to be exhibited as an exotic in royal gardens but not eaten. By 1618 the Duke of Burgundy banned the planting of potatoes because they were reputed to cause leprosy. Only in the late eighteenth century did potatoes overcome suspicion and become a popular food. Louis XVI accomplished this by various ruses and publicity stunts invented by Antoine-Auguste Parmetier. First, they planted land outside Paris with potatoes and set soldiers to guard the fields day and night. Then they gave the soldiers a night off, and local farmers, overcome with curiosity, stole the plants to put in their own fields. Finally, the king gave an all-potato dinner party at which Marie Antoinette wore potato flowers in her hair. (I didn't even know potatoes produced flowers.) Benjamin Franklin attended the royal potato feast. Soon potatoes were considered fashionable both by the court and by the general populace, and Parmetier published a book on how to grow and cook potatoes.

Viva les pommes frites!

Carolyn Blue, "Have Fork, Will Travel," *Cheyenne Gazette*

Carolyn

Honfleur is a lovely town; its harbor is crowded with yachts and sailing vessels whose masts reflect in the water like a leafless forest. Here, too, are reflected, seemingly a phantom city beneath the sea, the multistoried stone houses that wall in the harbor with their slate roofs sprouting chimneys and dormer windows. How lovely it would be to sit in one such window, I thought at the time, and stare out at the bustle of the Quai Sainte-Catherine or at the salt houses of the Quai Saint-Étienne, from which fishermen sailed to the rich and dangerous waters of the Newfoundland Banks. Or I could curl in a window seat and imagine the adventurers who sailed from Honfleur centuries ago to found Quebec, to reach Brazil, and to reconnoiter the Saint Lawrence Seaway.

On the other hand, those houses are narrow. They probably have no elevators. Would I have wanted to climb six, seven, eight stories to inhabit that dormered room of my imagination? Certainly not that day. I ached still, not unbearably, but I foresaw that the rest of this trip would involve continued personal discomfort accompanied by unease bordering on fear.

Still, I fell in love with Honfleur. Who could not after seeing Saint Catherine's Church, which was thrown up by sixteenth-century shipwrights in the form of a ship's hull? In this charming church, the builders, who were the bedrock of the town's economy, gathered to worship for many centuries.

And Honfleur has also been known for over a century and a half as an inspiration to artists. It still has many fine galleries, in one of which I saw an oil that I coveted, a portrait of a ghostly Mardi Gras girl in flowered hat and ribbon streamers, yet very young, pale, and sad. The saleswoman certainly thought I should buy it and offered a price reduction, free shipping, even financing. Ivan and Estrella were with us, I keeping a wary eye on that possible gangster disguised as an academic. He thought we should buy the portrait because the painter was Russian and because Ivan could not buy it himself, being a man looking forward to fatherhood and its many long-term expenses.

Estrella nodded approvingly. Wild expenditures were not for those who hoped to be parents, and the girl in the picture was too pasty-faced for her taste. Jason pointed out that he, too, was a father, one with two offspring in college, and extravagant expenditures were not to his taste at this time, although he did like the picture. Ah, well. I was feeling melancholy and didn't argue. The Frenchwoman did. She followed us out into the rain, elaborating on the growing fame of the artist and the probable increase in value of the painting in ten years' time.

Art as investment. That consideration hadn't occurred to me. If it had, I might have suggested to Jason that he was less than twenty years from retirement and needed to be on the lookout for such fine investments. Undoubtedly, Jason would have replied, "Who plans to retire? Not me. They'll have to carry me out of the lab in a pine box."

Mortuary salesmen tend to start calling one after the age of forty, our age, not theirs, with offers of elaborate prepaid funerals, early casket selection before inflation drives the prices beyond our means, and so forth.

Ghoulish telemarketers! We've formulated a marvelously discouraging reply: Whoever answers the telephone responds, "We'd be interested in a price quote on your least expensive pine box. Is there a discount for two? We could keep them in the garage. Oh, and do you actually have to convert to Judaism to be eligible for the day-after-death, unembalmed-corpse burial?" Even the children have taken part in this form of family entertainment.

After we fled the gallery with the saleswoman at our heels, Jason and Ivan walked ahead, so I was paired with Estrella, who gave me a perfect opening for a bit of sleuthing. She asked how I was feeling after my accident yesterday, and I replied that I was still in pain. Then I asked if she had seen it, and she replied that she had indeed. She had been one person away from Professor Childeric and seen him lurch forward into me.

My heart rate increased as I realized that had Ivan been standing with her, he might well have shoved Childeric into me, hoping to frighten or kill me while Childeric took the blame. My next question was critical. "Was Ivan with you? I wonder if either of you noticed who was behind Professor Childeric."

Estrella looked thoughtful. "Ivan must have been with Hugh or Jason. He *will* become involved in those scientific conversations." She smiled indulgently. "And I didn't notice anyone else. I assumed at the time that Professor Childeric tripped. He must be quite a clumsy person. Didn't I hear that he tripped at the airport, too?"

"Yes, Chris and I rescued him. You didn't see that one, I take it?"

"No, Ivan was getting the luggage while I looked for the tour representative."

"Did he see anyone push Professor Childeric?"

"I think he'd have mentioned it if he had, Carolyn. Isn't it strange that he insists on being called Professor? The rest of us are on a first-name basis by now, but he . . ." While I remembered, with a shudder, the professor imploring me to call him Jean-Claude, Estrella chatted on, saying that she preferred to be called Dr. or Mrs. I decided that I'd have to ask Jason and Hugh if Ivan had been with them when I was shoved in front of the bicycle. I soon found out that Jason hadn't been with either of them. I'd talk to Hugh next, although, of course, Childeric would say that it was Hugh who had pushed him.

We caught up with Hugh and Robbie several streets over. Ivan and Estrella had wandered off, so I could ask more questions without revealing that I was thinking of Ivan as the culprit in my injury. Since Hugh immediately fell into conversation with Jason, I asked Robbie first. She told me that Hugh had been with her when I was hurt, that she hadn't seen anyone push Childeric, and that she doubted anyone *had* pushed him. Then she added that, considering the things Childeric had said to her when she was trying to save him from pesticide poisoning at Giverny, she'd have been happy to give the man a push herself. However, she'd have made sure no one was in front of him, unless it was a horse doing its business, in which case she'd have pushed Childeric into the horse dung.

"There weren't any horses," I remarked. "Was Ivan with you and Hugh?"

"No."

"Was he near Childeric?"

"Actually, from where I stood, I couldn't see Childeric. And I didn't see Ivan either. Surely you're not thinking Ivan—"

"Oh, I'm just trying to find someone who might have seen Childeric pushed."

"Mark my words," said Robbie. "That man is a mean person. He probably pushed you because you were dodging him yesterday. You were, weren't you?"

"Well, I did promise Jason—"

"Good. Stay away from him. We'll all stay away from him. Serve him right." Then she spotted a jewelry shop and dragged Hugh in.

Could Robbie be right? I wondered. Would Childeric have given me a push in a fit of pique because I'd stopped providing him with an attentive audience? Was his visit to my room a last desperate attempt to prove to himself that I was, in fact, infatuated? If so, how could I explain the other attacks? Before Chris and I rescued him at the luggage carousel, he'd just met me. And he certainly couldn't have pushed the pot over on me because he'd been beside me. And whom could he have talked into doing it for him?

Back to Ivan. I still hadn't accounted for his whereabouts when I met with grief yesterday. More questions were needed.

21

Honfleur, Sailor's Delight

Carolyn

There were also delightful boutiques in Honfleur, which I had reason to visit that morning under less pleasant circumstances. We made the mistake of heading back toward the harbor to admire the boats. "Are you two still plotting an attack on mad cow disease?" I called ahead to Jason and Hugh. Jason replied that they were discussing which team had the best chance to win the NBA championship.

Hugh added, "I say the Lakers, but Jason—"

"Hugh's absolutely right," said Robbie and hustled ahead to take my husband's arm. I heard her suggesting a little bet as Hugh fell back to walk with me.

Time to see what I could find out about the attack on me. Not that I was interested in clearing the detestable Professor Childeric, but I did want to know who was responsible. First, I asked what Hugh had seen when the bicycle hit me, and he replied that he'd seen Childeric push me. "Gave you quite a whack with his good hand."

"You didn't see anyone push him?"

"I did not," said Hugh.

"Could you see behind him?"

"I didn't need to. I don't believe that nonsense about someone pushing him, any more than you should believe it when he says I pushed him. The man's paranoid, but that's no reason to take it out on you just because you and Jason are my friends."

There was a new motive. I suppressed a sigh and tried one more time. "Did you by any chance see Ivan when it happened?"

"Christ! Is he saying Ivan pushed him because Ivan's a friend of mine?"

"No, no, Hugh. I'm just trying to figure where people were when it happened, in case someone really did push him. If Ivan was closer, he might have seen something."

"So ask Ivan."

Hugh was getting irritated, so I changed the subject by inquiring after his children. He told me that his teenaged son didn't seem to be recovering from the death of his mother, that in fact, Sam's grades had dropped, and he was having a problem with what the school counselor called "anger management." "I guess that means he's pissed off all the time at school. He sure is at home." Looking woebegone, Hugh added, "God, I wish June were alive. She'd know what to do with him. But then if she were alive, he probably wouldn't be acting the way he is. He even seems to resent his sister and me, like we're getting over her death too fast."

"Maybe he needs grief therapy, Hugh," I suggested. Jason and Robbie had disappeared into a crowd at the wharf, where a boat was pulling in with much shouting of sailors, a scruffy-looking lot, in my opinion. All of them needed a shave. Or maybe they were espousing the popular unshaven look. Thank goodness Chris hasn't been tempted to go around looking mangy, and Jason's beard is always neatly clipped and, in my opinion, very attractive.

"What's grief therapy?" Hugh asked. "I'm ready to try anything."

"Well, you could send him to a therapist, or even get him into a group of young people who've lost loved ones. They meet with a therapist and—"

A shriek, a splash, and louder shouting interrupted my impromptu counseling session. According to people at the very edge of the crowd, Robbie had just fallen into the harbor. Neither Hugh nor I was close enough when she went in to see for ourselves. I could only hope Jason had been there. Hugh was muttering, "That damn Childeric," as he pushed his way forward with me following at his heels until I could see the water but not my friend.

The rain falling on my umbrella was cold (some of it had seeped down my neck during our walk to the wharf), and I'm sure the harbor water was even colder. It seemed to take forever for Robbie to surface, and I was terrified, remembering the horror of just such an event in my own recent past. Then she emerged between the two boats and, swimming powerfully, headed away from the quai, much to everyone's shock. We thought she must be disoriented and shouted for her to turn around, while Denis wrung his hands over yet another incident on his watch. As people milled about debating rescue options, Jason grabbed a life preserver and called to her. Since she didn't turn, he couldn't fling it out. Sailors on fishing boats to either side flourished life jackets and preservers and shouted advice in French, but still Robbie continued to swim, passing the end of the boat on her right.

More quick-witted and boat-oriented, Hugh saw what she was doing and ran down the wharf, from which he jumped off into a rowboat beside the fishing vessel that Robbie had circled. While he cut the dory loose from its mother boat and took up the oars, the sailors' shouts increased in volume. I presume they thought he was stealing their rowboat. Police arrived, and the tumult increased, added to by townsfolk and other tourists crowding in to witness the excitement. Gathering my wits, reasoning that Robbie wouldn't have jumped, I tried to memorize the names of those in the immediate area: the Macauleys, the Foxcrofts, and the Markarovs. They were the people nearest Jason.

Meanwhile Robbie swam past the end of a second boat, heading for the bow, or whatever, of the next. Hugh shouted to her. Him, she heard, for she turned her head at the last moment, reversed directions, and began to swim toward him as he rowed toward her. In less than a minute she was scrambling into the rowboat, her soaked clothes clinging fetchingly to her generous curves. Ingrid Jensen called out that someone should throw a blanket over Robbie. I'm not sure whether Ingrid was offended by the wet-clothing-on-voluptuous-woman display or afraid that Robbie would catch cold.

Robbie took up oars, and the two of them rowed back toward the wharf. The sailors, who had previously excoriated Hugh for stealing their dory, were now whistling and grinning and staring at Robbie as they lowered a rope ladder. They cheered her lustily as she climbed aboard, followed by Hugh, whom they pretty much ignored.

Within moments our friends had jumped ashore from the fishing boat. The mishap ended safely, thank God, but still someone had again been pushed into danger, the perpetrator unknown. Robbie verified that such was the case, although she denied being in danger. She and Hugh hadn't enough words of praise for each other, he for her "great crawl" and rowing, she for his quick-witted rescue, not that she needed it; there was a ladder up to the wharf several boats down, and she had been heading for that.

Ingrid may have called for a blanket, but Grace Unsell was the person who actually, with the help of Laura de Sorentino translating, borrowed one from a French woman in the crowd.

"Now I'll have to go out and buy a new outfit from the skin out and the toes up," said Robbie gaily. "I can't run around all day in wet clothes, or even this nice French lady's blanket. *Merci, madame,*" she said, smiling, to the French grandmother, who had been chatting with Grace after fetching the blanket. "Anyone seen a good boutique?"

"Oh, I saw a terrific place two streets over," said Hester, a person who peered into every window, no doubt looking for objects that would inspire a scary glass sculpture. Ultimately, there were four of us who visited the boutique: Robbie, Hester, myself, and the French grandmother, who wanted her blanket back.

22

Revelations in a Dressing Room

Carolyn

The proprietress of the boutique looked quite distressed when Robbie, dripping on the carpet, led our little group in. However, when my friend announced that she needed a whole new outfit, the lady placed her on a chair and offered various selections. Then they disappeared into a dressing room, the proprietress carrying an armload of Robbie's choices and a pressed linen towel so that my friend could dry off before trying on clothes. Finally the lady returned the soggy blanket to the French grandmother with ten dollars in francs for its rehabilitation and Robbie's thanks.

I, in the meantime, browsed the store's offerings and chose for myself a beautiful art deco hair clip, copied, according to the owner, from a Lalique brooch. It was so pretty that Jason didn't even ask the price. Having made my purchase and realized that Robbie hadn't reappeared after ten minutes or more, I became worried and hunted her down in a dressing room. There I found her sitting on a stool shivering.

"Oh, Robbie, you've caught cold. Let me help you out of those wet clothes," I offered.

"I caught a fright," she replied in a trembling voice. "Whoever pushed me wanted to make damn sure I didn't manage to keep my balance and stay dry."

I sat down on the carpet in front of her and took both her hands in mine. "And here I thought you were enjoying the whole thing. That was quite an act you put on out there."

She nodded. "Give me a minute, and I'll get back into the part."

"This tour is becoming a lot too scary for my taste," I said.

"Yeah, tell me about it. Can't believe what happened to you yesterday.

And what the hell could anyone have against the two of us? You think it's Childeric?"

"I don't know, but I won't be so quick to defend him from now on. He came to my room yesterday afternoon before Jason got back and made a pass at me."

"You're kidding!" My friend stopped looking shaken and said, "Tell all."

After I had described the scene, she exclaimed, "That lecherous old bastard! Man, I wish I hadn't saved his hide at Giverny. If I'd left that stuff on him, maybe his skin would have peeled off." Her eyes were narrowed angrily. "What shall we do to him?"

"For now, you should get out of those clothes, dry off, and find something to buy."

"Right. And then we'll get even." She jumped off the stool, stripped down with my help—wet clothes aren't easy to remove—dried off with the linen towel, and in less than five minutes had chosen tight moss green pants with matching boots and a high-collared blouse whose first button was fastened right in the middle of her cleavage. "Don't tell Hugh I was such a weenie," she murmured as we left the dressing room.

I suppose fellow kayakers want to be thought of as fearless. "I won't tell Hugh if you don't tell Jason about Childeric."

"Deal. We'll take care of the old fart ourselves."

I shuddered to think of what she might have in mind.

Hugh was bowled over by the newly outfitted Robbie, but by then she could have left the store wearing a burlap monk's robe, and he'd have been impressed. Hester bought a black dress that clung to her from ears to ankles. It had a slit on one side to the hip and crisscrossed ribbons in back to hold the bodice in place. She skipped out into the street where the men were drinking cassis with the Drummonds under a café umbrella and modeled it for Jeremy, who stammered, "Won't you catch cold?"

"I never catch cold as long as my neck is warm," she replied solemnly.

That was a theory I'd never heard. With her whole back and one leg exposed, she certainly wasn't following the keep-your-head-covered-and-the-trunk-of-your-body-layered-on-cold-days school of thought.

"And think how much my mother will hate it," Hester added. Jeremy nodded, evidently seeing benefit in that proposed poke to the maternal eye. Hester turned to me and explained, "My mother thinks my clothes are dreadful. She's of the Boston school that goes out and buys something expensive but dowdy and then lets it sit in her closet for three years, just to be sure she can't be accused of being fashionable."

I had to laugh. After my mother's death, my father had been friendly for a few years with a lady professor of that ilk. She specialized in Anglo-Saxon literature and linguistics. I'm happy to say he never married her, and she moved to the Pacific Northwest. However, before she left, she was in the habit of inviting us over for boiled New England dinners, which were quite dreadful. I'm sure she would have disapproved of French food, but I doubt that she ever ate any. On the other hand, she might have liked the food provided by the tour.

Macauley shouted with laughter at the remarks on catching cold and her mother's taste in clothes and told Hester that she looked delectable. His wife Nedda didn't seem to appreciate the compliment, Hester blushed, and Jeremy gave Drummond a blank look, as if he wasn't sure what was meant by that remark or who the fellow was who had made it. Nonetheless, Jeremy allowed himself and Hester to be whisked away by the Drummonds. I noticed as they departed that Jeremy found himself paired with Nedda. Hester was back in her gaily-colored gypsy togs and listening to Macauley.

Robbie had also purchased a dashing lined cloak and looked the picture of fashion as we made our way to lunch. We hadn't been invited to join the Drummonds—their loss, because we found a delightful second-floor café whose upstairs dining room overlooked the harbor. What could be more wonderful? The company of two good friends, a cozy table by a window with a charming view, and a large crab with a salmon pink shell and flesh so tender and sweet that one didn't really need anything to dip it in. Which is not to say that I resisted the horseradish mayonnaise that came with the crab. The French have a way with mayonnaise. You can buy the most expensive mayonnaise in the States or you can make your own, but it will never match the richness of French mayonnaise.

We even saw a hint of blue sky as we ate. Of course, now that we were inside a dry, warm café, the rain had stopped, leaving the patterned stones that paved the streets glistening. What period was it, I wonder, when towns took the time and money to have their streets paved in, say, intersecting arcs, one of the designs I've seen in Europe? At home we look underfoot (or under tire) only when the potholes catch our attention.

"I'll bet Childeric pushed you," said Hugh. "Did he? He's probably getting back at me because he thinks I'm harassing him."

"I wouldn't put it past him," said Robbie.

Hugh and Jason were devouring large bowls of fish soup. "The man's nuts," said Hugh bitterly. "I almost wish I'd never let them put me up for dean."

"Don't even think about dropping out," said Robbie. "I don't want that old bastard to be the dean of my college."

"And I don't want you to be injured," said Hugh seriously.

Robbie laughed. "Sweetie, whoever pushed me in, what good did it do them? I was wet before I got dunked, and then those sweet sailors gave me a cheer when I climbed the rope ladder. I think the whole thing was a hoot."

"But you didn't see who pushed you?" Hugh asked.

"Sorry. The shove came from behind." Robbie was feeding herself and Hugh French fries with hungry gusto.

"Jason?" I asked. "Did you see who pushed her?"

He shrugged. "I was standing beside her. The Markarovs were beside me, so they couldn't have done it."

Did that rule out Ivan? I wondered. And anyway, why would he attack Robbie?

"Hey, don't worry about it, folks," said Robbie. "I'm fine."

"You could have drowned," cried Hugh.

"Not a chance," she replied.

"What if you'd hit your head on the way down and gone in unconscious?"

"Why, you'd have rescued me. Carolyn, pass that mayonnaise, will you? It's delicious on these fantastic fries. Don't tell me you can make stuff like this."

"Not if I can help it," I replied. "I write about food. I don't cook it."

"Alas," added Jason.

"Cheer up, love. You can have the rest of my crab." It really was large enough for two people, and I didn't want to make a pig of myself. I dipped a last French fry in mayonnaise, then pushed the plate across to my eager husband, who can eat two entrées without the least discomfort or weight gain. The fries are as good as the mayonnaise in France, I mused as I chewed. Imagine ordering them with mayonnaise at some hamburger joint in the States. You'd gag.

23

Is Cheese Disease Fatal?

Jason

This tour was a rotten idea. After lunch in Honfleur, which was excellent, both Carolyn's crab and my fish soup and fresh oysters, we realized we had lost track of Chris and Edie, I suppose because we were so shocked by Robbie's mishap at the wharf. We found the kids together in a souvenir store, eating street food, Chris being solicited for opinions on various T-shirts that appealed to Edie. Carolyn was furious with herself for forgetting them. Anna Thomas-Smith looked grim because she had started searching for Edie before we did, and the departure from Honfleur was delayed by their disappearance, innocent as it had been. They could hardly seduce one another at a counter that displayed miniature brass sailing ships and busts of Samuel de Champlain.

And then there was the attack on Robbie—not my favorite woman, but I wouldn't want to see her come to harm. A gaggle of academics being attacked by persons unknown? Extremely unlikely, I would have said. Now Hugh Fauree, who is as calm and rational a man as I've met during my years in science, was accusing a noted, if irritating, medieval scholar of pushing his girlfriend off a pier. Hugh was convinced he'd become involved in an escalating feud over the deanship. Carolyn was still asking people questions about Ivan Markarov, although why she'd think the Russian Mafia had an interest in Robbie was beyond me. And I, on the way to a Calvados distillery, was trying to plot a strategy to protect my wife from Childeric.

Sitting behind me on the bus, Estrella Markarov provided counterpoint to my thoughts by telling one and all about Saint Teresa of Lisieux, some poor child who received so much indoctrination from her parents that she went to Rome to badger the Pope for permission to enter the local convent. The girl took vows at fifteen, lived eleven more years, wrote an autobiography, and specialized in small duties and miracles. All this information was offered because Estrella wanted to visit the saint's basilica and Denis insisted that the tour called for stops at a cheese factory and a Calvados distillery.

Denis won, and poor Ivan was left to comfort his drearily devout wife. I couldn't imagine what he saw in her. Meanwhile, Carolyn, although not asleep, was unusually uncommunicative. Maybe she was still fretting over her failure to keep tabs on Edie and Chris. As for Childeric, I didn't have to worry about him that afternoon. While we were having lunch, he, having received no invitations to dine, informed Denis that he couldn't be bothered with distilleries and cheese factories; he'd find something more interesting to do and rejoin the group in Caen that evening. When Estrella suggested that she join him for a visit to Saint Teresa's basilica, he refused; it was evidently too modern for his taste.

The Calvados distillery was actually fairly interesting, huge and smaller wooden vats banded with iron, a good explanation of the distillation process, and an amazingly primitive apple press in their museum. The size of a wooden screw incorporated in the apparatus was mind-boggling. Carolyn perked up and commented on the intriguing, musty smell of fermenting apples that pervaded the barnlike structure. Then we had a Calvados tasting. My wife tried all varieties and went back for seconds, which explained her long silences on the bus. She was in pain and admitted as much when I asked. Robbie provided more Tylenol, and other members of our group, who still blamed him for Carolyn's condition, made unfriendly comments about the absent Childeric. Another day of camaraderie on tour.

We went on to the cheese factory, which proved to be a large dairy farm with lathe and plaster buildings, a boarded-up estate château, and fields full of brown and white splotched cows with pendulous udders. Denis led us into a barn, where we watched from overhead as the cows jostled one another to get to the milking machines. It was a mildly entertaining exhibition, especially when one cow got its head stuck under the rails that separated its stall from the next. It shifted about uncomfortably, or so it seemed to me, the neighboring cow paid no attention whatever to the head protruding into its space, and Jensen speculated that mad cow disease might have infected the herd.

His remark was not well received. The company representative, who understood enough English to translate *mad cow disease,* became agitated. His exclamations in French resulted in an outcry among the employees supervising the mechanized milking operation, the gist of their remarks evidently being that there was no mad cow disease in their herd, nor in any cows of the Calvados district.

Before Jensen could get a conversation going with fellow bovine experts, Unsell approached the dairy representative and asked how the epidemic was affecting their business and that of French dairymen in general. Unpleasant remarks were made about Americans, and general ill will prevailed as we trailed after our flustered guide toward the cheese-making building. Evidently word of the American faux pas had spread there as well, for the explanation of the process was brusque.

When finally we attended the much-touted cheese tasting, the final break in international relations occurred. Several ladies refused the cheese samples for fear of contracting "the brain disease." No one could convince them that they would be safe. Edie announced loudly that she wasn't risking any fatal "cheese diseases," not after being exposed by Carolyn to "raw, mad-cow beef" in Paris.

A pretty young server, dressed quaintly as a milkmaid, burst into tears, and an older woman, possibly her mother, scolded Edie. Whatever she said, it must have been unpleasant because neither Denis nor Laura de Sorentino would translate. Unsell told his wife not to be a fool and to eat the "damn cheese."

"And have my grandchild catch some dangerous disease from me?" Grace demanded. "You eat my share if you think it's so safe, Manfred. Then you can stay away from our grandchild, just as you're ignoring her pregnant mother."

"Actually, Grace, the cheese isn't that good," whispered my wife. She had exhibited complete indifference to Edie's glares and complaints, inspired, no doubt, by the fact that Edie had not been allowed to sit with Chris after their Honfleur escapade. When offered cheese, Carolyn had shrugged, murmured "What the hell," and helped herself to four or five samples.

I assume that her uncharacteristic language devolved from her generous sampling of the Calvados at our last stop. She'd certainly been circulating through the group, both here and in the milking barn, asking questions about who'd seen what when she went down in front of the bicycle and Robbie into the harbor.

When she got to the Drummonds, Macauley asked loudly, "Are you suggesting that I was responsible for your injuries yesterday, Carolyn? Getting a bit paranoid, are we? Maybe you and your friend Robbie just fell."

"We did not," Carolyn snapped. "We were pushed."

"Then don't let your medieval fetish convince you that the eminent Professor Childeric wasn't responsible."

Carolyn flushed, Drummond looked pleased with himself, and various members of the tour group treated my wife as if she'd accused each one of a crime.

I hurried to her side as she was popping another piece of cheese into her mouth. "Are you all right?" I asked solicitously.

"Of course, I'm all right," she retorted. "I just happen to prefer Brie."

French Bruschetta

I had the most delicious and astounding bruschetta at a restaurant in the Caribbean. One expects to find garlic and tomatoes on a bit of toasty bread when ordering bruschetta, and it's usually very good. This bruschetta consisted of two narrow ovals of sliced, toasted bread, perhaps six inches long. On the toast were bits of ripe tomato, spread with a creamy avocado paste, rather salty and flavored with garlic, and topped by a thin slice of Brie. The whole must have been run rapidly under the broiler because the Brie was soft—slightly melted, in fact—and just a bit browned at the edges.

The dish is wonderful and easy to make at home, in a smaller size as an hors d'oeuvre or, as it was served to me, as a first course. What combination could be nicer? I do love Brie and adore avocados. Even though the dish was made by a Bahamian chef in a former English colony, this recipe is a sort of French bruschetta, which, believe me, is better than the French lasagna I had in Paris. It just goes to prove that cuisine has become a truly international art.

Carolyn Blue, "Have Fork Will Travel," *Oklahoma City Plains Courant*

24
Terrible Turkey

Peacock was a favorite meat during the Middle Ages, goodness knows why. The author of a cookbook in 1420, Chiquart Amicco, advised overcoming the toughness of peacock by boiling, larding, and roasting. After that, he suggested slicing the cooked peacock meat and allowing it to stand around for one or two months, then scraping off the mold before serving. His alternate suggestion was that the chef throw out the peacock, keep the plumage, and use it to dress a roast goose. Did gourmet noblemen realize that they were eating meat from which mold had been removed? When turkey was discovered in the New World and brought back, peacock began to be supplanted. After so many years, one would have expected the French to come up with wonderful recipes for turkey.

However, while traveling in Normandy, I had the worst turkey dinner imaginable. It featured the usual things: turkey, dressing, gravy, and so forth, but it was overcooked and thoroughly disappointing. Now, why would a restaurant in France, a country noted for its wonderful food, serve such a meal? Were they trying to please American tourists by re-creating Thanksgiving in Caen? It was April when our tour group visited that city, not November. Or maybe the meal was meant to illustrate that our national cuisine leaves something to be desired. If so, I'd have preferred that they treat us to some marvelous turkey recipe that put traditional American holiday fare in the shade.

Such recipes are to be had, even in America. My mother had one that an aunt had clipped from the old *New York Herald Tribune*. It featured an exotic dressing of fruits, meats, and an expensive array of herbs and spices, not to mention searing the turkey in mustard paste and then basting it with cider. That recipe would be perfect for Normans, who are so proud of their apples and cider production. Maybe that turkey was a sort of culinary joke. If so, no one in our group was amused.

Carolyn Blue, "Have Fork, Will Travel," *Naperville Voice*

Carolyn

By the time we finished our dinner in Caen, our destination for day six, I had begun to see our group as a society in miniature on the very edge of disintegration. People were getting hurt, or at least being attacked. Robbie hadn't actually been injured, but I had—twice. Now I had not only the healing cuts from pot shards but also my bruises, aches, and pains, which had, happily, abated somewhat with another application of Calvados and acetaminophen. If I don't watch out, Jason is going to think me in danger of falling into alcoholism.

France, by the way, has quite a high alcoholism rate: five million heavy drinkers, two million alcoholics, and seventeen quarts of pure alcohol consumed per year per person. Gracious! In France, they sell wine at highway service stations; remember that if you're driving on their highways. And really keep your eyes open in Paris; in 1979 the police stopped administering Breathalyzer tests because restaurants protested that the practice was hurting business, not surprising in a department that was founded to protect citizens going out to dinner. But I digress from my sociological analysis of our group.

In our little society, acquaintances and colleagues were accusing one another of plots and violence, husbands and wives were snarling at each other, and there was a shunning movement afoot against Childeric. Not that I didn't think he deserved it. Being around him both scared me because of my injuries and embarrassed me when I remembered his awful assumptions when he visited my room. Jason absolutely insisted that I avoid Childeric at all costs, and I was happy to do so.

At dinner in the tour-chosen restaurant, Jason accomplished that very neatly. We were to sit in two large, four-sided wooden booths. These booths had only a small opening on one end through which the dinner guest could slide. All that scooting while seated was awkward, and if one was seated in the middle and wanted to visit the facilities, five people had to wrestle themselves out. Jason quickly directed traffic so that our booth contained the kids, separated; Hugh and Robbie; Ivan and Estrella; Jeremy and Hester (although Jeremy arranged their inclusion, to keep Hester away from the Drummonds, I think); and Janice Petar. Childeric had to sit with the Jensens, Unsells, Drummonds, de Sorentinos, and Anna, who looked quite unhappy about her companions.

I suppose she'd have preferred to sit with Janice, but since Janice disliked Childeric, it was probably for the best. At least, the arrangement gave Anna a respite from Edie. I would have liked one, too, but felt I had to keep an eye on her. We could have sent Chris to the other table so that Janice could sit with Anna, but then Chris probably needed the respite from Childeric. Both of them had complained about the other to me. I was so incensed with Childeric that I pretended I didn't hear him. Oh, it was so complicated!

Anyway, some of the unfortunate things that happened as a result of Jason's seating arrangements were the altercations that ensued when Childeric wanted to find someone to share a bottle of wine with him. Unsell refused, against Grace's wishes, because he wanted a whole bottle to himself. The Jensens refused because they don't drink. The Drummonds refused because Nedda announced that they were over their budget and could only afford single glasses, which infuriated Macauley. He said she could skip wine, and he'd share with Childeric. Nedda retorted that she had as much right to her glass of wine as he. I gather they didn't speak to one another again that evening. But the worst refusal came from Lorenzo de Sorentino, after Laura generously offered to skip wine so Lorenzo and Childeric could share.

Lorenzo said, "If you're capable of pushing the girlfriend of one rival into the harbor, Childeric, you're capable of poisoning my wine because my wife is up for that job you obviously covet, out of all reason. After all, it's just a deanship. Who the hell cares about something that unimportant?"

Oh, my. Childeric was apoplectic. He shouted, loudly enough to be heard in our booth, that he had not pushed Robbie Hecht into the water.

Robbie muttered, "Much good it did you, you dirty old man."

Oh lord, I thought. *She's going to tell everyone what happened.* I sneaked a glance at Childeric, but he hadn't heard, and Robbie said nothing more, thank goodness.

Hugh murmured to Jason, "That man should be drummed out of the university. He's a menace!"

Childeric then, in what I considered an astonishing show of hypocrisy, gave a resounding peroration on the importance of deans and the necessity that they be eminent scholars and men of impeccable behavior. He mentioned the latter qualification while staring vindictively across the booth wall at Robbie and Hugh. Robbie gave him such a steely look that his eyes dropped and he flushed after glancing at me. However, Janice was the one who replied.

"Deans have to be men? Is that what you said, Childeric? Why not women? And any demand for impeccable behavior eliminates you, at least in my view."

Had Robbie told my story to Janice? Janice might well launch a feminist offensive on my behalf. Before she could say anything else, Laura tried to practice her peace-making talents, and Childeric told her brusquely that he didn't need any support from a rival candidate for dean, who, on the basis of recent attacks on his person, evidently did not wish him well. Then he harassed the waitress, a young girl who must have been new to her job. She did get the orders mixed up, and she brought him the wrong wine, and later she charged him for a bottle instead of two glasses. Each time he shouted at her, she became more incoherent, and the manager had to be called to adjudicate. It was a complete disintegration of civility. I imagine we would have been ejected from the restaurant if it weren't for Denis and the management's desire to secure returning tour business.

Of course, the dinner was practically inedible. Well, the salmon mousse with creamed lemon dill sauce was fair, the sauce a bit bland but the mousse quite good. While eating it, I had hopes that the next course would be acceptable. It wasn't. Turkey. The only thing that can be said for it is that it was probably better than peacock, its once popular predecessor, which was evidently dreadful in every respect but the feathers, which were put back on before serving. Edie wouldn't eat her turkey, I left most of mine as did Grace, but Hester, Robbie, and the men scarfed it down with minor complaints.

There was a dessert buffet at which I hoped to make up for missing the entrée, but we were slow getting there because it was so hard to exit the booths and I had to maneuver to avoid Childeric. Why couldn't he have skipped dinner as well as the Calvados and cheese tours? Surely, he was embarrassed after his overtures to me.

The buffet, when I managed to reach it, had some promising offerings, chocolate mousse, for instance. On the other hand, the tarts were disgusting. Soggy pastry and gelatinous fruit filling. Perhaps they had been made in the morning, then overheated in a microwave, and finally left to decompose on the table. I'm sure any Frenchwoman who cooks or just likes good food would back me up about that dinner. I'm not a Francophobe. I love French cooking, but I intend to send a complaint to the tour company.

25

Warfare: Modern or Medieval?

Jason

When Carolyn and I returned to our room in Caen after that contentious dinner (frankly, I thought Childeric was losing it), we had a largely fruitless discussion of who could have pushed Robbie off the wharf at Honfleur.

"Why Robbie?" Carolyn asked. "Why would anyone push her into the water? A boat propeller could have started up and cut her to pieces. Or one of the boats could have heeled over and hit her. It was a dangerous thing to do."

In reply I put my arms comfortingly around her. At least I hoped it was a comfort. "Are you still aching?"

"Some," she replied. "Janice Petar was really snippy yesterday at lunch when Robbie wanted to switch rooms around so she and Hugh could share. You don't think Janice—well, was she near Robbie on the wharf?"

"I don't know, but my candidate would be Childeric," I replied. "He was furious when she doused him with water at Giverny. Maybe he wanted to do the same to her."

"Sometimes I think people are being attacked at random. And we don't know why."

"Childeric seems to be the only link. The most we can do is avoid him and keep our eyes open."

"Well, that's another thing. Tomorrow we have the choice of a half-day at the Normandy beaches and a half-day at Bayeux or a whole day at Bayeux. I imagine you and Chris will want to visit the beaches."

"I would like to see the invasion sites. My great-uncle died on—"

"Exactly, and I don't like those war sites, especially the modern ones, but I'd love to spend the day at Bayeux."

"I know, but Childeric—"

"Will be sure to choose Bayeux." She shuddered.

Although I hate to see Carolyn upset, I was relieved that she was taking seriously the danger inherent in associating with Childeric.

"Another problem is Chris and Edie. We should try to keep them apart. If they're on the same tour, even both of us—well, look what happened yesterday. Not that I blame Chris. She plucked him off the street, dragged him into a shop, and they had lost the others entirely by the time he managed to get back outside. She's a . . . a minx."

I had to laugh. "Aren't you ashamed for calling Judith Atwater's daughter a—"

"Not at all," Carolyn retorted. "I suppose I'll have to take Edie to Bayeux while you take Chris to the invasion beaches."

"But you're too soft-hearted to brush Childeric off," I protested.

"No, Jason, I'm not," she said.

"Admit it. You feel half sorry for the man, even though he pushed you into that bicycle's path."

"Whatever happened, I'm staying away from him," said my wife. "In fact, I'm going to enlist Anna to stick with Edie and me. She doesn't think much of him, and the two of us should be able to keep Edie in line."

"Anna's not going to agree to spend the day with you if it means Edie tagging along," I protested.

"Oh yes, she will." Carolyn seemed surprisingly sure of that. "In fact, I think I'll go talk to Anna right now."

"By yourself?" I didn't like the idea of Carolyn wandering around the hotel on her own, especially with everyone in such a nasty mood. "Call her. You don't want to broach this proposal with Edie listening, do you?"

Evidently Anna was sympathetic to the problem, once Carolyn had explained it, and agreed readily to join her in minding Edie and fending off Jean-Claude Childeric.

"She's a nice woman!" Carolyn said with satisfaction as she hung up. "By the way, she said I was very lucky to have such a protective husband. Which I am." Carolyn sat up to give me a kiss. Too bad she was in no shape for anything more intimate.

Carolyn

Once Jason had plastered me with horse liniment, he went to sleep. I got up, wrote a column, and printed it out. I now have a small travel printer, which adds considerably to the weight of our luggage but makes Paul Fallon in New York happy; he doesn't like to receive faxes of handwritten columns. Having finished that chore, I pulled up my clue list and entered Robbie's mishap.

I looked over my list of suspects and couldn't see that Ivan would have

CLUE LIST

Day	Place	Victim	Injury	Means
6	Honfleur	Robbie	fell in harbor	push

any reason to attack Robbie, not if I was his target. And Hugh certainly hadn't, although Childeric had accused him of other attacks. Edie didn't seem a likely candidate; she seemed to approve of Robbie's affair with Hugh. I didn't think the de Sorentinos were a likely choice even if Childeric had once accused them of attacking him. That left Childeric, a target himself, Janice, or persons unknown. I shivered to think of the horrible things that could have happened to my friend while she was swimming to safety in that harbor full of boats. Then I shivered, remembering Childeric's visit to my room.

Anna, bless her, hadn't hesitated a moment to offer her assistance tomorrow. She hadn't even grumbled about Edie, although she had said that it would seem I hadn't told Jason about Childeric. Of course I hadn't. We didn't need any additional anger erupting on this tour, and Jason would not be happy to hear about unwanted advances to his wife. No, I wouldn't tell Jason unless I had to, but I would have to figure out why these things were happening. The violence, not the amorous attack.

If there really was an administration spy on the tour and I knew who, I'd certainly be tempted to tell that person about Childeric. He didn't deserve to be dean. He'd probably make sexual advances to the women in the college, if he were appointed. Hints from Janice indicated that he'd done such things before, although she had never been specific. Surely he hadn't tried anything with her! What a thought! She'd never have let it go the way I was doing. In fact, she'd be ashamed of me. On that thought I went to bed and slept badly, even though the liniment had eased my pain considerably.

Travel Journal
Day Six, Honfleur, Calvados, Caen

Shoving Roberta Hecht into the water didn't help much. It certainly didn't frighten her into leaving the tour. Instead she swam around with her nipples showing through her wet shirt.

Who'd have thought she could swim like that? Or row? Damn. She came out looking like a hero. Fauree's even more infatuated. Stupid fellow. Talking about dropping out of the race to keep his girlfriend safe. Can't have that. The fool will never be dean if he keeps sniffing after her.

But people think C. pushed her in. And he made a complete jackass of

CLUE LIST

Present	Suspect(s)	Motive
everyone	Childeric	revenge
	Janice	affair with H.

himself at dinner. Treated everyone badly. So I'm getting to him. And he's alienating the rest. Good.

I hope there is a spy from the selection committee with the tour. Someone to see what a bastard he is and report back.

An entertaining dinner. Bad food, though. What did they do to the turkey?

Blue won't let his wife near C. He can tell that C. wants to seduce her. And Carolyn's finally stopped feeling sorry for C. Small wonder. She's still limping after his attentions.

De Sorentino. There's another woman who needs to toughen up. She'll blow her chance at the position if she keeps trying to intervene on C.'s behalf. Doesn't she see that a user like C. doesn't deserve kindness?

Calvados tastes like fuel oil. And the cheese. I thought tastings were supposed to be tasty.

Only smart thing C.'s done is skip the afternoon.

But there's always tomorrow. I'll get him.

26

One-Upping a Philanderer

In 1809 white mushrooms were being cultivated in quarry tunnels outside Paris. Perhaps the people who now grow mushrooms in the multimillion-dollar tunnels originally built for a massive physics project in Texas got the idea from the French. However, I don't think the French taxpayer had to finance the mushroom tunnels. Does anyone know how much the Texas mushrooms would cost per pound if the congressional expenditure on tunnels was factored in?

An English botanist in the late sixteenth century said of mushrooms ". . . fewe of them are good to be eaten and most of them do suffocate and strangle the eater." I like mushrooms myself, especially in an omelet or buckwheat galette.

            Carolyn Blue, "Have Fork, Will Travel," *Evanston Observer*

Carolyn

Laura told me to try the buckwheat galettes, one of the delights of Normandy and particularly good in Bayeux, so at lunch I ordered the Gruyère and champignon variety (that's cheese and mushroom for non-French speakers). They were wonderful. The galette is a very thin, crispy-around-the-edges, nonsweet crepe sort of thing made of buckwheat instead of white flour. Gruyère is a mild cheese that melts nicely, and mushrooms need no explanation.

We'd had a fine morning in Bayeux, even considering the rain. The seventy-six-yard tapestry tells the story of Harold of England and William of Normandy, whose battle at Hastings changed the history of England for all time. Happily, there is a complete English translation of the French signs beneath the display to explain every panel.

Actually, it's not a tapestry at all, but a crudely embroidered story, wool yarn on linen, and it wasn't embroidered by William's queen, as Denis had told us on the bus before he went off to the beaches of Normandy with the others. William's half-brother, the Bishop of Bayeux, commissioned the Bayeux tapestry. This from Professor Childeric, who spoke very loudly because no one was talking to him. I found it particularly interesting to see that piece of history from the French point of view.

After a lovely morning, spent dry and warm under a roof, we ventured into the gale and arrived for lunch, pretty much soaked, at a creperie. It was then that Anna showed her mettle. She kept Edie and me from taking chairs until Childeric had been seated, the first person who was. Then she hustled us to another table under the puzzled eye of the waitress. The Drummonds and Foxcrofts sat with us, which left Childeric by himself. Shades of junior high school when cliques took joy in excluding lone students. I hate that sort of thing, but I wasn't going to sit with him myself. I needn't have worried. Before I could do anything to stop it, Edie got up and joined him.

I turned to Anna. "Should we—"

"He can't very well seduce the girl in a creperie under the eye of such a formidable proprietress," Anna murmured.

True. The black-clad woman at the cash register did look terrifying, and surely Childeric wouldn't even want to beguile Edie. "She's young enough to be his granddaughter," I remarked.

Evidently, Anna didn't think the age difference was a safeguard, but she did remark that Edie, being no part of the dean competition, shouldn't be in danger from another "accident." "And he'd be a fool to harm the only person in the group willing to sit with him," she added.

Meanwhile Edie was chattering merrily to Childeric, while casting competitive glances at me. That child was a ninny if she thought I'd be jealous. Such behavior makes one glad to have left the teenage years behind.

Nedda Drummond said to me, "Maybe you can explain, since you like medieval history, why they made Harold out to be the bad guy. After all, William invaded someone else's country, burning down cottages while women and children wept."

The weeping families were embroidered on one of the invasion panels.

"Harold even rescued a bunch of Normans when he was visiting William," Nedda continued. "At least, those are two stories the pictures told."

Professor Childeric heard and took it upon himself to answer. "That tapestry is the story of a broken oath. Harold took a sacred vow to support William's claim to the throne, which he broke when he ascended the throne himself upon the death of Edward the Confessor."

"Harold was tricked into the oath," I objected. "He didn't even know there was a sacred relic hidden—"

"Who cares, anyway?" Drummond interrupted.

"William the Conqueror was a great figure in history," Childeric proclaimed. "Harold was only—"

"—a guy who ended up with an arrow in his eye," Drummond finished.

"Harold might have won at Hastings if he hadn't had to march an exhausted army from a battle with the Vikings to face William," I murmured to Anna, as if she cared. I just couldn't let Childeric have the last word.

"Jeez," said Edie.

"I thought it was cunning—the way you could tell the Normans, who had funny hair, from the English, who had mustaches," Hester offered. "And all their heads were sort of skinny and lopsided."

"Absolutely," Drummond agreed. "And I rather enjoyed William's men rushing out of the coronation and setting fire to nearby houses. Not a very auspicious beginning."

"He was an excellent administrator and a great warrior," said Childeric testily.

"Who made the mistake of setting his sons against each other by dividing his lands between the two eldest, and giving the youngest only money." I just couldn't seem to resist one-upping Childeric.

"It was the custom of the time," said the professor haughtily.

"Too bad they didn't dramatize the story," said Nedda. "I'd teach a play like that, but I really detest those crude, farcical medieval church plays that—"

"Have you even read any of the great drama cycles of the Middle Ages?" Childeric demanded.

"Enough," Anna muttered.

Macauley Drummond, who had been whispering in Hester's ear, turned to Anna and asked, "What, Miss Smith-Thomas? Don't you home economists like academic debate? Too busy clipping recipes and making doilies?"

Reddening with anger, Anna gave him a look that would have cut steel, and I can't say that I blame her. Macauley Drummond had a penchant for gratuitous rudeness. Was he reacting to the stress of dangerous circumstances? I wondered. Or was he simply an unpleasant person?

"That's *Dr.* Thomas-Smith, not Smith-Thomas, and doilies are out of style, *Mr.* Drummond. Furthermore, my research is done in a laboratory, not in a kitchen," she retorted coldly.

And so it went. At least the lunch was tasty, although the cold and damp seemed to exacerbate my aches and pains. How I wished for Robbie and her bottle of Tylenol. I should have bought my own.

27
Watch Out for That Lunch Box

Carolyn

After lunch we wandered, guideless, toward the cathedral, where we were to meet those who had gone to the invasion beaches. Even in the rain, the cobbled streets and stone houses reinforced the atmosphere of ancient times. I particularly liked the old water mill site with flowers blooming in boxes on a stone wall. And the cathedral, originally built by the bishop to hold the tapestry, was an amazing conglomeration of styles and periods and alterations.

The original building, the west towers and the crypt with its rough carving and painted stone, the gorgeous fifteenth-century central tower, delicate with stone tracery but supporting a clumsy nineteenth-century top of the blob-and-spike variety, the Romanesque Norman sculpture of the eleven and twelve hundreds in the nave, Gothic influence in the chancel—I loved it all, took pictures, made notes, then watched with fascination a bit of contemporary byplay as workmen on scaffolding pulled to their high perches large iron pipes. What were the pipes for? Perhaps to drain off the pelting rain.

Later, the men hauled up, for their midday meal, heated pies and lunch boxes heavy enough to hold a four-course dinner. Jeremy, who had been sketching the round, arcaded façade and lawns outside, came in and stood gazing up toward the workmen who were feasting above us. He looked wistful, as if he'd like to join them and see the church from their lofty heights.

Then we heard the voices of our party as they entered the church, greetings exchanged, the chatter of compared experience. Jeremy turned to watch them. Above, the workmen began to lower their oversized lunch chests on the ropes. French voices drifted down to us, but we were absorbed with our own group until a hoarse shout pierced my consciousness, if no one else's, certainly not Jeremy's. One of the boxes, descending on its rope, began to rotate as it fell. It swung in a widening, falling arc.

"Jeremy!" My warning came too late. The arc intersected his thigh with a sickening crack, and Jeremy cried out and fell. From all over the cathedral the hum of tourist chatter stilled, and people began to stream toward the ugly sound of injury and pain. I reached Jeremy as quickly as anyone, and the poor man lay on the cathedral stones, blood soaking his trouser leg. He couldn't rise. De Sorentino was called upon to investigate, but he was

of little use. Jensen, however, pronounced the leg as broken as any cow's
he'd ever seen.

Gendarmes and ambulances arrived, priests offered prayers, gawkers
pressed too close. All of us on the tour shivered with new apprehension
even as we tried to be helpful to Hester, who was in tears, and Jeremy, who
was gray-white and sweating in an effort not to cry out again in pain.

While Childeric declared to the police that the attack had undoubtedly
been meant for him, and Laura de Sorentino told them in perfect French
what had happened, an unfortunate accident, preparations were made to
take Jeremy to a hospital. Soon he, Hester, and Denis were gone, but not
without Denis begging us to take care until he could return.

"Hit by a lunch box!" Macauley Drummond exclaimed. "Now there's
an embarrassingly mundane injury for you. I must remember to watch out
for such sinister weapons. Did it have Bugs Bunny painted on it? How did
you manage that, Childeric? And what could you possibly have against
someone as innocuous as Foxcroft? Did you think he was going to jump
into the dean's race? Or support someone else? Who would that be? Well,
Laura perhaps. She's prettier than you and not as alien to the arts as Fauree. And of course, she speaks better French."

Sharp words were exchanged between Drummond and Childeric, and
neither seemed to remember poor Jeremy.

I simply stopped listening because Jason was at my side by then, encircling
me in a protective arm, Chris in tow. "You all right?" my husband asked.

"Yes, fine," I murmured back. "It wasn't me this time. But poor
Jeremy—did you hear the sound of his leg breaking?"

"Nothing else happened this morning?"

"Isn't that enough? Truly, I'm fine, Jason. And that had to be a real accident, don't you think? How could anyone plan to hit Jeremy with a lunch
box?"

"Well, maybe that's it for today," said Chris.

"Where's Edie?" I had a sudden fear that she had escaped and—but I
was wrong. She was hanging on Childeric's arm.

And that was *not* it for the day, as my son had suggested. When we were
descending a hill on slick cobblestones, Macauley Drummond slipped,
bumping painfully and ignominiously from stone to stone for a good twelve
yards. People jumped out of his way. He had to rescue himself, and when
he did, he rose, reeling, and screamed up the hill at Childeric, "Don't think
I don't know who gave me that shove."

"If you mean me, Drummond, you're quite mistaken," said Childeric
with nervous dignity. "I do not—"

"Shove it, you asshole. You did it. And you'll be sorry. People don't
screw with me and get away with it. I'll be watching every move you make.
I don't need any poufy French police to defend me. I can beat you to a pulp
with my bare—"

"For heaven's sake, Macauley," hissed his wife. "I didn't see him—"

"Shut up, Nedda."

"It's slick," she persisted. "You probably fell on—"

"I said, shut up! Don't you understand English?"

Childeric looked pleased at Drummond's redirection of his fury. Nedda turned her back and walked away. And I felt a shudder of apprehension pass through me. *Had* Childeric pushed him? I had been ahead of them and couldn't say. Slipping my hand into Jason's, I leaned against him. "This is . . . is—"

"Surreal," he finished for me.

28

Tripe à la Mode de Caen

Tripe. The light-colored, rubbery lining of the stomach of a cow or other ruminant, used as food. (American Heritage Dictionary)

Doesn't that sound tasty? In El Paso tripe is very popular. Mexican restaurants advertise the days on which they serve menudo, a tripe soup. Sunday is popular because menudo is rumored to cure the hangover from Saturday night festivities. And the use of tripe in Mexican cooking is not a modern taste. Bernal Diaz de Castillo, a Spanish conquistador, mentions tripe as one of many foodstuffs he saw for sale in the market of the Aztec capital. That would have been tripe from wild deer, the only ruminant available at that time and place.

My husband likes menudo, which I, too, have tried. It's made with the less exotic cow tripe, and the broth was delicious, but the tripe? I'd sooner attempt to eat an inner tube.

In Caen, France, the signature dish is Tripe à la Mode de Caen. A culinary tome I read advised that if you have to eat tripe, Caen's is the best. Faint praise, indeed. And with good reason. It's cooked in cider. Even my husband didn't like it, but then maybe the restaurant hadn't done it properly. The sauce was black, which the author said was not a good thing. I quite agree.

Carolyn Blue, "Have Fork, Will Travel," *Syracuse Star-News*

Carolyn

We all ate together at a place suggested by Denis. Possibly we felt there was safety in numbers. Certainly we wanted to hear news of Jeremy as soon as any arrived. I'm embarrassed to say that I encouraged Jason to have the local specialty, tripe, and he agreed readily. Poor man, it was awful. I gave him part of my beef Bourguignonne, which is usually a safe choice and was in this instance. Childeric was not along, so we didn't have to make any effort to avoid him. Although he was being blamed for it, he couldn't have been responsible for Jeremy's accident. As for Drummond's ignominious slide downhill and his rude and profane reaction to it, Childeric might have been responsible for that, but Drummond had been so nasty to everyone, who could blame someone for giving him a shove?

Did I say that? Soon I'd be responding to aggravation and fear with violence. Not a happy thought. I like to see myself as more civilized. Indeed, I was beginning to feel that the whole trip was a nightmare for which none of us was to blame. Well, Childeric for pushing his way into my room and making a pass at me, as well as for his ludicrous declarations of affection and insulting assumption that I returned that interest. But enough of that. He'd stayed away from me since then.

Jason, however, brought up a matter that had been bothering me, too: the fact that our son was rooming with Childeric. I might be able to forget, if not forgive, Childeric's advances, or even my injuries in Rouen, especially because I wasn't hurting as much, but when it came to my son—well, I made no protest when Jason voiced his unease.

Chris shrugged. "I can take care of myself even if he is crazy, and believe me, he is. He never stops bitching"—Chris glanced at me guiltily—"complaining," he amended. "When I shave, I leave hair in the sink. I'm rumpled; I ought to iron my clothes. For Pete's sake. I'm living out of a suitcase. If he wants to iron *his* shirts, great. I'm not ironing mine. And he doesn't want me hanging out with Denis because Denis is a moron who doesn't know anything about French history. Like I care. He won't even let me listen to CNN on TV. He says in France, French is the language, so I should listen to French TV. Man, I've had it with him."

That was quite a long speech for Chris, who's not usually a complainer. My opinion of Dr. Childeric dropped even more. If he has children of his own, I feel sorry for them.

"Maybe we can make some other arrangement," Jason offered, although he didn't look very hopeful. Then he obviously had a thought. "If the Foxcrofts have to stay here in Caen or go home because of his leg, perhaps you could—"

"Listen, Dad, Denis has an extra bed in his room, and he says I'm welcome to it."

I looked a question at Jason while Chris said, "I've already told Childeric. He said, 'Good riddance.'"

Good riddance? That dreadful man! My son is a very nice young person. Professor Childeric should be so lucky as to have a son like Chris. "What do you think, Jason?" I asked, prepared to agree.

"It might be better," said my husband.

"I wish *I* could change rooms to someone more fun," said Edie, who was sharing the table with us. "In fact, I'd be more fun than Denis, Chris." She gave him what my grandmother would have called a come-hither look.

"This isn't a joking matter, Edie," I said.

"Who's joking?" she retorted.

"She's just putting you on, Mom."

"Okay," said Edie. "Maybe I'll move in with Professor Childeric."

Anna, who was sitting at the next table, leaned over and tapped Edie on the arm. "You are a shameless girl."

"And you're mean," Edie retorted.

"Edie," I scolded, "your mother would be—"

Anna, chin raised, said, "Carolyn, you really don't need to defend me from Edie. And anything her mother needs to be told, I can certainly do myself."

"Nobody likes a tattletale," said Edie.

Oh, my, I was so tired of angry people. I wanted to let my husband give me a good horse-liniment rubdown and then go to sleep in a quiet room. However, before I could fulfill my wish, I had to deal with Ingrid Jensen back at the hotel. Upon hearing Chris say that he'd go upstairs and move his belongings to Denis's room, she whispered to me, "You're not going to let your son room with that—that Denis, are you?"

"Why not?"

"Because he's a homosexual. I can always spot one. They prey on young boys, you know. Your son—"

"—isn't a young boy," I replied wearily, "and I believe homosexuals prefer to form liaisons with other homosexuals rather than approaching men who aren't of like mind. And furthermore, Ingrid, didn't I hear you telling your husband that you thought Janice and Anna were lovers? You really shouldn't spread rumors. People's feelings and reputations can be hurt."

"Well, I never!" Ingrid looked offended and flounced off.

Jason

We heard from Denis, before going to our room, that Jeremy would be in the hospital overnight, his leg definitely broken and already in a cast. The blood had been from a cut, not a compound fracture, which was good news. However, it occurred to me that the cut, even stitched, would be slow to heal under a cast. Perhaps I'd ask de Sorentino about that tomorrow. He'd been no help when Jeremy needed it, but he should at least be able to answer a question about the dangers of infection. Presumably Jeremy would be going home and Hester with him. Denis hadn't known any more than that Jeremy would be on crutches for some time, perhaps until the leg healed. Carolyn was very upset about his accident but had to agree that it *was* an accident. Neither of us could propose a scenario in which someone arranged for a workman's lunch box to strike a member of our tour group.

As for Drummond's fall, he said, as had others before him, including Carolyn, that he had been pushed, but by whom? Although he had accused Childeric, Carolyn pointed out quite rightly that the novelist seemed bent on offending everyone with whom he came in contact. Childeric was only the latest person he had attacked, but there were others who might have felt an overpowering urge to shove Drummond and had given in to the tenor of the times, as it were.

While I was preparing for bed and puzzling over the day's events, Carolyn was staring morosely at her "Clue List," something she'd started several days earlier in an attempt to track the series of attacks/accidents and come to some conclusion about the perpetrator. Finally, she closed her computer and said, "I can't tell what's happening. It could be anyone, or no one or everyone." Then she rose and said, "I'm going to brush my teeth."

When she returned, she'd had another idea: that someone might have a grudge against the tour company and be pursuing our group with the aim of ruining the company's reputation. "Look at the victims," she pointed out. "Childeric, me, Robbie, Jeremy, Drummond. How could one person have a grudge against all of us? And no one ever spots the person who does it. Maybe that's because it's someone none of us recognizes."

"And why would someone have a grudge against the tour company?" I asked for the sake of argument.

"The meals they provide certainly come to mind," Carolyn replied. "Remember the turkey? That was reason enough for just about any revenge."

"Granted," I replied, unable to suppress a grin. Most people wouldn't consider boring food cause for violence. "So the possibilities are that the tour has simply become a general free-for-all among a group of unpleasant and/or stressed-out people or that one stranger with a grudge against the tour company—"

"Unless it's Denis who's the target!" Carolyn exclaimed. "Remember. He told us to be careful in Rouen because he'd get in trouble if anyone were run down. Oh, Jason," she cried, "Chris is—"

"Denis himself hasn't been attacked. If we're postulating an attempt to get him fired, Chris should be safer in his company than elsewhere."

"Of course. Thank goodness." She gave me a hug. "There are certainly advantages to having someone around with an observant eye and a scientific mind."

"Glad you think so," I replied, "although I'd prefer that you loved me for my body."

"But I do, Jason. Both."

"So how are you feeling tonight?" I asked. "Any interest in—"

"Absolutely," said Carolyn, and slipped under the duvet.

Travel Journal
Day Seven, Bayeux, Caen

> *Worst piece of crap I've ever seen—that tapestry.*
>
> *C. got blamed for the lunch box accident. Stupid, because it couldn't have been planned, but just what he deserves, the thief! Stealing my research.*
>
> *Then he got blamed for Drummond, while I had the pleasure of sending that arrogant piece of shit bumping down the hill. I remember Mr. Bonheim, the father of a kid who never got to play, calling my dad, the big football coach, an arrogant piece of shit, which he was.*
>
> *And now C.'s lost his roommate. Let's see how he likes being absolutely alone. Night after night. Like I've been.*
>
> *Of course, the girl said she'd move in with him. Good idea. It would ruin him.*
>
> *He ruined me. She ruins him. I wouldn't mind some help in that direction.*
>
> *Doubt Carolyn would allow Edie to do it. That girl is a slut in training. And rude.*
>
> *Also, she's a wild card. Uncontrollable. My father would have said, "Drop her from the team before she screws up an important game."*

29

"Sweet Doggie"

Jason

On the eighth day of our tour, we left Caen and after a stop at the World War II Battle Memorial and a cafeteria lunch, headed for Saint-Malo, a seaport town in Brittany built on an island of granite and joined to the mainland by an old causeway.

Our hotel was far enough up a steep roadway to give us a view of the town ramparts and the sea beginning its rush toward the shore. Denis later told us that the ferocity and power of the forty-meter tides were second only to those of the Bay of Fundy, a rather frightening statistic. On our tour of the town we saw, of course, the cathedral; we admired the towers built by various rulers; we stared at the statue of a pirate/hero; and we walked the ramparts, some sections of which dated back nine centuries. It was a wind-and-water-buffeted place with, according to Denis, who is not always the most reliable source of information, a stirring history of privateers who preyed on British shipping in the seventeenth and eighteenth centuries and of warring nobles in earlier times.

Perhaps the most interesting tale was that of the English mastiffs, huge dogs that were kept penned and hungry until 10 P.M., then let loose to roam the streets attacking curfew breakers. In the morning the dogs were lured back and fed, if they were hungry. It seemed unlikely to me that either strangers or natives of the city would have been foolish enough to break curfew in those times. We were particularly lucky, Denis informed us, because there was actually a mastiff in residence, recently purchased by a history- and profit-minded citizen who kept the dog in his yard and allowed tourists to view the creature for a small fee, which Denis had arranged for the tour to pay.

So all of us crowded into the yard, standing back a respectful distance from the fence that separated Bishop Jean from the rest of the world. The dog was named after Bishop Jean de Chatillon, who, after taking refuge in Saint-Malo from unfriendly Normans, built the walls and cathedral in the twelfth century. Now, I had some notion of what an English mastiff looked like: square, dark, droopy face and powerful, short-furred body. But let me tell you, seeing a picture does not prepare you for this animal. He may not be as tall as a Saint Bernard or a Great Dane, but a full-grown male weighs more, 180 to 220 pounds, and he is very powerfully muscled.

His owner, Monsieur Broussais, a wizened little man wearing a beret and V-necked cardigan sweater, admitted proudly that he could not walk Bishop Jean on a leash unless he used a collar with spikes on the inside. Carolyn looked horrified. The owner, cackling, explained that the dog pulled him right off his feet and over the cobblestones without the proper collar, not that His Excellency was a mean dog, no indeed. He might be leery of strangers, but he was gentle with family and friends who were gentle with him.

Monsieur Broussais then went on to destroy that friend-of-the-family portrait with a history of the breed, which might have been brought to England by Phoenician sailors around 500 B.C. or bred by medieval lords to protect their forests and deer from hungry peasants. The breed had been used as war dogs by Roman armies and later human combatants and would die tearing an enemy apart in order to save their masters. During the Renaissance they participated in the notorious bull and bear baiting entertainments of England, but then what else could one expect of the thrice-damned English? asked the dog's owner rhetorically.

He concluded by assuring the ladies (and he claimed that Bishop Jean did love ladies) that a mastiff made a fine guard dog, was good with children, and in most cases would only clamp his jaws gently on the arm of an intruder or troublesome child. Watch the tail, the owner advised. Down, he's calm. Curved up, he's excited. Not that we'd see him on the streets tonight in either state, for Monsieur Broussais had his dinner at six and went to bed at seven, and Bishop Jean did the same. All this was said to us in a heavy French accent, but we did get the point. As we learned about him, the mastiff sat on his haunches studying us as if he were getting a lecture on humans.

"He looks like a nice enough dog," said Carolyn.

"Especially behind the fence," I replied, noting that when his mouth was closed, his teeth didn't show, which was a point in his favor.

Robbie was evidently enchanted, for she sidled up to the fence and began to speak to the dog—"Is he my sweet Bishy-wishy?" and other such endearments—while Hugh whispered urgent pleas for her to back up. She didn't; she extended her fingers through the gate. The dog stared, rose ponderously, and sidled toward her, watching the hand and listening to the voice. The rest of us held our breath, imagining the horror if he clamped those powerful teeth on her slender fingers with their brightly painted nails. Instead, he drooled on her.

"Oh, sweet doggie," she cooed. Bishop Jean rubbed his huge head against her hand. She had seduced the canine warrior even faster than she seduced poor Hugh Fauree.

The dog was our last stop on the walking tour; we then covered the short distance to our hotel and met Hester coming up the hill, all smiles and fluttering, brightly colored skirts.

"Ah, Madame Foxcroft, how is your husband?" Denis asked.

"Very well, thank you—considering. He has a huge cast on his leg, but still he got on the plane home with very little trouble. They have wheelchairs and people to carry you, and they even gave him an empty seat in first class. Wasn't that nice? And the construction company that was working on the cathedral paid for everything."

"You let him go by himself?" exclaimed Estrella.

"My mother's meeting him at the other end. He's taking her a picture of me in my new black dress." Delighted laughter bubbled from Hester, who evidently took an adolescent pleasure in tweaking her mother's conservative Boston sensibilities. "She loves to take care of people and boss them around. She's driving Jeremy straight home to Dedham, and then I'll meet him at the Boston airport after the tour ends to take him home with me, and—"

"He's your husband!" Estrella exclaimed. "It's your duty to take care of him yourself."

"But Jeremy's already seen France," Hester replied, astonished. "I haven't." Seeming sure that Estrella or anyone else would understand her point, she turned to Denis and said, "The clerk at the hotel told me you were going to see a huge, ferocious dog that used to eat people on the streets at night."

"Ah, but we have already been there, madame," said Denis apologetically.

Hester looked very disappointed. "Couldn't I go on my own?"

"I could not allow that, dear lady. Christopher and I will escort you."

And so the three of them went back up the hill, while Edie looked furious and Estrella muttered, "Just what you'd expect of a woman who'd leave her poor, injured husband to fend for himself. She can hardly wait to see a vicious dog."

"It was nice of Jeremy to insist that she complete the tour, don't you think?" Carolyn whispered to me. "Come along, Edie. You don't want to see that dog again."

"How do you know he insisted?" I asked. "Maybe she insisted."

"Don't be a pig," Carolyn whispered. "Did you notice that Professor Childeric hasn't said a word all afternoon? Not even to correct Denis, who undoubtedly made lots of mistakes, although I don't know what they were."

"A welcome silence," I responded as we climbed the stairs to avoid the rickety elevator. I've observed that many French elevators seem to be antiques, probably valued by the natives for their historical interest, as opposed to those of us, Philistines all, who would choose safety over history if given the choice. "Denis says we're eating at that fancy hotel down the street. Maybe we'll get a decent meal tonight."

"The Chateaubriand?" Carolyn's eyes lit up. "Do you think it's called that because their signature dish is a tenderloin of beef for two surrounded by delicious vegetables?"

"No, I think it's named for one of the city fathers."

"Is that the man who was ambassador to the court of Saint James and had the beef tenderloin dish named after him?"

"I have no idea, sweetheart. Why not ask Denis?"

"Now, that would be a waste of time. I wonder if I can work in a nap before dinner."

My wife does like to nap in the afternoon. She claims she got in the habit when the children were babies. While they napped, she napped to prepare herself for being awakened in the middle of the night. You'd think, to hear her tell it, that I never got up with the babies, yet I can remember several occasions when I did. I fell asleep in a faculty meeting, not a good idea for a new assistant professor, as a result of one such nocturnal fatherly stint. It must have been Gwen I walked the floor with. Lord, that child had a pair of lungs! No wonder she can make herself heard, without amplification, at the back of a large auditorium (a plus for a drama student). She began practicing early.

30
Finally a Good Meal

Carolyn

Maybe Denis had relayed the grumbling about the food because the restaurant in which we ate that night was regally appointed with linen tablecloths and chandeliers. It even had its namesake, Chateaubriand, on the menu, along with other tempting beef dishes.

Manfred Unsell, having been reminded of beef, remarked that the American Red Cross had announced a ban on blood donations from people who had spent ten of the last twenty years living in or traveling to Spain or Portugal. The ban related to putative exposure to mad cow disease. Dr. Unsell was not giving us a health warning; he was bemoaning what the news would do to the European economy, to American holders of European stocks, and to world trade in general. I just wished people would stop talking about it; I'd have loved a tasty piece of beef tenderloin in béarnaise sauce, not that we were offered that for dinner.

Still, our meal was quite acceptable: a crepe stuffed with seafood and cheese (no sand), chicken rolled in herbs with a rich gravy, lovely little green beans, potato galettes, and a chocolate éclair. Jason ordered a good light burgundy, and we were quite happy with our dining experience in Saint-Malo. That is pronounced "Sanmaloo," according to Denis.

Unfortunately, the company at dinner was not so pleasant. Macauley Drummond seated Hester between himself and his wife and talked only to Hester. Not surprisingly, Nedda took offense, while Hester seemed oblivious. She was too busy telling them both what a source of inspiration Bishop Jean was; she planned to do a glass sculpture, non-representational, of course, showing the dog in his warrior role, maybe even a piece depicting a bull baiting with mastiffs on the attack. She asked the table at large if pictures of those events were available in old books.

Before anyone could answer, and Professor Childeric seemed to be the only person inclined to, Nedda observed that Hester might find more customers for her sculptures if she produced something pretty instead of pursuing the macabre.

"Pretty!" hooted Macauley Drummond. "Since when have you turned into a stuffy, English professor type, Nedda? Pretty is not avant garde. Pretty is Philistine. No wonder you only teach drama up to George Bernard Shaw. What about the theater of the absurd? What about—"

"Shut up, Macauley. You don't know anything about drama. You're too wrapped up in your own novels to read anything you haven't written yourself," his wife retorted.

"Next you'll be pushing your syllabus back into the Middle Ages. You'll be consulting Childeric about *Gammer Gurton's Needle* and the like."

"An excellent idea!" said Childeric. "Although I'd call that play Renaissance. However, Professor Drummond couldn't do better than to solicit my input on medieval drama."

"*Dr.* Drummond," Nedda snapped. "To distinguish me from my *husband,* who never *got* his doctorate. The committee didn't understand his novel and turned him down." She cast her husband a malicious look.

"Which reflects badly on them, not me," he retorted.

"Goodness, I didn't mean to start a fight," said Hester. "It's just that I like red glass." Her eyes turned dreamy. "Drops of blood on fawn and black. Maybe flowing around the form."

Anna excused herself and headed toward the ladies'. I might have followed, but I hadn't yet been served my chocolate éclair and was afraid the waiter might skip me if I wasn't there. I do love chocolate éclairs, even those that contain pudding instead of cream, although at that moment I didn't yet know this one would.

"Perhaps we could agree that we all have different tastes," said Laura quietly, "and arguing about taste rarely changes anyone's mind."

"Ah, my wife, the peacemaker," said Lorenzo.

"After dinner, let's take an evening stroll on the ramparts," Laura suggested as if her husband had never spoken. "I've read that it is a thrilling sight—the waves breaking against the walls, especially when the moon—"

"There you go, Childeric," Lorenzo interrupted. "You've nothing to worry about from Laura. She's much too *nice* to be a dean. *Niceness* seems to be a genetic female trait that keeps womankind from accomplishing—"

"By God, Lorenzo," exclaimed Janice. "You really are a pig, as in male chauvinist. Females can be as aggressive and underhanded as men if they have to, and the accomplishments of women in the twentieth century have been . . ."

The arrival of dessert cut into the quarrel. Then Anna returned, but after so long a time that I asked discreetly if she was ill. She had pushed away her éclair as soon as she sat down, and she looked flushed.

"Too much rich food," she murmured. "I think I'll have an early night. If anything's planned for later, you'll see to Edie?"

"Of course," I replied. "Is there anything I can do for you? I think I have some Tums. They're good for both one's digestion and one's bones."

"And I, being postmenopausal, have to worry about my bones?" Anna asked dryly.

"I didn't mean—"

"It's quite all right. Very kind of you to offer. In return, let me suggest that Chris might eat a lower-fat diet. It prevents prostate cancer in later life."

I was quite taken aback. One never thinks of prostate cancer in terms of one's son, or even one's husband, if the thought can be avoided.

"I'm afraid I've upset you," Anna murmured. "Nutritionists should learn to keep their mouths shut, especially during meals. I'm as bad as those who were discussing mad cow disease while you were eating beef tartare."

"Don't think I didn't take that to heart," I responded. "I had a nightmare about my brain getting all spongy and full of holes, and Jason saying something about science being the guide to a good memory, only I couldn't remember his name. It was awful." I had fished the Tums from my purse and now held them out to her.

"It sounds awful," Anna agreed. "The dream. And put your Tums away. I'll be fine after a good night's sleep."

"But Nedda," Hester was saying, "I thought you *loved* Macauley's novels. *I* thought the one about the man who beheaded his mother and sent her head to New Guinea to be shriveled was amazing."

"I'll bet you did!" Nedda replied, rising from the table and leaving. She didn't even finish her éclair, although it was quite tasty for one with pudding inside. Maybe it was the chocolate flavor of the pudding that won me over.

Hester looked confused and stricken, Macauley told her to pay no attention, and Estrella whispered to Ivan, *"Menage à trois."*

He laughed. "Only if all of *trois* stay around, my pretty borscht beet. I think wife go to her room, maybe lock her door, and leave husband in hall."

Once the meal was over, we milled around outside the restaurant, discussing what route we'd take to the ramparts. Anna stayed with us that long, speaking to various people, which was a relief to me. She looked a bit better; nonetheless, she did start toward our hotel, and I suggested that Jason or Chris see her back, to which she replied, "Nonsense. It's just up the street."

Walking the ramparts was exciting. The half-moon silvered the tops of the waves, and the roar and swish of the breakers, rolling to the very walls and foaming white below us, was magical. However, a stiff wind, blowing like ice off the sea, soon turned us toward home. Although we had meant to walk the whole circuit of the walls, we were soon back on the cobblestone street climbing toward the hotel.

Jason was talking science to Ivan again, so the de Sorentinos invited me to walk with them. Given Lorenzo's remarks about women in general and his wife in particular, I'd have refused had Laura not been so eager for my company. I went for her sake, talked only to her, and even managed to maintain my sense of humor when he suggested that a laser peal might take care of the fine lines on my face.

What fine lines? I wondered, but said, rather politely I thought, "If I *have* any lines, they are badges earned in the lists of motherhood, and I'll just keep them, thank you."

Before he could urge some other operation on me, Bishop Jean, the English mastiff, suddenly loomed in the pool of light under an antique street lantern. He was unaccompanied! And he looked hungry!

31
Bad Doggie

Carolyn

If the dog is loose, it must be after curfew. No. What am I thinking? That I was centuries ago. Mastiffs no longer patrol the streets of Saint-Malo. Yet, there he is. My heart speeded up frantically when he produced a great, deep woof. Women screamed. Men shouted. Someone ran. The mastiff, mouth open, teeth displayed menacingly, sprang straight toward us. I was momentarily paralyzed with fear, yet my mind continued to function. Into my head popped an odd conversation with my postman, who often has to fend off unfriendly dogs. It seemed a flimsy weapon against such a huge creature, but I opened my umbrella in Bishop Jean's face.

He halted immediately. He whined and looked confused—I think. Dogs' expressions are not easy to interpret. Laura had gasped and cowered toward her husband. The dog raised his nose in the air, sniffed, gave a lower, but still frightening woof, and wheeled in another direction. Within seconds, Lorenzo was setting his wife on her feet, and the mastiff was thrusting his broad face at Childeric. The medievalist roared with fear and punched Bishop Jean in the nose. Tail curving promptly upward, the dog clamped his teeth on the professor's arm.

Oh lord, I thought. *The tail's up. That means he's agitated.* Childeric was caterwauling, "Help! Help!" He was agitated too.

"Shut up," Robbie hissed. She had dropped Hugh's arm and rushed toward dog and professor. Bishop Jean's ears twitched at the sound of her voice, and he turned his head toward her, widely set legs still braced against any move Childeric might make, the professor's arm still imprisoned.

"Sweet dog," she crooned, smoothing the mastiff's wrinkled brow.

"What do you mean, *sweet dog?*" Childeric moaned. "He's trying to eat my arm."

"Do be quiet, Professor," she cooed, looking into the dog's eyes, but speaking to Childeric. "Let go, Bishop. Umm. Let go of the nasty man's arm, little Jeanie Weenie." She leaned down to kiss the dog's ear.

I could see that Childeric was close to total panic. Sweat glistened on his forehead. "Don't move, Professor," she singsonged in a sweet voice. "Let go. Good dog. Good, sweet puppy dog."

The smitten mastiff rumbled, dropped Childeric's arm, and leaned against Robbie adoringly. Hugh had to shore her up to keep her from falling over. "Take off my shawl, Hugh," she murmured. "Good dog. Sweet puppy." Bishop Jean jumped up, paws on her shoulders, and licked her face. Robbie and Hugh both staggered, but Hugh managed to grab the scarf. "Hold me up, for God's sake, Hugh," she whispered soothingly.

"Can't you make him get down?" Hugh asked in a shaky voice.

Robbie rubbed her silky shawl against the dog's ears, then twisted it and tied it around his neck. The two were nose to nose as she did this, and I, for one, was terrified. What if he turned on her? What if Childeric did something stupid and irritated the dog again? What if—

She issued a command in French, and the dog, to the mystification of all, dropped his paws from her shoulders and allowed her to coax him, tied to the end of her silk shawl, toward his backyard enclosure. He listened to her cajoling as if she were a Siren luring him, a willing sailor, onto the rocks.

"We can't let her go alone," I whispered to Jason, who had hurried to my side when the dog appeared.

"Hugh's following behind, for all the good that will do," Jason replied quietly. "She's the one the dog likes. Anyone else might set him off again."

Our group, coming out of shock, began to stir. "I thought they weren't supposed to roam the streets anymore. How did it get loose?" asked Grace Unsell quite calmly.

"My God, he could have killed someone. That dog should be put down," said Macauley Drummond.

"He didn't hurt anyone. Not really," Hester protested. There was more excitement than fear in her voice.

"Carolyn, how did you know to put up your umbrella?" asked Laura. "I think you saved my life."

"My postman told me about it," I replied in a shaky voice.

"Don't think the dog meant any harm," said Carl Jensen. "Didn't seem dangerous until Childeric hit him on the nose. That's when the tail went up. Owner told us about the tail. Anyone'd looked at the tail first off would know he didn't mean any harm."

"You're saying it's my fault he tried to bite my arm off?" Childeric demanded.

"Haven't got any bite marks, have you?" Jensen asked. "Just a bit of drool on your sports jacket. Drool won't hurt you. Many a cow has—"

"But it wasn't a cow, Carl," his wife protested. "It was a huge, mean dog with big teeth. Cows aren't mean. But that dog—well, I wouldn't want him living on my street."

"The Chamber of Commerce should put a stop to such things," said

Manfred Unsell. "Killer dogs roaming the streets after dark may make a good story to tell the tourists, but the effect on tourism of the actuality is definitely poor economics."

"Oh, do be quiet, Manfred," said his wife. "You're so insensitive. We've all had a terrible fright, and here you're worrying about the gross national product or—"

"I didn't mention the gross national product," Unsell retorted. "If you'd been listening—"

"If I may be so bold as to point out who that dog went for," said Childeric. "The intended victims were Dr. de Sorentino and myself. Two dean candidates. You notice the dog wasn't interested in Fauree. That certainly tells us something about who was responsible for this vicious attack."

"For God's sake, Childeric," said Jason, "you're the one who provoked the dog. Roberta and Hugh rescued you."

"Indeed, which makes the ploy that much more clever. Who would suspect them of plotting against me when they are the ones who called the dog off? Utterly Machiavellian. But I am no fool. And Mrs. Blue, I must thank you for your quick thinking. You saved Dr. de Sorentino. Although your actions caused the dog to turn on me, I certainly don't blame you for putting me at risk." He gave me an unctuous smile, which I did not return.

"Perhaps you, Dr. Lorenzo de Sorentino, should rethink your remarks on the female sex. It was this fine, gallant woman, not you, who rescued your wife. If I should be so fortunate as to become dean, I certainly intend to show my esteem for our female faculty."

"I'll believe that when I see it," muttered Janice, "and I hope I don't have to."

We all, much shaken, resumed our walk toward the hotel. Jason put his arm around me. Chris took my hand, and Edie headed off to comfort Dr. Childeric, with many a resentful glance at us. "My lord, I was scared when I saw that dog heading for you," said Jason. "And me, off talking science with—"

"Let's not discuss it." I was shivering. "No one got hurt, and—"

"So speaks my cool-headed wife. I can't believe you fended him off with an umbrella."

I didn't tell Jason that I'd fended off worse opponents with an umbrella. I did explain the theory. "The postman told me that if you open a black umbrella in a dog's face, he gets confused because he thinks he's gone blind."

"Thank God it worked."

I could hear Hester asking Professor Childeric if there were any good medieval statues or paintings coming up. Estrella, overhearing, asked if Hester was Catholic.

"No," Hester replied cheerfully. "I just like those grisly crucifixions and saints being tortured. I did a prize-winning glass sculpture after spending a couple of hours in a Catholic church in Boston. It was the first prize I ever won."

Estrella looked dumbfounded at this revelation. "That's—that's sacrilegious."

"I beg to differ, Mrs. Markarov," Drummond put in. "Since Hester has no religion, how can anything she say be sacrilegious? At the least, it's an interesting philosophical point. Jean-Paul Sartre—"

At that point we reached the hotel and didn't have to hear what Jean-Paul Sartre would have said. Hugh and Robbie returned, and she announced, "The doggie's back at Mr. Broussais's, so all's well, although he wasn't too happy to be awakened or to hear that someone let the dog loose."

"Oh, indeed," snapped Childeric. "We can see why you'd think that all is well, having orchestrated the attack on myself and Mrs. de Sorentino."

"Dr.," said Laura.

"You, Fauree, and your hulking girlfriend—".

"What's that supposed to mean?" Hugh demanded. "You're blaming me? How the devil could I have orchestrated that if I'd had it in mind, which I didn't? You're dead crazy, Childeric."

"Hulking?" exclaimed Robbie.

"For heaven's sake, let's go upstairs," I whispered. "Thank goodness, you're no longer rooming with the professor, Chris. Edie, come along." She was still clinging to Childeric's arm. "We'll walk you to your room."

"You don't need to walk *me*," said Edie. "Dr. Childeric will do that, won't you?" She fluttered her eyelashes at him and, before I could intervene, dragged him off toward the balcony that looked out on the town. "First," she said, "let's check to be sure that mean old dog is really back in his dog house. What if he got into the hotel? It gives me the shivers, doesn't it you, Professor . . ."

I knew that I should go after her, but the thought of being on a balcony with Jean-Claude Childeric, even with Edie present, made me more nervous than the thought of Bishop Jean getting into the hotel. Instead of doing my duty, I dropped into a chair. I'd wait until she came back and see her safely to her room. When I told Jason, he offered to visit the bar and bring me back a snifter of Cointreau, which sounded like just what I needed.

32
That Nasty Old Man

Jason

The bar was more crowded that I'd expected; it must have been five minutes before I returned to the lobby where Carolyn had dropped, as if shot, onto the hotel's green brocade sofa. Other tour members were draped on the chairs in one of those "conversation groups" of furniture, talking about the mastiff attack. Robbie objected to the term *attack* as I handed the snifter of Cointreau to Carolyn.

"He may be a sweet dog, as you say, Robbie, but he certainly scared me," Carolyn murmured.

"You didn't act scared," Robbie retorted.

"Well, I was." Carolyn smiled her thanks to me and sipped some of the orange liqueur. "When you want a drink because you're upset or frightened or sad, is that a sign of alcoholism?" Carolyn mused.

"I don't think you need to worry, Caro," I assured her. "Now, if you were drinking in the daytime—"

"What about lunch after I got hit by the bicycle, and at the Calvados tasting? I don't even like Calvados, but . . ."

I'm not sure what my wife said after that because Edie appeared at the French doors that led to the hotel's scenic-view balcony. The first thing that caught my eye, oddly enough, was her navel. I hadn't noticed before that she was wearing a pair of slacks—more like tights—the waistband of which dipped below her belly button. Her top, some sort of snug-fitting knitted thing, was cut off several inches above that navel. A strange style. I remembered seeing coeds in such outfits, some with their navels pierced by rings. Edie didn't have a ring, but I thought the outfit unsuitable for a sixteen-year-old.

The second thing I noticed—the girl was crying. Carolyn evidently spotted that first because she rose from the sofa, pushing her snifter onto an end table. "What's wrong?" Carolyn asked. By then Edie had collapsed, weeping, into my wife's arms. "Edie? What happened?"

"He's . . . he's . . . disgusting," the girl hiccuped.

"Who?" My wife wore an expression—well, almost of dread. "Edie, what happened?" She had one arm around the weeping girl and patted her shoulder.

"He . . . he . . . that nasty old man . . . he—"

"Young woman, that's quite enough of that."

We turned toward Jean-Claude Childeric, who strode up, looking much more flustered than he sounded. My wife eyed him over Edie's shoulder with a dislike that would have withered a less self-important male. "What did you do to this child?" she demanded.

"Nothing. Believe me—"

"He kissed me," Edie wailed. "It was disgusting."

"I did not. I—I just patted her on the—the shoulder. As you're doing."

"Why were *you* patting her?" Carolyn asked through gritted teeth.

"She—we were supposed to be looking for the dog—and suddenly the girl just—just launched herself at me, babbling about how frightened she'd been—and—and what was I supposed to do? I tried to reassure her."

"How?" said Carolyn coldly.

"He hugged me," sniffled Edie. "Tight."

"I did not."

"Then what *did* you do when she—how did you put it?—launched herself at you?" my wife persisted. She sounded like a district attorney. Evidently her mothering instincts had kicked in on Edie's behalf, although I myself tended to take the girl's story with a grain of salt.

"Well, I may have—I mean I suppose I put my arms around her," stammered Childeric, "and gave her a—a pat or two—as I said. In a fatherly way."

"You kissed me on the mouth!" Edie peered at him accusingly from the safety of Carolyn's arms.

"I did no such—"

"You're saying you didn't kiss her?" Carolyn persisted.

"You don't believe me, do you, M-Mrs. Blue?" Edie stopped sniffling and burst into a fresh bout of hard crying.

"Yes, Edie, I do," said Carolyn.

She sounded quite grim, and I was rather surprised at her easy acceptance of the girl's story. I myself was still dubious. It had, after all, been Edie who dragged Childeric off to the balcony.

"So Professor Childeric, did you kiss this girl or not?"

"Well, I—I may have— Really, my dear Carolyn—"

"I am not your dear Carolyn," my wife snapped back. "I want to know exactly what happened out there."

"I—I may have brushed my lips against her forehead—but—but only as a—as a gesture of sympath—"

"My father never kisses me on the mouth. There's nothing s-sympathetic or f-fatherly about being kissed on the mouth by a disgusting old man who—who smells like wine and—and dog spit," Edie wailed. "He had his arm around my neck, and I could smell where the dog slobbered on his coat sleeve."

Childeric turned pale. The rest of the group stared at him with amazement and distaste. My wife said, "Professor, you should be ashamed of yourself."

"But I didn't . . ." His voice trailed away as Carolyn, Edie clasped firmly in the curve of her arm, led the girl toward the elevator, murmuring to her in a motherly fashion. I would have followed them, but Carolyn shook her head, and I backed off.

As there was only one elevator, the rest of us headed for the stairs, leaving Childeric, looking distraught, in the lobby. *Good lord,* I thought. The fool actually made a pass at a sixteen-year-old girl? I couldn't think of any more repugnant and self-destructive action in an educator. And how had Carolyn known that Edie was telling the truth? I suppose women have an instinct for that kind of thing.

33

Protecting Lolita

Carolyn

Edie was knuckling her eyes like a five-year-old as the elevator door closed. "Thank you for b-b-believing me," she said.

"You're welcome," I replied. I was experiencing a rush of guilt. If I hadn't been too embarrassed to tell anyone but Anna and Robbie about my own experience with Childeric, this might not have happened to Edie. "Anna's going to hear about this," I said gently. "Do you want to tell her, or shall I?"

"You." Edie began to cry again. "She won't believe you, though. She doesn't like me."

"I think she'll believe us. Now don't cry." I handed her a travel pack of Kleenex.

"No, she won't." Edie blew her nose but continued to weep as we stepped off the elevator. She hung back when I started toward their room.

"Come along." I took her hand. "You need a good night's sleep, and for that you have to go to bed." Edie followed obediently. "And Edie, tomorrow, and for the rest of the trip, please stay close to me." *If Childeric is exacting revenge for what he sees as dangers to his person, his reputation, and his chances at being dean, he'll see Edie as a threat after that scene downstairs,* I thought. *And he doesn't seem to be a man who accepts responsibility for his own actions.* "I can't protect you if you keep disappearing."

"I th-thought you didn't like me," she whimpered.

I sighed. "Why don't we start over?" I gave her a hug before I knocked at Anna's door. Edie hugged back.

"Thanks, Mrs. B. For sticking up for me with—with him. I hate him."

I almost said, "I know what you mean." Instead, I advised, "Best to stay away from him."

Edie nodded, not at all the rebellious girl she'd been through most of the trip.

At that instant, Anna, wearing a seersucker robe and a hair net, opened the door. "How are you feeling, Anna?" I asked. She looked pale.

"Tired," she replied, "but I'll survive. How was the walk on the ramparts?"

"You won't believe what happened," said Edie in a subdued tone.

"Have you been crying, child?" Anna asked.

Edie immediately began to weep again, and I told her to get ready for bed. With the girl in the bathroom, I told the story.

"Stupid child," Anna muttered. "Why did she throw herself at him out there?"

"I suppose she was frightened by the dog attack." Then I had to tell Anna that story, adding that I'd been pretty frightened myself.

"So he used the poor girl's fright to take advantage of her? Well, we shouldn't be surprised, should we? The man is completely without scruples."

"If only I hadn't been such a wimp when he grabbed me—"

"Don't blame yourself, Carolyn," said Anna. "You didn't do anything that any decent man would have taken as encouragement, any more than he can be excused for taking Edie's immature flirting as an invitation. The girl's only sixteen. And not that bright."

Edie appeared in the bathroom door, wearing a baby-doll nightie, all ruffles, bare legs, and shoulders. "I'm not dumb," she said resentfully. "I make good grades."

"Then show some intelligence when it comes to the male of the species," said Anna. "You can't go around flirting indiscriminately and expect that your age will protect your from a response you didn't anticipate."

"I told you she'd blame me," said Edie bitterly.

"Then you were wrong," Anna snapped back. "There's no excuse whatever for that miserable lecher's actions, and don't let him, or anyone, tell you there is. On the other hand, stay away from him, and everyone else in trousers."

"Mrs. Blue wears trousers," Edie ventured, trying to smile.

"And don't get smart with me," Anna retorted.

Edie flounced into bed and pulled the sheet over her head.

I could have wished that Anna had been a bit easier on the girl, but still, some things need to be said.

I was trudging back to my room when Hester Foxcroft stopped me in the hall. "I have something Jeremy wanted me to give you," she said.

Tired after a frightening evening, baffled at the idea that Jeremy, injured
and on his way back to the States, had left a present for me—or was it a
message? Or what?—I stared blankly at Hester.

"It's a drawing he did of Jason. In the Rodin gardens in Paris. You were
so kind to him when that lunch box hit him, he wanted you to have it. If
you want it. You don't have to—"

My eyes filled with tears. "That's so nice," I mumbled. "And poor Jeremy was so badly hurt. I'm surprised he thought of—"

"Oh, Jeremy's like that. He's as sweet as they come," said Hester. "And
they'd given him lots of painkillers by the time he told me to give you the
sketch. I had to tear it out of his sketchbook right there at the hospital. Do
you want it?"

"Of course I want it." I gave her a hug, and she gave me a large manila
envelope, then headed off to her own room. I walked to mine, double-
locked the door behind me and, remembering the mastiff attack, asked my
husband, "Was that dangerous, or not?"

"A man his age coming on to a girl Edie's age? I'd certainly—"

"I didn't mean that. I hope word gets back to the university and he gets
sacked."

"Carolyn, have you been crying?"

"Oh, not really. I was just so touched—"

"By what?" asked my husband, astonished. "I can't think of anything
touching that happened this evening, unless you're thinking of dinner. It
was pretty good."

"Hester Foxcroft just gave me that sketch Jeremy did of you. He wanted
us to have it." I set the envelope down on the bed. "In fact, I'm going to tell
Judith what Childeric did. But I was talking about the dog before. I can't
decide whether we were in danger or not. What do you think?"

"No idea," said Jason. "It certainly seemed dangerous at the time."

"And could someone have planned it?"

"I don't know how."

CLUE LIST

Day	Place	Victim	Injury	Means
8	Saint-Malo	Childeric	arm chomped	by dog
		Laura	attack	dog
		Me	attack	dog
8	Saint-Malo	Edie	attack	sexual

I nodded my agreement, unwound the cord that held the envelope flap, and pulled out the sketch. "Oh, my goodness. It's wonderful. Look at that." I held it out to my husband. Jeremy had caught Jason perfectly: the beard, the expression of excitement on his face—that was when he was talking about toxicity in paint, one hand raised to make his point, the other draped casually where his ankle rested on his knee, and behind him the vague outlines of the lovely garden. "I didn't even know he did portraits. I'm going to have this framed. Where shall we hang it?"

My husband admitted that it was a good likeness, said he was glad Jeremy had skipped the phase when he was fidgeting and feeling like a fool, and suggested that the Chemistry Department might like to hang it outside his office.

"Oh, go to bed," I said, laughing. "I think I'll have copies made for the children, too. And your mother. She'd—"

"I think I'll go to bed before you've got this sketch posted on the Internet and offered to the *Journal of the American Chemical Society.*"

Jason climbed in bed, laughing, and I put the sketch safely in my hard-sided, wheeled computer case and sat down to access my clue list, to which I added the day's events.

I looked over my list. Who would have reason to sic the mastiff on Childeric, Laura, and me? Or since I just happened to be by Laura, perhaps I could discount myself as a target, in which case, Laura and Childeric, being dean candidates—well, that left Hugh, but he had been with us, and Robbie had led the dog away. Of course, Hugh might have figured she'd be able to, so no harm would be done except a bad fright to Childeric and Laura. And Childeric had certainly made a fool of himself. And then gone himself one better by making a stupid, unconscionable pass at Edie, which couldn't help but make Hugh look like a more respectable candidate.

Oh me, Jason would be very unhappy if he knew that I was actually looking at Hugh as a possible culprit. And I had no idea how he, or anyone, could have arranged the dog incident.

CLUE LIST

Present	Suspect	Motive
everyone	Fauree	deanship
	Fauree	deanship
		couldn't have
		been planned
no one	Childeric	philanderer

Conclusions: (1) I'm no detective. (2) This tour is not only scary, but also an enigma. (3) There was nothing for it but to go to bed.

Travel Journal
Day Eight, Saint-Malo

> Not a bad dinner, and the chef was very cooperative about giving me raw meat chunks for my dog. The French love dogs. Someone's always letting his dog poop on the street. Or bringing a dog into a restaurant, making you think there's probably dog hair in the food.
>
> Who'd have thought it would be so easy to slip the meat into the pockets of Childeric and Lorenzo de Sorentino? Who doesn't think his wife is fit to be dean.
>
> No problem to let the dog loose either and set him off in the right direction. Too bad Laura saw fit to walk with her husband, and that Carolyn saw fit to save his hide. I was hoping he'd be so frightened by the dog that he'd leave the tour before he could slander a perfectly good dean candidate again.
>
> And C. No harm done, unfortunately, but again he made an ass of himself. Accusing Fauree. Too bad the dog didn't break skin. Or bone. Too bad C. didn't pee his pants. Dad used to say the cowards always did. Guess he was wrong. No big surprise there. He was just a loud-mouthed bully. Probably a coward himself. Had about the same opinion of women as de Sorentino.
>
> And C. making his speech about supporting women. Then putting a move on Edie. Now that, if it gets back home, should really screw him out of the dean's position. Must be sure the girl's parents hear about it.
>
> Contumacious conduct. Trying to seduce a sixteen-year-old faculty daughter would count as contumacious conduct. And even a tenured professor can be dumped for that.
>
> I'm definitely going to ruin the slimy bastard's life. And when he's out on his ass, I'll send him a letter, so he knows who did it.
>
> Can't think of when I've had more fun. Probably never. Not in years anyway. Not since C. screwed up my life.
>
> So what shall I do tomorrow? Seize the moment, I guess. That's what C. used to say, Carpe diem. He carpe diemed me out of a couple of years of research. It was all downhill after that. No full professorship. No family. There's nothing like being an aging, single nobody to make you invisible. Though invisibility has its uses. Carpe diem.

34

Mont-Saint-Michel

Savory Beans of Brittany

The salt marshes of Brittany and Normandy produce an excellent lamb, rarely available in the United States. Still, we can prepare a tasty bean dish in the fashion of the region to go with our own legs of lamb.

Heat *3 tbs. butter* in a frying pan and brown *1 chopped onion*, stirring frequently.

Add *4 minced cloves of garlic, ¼ cup tomato puree, 4 ripe chopped tomatoes that have been peeled and seeded, salt and pepper* to taste. Stir and simmer for 30 minutes before adding to *1 pound of canned flageolets or white northern beans*. Reheat and sprinkle with *1½ tbs. chopped parsley*.

Serve with roast leg of lamb and gravy.

> Carolyn Blue, "Have Fork, Will Travel," *Tuscaloosa Weekly Register*

Carolyn

Day nine contained the excursion to which I had most looked forward: Mont-Saint-Michel, that towering monastery and fortification thrusting up on a rocky promontory off the French coast. It embodies all the branches of medieval architecture from the Romanesque of the early Middle Ages to the Flamboyant Gothic as the era drew to a close, all the miracles a good Christian could imagine, and all the warfare any general or admiral could wish to relive in imagination. Until that day I had seen it only in pictures, but I loved it before I ever arrived over the causeway in a bus peopled by wrangling academics, a very subdued sixteen-year-old girl sitting beside me.

Two discoveries had been made the night before by Jean-Claude Childeric and Lorenzo de Sorentino, discoveries that explained the canine bishop's attraction to these particular people (evidently Laura and I hadn't been under attack). Each man found a piece of raw meat in his pocket when he arrived in his hotel room. The questions were: How did the meat get there? Placed by whom? Obtained from whom? Accusations flew. Childeric again accused Fauree. Lorenzo accused Childeric, without being able to explain why Childeric had the same irresistible item in his own pocket.

Maybe, I speculated, Childeric had meant to put the meat in Fauree's pocket and been unable to do that or to get rid of it before the dog arrived, nose on the scent. Janice Petar doubled over with laughter and was accused by both men. No one could explain how the dog had gotten loose, but Robbie said the gate to the enclosure was wide open, the owner asleep, and Bishop Jean perfectly amenable, after his brief adventure, to being returned. Hugh and Robbie insisted that they had closed that gate, not opened it, and they'd had no raw meat available as bait.

"Wonder if a dog can catch mad cow disease by eating beef?" mused Jensen. "Was it beef?" He addressed the latter question to Lorenzo.

"How the hell would I know?" Lorenzo snapped. "Ask Childeric. Maybe he tried it."

"I flushed it down the toilet," said Childeric angrily.

"That explains the plumbing problems this morning," said Grace Unsell. "The variety of things a person can reasonably flush down a toilet is limited, you know. I'm sure you inconvenienced not only the management but also many of us guests. I, for one, hate beginning my day with backed-up plumbing."

"I didn't have any trouble," said Hester. "How big was the piece of meat? Was it bloody?"

She pulled out a notebook and began to sketch as Lorenzo described his doggie treat, likening it to various human organs, which, as a plastic surgeon, he never had to deal with, thank God.

That was the gist of the conversation at breakfast and on the bus.

At least the wonders of Mont-Saint-Michel followed. Denis was particularly interested in the miracles associated with the island. Early Christian hermits had lit fires to signal the mainland when they needed supplies, which were then loaded by devout peasants onto a donkey. God directed the donkey to the island and the waiting hermits. When a wolf ate the donkey, so Denis's tale went, the wolf had to haul the supplies for the rest of his life. Then, there was the building of the first church on Mont Tombe, as the island was then known. Bishop Aubert had the church constructed at the request of the archangel himself, who appeared in a dream and later returned to remind the skeptical and/or dilatory cleric by poking an angelic finger into his forehead. Further miracles included the choice of the very site on which to build because the spot remained dry when dew covered the rest of the area; the removal of a large boulder by a toddler, who pushed it away with his foot; and the discovery of a freshwater spring at the foot of the boulder.

"Do you think those things really happened?" Edie whispered to me.

"I have no idea, Edie," I replied. "I just enjoy the stories and leave the question of authenticity to the theologians."

Estrella was ecstatic at these revelations; my son was highly amused, especially about the hungry wolf and the hole in Aubert's skull, still there when his bones were miraculously rediscovered. Chris's favorite was the stolen bull that miraculously appeared on top of Mont Tombe. My son said that wasn't a miracle; that was the ultimate fraternity prank.

Amid various disastrous collapses, the monastery was built, modified, added to, fortified, and even rebuilt by abbots, dukes, and kings until it became a huge labyrinthine complex of many layers that are a joy to explore. For me, at least. Edie wasn't that fascinated, although she did try to listen. It seems that the monks, too, were given to falling into decay, spiritual and intellectual in their case, and had to be expelled or reformed or educated from time to time, until finally they were ejected after the French Revolution and Mont-Saint-Michel became a prison. In our time the monks have returned, the monks and the tourists.

Pilgrims were coming to Mont-Saint-Michel as early as 860. Imagine! In the Middle Ages they walked across at low tide to expiate their sins, and children's crusades set off from as far away as Southern France to reach the archangel's citadel. Edie thought the children must have had a good time, roaming the countryside on their own. Lest she decide to follow their example, I remarked that most of them had died of disease, exposure, and hunger.

The island was also attacked by Vikings, then supported by their descendants, the Normans. Here the three sons of William the Conqueror faced one another over the water: Henry Beauclerc (later Henry I of England) holed up there while his brothers' armies waited ashore to starve him out. William Rufus, King of England, was touched to his chivalric soul (chivalry being one of his few virtues) by Henry's request to cross in surrender at low tide with his banners flying, so all ended well, although Henry later supplanted both brothers and took over Normandy and England.

During the Hundred Years' War, Mont-Saint-Michel fought off the English and provided sanctuary to those who remained true to France. In fact, at one point, a Breton fleet from Saint-Malo had to sail off to defend the citadel and drive away the pesky English ships. "That's where we're staying," Edie whispered.

"The very same." She was finally beginning to appreciate the delights of history.

"So the pirates sailed over to help the monks?"

"Even pirates were religious in the old days," I replied. A simplistic answer, but she seemed taken with the idea of pious pirates.

We did have a wonderful morning, following Denis from room to room, stair to stair. Then we went into the town for lunch, where we Blues and Edie consumed delicious omelets at Hotel Poullard. Mère Poullard was the mother of tourism at the site, for she sold her famous omelets to visitors once the island prison was closed in the early 1900s. I must say, Edie had been a model of propriety and good humor. She'd asked questions during Denis's lectures; she ate her lunch without complaint; and although she may have looked a bit sullen when Anna was within arm's length, she wasn't rude to her roommate. She didn't even ask for wine or flirt with Chris at the table, and we all stayed well away from Professor Childeric.

Although I had entertained the fantasy that he would be embarrassed enough to avoid the tour entirely, that proved to be too much to hope for. He was, after all, a dedicated medievalist. Even with Childeric tagging along, it was one of the best mornings we'd had. No one was hurt. Perhaps the culprit, or culprits, would finally be satisfied with all the fear and humiliation visited upon us and leave us alone.

35

Mont Tombe

Carolyn

After lunch we could wander at will, and the tour group was soon scattered by the complexity of the structure. I saw and took pictures of everything from the Artichoke House in town to the cannons left by the English. Once I had lost track of Chris and Jason, I explored with Edie, and in the company of whomever we met, the towers and ramparts, the soaring nave, crypts, cloisters, gardens high in the air, long stairways, chapels, refectories, halls built for great nobles and poor pilgrims, and the quarters of the monks, which were highest in the structure. Edie didn't see why the monks should get the best views since they were supposed to spend their time praying, not looking at the scenery.

"It was symbolic of the social order in the Middle Ages," I explained. "The religious orders were closest to heaven and God, the nobility next, then the peasants."

"I thought the poor were supposed to inherit the kingdom of heaven," she said. "That's what our minister says. Not that anyone I know wants to be poor."

"I think you've just put your finger on one of the paradoxes of Christianity, Edie." I hoped that I wouldn't be getting any irate telephones calls from her mother sometime in the future.

"I guess you mean we're all hypocrites," she said.

She'd been right last night when she told Anna that she wasn't dumb, and I decided to change the subject. "We haven't seen the great wheel yet. It was powered by serfs plodding around and around and was used to draw up supplies from sea level."

"Gross," said Edie. And somehow I lost her between the monks' quarters and the wheel. I did look for her. And I told others I came across, one of them Anna, to keep an eye out for Edie.

"Flown the coop again, has she?" said Anna and shook her head. She was sitting on a stone bench and didn't seem moved to rise and search for Edie.

The exploration of Mont-Saint-Michel was a breathtaking experience, literally (all those stairs) and figuratively, which left me once again at the lower levels, sans husband, son, and Edie, and gazing wistfully at the beaches as I imagined myself riding (not that I like horses) with Henry Beauclerc in the eleventh century to meet his brothers, Robert Curthose, Duke of Normandy, and William the Red of England.

"We should walk the beaches," said Macauley Drummond, who appeared unexpectedly at my side with Hester in tow.

"Oh, let's do," cried Hester. "I hate the Midwest. There's no sea."

"Wouldn't it be dangerous?" I asked, both yearning to go, even in his unpleasant company, yet wary after all the misfortune that had befallen the group.

"Not at all," Jean-Claude Childeric answered, having joined us. "The tide is receding. Forgotten who told me, but there's nothing to worry about. Can't you imagine the sons of William facing one another across the marshes?" He addressed this to me.

He'd read my mind, which did not please me. I didn't want to talk to him or be in his company. "I've just been thinking of that," I mumbled reluctantly, unable to stifle an honest reply, "of when Rufus allowed Henry to leave the island with all battle honors."

"Ah, those were honorable days," said Childeric wistfully.

I wanted to retort that he was a fine one to talk about honor, but then William Rufus had been a pretty disreputable character himself, although not where women were concerned. His romantic interests had evidently lain elsewhere.

"If you folks are thinking of walking out a bit, I'll join you," said Carl Jensen, who had entered our circle. "Like to see those salt marsh sheep."

"Well, let's go before it's time to catch the bus," said Drummond impatiently. "You better not bring down disaster on us, Childeric."

"Don't be a fool. I'm not responsible for anything that's happened. It's Fauree."

"I imagine they carried swords and lances," said Hester, "those sons of the king."

"Indeed," Childeric assured her and led the way. I hung back, but in the end I couldn't resist joining the group.

"The salt marsh sheep are famous," Jensen told me. "You'll want to taste those. Supposed to be the best lamb you ever ate."

"I've read about them. Will we see any?"

"Hope so," replied Jensen. "Sheep aren't the smartest of God's creatures. Like to see how they manage in a marsh."

Soon we were strolling on the hard-packed sand, staring back at the abbey, which loomed above us. Then we walked for a bit toward the mainland, and we could see sheep grazing, as well as cars and buses on the causeway and the little chapel of Saint Aubert with its stone stair and walkway, separated by water at high tide from the abbey.

Childeric, who was behind me, complained of all Denis's misinformation, Macauley chatted with Hester, who seemed oblivious to his interest,
and Jensen wondered if the sheep "out there a ways" were subject to the
scrapies that resulted in mad cow disease. "Doubt they're using sheep that
popular for feed," he added.

I nodded absently, for I was recalling favorite bits of history as they
came to mind. My pleasant musings were interrupted when Childeric suddenly appeared at my side and murmured, "Carolyn, I really would like a
word with you, if you don't mind."

I looked around for Jensen, but he had stopped to inspect a weedy
clump growing in the sand. Then he bent over, plucked a blade, and chewed
on it thoughtfully, as if it were some delectable tidbit offered for gourmet
consideration. "I do mind," I said to Childeric, silently berating my own
foolishness for walking out here. I increased my pace, hoping to get away
from him.

"Believe me, I would never—never have declared myself had I known
you wouldn't be receptive." His voice was low and urgent. "I misread the
signs. Unforgivable, I know, but, Carolyn, I didn't mean to offend you. I
hope you won't—"

"What? Tell other people? Isn't it a bit late to worry about that after you
made advances last night to Edie? I really can't forgive—"

"It wasn't at all what she made it out to be. I assure you—"

"What the hell!" cried Macauley Drummond, interrupting a conversation I desperately wanted to escape. We looked back to see that water was
swirling around his feet and Hester's.

"I thought you said it was low tide, Childeric," shrieked Drummond.

"I was—I asked and was told—" He stopped, frightened because the
tide was now at his feet and mine and frothing around the shins of Hester
and Macauley. Jensen, in between the four of us, stared down as if flummoxed by this unusual situation.

We all looked desperately toward the mainland, which was closer than
we'd meant to go but still farther than Mont—Tombe. It used to be called
Mont Tombe!

"Best head toward the monastery," said Jensen. "It's closer."

"But the tide—it's coming from that direction," Childeric protested.

I ignored him and waded after Dr. Jensen toward the island beach,
which was disappearing before my eyes as the water swelled around us.

"You idiot," screamed Macauley.

I glanced up in time to see him swept from his feet and grabbing for Hester, who cried, "I can swim. I can swim. Save yourself, Macauley."

"Thirteen miles an hour; that's how fast the tide comes in here," called
Jensen. "Best hustle, folks."

I was off my feet and trying to keep afloat among seemingly conflicting
tides. Nor was I doing well. I wasn't used to swimming in anything more

troubled than a crowded pool or a lake whose surface was now and then disturbed by the wake of a boat.

"Help!" cried Childeric. He caught up with me and proceeded to pull me under.

I fought my way to the surface. "Can't you swim?" I gasped. He threw both arms around my neck, and I went down, seeing, before the water closed over me, people on the shore, shouting. I was coughing up water when I resurfaced and whacked the struggling medievalist with my handbag. He let go, went under, and I managed to grasp his collar, determined that if he pulled me under again, I'd leave him to drown. Silly thought. We'd all drown.

"Childeric?" Jensen had slowed his efficient crawl and allowed the tide to wash him in our direction, while Drummond, with Hester following, swam ahead. I turned on my back to catch my breath, but waves broke over me, and Childeric's weight, suspended from my hand, pulled at me. "Think—I—knocked him—out," I gasped.

Jensen chuckled, took in a mouthful of water, sputtered, dove down, and brought Childeric up by the other arm.

"Boat," Hester called to us. She angled toward a row-boat, manned by two men, which, as I tried to keep it in view, seemed to go back as much as forward in the churning waters that had now obscured the beach.

"Just stay afloat, Miz Blue," said Jensen. "I'll tow Childeric along."

I tried, but the water kept breaking over my head. Childeric's head I couldn't see at all, although I still had him by the collar and tried to keep him above water.

"I've got him," Jensen gasped. "Let go. Use both arms."

I'm ashamed to say that I obeyed, much good it did me. I was sucked under, holding my breath, what little there was, for dear life, no idea how to fight free of a force I didn't understand. Mont Tombe! I was terrified. Sure I was about to drown.

36
Down the Abbot's Staircase

Jason

We were all to meet at the bus below the town at four. Somehow Chris and I had lost both Edie and Carolyn, who tends to stay looking at things without mentioning her intention. She, of course, maintains that it's the business of the person ahead to be sure that those trailing aren't left behind. Losing Edie was never a hard thing to do. If Chris wasn't paying enough attention to her, she tended to scamper off, usually in a huff. Neither of us was quite sure when she disappeared. Perhaps on the western side of the structure among the gloomy eleventh- and twelfth-century, barrel-vaulted rooms. Perhaps she had gone off with Carolyn, although I doubted it.

We noticed her absence several stories down where Chris discovered the "two twins," small dungeons that could be accessed only through holes in the pavement. Denis had told us dreary stories about occupants, one of whom, he had insisted, was a beautiful noblewoman whose husband didn't trust her and therefore left her in the care of the monks during the Hundred Years' War. As it turned out, Tiphaine, the lady in question, had her own house in the town. Chris decided that Edie could probably be found in a T-shirt shop in the town.

When we reached the bus, neither Edie nor Carolyn was there. Various people reported talking to Carolyn, so we assumed that she was still exploring, enraptured with Mont-Saint-Michel and forgetful of the time. Edie was another matter. Carolyn had asked other people to keep an eye out for the girl, but no one had seen her for some time. Denis muttered that those who were so rude as to be late should be left behind. Grace Unsell told him in no uncertain terms that any tour director irresponsible enough to suggest leaving a young girl behind in a strange country should be reported to his company.

Denis relented. Given the continuing problems that plagued his tour, he had probably been worried about losing his job before Edie disappeared. With various volunteers from the group, we searched the tourist area of the town, looking in shops, asking people if they had seen her. Our efforts were hampered by the lack of a photograph and the fact that no one could remember what picture had been printed on her T-shirt. She wasn't found.

Several of the women were now worried because no one thought Edie was so interested in Mont-Saint-Michel as to lose track of time. "I imagine she got lost," said Unsell. "Women get lost all the time."

"Maybe she met an attractive young man," suggested Laura de Sorentino. "Have you been avoiding her, Chris?" She smiled at Chris, who smiled back and said, "No, ma'am. I just try to hang out with my parents for protection."

"Where's Childeric?" demanded Janice Petar suspiciously.

We were all embarrassed to be reminded of events the night before, but no one had seen him either.

"Speaking of parents," I murmured to Chris, "your mother is still missing. Maybe she's found Edie and is regaling her with historical facts." Carolyn *would* lose track of time under those circumstances.

"Let's hope she's with Carolyn," said Anna. "Maybe we should see who else is missing."

"Professors Childeric, Foxcroft, and Drummond," said Denis.

Estrella nodded as if she had just discovered something significant. "Nedda, have you seen your husband with any of—"

"I lost track of him hours ago," Nedda snapped.

"Carl is missing, too," said Ingrid Jensen. "Now where did I see him? On one of those balconies that look out over the sea."

"Yes, he was talking about the sheep that feed in the salt marshes," said Unsell. "I remember asking if they are a popular French export, but he didn't seem to be interested in anything but the effect of marsh grass on the flavor of the meat. Tell me, Denis, has the tour planned to see that we sample this Norman delicacy?"

Denis looked uneasy, and I assumed that if we were to try salt marsh sheep, which Carolyn had mentioned, we'd have to pay for our own. The chicken and turkey we'd been fed heretofore were, no doubt, cheaper.

"We'll have to search the monastery," said Grace. "We can't let that child wander around on her own. She's too irresponsible."

"Grace, she's not *our* responsibility," her husband protested.

"What if she were your granddaughter, Manfred? Would you still—"

"She's not my granddaughter, thank God. I want to get back to the hotel. Denis, can't you send us back on the bus and—"

"I'm not leaving without Carl," said Ingrid. "What if some French criminal attacked him? In fact, the whole missing group may be terrorist hostages. Denis, you should contact the authorities."

Denis sighed. "There is a waiting period for missing persons before they are searched for. At worst, when the gates close for the day, they will have to leave. In the meantime, if some of you would be willing to help me . . ."

And so we spread out, searching the thinning crowds, stopping tourists who spoke English to ask if they'd seen Edie, keeping our eyes open for the adults. An hour later, Chris and I and Janice Petar found the girl at the bottom of a stone staircase that had, we later ascertained, been the entrance to the monastery in the twelfth century. Edie had obviously fallen, for she was bruised and unconscious, her head bleeding.

"She must have been with Childeric," said Chris. "When people get hurt, they're either Childeric or with him. And Mom's missing."

"Chris, can you find your way to the entrance?" I asked quickly.

"Of course," he replied, insulted that I'd think he was lost.

"Go for help. If you find an official before you reach the town, send him here." Fortunately, Janice had a guidebook, so we were able to tell him where we were exactly, the Abbot's Staircase. Chris loped off, taking the steps two at a time. "Be careful," I called after him.

Janice Petar, although almost as abrasive as my mother, was also as efficient. She took the girl's pulse, listened to her heart, lifted her eyelids, took off her shoes, and poked her feet and knees.

"Concussion. Probably no paralysis, definitely unconscious, maybe in a coma. Cover her central body with your coat, will you? I'll put my jacket over her legs. We don't want to move her at all."

"I wish I knew where my wife is," I mumbled unhappily, then felt abashed that I was worrying about Carolyn, who was probably fine, while this girl, who was more or less in our care, had been injured.

"If you're feeling guilty about Edie, don't," said Janice. "No one's been able to keep track of her since we left. No reason you should have any more luck than anyone else, especially since she resents being denied private access to your son."

Janice tucked my jacket about Edie's body and spread hers over the girl's legs. "She'll probably end up pregnant and puzzled about it before she ever graduates from high school. She's one of these hapless females who think, because they're pretty, bad things can't happen to them no matter what they do." Janice took the girl's pulse again. "You'd think her experience last night with Childeric would have taught her a thing or two. In fact, maybe we should ask ourselves whether he pushed her down these stairs. He was beside himself when she let everyone know what he'd been up to."

Surely the man hadn't—well, I wasn't guessing what anyone would or wouldn't do. Not anymore. We sat on the steps beside the unconscious girl, answering questions from the only two people who passed and wondering how long Edie had lain there unconscious. Finally, Chris returned with Denis and a French policeman. Denis said medical personnel would follow. I can't say that I've ever seen the ebullient Denis look more distressed, as well he might. Here we had yet another injury on his tour.

"Dad, listen," said Chris, drawing me aside. "People are saying two women and three men were caught in the incoming tide. A boat went after them, but no one seems to know—"

"Oh, my God." I don't think I've ever felt such dread. Besides Edie, five people had been missing from our group, Carolyn and Childeric among them. Wherever that pompous bastard went, disaster followed. She couldn't have taken a chance—who were the others mentioned before we went hunting Edie? Drummond. He would be too self-involved to help anyone but himself. Childeric, too.

Hester? A New Englander, but was she a strong enough swimmer to fight a riptide or a whirlpool, both reported to be features of the huge seas in the area?

Oh God, Carolyn couldn't have—wait, Jensen. He was missing. Ingrid had refused to leave without him. Jensen was a sensible man, but I had no idea whether he knew how to swim. Carolyn did, but—but it would be no ordinary situation out there.

I remembered one of Denis's stories. The pregnant peasant girl, who got caught in the tide and gave birth. It took a miracle to save her. Why would any of them have walked out—then I remembered. The sheep. Ingrid had mentioned her husband's interest in salt marsh sheep.

Surely, he wasn't foolish enough to—surely, Carolyn wouldn't have been interested in an expedition to look at—

"Dad?" Chris said sharply. "Dad? You're white as a sheet."

"She loves lamb," I mumbled, grabbed his arm, and headed up the stairs. "We've got to find your mother."

37
Bailing

Carolyn

The boat wasn't big enough for the five of us. They dragged me in and then Childeric. He had to be revived, no easy matter in the bottom of a boat. I was coughing up water as one of the fishermen pulled Hester in. She immediately turned Childeric over and pumped him, while Drummond demanded to be taken aboard next. As I hung over the side of the boat, still coughing and vomiting, Jensen was treading water and suggesting to the fishermen that they throw him a life preserver and let him cling to the stern. They didn't understand English. What a good man—even if he was obsessed with mad cow disease. He'd dived after me when I was being pulled down, dragged me up, and gone after Childeric.

Managing to edge away from the fisherman who was using oars in an attempt to keep the boat in place before it was driven away from those still in the water, I held a hand out to Jensen. Drummond tried to push him aside, but I withdrew my hand, for which I was roundly cursed. "You translate, Drummond," I ordered and grasped Carl's wrist. I wasn't saving Drummond. He hadn't done a thing for anyone but himself. Lucky that Hester was a good swimmer. He'd have let her drown.

"He's breathing," she said and propped Childeric up. He was also vomiting.

Drummond screamed broken phrases in French, clinging to a rope that Hester threw to him. Evidently he got some of the message across because the second fisherman gave me a life preserver and a rope for Carl, and I managed to get him tied. Meanwhile, Drummond shrieked, "Now, take me in."

Hester threw him a life preserver. "There's not enough room, Macauley. Hang on."

He shouted curses at her and at me. I slumped against the boat and sent a weak smile toward the oarsman. *"Merci. Merci,"* I whispered. They had given the only two life preservers to the men in the water. God help us all if the boat swamped. We were being buffeted by the waves and pulled this way and that by conflicting tides. The second fisherman, mumbling to himself, handed me a bucket, and took up the second pair of oars.

Hester was already bailing when I gathered almost nonexistent strength and wielded the bucket, keeping my eye on Carl, poor man. I don't know how he managed to get enough air to exist in those terrible seas, and I was terrified that the knot with which I had tied his preserver to the boat would give way and leave him stranded. A square knot. My father had taught me as a child to tie them, very impatient because I was so slow to learn. I remember a mathematician at a cocktail party. He studied knots, but in DNA rather than rope, and never when he was in danger of drowning. I was so frightened. And the boat seemed to take on more water than Hester and I could scoop out one-handed. I clung to the seat with the other hand.

38
Who Was Saved?

Jason

When Chris and I arrived in the town, we went straight to the bus. Carolyn wasn't there. Nor were any of those missing before we began to search for Edie. "Maybe they're in town having a drink," said Chris, who looked frightened.

"We'll find the police station," I responded, heading away from the parking lot.

Before we got there, we were hailed by members of our group who were sitting in a sidewalk café drinking Campari, Unsell among them. "Did you hear?" he called. "We think some of our people had to be rescued by local fishermen."

"Who?" I demanded, heart in my mouth.

"That's right. Your wife is among the missing. Now mine seems to be. Haven't seen her since she went off looking for that Atwater girl. Damned silly—"

"*Who—was—rescued?*" I demanded.

"No need to snap at me, Blue. We don't know. The boat headed in on the tide toward the mainland."

"How many were out there? How many were picked up?'

"Five," said Nedda Drummond sourly.

I breathed a sigh of relief. "Thank God."

"There were five on the beach. My husband and Hester. Your wife, I suppose. Childeric. Jensen."

"I can't believe Carl would be so foolish," said Ingrid plaintively. "But he *is* a strong swimmer."

"And they were all pulled in?" Chris asked, anxious for reassurance.

"Well, we don't know that, do we?" said Unsell. "Won't know until Denis lets us take the bus back to the mainland. I hope you found that silly girl so we can—"

"How can you not know whether they were rescued?" I demanded.

"The fishermen didn't come back here," Ingrid explained, "and none of us saw the rescue."

Chris and I exchanged agonized looks. "Let's try the police station," said Chris. "Dr. de Sorentino, could you ask someone where it is?"

"My wife's the French speaker, not I," said the plastic surgeon, waving to the waiter for a refill.

"Where's Robbie?" I asked. "And Hugh?"

"I think Dr. Fauree is still looking for the girl," said Ingrid, "and"—she sniffed disdainfully—"and Dr. Hecht came back here, heard about the tide catching Carl and the others, and went looking for news of your wife."

"We'll see if we can find Robbie," I said to Chris.

"Maybe you'd be so good as to tell me where my wife is before you leave," said Unsell.

"And Edie," added Anna.

"Fell down some stairs. An ambulance is coming for her," I called over my shoulder. "She's unconscious."

We met Robbie by the third gate. "No one knows who was picked up and taken to the mainland," she said. "Jason, what if she—well, she just has to be okay. I've asked everyone I could get to stop. I asked at the police station. There's just no news."

"Then we have to drive back. I'll drive the bus myself, if I have to."

"Good idea, but I can do it," said Robbie. "I drove a school bus when I was a graduate student. Anything to make money. I even tried topless dancing." She laughed, then said, "Sorry. Not funny. I'm whistling in the dark. Scared to death. Let's go."

39

Police Interrogations

Jason

The ambulance was gone, carrying Edie and Grace Unsell, who insisted on accompanying Edie. Grace had been an emergency room nurse before she married. Neither her husband nor the French ambulance attendants could convince her to stay behind. At Denis's insistence, the rest of us had to wait for the last of the searchers to straggle in. I kept Roberta on the telephone trying to get information from French bureaucrats on shore about the fate of the boat from Mont-Saint-Michel.

Even when the bus finally reached shore, there was no word. Police were there to interview us about Edie's accident but denied knowledge of a boat rescue. Not their business, I gathered. Try the coast guard, they said. But we couldn't try because we were not allowed to leave the police station. I did manage to get interviewed first. Chris and I separately, because we had found the "victim." Translators had to be found. Members of our own group could not be trusted to substitute, evidently.

Janice, furious when Laura's offer of help was turned down, launched into a diatribe on the French treatment of women, which she insisted that Laura translate. Laura evidently put the matter in such a way that the confused policemen misunderstood. They apologized profusely to the frustrated Janice, whom they thought wished to be questioned by a woman. Then they produced a policewoman, who not only had a marginal understanding of English but also provided a box of Kleenex to Janice and kept patting her on the shoulder as she escorted her away.

Then while I was being questioned, the cell phone given to me by Grace Unsell rang. When she insisted on accompanying the unconscious girl to the hospital, she had left the phone with me as the only person left of the couple charged with Edie's welfare.

"Word of Miss Atwater," I said to the protesting interrogator, who wanted to confiscate the phone. I backed away from him. The translator translated. "How is Edie?" I asked.

"Unconscious," Grace replied, "but they expect her to recover. I thought you'd want to know that the rest of our party is here."

"In the hospital? Carolyn?" The last was asked with both hope and dread.

"She's wet, frightened, and exhausted, but she's fine, Jason, and asking the doctors to let her see you."

I clicked off and rose to leave immediately. The interrogation officer tried to stop me. The translator tried to explain, presumably, my over-the-shoulder cry that my wife was in the hospital. On orders, a gendarme stopped me in the reception area. My fellow tour members stared as I tried to shake the policeman off, all the while bellowing, "Chris, they've found your mother."

Chris appeared at another door, trailing his own questioner and translator. General pandemonium ensued, but I did manage to convey the news that Edie was going to be all right and could be asked what had happened to her, something I did not know to be true.

A compromise was reached under which Chris and I were escorted to the hospital by our respective interrogators, while the other tour members remained behind protesting, especially Mrs. Jensen. I did notice that Nedda Drummond showed no interest in visiting her husband. In fact, I hadn't asked about the others. I simply said a fervent thanks to Grace and hung up. Carolyn would say that I should have been more thoughtful. However, panic and its sudden relief will overcome ordinary consideration for others. I was sorry, but I was also frantic to get to my wife.

40
French Health Care

Carolyn

Chris and Jason barged into the curtained-off room where I sat shivering in a hospital gown while a doctor applied a freezing stethoscope to my back and babbled from time to time in French.

"Carolyn!" Jason cried and embraced me.

"*Monsieur,*" the doctor protested, trying to extract his stethoscope from under my husband's tight grasp.

"Are you all right?" Jason asked.

I burst into tears. It was the first time I had done so since the water engulfed me, and it was a relief to cry. With one arm around Jason's neck and one hand clasped by my son, who looked pale and distraught, I sobbed, "It was Childeric's f-f-fault." My teeth had started to chatter.

"It was not," cried a voice from another cubicle.

"He s-s-said it was safe."

"Anna said it was," protested the voice.

"That's Ch-Ch-Childeric. He p-pulled me under when I tried to r-r-rescue him."

"Oh, sweetheart." Jason tightened his hold on me.

The doctor protested in French. A nurse bustled in and tried to remove Jason. She was young and pretty, so Chris said, "Hi, there."

She replied, "Eye, Yan-kee," and tossed her head.

"Dr. Jensen s-s-saved me," I chattered.

"For God's sake, can't someone get her a blanket?" Jason demanded. "She's freezing."

"I was so f-f-frightened," I sobbed. The nurse and Chris wrapped a blanket around me. The doctor snarled at her. French was tossed about. "Then two f-f-fishermen picked us up. J-J-Jensen and Drummond had to be dragged behind because there wasn't r-r-room in the b-b-boat."

"My God," said Jason.

"Drummond w-wanted to get in."

"I'll bet," said Chris. He was gazing at the young nurse while the doctor lectured her. Evidently there was some French hospital rule against wrapping freezing, traumatized victims of accidents at sea in warm blankets.

"What took you so long to get here?" I must have sounded weak-kneed and pathetic because my poor husband actually stammered out his explanation about Edie's disappearance and fall and the subsequent hunt for her.

"Oh, Jason. Is she all right?" I asked, now guilt-ridden because I was the one who had lost her.

"Unconscious in this hospital. She should recover."

"If you'd been looking after her as you were supposed to," croaked Childeric from beyond the curtain that separated us, "this wouldn't have happened."

Jason had to restrain me. I think I had in mind to stalk next door and attack that horrible man. At the risk of my own, I'd helped save his life, and he wasn't showing the least appreciation. "Too bad you didn't drown," I muttered.

Chris looked shocked. Childeric shouted that he'd heard me.

"You probably pushed Edie yourself to keep her from telling her mother what you did to her," I called back. "You're a nasty old man."

"He pushed Edie and almost drowned you?" Chris dropped my hand and started around the curtain.

"I was with your mother. How could I have done anything to that girl?" Childeric quavered.

"That's right. You tried to drown me," I said.

"Help!" Childeric wailed.

"Chris, come back here," said Jason and kissed my forehead. "Don't get yourself upset, sweetheart. I'll take care of Childeric later."

The young nurse tossed the folds of her nurse's headdress and went after my son, saying something like, "*Non,* Yan-kee," and other things in French. The doctor shouted at her, then at Chris, and finally at me, because I wouldn't let him remove my nice, warm blanket.

"I want to go home," I sniffled.

"To El Paso?" Jason asked. "Well, maybe we can leave tomorrow with Chris from Tours."

"Actually, I meant to Saint-Malo. Which reminds me"—I was beginning to feel better—well, warm at least—"I met a lady from Seattle in the Crypt of the Mighty Pillars. She told me that Saint-Malo has a wonderful dining room in a small hotel—I wrote down the name, but I suppose my note got all wet. Anyway, they serve Coquille Saint-Jacques. I'd like to go there for dinner."

"I think Mom's feeling better," said Chris.

41

Accusations

Carolyn

At last I was released from the hospital, dressed in my saltwater clothes, which Chris's nurse friend had put through a dryer. I'm sure I looked a fright, but we five survivors of the tide boarded the bus with the rest of the group and drove back to Saint-Malo. Childeric stopped by my seat and apologized for shouting at me in the hospital.

"I was distraught," he admitted. "And I hope that I didn't endanger you. If I did, my apologies."

His clothes were still soggy. I was pleased to see it, and I didn't forgive him, either. I was still distraught myself. Jason told him to leave me alone.

Looking chastened, the professor started farther back in the bus. People who were sitting alone moved to aisle seats to prevent him from sitting down by them. He didn't appear at dinner that night. Nor did he thank Professor Jensen or me for saving his life. Possibly he didn't remember much about what happened.

When he passed Drummond, the novelist said, "You might thank Hester for reviving you once they dragged you into the boat, taking up so much space that Jensen and I—"

"Don't apologize on my account, Childeric," interrupted Carl Jensen. "I'm none the worse for the dunking. A man needs a bit of excitement now and then. Can't spend a whole life with the cows."

"Excitement!" cried his wife. "I was terrified when I discovered you missing. I want to go home."

"We're on the way, Ingrid," said Jensen and readdressed himself to Childeric. "Glad to drag you up, Childeric, after Carolyn, here, had to hit you with her purse."

"Hit me with her purse?" Childeric looked dumbfounded and turned toward me.

"You were dragging her under after the water hit," said Jensen. "Some folks just naturally panic when they think they're going to drown."

"You hit me with your purse?"

"I hear he accused me of misleading him about the tides," Anna remarked from her place beside Janice at the front of the bus. "I distinctly heard Denis telling everyone to stay away from the water because of the tides." She turned to Childeric. "You were there, Professor. You must have heard him, too."

"I—I don't remember—"

"You were probably spouting some dull bit of medieval trivia," said Janice. "I've noticed that you rarely listen to anyone but yourself."

That was certainly the truth, I thought, but not as angrily as before, for I was so tired. I just wanted them to stop talking so that I could take a nap during the trip back.

"Professor Thomas-Smith *did* tell me that it was low tide that afternoon," said Childeric defensively. "I'd never have suggested walking out if I hadn't—"

Janice stood up and faced him. "Drummond says you claimed *someone* told you it was low tide. How is it that you've now decided it was Anna?"

"Well, I—" He looked toward Anna. "Anna, didn't you—"

Anna said quietly, "Professor Childeric, I knew the tide was coming in. Denis told us that."

"That's right, he did," said Nedda, who was not sitting with her husband. "Which makes me wonder why my husband was so stupid as to take Childeric's word for something so important."

"I'm the one who was nearly killed," snarled Drummond. "And I didn't hear Denis say anything about—"

"I told you all to stay off the beaches at high tide," Denis interrupted. "I told you the story of the pregnant peasant girl who—"

"Given the rank inaccuracy of everything you say," Childeric snapped, "you can hardly expect us to pay any attention to—"

"So you admit that you weren't paying any attention," Janice interrupted. "Then why should we believe you when you say Anna misled you? Why would she do that? And why would you listen to anything she said, given your attitude toward statements other than your own?"

"I wonder, Professor Childeric, whether Edie Atwater was with you when she came to grief," Anna asked softly. "Isn't it enough that you made advances to the poor child yesterday? Perhaps you were angry because she rejected you and embarrassed you in front of the others."

"You're saying I had something to do with her fall?" Childeric flushed red over his soggy woolen jacket with its puckered suede elbow patches. "On top of insinuating that there was something unseemly between that girl and myself? Her accusation was a lie. A vicious lie." He saw the disgust in the eyes of his fellow travelers and amended his accusation. "To put the best face on her story, she may have mistaken the kindness of an older man for . . ."

Wearily, I watched him working himself into a state of self-righteous indignation.

". . . and I don't have to put up with accusations of this sort. I was told that the tide was going out, whoever said it, and I did not try to drown Mrs. Blue, although she evidently tried to drown me by hitting me while I was struggling in the water. I don't, in fact, remember anything about that until I regained consciousness in the boat. And my relationship with Edie Atwater is entirely that of mentor to student. I thought the child had an interest in medieval history, which I've now begun to doubt. No matter what she or anyone else says, I have done nothing to be ashamed of. Nothing. If Miss Atwater is continuing to slander me—"

"She's unconscious," said Hester. "In the hospital unconscious."

"Took a terrible fall down some stairs," Janice added. "So how did that happen?"

"I was on the beach," said Childeric desperately.

"How convenient," Janice replied.

I didn't want to think about all the frightening things that had happened or who might be responsible. Rather than tax my poor, tired brain, I closed my eyes, and the clamor died away as the bus rolled toward Saint-Malo. I dreamed of a terrifying figure chasing me toward a restaurant where scallops were served in a delicious sauce. *If only I can get there before he catches me*, I thought. *I'm so hungry, and I don't want to die.* I woke feeling for my umbrella to defend myself. Jason was telling me that we'd arrived.

42

Exodus Dawning

Jason

Less than half of us ate dinner that night in the dining room about which Carolyn had heard from another tourist: the de Sorentinos, the Jensens, the Markarovs, a very sulky Unsell, Chris, Carolyn, and myself. Carolyn ordered not just one plate of Coquille Saint-Jacques but two. I didn't say a word, although I did wonder if she'd be surprised when the second order arrived.

I had the salt marsh lamb, which caused my wife to look distressed. I can't imagine why; she loves lamb, but she wouldn't even sample an offered bite when it came, and she evidently hadn't made a mistake in her order because she polished off both plates without comment. Of course, there were only two oyster shells per plate. She did try the Bretonne beans that came with my dinner and said that if she'd had the energy, she'd have asked for a recipe. However, the proprietress didn't look that friendly, and Carolyn didn't feel like an argument.

Not that Carolyn's reluctance prevented others from quarreling. First, Ingrid Jensen reiterated her desire to leave this "terrifying tour" and go home.

"Now Ingrid," said Jensen, his mouth full of fish in white sauce. "I'm the fellow who had the scare, not you. We paid a bundle for this vacation, and we're seeing it through. All those fancy châteaux. I know for a fact you want to see them." Ingrid subsided, but she was not a happy woman.

Then Lorenzo de Sorentino announced that he and Laura were leaving as soon as he could book a flight out.

"Why?" his wife asked mildly.

"Because it's foolish to expose oneself to danger."

"See there, Carl. *He* doesn't want to get *his* wife killed," said Ingrid.

"Phooey," said Carl. "You're not gonna get killed, Ingrid."

"Well, *we* can certainly afford to skip the rest of the tour," de Sorentino continued. "Not that I see any reason to lose money. I intend to demand that the company, which obviously cannot protect us, return a portion of our payment."

"Whatever you plan to demand in return, Lorenzo," said his wife, "cut that in half, because I'm not going."

"Of course you are."

"No, I'm not!" She took a sip of the Château la Tour he'd ordered with great fanfare and set her goblet down. "I am not fleeing. Is that tough enough for a dean candidate, or do you want me to go out and punch some-one?"

"Don't be ridiculous," he snapped.

A shocked Estrella Markarov whispered in Laura's ear, "It's a wife's duty to cleave to her husband."

"Is that in general or while on vacation?" Laura asked.

"At all times," said Estrella, forgetting to whisper.

At that moment the Unsells' telephone, which was still in my pocket, rang, and I answered. "Is that my cell phone?" Unsell demanded. He reached for it.

I waved him off. Grace was telling me that Edie had awakened and seemed to be progressing nicely. I relayed the news to the others. "But the poor child has amnesia. She can't remember how she came to fall down the stairs," said Grace. I passed that on. Unsell tried to get the telephone away from me again, but Grace mentioned Carolyn, so I held on tight. "Tell Carolyn not to worry about Edie," Grace said. "I'll stay here and take her home. She should be ready to travel tomorrow or the next day."

When I told Carolyn, Unsell shouted, "What? Give me that phone," and he knocked over Lorenzo's wine goblet yanking it away from me.

"You come straight back here, Grace," he ordered. "That girl's not your responsibility . . . Then let the tour company take care of her . . . Insensi-tive? The devil I am. You get yourself back here by tomorrow morning or I'll . . . Don't tell me that. Maddie always thinks she's about to deliver." Then he held the cell phone away and stared at it. "She hung up on me," he said, astounded. "She's worse over this grandchild than she was when she was carrying Maddie."

"I'm so sorry to hear that your wife won't be rejoining you, Professor Unsell," said Estrella Markarov, "but the coming of a child is a blessed event. Perhaps you should consider—"

"Mind your own business," muttered Unsell, his red nose shining like a beacon in the candlelight.

"Not talk to my sweet potato like that," said Ivan. "Is sweet potato right? Orange potato with sweet gummies melted on?"

"You're so smart, Ivan," said Estrella, beaming. "What a command of English! Our child will be trilingual. Isn't that exciting?"

"*You're* expecting a child?" said Unsell, looking at her with patent disbelief. "It's probably menopause."

"It is not," cried Estrella. "I'm pregnant." Laura, too, looked surprised. Estrella cried, "Well, I am, aren't I, Ivan?"

"You say baby coming. I celebrate. No cigars, but we drink toast to baby, no?"

"No," said Estrella. "Alcohol causes birth defects."

"Okay," he agreed. "I drink toast."

"You needn't look like that," Estrella said to Laura de Sorentino. "Maybe if you were a more dutiful wife and a better Christian, you could have a baby."

"Maybe if my husband had wanted a baby, I'd have had one," said Laura.

I could see that our group was moving from quarreling to exodus and wondered if Carolyn and I shouldn't leave tomorrow night with Chris.

Carolyn ordered a chocolate gâteau.

43
Could It Be Lorenzo?

Jason

Carolyn was too tired to write a column that night, but she did pull up her clue list and add Edie's fall. As a suspect she typed in Childeric, although I pointed out that Edie could have tripped. "He had reason to wish her harm," Carolyn replied. "He could be dropped from the dean's race or even fired for what he did to her yesterday."

"True, but I don't see that hurting Edie would help him. Everyone heard what she said. He's only off the hook if she decides not to tell her parents and no one else tells tales. And he was out on the beach with you. My God, Carolyn, how could you—"

"Are you blaming me because I nearly drowned?"

"No, but—"

"There were four other people, and we all thought it was safe. I suppose someone could have given him misinformation deliberately, but it seems more likely that he asked a question and didn't bother to listen to the answer. Men do that."

"I don't think I can be accused of not listening to you. I—"

"The really awful thing is that he panicked and nearly drowned me trying to save himself. And I was trying to help him. He didn't even say thank you."

"You want me to punch him?"

"Oh, don't be silly, Jason," she mumbled.

"I'm serious, Carolyn. I don't like the man, and I don't like the fact that he spent so much time hanging around you earlier in the tour, and I certainly don't like the fact that he could have killed you. I'll be glad to punch him in the nose."

"Oh, Jason." My wife started to giggle. "Professors don't punch each other."

"On this tour, I wouldn't be surprised to see it happen. I could give him a jab, and it would probably precipitate a free-for-all. No one would even notice I started it."

"I would, so don't do it." She then fell silent for a moment, looking thoughtful, and added, "It is strange that we never see who did any of these things. It's as if we have an invisible nemesis. One person hurt this afternoon and five of us in dire straits. Eleven incidents before that. I think." She glanced at her computer screen.

Later before we went to bed, Carolyn asked, "Why would Lorenzo de Sorentino decide to leave?" She was rubbing cream into her face.

"Maybe he was frightened by the dog last night."

"He didn't seem frightened. I wonder if he's the one causing all these *accidents*."

"Why would he?" I couldn't fathom her line of reasoning.

"I think he was around every time something happened. He could have pushed Edie. He wasn't with the five of us on the beach."

"Neither was I, Carolyn," I pointed out. I had been lying in bed, reading an article on toxicology, which mentioned that French bakers in the nineteenth century used copper sulfate and alum to whiten bread. Copper sulfate is highly poisonous and alum moderately toxic. I rolled sideways to tell Carolyn since the information intersected with her interests.

"I hope you're not saying that we can't eat white bread in France," my wife replied. "Surely their Food and Drug Administration wouldn't let the bakers use poisons in this day and age."

"We don't know if they have an FDA. Don't the French still allow the sale of absinthe? That's poisonous."

"Do they? I remember thinking I'd like to try an absinthe frappe when we were in New Orleans. Of course, they weren't available." She then returned to her new theory that Lorenzo de Sorentino might be the tour terrorist. "He could have been the one who told Childeric that it was low tide. Childeric obviously has no idea who said that. If anyone did."

"But why would Lorenzo—"

"I don't know, Jason, but the thought is especially dreadful since he's an M.D. He took an oath to do no harm."

"Doctors do harm all the time. Just putting someone in a hospital often does them harm. That's where the worst antibiotic-resistant bacteria reside. Did you read the statistics about—"

"No, and I don't think I want to hear them." Then she eyed me with new alarm. "Are you saying I might have picked up a fatal disease because they took me to that hospital today?"

"Of course not. You didn't have any invasive procedures. A lot of the infections—"

"Maybe Lorenzo's doing these things to control Laura. To make her go home when she wants to stay."

"Come to bed, sweetheart."

Carolyn removed the cream she'd applied to her face, turned out the light, and slid into bed beside me. "He definitely doesn't want her to be dean," she said, her voice drowsy.

"Then making Childeric look bad wouldn't be a good move." I could have saved my breath. Carolyn had fallen asleep. She didn't even wake up when Chris came by to suggest that it would be a good idea if we left France tomorrow with him, even though our spring break allowed us to finish the tour.

"And if we don't, you might have to sit with de Sorentino on the way home," I said dryly. "He'll tell you about the plastic surgery you'll be needing in twenty years or so."

"Great. Mom told me that Professor Thomas-Smith said I should cut down on fats so I won't get prostrate cancer."

"Prostate," I corrected.

"And Mrs. Jensen said I shouldn't room with Denis because he's queer. Of course, she thinks half the world is. When I didn't pay any attention, she looked at me like I was."

I'm afraid I chuckled at my son's complaints. And it was a relief to hear about problems that evoked laughter instead of dread.

"I'll tell you, Dad, it'll be good to get back to the fraternity: no high school girls and no advice from weird adults."

Travel Journal
Day Nine, Mount St. Michael

Dark and dank. Stone and stairs and dungeons. Perfect setting for skulking around, setting people up.

So Laura de Sorentino's husband's leaving? Good. He was ruining her chances of beating out C. for dean.

And Edie Atwater. Not my favorite person. Now people are whispering that C. might have pushed her. Wouldn't surprise me. No question he's scared the story about him and Edie will get around back home. So he should be. If no one else spreads it, I will.

And C. so panicked in the water he almost drowned Carolyn Blue. Good again. Now everyone's scared of him.

No one sat with him on the bus. No one ate dinner with him.

Let him see how it feels to be alone. A nobody in a crowd.

44

A Reading over Croissants

Carolyn

Still wobble-kneed on my way to breakfast the next morning and having forgotten to put my bag out the night before, for which I think I can be forgiven under the circumstances, I ran into Ingrid Jensen and told her how much I appreciated her husband's bravery yesterday afternoon. She told me that she'd heard Chris come to our room last night and commiserated with me over the reason. I must have looked blank.

"Well," she said, a bit huffy, "you don't have to tell me if you don't want to."

"Tell you what?"

"Obviously, Denis made a pass at him. I did warn you not to let him room with that man."

"Chris didn't—"

"Didn't tell you? I suppose he was embarrassed to admit such a thing to his mother. You'll find he told Jason. Unless, of course, he didn't mind."

I was beginning to take offense. "If Chris told Jason something while I was asleep, Jason would have told me this morning. And what do you mean about not minding? If you're implying that Chris is—not that there's anything wrong with that—"

"Nothing wrong?" Ingrid looked shocked. "It's against God's—"

"—but it happens that my son likes girls," I continued before she could say anything more irritating.

"Yes, I noticed him pursuing that little high school girl. I've heard some people go both ways, as they say."

"He doesn't—he didn't—"

"I wonder if he got her pregnant? That would explain her timely fall down the stairs. She probably miscarried last night at that French hospital."

"Have you ever considered writing for soap operas, Ingrid?" I asked and headed for the breakfast room. To think I had started the conversation by saying something nice.

Having collected my croissant, coffee, and fruit juice, I had no more than sat down beside Jason, bent on telling him about Ingrid Jensen's penchant for gossip, when Nedda Drummond spotted her husband entering the breakfast room behind Hester Foxcroft. "Well, the errant lovers show up for breakfast after a night of wild, illicit sex," Nedda said. Everyone gaped. Some even slopped coffee into their saucers.

"If you're addressing me, Nedda, you're talking absolute rot," said Drummond as he mixed coffee and hot milk in his cup.

Nedda stood up, her hand closed so tightly around her juice glass that the knuckles were white. I waited for her to hurl the glass at him, if it didn't break in her hand first. "You weren't in *our* room last night," she said.

"What if I wasn't?" he retorted.

"Well, he wasn't in mine," Hester added. She had been contemplating the croissants as if she thought something different might appear if she waited. "I'm sleeping in Hugh's—"

Estrella had just entered and gasped.

"—single," Hester continued, "so he and Robbie can have my double now that Jeremy's gone home."

"Not that you can't have fun in the single," added Robbie, laughing. "We put it to good use. Of course, I'm not accusing anyone—" Everyone was glaring at her now. "Oh, poof!" she said and sat down.

"By the way, if anyone cares, Jeremy's doctor in Boston says his leg is healing nicely, and he should be out of the cast in two months," said Hester, her tone that of a woman mildly offended by the preceding remarks, "and I've never been unfaithful to Jeremy, so you have nothing to worry about, Nedda. At least, not where I'm concerned."

"While I," said Macauley Drummond, "do not appreciate having my comings and goings monitored as if I were some schoolboy. A man without freedom is a man whose marriage has become an impediment to his creative expression."

"Really?" His wife pulled a shirt box from under her chair. "Creative expression? While I was waiting for you to show up last night, Macauley, I entertained myself with your latest effort at creative expression. Not quite up to your usual obscure standards, but I'm sure our fellow travelers would be delighted to hear a reading."

Drummond shrugged. "Don't be a fool, Nedda. No one wants to hear a first draft." He sat down across the table and reached to take the manuscript from her.

She jerked it away. "Don't be modest, Macauley. People love to recognize themselves in a novel, especially by such a *famous* writer." Backing away from his grasp, she ran her eyes around the table that seated our group, what was left of it. Three had already departed. "He's writing a novel about the tour," she said. "I thought I'd share some of it with you before I leave this evening on the plane from Tours."

Macauley looked shocked, then readjusted his expression to one of amusement. "You're doing no such thing," he said. "Don't be a fool."

"Leaving you is the least foolish thing I've ever proposed in my life," she replied and began to thumb through the manuscript after putting on her reading glasses. "Let's see. Here's a passage that just has to refer to Dr. de Sorentino, the medical one: 'The aging Pygmalion, whose power over his creation was fading with his virility, turned to the woman he referred to as Brillo-Head'—that's me, wouldn't you say?—'and thrust the dull blade of his wit into her ill-defended ego.' My ego's in better shape than you might think, Macauley . . . Ah, here's another. It's about the lovely Estrella, I'd say. 'She wanted a child as a boa constrictor lusts after a tasty rabbit or a young goat, so that she could consume it utterly.' "

Estrella began to cry and had to be led from the room by her husband, who could be heard saying in the hall, "Is nothing to cry on. He have no baby to see that is baby eating mother, not mother eating . . ." Estrella wailed with anguish at that piece of presumably well-meant, if ill-stated, consolation.

"Goodness, Macauley, that one didn't go over very well," said Nedda to her stone-faced husband. "Well, here's a nice scene. The character says, 'Look at that cow! Got an udder that makes a man's hands itch to grab it.' The character's wife says, 'I wish you'd spend as much time looking at my udders as you do at . . .' and so forth. I won't trouble you with the boring and pornographic witticisms that follow or the peculiar comparison to the begetting of the Minotaur."

Not surprisingly, more people began to leave. As Jason and I dragged Chris out, Nedda was saying, "Goodness, Macauley, you seem to be losing your audience, not that you ever had a very big one. How many copies did your last book sell? Fifteen hundred? Well, let's hope this one does better because I'm hoping to get the royalties in the divorce settlement."

Hester murmured, "That's not nearly as good as your last book, Macauley."

"See, even your newest bimbo doesn't like it," Nedda exclaimed. "Let me read what he has to say about you, Hester. I believe he calls you an 'oversexed, bloody-minded pseudo artist.' "

Hester laughed. "Bostonians are never oversexed. So I guess your—well, your soon-to-be ex—has an overactive fantasy life." Then she looked thoughtful. "I wonder what the id would look like in glass."

45
Launched by Bubbles

Carolyn

No one spoke to Macauley Drummond on the bus that day, and Nedda refused to give back his manuscript. Instead she perched by various people and read choice bits to them. Before long, no one was speaking to her either. The last person to do so was Laura de Sorentino, who, unwilling to sit with her husband, had joined Anna. Having leafed through the manuscript to another flagged passage, Nedda stopped by Anna to say, "He calls you the 'portly virgin, patron saint of sexually deprived homemakers.' He's got you trying out one of those shake mixers as a—"

Laura leaned forward and cut off the rest. "Nedda," she said quietly, "put that spiteful manuscript away. You have a good reputation in the college. Don't ruin things for yourself because you married the wrong man. Lots of us make that mistake."

Nedda looked startled. Then she walked up the aisle and dropped the manuscript on her husband's lap, from which it slipped and spread out on the bus floor. Turning, kicking a few pages aside, and walking over others, Nedda returned to sit beside Janice Petar. "Now about this feminist point of view . . ." she said, and they fell into conversation.

The last thing I heard before I dozed off was Childeric saying, "You two are plotting against me, aren't you?" He had risen and leaned forward between Laura and Anna. They ignored him, but from behind came Janice's amused declaration, "No, but Nedda and I are." I carried that voice and the dread it caused into sleep, for it reminded me that Janice, who made no secret of her dislike for Childeric, was someone else whom I had suspected.

This uneasy premonition was still with me when we reached our destination, the château of Angers, part fortification built by Saint Louis to hold off the English, part pleasure palace of the Dukes of Anjou, and most interesting, home of the Tapestry of the Apocalypse. Since Denis had warned that some climbing was involved, Jason asked if I really felt up to this exploration. However, I was inspired by the great castle with its eighteen round towers and my somewhat morbid desire to see the famous tapestry depicting the last great battle of good and evil. I insisted on going, even though I was, in fact, exhausted from the struggle in the tide the day before and still experiencing pain from my collision with the bicycle in Rouen.

After the escalation of violence and the bickering that characterized this tour of seemingly ordinary people, the tapestry affected me with admiration as well as trepidation. Finished in 1382, it had survived all these years, a huge work of art both grim and glorious, as had been the vision of Saint John, who wrote the biblical book from which the tapestry was taken. Some parts were gone, some damaged, but the original bold colors still survived on the back, which had been lined.

And the scenes were amazing: the graceful, flowing robes of the Four Winds, the decorative beauty of the trees with their individual leaves, the simple lines of the palaces, and the horror engendered by such figures as skeletal death riding his pale horse against a blood red background with lovely trees whose leaves are beginning to wither; the bat-winged Angel of the Abyss riding a mailed horse with a king's head and scorpion's tail; the contrast of the hideous little demon with the graceful angel in the panel depicting the overflow of the wine press. So many visions of evil. In the end I was glad to get away from this vivid medieval depiction of the struggle between God and Satan, but I think Hester had found her favorite work of art. She had to be coaxed away by poor Denis, who wasn't nearly as sprightly as he had once been.

We stopped at a patisserie for lunch, mushroom quiche and a lovely chocolate-covered cigar shape filled with a pistachio-coconut filling for me. In a stab at normality I took notes and planned a column. After lunch, the visit to a Saumur vineyard and winery was an anticlimax—steel towers, oak vats, automated wine racks that flipped a half-turn a day until all the sediment had gathered in a metal cap, freezing to blow off cap and sediment, two infusions of bubbles, and voilà! Sparkling whites, rosés, and reds. The owner explained the modern processes and equipment to us with great pride. His was the winery of the future.

I don't suppose the man expected that a cap would actually blow off during his speech, but it did and hit Childeric in the forehead, both cap and wine sludge, which ran down his face. Comic relief. Childeric was unhurt but also unamused. Hester, to whom he had been chatting about the ugly tapestry images of evil, started to giggle. Drummond seemed to have deserted her in an attempt to attract the interest of Laura de Sorentino. Although Laura listened to him politely, probably as a means of ignoring her husband's mutters and glares, she was obviously unimpressed with her new admirer.

Meanwhile, Childeric decided that the wine cap incident had been a planned attack on him and ranted about it during the wine tasting that followed. No one listened. Unfortunately, the high-tech wine of the future was only fair. We sipped politely while Denis went from tourist to tourist dithering nervously. The explosive wine bottle was evidently the last straw for him, although hardly the worst thing that had happened. Still, who could blame him?

Then we moved on to Tours, where Chris would fly home, not to mention Lorenzo de Sorentino and Nedda Drummond. By tomorrow we would be missing six of the original twenty-two, with Chris's early departure the only one planned in advance of the tour.

46

Edie's Message

Carolyn

We traveled to Tours beside the Loire River through a pretty green countryside with odd dwellings built into the tufu stone of hillsides. The hotel in Tours, a Best Western, sounded reassuringly like home, and our room was larger than those we had been assigned in past days. It had floor space. It had the toilet in one room and the sink and shower in another. There was an armoire and desk and a ceiling that curved down to a white, leaf-carved molding. Although the weather had turned cold and the sky filled with dark clouds, it was not raining. All in all I felt more comfortable than I had all day.

Although the tour company was to provide dinner in the hotel, which did not augur well, Jason suggested that our meals would probably improve because the company would want to leave us with a good impression. Remembering the meal at the Chateaubriand in Saint-Malo, I again wondered if Denis had heeded our complaints or, perhaps, noticed me taking notes and ascertained that I was a food columnist. Whatever the reason, another good meal would be welcome. That chocolate-coconut-pistachio cigar at lunch had cheered me up.

I was just settling down for a before-dinner nap when the telephone rang. I stared at it, astonished. The only telephone ringing for us since we arrived in France had been Grace Unsell's cell phone, and we no longer had that. What if our daughter was ill? Or our maid was calling to say that it had actually rained in El Paso and our roof had collapsed. Gingerly, I picked up the receiver. Had Jason not been downstairs with Ivan and Hugh, I'd have made him pick it up.

"Carolyn? Is this Carolyn?"

"Yes," I said cautiously.

"This is Grace Unsell."

"Oh dear, has Edie taken a turn for the—"

"No, no. She's fine. We're in Chicago waiting for her parents to arrive. She's claiming to have regained her memory."

"Oh? Oh my goodness, does she remember who pushed her?" Now that the information might be at hand, I was afraid to hear it. "Or did she simply fall?"

"She says not."

"Then who—who did she say—"

"Well, first she said it was Professor Childeric."

I sighed. "I was afraid of that, Grace. After the scene in Saint-Malo, and given how much he has to lose—"

"But, Carolyn, he was out in the bay with you. The five of you almost drowned."

"Yes, but he could have pushed her before that, Grace. Maybe he went out on the beach to get away from—from the scene of his crime."

"Well, I didn't think of that, and I doubt that it was the case. At any rate, I pointed out to her that he himself had been in danger elsewhere."

"And what did she say?"

"She said that maybe it was Anna, that she'd seen Anna."

"Anna? You can't be serious."

"My reaction exactly, but Edie insisted when I expressed doubt. She was looking a bit confused, but she said, 'I'm sure it was Anna. I saw her. She doesn't like me,' and more of that sort of thing."

Of all the people I might have guessed, Anna would be a last choice, although it was true that the two hadn't gotten along. However, if one, indeed, had pushed the other down a flight of stairs, it seemed more likely that it would have been Edie pushing Anna. "I can't believe that," I said to Grace.

"Exactly. The girl is obviously lying, but what if she tells that story to her parents? She's probably trying to head off anything Anna might report about her—the flirtation with your boy, throwing herself at Professor Childeric, not that her behavior excuses his. Anyway, I thought I should warn you about what she's saying." There was a silence while I tried to take it in. Then Grace continued rather sadly, "And I missed the birth of my grandchild."

"Oh, Grace, I'm so sorry. I know how much you wanted to be there. Did everything go well?"

"Yes, it did. In fact, I was talking to Maddie when the baby crowned and she had to hang up. I bought another cell phone in Paris when we were changing planes. Manfred won't be pleased. Not that I care. Maddie had a little girl. Six and a half pounds, twenty inches. As pretty as her mother, my son-in-law tells me. You might pass the news on to Manfred if he seems interested."

We rang off with promises to keep in touch, and I forced myself to consider the implications of Edie's claim. Was she speaking out of vindictiveness or confusion? Well, I had to warn Anna. I couldn't let her go home unprepared for such a damaging accusation. Good grief, the Atwaters might actually believe Edie and contact the French police. I took off my robe, dressed for dinner, and called Anna to tell her we needed to talk. She was surprised, but she gave me her room number.

After I'd explained the situation, Anna sighed. "What's that saying about good deeds coming back to haunt you? If I'd never tried to keep track of her and had managed to farm her off as a roommate to someone else, I suppose she wouldn't have come to hate me so much. Not that I like her, but I did pity her, especially after the incident with Childeric."

"Anna, I'm so sorry. I'm the one who lost track of her at Mont-Saint-

Michel. If I'd been a better minder and kept up with her, she could never have blamed you for anything. For that matter, I'd never have been out on that beach."

"Actually, she was with me for a while and completely uninterested in sightseeing, but she got away, so you needn't blame yourself, Carolyn. She was probably running headlong down some staircase, trying to find a T-shirt shop, and fell over her own feet."

"Well, anyway, I thought I should warn you about what she's saying. Of course, Grace doesn't believe her, and neither do I. I'm sure nothing will come of it, but if—well—"

I smiled at her, embarrassed. "You can always call on me as a character witness."

My goodness. Our first course was a lovely, light puff pastry filled with creamed asparagus, and the entrée was Coq au Vin, very good too, followed by a cheese plate and pears poached in wine. Only two unpleasant notes were struck during dinner. The first was the acidic carafe of gamay we ordered; it was so nasty that Jason wouldn't drink it. I did. I do like wine with dinner and sipped my way through the half-liter with no effect whatever. It must have been watered. Jason ordered beer and complained to the headwaiter about the wine. The management did try to make amends. We found a half-carafe of a good local red when we returned to our room from the airport, but by then it was time for bed and we left it on the dresser, tasted but not drunk.

The second source of unpleasantness came from Lorenzo de Sorentino. Laura was ignoring him, and Macauley Drummond was still trying to attract her attention when I heard Lorenzo hiss into her ear, "My leaving is not meant as an invitation to take up with Drummond, Laura."

She replied, "Don't be ridiculous, Lorenzo," and went to her room instead of seeing him off at the airport.

47

Farewells

Jason

For the first time in my life I was glad to send my son away. I know that Carolyn was reassured by a relatively uneventful day, a good dinner, and the prospect of less marital turmoil tomorrow when the two bitterest couples were separated—quite possibly for good, although only Estrella

Markarov was obsessing over that. Chris seemed torn between a desire to get back to school and the feeling that I needed him here to protect his mother. He also seemed worried about Edie Atwater, for he asked if any word of her condition had been received.

"I imagine she's back with her family even as we speak, Chris," his mother replied. "And having been able to make the trip home, she's evidently on the road to recovery."

"I'm really sorry that I didn't handle the situation with her better, Mom." Chris shifted self-consciously and readjusted his backpack. "If I'd told her to knock off the flirting and kept a better eye on her," he mumbled, "I expect she wouldn't have had that trouble with Childeric or even fallen down the stairs and hurt herself. All in all, it must have been a pretty miserable trip for her."

My wife sighed. "Don't blame yourself, Chris. I lost track of her after you last saw her. Even Anna did. Edie's going through that confused, rebellious stage."

Chris grinned. "Who isn't at sixteen? Anyway, Mom, I'm sorry your vacation was spoiled by all this." I noticed that he gave Carolyn an extralong hug before boarding his plane, and Carolyn, as always, cried. She used to cry when one of the children went away to camp, even if it was only for a week. Yet she seems to enjoy the traveling and the time alone we now have. I certainly do. Well, what man can understand women?

I heard an offer that should prove my point about the mysterious nature of women. Lorenzo de Sorentino was giving Nedda Drummond (neither of their spouses came to see them off) advice about her hair and suggesting that he could improve her looks "one hundred percent if you let me do a nose job on you."

Instead of biting his head off, as I would have expected, she said, "Fine. I'll use the royalties from Macauley's book, from all his books, plus the alimony I plan to get in the divorce settlement. If he coughs up enough money, I won't even have to ask you for a tour discount."

De Sorentino laughed and took her arm as they boarded. Maybe he thought she was kidding. If his departure meant an end to the accidents and injuries, so much the better. Carolyn would be delighted to have the latest of her theories proved right, and I could enjoy a carefree and safe end-of-tour with my wife.

As we turned to leave the airport, we were caught by surprise at the sight of Professor Childeric, who hadn't appeared at dinner, walking away from an arrival gate accompanied by a stocky woman with black hair braided around her head.

"Ah, Dr. Blue, and Mrs. Blue, let me introduce you to my wife, Astarte."

Astarte? Wasn't that some prehistoric moon goddess? I'd have to ask Carolyn, who is the family keeper of arcane information. In her full-cut, nononsense suit and sensible heels, this woman did not look like a goddess. I remember Carolyn describing that shoe type as "a court pump." Mrs. Childeric didn't look like a courtier either, or whatever the female of courtier is. Both Carolyn and Childeric would know that. Actually, Mrs. Childeric looked like an uncompromising battle-ax.

"My dear wife has been so kind as to join me for the last days of the tour. One does miss the companionship of one's spouse, doesn't one?" said Childeric.

Mrs. Childeric looked rather surprised and suspicious to hear this paean to her company. "Well, you know I wouldn't have come, Jean-Claude, if I hadn't played that ace of diamonds and dropped myself right out of contention. My opponent, the dummy hand actually, knocked his coffee into my lap or I'd never have made that mistake. I did complain to the judges, but—"

"Yes, yes," said Childeric. "Most unfortunate, but still it gave me the pleasure of your companionship, my dear." Again she looked at him askance. "And I know that you'll enjoy seeing the châteaux of the Loire Valley. Shall we share a taxi to the hotel?"

The last was addressed to us, and I'd rather not have, but it would have been rude to refuse in front of his wife, who, after all, hadn't tried to drown mine at Mont-Saint-Michel.

"You'll love the hotel, my dear," he said to the doughty Astarte.

That's what she looked like. A Wagnerian soprano.

"Excellent woodwork in the rooms," Childeric chatted on.

I think he was afraid that we'd do just what I wanted to do, refuse to ride with them, if we managed to get a word in.

"Well, I hope we're not paying extra for the woodwork," said Mrs. Childeric. "Last-minute tickets to Europe are expensive, you know."

"But worth every penny," said Childeric.

"Jean-Claude." She eyed him suspiciously. "Is something wrong with you?"

"Nothing that your company won't remedy, my dear."

Once in our room, Carolyn remarked that Childeric must have been very unhappy about being treated as a pariah by the tour group. "Now he'll have someone to talk to."

I shrugged and climbed into bed. "At least he can't lure anyone into danger or try to seduce any teenaged girls if his wife's with him."

"A comforting thought," Carolyn agreed. "Perhaps tomorrow will be a trouble-free day. I, for one, would welcome a bit of peaceful touring. And do you know, I'm not aching as much as I was? I only took four pills today. Maybe there's hope for my liver, after all."

"That wine you drank tonight would put holes in any liver, much less one already weakened by several days of acetaminophen. Still, if you're feeling better—"

"Yes," said Carolyn. "Let's," and she scooted over to my side of the bed.

Travel Journal
Day Ten, Tours

    I actually enjoyed dinner tonight. The food was good, and C. had made a fool of himself over a flying wine cap. Everyone decided by the time we left Saumur that the bastard's paranoid, as well as dangerous and immoral.

    He didn't even show up for dinner, which made it the best meal of the tour. I thought I'd succeeded. Isolated him, and no one the wiser.

    Should have known better. He brought his wife in to keep him company. I'd almost forgotten about her. He's married. If Edie keeps her mouth shut, he's still got it all, spouse, reputation, a full professorship. Maybe even the deanship. He could be appointed before we get back and I can spread rumors about him. God, I hate him.

    And I've got to get him. While there's still time. All the other things I did—they weren't enough. Not nearly enough.

48

A Birth Announcement

Carolyn

At breakfast on the eleventh day, we were a subdued group. Six of our number had left the tour, two injured, two willingly, two in a snit. That left seventeen, since Mrs. Childeric had joined us. She and her husband had a peculiar relationship in that they talked to each other but usually speaking at the same time, neither listening to or even interested in what the other had to say. She described bridge hands and strategies, and that morning he held forth on Renaissance French history as it related to the châteaux we were about to visit, Chenonceau, Azay le Rideau, and the gardens at Villandry. I wonder if she knew what he'd been up to in her absence. And if she noticed that people on the tour were avoiding him. Her arrival was certainly a relief to me.

This attention to the Renaissance was motivated by Childeric's desire to point out Denis's mistakes when the guide attempted to give us pretour information. Usually quite immune to such carping insistence on accuracy, Denis on this day gave up with hardly a fight. He had been accused in the lobby before breakfast of causing Chris's abrupt departure, the accuser Ingrid Jensen, who mentioned "unnatural attentions" and "unchristian perversions." At least she was fairly discreet. I wouldn't have heard the beginning if I hadn't been at the front desk asking to have extra towels left in my room so that I could wash my hair when I returned from the day's activities. Denis was confused by her lecture at first. To me she seemed intent on converting him to heterosexuality. Finally, he caught on, went very pale, and broke into a stream of French invective.

Everyone heard what followed. "He's saying, in essence, that you are a woman with a nasty mind and slanderous tongue," Robbie translated for Ingrid, who had backed away when Denis took her remarks amiss. "Not to mention a liar for calling into question the manhood of one who has enjoyed many women and no men in sexual liaisons. Am I getting that right, Laura?"

"I think this is a subject best dropped," said Laura.

"Mon Dieu!" Denis exclaimed. "My honor has been—" Flushed, he turned to us. "Has your son—"

"Not at all," said Jason hastily. "Chris is not gay, and he has not accused you of anything, Denis. He went home because his spring break is over." To Ingrid, Jason said, "We've already told you that, Ingrid. Please don't make accusations of this sort again."

"Don't know why you get these bees in your bonnet, Ingrid," said Carl.

"I told you we should go home," retorted his wife, now as flushed and angry as Denis. "Decent people shouldn't have to—"

"That's enough, Ingrid. I want my breakfast, not some big to-do that's likely to gave me pains in the gut, maybe even the trots."

"Carl, how can you mention your bowels in public?" Her voice was by then almost inaudible because her husband had hustled her away to the breakfast room.

That morning no one sat with the Jensens, and I felt the demise of hopes that this might prove to be a less contentious segment of the tour. Most people in our group were embarrassed enough to keep their eyes on their croissants and their mouths shut at the table, except for Janice, who was excited about the visit to Chenonceau. According to her, the château had been the home of many strong and influential women. "Admittedly, they prostituted themselves through marriage and—"

"What?" Estrella looked horrified. "Marriage is a Holy Sacrament of the Church, not—"

"Maybe you should read some Roman Catholic history," Janice interrupted dryly. "The Church didn't always approve of married sex. Priests didn't even perform the ceremonies for some time—before the tenth century, I believe."

"There's some truth in that," Childeric agreed but was drowned out by his wife, who thought we might like to hear interesting statistics on the success in tournament bridge of married partners as opposed to unmarried partners.

"As I was saying," Janice cut in, "Chenonceau was ruled by mistresses, wives, and widows, and although they may have used sexual favors as stepping-stones to power, they were, at least, women of intelligence."

As Janice talked, my eyes wandered from face to face, thinking of all the people I had suspected of the violence that plagued our group: Ivan, whom I had thought might be a Russian hit man out to get me or Jason; Janice, who hated Childeric (she seemed to think him guilty of crimes against women, and I now understood why); Childeric himself (he certainly had put me in danger more than once); Hester, who seemed to have an unnatural interest in violent art; Macauley Drummond, who was unpleasant by nature; and Lorenzo de Sorentino, who was now gone. Oh goodness, I really had no idea what was going on. I could only hope that it stopped.

"By the way, Dr. Unsell," I said during a break in Janice's lecture, "congratulations on being a grandfather."

Unsell looked at me with real dislike. Was he the attacker? I wondered.

"May I ask why you think that my grandchild has been born?" he demanded.

"Grace told me last night." Had Grace asked me to tell him? I had been so upset about the accusations Edie made against Anna that I couldn't remember.

"She called *you* with the news instead of me!" The man's face turned as red as his nose.

"Actually, she called on another matter." I glanced nervously at Anna. "Of a more personal nature," I mumbled.

"What could be more personal than the birth of my grandchild? Possibly Grace was trying to call me and failing to reach me, called you to relay the message, after which you picked the most embarrassing time and manner possible to—"

"Look, Dr. Unsell, Grace called about something else and mentioned the baby, and now I remember. She said to tell you if you seemed interested, which obviously you're not. You haven't even asked the sex of the child, or whether mother and daughter are doing well. So please don't raise your voice to me."

Jason was tapping my hand, presumably to get my attention, when Laura broke in, "A granddaughter. How lovely. Congratulations, Dr. Unsell. I'm sure you'll want to go call Grace. What luck that you still have the cell phone."

Now there, I thought, *is a diplomatic woman. She not only headed him off but also reminded him in a subtle way that he had a cell phone, the number of which his wife knew, so that Grace could have called him if she'd really wanted to.* In deference to Laura's exercise in tact, I restrained myself. I must admit that I had been quite irritated with Dr. Unsell for yelling at me and not caring about—well. I took a deep breath and glanced sideways at Jason. That rat. He had his hand over his mouth, and his shoulders were shaking. "Stop that," I whispered and gave him a poke.

"You're so cute when you're mad," he whispered back, starting to laugh again.

"Women my age aren't cute," I murmured. "We can be charming or handsome or well preserved or—" Now I had to suppress my own laughter, and both of us were getting disapproving looks from our fellow tour members, not the least of whom was Manfred Unsell, who gave me an absolutely vicious glare as he left the room.

Then I noticed that Anna had risen to leave. I jumped up and followed her into the lobby to assure her that I would not be mentioning Edie or Grace or the conversation we'd had the night before.

She nodded. "Very kind of you, Carolyn. Given the unpleasant mood everyone seems to be in, I'd hate to become the focus of their ill will."

I sighed. "I've obviously managed to enrage Dr. Unsell, although I didn't mean to. I expected that he'd have talked to Grace by now. Why wouldn't he?"

Anna shrugged. She seemed distracted.

"The tour today should be interesting, don't you think? All those 'Amazons,' as Janice called them."

"Yes, I'll be sorry to miss it," said Anna.

"You're not going?" She'd caught me by surprise. "But—"

"I'm afraid all this rich French food is catching up with me again," she said ruefully. "My stomach was happier when the offerings were plain and boring."

"Oh, Anna, I'm so sorry. Is there anything I can do for you?"

"Enjoy the tour and tell me all about it at dinner," she replied. "A day of rest and simple food should revive me. Then I can enjoy Chartres tomorrow. Janice tells me she was there in the spring once and saw flowers growing out of the stones high on the cathedral walls. That would be something to see."

"Oh, it is," I replied. "They looked like daisies." She sounded almost wistful, as if afraid she might not be well enough to see Chartres either.

Later, when I told Janice that Anna had stayed behind because she felt ill, Janice said that the tour had been very stressful for Anna. *As it has for us all,* I thought, although I was very sorry that the stress had made Anna sick, and very resentful against whoever was causing all this misery. I myself, rather than the rich food, might be responsible for Anna's illness. Perhaps I shouldn't have told her about Edie. Still, I couldn't let her be caught unprepared by Edie's accusation. Such a situation could ruin a career if the girl's parents believed it. Poor Anna. And Edie—was it confusion resulting from the fall or resentment against Anna that had triggered that allegation?

49
Le Château des Dames

Artichokes

The great châteaux of the Loire are known for both their architectural beauty and their gardens. Chenonceau, for instance, was first provided with an elaborate Renaissance garden by Diane de Poitiers, famous beauty and mistress of Henri II. These gardens featured flowers, shrubs, and trees, as well as orchards, fruits, and vegetables. Diane received as gifts rare melons and artichokes. One wonders if they were considered ornamentals, as potatoes had been. Or perhaps her chef prepared them as hors d'oeuvres for the nobility while they drank champagne at the festive parties.

Did the king demand that his queen, Catherine de Medici, who not surprisingly hated her rival, provide prosciutto from her native Italy to wrap the melon slices? Maybe the artichokes were served with melted Norman butter. Incidentally, Pliny the Elder in his natural history called artichokes a monstrosity, but the Roman nobility loved them. Small wonder. Today's Romans fix the world's most delicious artichokes. For those of us less talented, artichokes are still an easy first course to prepare:

Cut off the tough part of the *artichoke stem.*

Strip away the tough outer leaves.

Shear the sharp tips.

Boil, covered, in lemon-flavored water for 40 minutes.

Drain and chill.

Serve one per diner with *melted butter* or *mayonnaise* for dipping

Not only did the royal mistress, Diane de Poitiers, have exotic edibles in her garden, she had an interesting beauty regime. It seems to have worked amazingly well since she managed to hold, until his death in a tournament, the affections of a king twenty years her junior, and she was reputed to have been as beautiful as ever when she died at the age of sixty-seven. Here is the lady's beauty recipe:

Recipe for Enduring Beauty

Rise early.   Then retire and sleep until noon.

Bathe in cold water.   Never wear makeup.

Go for a brisk horseback ride.

It probably helps to start out beautiful, as well.

Carolyn Blue, "Have Fork, Will Travel," *St. Paul Star-Register*

Jason

The more I see of Ivan and Estrella, the less I understand how he could have married the woman. If he didn't seem so smitten, I'd have guessed that the marriage was a ploy to avoid deportation. Be that as it may, our day exploring châteaux should have been very pleasant. Although I'm not necessarily a fan of elaborate country houses and mind-boggling gardens, the goings-on in these places over the centuries were enough to keep society in a state of continual overstimulation.

Our group paid closer attention to the remarks of the guide, who was a graduate student in history, than they ever had to Denis. Carolyn wondered in my ear if Denis had called the fellow in to relieve himself from another day of Childeric corrections. After ten days of shepherding our group, Denis was probably reconsidering his choice of profession.

First, we admired Chenonceau from afar. It bridged a river with forests on one side and gardens on the other—Frank Lloyd Wright's "Falling Water" on a much grander and more traditional scale. The new guide, Maurice, called Chenonceau *le château des dames*, and explained that a mill and keep owned since the Middle Ages by the lords of Marques had to be sold for debt. The new owner left his wife Catherine Briconnet, the first *dame* of Chenonceau, to build the château beginning in 1521 while he flitted around France and Europe on the king's business.

Manfred Unsell remarked gloomily that bankruptcy had a long history, but none so unscrupulous as contemporary bankruptcies, whose losses were imposed on businessmen by laws that allowed ordinary people to run up huge debts and then wriggle out of them with no damage, except to their credit ratings. Evidently, there were no bankrupts among us because no one took offense, although Carolyn whispered to me that the European nobility had, for centuries, been in the habit of running up debts with tradesmen, which could never be collected.

Unfortunately for the Briconnet family, Frances I liked Catherine's château so much that as soon as she and her husband died, the king announced that royal funds had been mismanaged by the late Collector of

Taxes; accordingly, the Briconnet son and heir was forced to hand over Chenonceau in lieu of paying a huge fine for his father's alleged embezzlement, and Frances became the owner of an estate he had coveted. The second dame, Diane de Poitiers, took over in 1547 when Frances's son Henri II came to the throne and gave his mistress the château.

Carl Jensen was pleased at a description of Diane's interest in agriculture and said he liked to see land put to good use. Ingrid was less pleased with the life of the royal mistress; however, the thought of the king and Diane living in sin, and in such luxurious surroundings, was more than Estrella Markarov could stomach. She compared the beautiful Diane to Robbie. Robbie thanked her for the compliment. Estrella retorted that she had meant no compliment, that the comparison was between couples living in sin.

Ivan laughed, cuddled his wife affectionately, and said, "Sin—it can be much funs, no, my little samovar?"

His wife pulled away, eyed him with disappointment, and told him that as an expectant father, he was obligated to take a strong moral stance against sin and sinners. Robbie then told Estrella to mind her own business, and Estrella told Robbie that her seduction of Hugh and blatant sexual misconduct were ruining his chances of becoming dean, to which Robbie retorted, "Bull!"

"Obviously," Estrella continued, "a college cannot afford to have an immoral dean." Hand in hand with his legal spouse, Childeric had listened to this interplay with smug satisfaction while nodding his head in agreement.

Robbie began to laugh. "Well, you're in the College of Education, Estrella, and education professors are either stupid or dorky or both, so you'd probably be right if we were talking about deans of education."

Maurice, the new guide, had been staring open-mouthed during this argument but then recollected his duties and said, "The sublime Diane commissioned the bridge that links the château designed by Catherine Briconnet with the woods across the River Cher. After that, the court spent more and more time at this beautiful place. Shall we look at—"

"Sublime?" exclaimed Estrella. "That is a word better used for angels and saints, not—not—women of ill repute. This *Poitiers* person was a courtesan and an adulteress. Marriage vows are sacred."

"She was a widow, Estrella," murmured Laura. Perhaps she thought that would pacify the education professor.

"A widow? My goodness, I suppose you think that makes everything all right. Well, I was a widow before I married my dear Ivan, and I assure you that I did not become anyone's mistress. And the king was married—to someone or other."

"Catherine de Medici," said Childeric helpfully. I imagine he wanted to keep the skirmish going as long as possible now that Estrella seemed ready to attack a second runner in the race for dean.

"They were committing adultery." She glared at Laura. "A woman's place is by her husband, not in someone else's bed."

Laura's eyebrows lifted inquiringly. "If you're insinuating that, because my husband has gone back home, I am jumping into some other man's bed, Estrella, you're quite wrong."

"And I'm not either," said Hester, "if you've got me in mind. And I'm not a widow. Jeremy is definitely alive and in a walking cast now. And I am not sleeping with Macauley. Laura isn't either, are you, Laura?"

Laura looked somewhat embarrassed, but Macauley Drummond jumped in with relish. "Ladies, pay no attention to this woman. Professors of education have very small minds in matters both social and intellectual."

"But bigging tummies," Ivan chimed in, patting his wife where their child was presumably growing. I could tell that my friend had missed the point of Macauley's insult. Estrella had not. She scowled at Macauley, then at her husband, and poor Ivan looked crestfallen.

Maurice led us hurriedly toward the bedroom of Louise de Lorraine, perhaps thinking to pacify Estrella. Louise had received Chenonceau from her mother-in-law, Catherine de Medici, after her marriage to Catherine's son Henri III, and retired to that bedroom when an assassin killed her husband.

"Of course," said Carolyn, pink with excitement. "He was assassinated in the great market, Les Halles, while trapped between two overturned vegetable carts. The market was founded by Phillip the Fat centuries earlier."

"Henri III, while besieging Paris, was assassinated by a Jacobin friar," said Childeric. "Where in the world did you get that bizarre idea about food carts and Les Halles?"

"From a book about food," said Carolyn, crestfallen.

"Pardon, madame," said Maurice politely. "You are thinking of Henri IV, who had been King Henri III of Navarre before he became King of France. *He* was killed in the food market. Now back to Henri III."

Then Maurice told us that Queen Louise was so grief stricken at the death of her husband that she spent the rest of her life wearing mourning white and living in that bedroom, which she draped in black velvet and decorated with silver tears.

"An excellent example of a woman who *honored* her vows," said Estrella.

"Unlike you," snapped Robbie. "When your first husband got clubbed, you kept right on preaching bilingual education and snagged Ivan, right?"

Estrella burst into tears. Ivan said, "Is nice she choose me instead of black room."

By the time Maurice mentioned the second-to-last dame, the intellectual Madame Dupin, none of us had much to say. Things livened up a bit when Denis returned to the group and, seeing the grim faces, entertained us as we explored the gallery over the river with the exploits of Catherine de Medici who, once her husband Henri II died, was able to wrest Chenonceau and a quantity of jewels from her rival Diane and then rule France during the reigns of three sons.

I, for one, was interested to learn that young, bare-breasted noblewomen served refreshments at Catherine's balls, posed on the riverbanks singing, and sold their "favors" on spying missions for the Queen Mother. Estrella demanded that Ivan take her back to Tours before any more scandalous stories were told, so the Markarovs missed Azay-le-Rideau and Villandry, where Carolyn was interested in the decorative cabbages that filled the vegetable gardens.

"They look like posies," she said. "I wonder if they're edible, and if they were served during the Renaissance. Cabbage, even pretty cabbage, doesn't sound like food for a royal feast."

Thank God, there had been no incidents of violence, other than verbal, during the day, and my wife was back to thinking about food. She did ask, once we were seated in the bus returning to Tours, whether I thought Estrella could be the spy sent by the selection committee to check out the dean candidates.

"What spy?" I asked.

"People are saying there is one. I thought maybe it was Anna, but now— well, if it's Estrella, I'm afraid Hugh and Laura are out of the running. Professor Childeric *appears* to be the only candidate left who's not living in sin or failing to cling to his spouse. I hope Estrella hasn't forgotten his conduct with Edie." Carolyn looked quite upset at the thought of Childeric becoming dean.

"Be a pity if he got the post," I replied, glancing at Childeric. He was sitting by his wife, looking self-satisfied, and talking in counterpoint to her bridge tales.

50

Duck à l'Orange

Duck à l'Orange

A favorite meat in Normandy is duck, and a duck raised in Normandy is a treat indeed. Take that Norman duck and treat it Provençal style (Canard à l'Orange), and you have a culinary delight. Here is a recipe:

Remove anything found in the cavity of a *duckling*, and cut away excess fat inside and at the neck and tail; bind the wings, legs, and neck skin to the body with kitchen *twine or skewers*; and prick the skin here and there to let the extra fat seep out while the duck is cooking.

Paint the skin very lightly with *butter*, and roast to medium rare: 15 minutes per pound at 450° F.

Do not salt the uncooked duck. Do *salt* the cooking juices and baste often with them.

In the meantime, peel the zest (only the colored part) from *2 tart oranges and 1 lemon,* cut julienne style, cook 1 minute in boiling water, and drain.

Reduce *3 tbs. wine vinegar* with *2 tsp. sugar* in a small pan until caramelization begins.

Add juices of the oranges and lemon, reduce a bit, and add zest.

Place the roasted duck on a heated platter, drain the fat from the roasting pan, and dissolve the brown juices with a little *Cointreau or brandy.*

Add this to the sauce and simmer for several minutes.

Garnish the duck with *orange slices* and serve the sauce separately.

SERVES 4 OR 5 PEOPLE.

Carolyn Blue, "Have Fork, Will Travel," *Biloxi News-Courant*

Carolyn

At last, a day without physical violence, and soon we would be flying home—not even on the same plane with these people. I understood that the tour had been difficult for everyone, frightening, in fact. But I don't see that anyone else had been in more danger than I had, and I didn't indulge in rude remarks. Well, perhaps about Professor Childeric, but he deserved them.

Although the tour was not providing dinner that night, Denis had suggested that we meet in the lobby so that he could suggest several restaurants that were both excellent and reasonable in price. I, for one, would have been happy to ignore our guide's restaurant suggestions, but Jason liked the sound of "reasonable in price."

"I have not yet provided you with the opportunity to sample the delicious *canard* of Normandy," Denis told us. "Therefore I offer two suggestions. One café has in Tours the best *canard à la rouennaise.*"

My gourmet sensibilities sharpened with interest, for I had read that *canard à la rouennaise* is the very best way to cook duck. Since I had not had the opportunity to sample this delicacy in Rouen, I nudged Jason and nodded, as if to say, "That's what we want to try."

"The second café offers a sumptuous *canard à l'orange,* one the finest dishes of Provence. I leave it to you." Denis gave us his winning smile.

"Why don't we vote?" suggested Carl Jensen. Alas, they went with the dish they'd heard of, rather than the one I tried to recommend. I suppose Jason and I could have refused to surrender ourselves to the democratic process and gone off on our own in a show of elitist rebellion, but Jason said, "Well, that's settled."

Once in the café, a long, narrow, noisy place with wall benches and rush-bottomed chairs, we all ordered duck à l'orange, like so many ducklings, waddling mindlessly after Mama. Since I happen to like duck à l'orange and this might be my only chance to sample the local duck, I too acquiesced. It was, in fact, delicious, the dark, rich meat contrasting nicely with the tart-sweet, orange-flavored sauce and the fruit slices.

Surprisingly oranges from Seville are favored for this dish. Jason and I once picked an orange from one of the beautiful trees that grow everywhere in that lovely Andalusian city. My goodness, it was sour. Maybe we had taken up orange theft in the wrong season, although our choice certainly looked round, colorful, and tasty.

The surprise of a wonderful meal seemed to quell the animosity that had plagued our group for days. People were generally polite, sometimes even friendly to one another, and when tempers flared, Laura jumped in with diplomatic words to turn the would-be attacker's wrath aside. Diners less historically and religiously inclined listened with tolerance when Denis told us how Saint Martin, then a young soldier in a Roman legion, cut his cape in half to share with a beggar, after which, seeing Christ in a dream clothed in the half-cloak, Martin sought baptism and began his holy life. Estrella offered the story of the transport of Saint Martin's corpse by river to Tours and the greening of the trees out of season as he passed.

Drummond, for once, managed to repress his usual offensive remarks, and Janice refrained from denouncing the patriarchal ways of the Church. When Childeric described in detail the Viking depredations in Tours, no one protested, and Hester showed an interest in the arson and slaughter.

Many of us asked solicitously after Anna's health and described the sights of the day to her, leaving out the arguments that had darkened the beauty of the tour. Anna said she felt much better, and she certainly looked better. That morning she had seemed ill and uncharacteristically nervous. Now there was color in her face, and she ate her duck with appetite. I didn't have the heart to suggest that, if rich food had been her problem, duck à l'orange was not a good choice. She seemed so calm, even peaceful, although when Childeric held forth, talking over the interruptions of his wife, Anna eyed them both coldly.

I couldn't blame her. I was heartily tired of the man myself, and his wife was simply a tiresome person of another color. Playing bridge can be entertaining, but surely she had some other interest she could talk about.

When dinner was over and even the grumpiest among us were mellow with good food and wine, Denis announced that he had a surprise; he hoped that we'd all follow him to see it. Janice said that she'd have to forgo the surprise since she was expecting a call from the States. She suggested that she and Anna walk back to the hotel together. Still becalmed on some mental island, Anna murmured that she thought she'd go along for the surprise. Although Janice seemed taken aback at the refusal, and I'm sure that I heard Ingrid make a tasteless remark about "trouble in fairyland," most of us paid our bills and trailed away after Denis through quiet, dark streets.

"Are you ready for the surprise?" our guide called gaily. We saw nothing but one more shadowed street. Then suddenly he waved us around a corner, and looming ahead was a magnificent cathedral, glowing in the darkness.

I swear that it looked like a magical vision floating in the night air, all ornate tracery and mellow stone with lovely stone lanterns topping its twin spires. Flamboyant Gothic architecture at its most glorious. It was so beautiful a sight that, for a moment, I could hardly breathe and wished that I had brought my camera.

Denis said triumphantly, "Cathedrale Saint Gatien!"

"Ah," said Professor Childeric, "a Gallo-Roman foundation, a Romanesque thirteenth-century base with a chancel designed, in all probability, by the genius of Sainte-Chapelle in Paris, stained glass of the same period, and upon the Roman wall the elaborate decoration of—"

"I do believe that cathedral was pictured on the decks of cards we used at a tournament in Cleveland," said Mrs. Childeric.

"—and topping this fine example of flamboyant Gothic, the charming Renaissance lantern domes that signal the church's completion in the sixteenth century."

"Yes, I'm sure it's the very same cathedral," said Mrs. Childeric. "I bid and made an amazing six clubs at that tournament. Everyone was quite impressed."

"Although Saint Gatien's is a cathedral of the second rank, still I find it very pleasing," said Professor Childeric. "Most graceful and—"

"*Anna!*" I cried. We were scattered in a loose group with the golden light of the church falling on us. By that light I saw something I could hardly believe: Anna Thomas-Smith had pulled a pistol from her purse and, holding it in both hands, was moving forward. "Anna! What are you doing?" She continued quite steadily, quite calmly toward the Childerics.

51

Murder at a Cathedral

Jason

When Carolyn cried out, my attention was diverted from the cathedral, a very impressive sight, to Anna Thomas-Smith, a sight that made me question my vision. The woman had a pistol in her hand. Had someone threatened her? And if so, where had she gotten the pistol? One can't bring weapons on board a plane. And I doubted that a pistol would be easy to buy, especially in a foreign country, especially by a middle-aged home economist or whatever she was, an unmarried, middle-aged—well, I was struck dumb, frozen in my tracks when I saw the gun in Anna's hand.

Hugh had been beside Anna when Carolyn called out. He turned and, seeing the weapon, reached toward her, crying, "My God, she's got a gun!"

Anna pulled away from him and fired. Stunned silence fell over our group. "I missed," Anna said, her tone one of shocked lament.

Thank God! I thought as I lurched, belatedly, in her direction. Hugh actually got a hand on her arm, but she now held the weapon tighter, still in both hands, and fired a second time. As I grasped her left arm, I heard Professor Childeric wail, "I've been shot!" as he crumpled to the ground, blood spreading in rosy blossom on his pant leg.

Hugh and I immobilized Anna and wrestled the gun from her, as Childeric, trying to stem the flow of blood from his leg, screamed, "You tried to kill me, Fauree, but it won't help you get the deanship. I'm still alive, and I know you—"

"You stupid bastard," Hugh shouted back. "This isn't my gun." He waved it at Childeric.

"Give it to me," I said. "It may have more bullets in it."

"He's still alive?" Anna was shivering uncontrollably in our grasp. "Give the gun back." We didn't, of course, and she burst into tears, saying, "I can't seem to do anything right."

I shoved the revolver into my pocket and tightened my grasp on Anna who, although I could hardly believe it, had evidently meant to kill Childeric. Carl Jensen left the shocked crowd and attempted to stanch the flow of blood from the medievalist's leg. After commandeering neckties from all of us, Jensen balled several up, pressed them against the wound, and used the rest to tie the packing in place. "Well, that's better," said Jensen. "Now stop jerking around, Childeric. You'll dislodge the bandage."

A good man, Jensen, I thought. *Quicker thinking than the rest of us.* I'd have to remember to thank him again for saving Carolyn from the tides off Mont-Saint-Michel.

"Anna, what were you thinking of? Why would you—" My wife was now standing beside Hugh and our prisoner. Anna continued to weep.

"Anna?" Carolyn touched her cheek. "What happened?"

Anna sniffled, her attention caught by my wife's gentle words. "Oh, it happened years ago. If he just hadn't come on this trip. If I hadn't had to see him and listen to him every day."

"Anna, you shot me?" Childeric whined. "I thought we were—"

"Friends?" she asked bitterly. "In love? That's what I thought, Jean-Claude. That's what you told me."

"But that was years ago," he protested. "I mean . . ." He looked around at the staring crowd. "I mean you obviously misinterpreted some little—"

"I just wanted to ruin your life, Jean-Claude. The way you ruined mine. But I couldn't even manage that."

"Robbie, do you think you could call the police?" Hugh whispered to his lover.

"And before everyone gets going again with the recriminations, someone should look at Mrs. Childeric. She hasn't moved at all," said Hester. "I think something might be wrong with her."

Jensen looked around, spotted Mrs. Childeric lying, face up, on the cobblestones of the open area in front of the cathedral, and ordered his wife to keep pressure on the professor's wound. Childeric was keening to himself when Ingrid took over while Jensen knelt beside Astarte Childeric. He lifted her eyelid, then felt the artery in her neck.

"Mad cow disease?" asked Macauley Drummond sardonically.

"Dead," said Jensen. "Bullet in the chest. Better get an ambulance, too, Ms. Hecht," he called after Robbie, who had found a telephone and was making the call to the police. She held up her hand to indicate that she had heard.

Anna's legs had given way when she heard that Childeric's wife was dead. "That's not what I meant to do," she mumbled. Since she seemed unable to stand, we lowered her to the cobblestones.

Carolyn sat down beside her, legs tucked neatly to the side. I'll never know how women manage such things in skirts, especially narrow skirts like the one my wife was wearing.

"Anna, you must still be sick," Carolyn suggested.

"I wasn't sick," Anna replied wearily. "I was out buying a gun. It's hard to do when you don't speak much French. And very costly."

"But why would you—"

"I don't want to talk about it, Carolyn. I'm sorry you had to see this. You're a nice woman. And I'm sorry you got caught in the cross-fire."

"I didn't." Carolyn looked surprised. "I wasn't hit."

"Bad choice of words. The push in Rouen was meant for him." She nodded toward Childeric. "And the tide thing—I never dreamed you'd walk out on that beach with him, not after—"

"It was stupid," Carolyn agreed. "I was caught up in the romance of the Middle Ages—Henry, William Rufus, Robert of Normandy—well, it was stupid of me. The police will be coming, Anna. Do you want me to go with you?"

"I can't believe you said that, Carolyn," Childeric cried. He had raised his head and caught the end of the conversation. "I'm the one who was shot, and she's the one who shot me. Why are you being so nice to her? I can understand that Janice Petar hates me, although she has no reason except that she hates all men, but you! I had a tender regard for you. I—"

"Dr. Childeric, you've been shot," said Carolyn. "Just shot. That's all."

"All?"

"Your wife is dead, or doesn't that matter to you?"

Childeric looked at Carolyn with puzzlement, then glanced aside and noticed, evidently for the first time, the body of his wife. "Astarte?"

The police and hospital vans, sirens blaring, arrived at the same time. Childeric, while being placed on a stretcher, saw his wife's body covered with a blanket and said, "Oh, my God," as if he'd just realized she was actually dead. After listening to an explanation in their native language from Laura, the police took charge of Anna. Again my wife offered to go along.

"I think I'd be of more use, Carolyn," said Laura. "She'll need a translator."

"There's a journal in my room," Anna said to Carolyn. "You can read it if you like. Then give it to Janice. She can send it to my father."

As it turned out, no one was allowed to go with Anna. After the police car pulled away, Carolyn stood forlornly on the cobblestones, watching its lights disappear around the corner. "This is all my fault," she said.

"Now, Carolyn," I protested.

"No, it really is, Jason." She looked to. be on the verge of tears. "Edie told Grace, who told me yesterday, that Anna had pushed her down the stairs at Mont-Saint-Michel, and what did I do? I thought Edie was lying. So did Grace. And I warned Anna. She probably panicked. She must have thought she was about to be arrested, and that's why she—why she bought a gun—and—and . . ."

Carolyn started to cry, and I put one arm around her while I fished for a handkerchief. I didn't have one. "If you'll let go of your purse, I'll find you a Kleenex, sweetheart."

"Why is it that only Southern men carry handkerchiefs?" she sobbed as she relinquished her purse.

Ah well, women say strange things when they're upset. I found her a Kleenex and let her odd remark go.

52

Best Western Revelations

Carolyn

Except for Denis and Laura, who followed Anna to wherever the police take prisoners, the rest of us staggered back to the hotel and headed, without even discussing it, toward the bar. I certainly needed a drink. I was horrified and confused and saddened. One wounded, one dead, not to mention all the other "accidents." Could Anna really have been behind all these things? Well, not the lunch box that broke Jeremy's leg. Not the wine cork that hit Childeric's forehead. I ordered a double Kir Royale.

Laura arrived twenty minutes later and ordered a double bourbon.

"Denis is getting her a lawyer, and she didn't want to talk to me, so I came back." She looked depressed. "What an awful trip this has been. Has anyone thought to tell Janice what's happened? She obviously knew Anna better than the rest of us."

Hester said she'd make the call and left to do so.

"Isn't that just what I've been saying?" demanded Ingrid. "Perversions and—and illicit sex are a sign of moral decay. We shouldn't be surprised that—"

"Ingrid," said Carl sharply, "I don't want to hear any more of that kind of talk. Jesus told us not to be casting the first stone."

"He said, 'He who is without sin,' " she cried indignantly. "I've certainly never practiced perversions or illicit sex—or murdered anyone."

"We don't know the whole story," said Carl stubbornly.

Janice joined us, pulling up an extra chair, and listened to the account of the night's events. Then she said sadly, "If only she'd come back with me. I knew she was upset. I should have—"

"I'm sorry to say this, Professor Petar, but Anna didn't seem at all upset," Estrella interrupted. "She was perfectly calm until she realized she'd shot the wrong person or hadn't killed them both or whatever it was. Then she started to cry. I think that's terrible. It's bad enough to shoot someone, but to cry because you didn't kill them!"

"This tour was the first thing Anna had looked forward to in years, and having him here ruined it for her. She'd never have booked if she'd known Childeric had tickets, and he only came at the last minute because someone else dropped out." Janice shook her head. "It's really sad, when you think about it. She's always been such a gentle person, but this was just too much for her."

"Too much what?" asked Hester. "He is pretty boring, but most people don't shoot someone for being boring."

"Oh, he got what he deserved," said Janice.

"No one deserves—" Estrella protested, but was cut off.

"You don't know anything about them, Estrella, so there's no use your judging them," snapped Janice.

We all looked at her expectantly.

"Anna once had a good career building," Janice explained. "She'd probably have been promoted to full professor in a year or so. Before she was forty, which is extraordinary for a woman. The old boys' club pretty much tries to keep women in the lower echelons of—"

"I don't think we need a feminist lecture," said Macauley sardonically.

"I expect that you, of all people, do need one, Drummond. At any rate, Anna was doing well, and then she met Childeric, who was interested in the changes in quality and length of life that could be attributed to changing diet during the Middle Ages. He got her interested, and she started doing research and even lab work on his project. Pretty soon she was devoting all her nonteaching time to Childeric's research, and she was in love. He said he was, too. He said he was going to leave his wife and marry Anna. They had an affair, which I doubt that Anna had ever done before. I don't know that. She's a reserved woman about sexual matters, but—"

"They committed adultery?" Estrella interrupted.

"That they did. It's fairly common in universities, in case you didn't know it, Estrella. Better watch your own husband, especially when you're further along in your pregnancy. That's a time, so I've heard, when men are particularly prone to straying, not that they don't at other times, too."

Estrella looked alarmed.

Janice continued imperturbably, "Childeric strung her along for almost two years, and then he dumped her. He said he'd discovered that he couldn't leave his wife, after all. Anna was devastated, but at that point she didn't know the full scope of his betrayal. That came later, when the article on their work was published. Her name wasn't even mentioned. She'd given the man her love, her loyalty, and two years of research on something that benefited only Childeric. He was given a research award and a chaired professorship, and she was passed over for promotion.

"I don't think she ever dated again, certainly never married, although she'd wanted to be married. She had enough trouble with depression after the affair with Childeric that her department would probably have fired her if she hadn't had tenure. So she kept her job, but she sort of faded into the woodwork, academically speaking. I wish she'd spoken up at the time, but she was humiliated, and she thought if people knew about the affair, she might get sacked for moral turpitude. Hell, maybe she was right. We'll never know.

"So he got away with it, and her life was wrecked. The best she could do was stay away from him, which she did. Anna stopped attending university convocations. She never went to social events. Then he turned up on this tour, and I think she just went a little crazy when she had to see him every day. It was too much for her. I only hope a French court will see it that way."

"I'm afraid that's unlikely," said Manfred Unsell. "In France, one is guilty until proven innocent. The Napoleonic Code. Nor do I think that a broken heart is considered mitigation for murder."

"Right," said Janice. "But then how would you know about broken hearts? As far as I can see, the only thing that flips your switch, Manfred, is the European Common Market." She stood up and slung a heavy handbag cum briefcase on her shoulder. "Well, I've got a couple of visits to make. One to Anna, if they'll let me see her. I want to tell her that she may have gotten her revenge, after all. And then I'm going to pay a call on Childeric."

Jason looked startled. "I hope you're not thinking of—"

"Finishing off the job? No, but I'm going to give him a bit of news that will ruin his day. In fact, I might as well tell the rest of you since at least two of you have a stake in this. The selection committee met today and named the new dean."

"And it's not Childeric," Hugh guessed.

"That's right, it's not."

"Then who is it?" Hester asked. "After all, it's my college too. And Jeremy's. He'll want to know."

"Laura, congratulations." Janice nodded to her.

"*Me?*" For once, Laura de Sorentino lost her amazing calm.

"Yes, congratulations," said Hugh, rising to shake Laura's hand. "If you ever need input on the scientific mind, feel free to call on me." He grinned cheerfully.

"That's very gracious of you, Hugh. You don't mind?"

"Hell, as long as it's not that ass, Childeric, I'm as happy to see you get it as not. I've got an announcement of my own to make." He reached for Robbie's hand and pulled her up. "Robbie and I are getting married. We thought we'd try to do it tomorrow or the next day in Paris. The city of romance." He dropped a kiss on Robbie's lips.

"Ah, my friend, is very romantic," said Ivan, "but takes many months for French wedding. Papers for divorce. Papers for showing spouse is dead. Many papers, all with many stamps of officials. Many, many months."

Robbie laughed. "Well, that's all right. We can get married at home. I know your kids'll want to be there, Hugh."

I wasn't so sure that Hugh's children would want to attend the wedding, no matter where it was held, and Jason looked flabbergasted.

"A few more days of living in sin won't hurt us," said Robbie gaily. "Right, Estrella?"

Estrella shrugged. "Since you're not Catholic, your marriage won't be any more valid in God's eyes than your sinful conduct is excusable."

"How do you happen to know who was appointed, Janice?" Hugh asked.

"What? You think I'm making it up? I'm the selection committee's spy."

"Goodness, I thought Anna was." The words just slipped out of my mouth.

"Nope. I am. Won't Childeric hate to hear that. He'll think of all the nasty things he's said to me and wish he'd sucked up instead. Well, I'd better get moving. It's a shame about his wife, though. Bad enough to spend all those years with him, but then to die because of him. He's the one who should have died."

"He's the one she meant to kill," I said.

"That I can understand. I mean, why she'd want to. It's just hard to believe that she did all the other stuff." Janice seemed baffled. "She really is a nice woman."

"It's hard to believe none of us ever *saw* her do anything," I said. "Well, until tonight. Except for Edie's fall, we were all *there* when these things happened."

"She didn't push Edie," said Laura. "She told me that she'd been lecturing Edie for being rude to some tourist, and Edie ran off, laughing. She must have tripped."

"You wonder why you never saw Anna pushing anyone? Or why no one heard her give Childeric the wrong information about the tides—if she did that. I don't know; maybe he just misunderstood." Janice addressed this to me. "It's because no one notices older women. Unless you're beautiful like Laura, or pushy like me, or really famous in your field, no one sees you or listens to you. Give yourself ten or twenty years, Carolyn, and you'll see for yourself. When we're old and plain, we become invisible."

Epilogue

Carolyn

Jason and I left the bar shortly after Janice. Guilt ate at me as I thought of the clues I'd missed that might have told me Anna had an ominous interest in Jean-Claude Childeric. From the first night when she kept asking me questions about him and about our relationship to last night when I heard that Edie had accused Anna of pushing her, there had been clues, and I had missed them or ignored them. She'd wanted me to tell everyone when he came to my room; she'd hinted that his behavior that afternoon wasn't unusual; she'd believed Edie, whom she didn't like, when she heard that Childeric had kissed the girl; she'd disappeared from the dinner table right before the beef snacks for the mastiff appeared in people's pockets. So many clues, and I'd ignored them.

And her own story was heartbreaking, a shy, lonely woman preyed on by an unscrupulous man. "What a sad tale that was," I said to Jason as I began to prepare for bed.

"Anna's?" Jason stared out the window of the hotel room, his back to me. "It was sad, but if she'd handled the situation better when she first faced it—"

"She was seriously depressed, Jason. Childeric ruined her life."

"There are psychiatrists for depression, not to mention excellent drugs."

"Yes," I had to agree. "Laura thinks Prozac is a miracle drug."

"Laura de Sorentino takes Prozac?" Jason looked surprised. "I wonder if the selection committee knows that?"

"You're just upset because she was chosen over Hugh."

"I'm a lot more upset about this marriage he's jumping into. Robbie's had four husbands, and Hugh has children."

"Keep in mind that Robbie is a friend of mine," I reminded him. "Hugh knows how many husbands she's had, and he's a grown man. They're in love."

"That's what Anna thought, and now Childeric's wife is dead."

"Anna didn't mean to kill Mrs. Childeric. You heard what she said."

"What about all the others she attacked? Your friend Robbie, for instance."

"I don't know. That was after Robbie talked in front of her about the affair with Hugh. I'm sure Anna didn't want to see Childeric become dean. Maybe she thought she could frighten Robbie away before she ruined Hugh's chances. And the meat in Lorenzo's pocket, that did frighten him away, and he was certainly undermining Laura."

"What about Drummond? He said he was pushed."

"After Nedda read those passages from his book, I'm surprised the whole tour didn't attack him. He said something really mean to Anna at lunch before we went to the Bayeux Cathedral. But he was horrible to Childeric, too. Do you think Childeric pushed him? Drummond thought so."

"No idea," Jason replied.

"I'll bet he did. He was a bad person." Jason was frowning at me. "Well, I do realize that what Anna did was wrong, Jason. I just feel sorry for the miserable life the poor woman had, and now she's in jail. It doesn't look like things are going to improve for her."

"You're right, sweetheart. And I don't even like Childeric, but she put you in danger, too. Twice."

"Not on purpose," I replied defensively.

"Not on purpose doesn't count. You could have drowned."

"Well, it would have saved me from becoming invisible," I retorted, shivering at that depressing statement that Janice made about the prospects of older women.

"Carolyn, as long as I'm alive, you will never be invisible—or plain—or old. Love has very clear eyes about things like that."

While I was giving Jason a hug, which ended with me sitting on his lap, I thought how very lucky I was to have married such a sweet man. "You know, Jason, maybe we should stop traveling so much. We haven't been very lucky this year, at least when we're away from home."

Jason laughed. "That being the case, we're due for a run of better luck, sweetheart. It's like the man who takes a bomb on an airplane. His reasoning is: What are the chances of there being two bombs on the same plane?"

"How did he get the bomb on in the first place? If my wristwatch will set off the metal detectors, surely a bomb—"

"It's a joke, Carolyn."

"I don't think it's funny. Bombs are very—"

"—rare on domestic flights, thank God."

Jason gave me a kiss and pushed me off his lap, much to my surprise. Just because I hadn't liked his joke—

"Now I want you to take a deep breath, Carolyn, get out your computer, and write about eating Duck à l'Orange in Tours."

And I did just that.

Travel Journal
Day Eleven, Twelve? Whatever, Tours

They've actually been very kind to me considering that I just killed someone. I do feel badly about Mrs. Childeric. I hated her when I thought Jean-Claude was going to marry me. He kept saying that she didn't love him but still she refused to give him a divorce.

They gave me paper and a pencil, and they let Janice come to see me. He won't be dean. Well, that's good news. Maybe I won, after all. Everyone will know what he did to me, and I won't have to put up with their pity or disapproval. I'll be here.

And he'll never be dean, and probably no one will ever love him. He'll be all by himself. Growing old. Losing the respect of his colleagues, maybe even fired for taking up with Edie. Maybe he'll become invisible. Just like me.

It's been so strange. Like a dream. Ever since I heard that Edie had accused me of pushing her downstairs. I wouldn't have minded doing it early on. I'm surprised I didn't. But the point is that I didn't do anything. Not that time. But when Carolyn told me what Edie was saying, I knew I had to act. Before people figured out that I was the one and stopped me from getting my revenge on Jean-Claude.

I wonder if I'm crazy. I don't think so. He just shouldn't have come on this trip.

My father. He'll be surprised when he hears about this. Mr. Tough Guy. Yelling at kids. Yelling at me. He never killed anyone. Big surprise, Dad. Your daughter's a murderer.

Do they still guillotine criminals in France? I don't expect that I'll feel invisible when they're cutting off my head. And maybe I can learn some French while I'm waiting. Maybe I can make some friends. At least I don't seem to be invisible anymore.

Anna Thomas-Smith

Recipe Index

＊Taken from *Great Chefs: The Louisiana New Garde* by Nancy Ross Ryan with Chan Patterson,
New Orleans: Great Chefs Television & Publishing, G.S.I., Inc., 1994.
°Recipes are reprinted with permission from *Dining and the Opera in Manhattan* by Sharon O'-
Connor, Menus and Music Productions, Emeryville, California, 1994.